Volume II of the fictional biography

BENJAMIN BLACKIE

Nice Day For a War:
The Unstoppable Warpath of the Unkillable Jack Churchill

Typeset: 20, 12, 11.5 pt Baskerville Old Face
11.5 pt Rainydays by *bruag*
11.5 pt Arial Narrow
10 pt Times New Roman

FIC014050

1. Historical - Fiction. 2. World War, 1939-1945 - Fiction.

I. Title.

A823.3

ISBN: 978-0-6486321-4-6

Published by Kindle Direct Publishing
2024

A word from the Author.

The idea of this war story was originally planned to be a nonfictional, unauthorized memoir - historically referenced, explicated accurate true tale that Jack Churchill is perhaps best deserving. It was intended to be served in its fullest and most autobiographical form. In many ways, it is still very much incorporated into the final product, albeit with a dash more flamboyancy for flavouring.

I delved deep into the historic abyss of significant and trivial detail alike, researching anything and everything remotely related to Jack Churchill primarily during the Second World War. During this process, I had a spellbinding epiphany that would drastically divert the direction of my manuscript. I flexed my artistic licence and remodelled the adjective, fact-based documentation, striving to still deliver the details amongst the type of entertainment that would now be categorized as fictional action/adventure. What better way is there nowadays for being informative than through the artform of storytelling? The revelation came whilst exhuming those buried accounts, hearing those firsthand versions and unsung war stories documented in soldier diaries, video documentaries, and recorded cassettes made by the families in their elder's twilight years. I peeled back layers of history, uncovering for me what I believed to be the quintessence of the man himself, especially the eccentric archetype. He was built different … why not tell his tale differently? It became evident that Mad Jack Churchill was anything but as colourless as the black and whites depicted him to be in old photographs, not that that was ever thought to be the case. Consequently so, I supposed him to be deserving of something more stimulating and amusing than another run-of-the-mill nonfiction publication. He was more than just history, he was legend. After all, what is believable about a commando charging onto a beach during the Second World War with a sword and longbow? Any form of chronicle would be deemed doubtful by any audience and branded fabricated and untrue … so I took it that step further from the beginning and just ran with it.

Thus, my intention became to make this book (and any subsequent books) just as action-packed, saucy, and humorous as they were hard-hitting, historically accurate, and to pay heartfelt respects to what transpired all those years ago. I aspired to tick all the boxes, pull out all the stops, and leave no stone unturned whilst retelling the true story.

As a result, born out of a playful and fictitious gambit, the final draft of the novel based on this man's extraordinary life shaped up as more of an action-packed and extravagant fictional biography rather than a stale history lesson. An entertaining bedtime story instead of a monotonous research article. And why not have fun with it? If you are a staid history buff, allow for the mere prologue of this novel to act as your assessment of what is to come and how to receive it. If your nose turns at this notice, don't bother turning any more pages … because yes, I allowed myself to have a blast telling this story, as I believe Mad Jack himself would. Not as a form of gloat, but for the entertaining factor that one could not doubt coursed through his veins along with pure heroism.

Although a work of fiction, _The Unstoppable Warpath of the Unkillable Jack Churchill_ is built on a solid foundation of true historical fact, down to names, quotes, dates, and locations. This has been done intentionally to recreate as accurate a retelling as possible and to help respectfully keep the memories alive of those long since gone from this world. A vast amount of research went into the development of the setting for the saga. Irrespective to the improvisation in this fictitious retelling, pages drenched with additional palates of detail constructed by the author's overactive imagination, Churchill's story was born from a thorough understanding of the legend through the method of true accounts dated and written by those closest to him at the time.

So here it is - a glass raised to the man.

This literature, however fictitious as it may harmlessly digress, is a celebration of a gentleman born from the stuff legends are made of.

A fête of his fate, a bit of fun, action, romance, and war - in its dubitable inexplicitness - lays a sincerity paralleled with the eccentric essence of Mad Jack Churchill. I hope this is conveyed entertainingly and with all due respect.

<u>You have now been cautioned of the fictitious recounting that threatens to entertain as well as enlighten. Enjoy.</u>

O.K., go.

PROLOGUE
Thrills, Kills, and Mad Jack Churchill

1940, May
L'Épinette
Nord Pas-de-Calais, France

Adrenaline still laced his blood.

Eardrums resonating from the brisk gunshots ...

Within his chest, his heart pumped loud from the action ...

From the chase. From the thrill of the kill.

Captain Jack Churchill orchestrated a few of his men of the loyal Second Manchester Regiment D section whilst they stood in the rain, drenched and dripping. Their position upon the south-most outskirts of the small French town called *L'Épinette* followed the daring ambush of an enemy scout party, and subsequent excitement of a second wave of action resulting in the dispatch of two German moto-scouts.

Churchill had just given the order to return to the town, pre-empting an additional enemy advance from beyond the southern boundaries, from the east.

Enduring the light rainfall, smoke still rose from the flickering spot fire of the mangled motobicyclette wrapped along with its previous occupant, around an oak tree.

His maroon beret dark with moisture, Churchill lingered behind his dismissal of the others, still standing over the final deceased enemy scout. The dispatched was freshly crushed underneath his Werner Brothers-branded motobicyclette, from which he had been dethroned during a high-speed slip.

However, it had not been the crash that killed him ...

Nor the strike from a bullet impact in his speeding wake ...

It was the medieval war arrow.

The feathery tail of the lodged arrow protruded from the carcass ...

... the signature of a self-proclaimed toxophilite enthusiast.

This soldier was killed by a modern-day archer, who now stood over his corpse with his six-foot strung longbow in hand.

While the rain continued to douse France with a misty dew, Churchill swapped hands with his bow in order to properly adjust his maroon beret upon his dome whilst he laid eyes on the dead soldier partially wedged under his toppled motobicyclette.

The deceased man's uniform tags read *SS (Schutzstaffel)*, like all the others they had encountered throughout the extended L'Épinette ambush on the outskirts of this nothing town. The fact that these scouts were a part of Hitler's cruel and despotic fanatical assault division sourced even less sympathy for the fallen, however Churchill's loitering upon this man's fresh cadaver was not out of any self-reflection or forced moral inquisition. The man known as Mad Jack saw no value held in such regard.

More specifically, the Nazi insignia indicated that he was from a specific unit: *the 3rd SS Panzer Division Totenkopf.* This was an unambiguous response to his men's prior inquiry to the probability of looming doom in the form of German armoured tanks, of which there was now an ominous hum in the closing distance, hence their sudden retreat into L'Épinette.

Churchill focused on the feathery flights on the end of the arrow protruding from the man's skull. The war arrow had grotesquely penetrated through his open mouth, piercing between his grimacing and now broken teeth. The acute bodkin tip of the arrow had punctured his brain, fractured his skull, and finally ended its flight path midway out the top of his forehead, making him the world's first fascist unicorn.

Squinting with mild displeasure, Jack inadvertently attested to the ghastly sight upon the intention of interacting with the dead. In doing so, he recalled a recent quote from a powerful Englishman and new Prime Minister (of non-relation) about politeness on the battlefield.

"Sorry, chap, I think I may need this back if it's all the same to you," Churchill said with respect, forever well-mannered. He reached down and tensely gripped the end of his bodkin-tipped arrow by the stem, placing a firm boot against the cold Nazi's breastbone to hold the dead body stable. Employing a firm hold, he pushed and twisted to release the tip from the corpse's meaty hold, then retracted the arrow with the type of strident wrench one would apply in taking a well-rooted stump from a cricket pitch.

A gruesome *squish* accompanied the withdrawal as he pulled the arrow clear from the man's hollowed cranium, leaving him to eternally rest in the mud. The arrow was fully intact and whole, and so Churchill gave it a wipe on his trouser leg before simply reinserting it into the cylindrical leather quiver that hung aslant over his right shoulder. Due to years of practice, he was able to blindly stow the ammunition like a seamless hole-in-one.

Before he departed, and trail the others back to their defensive defilade along the outskirts of L'Épinette, Churchill's sterling stare scanned south and towards the source of the incoming enemy armada ...

... and then up to the dreary and otherwise depressing sky high above as the clouds groaned with roaring thunder.

His eyes softly closed, feeling the radiance of conflict to come against his skin like the invigoration of sunshine, and a delicate smile curled beneath his neat pencil-thin moustache.

His blue eyes reopened, evaluating the scene from behind his steely stare.

From seemingly nowhere, a peculiar figure in military service dress representing the *Queen's Own Cameron Highlanders* materialized and stepped into focus from over Churchill's shoulder. The uniform was complete with a heavy Scottish kilt patterned with regimental earthly colours of the *Cameron of Erracht.* To top off the eccentricity of the attire, a pom-pom bonnet was aslant this character's head.

It was none other than *Lieutenant-Colonel Sloan MacLeòid,* aka *the Angry Scotsman.* A man long since retired from life when he was killed in action ten years ago in *Burma.* Even in death, the highlander haunt still frequented his finest lad—however unsolicited by Churchill as it may have been. He seemed forever the Sawney conscience on his shoulder.

Sidling up to Churchill from the unknown vicinity of his imagination, MacLeòid took in a lung full of air, smelling the scent of warfare in the atmosphere. He couldn't agree more with Jack's sentiment, vocalizing with a Glaswegian growl:

"*Storm's comin', laddie ...*"

Accepting the impending fate, Churchill's expression gestured understandingly. He was at peace with this pending war.

Mad Jack Churchill declared unto himself:

"It's a nice day for a war."

From his serious stare, MacLeòid's crooked grin beamed.

"*Aye.*"

Unafraid to be visited by this celestial being and an arguable figment of his imagination, Churchill firmly acknowledged his local apparition. Even though MacLeòid's visits were visible only to Mad Jack's own fractured psychosis, in the interest of protecting integrity, Churchill cast a glance to the men of his section, ensuring their distance was out of eavesdropping range.

Colonel MacLeòid cast him his signature scowl.

"Sir, you've got to stop showing up like this ..." knowing it safe to effectively *talk-to-himself,* Churchill responded to his friendly ghost with a discreet simper. "Me lads are going to think me mad."

Churchill lingered a moment longer before pursuing his men.

His soldiers were ahead of him by now, crossing the tall grass field of the clearing. As ordered, they headed back to regroup at the town in the distant view, L'Épinette, approximately 300-feet in range.

After all the running in wet and heavy clothing, Jack found himself rather bushed. He shifted the bagpipes from his hip in order to step over the discarded scout motobicyclette, lifting it from off the deceased German scout. After rolling it out from the corpse, he tested the stability and that the suspension of the vehicle had not been compromised during the crash. Other than being a little scuffed and muddy from the collapse, it seemed operable.

Churchill offered a furthermore to the fallen, effortlessly maintaining his forever well-mannered nature whilst he taxed the German motorbike.

"I shall require this also, old boy. Hope it's no bother."

It surely was not.

Dead as a doornail, he sure as shit no longer needed it.

Over his shoulder, Churchill bore a grin as he throttled the clutch and the bike engine kicked over. The audio was loud and triumphant, as he was in this moment. The reverberations felt through his arms accorded with the adrenaline.

In true Mad Jack style, he rode it adjacent to the tall grass field and into the small town of L'Épinette to meet with his men.

NICE DAY FOR A WAR

The Unstoppable Warpath of the Unkillable Jack Churchill

' No prince or lord has tomb so proud,
        as he whose flag becomes his shroud. '
                                - Thomas Francis Meagher

"Let me know when you're ready for more ..." the hoarse voice of a battle-hardened 1944 Jack Churchill delivered. He sat inside the bottom bunk of his wire double-storey bed in the prisoner barracks within the *Sachsenhausen Concentration Camp* in *Oranienburg*.

They had taken a breather from the man's interminable memoir.

A continuation of the same seemingly endless nocturnal, it remained dark and quiet. Being the middle of the night, their biographical seminar was undisturbed by any of the other prisoners.

Penning through cracked and murky spectacles, *Felix Hardy* was approximately an eighth of the way through scribing the detailed chronicle of this infamous British prisoner of war, obtaining the story of a lifetime.

"Oh, I'm ready when you are ..."

Across from Churchill's bunk on the opposite side, Hardy was also on the lower level of a rusted and squeaky, wireframed hammock, beneath a heavy sleeper above who sagged like dark shade. They occupied the last rows against the back wall of the wooden barracks block, where the countless malnourished POWs existed, packed into the shed like sticks in a matchbox.

The Sachsenhausen was designated inversely to most generalized POW camps, primarily for those regarded the highest offenders of value to the oppressors. These high-profile or political prisoners of war were referred to as *prominenten*—men like Mad Jack and, seemingly, his tagalong American cohort, journalist Felix Hardy.

The wooden-framed wire beds were stacked so close together, most were only accessible from the open ends. The barracks they occupied inside the Sachsenhausen-Oranienburg were home for prisoners of war from all over the globe of Allied nations, including British and American soldiers (typically officers or NCOs of higher ranks) and captured intelligence operatives, Norwegian Labor Party members, Russian and Ukrainian nationalist leaders from the Red Army, as well as anyone with a halfway celebrity status. The Spanish Prime Minister *Francisco Largo Caballero* resided within, a dark man from Tanganyika, several Danish Communist leaders, various pilots from all walks of war, freedom fighters and resistance members, both of alleged and actual status of condemnation. Non-military prisoners also resided, such as teachers, poets, artists, and numerous other men of various other vocal and social political reputations who the Germans deemed too important to execute for fear of loss of intelligence.

Crammed tight in the barracks, the camp was ghastly silent at night.

Bodies occasionally stirred, breathed heavily, or snored. Any movement or shifting of their weight on the wire supports beneath the double-folded blanket mattresses of their extremely uncomfortable beds conducted an orchestra of wretched screeching. At this hour, most people were either sound asleep, sadly deceased, or, entombed in a place worse than death. Some of the men were so utterly depressed that they were stuck in an endless delusion of reminiscing about better days. In these cases, throughout the aligned bunk beds, the only sounds other than snoozing were of these distraught and inconsolable heartfelt weeping wails. Some men preferred the muddy floorboards on the ground to the often-broken timber slat or sagging wire mesh beds, lined with nothing but rags. If any prisoner was lucky, an old boot or balled tatter qualified for a luxury pillow.

It was an absolute permanence of misery, but over time, the men oddly found a bizarre coziness to their predicament at the Sachsenhausen.

In the harrowing gloom, Hardy ceased scribbling in his frayed and torn notepad with his broken stub of a wooden lead pencil and turned the page, ready to continue recording more of Churchill's dictated narrative ...

From his at-ease position upon a rugged hessian sack sleeping swag with a pair of squalid, laceless shoes as a backrest, he browsed towards his friend and held an absorptive gaze.

The journalist enquired from his storyteller. "Where were we up to?"

With a thousand uneasy creaks and torquing wire, the aged envisionment of a weary and bearded Jack Churchill shifted in the shadows of night, alit as an embossed silhouette by the moonlight shining in through their only window.

Unshaven and battle-scarred, this incarnation of Lieutenant-Colonel Jack Churchill was a sight to behold. The wars had aged him, however being imprisoned seemed to have aged him more. Recent indentations of scarring were prominent across his cheek and eyebrow. Fresh uncleaned sores littered his weathered skin.

It was then that Churchill caught Hardy up with just one word.

It was the most relevant word to the entire saga of which the journalist had set upon chronicling, a wordsmith to the imprisoned gunsmith—or more accurately, *swordsmith.*

" *War.*"

Hardy cocked his head, pencil at the ready. "O.K., go."

I
Faultline

1940, May
L'Épinette
Nord Pas-de-Calais, France

Bam!
    Bam! Click-clunk ... bam!
    In defensive positions, British soldiers cycled round after round from their Lee-Enfield bolt-action rifles. To the fullest utilization of precision accuracy and tactical expertise, the men of the Second Manchester Regiment D section held their ground beneath the dreary clouds of a rainy morning against a surfeit of advancing enemy soldiers.
    Leagues of German soldiers, dressed in similar polyspot plane tree camouflage smocks to the scout party they had very recently denied access to the village, trickled through the far-southern tree line. The increasing detachments would immediately obtain offensive positions and engage those asserted within the petite and peaceful French town known as L'Épinette.
    The enemy clutched with a purpose stronger than merely avenging their fallen kamerads in the grass clearing between defilades. They wanted this town like they wanted France: absolute, and in domineering control.
    The brodie-helmeted British peered out from behind strategic elements of concealment across the southern locale of L'Épinette, a once peaceful and untouched landscape of French life turned into a violent riot of carnage, flames, and bloodshed.
    With cracks of force, grenade explosions detonated in the field between the forces, sending brown masses of dirt and smoke upwards, blanketing the land in ash and dust vapour. The deep bass of the explosions were a contrast to the constant exchange of lateral potshot gunfire across the battlefield clearing.
    The once quiet and out-of-the-way town had now become another victim of the ever-growing collateral damage from the vicious whirlwind that was the Second World War. This space south of L'Épinette was an

etched line in the sand drawn of cataclysmic effect. It was in fact regarded as a *faultline* to the impending earthquake of a German armada presently lurking yonder south.

Defending the town's virtue, a scarcity of British soldiers laid between partially destroyed brickwork and walls, amongst spoiled garden beds, and down low on tall grass mounds. They leant out from behind quaint real estates, inadvertently turning what was once *picturesque* into *pockmarks*, and scenes of devastation.

Scattered soldiers everywhere soon became buried in their own brass from spent ammunition casings. Their muddy boots stomped them into the earth as they relocated and repositioned themselves on the active defensive, inhaling their own gun smoke as chain smokers do tobacco.

Panic was present, however, their ability to maintain composure prevailed. The soldiers maintained a stiff upper lip in the face of the German upsurge.

Like the thrashing waves of an inescapable rising tide, the enemy forces crashed against these immovable rocks of the shoreline.

Unstoppable in its strides.

Unrelenting in its purpose.

These men of D section, Second Manchester Regiment *(Second Chesters),* would hold until death or until their fearless leader said otherwise.

Follow him into Hell, they would ...

And on this day, they just might have.

'Good day, readers. Felix Hardy here, again, signing on to bring you more of the unbiased, raw war. Truth be told, it feels like I had barely even signed off. Since 10 a.m., May 27, the very minute we all stepped foot into the minor French town of L'Épinette, I watched the brave men of the Second Manchester Regiment D section in untameable, visceral battle as they bravely held their ground against the assemblages of the advancing German army. Serving under the command of Captain Jack Churchill, the troops are engaged in frequent onslaught with the enemy forces. For weeks, Germany had been looming from the west ... and now, the clash of titans had commenced.

My paid shutterbug, Omar Ny, and myself were right there to witness and record every intense second *of it ... right up until the British could hold on no longer. Retreat was always inevitable, even if Mad Jack refused to see it at the time ...'*

Resident 'Noirs de France', *Omar Ny*, fought his nerves well to perform his job of photographer, employed by American journalist Felix Hardy. The gangly tall, dark-skinned Frenchman was under constant pressure during the tumultuous gunfight, fighting the urge to hide in order to snap pictures of nearby soldiers in combat. He captured many glorious shots of the men as they cycled rounds from their rifles downrange at the enemy across the open field, took cover, and inescapably returned the fire from the distant tree line. A continual match point, the opposing forces were locked in a perpetual quarrel until someone eventually lucked-out. With which, it was then simply onto the next.

A soldier with a chimney plume of smoke pouring from his Thompson submachine gun after expelling magazine after magazine at the German foes was located behind the refuge, close to Ny. Mid-reload, he shouted at the photographer to *'get back'* and to *'take cover'* while the dark Frenchman peeked closer to danger—in order to get the perfect war snapshot. Breaking a sweat, Ny complied. It was insanely dangerous, but part of his job.

The situation was dire and intense.

Soldiers shouted, shot, and reloaded ...

Displaced, discharged, and endured ...

The sound of war was deafening, and the heat was on.

Ricochets and near-misses chipped and flaked at brickwork, fractured ligneous framework and palings, generating clouds of scatter. The raining debris caused splinters to shower down upon the brims of soldiers' Mk. II steel brodie helmets and khaki-clad shoulders.

In lurid cries of invaluable communication, the British men relayed enemy positions, keeping their heads level whilst under fire. Holding their own, they inflicted consistent casualties on the faraway combatants, evident across the distance as enemy soldiers visibly slumped, dropping weaponry where they lay and dropped stahlhelms from their domes.

For elongated portions of time, they started to conceal themselves behind respective cover. Proving to be decent shots, the enemy established firing positions amongst the sporadic array of tree trunks and fallen logs beyond the foliage of the tree line.

They battled the British fiercely and persistently, eventually inflicting several perceptible injuries and casualties.

Across the L'Épinette line, some men discarded their guns, clenching at their bloody wounds with their bare hands and with clenched jaws. They gritted their teeth as they braced under a ferocious fusillade of constant enemy fire whilst their mates dashed in with assistance. Men cried in agony as the burning sensations from their bodily wounds flooded their ability to fight. Warm blood began to flow, pouring from fresh wounds as crimson gore-stained khaki thread.

Across various positions in the town, the British soldiers of the Second Chesters carried on, finally in the diabolic fray of war they had been both equal parts longing for and dreading during the *Phoney War* period.

To them, the war was becoming extremely real.

Out of the frying pan and into the fire, they were burning brighter than ever.

Smash!

Upstairs, in the double-storey building of the French house located closest to the foray, tinkling fragments of heavy glass from a completely shattered window rained down onto the rug-lined floorboards of the home-turned-warzone.

From the upper windows in neighbouring rooms, a duo of loud Bren machine gunners pounded away downrange at the tree line. Shells from their top-fed suppressive machine gun expenditure littered the timber floor, rolling and sinking between slats, in turn causing hot brass to shower down upon the heads of any soldiers on the ground floor.

Retaliatory fire from the distant enemy followed.

Rounds punched into the outer surface. Projectiles chipped away edges of the painted wooden windowsills, causing debris to scatter. Bullets blasted apart the plasterboard as though it were compiled of sand, impacting within the indoors of the household, detonating decorations and shredding paper-plastered walls with a sudden loudening.

The constant onslaught shook the interior, causing a hanging picture frame to crash down onto a wardrobe lining a wall. Enemy fire struck the wooden furniture, causing it to collapse onto the cowering men inside as they attempted to shield their faces from flying fragments.

Down on the lower level of the chaotic double-storey house full of fighting tin hat-wearing soldiers, the maroon beret-clad Captain Jack Churchill emerged from a connecting hall, fearlessly strutting into the dusty space in lieu of the immense gunfire. Squinting, he waved his hand through the vapour of dust and debris. The man seemed undaunted by the hail of incoming bullets as walls still detonated in proximity.

Casually, he temporarily stacked his six-foot longbow by a doorframe, taking the time to adjust his belt strap across his chest and pull taut his sleeves to level. It was for no other reason than to look good.

"The Huns aren't having any!" he stated to the few nearby riflemen seeking refuge within these parts. Thankfully, D section was yet to see the predicted enemy armour they had heard away down the road ...

... but they weren't in the clear yet. Far from it.

"*Sir! This is fucked!*" a soldier by the title of *Corporal Ernest 'Knocker' White* commented loudly, right as the enemy fire in their direction conveniently settled slightly. His voice was a squeal, having been located beneath the window which had just unwillingly accepted an offering of incoming fire. He uncoiled a bloody right fist as he nursed it above his jammed bolt-action rifle, observing the minor ricochet injury he had sustained across his knuckles when the fight first broke out. The injury was now affecting his ability to reload his weapon and, like the rest of Churchill's proclaimed *Merry Men*, his calm was beginning to dwindle in the face of this unrelenting enemy—as well as the pending arrival of a rumoured armoured division convoy.

Churchill cocked his head with regard.

"Isn't it beautiful."

More of his men who were present, alongside Knocker White, stopped and stared confounded. It was as though they had only just come to the realization that their commanding officer was monikered *Mad Jack* for a reason ...

"Got any gum left to clog the hole, Corporal?" Churchill queried, coming back to earth and calming their unsettled nerves slightly with his show of compassion during conflict.

Knocker White had an undying oral fixation with gnawing on chewing gum. No matter the circumstance, he was forever with a piece of flavoured sticky in his gob, however right now he seemed to be uncharacteristically without.

Perhaps he had swallowed it when the shooting began?

"Only joking," Churchill finally regarded, stepping into the hazardous room from the connecting hall and kneeling to wrap a bandage around White's hand. He dressed the wound messily, but tight, essentially putting his man back in the fight.

"Thank you, sir!" Knocker shouted, watching his maimed limb become dressed firm. "If it's all the same, I suggest we fall back and get out of here before that armour rolls up!"

Churchill's brow raised. "You want to leave before the party starts?"

"*Armour?!* What *armour?!*" from his position adjacent in the room D section second-in-command *Lieutenant Gordon 'Gin' Parker* questioned suddenly alarmed. Keeping low from the mayhem, he collected his Lee-Enfield and migrated position, crouching nearby. There was a degree of heightening anxiety present within his tenor, but to be fair, this was the first he was hearing about this new intelligence.

Moments ago, Churchill, along with a confiscated German scout motobicyclette beneath his arms, had returned with a few others from the southern tree line where they had just eliminated the threats of the enemy moto-scouts. This was just *minutes* before advancing enemy movement was spotted in the same tree line and their defending line had become engaged—bringing them to their present situation where a firefight had existed ever since.

Before their return to L'Épinette, Churchill and his forward men had heard the distinct reverberation and tremble of what they deduced to be a large German vehicle: potentially an armoured tank. It appeared to be materializing somewhere farther south of the tree line, and was conceivably a part of a Panzer convoy for which the late scout party acted as a forward reconnoitre.

There was a sudden surge of haste in Parker's voice.

"*What armour, Jack?! What's he talking about?!*"

"Relax, Gin!" Churchill commented at the worry wart, gesturing an open palm and lowering his voice. Straightening his tilt.

The ever-tilted Gin Parker's wide eyes of concern simply traced the seemingly fearless Captain Churchill as he casually strode across the exposure through a shot-out window and squatted close. The odd bullet ricochet punched a hole in the wall nearby, but he paid it no mind. Once down and comfy at a knee, he drew his Webley pistol from his WWI-era leather *Sam Browne* hip holster and crept up higher to spy into the warzone from a windowsill. With a certain elegance, Jack revolved with his arm fully outstretched, and unloaded his revolver out of the broken window and at the distant tree line, aiming nonchalantly towards various targets. He wrestled the kick of the recoil from the six shots before retracting. Sporadic, incoming fire chased his mark.

Under the fretful, watchful eyes of his few men, intervals of returning gunfire scored the shelter by his exposed position, causing him to casually tip his maroon-beret covered head as he carelessly popped the snap clasp on his heavy black Webley, ejecting six empty casings to the floor in order to reload fresh from a primed speed-loader.

Under fire, he was calm and collected as he spoke. "These Huns must be from the *3rd SS Panzer Division.* They ride with balls of steel and tanks made from the chode of a juggernaut."

Contemplating that remark, Gin Parker's expression said it all.

"Why haven't we seen them yet?" he stubbornly asked, disbelieving out of desire, not just because he disdained his CO's perception. The man had a permanent contempt for Churchill's living eccentricities, and his lack of urgency right now was not ameliorating that disfavour.

"Tanks are a lot slower, snaking along winding roads. Meanwhile the knackwurst knobheads on foot can arrive through flat terrain, slotting between trees."

After rolling the loaded revolver cylinder with his spare hand so that it clacked like an overwound clock, Churchill accompanied his wisdom with a flip of the wrist that shut the clasp of his pistol, and he ogled his men. He observed a lingering trepidation in their gazes at the thought of battlefield inferiority to German tanks. It was understandable, but their holding of this defensive line was as dutiful as it was doable—for now. Eviction was likely inevitable.

"Don't worry, lads. The armour isn't coming—*yet!*"

"How could you possibly know that?!" Gin, again, with the probe.

Churchill's expression browsed back onto him.

"Because they would have rolled those noisy tin cans up the main drag already! It's why they're holding at the tree line. Huns tactically lead with tanks; they don't use them as backup. They're waiting for their bullet sponges to arrive before they advance on the town. They must have halt orders to hang back ..." Churchill clarified his stratagem, backing his logic with a familiar Gerry narration of recent publicity and controversy concerning the mysterious *Halt Order.*

His inconsequential explanation was not sound or even elaborated on, regardless it was not questioned by his men—not even the fickle Gin Parker, which was a rarity. Honestly, they had no time to argue with Mad Jack's reasoning past a certain point, not to mention dare disobey an order. The time had come for them to completely trust in the man's superlative. They had done so thus far, finally finding them in the fray.

"Well, what about these numbers, sir?" Knocker White queried reasonably from his new position leaning through the doorway from the hall, kneeling on the stairs that headed up and to the second storey that housed the noisy machine gunners which included the section's heavy gun: the Vickers. He took a second to prepare fresh gum from a coated paper packaging with his quaking hands whilst he cradled his gun across his folded elbows.

Churchill raised his chin. "What about them?"

"They just keep stacking up!"

"Numbers aren't everything, lads," Churchill denoted as he pushed off the wall with his pistol down guarded, relocating his position and about to leave the vicinity to do the rounds and check on other men of the section. "They won't advance. Even if they did, there is too much open ground. They'll take too many casualties from our guns, and they know it, so just keep pouring it on them!"

Just then, one of the machine guns up above them on the second floor of the double-storey house boomed to life after being absent for a few seconds, likely to reload or cool down.

The distinctive bass of the shooting identified the Vickers heavy machine gun and who it belonged to—the loud section Scotsman, *Private George MacWilliam*, or just *MacWilly*. He was a stereotypical Scot: muscular, with bright red hair and pale freckled flesh, rather vocal. It was a two-man deployable tubular machine gun he had the muscle to operate solo. Betraying an uncanny and potentially unhealthy connection to the weapon, MacWilly had named *her* 'Vicky'.

Upstairs in a bedroom of his own, he used the water-cooled turret weapon wisely, sweeping in controlled bursts across the enemies in the tree line, so as not to overheat the gun or rupture a barrel for there were no spares present.

The constant barrage from his machine gun, along with the two light Bren machine guns in neighbouring window positions were what was predominantly holding the enemy masses back. They had made for themselves a chokehold on L'Épinette, that was until either the enemy thought to circumnavigate the front and flank the position, or the armoured units of a mechanized column arrived to shake the tree.

"And if they *do* move up?" grilled Parker from the same crowded downstairs room, shouting over the constant cacophony. "They will take L'Épinette!"

"Of that, I am certain. Our job is to hold the line, gentlemen. Not win the war ..." Churchill rationalized, reconsidering his wording on the last bit. "Well, *not right at this minute,* anyhow."

"Jack, D section is built for running *recon,* not ground defence! We're not stocked for this sort of prolonged engagement! We will run out of bullets!" Parker implored with an abundance of logic. The two always butted heads over how to steer the section driving wheel. This was just another day in the life.

"Gin has a point, sir," Knocker White inserted with all due respect. "My hand's seen better days, I'm low on ammo, and I'm almost out of chewy!"

Humour in a time of peril was a unique attribute; a D section custom shared if not instigated by Mad Jack. It caught Churchill momentarily off-guard.

"Pardon?"

"I'm on my last stick, sir!"

Churchill maintained a look as Knocker White formed a grin.

Gin Parker made an interjection with importance. "I've been given sit-reps of a half-dozen men already wounded out there ... we only had a bit over twenty to start with, whereas it seems the enemy has likely got hundreds," and specifically at Churchill: "We need to at least be considering our fall-back options!"

The men within proximity flinched as a stray round from an enemy weapon shot in through the wall, past Knocker White's head, missing him by an inch. It cracked the wooden hand railing that lined the ascending staircase beside him, powerful enough to shatter it to splinters.

A perplexed moment transpired.

Knocker White leaned forward, tipping his cowering view upright at the others. "Did you guys just bloody see that? I just nearly lost me head!"

The decision made; Churchill sauntered towards the hall. Without a care about being exposed to any incoming enemy fire, he strolled across the shot-to-shit room to delegate some fresh orders. In doing so, he stepped up and over a collapsed dining table, fragments of porcelain plates crunching beneath his boots.

"Locate the medic and load the wounded on the truck," Churchill proposed, referring to the big Bedford lorry the retreating men of the *4th Wiltshire Regiment* arrived in just prior to the attack—this was just after their halfwit of a sergeant elected to move his men in a premature advance toward the enemy. They had appeared under volatile fire from these same enemy combatants. With the aid of the Second Chesters, they had flipped the heavy transport back onto what was left of its six wheels and flushed the flooded engine, revving the vehicle back into life. The transport truck had been parked just out of sight, almost midway down the central strip known as the *Rue du L'Épinette*, ready to use in a quick retreat if they so ever needed. It was their ticket out of harm's way.

"Get the wounded ready for evac!" he ordered. "But we must hold out as long as possible!"

As much as these orders were music to his ears, Gin Parker disagreed with prolonging their stay any longer. "Where are you going?"

"To visit the men!" Churchill exclaimed, as though it were gospel for a CO to do such rounds of the frontline. "Never stop fighting, gentlemen!"

After Churchill's added mantra, he slapped Knocker White on the back as he moved about the war-torn home, exiting the room and preparing to call on other men in his section that were scattered throughout the large double-storey house. Bullets smashed randomly into the drywalls as he passed them. Churchill stood tall and without a care as his men stayed low and out of sight.

Right as Gin Parker stepped in next to him, there was a sudden sense of shock. Knocker White appeared to be choking. It called his concern, and he leaned in to view him closer.

"Oi! Are you alright?!"

Red in the cheeks, White mildly shook his head as he recovered from whatever had just ailed him.

"Yeah. I just swallowed me gum ..."

Conveniently, the articulation of the words in Churchill's speech seemed to sound loudly between bursts of gunfire, and his voice reached them upstairs.

On the second level of that same building, young Cockney privates *Wand* and *Macken* heard their captain's sermon and were immediately invigorated with more self-confidence during this battle. After an exchanged look of determination, they bolted their rifles and peered from their positions by upstairs windows, quickly targeting and letting loose more shots at the distant stahlhelms lurking within the shaded tree trunks.

Beside them in the neighbouring rooms, Bren guns roared to life, bravely fighting the good fight.

Not that he had ever intended to cease firing or stop fighting, the carrot-top Scot MacWilly heard the address of his eccentric commanding officer down the stairs.

With a growl that sounded a lot like a pirate, the heavy gunner cried "*Aye!*" in concurrence before homing his winking eye down the battle sights and squeezing the trigger of his large Vickers machine gun in controlled rhythms, as did the milder Bren gun boys next door.

From midway up the stairs, Churchill added:

"Once you all hear *the Cock o' the North,* it's time to retreat. Until then, we hold! If you become low on ammo, make 'em sing for their supper!" he shouted to all those in the surrounds. "We'll make 'em fight bloody hard if they want to take this town!"

"Yes, sir!" Knocker White responded before cautiously leaving the house and entering the street to begin rounding up the wounded men into the truck.

Remaining in the room, the look on Parker's face expressed again his displeasure in learning that their signal for retreat was again about to be triggered by another one of Mad Jack Churchill's eccentric oddities. In this case, a tune from his bagpipes. However, it was at least apparent that retreating to live to fight another day was his preferred next direction.

Parker solemnly nodded towards his questionably sane but unquestionably courageous captain before approaching his junction of fire with his rifle, gaining a solid bead on enemy locations and engaging with distinction.

After watching Parker resume combat, Churchill's head waggled an endorsement unto himself. He was content with this foothold, as loose as the ground was becoming.

To further embolden his Merry Men, Mad Jack collected his resting six-foot-tall longbow before exiting the house. Hands free, he strapped it firm across his shoulder using the strung bowstring and headed outside.

Once outdoors, the volume of the fight increased.

To him, it never sounded sweeter.

Within the perimeter of L'Épinette, the British traded shot for shot with the Germans in the seclusion of the tree line. Exchanging rifles for rackets, the tall grass in the clearing between resembled a tennis green, although this game had several hundred balls in play. Instead of balls, they were bullets.

The morale boost was graciously received by those near him as their captain patrolled the dregs of the defending line, shouting words of encouragement from between cover.

Dashing out in the open to cross the street with nothing but a pistol in his hand, arrows in a shoulder quiver, a bow bound on his back, and a sword at his hip, the sight of the beret-clad Jack Churchill prancing about the danger zone was one to behold.

Exiting each stature of concealment, he extended his arm and fired an aimless pistol shot at the enemy in the tree line in an attempt to cover himself and show formidability.

He moved with conviction and courage, a monument for all those underneath a tin hat to bear witness, and they did. The soldiers watched as their plucky captain frolicked between elements of cover, somehow immune to bullets and enemy fire.

It was hard to tell where the men saw Mad Jack in the same centre-stage spotlight that he saw himself, or if they were just amazed at how brazenly mad this guy was for thinking himself indestructible. Either way, Churchill's methods of inspiration told a tale—perhaps soon to be one of caution.

He relayed word of their fall-back strategy after an arduous occupancy of the town of L'Épinette to his men. However, during his tour, Churchill became targeted by the afar enemy.

He kicked his legs up like a startled horse at a serpent as a line of long-distance, automatic machine gun rounds nibbled at the mud road near his shuffling feet.

Visible and attracting some incoming fire, bullets started to *ping* and *puff* behind Jack's boots as he paraded like a show pony, though he kept his chin up and his head down, and somehow the enemy miraculously continuously missed him.

Moving low, he came in close behind another group of his Merry Men. From the grime of the muddy floor, they glanced upwards upon his sudden arrival, with looks of awe at how he could just simply kneel there, semi-upright and exposed whilst they all lied prone in the bushes.

"How are you lads faring?!" Churchill shouted over their gunfire as he squatted, barely behind shelter. Incoming rebounds and bullets overshot their heads and tore up the wet grass nearby, even chipped away at the stone garden wall cover that protected them.

For some inexplicable reason, all the bullets still missed Jack.

It was almost as if he was protected by a magical forcefield ...

... like some divine intervention prevented his untimely death at the reception of enemy gunfire. Although, he was crouched down, his maroon beret would have stuck out like a sore thumb to the enemy across the way. The iron-sights of their many Karabiners would have certainly traced him across the frontline like a jack rabbit for the greyhounds.

The D section soldiers nodded and gave hand gestures, signalling to their captain that they were okay. This prompted completion and, after a few seconds, Churchill picked up the pace and galloped off to the next group of troops, seeing to them as two of the three riflemen assisted a wounded soldier who had been shot in the abdomen and was writhing in pain.

Churchill slid in close on a knee on the wet grass, keeping his head down as he took in the scene. He kept emotion detached after noticing that it was the young *Private Jett* who had been maimed, a man he knew slightly deeper than most. Jett had been shot in the gut—a little off centre, but not far enough for it to be in any way a relief. Knowing their section medic was at the truck, Churchill ordered the two men to temporarily abandon their position and carry him to the evacuation truck. He would personally maintain their firing position until they returned.

Whilst they prepared to carry him off amid the hailstorm of sporadic gunfire that either whizzed over their heads or damaged scenery, Churchill detached Jett's ammunition pouch and weapon strap, collecting the blood-slicked rifle with both hands as he meandered to the frontline.

Before dropping completely down low with the remaining riflemen nearby, Churchill reached down to his groin area and took the time to arrange himself for comfort during the squat. The soldier and another just beyond him were entranced at their captain's chilled composure whilst joining them in the heat of the battle, unsure whether to accept his unconcerned state as a type of limbering-up and not straight-up naïveté.

Churchill had loaded Jett's Lee-Enfield with fresh stripper clips; two stacks of five from what was known as a speed charger, and he leaned on the low stone wall, gaining a wide angle down range.

Now prepared for this objective, he shouted across the volume to his men. "O.K., lads! Let's give 'em some covering fire on *three, two, now!*"

Joyous to comply, the surrounding riflemen peeked from concealment and conjoined their fire. Unafraid, as was their captain, the men strayed out from concealment a little longer than what felt comfortable.

They pumped round after round at the tree line, cycling fast as they could between fresh targets. The instance resembled target practice.

Aided by that saturation of covering fire, the two men upped the wounded Jett and moved fast to seize the opportunity. In the background, they bolted down the main strip, risking becoming fatalities themselves as the enemies in the hind distance issued shots in their direction. They balanced the wounded and bloodied Private Jett as they ran, shaking him uncomfortably and inflicting necessary pain to the already agonized soldier in order to help try and save him. They would eventually reach the evac truck successfully.

Holding the weapon in firing position, Churchill propped his position higher. With a single eye, scanning across the weapon's sights at the distant tree line, sweeping slowly for motion. Zeroing in, he locked onto a target: a grey-uniformed German rifleman who was doing the same thing, cycling round after round at the enemy.

Bam!

Barely witnessing the soldier take the hit, Churchill recoiled back behind shelter, operating the lever to eject the shell and load a fresh round in the chamber. He envisioned that the enemy rifleman he targeted received that well-placed round through the chest and collapsed to his rear out of sight.

After three seconds of pause amidst the constant rifles firing around him, Jack's beret-clad head popped up again. His piercing baby blues were locked in an intense and tight gaze across the sight of his rifle, and he scanned the tree line furthermore, in search for an exposed target. Whilst doing so, he ignored the ricochets of retaliatory fire against the stone wall at his front cover as puffs of dust blew up before his face.

Mere near-misses ... *not hits.*

It didn't take long for him to find another mark.

He pinched one eye closed, lining up the sights.

Bam!

Another kill.

Churchill withdrew behind cover, repeating like before and charging a fresh golden bullet. He did this again and again amidst a few of his men, racking an emergent tally against the enemy.

After expelling the total rounds left of Jett's rifle, Churchill distributed the remainder of the ammo bag amongst the men at his sides who were starting to run low. He wished the soldiers luck before pushing up from behind the low wall and continuing his errand. Under constant fire, he zipped further left across the battlefield frontline they had created along the skirt of L'Épinette.

He cleared a long twenty-five-foot stretch of exposed area, aiming to skid in low into the bottom level of the southwest granary—where his war had originally begun, and he had loosed the arrow to signal the ambush.

Where he had made history.

Churchill made the distance, outrunning a shower of erratic enemy fire from what appeared to be a freshly established portable heavy machine gun, likely a *maschinengewehr-34 (MG34)* judging by the distinguishable and audible short-recoil rotating-bolt clattering sound that coincided with the shooting, perhaps bolstered by a wide muzzle booster.

They were surprisingly accurate shots across the distance.

Churchill could tell by the rate of fire and velocity at which the bullets chewed up the earth after his feet that the Germans now had a proper machine gun established amongst those trees. This was bad, as it meant they were rooting in for the long haul.

Rounds that overshot him made demonic matter-warping *whoop-whoop* sounds as the projectiles shot like barbs through the air at a subsonic rate. Some of the rounds had phosphorus tracers loaded within them, sketching their trajectories with a golden beam through the air. This showed just how close the bullets came to hitting their fearless captain as he strafed the battlefield, somehow outrunning the Grim Reaper with a relative ease that left onlookers shaking their head in wonderment.

Outrunning the gunfire, Churchill came into the pile of cover beneath the granary at a full speed slide into shelter.

"*Machine gun!*" now swathed in mud and grain from the skid behind concealment, Churchill shouted aloud to those nearby. He propped himself against the rusting metal cover of the parked tractor at the bottom of the granary as it took fire from said machine gun, erupting in a firework display of pinwheel sparks and smoke scatter as bullets pounded it.

Adjoining this position, journalist Felix Hardy cautiously observed everything with eyes the size of saucers, both stunned and amazed.

Nervous and in complete awe after watching the death-defying British captain in action, his pencil had momentarily paused from scratching on the tiny notepad in his sweaty palm.

"Oi, Sinclair?" after the prolonged barrage by the angry machine gun, Churchill probed upwards and at the elevated granary structure. Mud filling the dimple in his cleft chin, he grimaced with mild breathlessness from all the sprinting. He tapped on the metal chassis as though he was room service, desiring the attention of his trusted marksman above in the high tower that stood two-stories high. "Oi, anybody home up there?"

"Yes, sir?"

"Gerry's got a gun. Do something about that, eh?"

"Yes, I see him," the serene voice of section sniper *Private Perry Sinclair* finally responded from the top of his somewhat solitary birdhouse. He was laying low behind established feed bags for concealment, firing selectively to remain as untargeted for as long as possible.

Fast paced, he gained view of the gunner within the sights of the telescopic zoom scope mounted upon his sniper rifle variant of the Lee-Enfield, and reported as he saw it:

"*MG34 ... tripod mount ... single gunner ...*"

"Flick his bellend for me, would you?" Churchill remarked casually, brushing some hay from his sleeves in the process of tiding himself up. Coincidentally after issuing the descriptive order, he *flicked* a strand of debris from his wrist.

"With pleasure, sir."

A view through his mounted telescope across the distance, the lurid resonations from blaring bursts from the MG34 matched the visible muzzle flashes from the machine gun ...

... *wwhizz-THWACK!*

With a brutal hit like a horse kick to the melon, the British sniper put a bullet through his face. Thereafter, the thunderous marksman gunshot echoed.

The German soldier's *bellend*-shaped stahlhelm helmet bounded off and into the background of the tree line, and his head reeled back as though he had been rear-ended at a traffic light. Finally arcing forward from the whiplash, he slumped forwards onto his ceased machine gun, deceased.

From a gory cavity, his head gushed an unexpected fountain of oozing blood like a leaking faucet. The exit wound from the shot had blown out the back of the gunner's noggin, taking with it the soldier's stahlhelm, punctured through as though it were made of mere tinfoil.

Dark discharge leaked out of the newly gained smoking orifice as a pair of neighbouring soldiers observed in utter dismay the sight of their fallen comrade. Whilst they attempted to remove the body from the machine gunner position, blood sprayed out of him like a broken faucet in a rest room, drenching the other candidates for the machine gun position. Disgusted and appalled, the dutiful Germans wrestled to move him from the occupied space, becoming covered in cranial contents and claret slickening. One of the men almost vomited from witnessing the display.

As a result of the thrown spanner in the works of the offensive, the once dominant automatic gunshots from the German line had momentarily ceased.

In the humble granary tower, Sinclair peeled his eye away from his sniper scope after observing the aftermath of his sniper shot, cranking the bolt to eject the smoking brass.

"Done."

"Cheers, lad!" Churchill commented down below, not bothering to rubberneck the takedown. He immediately noticed the absence of pounding automatic fire across the field which accompanied the successful mark. He next eyed Hardy, who was cowering low and tight behind the steel cover of the tractor. He paid mind his shiver and disinclination at present, daring to target him in ridicule.

"You having fun yet over there?"

"Are you kiddin' me, pal? I live for this shit!" Hardy replied, somewhat authentic with the gallantry of his response, however, the out-of-place journalist was hopeless at masking the tremble of his quaking distress and thus Churchill saw right through his charade.

"Yeah, right'o," he derided, revolving around, and peeking over the tractor and across the chaotic battlefront ... and he beamed imperceptibly to himself, talking under his breath at the exhilarating realization:

"*Me too, lad ... me too.*"

Jack Churchill. A rare breed of man. After a few minutes with us by the granary, Jack informed Sinclair and I that when he gave the signal, which was the tune 'Cock o' the North' on his bagpipes, we would evacuate onto or in formation beside the transport truck and depart L'Épinette. After outlining the plan, I watched him in awe as the fearless mad man ran back out into battle, flitting between components of cover, some barely big enough to shield his body from the enemy. A constant onslaught of projectiles whizzed and snapped around him, but his focus was forever unwaveringly stern. Relaying his order to his Merry Men, Mad Jack kept winnowing the frontline, checking in with each of his boys, all the while unconsciously boosting their morale with his unending courage and valour.'

Spread out throughout the tree line, the infantrymen of the 3rd SS Panzer Division Totenkopf filled out in a stretched line formation, taking up firing positions that confronted L'Épinette.

With ample open ground and barely any cover, a frontal advance was still too risky. They took many casualties holding positions between the frail tree line and even more attempting displacements further west around the tree line in a crescent pattern.

The majority of the force held firm stances at the tree line, peering out from behind the battered trunks as the bark disintegrated into wood chipping from the bout of every British .303 sent their way. Suited, they gained decent visibility across the high grass and opened fire at British enemy directions with their Karabiner-98k rifles and MP38 submachine guns, spending thousands of rounds of ammunition and turning the southern façade of L'Épinette into bullet-riddled ruins and decay.

In an attempted advance for stronger footholds, some sneaky soldiers crawled through the long, wet grass reeds, mimicking the serpents that they were. They managed to slither into prone positions in the dips of the field, some partially behind fallen logs.

When more men befell bullet wounds or were killed from the fight, the kommandierender offizier *(commanding officer)* of the opposing forces became compelled to consider breaking their halt orders in this portion of the grid and roll up the tanks. Germany had strict orders not to advance past certain points, and these orders were directly from the upmost top of command; from *Adolf Hitler* himself.

As a compromise, the kommandierender offizier decided that the visible presence of their Panzer tanks may deter the British soldiers from withholding the town. This was a presence, not an engagement, therefore not breaking their Führer's Halt Order. He was bending the rules to suit the circumstances.

Ultimately, a läufer *(runner)* was given the order to relay to advance the tank crews who would presumably comply.

He nodded, picking himself up from the foliage-scattered forest floor with his Mauser pistol in hand, and he dashed past a dozen branch-snapping ricochets, falling back south and away from the boisterously resounding battle zone.

The orders from his kommandierender offizier charged, the läufer sprinted around the bend and towards the nearest town ...

... and towards their parked Panzer armada.

It was time to bring the thunder for this drizzle.

The smell of gunpowder and petrichor scented the air.

In town, Churchill crossed a gap of enemy exposure with a gradual stride. He was barely behind concealment when he stopped moving, red-cheeked and exhausted from all the hasty scampering.

Forever well-mannered, he took the time to kick some excess mud from his boots before returning into the double-storey premises. He pushed open the door to the house for a recess of recovery.

"Captain!" rifleman Private Macken commented from inside the bottom level of the house right as Churchill entered. Lieutenant Parker and Private Wand maintained a firing position in this ground-level room as well. The second-in-command cast his captain a look up and down, taking in his muddy and clammy condition with a look of utter bewilderment, still unable to fathom why on earth a commanding officer would willingly expose himself to such dangers.

"'ave a slip did we, sir?" Macken furthered.

"Whoa, shite! Oi, you okay, sir?" Private Wand questioned in his Cockney accent from beside Macken, noticing Churchill's filthy state as he stepped into the house foyer near the staircase. These two were rather smitten with their captain.

Churchill met their remarks upright though with a grimace at the stitches in his side from the overload of ballistic cardiovascular exercise. "Truth be told, lads ... I'm absolutely fucking spent after that."

In the heat of absolute battle, the soldiers took a second to chuckle at their captain's seemingly irrelevant predicament during war.

With the laugh, Macken and Wand acknowledged his response with confident esteem before they continued into another room to maintain fire support on the enemy.

"Keep up the fire!" Churchill relayed to them and, as well, to the others in the holding household. "Inform me when ammunition is scarce! Allow for some to cover our way out!"

Over by a wall near a shot-out sill, Parker and the other rifleman's ears perked, loving the sound of a possible evacuation from the hellish warfare here in the town.

Jack added, "We will be rendezvousing by the transport truck on my signal."

Parker exclaimed, keen for an exfil. "Yes, sir!"

Incoming ricochets from enemy fire spiked into the walls of the interior of the building right as Churchill climbed the stairs to the second-storey. The collateral barrage of enemy gunfire cut through the plaster wall above his head, and he casually let up a moment and allowed for it to die down before entering the top level, remaining more hidden than usual to the multiple southern exposures.

Private MacWilly was central in the war-torn room, seeking shelter beside a windowsill that had more holes shining light through it than a block of Swiss cheese backlit by a solar flare. The floor was absolutely littered with bronze casings from his heavy Vickers machine gun expel, of which he was in the middle of reloading with a fresh belt from another one-hundred-round ammunition crate. He had gone through two whole boxes already, and this was his final ordnance store. Unbuckled from the tripod mount, he now wielded the gun by force and strength, slamming the piece on windowsills and on propped-up shelves of furniture, man-handling Vicky the way she supposedly liked it.

A sudden onslaught of distant enemy machine gun fire streamed into their direction in the house, punching holes through the drywall and shining white lines of light, tracing stitches overhead MacWilly's position and into the neighbouring room where two light-machine gunners, Privates *Logen* and *Royall*, were both located with their Bren guns.

The continuous pulverizing by the faraway enemy chomped away at the face of the building across the clearing, sweeping back the opposite way after tracing the entire plane. The returning stretch caused Churchill to duck for cover near a toppled wooden wardrobe in the debris-filled bedroom.

"Hullo, sir!" in his Scottish tone, MacWilly merrily commented after the chaos quieted a pinch.

"Hullo, Mac! How goes it up here?" Churchill questioned his loyal Second Chester, prepping his longbow from off his back and examining it for damage from all the running around. Other than it being a little muddy, it was fine. He noted that his customized quiver had now finally been fully stress-tested in the field. Due to the specifically designed magnetic device that was sewn into the reservoir lining, the cylindrical pouch had held his bundle of arrows in place and successfully prevented them shaking out during Jack's erratic movements and dancing about. Perhaps a creator's signature, the ambiguous words *'MD-1, 1939'* were soldered into the leather.

Scotsman MacWilly shouted in report over the noise. "She's a thirsty wench, sir! Gotta keep her guzzling!"

"Glad to hear it! Lads!" Churchill nodded respectfully, noticing Logen and Royall were facing his way through a connecting doorway. They were also taking cover from the machine gun assault. He could see both rooms from his position in the hall.

"*Sir!*" they both nodded in retort. These two were just about buried knee deep in brass casings and empty top-fed thirty-round magazines from all the support they had provided from their Bren guns. When they shifted in their kneeling stances behind concealment, a dozen shells each rolled and tinkered from out of the folds in their uniforms. These blokes would be receiving MVP merits for this battle, for sure.

"How goes ammo?" Churchill requested a report.

"Last belt!" MacWilly grunted as he pushed the lid of Vicky's receiver shut, ready for fire.

Royall and Logen both remarked as follows:

"*Two more mags, sir!*"

"*One more after this,*" Royall reported with haste. "*Permission to get the absolute* fuck *outta here soon, sir?*"

"*Yeah,*" added Logen with an uneasy jitter cloaked unconvincingly behind a gleeful grin. "*We're just abou—*"

Like flicking off a switch, Logen's lights suddenly went out.

The soldier went from alive to dead in a half-second.

With focus upon him whilst he had been communicating to those around him, a bullet unexpectedly passed through the back of his head and out through his cheek, pushing his suddenly limp body over forwards.

...wwhizz-THWACK!

The stray round penetrated the plaster wall across the room.

It caused him to clench his teeth and chomp his tongue. Lifeless, his body simply toppled forward, collapsing with a generous *thud* head-first onto his tipped brodie helmet. The gun and fresh magazine in his lethargic hands spilled onto the floor as a pool of shiny blood began pouring from beneath like a dropped bottle of red wine. The liquid leaked rapidly through the slats of wood beneath the rug that lined the floor, and would be ominously oozing into the room below from above.

Around him, the soldiers blinked, taken aback for a moment.

The gleeful private had abruptly terminated his talking mid-sentence.

"Oh, *fuck!*" Royall cursed, shocked and plunging onto his backside, pushing frantically away from the fatality as Logen's cadaver started to spasm and involuntarily shutter as though his nerve endings were having a spasmodic fit.

Churchill's eyes went wide with numbness and slight dismay.

Eliciting his officer's training, this emotion was fast subdued.

He recalled all sentiment and buried it deep inside.

Quickly, he pressed up from his kneeling position, charging low into the room as Royall sat in stunted disbelief that his long-time service mate had just been killed before his eyes. Churchill placed his longbow down on the floor and prepared to check for a life sign. He halted at the last second, for it was obviously too late. The body finished convulsing as Churchill arrived, and a blank stare declared that Logen was gone, killed by the fateful headshot.

"*What's happenen' in dere?!*" MacWilly queried aloud from the connecting room, just out of view. Too busy to wait around for an answer, he brought up his heavy Vickers machine gun onto the toppled wooden wardrobe he had been using for protection and dished out a few bursts of fire at sporadic targets down in the trees.

He recoiled when a few volleys were returned close his way, and he dropped low behind the cupboard, cradling the big unit of a gun. From his new position, he listened out for an extended moment before shouting aloud. "*Oi! What's goin' on in there?!*"

"Logen's ... Logen's ..." Royall stuttered, barely audible as he clenched his empty Bren gun in close across his chest.

Churchill's focus raised from the deceased man and onto his speechless soldier, completing his sentence because he was unable.

"Logen is dead!"

Churchill returned his view from Royall to Logen.

Carefully using his fingers to close the eyelids of the man's dead stare, he noticed in his peripherals as the blood pool from the body spread and consumed his longbow. The thick crimson liquid coated some of the handle grip and wood of his yew bow. After a brief moment's captivation, Churchill removed it from the puddle as he stood himself up.

In the next room, the report was heard.

A few seconds of silence had followed before ...

"*Proper dog cunts!*" MacWilly breathed fire as he repositioned the hefty tubular barrel of the Vickers back along the thrashed windowsill, again opening incessant fire at the enemy. What was before a steady, cautious, and controlled aim, was now an abrupt, rage-fuelled intensity, shooting extended volleys of hot tracers barbing across the distance. The barrage of machine gun fire crossed the distance and shredded tree trunks, erupted geysers of dirt, even collected a kraut or two or three, mincing them up and even mutilating already fallen dead bodies.

He was throwing back what they had given.

Drunk on the bloodshed, the six-foot-tall Scotsman stood from the partially concealed position as the German's return fire seemed to push him from the windowsill. He lifted the big gun up, supporting it with his hand and continued to push the trigger with his thumb, somehow maintaining the fire through sheer strength.

No longer did MacWilly conserve controlled, short bursts as not to overheat the machine gun and preserve ammunition. Instead, he held in that spade-grip trigger, clutching with all his might and raining down an ungodly distribution of fully automatic gunfire at the enemy in a barbaric sweeping motion, hosing across their frontline like a firefighter dowsing a blaze.

The heavy gun drowned out all other sounds of war, including nearby rifle fire and incoming enemy ricochets. The ear-splitting, thunderous Vickers lit up the battlefield with golden tracer rounds, carving up visible enemy kills in the distance as MacWilly sought enough courage to stand tall and exposed in the open, maintaining a continuous chain of gunfire that drew a streak across the tree line in the distance. His gunfire even dulled out his own battle cry as he roared uncontainable Scottish fury.

The fiery fusillade rained down from the double-storey window and into the enemy line, tracking targets as they hopped from cover and even pulverizing wooden trees to hit those who sought concealment behind a line of sight.

Whole fucking trees collapsed in clouds of ruckus, absolutely laid to waste.

The volley trimmed the tall grass, killing anything hiding in it with upward bursts of red mist.

Foliage greens snipped, dirt exploded in puffs, as did the heads and chests of German soldiers. Limbs were separated by the power of the unrelenting machine gun fire. One particular volley corked a German's leg in the worst way, severing it at the hip as he dashed from cover.

Struck with fear, SS soldiers stooped low in the grass and launched themselves behind cover as the deadly British machine gun over-performed, miraculously without overheating, obliterating their line.

It was right as Churchill was pondering yet another memorable quote of Sun Tzu *'it is the unemotional, reserved, calm, detached warrior who wins, not the hothead seeking vengeance'* that it happened ...

THWisch!

Out of nowhere, a well-placed round from a distant sharpshooter struck MacWilly in the face—specifically, the eye—and he bellowed in agony from the sting as he subsided backwards like a lopped tree trunk, landing with a weighty *thump!* across the casing-littered floorboards.

The subdued Scot's now spent and smoking Vickers machine gun dropped to the floor with a significant collapse. The rim of its thick, tubular water-cooled barrel glowed a vibrant red hue, heated from continuous fire. Overheating, the idle weapon hissed like a boiled kettle.

After the initial shock, MacWilly suddenly writhed with pain, clutching at the bullet wound to his face. Somehow, what could have been perceived as a fatal wound had not killed him outright, even though it probably should have.

Low, Churchill entered the room, eager to assist if he could.

The soldier was in his midst squirming and shrieking as though he was on fire, wrapping his big hands over his stinging eye wound.

No thanks to MacWilly's barrage of suspenseful gunfire from the space in the top storey of the overly exposed house, the wall and window was now the main source for reciprocal discharge by the enemy. Chunks of wooden splinters and dust rained upon them as the building became ground zero for the entire German force to unload their weapons upon, in one conjoined counter-attack of retaliatory fire.

"Mac! Mac!" Churchill called over the onslaught as flying fragments rained down upon their heads like a cloudburst below which they had no umbrella.

Due to all the loose debris and metal casings, Jack was able to grapple deep within the big man's webbing straps and tow, sliding him across the well-greased floor just as the ground gave out beneath them. Due to instability, the floor of the second-storey room gave out, swallowed by the fire below. Light spewed into the room from outside now that the can had been cracked open.

With all his might, Churchill pulled MacWilly into the much quieter connecting hallway right as the cloud of smoke from the big collapse enveloped the area, chasing them. Once clear of the chaos, he next attempted to remove his soldier's hands from the injury to examine the damage dealt.

It was bad and bloody.

The eyeball was gone.

Churchill was no medic, but perhaps it had been sucked in through the entry wound, consumed by suction pressures within the skull. It was a wet, gaping, visceral slurry, hollow and horrible.

Perhaps luckily for MacWilly, there was seemingly no exit wound along the circumference of his head, meaning his brain was intact. Shit thing was, there was likely a bullet rattling around inside his skull. But, for now, he was alive.

Churchill was fast to tear an article from his attire in order to plug the leaking eye socket, replacing MacWilly's squirming hands back upon it to apply pressure. He wrestled with the Scottish goliath to hoist him forward and tie it off behind his head as a makeshift bandage.

They probably couldn't hear it over the blazing machine gun and agonized screaming, but there was now a very distinct reverberation growing in the ambiance ...

One of an ominous, queer foreboding ...

Then they heard the rumble.

Tanks!

"*Jack!*" the voice of Lieutenant Parker shouted with a fresh level of anxiety. He had now upped a few steps from the bottom level of the once humble, now holy French house. "*Jack?!*" he repeated louder.

"What is it, Gin?!"

"*Can you not bloody hear that?!*"

"I've been a little busy!" Churchill froze for a second, able to listen now that MacWilly had quietened down to thrashing squirms and groans as he clutched his blood-glazed face firmly. He grunted firm and tense, maintaining pressure on his head.

Churchill's gaze fell flat and his eyes narrowed ...

Yeah ... he fucking heard it!

Parker implored—and for once, rightfully so. "*It's time to go!*"

Remaining low and allowing for Royall to take over with medic duties, Churchill shuffled over to a perforated wall facing south. From the height, he spied through a cluster of bullet holes down the southern road out of L'Épinette as a queue of huge grey Panzer III heavy tanks crawled up the road in a cloud of dust and chugging mechanical smoke. The monstrous tremble of their three-hundred horsepower engines boomed constantly.

Once heard, the resonance overpowered all other sound.

The clunking of the cumbersome distinct caterpillar treads shook the earth, along with the monstrous throttle of the twenty-tonne Panzer tank. The hydraulics could even be heard faintly buzzing as the turret atop of the unit shifted and panned, directing its 75mm KwK 36 *Ausf.* A-F cannon their way ...

"You know what, Gin ...?" Churchill faced the hall, now showing his exasperation at remaining calm. "This time, you've never been more right."

With assistance from Royall and another nearby soldier, Churchill upped and navigated the vision-impaired, wounded MacWilly towards the door and down the staircase as the room continued to be riddled with bullets in their wake.

"No, wait!" MacWilly cried and fought them with despair, even latching onto the wooden railing as the men escorted him to safety. He glared backwards with his one good eye, scanning for her ...

"Come on, Mac!" brodie-helmeted Royall responded, pulling his cooperation as well as trying to carry his Bren gun.

"No!" MacWilly cried. "Not without Vicky!"

In the chaos, Churchill glanced back in the room, spying the discarded Vickers machine gun and MacWilly's prized possession on a piece of floorboard that still remained. It was unreachable. This unhealthy relationship unfortunately ended now. The gun was heavy, out of bullets, and thus now a surplus.

He relayed the news the best way he knew how.

"My condolences, lad. She's done for ..."

"*Noooo!*" MacWilly whimpered as they pulled him away, shedding bloody tears. Perhaps a coping mechanism to hide from the physical pain, MacWilly whimpered and sobbed furiously for his loss.

The newly asserted presence of German Panzer III tanks humming along the southern outskirts of L'Épinette instigated an order to fall back for the surviving soldiers of the Second Manchester Regiment by their commanding officer.

And so, in true Mad Jack fashion ...

In the double-storey building, an intact upstairs window that faced north became suddenly kicked out by Churchill. The clink of shattering glass was audible above the deep rumble of the arriving tanks, still 350-feet away to the southern outskirts of L'Épinette.

The continual shooting from the German forces had begun to die down, as had the stonewalling resistance by the British troops. This was both due to minimal remaining ammunition and now, their fearful retreat before the arrival of the dominant mechanized column coming their way.

Up on the window ledge that surveyed the small French town, overlooking the parked troop carrier that was full of the wounded and sentries, Churchill got on his bagpipes—always ready for a song at a moment's notice—and started blasting away their signal for retreat. The Scottish bagpipes were a 1931 edition *Robertson of Edinburgh*, housed in a dark red and black tartan bag stowed within a 37 pattern khaki haversack. They were custom constructed and comprised of African blackwood, engraved and hallmarked in full silver. The set was arguably too heavy to take to war ... but that hadn't stopped Mad Jack so far.

Soldiers everywhere heard the hum of the Scottish instrument's purr as it blocked every earhole like a build-up of pressure. The oscillation was followed promptly by the pitching skirl that cut through the deaf tone like a razor-sharp knife through the brain sponge.

Albeit an obnoxious sound, it was music to the ears of the British troops for multiple reasons, though mainly the one that it was the fall-back signal they each furtively forestalled.

It was *the Cock o' the North*, a somewhat familiar tune, and it couldn't have come at a better time, considering most of them had started clicking empty of bullets or were down to their final few rounds. The arrival of the enemy's armoured tanks was yet another dire strait placed upon the camel's quaking back.

Upon hearing the skirl of the bagpipes, men everywhere pushed up from their defensive positions across the southern facing of L'Épinette and hauled ass back onto the main strip of town—often chased by enemy gunfire and pot-shots. Around a short bend from the action of the line, a repaired Bedford OYD open air troop carrier idled in wait to ferry them into retreat.

Wounded soldiers had already been piled onto the floor of its open tray along with section medic, *Corporal Charles Greene*, a recent addition to the section inherited from *Captain Mason's* Second Manchester Regiment C section after the battle along the Dyle River, where they sustained heavy losses. Greene was tending to those who needed aid, as were those who were only mildly incapacitated. The truck was practically a mobile triage.

Also assisting was D section military chaplain, *Lieutenant Jos Nicholl.* The supposedly non-combatant army preacher, Padre Nicholl, was a somewhat gaunt fellow, pale in appearance, and with thin-frame spectacles. Due to years of analysing tiny bible print without the aid of a loupe, his pointy face would be forever enveloped in a pair of wraparound eyeglasses with substantial magnification. Churchill had often contemplated if his enhanced spectacle zoom allowed him to see *Jesus Christ* amongst the clouds. The man was a walking telescope, but also a great, generous, and loyal member of the Second Chesters, one of whom Churchill deemed worthy of referencing as one of his Merry Men.

Padre Nicholl was with the wounded at the truck and had been the entire time, overseeing the loading of the injured soldiers. He was now supervising the loading of anybody who couldn't evacuate L'Épinette on their own two feet.

The pipes caused a vacuum of volume through the streets, and Padre Nicholl's acute features turned to observe the ersatz musician, noticing Mad Jack up high and serenading L'Épinette like a parishioner would on Sunday.

He next witnessed as almost all the Second Chester soldiers came running towards them from the active vanguard. They had retreated in-full upon hearing the horn-substitute sound.

Men charged, outrunning the pursuing off-shoots of enemy gunfire. Conceivably from their positions across the clearing, the sights of scrambling men in a full-blown retreat turned the situation into a relative turkey shoot for the Germans in the distance.

An unfortunate byproduct of the withdrawal was a culmination of casualties to the British. Men were struck in the backs as they ran, some collapsed dead to the mud while others were able to hobble away with flesh wounds.

Men nearby intended to quickly bolt from cover to assist those struggling. They were halted by Corporal Knocker White, who cautiously peeked out from the edge of a building to survey the incoming fresh hell from the enemy across the clearing. The only movement over his deadpan expression was the waggle of his jaw as he masticated his chewing gum.

"*Sir?!*" a soldier asked, eager to leave.

"Wait!" White insisted, holding the man and another back with his arm so that they did not aimlessly wander into the incoming fire. He knew something they didn't of their captain's plan. "Wait for the smoke ..."

"*Smoke?*"

Up above them, still leaning out of a window of the double-storey building, Jack Churchill tossed a smoke grenade can into the street. Thick white smoke puffed and fizzed from the head of the compressed container, creating a visibility impairment, especially for the Germans in the distance. There was now a rising vapour wall growing within the vicinity of the L'Épinette central strip, concealing their motives and movements.

The cloud grew thick and dense, ranging from wall to wall of the houses on either side of the main street, providing ideal concealment for the men to run out and assist the downed squad members.

Churchill continued the bagpipes as he oversaw the amassing numbers for the retreat below. Almost everybody had fallen back to the truck, and it was nearly time to go.

From ground level, Padre Nicholl shook his head as his beady peepers raised onto him. Jack Churchill with that bagpipe was essentially the *Pied Piper of Hamelin* right now, bringing in the troops for retreat.

The man was absolutely mad ...

"What is that? Th-that sound?!" still by the granary, Hardy questioned, wide-eyed and squeamish at the sound of the Scottish instrument in the hands of Mad Jack Churchill.

"Hope you can run fast, Yank," Sinclair stated after quickly shuffling down the wooden ladder of the granary shaft with his sniper rifle strapped onto his back for balance. He was done shooting. Once low, he positioned himself like a sprinter behind the shared concealment of the tractor.

"Huh?" Hardy probed, almost grappling onto the soldier as Sinclair prepared to make a dash out in the open from their position under the heavily battered granary tower and towards the Rue du L'Épinette. There was about thirty to forty feet of flat, open land and a garden bed with a low wall which they would need to hurdle, all whilst, most probably, under fire by the distant enemy who had a bead on them.

"Let's dance!" cockily, Sinclair stated, and he sprinted off the mark.

"No, *wait!*" Hardy pleaded, likely too scared to run anywhere whilst the Germans were able to see and shoot at them. Fact was, there was no time but the present and the incoming high tide would only get deeper for them to stand. The deluge would consume them.

A step out from concealment and Sinclair heard the desperation in Hardy's voice, beckoning that the civilian journalist could not make the journey on his own or without further guidance. The marksmen slowed and twisted, staying low and still partially behind cover as to offer a hand of support to Hardy.

Hardy's brown eyes befell his offering, and it was then that he realized that there was truly no way around this. He would have to make the same death-defying dash, and he would be shot at by the Germans as though he was any other British belligerent, spared no altruism.

"Come on, mate. Ready? One, two, th—"

Thwack!

From out of nowhere, the random slug from an enemy rifle struck Private Sinclair in the side of the abdomen. It jabbed him like a surprise uppercut, winded him, and causing him to wobble as though he were sapped of all his energy charge. Growing pale in the face as he discovered the wound, he abruptly keeled over and grimaced in a combination of pain and shock as the reality fully overcame him.

Though untouched, Felix Hardy wore a similar expression of dismay. He had just witnessed the man who had risked everything to try and help him be mortally maimed. His mind may have contained every verse in the glossary, every stock phrase, and every platitude when it came to putting pencil to paper, but right now, he was speechless and utterly mortified at the aghast sight. Unknowing what to say, what to do, how to comprehend this shocking circumstance.

Breaking the moment, a bullet pinged loudly against the frame of the metal tractor that Hardy used for cover, and the sudden interruption tore away his vision of the wounded British soldier. He retracted further out of sight, bewildered, and seemingly petrified.

Another round hit the metal tractor again, this time snapping something off, and another hit one of the large rubber tyres, causing it to deflate on one side, minorly shifting Hardy's propped stance.

The seconds here felt like minutes.

Hardy finally brought his view upon Perry Sinclair, who was on his knees, coiled over in the wet grass and mud slick, clutching at his bloody gut with an awkward grimace as his life departed. Sinclair's weight toppled and he leant forward, finally tumbling onto his side where he rested immobile in the mire beneath the shadow of the granary ... to die ...

After a prolonged moment of reflection, Felix Hardy's eyeline clambered slowly upwards. From his position, he could see the thick, white smoke cloud that covered the fall-back of the Second Manchester Regiment section, and he knew where he had to be in order to not get left behind. And to not get killed.

Heart pounding deafeningly in his temples, causing his eyes to ripple, the American journalist steadied his composure to dash as though the Devil was chasing him. Clutching his notepad and his pencil, he took off the mark like an athlete in a sprint, panting before he had even begun running.

The view of the granary ... of Sinclair's body ... it all faded in the background as he ran like the wind, careful not to slip in the mud. A heavy stomp with utter disregard to the flowerbed in the garden, and he hurdled over the stone wall, disappearing into the smoke as bullets whizzed through the air about his person.

It then became known to him that there was nothing more exhilarating than to be shot at without result.

Claret in the cheeks from puffing the pipes, Churchill twirled from his orchestral position up the top of the town and started down the stairs. Enough of his unique and unorthodox signalling had been accomplished, and although the men had accumulated down before for extraction, Mad Jack was determined to play the entirety of the song as *the Cock o' the North* traditionally only held a duration of 01:48.

He'd be damned if he wasn't able to finish such a brief, reverential tune.

Blowstick between his lips and chanter in his midst, Churchill returned inside from the window, rounded the stairs, and reached the bottom of the ruined and partly demolished, abandoned French home. With a single hand, he managed to prime and lob another smoke grenade out of one of the front windows to further compromise the sights of the enemy on L'Épinette. After a second, the gas can spat and chugged from the tossed device, wheezing thick white smoke into the air, further minimizing visibility for those at the tree line offensive.

Eventually, he rounded a lower-level doorframe that destined outdoors, facing him out into the chaotic connected street right as the sounds of hurrying combat boots trotted in a fast pace up the Rue du L'Épinette to join the exodus.

As they endured a full retreat, random potshots of blind fire from the distant enemy forces penetrated the smoke and either gnawed the street or impacted against the sides of nearby structures. The Huns could not see a thing through the cloud; however, they maintained suppressive fire in their general direction, aiming at the vast smoke-screen and effectively stabbing in the dark.

Churchill casually strode into the open, following after the men who had passed with haste. Nevertheless, he played his tune whilst embarking in leisurely strides as more retreating, panicking men swarmed around him through the smoke, desperate to get away from the impeding enemy aggression behind them.

He finally pulled up to the side of the street, allowing for his men to pass and gain access to the truck as one of the new additions from the 4th Wiltshire climbed in behind the wheel along with a member from the Second Chesters riding shotgun. A grimacing lad sat in the middle, clutching at a wrapped shoulder wound.

Emerging from the smoke cloud last and least, Felix Hardy made eye contact with Churchill as he scampered past, casting a look of angst and dreadfulness over his face, pallid and like he had seen a ghost out there in the man-made mist.

"Come on, come on!" Knocker White hustled at the rear tray of the truck, assisting the wounded. Their lone lorry was now beyond capacity. They had organized for it to carry only those who were wounded or unable to run or walk. Everybody else was about to be in a formation jog alongside of it as they travelled out and away from L'Épinette, lugging behind on foot.

"You! Oi, are you injured?"

"*Wot?*" "*You wot, sir?*" Macken and Wand each questioned, rather confounded as they attempted to leap up and squeeze onto the rear tray of the Bedford.

"Privates, are you injured?" White sternly asked again, obstructing their progression to board with a flat palm.

Cock-legged, the two exchanged a look.

"*Nup.*" "*Nope.*"

"Well, you're on this side then! We're legging it out!" White directed as he jumped down, himself. He adjusted his slanted brodie with his bandaged hand. "The truck is for the wounded."

"Serious, sir?" Wand complained, carting his rifle.

"You mean we gotta *walk?*" Macken asked in a similar tone.

"Yes! Now *move! Move!*" Knocker White ordered, guiding them along. Straight after, he spotted Hardy incoming, holding a hand up towards him as he inspected his form. He seemed injured ... but may have just been fucked from running. "Whoa, whoa, you alright, mate? Where are you hit?"

" *What?*" Hardy contorted, breathless.

"Are you shot?"

Rattled, the yank shivered his head. "N-no ..."

Over him, Knocker's frown formed into a beam. "You look like you've been proper shat on, mate!"

"Felix!" the deep voice of Omar Ny called from up on the tray already. He had managed to secure a seat by offering to help with the wounded. The photographer had put down his camera in order to get his hands dirty, which they truly were. "Felix! Up here! *Allons-y!*" the Frenchman called.

"Get this man onboard before he drops!" Knocker ordered, pushing the civilian journalist up rather coarsely.

"*Oi, sir, what the fock, aye?!*" Macken disputed, distraught.

"You lot wanna carry the lard when he keels over?!"

Both Macken and Wand withdrew, stubbornly unwilling.

"Didn't think so."

Once Hardy was safe onboard and amidst the busy truck tray, the vehicle shifted as from idle, the engine was put into gear and shuddered to life. She was raring to go and to move out.

"*Captain!*" a voice called from beside the truck as the Bedford started to shuttle out, turning right onto the Rue du L'Épinette, headed north and away from the Panzer division and away from the sound of action. The rear smoke cloud mostly covered their departure, however stray shots still punched through obscurity causing droplets of mud to pop and sparks against brickworks to ignite. One hit even rebounded from the rear tray of the truck, causing its occupants to curse and start shielding their heads with their tensed arms and brimmed tin hats.

"*Sir!*" weapon in hand, Lieutenant Gin Parker called, leading the jog on foot alongside the rolling vehicle with a little over a dozen able men while the rest rode in the truck. He was casting an eye backward, spying he who remained: Mad Jack. "*Let's go! We're all here!*"

Down the street aways, Churchill took an extra second to finish his doodlesack tune before walking over to join them as the lorry taxied around the sharp bend at a slow speed, preparing to shift gear and floor it along the strait. When he began to fade in the growing distance of their slow departure, those aboard the open air tray all watched as Churchill waved as if to gesticulate *go on without him.* The bloke seemed more interested in his bagpipes than the retreat.

Didn't have to ask Gin Parker twice.

He'd leave Jack Churchill behind in a heartbeat.

"*Let's go, then!*" Parker slapped the side of the truck and began to hobble after the men. He did not bother to second-guess or argue with their commanding officer. As far as Gin Parker was concerned, if mad lad Mad Jack wanted to hang around and choke on smoke before eventually being captured by the invading enemy then that was up to him, but they were leaving.

Shortly, Churchill concluded the tune with a final burst of air and removed the blowstick from his mouth prior to once again casting them another wave to move out.

The rosy-cheeked captain caught his breath ...

"Press on! Go on! I'll catch up!"

Passing Padre Nicholl in the emptying street, Parker mildly shook his head before revolving around to follow suit with the rest of the men on-foot after the Bedford. He mumbled beneath his breath, "Bloody nutter."

Nicholl shook his head in incredulity.

The last thing he saw before turning his back to follow the retreat was Jack Churchill begin to plod along behind them in an excessively slow pace—

Thwip!

Out of the blue, in a reaction not dissimilar to that of a snake lashing out and biting him, something nipped Mad Jack in the ear whilst he faced downwards, arranging the stowing of his doodlesack over his left hip.

With a tense pout, Churchill winced as whatever it was had stung his ear, drawing blood that subsequently warmly trickled down his nape.

He reached up and touched the tender point on his left ear. There was now a gash and a small groove in his cartilage. The thing warmed like it was fresh out of the oven.

He'd just been shot in the damned ear!

"Ouch," Churchill commented half-heartedly, examining the tack on his fingers after touching the source. His ear and neck now glistened red, and his lobe throbbed like a stricken knob.

"*Jack!*" the voice of Nicholl called back one last time, noticing a sudden decline in his pursuit of their exodus.

"*Come on!*" "*Run!*" called other Brits from the back of the truck.

The crowd support was immense.

Churchill glanced out to them as the lorry faded in the distance and in the smoke of their retreating artificial cloud ... but then he remembered something important. Important to *him*, at least.

Jack held up a finger, indicating them to give him a moment while he stepped across the street, as if he had forgotten something. He disappeared deeper *into* the cloud, seemingly heading back into the fray.

"What the ..." Nicholl murmured.

"Forget him! Suicidal git ..." Parker growled under his breath, bringing his and their attentions forward. "We've got to go! We've got to get out of here!"

Unable to simply turn a blind eye to the madness, they cast the odd glimpse back at the southern end of L'Épinette as they grew farther in distance, almost out of town.

The others on the truck tray sat and watched in awe ...

It couldn't be ...

Would this be the last time they laid eyes on their captain ...?

Swiftly, appearing out from the white smoke cloud, Churchill began to jog with a motobicyclette under his arms. Whilst he plodded along, he would gallop fast enough to try and kickstart the clutch with his heel. The four-stroke, single-cylinder engine of the small motorcycle finally choked to life, and Churchill revved the shit out of it for an instant before hiking a hoof over and leaping onboard.

Looking over his shoulder at the French town of L'Épinette as he left it in his rearview, the nothing town-turned-battleground grew smaller and smaller as he followed the truck north and away from harm's way. He was able to see in the distance, through the dying white smoke he had popped earlier, as movement from the tree line began to stir.

The Germans were moving up.

Due to the apparent Halt Order issued to them by their Führer, he had doubted that they would have used the Panzer tanks against such a small resistance. The Panzer III tanks were just for show, and Churchill would have called that bluff if the circumstances were different ...

Would 'a fought them with his bow and arrow ...

With that, Jack Churchill pulled the pin on his last can of smoke and let it drop with a metal tinkle to the road as he passed over it. It would provide some level of protection for their retreat.

He hit the gas of the bicyclette, chasing after his men of the Second Chesters inside of and around the truck up ahead on their successful evacuation of L'Épinette.

Eventually, he exploded from the visual disruption of the smoke cloud, and appeared behind the Bedford truck and marching infantry.

Most of them were enthralled and glad to see him survive.

Gin Parker's expression fell flat.

Mother fucker.

'I was one of those guys watching Churchill tail us on his petite 216-cc bicyclette—a vehicle borrowed from the enemy of which he now eluded. Omar was beside me, taking some utterly amazing photographs of him on the bike with the backdrop of the smoke rising into the sky above L'Épinette as the Nazis moved into it in our wake. Mad Jack and his Merry Men had fought hard to keep them out for as long as possible and, evidently, Jack would be cited for his duties that day. The bicycle was tiny but surprised us all with its nimble speed, likely a credit deserving of the man who manipulated it.

Jack caught up quickly, remaining behind as we travelled up north and into Richebourg l'Avoué, where we discovered several groups from the BEF (British Expeditionary Force) had congregated. We discovered that of Jack Churchill's section of twenty-eight men, eight had been severely wounded, five killed or presumed dead. One missing-in-action (MIA) soldier, Sinclair, of whom I had the misfortune of relaying to Jack, had been killed-in-action (KIA). I witnessed his demise in the eleventh hour of the fight, and I informed him of his soldier's passing with seemingly more empathy than his commanding officer could muster. Jack's section had been through a rough day. They either slept well that night ... or not at all.'

'The next morning, word came through that the Germans' 'Halt Order' had been lifted, and units of the British war office had therefore declared 'Operation Dynamo' to full effect. The time-sensitive objective of this operation was for the entire BEF to evacuate France via Dunkirk before the Germans could capture the rest of Europe ... and the clock was ticking. The French, Polish, and Belgian troops, together with a small number of Dutch soldiers, were amongst the immense crowds stampeding towards the shore behind the English, climbing aboard the bows of some 800 vessels. These boats were mostly those of the Royal Navy, but also civilian 'little ships' were eventually commandeered to help bring men back to England across the channel. The vessels ranged from fishing boats to private pleasure cruisers which belonged to citizens of England. Commercial vessels such as ferries also aided the force in the end, contributing crucially to the evacuation process.

In the days before what became monikered by history as the Battle of Dunkirk, Jack's section said their farewells to the wounded, putting them onto a truck which was part of a first aid convoy with priority headed towards Dunkirk for evacuation to England. The beloved Second Chester George MacWilly was a part of this wounded rollcall on his way home, at this stage nursing a nasty bullet wound to the eye, yet he would somehow survive to fight a number of great battles with Mad Jack in the future. Other than Jack

Churchill himself, all that remained of the section were officers Gin Parker and Padre Nicholl, then Knocker White, the inseparable Privates Macken and Wand, Royall, Doc Greene, Butler, and a handful of other brave and loyal riflemen.

The Second Manchester Regiment D section took a ticket and got in line for their number to be called to the Dunkirk shores ...'

II
Operation Dynamo

1940, May 28
Hennelle Flanders Fields
Nord Pas-de-Calais, France

The following morning, far away from all the action, *Captain Rex King-Clark* was enjoying his morning tea.

He rested upon a set of questionable chairs and an even wobblier table salvaged from the rubble of an abandoned French café known locally as an estaminet. Since the war, the once humble establishment had been ransacked and picked clean, as were most of the French towns. Entire buildings and houses were left abandoned, possessions up for grabs in bracing for the incoming invasion from the east. The swastika bled red out from the heart of Europe, sending an unavoidable tidal wave France's way, and those walls were now closing in tighter than ever. Total consumption was imminent.

King-Clark was the CO of Second Manchester Regiment B section, and an old friend of Jack Churchill. Best friend, even. He was of medium athletic build and similar age, clean shaven, and recognizable in a crowd due to a persistent and untameable cowlick through his golden fringe line.

This morning was especially delightful for this jolly Brit and his second-in-command, who was lucky enough to be seated with him for breakfast. They were located along the *Rue Hennelle*, soaking up the early morning rays within the vicinity of the rest of his section who had made camp nearby.

King-Clark had also served up to share some plain starch biscuits scrounged from a nearby abandoned home. They were *arrowroot-esque* in appearance, which was a nice familiarity to home. They were a little stale, but enjoyable nonetheless with a slither of butter from what was left in a 4-ounce block he had acquired whilst surviving on tour in France. King-Clark was quite the opportunist when it came to comfort.

Beneath his woollen maroon beret that he preferred to wear in the combat zone rather than his steel brodie helmet (not unlike his eccentric best friend), his brown eyes scanned into the clouds above as they again blocked the morning sun. This was a clear day for what they had been used to so far in typical dreary France. He twiddled a lead pencil between his fingers, searching his mental vocabulary for a word best to describe this morning's events for his diary. There were very few days that eluded his intellectual capture within his autobiographical chronicle, as King-Clark was a keen diarist and life storyteller.

"Lieutenant, what is another word for *'delightful'?"* he asked the officer who shared his ration banquet feast, reaching in and taking a biscuit from the clean serving plate, another useful item of luscious comfort he had acquired by opportunity.

" *'Good'?"*

King-Clark eyed him sharply. "Something with more than one syllable of pronunciation?"

" *'Enchanting'?"* the man finally responded.

King-Clark pondered. "Too *fairytale."*

" *'Nice'?"*

"Too *simple."*

"I dunno then. What about just *'pretty'?"*

King-Clark eyeballed him again. "Bloody hell, lad, why don't I just make it a picture book with that calibre of description?"

The officer across from him shrugged without care, staring down into his breakfast.

A few seconds of silence after, King-Clark's fingers snapped, delivering his following words with a profound nod. " *'Pleasant'."*

In the following moment and as King-Clark's pencil hand scribed in his diary, both seated men swapped a frown before drawing their attention along the road and towards the growing reverberation of an incoming automobile. It was a motorbike approaching from the west, therefore not a cause for alarm, as it could not be the enemy.

The small, overworked motobicyclette came puttering towards them from the drawn-out road running through the flat and deserted *Hennelle Flanders Fields.* An educated guess would perceive the rider originating from the likes of *Richebourg,* which, moreover, presented them as a friendly visitor.

Unannounced, the lone driver of the bike received a partially unwelcome reception from the nearby guarding soldiers of King-Clark's Second Manchester Regiment section until, up-close, the rider became confirmed as non-hostile. Until that moment, the prepared sentries of the camp traced the visitor's entry along the road down the barrel of half a dozen rifles.

As the rider slowed, braked, and parked just off the road aways, King-Clark recognized the motorist. And of course, he should have. It could have been only one man to have made such an entrance.

Jack Churchill.

"Hullo, Jack!" upstanding from his rickety table, King-Clark broadly announced as the engine drone of the motobicyclette snipped silent. Churchill rode the unit in on a playful trundle before braking dead still diagonal from their quaint little set-up. It resembled a war-time picnic on the side of the street.

Churchill had his strung six-foot longbow strapped across the length of the handlebars of the motobicyclette. Mounted over the busted headlamp slung a German officer's cap—*a relic,* so he later put it.

"Hullo, Clark," Churchill aptly responded, flicking out the kickstand with his boot, then stepping over and observing their tabletop feast. "Heard from a little birdy in Richebourg that you twats were camped along this route. Thought I'd sneak out for a wee visit now that Dickey's watching my lads."

King-Clark bowed to the resolve of their overall commanding officer, Major Dickey Allen, maintaining Jack's section while he was gone. It meant he could visit, and he was glad to see him.

Churchill eyed him. "Got anything to drink? I'm rather parched."

"Of course," King-Clark replied after firmly shaking his friend's hand and offering him a seat—the only other seat, currently occupied by a lieutenant from King-Clark's section, who was happily reading an outdated newspaper. The officer who had been comfortably seated understood this as his cue to abscond and did so promptly and without questioning his superiors, taking with him his steel mug of steaming earl grey, and snatching an arrowroot biscuit for the road.

"Word is that we're to ration further; the Germans are making it tricky by flying ahead and bombing all the blasted waterworks ..." Churchill mentioned, staring at their beverages.

"So I've heard. But I'll be damned if I'm not having a cuppa in the morning. An Englishman might as well let the bloody boche have them at that point. Besides, you know better than to challenge my guile. Or cunning ..." his eyes danced around in his mental dictionary deciding on the more applicable word for his penchant for acquisitions. King-Clark offered, "Tea or coffee? Your choice, old boy. BYO cup, though."

"Cheers, lad," said Churchill, accepting the empty space across from King-Clark and the two sat simultaneously, forever upholding good etiquette.

The two captains were quite in contrast of one another at this point in time. King-Clark was yet to see any action pre-Halt Order, and of what he did, he had not gotten his hands overly dirty, metaphorically and figuratively. Churchill on the other hand had done quite the opposite.

He took up the seat at the table, helping himself to the kettle of recently heated water and a metal mug from off his own rucksack webbing. King-Clark paid note to his darkened fingernails and how Churchill's skin was putridly tanned with dust. He grasped the small sachet of coffee grounds from King-Clark's table stash and gave it a tap to tremor compacted grinds.

King-Clark found his state rather humorous, for he had known Churchill for some time, and knew he was habitually particular concerning his personal appearance, exceptionally so. In the past, it had amused King-Clark to watch him fuss in his vanity. He often travelled with a rather large toiletries bag, loaded with nail clippers, files, a razor, and colognes. Fond memories prevailed when they were on their tour of Europe together, when he would watch Jack out of the corner of his eye as they approached some village or town in their automobile. The rearview mirror of their ride would be pulled around and Churchill would check the angle of his bonnet and the sweep of his moustache. He would then straighten his clothes and the set of his bright Macmillan plaid across his shoulder, always sure that his cuffs were of equal length and visible. Everything to utter perfection. Evidently, deep in war, it seemed he cared less about his appearance.

King-Clark observed him savour every slurp of the fresh coffee.

He pushed forward the plate of biscuits, making sure his man was fed and fighting fit.

"You look a state. I always knew you were a grub, but I've never seen you be a dirty bugger."

Churchill sneered. It was a good call, and he was putrid after yesterday's shenanigans in L'Épinette. He was still yet to bathe or change.

"Richebourg's laundry service is terrible," Churchill joshed in retort as he leant in and helped himself to the stick of butter, preparing a perfect spread across the flat surface of one of the wheat biscuit crusts. Absorbing the tranquil moment of the morning, Jack took in the nearby surroundings, namely the estaminet beside them had been slightly ransacked. Perhaps by King-Clark's B section or by the desperate locals when the war had broken out, all the same, Churchill planned on conjuring a witty jab in which he could blame it upon his friend in a tongue-in-cheek fashion.

In a *change-of-topic* manner, Jack kidded whilst surveying the stability of the table of which they dined. "Nice furniture, Clark ... is it not supposed to be reserved for paying patrons, only?"

" *'In times of war, the law falls silent'*," with a lighthearted grin, King-Clark responded poetically, accurately testing Churchill's intellect, where he easily recalled the quote just not quite the author.

The hourglass emptied and King-Clark gave an answer to the puzzle after quizzing his brain-drained friend.

" *Cicero.*"

Mouth full of arrowroot, Churchill clicked his fingers and pointed, quick to issue his excuse with a hoot, hinting insistently that the quiz was not fair because he hadn't had his caffeine yet.

"Cheers for the brew," said Churchill as he brought up the cup.

"Cheers for the visit," King-Clark correspondingly toasted.

The two toasted with metal mugs, keeping the civility real, and it was then King-Clark noticed a smeared line of dry blood which had trickled down his friend's neck from his ear, and had stained the collar of his uniform.

"You all right?" he asked, analysing the wound and gesturing a hand towards it. "Nip yourself shaving, eh?"

"Oh," Churchill bobbed, acting as if he had forgotten about the injury on his left ear. It had dried and scabbed over, but as he ran his fingers tenderly across the wound, he was reminded of how there was a little chunk missing, blown off by a vagrant bullet. With a haphazard tone, he explained it willy-nilly, "Stray round from an enemy machine gun yesterday ... clipped me."

King-Clark stressed, concerned and bewildered. "Wait, really?"

"Yes. 'tis nothing but a graze. My lads told me to run, but I was too tired."

The two shared a chortle at Churchill's carefree remark to the incident of almost getting his head blown off whilst they enjoyed their hot beverages.

"Yes, I heard about L'Épinette," said King-Clark, axing the mild eeriness that followed. "Textbook ambush followed by a stellar hold, as I understand it. So do the chiefs upstairs."

"Eh," Churchill scoffed modestly, figuring word would have gotten around about D section's encounter with the enemy the previous day. "Simply did my job, was all. The men did theirs."

King-Clark agreed with a nod of consideration, then eventually slinking into the hard question. "How many men did you lose?"

"Eight wounded. Five dead," Churchill reported with a noticeable degree of anguish towards the losses. He dwelled for a moment, unable to remain as desensitized to the reality of death as he could at times, especially on the battlefield. "All good men."

"The best," King-Clark nodded, unequivocally agreeing. "So, I take it you've heard about *Dynamo?*"

"Eh. Load of bollocks, is it not?"

Regrettably, King-Clark shook his head. "Apparently not. *General Gort* wrote the PM just days ago. Press says he's leaning towards a total evacuation of our armies from France and back to England. The official codename *Operation Dynamo* ... It's true as of yesterday, and fully authorized. Anyone left will be pulled off the front when their ticket's up, and soon. That means us, old boy. We're going home."

Churchill's expression was priceless. One of repugnance and utter mystification, numbed by the sorrow of depression in the knowledge that this war, his war, might come to an abrupt end ...

"Why?" he questioned with heart.

" *Why?* " King-Clark lurched forward, entertaining the seriousness in his dear friend's misunderstanding of the overall point. "Because if we don't retreat, we'll die. Then England will follow. We've lost this war, Jack. At least this battle of it. What matters now is *how badly* we lose."

Churchill visibly recoiled.

He did not enjoy comprehending this.

"Deutschland has got us by the bollocks ... we have no other option but to return across the channel and lick our wounds, regroup, and defend the King's land if necessary. We can't do that if we're dead."

"Defend? Then what?"

"Wait for the Americans, maybe? I don't know ..."

" *The Americans,* " Churchill scoffed. "Clark, please, that tickles. And in the meantime, what happens to lady France and her people, eh ...?"

King-Clark forlornly shrugged. "History happens."

Waiting for a punchline that never came, Churchill snorted.

What a sad truth that was.

What a miserable actuality King-Clark's simple answer conveyed.

"The frogs will survive, they always do. What choice do they have? They'll surrender and obey their new overlords—for now. There will be little resistances, even smaller ounces of hope, but they will endure as long as they need. However, waving a white flag is a luxury we don't have. Jack, get your section prepared to retreat at a moment's notice. Keep them nimble. Pack light. Most forward defence platoon and company COs have already begun to pull their units back towards the coast, pre-empting the naval evacuation. I imagine the ships will be upon the horizon any day now. Troops are forming queues on the shores as we speak. With all the kerfuffle, it'll be a *first-in-best-dressed* sort of deal ... We should convince Dickey to do the same with the Second Chesters, and pre-empt the order before they sound the horn ..."

King-Clark's latter words fell upon deaf ears.

Jack Churchill was absolutely mystified at the comprehension that the excitement of war might actually be coming to an epically premature end.

"... I'm not even sure why the Second Chesters haven't been given the order to retreat yet. All we're doing is reinforcing a dying frontline, sitting around along the supposed 'faultline', waiting for the earth to start giving out from under our boots. Let's face it, a line of infantry defence is utterly pointless against waves of armoured divisions—an extremely *thin line* at that. Waste of bloody time and men if you ask me. For example, you and your boys in L'Épinette yesterday, fighting a losing battle. They already knew that the Huns weren't pushing up. That fight could have been mostly avoided."

Churchill snapped from his distant gaze, paying attention, at least to the last bit, of which he seemed to take mild offence.

"You think I made a bad call by staying? By fighting?"

"No. God no," King-Clark confirmed, preparing to sip his brew. "I meant *on the whole*. They'll probably give you a bloody medal for that job. A pat on the back from old matey Gort, well-done, jolly good."

Churchill bobbed his head, sure at King-Clark's sincerity.

"No, what I was referring to was instances such as *Le Paradis.*"

"*Le Paradis?*" Jack frowned.

"The massacre? You haven't heard?"

Churchill shook his head. "Been a little busy."

"The news has got every King's man and his canine clenching their fists at the Nazis, showing more brunt than ever, but then old matey Winston is trying to pull us onto the boats."

"What happened in Le Paradis?"

King-Clark further explained after a short pause to drink. "Well, the reports are still coming in and they're unconfirmed for the most part, but, initial word says that it was a group from the *Royal Norfolk Regiment* attempting to defend a small town: Le Paradis. Due to our scarceness in these parts, they quickly found themselves out manned and out gunned. Naturally."

"*Naturally.*"

"Sounds all too familiar, right?"

Churchill nodded, however he partially disagreed with the sympathy sentiment. The Brits knew what they were signing up for in standing up against Nazi Germany. They knew how few bullets and bombs they had going in. Righteousness of this country-sized calibre was never going to be a cakewalk.

"Yes, well, an element within the 3rd SS Panzer Division won that arm-wrestle and captured almost a hundred of our boys, lined them up ... and then shot them. They took no prisoners."

Churchill cocked his head. "But what of the *Geneva Convention?*" he questioned. "Are we not following rules for this warfare?"

"Apparently not. Horrible stuff. A nightmare, really. It's the wild west out here."

"Bastards," Churchill labelled punitively, and deservingly so.

An element of the story caught him off-guard slightly.

"Did you say the *3rd SS Panzer Division?*"

"Yes, yes, 3rd SS," King-Clark confirmed as one of his section soldiers came running over from their nearby established campsite. "There are rumours beginning to circulate of several of these incidents. Le Paradis wasn't the only massacre."

King-Clark spoke to his man about a communique intercepted via radio, and Churchill's mind speculated about the culprits behind this Le Paradis massacre, the 3rd SS Panzer Division ...

... had they been the same men of whom he had relinquished hold of L'Épinette to?

Maybe if he had just held out longer ...

Maybe if he had gotten his men to fight harder ...

"Jack? Oi, *Jack?*" King-Clark called, breaking Churchill from a mindless stare. "You okay? Boy, you really didn't get much kip in last night, did you?"

"The fact I allowed myself to sleep at all is the only real crime here, Clark. We should have all been out there, making a difference. *'Bad men need nothing more to compass their ends, than that good men should look on and do nothing',*" Churchill stated, angrily.

He pushed out the chair, suddenly determined and furious.

"*Burke?*"

"*Mill,*" Churchill corrected King-Clark's literature-rusty brain. They were both educated men, often tossing philosophical quotes at one another, playing the guessing game. "Clark, what are we all even doing?

Sitting here, our thumbs up our bums like a bunch of limp sissies. We should be out there flexing; holding back the Huns as best we can!"

"Well, maybe this news will change your mind," King-Clark started, about to relay the information that was just delivered to him by his man from the camp. There was a transcript, highlighting specific orders for the remaining men of the Second Manchester Regiment in the Nord Pas-de-Calais.

King-Clark paraphrased from it ...

He sighed first after reading the first line.

"Pull out order ..."

Post a sip of his coffee, Churchill said with a grin as though he were promoting a brand advertisement. "Dear sir, I *always* pull out."

"No, Jack, this is serious ..." King-Clark announced, joining his friend in standing at the table. "They're pulling the Second Chesters out. They're pulling us all out, and back to the coast."

Churchill swallowed. "Pardon?"

It was over.

"Operation Dynamo is in full effect. Evacuation will be by the ships of the Royal Navy from the shores of Dunkirk, effective immediately. Every single unit of the BEF."

"So, it's over? Just like *that?*" Jack questioned, plonking down his mug with a mopey frown.

King-Clark downed the rest of his tea and pushed out his chair. On rough terrain, it fell over behind him, and he twisted to view it, finding himself a little uncertain. He pointed, confused by wartime etiquette. "I ... I don't even know if I should pick that up or just ... leave it?"

Churchill shrugged. "Leave it for the Huns to pick up, I guess. Maybe one of the bastards will get a splinter."

Preparing to immediately pack and march on with the new orders to head towards Dunkirk and join the Dynamo queue, King-Clark rounded the table and met Churchill who remained partially lost and in shock from the abrupt news.

"Don't be so melodramatic, Jack. I doubt the war is over ... far from. Remember old mate *Plato* and what he said about it?"

Churchill's blue eyes flickered, instantly reminded of the classical Greek's cite, and instantly discerned, concluding in paraphrase, " *'Only the dead have seen the end of war'.*"

King-Clark collected his belongings from the table. "Best collect your doodlesack and round up your *Merry Men, Robin Hood.* It's time to *book,* as the youths would say."

"By God, Clark," retorted Churchill in disgrace. "You say that as if we've reached the ranks of old men."

"Have we not?"

"Isn't it *old men declare war* and *the youth fight and die?* Take solace in that sentiment, as we're indubitably the latter."

The next twenty-four-plus hours were especially tedious and laborious for the entirety of the British Expeditionary Force (BEF). Nearing night, the men of the Second Manchester Regiment present in or around the Nord Pas-de-Calais in southern France suddenly found themselves focused on terminating all current operations and defensive stations and were immediately falling back to several rendezvous points.

Existing patrols were retracted. Transportation was organized for entire platoons and various supplies to Dunkirk. Coordination of some semblance of an evacuation queue system commenced.

Naturally, Churchill volunteered his section for one of the last tickets, allowing for a multitude of other platoons and battalions to inarguably go ahead.

Churchill's section of Second Chesters, even after becoming amalgamated into Dickey Allen's larger section, remained close-knit to their intrepid leader on this uneventful evening.

Now, more than ever before, they were more indulged and reinforcing of his leadership approach. Although remaining dutiful, his spirited unwillingness to give up the fight was contagious.

"Look at these sad sods," after the deflation of a blown gum bubble, Corporal Knocker White commented from his seated position between the building ruins of a crumbled victim of shelling that overlooked a busy town square within the French commune of *Richebourg l'Avoué.*

He looked as tired as any other of the group of beaten, sullied, and exhausted stray soldiers sitting slouched and speechless as they waited for their CO to gain new orders. There was nothing left to pack up and nothing left to escort along the roads towards Dunkirk.

As trucks and bands of platoons marched north towards the coast, several truckloads of battle-battered soldiers started drifting in from areas to the south. Towns like Richebourg l'Avoué became a halfway point of coordination for a great many men's evacuations to salvation.

At present, the Allies were in a vanguard interlaced with the Axis. There were countless tales of random battles breaking out in all frontline directions, where enemy patrols had unknowingly broken Allied lines and ended up above them on the map, and vice-versa. Confusion and disorientation had started to set in, the enemy inadvertently striking blows between chinks in the armour as the disarray of the pull-back left some regiments in a tailspin.

The front*line* was becoming a smudged *blur.*

After Knocker White had released the comment, nearby him, Privates Macken, Wand and Padre Nicholl lurched their views forwards. They witnessed the retreating soldiers; their masks of grime-layered faces with darkened creases. Their eyes were red and much more sunken. Their cheeks were gaunt and seemed slightly undernourished, as did their energy levels and mentalities on every subject. They each possessed thousand-yard stares, completely zombified.

"Jesus Christ," Macken cursed as he observed the group of shattered souls as they trotted into town. Their gazes barely blinked, tracing the ground before them with an aimless gawk. Their skeletal claws barely able to clench the rifles in their lanky grasps, hunched like numb, old beggars. Their uniforms were darkened with soot and dried crustily by mud and blood, and frayed and torn over the elbows and knees. Their proudly worn country insignias were stonewashed—a reflection of their tattered souls.

"That's blasphemy," Padre Nicholl condemned droningly after adjusting his wraparound spectacles, finding the energy to discipline via the strength of his belief—however, even he could not agree more with the lad.

The men of the Second Chesters watched on with wretched, saddened eyes, full of sorrow and remorse for these men. They, themselves, had had it rough ... but this lot had emerged from Hell. They were distant brothers and cousins in the King's armies. They knew how they felt. Exactly how.

"Cheer up, lads. You've made it through," an Englishman down amongst the crowd of uniformed soldiers bellowed, starting a slow clap. Others joined in applause, and a few of the faces of these new arrivals gleamed about the town square ...

Yet it was not enough to win even a smile.

On the opposite side of the square to where the Second Chesters sections were positioned, Major Allen, Captain Churchill, and Captain King-Clark were standing in a congregation of other commanding officers from other units, listening to orders from a nearby group of radiomen who were drawing on maps. Naturally, they sipped at mugs of served tea and picked from a tray of crackers as they pivoted upon noticing the grand entrance of yet another shot-to-shit band of soldiers.

"Bloody hell," Dickey Allen commented, leaning past Churchill and another officer. Due to his leggy, lanky body shape, it was not a difficult task to see around the other men.

"They're the men of the *Royal Highland Regiment.* That's Jim Reynolds' section, is it not?" King-Clark commented, casting an eye to Churchill. They vaguely knew the man.

"I believe so ..." brow askew, Churchill responded. He was barely able to recognize the man as he strode amongst his soldiers. Downtrodden, shattered, and begrimed from what was obviously tolling subsequent battles with the enemy somewhere southeast, his appearance was quite astonishing. He had literally been through the wringer. He seemed merely a shadow of his previous self.

"Where do you think they've come from?" Allen questioned.

Churchill stood fast, taking in the appearance of the poor lads.

They were nursing injuries, carrying stretchers of the injured and even some dead men from their units. This march was one compiled literally of the walking dead who had seen the worst of war. His response was as real as it was fact.

"France, 1940."

On that depressing note, Churchill decided he was no longer in the mood. He handed King-Clark his unfinished mug of tea and broke rank. He was one of the only soldiers in that square of partitioned onlookers who dared move whilst the men of the Royal Highland Regiment strode into town. Frozen stiff, all those present in the square observed as a more rested unit made way for the broken, tired Highlanders, giving them a truck to load into seeing how they obviously needed it more. The gesture was done without words; the evacuation ticket which had been reserved for these various men, forfeited, for sake of lending a hand to their brothers in arms who needed it more.

As the Royal Highland boys moved in, realizing and thanking the men who made way for their arrival at the base of a Bedford troop carrier, an unexpected skirling tune broke the mood, cutting the overarching tension ...

Jack Churchill's bagpipes.

The beret-clad man strode out softly, marching alongside them, piping a low and gentle pitch. One that was familiar and heartfelt to those who hailed from the United Kingdom.

As did all heads in the town square, the heads of the many crippled men of the Royal Highland Regiment finally began to uplift, hearing the customary skirl as Mad Jack carried the traditional sound of Scotland.

A simple tune he played; a border ballad made famous by *Sir Walter Scott* from the collection *the Minstrelsy of the Scottish Border*.

A reveille of types, Churchill's pipes were received well by all gents present in Richebourg.

'It was the first time I had heard Jack on the bagpipes with my own ears since L'Épinette, where I'll admit I was not paying attention. When the timbre of the instrument's skirl commenced, myself and Omar gave each other a look of hilarity. The bagpipes sounded so foreign and abstract to us. So Scottish. The instrument played by such a skilled musician was more than a well-received notion of ambience or celebration to the British soldiers. The song Churchill had selected at the drop of a dime was heartening, cheery, and quite uplifting on a spiritual and emotional level. It elevated all those troops in the Richebourg l'Avoué town square.

I recall, at first, almost laughing out loud at the scene of the eccentric Englishman busting out his bagpipes and serenading the war-torn area with Scottish folk music ... but as my view panned about that open square, I remember engrossing the looks on everybody's faces. Not a single one was borne of mocking Mad Jack. They were totally absorbed, captivated, and above all, gratified. It was the perfect presentation for that dull atmosphere. He had not intended to 'brighten' or 'make it all better' for those troops of the Royal Highland Regiment, or even all of those arbitrary assortments of British soldiers within the Richebourg congregation ... what he did do, however, was plant a seed of hope and give a much-needed reminder to their foundation as modern-day British frontiersmen.'

1940, May 31
Richebourg l'Avoué
Nord Pas-de-Calais, France

Distant gunshots cracked at intervals ...
  Tanks firing their guns with bass-filled, rippling booming ...
  Fighter planes roared through the navy-blue heavens above, chasing one another, shooting aimlessly into the dawn sky with firework displays of yellow tracer volleys ...
  Explosions detonated in the distance, close enough to bloom upon the dark horizon, visible as dawn broke and warmth began to illuminate the overcast skyline of France on the Friday morning of 31 May 1940.
  Warfare trembled, ready to pounce.
  Faultlines had faltered.
  The enemy progressed and were now a stone's throw away from the British grand congregation at Richebourg. It was now time for those who remained within the refuge to depart and disperse. The eleventh hour of the countdown had been reached before the dial struck war o'clock.
  Operation Dynamo was in continual effect, and the evacuation of the total BEF out of Dunkirk at the coast was ongoing.
  The men of Churchill's Second Manchester Regiment section were one of the last military companies to vacate the town in what had seen days of departures, minimalizing the BEF from France like a draining sink. Reports of perimeter defences and morning patrols encountering heavy enemy advancements were pouring in through both word of mouth and blasting over the radio wire, as were the casualties rolling into town, visual aftermaths of the fact. The retreat horn for those forward units had sounded, reeling them all in for the mass withdrawal.
  Not that many of the soldiers holed up in the town slept well through any of the nights, most of the men of the Second Chesters were already awake, packed, and ready to go at the break of dawn. Their sunken bloodshot eyes gawked at the southern horizons out of town, ears constantly pricked and glued to the skies above. A squadron of nimble Supermarine Spitfires from the No. 222 Squadron out of *RAF Duxford*

engaged with units from an unknown *Luftwaffe* squad of fighters nearby, contesting in an amazing display of aerial combat, attempting to prevent the German air force from attacking Dunkirk like birds of prey. So far, they had proved successful at keeping any Stuka bombers well at bay, turning any formations back towards Germany.

Machine guns on planes buzzed and chewed through the air as crafts zoomed by sporadically, dogfighting with stubborn enemy fighter planes.

Their formations and battles were visible over France.

The sections pulled their attention from the mesmerizing sight in the sky to welcome a string of returning Bedford transport trucks as the cavalcade rolled back into town along with a motorbike escort, bringing with them the brightness of day and the rising sunlight. These six flatbed transports were ferrying load after load of infantrymen north to Dunkirk, where the Royal Navy had berthed many ships to ferry the masses. They would, in turn, load up and convey units across the English Channel and then back again in as many times as they were able. Until time ran out.

Right as soon as the trucks entered the square and constructed a queue for loading up, soldiers from all the few remaining sections emerged from their hiding holes and entered various organized formations.

This included D section, Second Chesters.

After days of waiting, their time had come.

Cockney Privates Macken and Wand, and Corporal White were among the first of the section to emerge from their overnight accommodation inside of an old church in the centre of town. They were surprised to see, again, the stalwart French residents of Richebourg out front of their residences and various holding sites. Their eyes were all up helplessly watching the sky as planes *whirred* about, dogfighting, locked in furious battle. That, or they were scanning the roads out of town, waiting for the street skirmishing to begin, listening for the German march to tremble the cobblestone; for the deep bass of droning tanks to shake the earth beneath their feet as they rolled into town, causing the inevitable unprecedented destruction and mayhem.

Invasion was certain, and resistance was futile.

Churchill met his men as Lieutenants Gin Parker and Padre Nicholl joined them by the trucks just as the vehicles turned and parked in convoy formation. Refuelling, they dropped their rear trays so that the desperate men could clamber aboard.

The rev-head in Churchill could not help but pay note to sets of beautiful Norton WD16H bikes as they rolled in amongst the parking Bedford lorries; the riders providing support by scouting the roads ahead of their journeys. Their riders were in goofy leather caps and large bug-eyed goggle masks, strapped with Thompson submachine guns across the shoulder. Their 500cc engines thundered away, overlapping the bass from the louder trucks as they circled the town square, pulling up near one of the tankers to refuel.

"*The last truck on the end is ours! Mount up!*" Churchill announced above all the engine noise, set on the task of getting what remained of his section out of France now their ticket was pulled, and their number was up.

His tired men quickly fell into line, queuing to mount the tray carrying all their gear, packs, and rifles. They stacked onto the troop carrier quickly and with much haste, anxious to get out of Richebourg and out of Dodge. It was a sensation to cause a shudder, but it had been suggested that the Germans would occupy this town before the day's end.

Padre Nicholl was up first along with Doc Greene, and Macken and Wand, and the chaplain remained at the end of the tray to assist the others of the section aboard with their heavy bags and gear. One after the other he took their hands, pulling them up as they hiked the steep ascension into the Bedford tray and found a seat on the side, filling front to end. Last onboard the truck would be Butler and Royall, followed by Gin Parker, who were still in the process of passing up the bags and extra gear they had been tasked with bringing to Dunkirk.

It was an estimated six-to-eight-hour drive to Dunkirk, not to mention the expectations of delays by either (or both) en route hazard or the wait to even get into the coastal city. Apparently, the roads were backed up.

Churchill stepped up and cranked open the passenger's side door to the tall Bedford truck, the last on this convoy. Lingering a moment outside, his pondering blues scanned the crowds of huddling French residents on the sidewalk as his men boarded, causing the vehicle to wobble and tilt. The civilians all looked the same: men, women, children, all cowered and clustered together on the raggedy edge of what would become an unfortunate existence living a life of occupation. They weren't entirely lifeless, but were certainly entirely directionless. Some grouped together as families, gathered on the front steps of their premises. Others hung out of top-storey windows of the houses, utterly powerless and vulnerable. Some had their bags packed, their lifelong belongings confined to mere baggage, perhaps praying for a ride out of town but too afraid to beg—not that they could afford to take them, anyhow. Their eyes were empty of panic and alarm, constrained by their own ineffectuality. There existed the realization that even if they wanted to, the British could not afford to provide their transportation. All that remained for them now was destitution, dread, and wait. And hopefully, survival. Anxious looks inverted their brows as they held each other with despair, watching the British vacate their town, remaining unprepared for whatever came next along with the rolling treads of German Panzer Divisions. They had no choice but to concede, completely at the mercy of Adolf Hitler and the merciless Nazis of the Third Reich.

These people on the pavement cast desperate pleading eyes upon the British as they piled into their escape vehicles, unable to stay and protect them. Unable to save them.

In amongst the onset of growing pandemonium, Churchill's stare locked onto a particular pair of familiar civilians. They were not residents of Richebourg, just visitors, which he knew personally.

"*Oi!*" he shouted—loud, above the aerial chaos of the planes fighting and the truck engines. "*Oi! Hardy!*"

On the side of the street, just before the steps of the church, stood American journalist Felix Hardy cradling his fedora hat and his dirty dark jacket. By his side was his tall photographer mate, Omar Ny. The two seemed to have been forgotten in all this and left behind. As it turned out, not by accident.

Their views cast towards the truck and the man standing on the metal lip of its footing, clutching to the open door: Jack Churchill. For the first time ever towards the two nuisances, the captain showed compassion with a thumb over his shoulder, signalling the truck's rear tray and his men loading into it. "Jump in, ya pair of sissies. We'll get you out of here."

Hardy took a few steps closer, putting on his lucky leather jacket from a rolled-up ball under his arm and his hat on his head. The trusty article had doubled as his pillow the previous night.

"We're not going," the American announced, yelling loud.

"Pardon?" Churchill glowered. It sounded like he said he *wasn't going*, but that could not be right. He must have misheard him over the noise of the dogfighting and pending war that soaked the atmosphere around Richebourg.

"I said, *we're not going!*"

Churchill dismounted for a minute. It wasn't go-time just yet, as there were still a few of his men loading into the rear tray and casting up supplies to take with them. He stepped nearer to Hardy, but even then, they still had to raise their voices.

"What do you mean, *you're not going*?!"

"We're staying, Captain!" explained Hardy, inclusive of Ny's concurring desire. The tall, dark-skinned Frenchman was basically trembling where he stood in the shade of the huge church, clutching his camera with unmaskable trepidation. "We've got a job to do!"

"You're off your rocker, mate!" Churchill exclaimed.

Hardy shrugged, forming an uneasy smile.

"You're gonna die if you stay ... you know that, right?"

Felix grimaced and flinched as, low in the sky, a German Messerschmitt fell victim to a RAF fighter, which scored hits along its starboard quarter with its crackling machine guns. The propeller engine of the Messerschmitt Bf-109 must have also been struck or imploded due to the impairment as with a loud *pop* and *bang*, and a flurry of smoke poured from out of its nosecone as the fighter begun to spiral and twirl, completely out of control in the airspace above Richebourg l'Avoué for all to witness and cheer at the victory.

Macho British soldiers threw their fists and rifles into the air above their heads as they watched the German fighter bite the dust. The plane was strafed by a Spitfire which shook the ground as it screamed overhead marking the Messerschmitt, which after a plummeting *whiiiiiiir* erupted into a blazing fireball across a patch of field not four hundred feet from the city limits.

Churchill's focus whipped back around to Hardy.

"You *will* die."

"Maybe," Hardy replied humourlessly. "But this is my job, and I know the risks. Can't exactly take photos or write stories of the frontline battlefield from England now, can I?"

"No, I suppose not."

Churchill's view held on him.

Though, it wasn't of animosity, rather, admiration.

When he had first met him, he had never imagined that the American possessed an iota of heroism or bravery. For the first time, Jack Churchill saw Felix Hardy in a different light, the same way Hardy had with him during the ambush in L'Épinette four days ago. It would appear they had both fallen victim to either *stereotypes* or *judging a book by its cover,* or both—only, they'd swapped.

The two men nodded with understanding and certainty, looking each other square in the eye. They shook hands, firm and with nothing less than total admiration and respect for one another held in utter regard.

"Good luck, Felix."

"You too, Captain."

"Call me *Jack*."

Hardy nodded respectfully, but with disagreement. "Captain."

Churchill eyed Ny, in turn casting him a nod with the same esteem before turning to depart.

Hardy watched as Churchill took a few short strides back to the truck and launched himself up into the doorframe, throwing one more look of apprehension about the town of Richebourg and its population as they hustled and hoisted, reflecting nothing but trepidation and hopelessness at this lost cause.

The journalist caught a sense of sorrow beneath the captain's brow.

Subliminally, he put two and two together, recognizing that that local French family—the *DuPonts*—would be left behind in all of this. Prior to L'Épinette, they had allowed for the British to camp on their property and had been very hospitable to the troops. Churchill and his unit had become fond of them—Jack, *more than most.* By abandoning the people of Richebourg, they were forsaking them, too. The war and the BEF's evacuation were all the more real for him in that repute ... it became obvious in Churchill's stare.

"Captain!" Hardy bellowed, catching Churchill before he could close the door, now sitting, facing out of the cabin. He made sure that he could see and hear him before continuing. "It's not a desertion! You're not abandoning anyone here, y'know ..."

Not only did he hear him, but Churchill listened.

Hardy added a much-needed sentiment along with a waving salute. "*'For he that fights and runs away, may live to fight another day'.*"

Jack pulled shut the heavy door, leaning out of the window to catch the quote that Hardy pitched, rather surprised at the intellect. Another reminder about how he may have been wrong about the man.

"*Goldsmith,*" he answered correctly.

An apparent intellectual, Hardy bowed then turned away.

Churchill took a breath, bringing his eyes forward and into the cabin of the truck as the loud throttles of the Norton bike escorts all kick-started, revving the stalling ambiance with the sound of preparation.

A deep cut in its linger, Churchill caught the connotation Hardy meant with the added intent of the quote, too, referring largely to the afterglow state of the DuPont family, particularly eldest brown-eyed daughter, *Ève.* In typical Jack Churchill form, he had allowed himself to share intimacy for her character; that was a nice way of his mental rationale framing that he had shagged her.

Perhaps it would be a non-event ... perhaps it would haunt him ...

In all sincerity, the DuPonts were a perfect example of how Churchill felt about the French, in general and as a whole. Britain had let them down by neglecting them with the withdrawal. At the risk of further romanticism, he felt like he had *failed* France on a personal level, and it was now going to eat him up inside ...

"Eyy, Mad Jack!" a familiar voice shouted from right beside him in the truck cabin. It was a welcome distraction from heavy thoughts weighing down a dismayed mind.

Churchill tore himself away from the helpless views of sentimentality, noticing that his driver was the same sapper from the *555th Field Company Royal Engineers* who had driven his section *to* the Richebourg hub from Dunkirk two weeks ago—what felt like the turning of a world ago. He even recalled his name after the pause and recollection.

"*Cocky Charlie!*"

Churchill scooted his rear end across in the seat and grappled the gent's hand, glad to see him.

"Hey! Hey!" Charlie intervened all pleasantries to draw attention to his own pencil moustache, which Churchill had inspired and given advice on how to groom on their previous, and *only*, encounter. The result was as equally strange as it was unique. "Ya like?"

No wonder they called this bloke 'Cocky' Charlie.

"Charlie, that is one fine caterpillar! I commend you!"

"*Ha-ha!* Ready to get the bloody hell out of this place, Captain Churchill?" Charlie asked, keying the engine. Their engine purred to life like had all the others.

"Thought you'd never ask," Churchill said, polite and chivalrously calm.

"*Ha-ha!* Me too! You're actually my last trip, Mad Jack!"

"Really?" Churchill frowned in all seriousness. He looked out past the filthy windshield of the truck at the remainder of the British presence in Richebourg l'Avoué. All units were either loaded or queued up at the trays of this final division of troop carriers. It was hard to believe, and he thought this day would never come, but this really was the final trip for this, and probably all, transport divisions ferrying men to Dunkirk.

"Fuck oath!" Charlie scoffed. "And thank God! Let's make tracks before one of those bloody fighters bombs us, what do ya reckon?"

Churchill nodded, pushing the DuPonts and France to the back of his mind; Ève DuPont, specifically. Of recent memory of the circumstances, her face, her stare, haunted his mind. Her *amber brown* with a *hazelnut* blush, *honey* glowing eyes silently stared through his soul. The thought of times spent and the level of his adoration of her caused his heart to throb comprehensively with the action of the departure, becoming overwrought with a tremendous sense of guilt.

The truth about this path was, he would possibly never actually see her again. The guilt of his pledge to her weighed the heaviest beside the thought of a lost love.

She was France, and he was the BEF, leaving her damned.

"Let's."

While the pending earthquake of war trembled the cobblestone beneath their feet, Hardy collected his shoulder bag of minimal possessions and conversed about the next step of their plan with Ny.

The two looked about the hopeless surroundings, as Churchill once had, comprehending the melancholy of war for possibly the first actual time.

"Ready?" Hardy asked, after the two watched the last convoy of trucks take what remained of the British infantry presence away from the frontline. These Western outcasts were now completely alone in a dangerous land.

Ny shrugged, unsure.

"This is my last roll," Hardy announced, handing Ny a tube of film. "Make every shot count."

Ny took it, pocketed it. Judging by what was coming, the two would no doubt spend that within a day, then they, too, would attempt to fall back. As non-combatants, they hoped for leniency from the Germanic overlords ... but they did not expect it.

"You don't think we should have left with them?" Ny questioned in his French accent as Hardy collected his things from the ground, becoming laden with his effects.

Hardy thought hard on the topic. The likelihood of their death right now was quite probable, as they had never been farther out in harm's way.

"Oh, undoubtedly," he responded, taking point on their journey's continuation, which was now an eerie one, and without an armed escort. Over his shoulder, he added with a smirk:

"But someone's gotta tell the world this story ..."

Minutes into their retreat from Richebourg, the rolling convoy hit the first of many delays.

One of the multiple transport trucks midway along in the cavalcade on the thin one-way strip of raised earth between sunken marshland fields, overheated and stalled. Men dismounted and the hood was popped open. Smoke poured from the cooked engine, blowing heat in the faces of the driver and unit CO as the two peered to observe the bake like two cooks over a burning roast. The men on its rear tray all stood and watched, unable to do a thing but rubberneck.

"Fucker!" Charlie cursed, slapping the wide steering wheel with an angry palm as they coasted, dropping speed. He brought their trundling truck to a halt behind another three full transports who were all now trapped behind the broken-down unit on the narrow road. "What a cunt of a place to break down!"

Churchill excused his French and lent out the window as the rear bike escort from behind them sped up, zooming past with a thunderously loud throttle that he admired.

He paid note: the reasoning why the trucks didn't attempt to go around the stalled unit was because of the moist marshland on either side of the route. The fields were so wet, they would certainly become bogged under the weight of the trucks and swallow their tyres like quicksand. And evidently so, as up ahead there was a smaller civilian truck left abandoned after peeling from the road, stuck in the sludge.

If the vehicle could not be fixed, the trucks could get around the stalled unit by either unloading its men to reduce the weight and then attempt to dive around the obstacle through the marshland, risking submersion. Or, worst-case scenario, they write the dead truck off and send it into the swamps. This had also been done before during the fast-paced evacuation. Whatever men were onboard it would be forced to march the remainder of the distance.

Regardless, delay was inevitable.

Either method would take time ...

Time they didn't have.

"This happened yesterday as well," commented Charlie. The knowledge of such only added to his disillusionment.

"Oh?" Jack eyed him with a raised brow.

"Aye. These trucks have had quite the workout these past few days, lemme tell ya. Nonstop for over fifty hours now. They're right to keel over like dehydrated mules."

"Will they get it started again?"

"Probably. They'll have to cool it down and give it a rest first, though. Don't worry, Mad Jack, we'll be up and moving again in no time."

"How much time?" Churchill asked, eyeing the side-mirror, where the town of Richebourg was still within eyesight. His concern was valid, as the German Panzer Divisions could be rolling into and possibly through that town any minute now ...

Their Bedford transport truck was the last in the queue, which meant being the first in line to cop a HE shell in the backside.

"Maybe an hour," Charlie guestimated calmly. "Maybe two. Or three."

Churchill sighed.

It was an hour—or two, or three—that they did *not* have.

"What say you about taking a detour, Cocky Charlie?" Churchill opted, gesturing out and to their eastern flank, where there was a farmstead and a property, connected by what appeared to be back-end roads. It was likely that it connected up to another main road and could possibly take them on the route via the town of *Béthune, Bailleul,* and then *Hazebrouck*—the reverse order of side towns that Cocky Charlie had taken them along on their way to Richebourg two weeks ago.

Charlie followed Churchill's gaze across the window, referring to his mental top-down map of this section of France, plotting their route. A skilled driver and navigator, the man knew every route through the Nord Pas-de-Calais portion of France.

"It's risky ... but doable," he gazed at the cunning captain.

"*Risky?*"

"Aye. German units have been spotted around Béthune. With no scout escorts, we could drive right up the fanny of a Panzer Division on its way to Dunkirk. That's just how jumbled everything is around these parts at the moment. Bloody people everywhere. It's madness, Jack."

Churchill rotated around, antsy about their rear exposure to Richebourg. "Well, at least we'd see it coming."

Cocky Charlie cocked his neck. "Touché."

"Let me ask my CO," Churchill said before cranking open the heavy door of the truck and standing outdoors on its frame, where he could speak with his men. In the open bed tray, one of the men closest to the cabin was Lieutenant Parker.

"Someone broken down?" Parker questioned rhetorically, looking past Churchill along with the other twenty men in the open rear tray, eager to progress.

"Yes," Churchill informed, running his idea past his lieutenant, as well as ordering a runner to get Major Dickey Allen's sanctioning on an alternate route. He picked a man nearby to do his bidding. "Private Wand. Jump down and run ahead. Find Major Allen's cabin. Ask him if he wants to get moving ..."

"Sir?" Wand stood in the confines of the sardine-packed tray. The men were packed so tight, they all touched knees.

"Tell him that *if so*, my driver knows an alternate route to Dunkirk to the east. Tell him, if he asks, that it's safe ..."

"Sir!" Wand complied, energetically stepping over and off the rear tray and into open air where he dropped onto the dirt road. He jogged on up ahead to the next truck in the convoy, which was the only other one loaded with men of the Second Manchester Regiment.

"*Safe,* huh?" beside Parker, Padre Nicholl questioned with a raised brow, rightfully questioning the statement.

"It's about as *safe* as sitting here waiting to receive a Panzer tank up the flaps, Padre," Churchill responded, his eyes grazing across their background and the town of Richebourg as it dwindled in distance and in neutrality. He climbed back into the cabin with his focus on the road ahead of the stopped traffic, watching as Wand spoke with Dickey Allen.

Allen eventually leant out and gave them a thumbs up.

Having given the signal, Wand ran back and boarded the truck.

Cocky Charlie keyed the engine and put her into reverse gear, skilfully backing the three-tonne, twenty-foot-long troop carrier over forty feet of single-lane throughfare and to where the side road connected, and they were able to make the turn.

Now trailing behind, Allen's truck followed Churchill's, in which driver Charlie boldly improvised the route the rest of the way.

Slowly, they went off-road for almost two hundred feet, but the land was higher and mostly dry. The trucks then picked up speed on an easterly approach to Dunkirk, which took them along the outskirts of Béthune.

With vigilant sets of eyes, they passed the large French town along its quiet and uncharted northerly peripheries.

Charlie kept them at a safe speed but not excessive, as not to gain unwanted attention due to their tyres screeching or engine revving.

They eventually passed the suspected enemy-occupied town and, finally, the men onboard could allow for their hearts to sink back down into their chests and enjoy the rest of the ride to the coast ...

"Good call, Mad Jack," Cocky Charlie said after they took the gamble and the route paid off. "I think we're ahead of the curve again. Gerry is yet to wreak havoc through this sector."

Churchill lurched to the right in his seat, staring out the window at something grand as they passed by it ...

In the rear tray, commotion started. It was so loud they could hear it in the cabin as men on the right side turned in their benched seat in order to observe what the fuss was about.

"I think you might have jinxed it, mate ..." Churchill responded quietly, fixed on what it was they passed.

The two trucks slowed as they passed the roadside farmstead.

What was once a brown, wooden barn side wall was now coated in splatters of crimson blood and absolutely raked with drilled bullet holes. The back end of the farm had been set alight and was now a charred wreckage, still partially smouldering and gusting smoke wafts.

Lining the wall was a genocide of collapsed carcasses.

The dead were in familiar khaki uniforms.

It was another massacre ...

"Shit!" Charlie swore, heavy on the breaks.

Their eyes immediately sought for shooters lurking in the outskirts, and their rear truck grinded to a halt. Some of the alert men dismounted or stood in the tray, rifles in hand and ready to charge in assistance to those who had fallen ... only, as they gained a stationary view on the slaughter, they knew it would be pointless.

They were all deceased.

Every single man, dead.

Jack Churchill pushed open the door and stood half out the truck cabin, observing the carnage from up high.

Without words, all he could do was breathe heavily.

He cast a quick glimpse at his men in the rear tray, who were upstanding and equally aghast at the sight of the slaughter. It was a war crime in the finest.

"*What the fuck?! ...*"

"*Oh my God ...*"

"*Jesus Christ ...*"

"Stay by the truck!" Churchill ordered, fully dismounting and taking strides towards the scene at the farm. His hand rested upon his holstered sword as he moved up, ordering his men again to stay as he ventured on.

Distraught, the men watched on.

They were shocked and disgusted, distressed and fuelled by a bitter new rage ...

About halfway there, Dickey Allen met Churchill on what felt like cursed, unholy ground, literally twenty paces from off the back road. As the two officers paused, taking in the sight, they paid note to the hundreds of nine-millimetre parabellum casings that littered the short grass at their feet—a common German ordinance cartridge.

Churchill envisioned a couple of Germans with submachine guns standing where they were now, hosing down the line-up of unarmed British prisoners of war as they stood in front of the barn house. The executioners had been standing precisely where he and Major Allen were positioned, not thirty feet away.

"Jesus-fucking-Christ," Allen commented with a severe lack of words striking the scholar. He held a hand up over his mouth as the smell of the dozens of carcasses hit their nostrils and the buzzing of flies was suddenly audible. This atrocity of human slaughter was recent, having most likely occurred within the last day or two.

"There have been reports of this everywhere lately," Churchill remarked.

"This is ... this is *wrong! Unprecedented!* Th-they can't j-just ...? It's against the rules of warfare! It's against the Convention!"

Churchill cast the stuttering Allen a look.

His face read an expression beyond disgust.

Beyond hatred or anger. Even beyond vengeance.

Rather, it held reservation ...

"The Nazis aren't taking prisoners with this invasion," Churchill quantified to his superior. "Why even bother to issue *the Halt Order* and let us fall back in the first place? Why not just hit us with everything, without remorse? If annihilation was always their endgame, then what's the difference here ...?"

"Animals. Bloody animals," Allen remarked as he turned away, back towards their trucks. They could do nothing here but mourn, and they had to keep moving.

His steel gaze tensed as he took in the awful sight of the dead bodies within the massacre. The blood-stained uniforms, the vacant, hollow stares of the departed brethren as they lay amongst the beige grass reeds and mud.

Speechless, Churchill lingered a few seconds after Allen vacated and joined the others at the trucks before a Scottish voice over his shoulder gave voice.

This enemy was ...

"Farken' cunts. E'ry farken' one ov 'em."

Churchill did not have to look to see who the ceremonial uniformed seven-foot-tall haunt was now lurching by his side with a pom-pom bonnet. He knew it was his invisible Scottish friend, MacLeòid.

"Et's what happens when men stop fechtin', laddie ..."

His words of wisdom fell upon Churchill's ears. But there was an offence. "These men hadn't stopped fighting. They were retreating."

MacLeòid's brow raised. *"Exactly."*

Churchill focused forward.

Arguable semantics and tactical predispositions aside, this was a cause for reflection.

"Ne'ver let dis become yoo, Jackie ..."

Finally pulling himself clear from the view, he passed the visiting undead Scot a look of detestation with a hint of planned retribution.

"When tha time comes, yoo git mad, or yoo git dead, aye?"

Jack nodded incontestably.

"Aye."

Lesson learned.

1940, June 1
Dunkirk
Nord-Pas-de-Calais, France

The following day saw the trucks of the Second Chesters finally arrive in the seafront city of Dunkirk. Due to the enormity of the scale of the retreat, many units parked for the night on the outskirts of the town of *Bourbourg,* located southwest of Dunkirk, where they queued for almost a full day. The convoys moved at a snail's pace before finally reaching the outer rim of Dunkirk the next day, the 1st of June. It took all day just to enter from the city limits.

The view of the port resembled something biblical.

Churchill's truck travelled inwards, approaching Dunkirk from atop a slope from a southeast route. The men aboard bore witness to the evacuation process. They winded the streets and passed several French army fortifications in the roads before reaching the tail ends of the queues leading to the docks and the beaches.

Entryways to the coastal town were choked with the horrifying afterthoughts of human mass departure mentality.

Heavy vehicles and artillery tows which would not be making the trip across the channel were abandoned by the side of the road, and made useless so as to hinder the Germans' momentum. Horses which had loyally dragged carts full of refugees since the Blitzkrieg had begun were mercifully put down, and showed signs of butchery from starving troops with no rations left. Piles of civilian luggage and belongings were scattered and strewn about the streets; thoughtlessly lugged the distance by oblivious inhabitants who thought of the evacuation like a coastal trip, uncomprehending that the vessels barely had room for them alone.

And finally, those poor British nationals who had made the distance and succumbed to injuries sustained or victims of the occasional cruel targeting from the Luftwaffe lay under billowing bed sheets and linen, weighed down by whatever was nearby and hefty. Sadly, they would never make it home.

The amass of commotion was frenzied and overflowing with alacrity and potential disorder, yet somehow the British mobilization remained intact. The drilled discipline of the thousands of soldiers in the town and lined up through its streets and along its coastal shore was the only thing keeping order from turning into chaos.

The ocean beyond the land was littered with boats of all shapes and sizes, both military (navy) and non-military. There seemed to be no real rite of passage. It was simply every ship for themselves, taxiing voyages into the docks and pier areas to fill up and then embark back across the English Channel.

The town was a hive of activity, all things military.

Hundreds of armoured tanks and armoured cars cruised the many wide streets, with flocks of a dozen noisy motorbikes tearing through the thoroughfares with grossly reverberating engines, messengers carrying messages and relaying orders.

Almost a thousand transport trucks were stacked in seemingly endless queues, all facing the coast like a giant bottleneck. The line for the ride would be well worth it, as it led to the only salvation available.

Over a hundred thousand soldiers belonging to dozens of different platoons and companies within the British Expeditionary Force, as well as those civilians fortunate enough to have British passports, crowded the evacuation venue.

A string of queued vehicles clogged the main road through the town, proceeding what lingered of the BEF on foot towards the many piers and beach of Dunkirk, where the Royal Navy had banked several large ships along with smaller vessels taxiing in between.

The sight was behemoth and gargantuan.

Joining the queue, their two trucks fell into line midway through the manic city streets. From here, they could see at least fifty vehicles before them, in line, before they could see the harbour and dozens of grey navy ships mooring idly.

They could see the ocean. Beyond that, somewhere through the distant haze ... was *home.*

"Well," Charlie commented, killing the engine. As the sound of theirs died, there was still the ambiance of a hundred different engines and motorbikes about the sunset atmosphere. "Here we are. Dunkirk."

"What now?" Churchill questioned, scanning the impenetrable vehicle and foot traffic in the street, as well as neighbouring streets adjacent.

"Now, we wait. Stretch your legs if you'd like, Captain. We might be here a while before your boys get called up to board a vessel."

Churchill frowned, pressed his head against the cabin rear and sighed. He had been quiet for the remainder of the trip, as had most of the other soldiers aboard both of the trucks in their dual convoy, ever since they had witnessed the massacre at the farmstead yesterday.

In the trucks ahead, men were either seated in the rear trays or out and standing about them, waiting patiently. Judging by their efforts at comfort, such as arranged bags on which to lay and rest, placed down, stacked weapons. Their helmets were mostly off and cigarettes lit. Card games were in their midst, as well as joke recounting and storytelling. Some men even snoozed.

There was nothing else anyone could do but linger in wait.

From the truck behind, Major Dickey Allen appeared by their cabin and stepped up the side footing, peering through the open window to address Jack.

"Section heads say it'll be hours before we're aboard a ship. Better make ourselves comfy. Might even be overnight at this rate."

"Aye," Charlie commented with a snicker. "See that trawler out there with the blue skirting? That was there yesterday ... it would'a started loading this morning, an' it's still there, not even full. Those lads boarding now I probably dropped off two days ago."

Churchill blinked wide.

That information was a real eye opener.

They could be here for *days* at this rate.

"The organization of Dynamo is as good as can be, but slow."

Churchill and Allen took the driver's words onboard, and they both dismounted the truck beneath the dusk setting of Dunkirk. It was a strange vibe beneath the atmosphere. Around their proximity were hundreds of soldiers carrying their coats, guns, and gear, either shuffling in lines or sitting in gutters, smoking, leaning on buildings, conversing with civilian refugees who were still present during all the commotion. Some even slept on the ground, wrote letters or read from dog-eared books using their bags, helmets, or gear as cushion comfort. Some of the more scarred veterans just stared blankly, cradling their rifles, tortured by reminiscing the hard times passed. They could literally do nothing but wait their turn as they gradually moved up the line towards the harbour.

"Well, old boy, I guess we'll be here for a while," Major Allen commented, pressing on his hips, sore from the long drive. "Thank God for Hitler's *Halt Order*, then."

Churchill strained a quick stretch. "Pardon?"

"*The Halt Order?*" Allen elaborated. "If they hadn't given us the time to start preparing this evacuation, God only knows where we'd be at—"

"Ah, yes, *thank God* for Hitler. What a generous fellow," Churchill scoffed with a hint of resentment. The degree of insubordination was rarely shown by the loyal captain.

Major Dickey Allen held a stare upon him, seeing Churchill realize the error in his tone.

"Apologies," Churchill replied. The man was worn, tired, and rightfully so. "I've got a lot on my plate."

Allen nodded, understanding.

"Haven't we all."

Disciplining Jack Churchill was not a rare occurrence, but never for disobedience or defiance. His tone had been offbeat, even for him, and they went back a long way. The two had been cadets together in Burma.

Allen padded him on the shoulder as he stepped over towards their men of the Second Chesters. Some were dismounting the tray of the Bedford while others stayed seated and spread out. "I'll inform the men of the delay. Tomorrow, try and find Clark and B section in this mess, and tee some sort of a rendezvous. Hopefully we can get us Second Chester lads together and on the same ship, yeah?"

"Fine-o-fine."

"In the meantime, Jack, be sure to get a kip in. I haven't seen you sleep since that first night in Richebourg."

They held their words as a noisy Norton motorbike and single rider with leather cap and bug-eye goggles cruised alongside the trucks, probably carrying a message from one end of the queue to the other. All soldiers watched as the bike zoomed by loudly. The rattle of the compact 500cc engines reverberated loudly against the cobblestone streets and narrow architecture of the stone buildings.

"I'll sleep when our boys are safe across the channel."

"It wasn't a suggestion, Jack."

Churchill's bloodshot blues focused on Allen, noting the seriousness of his stare.

It was an order.

Jack finally nodded in accord, turning to step back up into Cocky Charlie's truck cabin to gain some rest. The 555th sapper had since left the cabin, most probably to stretch his legs and smoke a fag cadged from one of the groups of lads spread around the city.

In the solitary cabin, Churchill closed the door, suddenly gifted ... *burdened* ... with silence.

Alone in the quieter truck cabin, Jack stared driftingly.

What was this sensation?

Rest?

His head began to tilt, magnetizing itself towards a comfortable spot as he shimmed down in the seat, finding serenity, and his eyelids subdued to heaviness.

Even at this moment, he was unable was he to deny his thoughts from drifting onto Ève and the DuPont family, and where they could possibly be at in this moment of time. Churchill entertained the thought; the thought of them on their farm, becoming overrun by German forces as they passed by within the next few days, realistically, at any second now, if they had not been already, on their way across this final pitch of European land before driving the BEF off the coast.

He thought about them dreading for him in particular. About his safety, about his well-being. Questioning why Jack Churchill never returned to them like he had promised. Why he never killed all the Nazis and came back for them; for Ève, whom he adored intimately ...

Their vowed knight in shining armour, nevermore.

Evil thoughts haunted him like a bad dream surfacing.

Churchill shook them clear, unable to steer the overthinking considerations away in order to relax his stressed mind. Hopefully, due to his sleep-deprived state, slumber would win the arm-wrestle and he would fall asleep momen ... *momen ...*

Churchill's eyelids fluttered, unable to stay awake.

Lights out.

III
Their Knight in Shining Armour

1940, June 1
Dunkirk
Nord-Pas-de-Calais, France

Awoken from a deep dream, Jack Churchill's bloodshot blues blinked open. Reality shifted, and he was all of a sudden back in the parked Bedford truck, queued through the streets of Dunkirk during the evacuations of Operation Dynamo.

It was night-time, and dark outside the lorry cabin.

Somewhat tranquil, all things considered.

The momentary disorientation was all too real for Churchill. The setting seemed somewhat familiar and how he had last seen it, however a starry night had shifted the orbital scape.

The avenues of the coastal city were mostly lit by bonfires, vehicle-powered headlamps, and decorative but dull Yablochkov candles (a type of electric carbon arc lamp) erected throughout the coastal city.

British soldiers huddled on street corners quietly chatting. Others were sleeping against cold stone walls with eyelines shaded beneath tipped brimmed helmets. Most men stayed in groups and kept confined within the rear trays of the parked trucks. Some were even lucky enough to shotgun a seat in the cozier cabins by the driver's wheel, where many poor souls had no choice but to line the gutters, using their sacks as blankets and their helmets as pillows, lying filthy in torn clothing, a resemblance of glorified homelessness. The soldiers could do nothing but wait, stuck in a type of war limbo between battle and retreat.

Through the grimy windshield of the truck cabin he occupied, Churchill shifted abruptly from his seated slumber, squinting to see through the sullied backlit glass and into the darkened street vicinity. Their position seemed to be exactly the same as when he had shut his eyes, but he could not be certain. The location outside the truck seemed altered since he had fallen asleep. During his deep doze, he mustn't have woken when sapper Cocky Charlie had keyed the engine and crept them up almost an entire block, even around a corner.

Upon a longer examination, he noted that their position in the evacuation queue had moved along. They were now along a street labelled the *Rue de Lille* as Jack read it. The biggest reveal was of locale. This road ran parallel to a shallow canal, and they were literally now within eyeshot of the docks. From here, sound travelled, and he could hear the waves breaking in the night and smell the ocean much clearer than before. Still approximately three or four kilometres from the port, the Second Manchester Regiment still had no certain estimation time for naval departure back to England.

From the illumination of the warm electric hue of nearby sconce streetlight through the clouded windshield, Churchill was able to check his wristwatch. The radiance was faint, but bright enough to read the time:

10:56 p.m.

He had slept about four hours.

Out in the street, commotion stirred alongside the parked convoy and aroused Churchill's attention. He shot a glimmer via the cracked exterior side-mirror on the driver's side. There was a boisterous tone of anger within the tenors of British soldiers as they spoke with heightened abhorrence and ire, and Churchill recognized at least one of the men from his section.

Now conscious, Churchill cranked the metal door and dismounted the truck, dropping his boots to the cobblestone street. The nightscape ambiance of Dunkirk was one of calm serenity, harmonious with the underlining mechanics of labour from the port where ships moored, as units were actively ferried to them. The evacuation may have decelerated for night-time, but it was still in progress, albeit at a much slower and restricted pace.

"Private," Churchill called, closing the truck door and strolling over to the group of soldiers to access the validity of this ruckus. The group of men were a mix of outfits, some from the Second Manchester Regiment, some from another infantry division. The layout of the crowds of soldiers in the queue was chaotic. The familiar soldier he addressed was Private Royall, a machine gunner from his own section. "What's going on here?"

"Fuckin' Gerrys, Captain," Royall partly explained the tone, tearing away from the other angry soldiers who continued on past the convoy and further down the line, relaying some sort of horrible news. As Royall approached, he neglected to keep his voice down, and a clue of disrupt emotion underlined his breath. Others from within the section who were standing within proximity or lounging about in the rear tray sat up and leant over the side, listening intently. "Fuckin' cunts, all of them. Filfy fuckin' cunts!"

Churchill detected the degree of passionate instability within his man's voice. He grappled onto his shoulder, lowering his tone in order to inculcate such with Royall, and the reflection worked. "Oi, oi ... calm down, okay? Look at me. Now, tell me what is it? What news have you learned?"

He took a breath. "Another massacre, sir ..."

"*Another?!*" Churchill's eyebrows rose.

"Where?!" Lieutenant Parker questioned from above them, hanging off the tray of their parked Bedford. He had sleepy eyes but didn't appear to have fully woken from inertia.

"Southwest of Le Paradis."

"*Le Paradis?*" another nearby soldier repeated, turning to somebody next to him in the rear tray of their parked truck. "We passed that on the way here!"

"We did," Parker concurred, recalling. "Are you saying they found more massacres around there?"

Royall aversely bobbed his head.

"This is insane ... How can they get away with this?" Corporal Knocker White added, approaching on foot from a nearby oil drum along with Padre Nicholl, rifles slung on their shoulder via their straps. They, too, had heard the news that was flooding in.

"Initial reports are saying almost a hundred dead."

Churchill breathed in disbelief.

"Yup," Knocker White intensified, quite irritable. "Oh, it gets better; they were all surrendered POWs, too. Not casualties of war, but prisoners."

"So, these guys *surrendered* and were then *executed?*" Gin Parker shook his head, his hatred towards their enemy ever so strong, caressing his unshaven stubble. Execution of surrendered soldiers was absolutely against the rules of the Geneva Convention that outlined the treatment of prisoners in a time of war—a code that Germany still apparently abided by. "They *are* fucking cunts. Sorry, Padre."

"It's okay," Padre Nicholl nodded, tolerantly.

"Shit ..." Churchill stated in utter astonishment, caressing his own chin growth. If he hadn't seen such an atrocity earlier today with his own eyes as they passed that farmstead, and also heard about similar atrocities from his friend Rex King-Clark days earlier, he would have been fairly sceptical at the resolve of their enemy ... but in actual fact, they truly were that malicious. Pure evil.

Royall added, "Le Paradis ain't the only reported massacres. *La Plaine,* near *Wormhout, Esquelbecq,* a town outside of *Lille,* literally a dozen different locations across the region."

"Yeah," Knocker White concurred matter-of-factly, hearing similar stories. "Not just soldiers, either. Civilians, too. Anywhere shadowed by the BEF retreat."

"These bastards are taking it out on the French because they missed the fight ..." Churchill stewed, disheartened. He then quantified, "Fascist fuckwits throwing a tantrum."

Knocker White passed an indeterminate expression around the discussion group. "Makes you think what's going to happen to us if we don't make it on a boat an' out of here in time, lads ...?"

"Not even surrender will save us ..." Royall proclaimed in retort.

"There are endless stories of this sort of shit flowing down the grapevine ..." White added. "Padre and I just met a passerby who was in the unit that found the new one at Le Paradis. They were a section from the 2nd Battalion of the Royal Norfolk. He said it seemed that they had been detached from their regiment during the evacuation order and were falling back. They were pursued by Germans for a stretch before they ended up having no choice but to defend a small farmhouse against an attack by *Waffen-SS* forces."

Churchill silently brooded. Simmering beneath the surface upon hearing the involvement of the Schutzstaffel. He tossed a subliminal glower in the direction of the distant horizon—towards the south-east, towards the enemy. His nostrils flared.

"We haven't been restocked for weeks ... would've been the same for those men. They would have run out of bullets quick and had to surrender to the Gerrys who took them prisoner. Shortly after, they'd have led them across the road to a wall to do a headcount of the POWs, or so they thought ..."

They each listened while Knocker White painted a picture.

"They stacked the prisoners in a line for what they thought would be due processing ... and then proceeded to gun them down."

"Ninety-seven," a voice added from off-side. It was Major Allen, their commanding officer. He possessed insider information, undoubtedly issued in confidence by higher-ups. Beside him in step was Captain Rex King-Clark, who Churchill specifically embraced with a firm handshake.

"Hullo, Clark."

"Jack."

"Ninety-seven. Ninety-seven, confirmed dead," Allen continued amongst all the soldiers, delivering the exact figures. "And that's just what units discovered on their way to Dunkirk. The blokes who found them gave up searching for any supposed survivors from the massacre, but some are believed to have run off into nearby woods."

"*Survivors?*" Churchill whispered, eyeing King-Clark.

"*Supposed,*" on behalf of Allen, King-Clark grimly replied to his friend, then under his breath so that only Mad Jack could hear. "Don't *you* get any ideas ..."

Little promise that cautionary whisper held.

Not when the men under Mad Jack were just as crazy.

The madness was contagious.

"Survivors?" Private Wand commented, eyeing his best mate, the more reserved Private Macken. "What are we waitin' for, Major? Let's go 'n see if we can find 'em!"

He dismounted the truck with his rifle and barely anything else, including common sense, which he always seemed to forget.

"Leave no man behind, right bruv? You can hold our place in the queue ..."

"Too right," Private Royall nodded, ready to gear up with the two loose Cockney cannons. He dropped everything that was not his rifle and spare ammunition. "I had mates of mates in the Royal Norfolk. This is personal."

"I'm with ya, too," another rifleman stated enthusiastically, gaining a slight bit of unwanted attention from nearby soldiers from an unknown unit as they strolled by with their rifles slung and a cigarette in their lips. They cast a glance with interest. They were likely just potential volunteers to this rebellious revenge raid ... though they strolled on after a brief linger.

"Captain?" Wand questioned, keen to move out and go on an adventure, knowing damn well Jack Churchill would be another man mad enough to go with, even hopefully lead.

"Private ... stand down," Churchill ordered, static under the gawk of his CO, Major Dickey Allen.

There was an unusual pause.

Quite the divergent, Mad Jack shied away from exploit and certain excitement. Even the equal ranking Captain King-Clark thought it so, mildly taken aback. There were a few men who had either grown bored of the wait or eager for more action so close to departure who were keen to lock and load and move out at a final chance to punch a Nazi in the face. Besides, serving under Mad Jack Churchill for over the better half of a year, they had inherited his bravery and leap before looking heroism.

Wand questioned, looking a bit miffed. "Sir?"

"I said, stand down," Churchill reiterated, feeling the eyes of his superior officer upon him. He followed up with a quote from *G.K. Chesterton* to all those around him who so obviously sought vengeance for those lives lost in the massacres. "Gentleman, *'a true soldier fights not because he hates what is in front of him, but because he loves what is behind him'.* We must stay true to our objective here in Dunkirk, which is to see us pulled back safely across the channel. We are this close to Blighty, lads. Once home, we will undoubtedly re-stock, re-arm, re-load, and re-plan for an attack against the Nazis, all whilst defending our own soil. We will get our chance at retribution ... but sadly, that chance shan't be tonight ..." in the dissatisfied silence that followed, comprehension by the men could be felt as the words fell upon their ears. Churchill eyed King-Clark and firmly added in a paraphrase of his own fruition. "We live to war another day."

The men about the truck lowered their tempers and, eventually, their guard, settling their vengeful spirits.

Churchill then glanced at the lurking major, who gave him a subtle impressed gesture at how he defused the sudden situation of heightened testosterone emitted from his emotionally distraught men. His best friend, King-Clark, did the same, though not as enthralled. He knew what Jack was capable of, both in war and out of it.

Churchill again faced his congregation of unmerry men, seeing the underlining composite in their eyes. Through his stare, he made sure they knew he was sincere, and they were in esteem.

Little did they know, Jack Churchill was soon to be a hypocrite to such sentiment ...

He placed a hand on Wand's shoulder, soothing him in particular as the others turned away and dowsed their embers.

"We'll get our chance, Private."

Wordlessly, Wand's head bobbed, accepting the directive.

With the assistance of his mate Macken, he tossed his rifle and bag back into the rear tray of the truck and clambered aboard, leaving sleeping dogs to lie.

Before departing the vicinity of the section, Major Allen addressed the surrounding Second Manchesters:

"I recognize the enthusiasm, lads, truly. But as your captain stated: *not today.* I'll give you an update when I hear more, but for now, get some rest."

King-Clark loitered a moment longer until all likely overhearing ears departed from the crowd, and he and Churchill spoke quietly by the Bedford.

"Wasn't it you quoting Mill three days ago? *'Bad men need nothing more to compass their ends than that good men shou'*—

"—*'should look on and do nothing'*, yes, yes, it was, Clark," Churchill sneered, affrontingly. "I simply told them *'do as I say'*, not *'do as I do'* ..."

King-Clark's tense brow loosened as his attention pricked.

"Jack ... what are you scheming?"

"Nothing, Clark," Churchill hissed, silencing his questioning as he stepped away, dragging him under the elbow and away from any prying ears of his men—such as the dirty rat Gin Parker or churchy goodie-goodie Padre Nicholl. Either of those men would gladly see to any form of lone wolf act being annulled immediately.

In those moments, Churchill postponed a more expanded explanation, and King-Clark gave adequate time in which to answer but the forthcoming felt delayed.

Truth was, Churchill was still in the process of planning it.

They halted their waltz far enough away to not be heard.

"Jack?"

"Clark, listen, we're going to be in this queue for a whole nother day, perhaps longer ... I need you to cover for me."

King-Clark rolled his head, "You're not seriously considering running off on your own to try and find these *survivors*, are you? Germany is a high tide washing over France, Jack. Not even *you* can possibly sail through that shit storm."

"I am not afraid of storms, for I *know* how to sail my ship."

"You're quoting *Little Women ... really?"* King-Clark scoffed after identifying the wordplay on the quote from the famous literature. He was surprised he would even know a quote from such a novel.

Jack scoffed, eyeing him up and down. "Why do you know the quote?"

"I don't!"

"Well, clearly, you do?"

"Piss off. Look, Jack, it's mad. I don't want to know the reason—"

Churchill homed in more seriously. "If I don't return within an ostensible timeframe, I wish it to be what you leak as the reason behind my MIA status."

King-Clark sighed and rubbed his tired eyes.

His grimaced teeth and tense jaw were an obvious sign of his frustration aimed at his best friend. "Jack ..."

"Also, I do not wish for any of the Second Chesters—or *anyone,* for that matter—to hold in Dunkirk and wait for my return. Worst case, if I'm late, I'll find my own way back to England ... understood?"

King-Clark stared him down, deadpan.

"And what makes you think *I'm* going to let you go?"

Churchill issued his winning smile as he playfully cupped the cheek of his best buddy, forcing an accord.

Churchill instantly dismissed his friend's valiant attempt at preventing his endeavour. "Clark, please."

"Is there any point in me even *trying* to talk you out of this?" King-Clark asked, discouragingly serious. It was one hundred percent rhetorical as he already knew the answer.

"None at all!" Churchill stated in a confident stride towards the side door of the Bedford truck. Inside rested his bundle of effects.

"Not even tree sap?"

Huh?

Churchill frowned through his holding smile of confidence and giddiness. Whatever that reference was by King-Clark, it had lost him.

"*Burma,* remember? *Excalibur?*" King-Clark questioned, baiting him to recall the comment with some clues.

Churchill stood up straight, thinking, reminiscing.

"Training in Phyu. Colonel MacLeòid. 1930. Nobody bloody knew what you were on about then, either."

Churchill's eyes blinked and scanned over his shoulder. He almost asked *where* he believed so much that King-Clark may have seen his ghost, too ... and then he remembered. "Excalibur, right. That was a secret *the Angry Scotsman* took to his grave, was it not?"

"It was ... until some second leftenant worked it out afterwards, and it spread through the grapevine. The tree sap acted as glue, did it not? It's why all the others failed the test—and why you never tried. It wasn't *brute strength* that could remove that knife from the tree. MacLeòid knew when he stabbed the blade into the tree that overnight, the sap would resin act as an adhesive. There was no way any of us were going to be able to remove that with force, and *you* knew it, even back then. You were the *only one* that day who used his *brain* rather than his *brawn*. You stopped and you thought about it, and you won. Alas, you used your head, Jack, not your brute strength."

Churchill bobbed his head attentively.

He heard the words and read between the lines, seeing what his friend was getting at here with this straight talk.

"Unlike now."

"I *am* using my head, Clark."

Churchill smiled, reefing open the truck door where inside on the seat and across the dashboard rested his six-foot longbow, quiver of war arrows and holstered claybeg sword ... and of course, his doodlesack.

Jack Churchill returned to ground level, handling his possessions to gear up. He said not a word, and just held his winning smile at King-Clark, ready for his own private war.

"I ride at first light."

1940, June 2
Dunkirk
Nord-Pas-de-Calais, France

An astounding sight for dreary France for the time of year, the sun was out during the morning of Sunday, the 2nd of June. The warm glow raised high overhead, parting clouds above the seafront city of Dunkirk.

As soon as daylight broke the town was again a fluster of activity. Soldiers were scattered like ants throughout the streets and the momentum of the evacuation onto the floating ships in the port-side harbour and beyond in the basin was back in transition.

Located on the side of the street alongside the parked queue of transport trucks, Jack Churchill and Rex King-Clark sat over a turned-up wooden crate, sharing a breakfast of whatever little rations remained and a desperate cup of coffee—a welcome parting meal for the lone soldier before his foray back into France, which was now heavily regarded as enemy territory.

King-Clark implored one last time.

"You *do* realize that the evacuation ships will not wait for you? T-minus twenty-four hours, we'll undoubtedly all be gone from here. There is a deadline. Operation Dynamo will conclude tomorrow."

Churchill nodded. "I'm well aware."

King-Clark slowly bowed his head, knowing that his friend knew the risks of the time constraints. Humouring Churchill's proposal as they attempted to chew the notoriously unyielding army biscuits he offered further suggestions.

"You're going to need wheels ..."

"Covered."

He saw Churchill's gaze pan as, just at the right time, a messenger bike wreaked havoc through the streets. Its nimble, noisy engine kicked up volume, drowning out all speech for a moment as it rocketed by.

Churchill's intent regarding the two-wheeled vehicle was apparent.

"You're going to steal a messenger's bike?"

"Clark, no. I'm going to *borrow* a messenger's bike."

Churchill held his grin.

King-Clark blinked and shook his head.

Of course.

"I have full intention of bringing it back," Churchill elaborated, however truthful. With King-Clark now onboard for planning, Churchill's strategic mind blazed. "Besides, I need something sprightly to get me out of Dunkirk. Something fast to get me from *A* to *B* in the least amount of time possible, as well as be able to dodge any German patrols I may encounter along the way. A truck is not nimble enough to perform either one of those two things."

"Fair enough. But what about transport back?"

"Hmm?" Churchill frowned, tipping back what was left of his lukewarm morning brew.

"You're going to potentially have more bodies with you on your return, correct? They won't all fit on the rear of your borrowed messenger's bike with their hands around your waist."

Churchill granted with a bow. "I'll think of something."

"Oh, of that I have no doubt," King-Clark responded coyly, swirling his dented grey mug. "Perhaps if you ask a Hun nicely, they'll give you a lift back to Dunkirk. They're on their way here anyway."

Churchill, also sardonic, nodded in accord with that plan.

What a great idea.

The two struggled chewing and swallowing their breakfasts, finishing up. King-Clark lurched back, patting the corners of his lips with a handkerchief. "What about guns—"

He abruptly silenced as a soldier walked past them within earshot. The method of their plan as well as Jack Churchill's imminent departure must, for now, stay a secret.

"What about guns, Jack?"

"None. They'll weigh me down."

King-Clark's brow narrowed at the response.

"You're not taking any weapons?" he asked in a reiterative tone, emphasizing the likelihood. "What if you run into trouble?"

"Oh, I thought you meant firearms. Of course, old boy. I'll take all I need; my sword, my bow, and a pistol in my utility belt."

"You're going to take on Hitler's army with a loaded revolver and chanting your favourite Meagher quote?"

Today, even King-Clark challenged the man's typical outlandish choice of armament.

Ever since his return to regular service after a stretch in the mysterious and clandestine *aux-ops* (Auxiliary Operations), Churchill had no longer armed himself with a standard shiny silver basket-hilted claybeg sword. Mad Jack's symbolic sidearm had been seriously upgraded.

The reissuance was a more lethal and intense looking weapon, customized with a hilt that resembled the menacing US M1918 compact trench knife. Shaped with the brass knuckleduster-style eyelet handle, the design had been purposefully adapted onto the body of a claybeg sword. The brass grip was bored out and welded to the tang right below the compacted cross hilt of the double-edged blade. The custom weapon looked amazingly lethal.

To a few entrusted allies upon his return to the Second Manchester Regiment, Churchill had mentioned that the blade was a gift to him by his collaborators during that short spell in Switzerland, who shall remain nameless, and had gone into detail only in that the acquisition and development of the weapon were a story in and of itself. Anybody who had seen the claybeg unsheathed and up close would have noticed the blade's unique and traditional finish which caused miniscule meandering variations in silver tone, hinting that a thirteenth-century-style Damascus steel had been used during the forging.

Damascus steel was a blend of two dissimilar alloys of metal. Depending on which metals were selected by the forger and how they were treated, the rigidity and durability of the material varied with the goal being performance and longevity. A technique known as 'hybrid' Damascus was hereby incorporated at the request of the sword procurers and for the issuance of the esteemed Mad Jack Churchill. A blend of austenitic stainless steel and high carbon steel had been selected, obtaining an overall hardness akin to *C47 Rockwell.*

The sword was considerably lightweight and adaptable to the user, and the metal was rumoured to be nigh on indestructible.

With all due respect to the sword of Jack Churchill and his express choice of the sidearm armament of a firearm, King-Clark implored a differing stratagem:

"Let's be realistic here, Jack. I'll see about finding you a Tommy gun at the minimum—"

"It's okay, Clark. I have all I need," Churchill stated.

"Jack, you have a sword."

"Any officer who goes into action without his sword is impr—"

"—is improperly dressed, yes, yes, I know," King-Clark dismissively finished the line Jack Churchill wished to make famous.

Both men became upstanding.

"Thought you were going to say, *'No prince or lord has tomb so proud, as he whose flag becomes his shroud'* ...?" King-Clark cited an excerpt from one of Jack's favourites: *Thomas Francis Meagher*. The quote referenced a proud soldier's honourable burial after valiantly sacrificing himself on the battlefield for his country—an outcome Mad Jack seemed to aspire towards.

Churchill bobbed his head in acceptance.

Although that saying was still true and dear to his heart, it would be an unintentional outcome of the course of action this day.

"It's feasible."

"Well, then," King-Clark queried, now that it was daylight and Jack's hunger satisfied. "Now that you've had your last supper, what remains of your plans, other than obtaining vehicular transport?"

"Attire," Churchill answered curiously, casting a look to his friend, a glint in his eye and a smirk on his face. "And, perhaps, a shave."

A moment later, the two men shook hands, and King-Clark wished Churchill good luck before departing.

Churchill straightened his maroon beret and took to foot with his longbow strung, arrow feathers exposed in their shoulder quiver, sword holstered upon his side hip, and weighted doodlesack and bag with minimal other effects slung over his shoulder.

He approached a humble Frenchman who was seated outside of his shop.

"Good sir, are you open for business?" he questioned mysteriously to the old man, who was looking up at Churchill with the most peculiar of looks.

This man was a barber by trade and, although the present situation had rendered his hair cutting business moot, he still occupied the establishment.

"Do you own a razor? I seem to have misplaced mine and am in need of a close shear."

Considering business had been non-existent during this recent crisis and the outbreak of war, the old man was perplexed at the bid, however he nodded in approval all the same, welcoming him inside.

Soon after, Churchill emerged with another box on his list ticked. Shorn and shaved, washed and with hair slicked and combed and dowsed with extra cologne, he placed his maroon officer's cap firmly upon his dome. His uniform was pressed and buttoned, with pins in his collar and cufflinks presentable. Abnormal for the situation, his strange statement drew the focuses of several soldiers who were standing and sitting about the vicinity, waiting with their units in line.

Churchill stepped out into the street at his own pace, with timing unintentional of a perfect essence, stopping an incoming messenger bike as it zoomed along the queue of parked trucks.

Unorthodox in armament—longbow bound about his shoulder and arrow flights erect from his shoulder quiver—the eccentric fellow stood directly in its path where all others dissipated to make way.

The bike drew to an abrupt and undesired halt.

"*Oi!*" the irritated bug-eyed rider yelled after having to stop, peeved at the delay. Bike messaging was no doubt incredibly important and highly time-sensitive given the dire circumstances.

He stopped for no man ...

Rather than respond verbally, Churchill instead drew his claybeg sword from his side, presenting the motorcyclist with an additional unavoidable obstacle—and one that took his eye with such oddness. The customized double-edged sword turned many heads.

Expressionless, the wide-eyed rider raised his gloved hands from the throttle in surrender.

Unmoving, Churchill's freshly shaved maw sprouted an unhidable grin.

Beneath the hum of the idling army-green Norton WD16H motorbike, the beret-clad mad man pointed the tip of his sword up under the rider's chinstrap, causing the messenger to calmly rise off it with his palms outwards, reaching for the sky. Awfully confused by the banditry by a superior officer who could have very well ordered the messenger off in order to commandeer it, the rider begrudgingly abided and stepped away.

"Sorry, lad. But I require this magnificent motorcycle for a matter of the upmost importance. I'm sure you understand?"

The rider gesticulated, scared for his life.

"Fuck no, I don't. But she's all yours ..."

With little to no interference, Churchill commandeered the Norton WD16H motorcycle from the confused and defenceless messenger and within seconds, blasted off the mark with a squealing 180-degree turn-around.

At absolute full pelt and under a hundred vigilant glares of British soldiers queueing up for the evacuation, Churchill sped through the stalled city streets of Dunkirk. He was the only one mad enough to head in the direction from which they all had come.

He twisted the throttle and sounded the horn, carving up speed as he zoomed past the never-ending convoy of jettisoned and queued transport trucks and towards the end of town, even passing a few elements of British armour, such as several small tankettes, cruiser tanks, and a couple of *Matilda II (A12)* infantry tanks. They all cast a gleam as he sped past them like a bat *towards* Hell.

All soldiers bearing witness to Churchill's noisy exit were flabbergasted and a little confused as the lone wolf shot out of the city streets, headed southwest and in the direction of the enemy, leaving Dunkirk behind his trail of smoke.

'While Jack was on the road the morning of June 2, Omar and I were truly in the thick of it. The deadly uniformed and gun-toting, barbaric fascists arrived in Richebourg l'Avoué on the Friday at approximately 2:15 in the afternoon—mere hours after the British soldiers had vacated. We humble reporters made ourselves scarce and watched from secluded dwellings as wave after wave of German infantry units intimidatingly funnelled into the town, marching through the city streets, setting up command posts, even booting French families out of their homes so that they could establish their own lodgings. There weren't many that resisted, but any who did were made examples of and shot dead in the streets.

We took multiple photographs as their military numbers, which included vehicles and armoured tanks, rolled through the town, crumbling brickworks, fracturing sewage systems and cobblestone gutters beneath their quake. They destroyed homes and demolished houses for advantageous positions. They parked Panzer tanks inside so that they were invisible from the air, facing their turrets north, towards the enemy in case the BEF retaliated instead of retreated. By dusk of that same day, about five hundred yards east of where we were situated that night in Richebourg, the Nazis brought in large anti-air cannons, and set them up facing the night sky, where they could make an effort to shoot down any RAF fighters and attempted so on numerous occasions. Quiet as mice, Omar and I spent the night in the dusty attic of a double-storey home about a block from the town square. We were up all night, questioning our decision to stay, listening to the sporadic blasting of the AA guns and the transit of mobilizing armoured divisions, as well as the marching of thousands of German soldiers through the city, headed for the frontline, chasing after Great Britain and what was left of the French army, by now all reaching Dunkirk.

Without a wink of sleep and now out of film for our only camera, we decided at dawn to make a move and attempt to get out of the city. As we prepared to make this wild dash under the cover of what remained of the early morning fog and gloom, an element of some form of French resistance attacked the Germans in the city. It sounded quite pitiful against these bulletproof Nazis, but a gallant strike, nonetheless. In immediate hindsight, I would have loved to have been able to witness such an event or even record it, however, we probably would not have been able to escape the city as scot-free as we did without the distraction on the opposite end of Richebourg, which saw to most of the German occupation relocating during the excitement. It was as if Moses himself had parted the German seas for our escape, and we were grateful.

Out of the frying pan and into the fire, we were, as the only direction we could travel in safely was east—and further behind enemy lines. We were a leaf on the wind, adrift of the ocean, unable for now to choose our final destination. We kept moving and hoped for the best ...'

1940, June 2
Route de Lynck
Nord Pas-de-Calais, France

Racing against the very momentum of history ...

Churchill's Norton military motorcycle bellowed a throttling squawk as it tore along the *Route de Lynck,* not a quarter hour out of Dunkirk, where the smell of the sea dissipated from the air and was replaced by repugnance.

Sharp as the determination set to his purpose, Churchill's steely stare squinted tight as the air rushed into his face. Wind resistance pressed his maroon beret against his straw-coloured dome. Maintaining maximum speed, he hunched low over the handlebars, scanning the road ahead for turns and, especially, for the enemy.

So far, so good.

Upon the nimble vehicle's procurement, he was happy to see its fuel gauge at near maximum.

Contemplating that it would be the most vacant areas concerning enemy movements, Churchill decided to take a route as westerly as he could, leading away from Dunkirk, slingshotting above *Craywick* and then south beside the town of *Bourbourg.* On this course, he then headed in the direction of the large Christian commune known as *Saint-Omer* and onwards through a section of the Pas-de-Calais area called the *Caps et Marais d'Opale* Natural Regional Park.

He reached the peacefulness of the natural regional park backroads by late morning. From here, he planned to hook east and in the direction of Hazebrouck. The town of Hazebrouck was a familiar burg which he had passed through twice in the past week and a half, and he hoped he could then find the same alternate route Cocky Charlie had steered them through from Richebourg, and reverse it.

Although he would stop to assist any BEF survivors he encountered along the way, as per his mission parameter, his terminus was and always would be the DuPont Dairy Farm ... *his endgame.*

At this level of speed, and if delays continued to remain non-existent, Churchill could reach the farm in just under two hours.

Potentially, he could get there before the Germans ...

He could still save the DuPonts; save Ève, the girl whom he had accidentally grown to adore whilst on tour. At least then he could sleep at night knowing he saved at least a little piece of France.

He could be their knight in shining armour ...

With a determined scowl, Jack's white-knuckled squeeze twisted the throttle an inch more ...

The British motorcycle absolutely *thundered* along the road.

A blunt blade tearing a hole through eerie tranquillity.

When Churchill reached Hazebrouck, his heart skipped a beat as the road ahead literally blackened with the occupation of incoming Nazi troops and vehicles.

The fucking enemy.

Before his position was noticed by them on the distant horizon, he slowed and banked left off-road and onto a dry field, cutting across the flat surface and reaching a partial tree line.

Once there, Churchill allowed the bike to roll to idle.

He twisted at the waist to bring his pair of binoculars up around to his eyes, bravely spying on the travelling enemy force up the road.

With the idle hum of the hot metal between his thighs, Churchill held his breath as he examined the convoy. He spotted four Sd.Kfz. 251 half-tracks and four ZV-Model Einheitsdiesel troop transport trucks, each fully stocked with about fifteen to twenty infantrymen per unit.

It was a whole battalion.

Amongst the convoy were some smaller cars carrying German officers and important radiomen, usually at the rear of such a heavy line.

This army was advancing ahead of an armoured position, almost certainly aiming to set up a forward operating base closer to Dunkirk before nightfall.

Churchill checked his wristwatch.

Tactically speaking, if these guys were about to occupy either Bourbourg or another town north of that, it would take about another five to eight hours to fully mobilize their Panzer divisions. This meant that the Germans would be knocking on Dunkirk's door by dusk this very next evening, and probably marching an assault the following break of day.

Churchill lowered his binoculars around his neck and faced forwards. What he should have been contemplating was turning back. Doing so would at least ensure his own escape from France ... but instead, he was pondering an alternate route to the DuPont farm now that the road he travelled was deemed cautionary.

Disappointed at his deficient new options but accepting them nonetheless, the courageous captain skidded off the dirt mark and through the small collection of trees headed south, chomping off-road terrain in order to circumvent the masses.

If the Germans were this far across on the most westerly side of the Nord Pas-de-Calais, further east would by now surely be absolutely swathed in the swastika.

He would have to ride vigilantly and stay in the peripheries.

Keeping off main roads would double if not triple his arrival time at the DuPont Dairy Farm ...

...but at least he would get there in one piece, and not risk literally driving into the cannon of a Panzer tank afoot of an entire armoured division.

'By that same time on Sunday when Jack had stolen— apologies, 'borrowed'—the messenger's bike and puttered back inland, Omar and I had stumbled onto a sight I will never forget: the Alamric family farm. Situated northeast of the DuPont Dairy Farm, Omar and myself discovered another of the war crime atrocities performed by the SS, ranking as high as such with the Le Paradis or the Wormhout massacres: both genocides of history we learned of later. What we had found at the Alamric property were the blood-spattered, hole-ridden, rotting corpses of at least a dozen British soldiers. They had been stripped of their weapons and gear prior to their executions, apparent as they were unloaded and tossed into a bonfire and set alight. The men had then been made to kneel in a line where they were shot, execution-style. As for the residents of the Alamric farmstead (two teenage boys and parents), who had obviously accommodated the lost and battle worn British soldiers (not unlike the DuPont's had accommodated D section), had also been executed on the front steps of their family home. The house had then been set ablaze, leaving their carcasses as mostly charred skeletons.

I recall so vividly the look of panic and surge of fear in the tone I gave to Omar when I realized the residents of the neighbouring property to the Alamrics were the DuPonts, whom I'd met just days ago. Gérard, the nice old man, and his lovely wife and three daughters. Little did I know that, at that point in time, myself and the great and fearless Jack Churchill shared this same heroic vendetta ...

This makes me feel both humble and proud.'

Dusk.

What had intended to be a two-hour journey plotted for Churchill on his motorbike took almost the entirety of the day, no thanks to sporadic setbacks. These consisted of needing to take alternate roads and dodging enemy patrols—innumerable amounts of enemy patrols—as they flooded in through northern France, occupying almost all main routes. The Nazis were absolutely swarming over France like cockroaches on a discarded croissant.

A direct result of the delays, he had burned too much time and too much fuel. Sun setting behind him, Churchill finally arrived at the dairy farm ... only to have his heart torn from his chest.

While Churchill rounded off the road just south of the farm and onto the long driveway of the property past a pasture of grazing cows belonging to one of Gérard DuPont's free-range herd, he was stunned to witness a commotion of German infantry in the near distance.

They were at the farm.

He was too late.

Thankfully, his bike engine was just out of earshot of the location, and he had not yet been spotted by the dozen German soldiers on the DuPont premises. The Gerrys were heavily armed and clad in the stahlhelm, dressed in similar polyspot plane tree camouflage smock to the ones he had encountered in L'Épinette days earlier.

The bulk of the section, about half a dozen soldiers, were assembled in the sludge out the front of the main house. There were another two or three sharing a cigarette near an Einheitsdiesel troop transporter truck parked beside the old green Renault tractor out the front of the large barn.

This situation was not at all how Jack had pictured it.

On the ride over, he had envisioned in his mind's eye that he would be their knight in shining armour, and arrive in the nick of time to pull Ève clear as the black and red walls of the swastika caved in all around them ... but the Germans had beat him there.

With his heart hurting and his stomach sick from anxiety, it was with a solid grimace of dread Churchill unobtrusively navigated his bike off the narrow dirt driveway and into the trees to the east of the farmstead outskirts. There was a slight hill connecting along these limits which overlooked the entire flat greens and the property, and it would give him a vantage point to oversee the area and his options, or lack thereof.

Killing the hungry engine, Jack wheeled the bike on foot halfway up the slope before allowing for it to collapse on its side, toppling gently into some light foliage and tall weeds.

Staying low, Churchill slung his longbow from across his chest and drew a single arrow, nocking it to the drawstring. He advanced on what could be considered a principle reconnoitre to the top summit of the eight-foot-high slope where he knelt low, eventually going prone between larger grass tufts.

With his binoculars, Churchill gained a close-up inaudible live image of the hostile situation approximately two hundred feet across a clearing of spotty marshland.

Behind the binocular lenses, he patiently observed ...

"*I though yoo didn't wanna buy tha cow, Jackie?*" the Scottish tone of the ghost of Colonel MacLeòid jeered from a position alongside Churchill, also lying face down on his elbows in the mud of the sloped summit. If it were not for the fact that the kilted dweller was a ghost and therefore incorporeal, he would be doing a nasty job at getting his Cameron Highlander's ceremonial suit proper filthy in the mud.

Churchill ignored his mockery regarding the DuPont daughter with which MacLeòid knew he had marital relations, let alone an existent emotional attachment. Jack was unphased by his unexpected company, and he had come to expect visits from this Highlander haunt whenever he was alone.

MacLeòid crept in tight beside Churchill, surveying the ground. "*Looks like yoo're en a wee bit o' a pickle, dere, laddie ...*"

"Aye," Churchill agreed, still wearing the binoculars.

He performed a headcount of the Germans.

Nine—no, *ten.* All armed.

But worst of all, he saw their uniform insignia ...

The *Totenkopf skull* and *crossbones* ...

Schutzstaffel.

"*Farken' SS poofters, ey?*" added MacLeòid, watching onwards. He was without a pair of eyeglasses, but could see everything clearly, sparing no detail. He added with the upmost hack from his Glaswegian patter: "*Farken' hate deez Nazi sissies.*"

And he was right.

Churchill hated the SS, too—on a personal level.

Not only did these men belong to the same outfit who had driven him and his section out of L'Épinette a few days ago, resulting in the deaths of a few of his beloved servicemen and a defeat on Churchill's battle tally, but they were also presumed to be the same relentless bastards responsible for the war crimes of late. They were an army without remorse.

Causing him to suddenly dip his head slightly, the sound of a healthy motorbike came roaring onto the scene, taking the bend from the main road of which Churchill had just minutes ago. Without a worry, the German rider tore down the dirt strip and onto the DuPont driveway, flicking up rocks and summoning an angry dust cloud in wake.

There were two occupants: a driver and a passenger in an attached sidecar.

"*Moor Huns ta join tha party,*" MacLeòid commented morosely. "*A messenger, bey tha looks. Nice bike, though ...*"

Certain that they would not spot him on their entry now that they had passed, Churchill raised his view, and couldn't help but admire the vehicle which the botenmeister *(messenger)* rode in along with his driver.

Churchill added, well educated in automobiles, "*1938 BMW-R71 ...* jet-black ... chromed trimmings," he surveyed and labelled, taking in the view closer with his binoculars' zoom. "Four-speed, twenty-two-horsepower, seven-fifty-cc flathead side valve ... very nice, indeed."

"*Oh, aye?*" MacLeòid feigned a knowledge of such things, even though he only knew because Jack knew.

They tracked the unit as it thundered through to the gathering by the house. It was visible that the particular model had an attached sidecar on its left side: referred to as a pod, which the supposed messenger rode along with a rider carrying the news to relay. It was perhaps how the frontline soldiers gathered their orders from Germany across France.

Churchill scanned through his enhanced optics, identifying the officer in amongst the SS soldiers at the farm, a *Feldwebel (staff sergeant)*.

After the bike arrived out front of the DuPont family house, the feldwebel approached the messenger after he climbed out of the sidecar pod of the BMW motorcycle. The driver also dismounted, removing his goggles and head gear in order to break and enjoy a cigarette, standing guard near the bike.

"*What en tha fark kinda messenger es that?*"

Hearing MacLeòid, Churchill's zoom returned to the passenger from the sidecar, where he realized that it was not a messenger at all. It was another Schutzstaffel officer, and one of some foreign, obnoxious designation in the Nazi craze of radical hierarchy.

This newcomer bigwig nodded to the lower ranking feldwebel as he stood in salute, acknowledging the pecking order.

This high-ranking Schutzstaffel officer wore slightly different attire and was clearly their commanding officer to some degree. To Jack's knowledge, he looked as though he was a German military chaplain (a military *Field Bishop,* known as a *Feldbischof)* but that couldn't have been right ...

In fact, this whole legion of SS seemed a little ... *off.*

Whereas the multiple other soldiers were an assortment of riflemen and assault gunners dressed in grey SS uniforms under camouflage smocks, this fellow wore a knee-length leather trench coat and a cap with differing insignia which included some Christian crosses. Upon his head was a *feldmütze (field cap)* which differed only slightly to an officer's standard-issue cap, with silver pipings and a violet soutache as the *waffenfarbe (colours).* Between the national eagle and cockade, this man had a small gothic cross embroidered upon his cap. Outside of his numerous religious insignia, Churchill also spotted some of militaristic origin, signifying that he was an *SS-Sturmhauptführer (storm chief leader)* and a war veteran to some degree.

Who the actual fuck was this character?

Churchill marked him as their leader.

Through the circular zoom, he watched as the field bishop was immediately and enthusiastically saluted by the other soldiers. They seemed to really respect—or fear—this *feldbischof.*

The feldbischof was then verbally issued with what must have been a situation report regarding the farmstead and its occupants by the feldwebel in charge of the SS unit. He seemed pleased by the news, especially when the feldwebel talked about the prisoners inside, of the female variety.

"*Yoor mate's doon dere,*" MacLeòid denounced without much certainty. The suggestion was enough to get Churchill's hackles up.

"Who?" Jack questioned, pulling his face from his lenses.

"*Yoor enemy ... Friedrich Feind.*"

Churchill squashed his face with bafflement. "Pardon ...?"

Churchill's sterling stare quickly began to survey the soldiers, hunting for his archnemesis, an old enemy being a German by the name of Friedrich Feind. He had not encountered the man since before the war, however MacLeòid always liked to play with his food, toying with Churchill that he was always lurking about.

"No, he's not."

"He coold be. Have yoo even checked ...?"

Churchill caught MacLeòid at a fib and affirmed.

"He's not here ..."

"So sure, are yoo ...?"

A slanted frown developed above Churchill's stare as he scanned the enemies by the farm. They were probably too distant, so he assisted his exploration with his binoculars once again.

Across the silent distance, his view went from soldier to soldier, carefully examining their facial features as best he could, moving on as soon as he differentiated them from being anyone but his rival opponent from Oslo, Friedrich Feind.

Churchill's mouth breathed tensely from below the held binoculars as his stare continued to scan the faces of the soldiers, almost halfway hopeful that Feind was actually amongst them, to rekindle their feud.

And then ... Churchill's scanning halted.

Deep in concentration, his physique suddenly altered from being prone on the slope, and he abruptly brought his view higher. Something drastic had caught his view ... it was as if ... as if ...

Through the circular zoomed image of the binoculars, Churchill blinked as he toggled the focus. The maintained vision he held over one particular German troop within the ranks of the Schutzstaffel soldiers seemed to be the *doppelgänger* of Friedrich Feind, if not actually the fiend himself ...

The man's head shifted. His identity faltered.

It was not Feind.

Sinister laughter from Colonel MacLeòid could be heard from beside Churchill in their horizontal position overlooking the DuPont farm. Jack's steady view peeled away from the binoculars and his deathly stare found its way onto his friendly ghost, his benevolent spirit, his guardian angel ...

... more like malevolent trickster ghoul.

He was beginning to see this evil side in MacLeòid more often as the years went on, casting his presence in a whole new light.

"The only *fiend* here is you!" Churchill stated insultingly.

"*Sorry, laddie, ha-ha ... phew ...*" MacLeòid giggled, catching a breath from all the laughter he had just had with Churchill, again, the butt of a joke. "*I had ta do et. Had ta get yoo riled up, ya knoe? Tickle ya jimmies. Ruffle ya pubes.*"

Churchill sighed with relief.

He brought his face back into the binoculars, tactfully weighing his options to formulate a plan ...

"*I hate ta burst yoor booble, but dese sissy-boys aren't jus' yoor run ov da mill Huns, Jackie. Dey're SS twats. Top-shelf cuntage. Therefore, I fear da possibility ov enmity an' mistreatment towards ya DuPont mates an' ya missus ta be all tha moor real,*" MacLeòid informed with a natural roll of the tongue. "*A shoorefire freat.*"

"You think I don't know that?"

"*Dey're probably gonna kill an' fuck tha shit outta 'em!*" he added sickeningly blunt. "*And hopefully, fur dem, en dat order.*"

Churchill's jaw tensed ...

MacLeòid whacked him on the shoulder.

"*Jackie-boy, please! I'm jus' tryin' ta git yoo ready. Git yoo mad.*"

"Trust me, I am already mad. What you're doing is just pissing me off ..."

"*Et's like I've always sed ta yoo, laddie,*" the Scottish wizard of wit postured to further his donation of wisdom. "*Yoo wanna take somethin' from this war, eh ...? Yoo wanna win et? Win this fecht?*"

Churchill's stare peeled from the focus through the binoculars and blurred to the side, attaining a solemn view of MacLeòid as he spoke.

Jack took his spiel onboard.

"*Yoo wanna life beyond tha depths with this lassie or the next, yoo got'a be prepared ta give et somethin' en return. Yoo're gon' 'ave to fecht, an' ne'er stop. Tha war demands yoor sacrifice!*"

"I know it does."

"*Git mad, lad! Doon git scared!*"

"I know!"

"*Git mad!*"

"I am!—"

Churchill's fists clenched the binoculars ...

Suddenly, there was the sound of twigs breaking directly behind their position ...

"Did you hear that?" Churchill whispered as his wide eyes scanned the hill behind them. He faced MacLeòid amid a response to confirm his suspicions, but the figure was no longer present. He was alone. One might argue, he always had been.

There it was again: more snaps of motion.

It was discreet, barely audible.

... and close!

Like lightning, Jack Churchill reacted.

He twisted in his position, bringing about his longbow outstretched at its fullest fistmele and with a drawn arrow up to his chin, pinpointing a bead on the lone German scout who would dare attempt sneaking up on him, only ... *it was no German scout.*

Churchill exhaled after he saw who it was.

Carefully, he moved the bow far left of his target and relaxed the pull on the tense anchor point draw. It was like de-cocking the hammer of a loaded gun.

He cursed. "Jesus Christ! *You?!*"

The man revealed: *Felix Hardy.*

"Fuckin' hell, pal!" the American journalist retorted, clutching at his chest and allowing for himself to hunch over, scared shitless from that reaction—one that almost got him killed. Though it was by chance, he should have known better than to sneak up on a trained soldier.

"You gave me a bloody heart attack, you stupid bellend!" Churchill complained, spinning back around to check on the scene. It seemed unchanged since he had taken his eyes off it.

"Gave *you* a heart attack?!" Hardy scoffed, still catching his breath. In a controlled collapse, he lowered onto the same slope behind Churchill. His leather jacket was covered in grime, and his fedora was putrid and damp from sweat. Since the last time he had a chance to shave, the yank had sprouted some lengthy five o'clock shadow.

"I damn-near shit my fuckin' pants just now!" Hardy exclaimed with an element of truth. "And mind you, that would have been a blessing as I've been unable to shit for days now ..."

There was the echoic surge of a German accent from the distance.

"*Shh! Get down! Down!*" Churchill hissed in a harsh whisper, suddenly lunging out and grappling onto a fist full of Hardy's rugged leather jacket to tear him down lower, joining him out of sight in the grass of the foliage-littered ground along with him.

Fast to examine for their detection, Churchill scanned over the top of the hill at the farmstead and the enemy located within it, finally certain after a moment's gaze that they were still undetected and their position on the foothill was still secluded.

"What in the bloody hell are you doing out here?"

"What am *I* doing here? What are *you* doing here?!" Hardy replied sternly. "I thought you lot pulled out to the coast?"

"We did," Churchill explained, facing the farm and watching the Germans from two hundred feet away. "We reached Dunkirk. The men should be loading up for England as we speak."

"So, why aren't you with them? Why did you come back?"

Churchill glowered over the armed men, deep in contemplation, rendering his answers to the man's questions was secondary. "Why do you think?"

"The DuPonts," Hardy bobbed, assuming that answer. It was obvious that Jack Churchill had some kind of personal connection to the family, or possibly a certain member within it. Hardy didn't let it linger for too long, but he was more perceptive than what he was generally credited for. "Sure. I get it. France was always just a country to your type. Now that their population is being *culled* you suddenly wanna try and hang onto the people you know, huh?"

"Sure, something like that."

There was something in Churchill's delivery that perked Hardy's reporter's instincts, pointing him towards an ulterior motive behind his crusade here. Considering a paucity of prized possessions regarding this type of man, as well as a lack of kindness typically due to the desensitization of soldiers, it had to be something far more valuable ...

"Pussy, huh?"

"Pardon?" Churchill glared. Of course, the gentleman in him was appalled, though, in a way, Hardy was spot-on. Fact was that either way Jack didn't have the time right now to argue with the journalistic git.

"Yeah, sure, that French chick. The farmer's daughter," the American revealed, exposing Churchill's true motivation. "Yeah. I remember the way she was eye-fucking you that last night at the dinner table ... I knew there was something there ..."

Churchill glared away from him, shaking his head.

Hardy's schoolyard humour seemed to quieten.

He nodded, clearing his throat. "Yeah, well, it's why we came to this farm, too. Me and Omar."

Churchill corrected again. "*Omar and I.*"

"Whatever!" Hardy briefly issued him dagger eyes. "Well, not for *her* exactly, but y'know what I mean ... we thought we could try and make a difference—"

"Omar?" Churchill then frowned. "The dark Frenchie? Where is he?"

Hardy jerked his head off into their focal distance. "Down there in the fray somewhere ..."

Using the *Colmont Norma* field glasses he took from his leather case, Churchill took a minute to properly examine the entire situation once again through an optic zoom. This time, he noticed that the German soldiers were not the only people down and outside the DuPont family home. As some of the patrol cleared in their stances, he could see that there were also two other men: father of the house, Gérard DuPont, and the dark-skinned Frenchman, Omar Ny. They were slouched on their knees in the mud beside the front door, under the guard of several German soldiers.

Churchill continued to examine the area through his binoculars. Standing in the open front door to the home was another armed soldier. Beyond him, from this angle, Churchill could see movement *inside* the shade of the interior of the house. It was a mix of uniformed men and plain-clothed civilians, and likely the rest of the DuPont family held captive; mother, *Sophie*, and brunette-haired younger daughters *Audréy* and *Yana,* and eldest daughter *Ève*—his main objective, and whom he was itching to lay eyes on.

"We arrived an hour ago, just before the Germans did," Hardy explained. "I was up at the house for a bit."

"You were there?" Jack confirmed. "You saw *Ève?*"

Hardy bowed.

"Was she okay?"

Hardy shrugged. "She's terrified. They all were."

Churchill felt his heart sink.

"We spoke for a bit and then planned I was gonna keep an eye out along the road. I was on my way over, when ... well, they arrived in a truck ... I couldn't get back in time, so I hid."

Churchill's eyes sealed.

An hour ago ...

One hour.

One fucking hour!

If he had not been so delayed, he could have made it before the Germans. This whole thing would be vastly different. That ... or he would be just another prisoner under armed guard down there on the front step.

"I couldn't warn them ... I barely even made it across the field before they pulled in the drive and tore ass up it. They stopped short and the soldiers all leapt out with guns, shouting, and being dickheads. I hid over there in the bushes ... I was about to go and turn myself in, so I could at least be with Omar, and then I heard your bike in the distance and saw you come off the road. Watched you pull up ... and now here we are ..."

Churchill's beret-clad head bobbed.

His story checked out.

"Well, do we have a plan here, Captain? When are the rest of your pals gettin' here?" Hardy asked, so innocuously assuming that there was no way Jack Churchill was this far out on his own.

"They're not," Churchill said after a small delay, again watching the farm through his zoomed eyeglasses.

"You're here on your own?"

"I am."

Hardy's view froze upon Churchill, growing wide and losing focus ... and hope. "So ... what, then? What do we do?"

Churchill took a breath, removing the glasses from his face. "We concoct a clever, strategic, ballsy plan of attack where the two of us can successfully gain access to the DuPont farmstead and efficiently rid them of those soldiers, preferably by distraction due to our lack of arms and numbers for an anterior assault, so that we may sneak in and exfil the prisoners, and save the blasted day ..."

Hardy stared blankly.

"What say you, old boy?"

"*We?*"

Churchill scanned the trees about them. "Well, unless you've got any other French negroes hiding in wait about these parts ...?"

Hardy shook his head. "I do not."

"Didn't think so."

"We really got time to *concoct a plan,* here, Captain? I've seen what these assholes can do on a farm just down the road aways ... believe me when I say, things are about to escalate *extremely* fucking quickly here," Hardy denoted. "Suggest we, like, *go in* and *bluff 'em* into thinking we got more numbers or something. Take a non-violent approach. Y'know, try and scare 'em off?"

Churchill shook his head at the plan.

"Numbers? You want to see numbers, Felix, take a walk up the road. Look in any direction and you'll see literally thousands of Huns up every avenue. They're clogging the thoroughfares. It's congested with kraut like a bloody constipation of France. We've got to be smart about how we do this, or not at all ..."

"What's the *not at all* strategy, then?"

Jack nodded modestly. "I see how many I can dispatch one-by-one with my bow ..."

"Guns blazin', huh?"

"So-to-speak."

Hardy grunted with anxiousness, rolling fully onto his chest and crawling closer to peek at the farmstead. He threw out another suggestion aloud while Churchill pondered internally.

"O.K., so what about the distraction? You got weapons, yeah? Gimme a gun, I'll start shooting from here, make lots'a noise, then run away. That aught'a peel a few off from the house. Meanwhile, you roam around wide, sneak in through the back, kill those assholes that are left, save the broads, and bail ..."

After giving some consideration to certain elements of Hardy's plan, Churchill shook his head again. It was not a terrible plan of attack, but he thought against it in sight of another idea berthing upon the tip of his mind.

"Not enough time. I'd have to circle the whole way around to the neighbouring property just to ensure I'm not spotted. It could take hours."

"Good, by then it'll be dark. They won't see you coming at all."

"*By then*, it'll be too late, Hardy. You've got a group of unarmed, defenceless young females cornered in a house by a dozen testosterone-filled fuckwits with a thorough understanding of their shortened life expectancies, and who have been starved of female companionship for God-knows how long. They're in a lawless time zone of organizational chaos with no morals and no witnesses, and are well aware of their immoral actions having zero ramifications. In fact, the heinous mistreatment of the foreigners they conquer is apparently sickeningly endorsed by their superiors. Men are savages at their most basic of instincts and right here, right now, it's a sure spectacle. We need to plan for the worst. Believe me, that family has no time left as it is. And even then, what about you? How do I get *you* back safe?"

"I'll be fine on my own."

"Bollocks," Churchill denied the idea. "This is no longer some *Phoney War* backdrop that you can prance around within, with a camera and notepad and a falsified sense of immunity. This here is a proper war, lad. One the likes to which the world has never seen. All bets are off. Out here, men like that will shoot you in the face for a laugh and nobody will ever care to find the body. There are no repercussions to their actions at this juncture."

Hardy eyed Churchill with an ounce of contempt.

"So, good idea, but no, your sacrifice is not an option. We all get out of this alive and safe or none at all. Welcome to the conscription. There has been too much death dealt already on these few eves."

"So, what then?"

Crack ...

The distant echo of the tiny pistol shot hushed their debacle.

The gun had sounded so far away it resembled a thunderclap.

Churchill was fast to examine the farmstead through the zoom of his binoculars under the dimming of the dusk light ...

His mouth whispered with a quiver of emotion. *"No ... no, no, no!"*

"What? What is it?" Hardy glowered, worried, barely able to see any detail with his naked eyes through the shade of the dimming setting ... but what he could see, was that one of the men who were on their knees as prisoners were now lying flat in the mud ...

Churchill's zoomed image of the interaction saw the aftermath of Omar Ny being shot point-blank in the sternum. His pale button-up shirt had erupted with a splotch of red and he was now face down in the mud, lifeless.

On his knees in the mud, Gérard DuPont was stunned by the execution of the man right beside him. He sheepishly glanced at the shooter with utter, hysterical besought. There were tears in his eyes as he cringed and pleaded. His cheeks were pink from the blush of shock as he clenched at the leather trench coat of the feldbischof amongst the SS grunts. Up by his head, the smiling field bishop was holding a smoking Luger pistol in his gloved hand. He had obviously been the one to pull the trigger on Ny.

Gérard was begging, imploring—but not for his life ...

... he made gestures to the house.

... for his family, and their lives.

This was as the German feldbischof took a step towards it, towards the girls inside. They were now present, huddled in the doorframe and crying, squirming whilst being restrained by a big soldier with a gun.

Churchill could see them clearly.

He could make out Yana, Audréy, and their mother, Sophie DuPont ... and then finally, he could see Ève. Tears swelled as shock weakened them under the firm, strong grip of the German guards. They were numbed and paralysed by this trauma.

Alarmed by the shot that killed the kind French photographer, they fretted for the safety of their father and husband and fought to lay dreadful eyes upon him. They no doubt begged for his life as he did theirs. He pleaded not for what the German soldiers predictably had in store for an empty house with defenceless women and an overbearing sense of lawlessness. He begged for mercy.

"Shit," Churchill cursed, witnessing the pandemonium unfold. It was kicking off prematurely to his plans. The end was nigh.

"Omar ..." Hardy muttered as his view fell out of focus and he retracted from his position a little, stomaching the loss of his friend as the shock set in. He held his face with his dirty palms.

"Your mate ... they've just shot him. He's gone," Churchill commented with anguish, wanting to gear up and intervene, but reserved by a lack of options.

He watched as Gérard begged at the foot of the feldbischof, who attempted to shake him free from his coat, only to have the pistol intimidatingly and tormentingly waved in his face ...

"This bellend is a bloody field bishop ... what is he doing killing?"

Churchill pulled the binoculars down from his face, scanning to his left, to his right, searching for options—any options.

He was out of time ...

He broke a sweat.

He bit his lip.

Angry, he cursed.

"*Shit! Fuck!*"

Crack ...

Another gunshot.

... he froze stiff.

His body, his mind, his eyes, all froze stagnantly.

Churchill's mouth closed shut and he calmly took a deep breath, bringing the binoculars up to his face to examine the fatal scene.

He saw Gérard DuPont on his side in the mud, unmoving.

Dead.

He was gone.

His head resting on its side, a single red dot could be seen just above his left eye and, even from this distance and with this dying light, Churchill could see a thin trickle of blood bleed from the bullet hole.

In that moment, a rush of desolation overcame Churchill.

It felt as if a piece of hope had been fractured. Unrecoverable.

Lackadaisical in his demeanour and with unsympathetic disregard to those deceased, the SS feldbischof swapped hands with his gun to perform a feeble holy trinity gesture upon the fallen. Cavalier to the calamity he created, he then stepped up the front step and into the house, anxious to partake in this new rape rally tonight and judging by their organization skills in herding the women, it wasn't their first. There were several muffled screams as the women were forcefully separated inside of the house, restrained by the men inside. They would be taken into separate rooms, sexually assaulted, and improperly, gravely injured ... and then eventually killed.

Afterwards, the Germans would typically burn down the houses via means of the combustible thatched roofing and mostly wooden constraints, which would blaze like kindle. The fire would dissolve all evidence of the atrocity ever taking place, not that Nazi Germany wasn't already beyond reproach.

Across the echoic distance of the farm plane, the cries by the girls were audible as they were forced around inside the house.

Ornaments within the DuPont family home smashed in distinct breakages, furniture budged with squeaks as brute soldiers forced their way inside of the house.

Furthermore, the unsettling cries of girls screaming persisted.

There were brief elements of distraught non-compliance immediately after the Germans entered the house by force, making themselves at home. Without the man of the house alive to defend his family, there was little to no real resistance.

The front door closed over.

Their view from over the property grounds was barely audible, however muffled screams and slaps against bare skin were distinguishable as the evil Nazis imposed the DuPont women's submission. Malevolent laughter abruptly persisted.

There would likely be foul play before the foreplay.

These hungry soldiers would undoubtedly want a warm meal and service before whatever dessert plans took full effect, meaning consequently, they were in a type of overtime for this charade. The sun was setting both in the sky, and on the lives of an innocent French family.

Even from this far away, Churchill and Hardy could hear the violence as it commenced inside the four walls.

Hardy breathed heavily, seemingly sulking in pain at the loss of his friend. He asked Churchill not what had transpired, only read it from his expression and emotion as Jack allowed for his gaze to peel away from the stationary binoculars and he stared into nothingness.

"We're too late ... aren't we?" stated Hardy after steadying, shaking his head in despair. There was an underlying intention present in his tone, one that understandably resembled them vacating the premises and falling back.

Churchill repeated unto himself. "*We're too late ...*"

It was spoken with a sense of doubt, as if he refused to fully believe what had just happened and what was about to happen, absent his control. And then, suddenly, through the shock of the executions and pending failure, an idea surged through his mind, charging the mind behind his piercing blue eyes like lightning.

"... but this can't be it."

Hardy observed his chain of thought, still with a heavy brow.

"It can't end like this," Jack muttered, his stare pacing in the mud before his short-sighted stare. " *'Bad men need nothing more to compass their ends, than that good men should look on and do nothing'.*"

Refusing to believe he had failed, Churchill suddenly shifted his posture and spun around, remaining low to scan the leaf-covered earth around them, scouring the rustling foliage like a nestling bird.

It was as if he were searching for something hidden, he portrayed a mad man, digging like a wild animal, rummaging around with his bare hands in the grass, frolicking, digging through the dirt, burrowing ...

He paused and cast a view back to Hardy.

"Come, quickly. Help me dig."

A little lost, Hardy inched forward, watching Churchill's erratic behaviour. "Dig? What the *hell* are you looking for?"

Mad Jack paused to face him with a contagious, inspiring look of determination reborn in his sparkling blue stare. "That *plan* you wanted ... it's here somewhere. Now *dig.*"

IV
Nicht Schießen

Dusk dimmed a lateral shadow over France.

Precious minutes dropping like the grains of sand in an hourglass, time was running out for the DuPont family rescue.

Right now, Churchill was living up to the epithet of *Mad Jack.*

Rising to his feet since they had slid lower behind the mound and become visually concealed from the DuPont farmhouse and the enemy Germans occupying it, Felix Hardy understood the reasoning of the nickname precisely as he watched the crazy Brit scurrying about in the mud. Before his eyes, Churchill was witlessly excavating the ground with his bare hands. He felt around piles of leaves and littered foliage, kicking over logs, upturning rocks.

There was apparently a method to his madness, for he was looking for where the two men from the 4th Wiltshire Regiment had stashed a collection of confiscated German gear a few days ago ... in other words, he was *looking for a miracle.* A longish story short, back when D section was patrolling these parts and boarding on the DuPont family farm grounds, they had come across two young Wiltshiremen who had successfully counter-ambushed a German patrol compiled of two scouts. They had confiscated their gear and weapons, and Captain Churchill utilized the dressage to play a nasty trick on two privates in his section with the goal of teaching them a lesson in preparedness. Not long after, they discarded the affects by burying them somewhere in these hills surrounding the property. The only downside was that Churchill had never actually seen where, only that they were around this vicinity as per his direction.

"... they *should* be around here somewhere," Churchill added while searching hastily on his hands and knees, digging like a dog for a bone.

Hardy stood perplexed. He hissed, "... what?"

Jack halted for a moment, scanning about.

There was buried treasure here somewhere, only there was no *X* to mark the spot and he had no map.

"Two pairs of Hun gear and guns! This is where I told them to bury them ... I saw them go up this way ... past the dead tree ..." Churchill pointed at the landmark with a grimy finger. "They have *got* to be here somewhere!"

"Yeah, O.K.," Hardy replied, still very much lost. "Say you even find the gear, what makes you really think a couple of functioning guns are going to help turn the tables? They've got *a dozen* guns down there. We'd barely get close."

Churchill stopped for a second, upstanding, scanning about the area in the search for a clue: perhaps some discoloured dirt, a recently moved log—or just anywhere apparent. The men who performed the task were not overly bright, and the chances that they stashed them in the most obvious place imaginable was feasible.

His response to Hardy's pessimism was belated.

"I never said they were *functioning* ..."

Hardy gave up before even beginning to assist the British looney, coming to stand over Churchill's toppled over Norton motorcycle. He put his hands on his hips. "Oh, good! Even better odds, then!"

"It's not exactly the *guns* I'm interested in, chap," Churchill added beneath his breath. "*Brains over brawn.*"

Ignoring his reply, Hardy broke some of the vegetation away that had fallen over the bike, attempting to stand it upright.

"I hate to say this, but ... we should probably just go, Captain," he stated, heaving the vehicle upright. The handlebars and metal were still warm from Churchill's trip from Dunkirk. Dirt, leaves, and grime poured off and over its metal components. "This is war. This sort of shit ... it just happens. All we can do is ... survive."

Churchill's stare of concentration faltered for an instance, and he looked to Hardy objectively. He was tired of resorting to platitudes, even if they did seem rather relevant of late.

"Live to fight another day, huh?"

"Something like that, yeah ..."

"And what of he who is battle slain? You're implying *war* ... *that* isn't war," Jack responded rationally and with a pointed finger. "When we find this gear, we're going to show them *war* ..."

Hardy observed as Churchill continued to turn soil, rapidly probing the foliage-littered floor, mining earth with his bare hands like a crazy person.

"Besides," Churchill added with his head down and rummaging. This new sentence was in direct reference to Hardy's idea with the bike. "We aren't going anywhere on that ... it's out of petrol."

Hardy looked down over the bike and at the fuel gauge and tapped it with his fingertip. The gas was on empty.

"Fuck me," he cursed with frustration. He let the heavy motorbike drop back to the bushes that would likely be its forever resting place, discarded to rust and into history.

A few more minutes passed, and Churchill continued searching, finally discovering his treasure located behind a rather large fallen, putrefied log. It was suddenly an obvious shallow grave, but only after he had found it.

Wrapped in a weatherproof polyspot pattern plane tree camouflage smock from the uniform, the pile was partially entombed in leaves, twigs, and soil. It was true, the Wiltshire lads hadn't really done a great job burying the evidence, but in hindsight, Churchill probably would not have found it otherwise.

"Ah-*huh!*" he said with gumption, reefing it out of the dug cavity.

The treasure trove was balled in the camouflage smock, rolled, and tied up with hay bale-binding from out of Gérard DuPont's barn.

Intrigued, Hardy stepped over, watching past Churchill's shoulder as he unravelled the dormant gear. Dampness and dirt had seeped through the wrapped layers, coating everything, but it seemed to be mostly in good nick.

Inside the bundle was a pair of stahlhelms with pelt chinstraps, wound belts, and pocket pouches made of brown leather, all wrapped in what remained of the smock jackets. Most importantly, there were two sets of nine-millimetre maschinenpistoles *(submachine guns)* with limited ammunition.

"Schmeissers!" Churchill affirmed at the guns.

Hardy's brow raised. "Um ... *bless you?*"

Churchill reached in and grabbed one of the steel stamped MP38 maschinenpistoles, holding it up for focus. The term *Schmeisser* was a British colloquialism monikered after *Hugo Schmeisser,* the creator of the MP18 submachine gun. Funnily enough, he was not involved in the design or production of the MP38 at all, but the name stuck like a genetic appellation.

The metal clacked as Churchill shook it free of dirt.

"Swell," eyebrows raised at the realization, Hardy commented. With both hands, he collected one of the squalid submachine guns, eyeing it over as if it were the first time he had ever handled such a weapon before.

There was a pink worm crawling on his one, which he flicked clear and blew off the dirt from the cold metal while he examined the weapon, getting a feel for the weight. It had no magazine inserted, thus was unloaded. He found the obvious receiver bolt and touched it, unable to confidently navigate the killing contraption and making it obvious this was not his forte.

Jack snatched the empty weapon from him, harshly pinching the bolt back and forth several times to clear it of debris. He then squeezed the trigger of the gun to close the breach with a discernible *chik* that proved it was still functional.

Hardy nodded his head, observing this instance.

It fuelled his unthinkingly enthusiastic mentality.

"Alright, gimme the other one and some bullets, let's go—"

"Not so fast," Churchill instructed with a calculated mind. He poised with the two MP38s up by his shoulders, jerking his head at Hardy who stared blankly. "Say: *'Nicht schießen'.*"

Hardy squinted. "*Nikked scheessan?*"

"It means *don't shoot* in German," Churchill informed whilst they prepared for their impromptu last-ditch infiltration mission, in which a classic Churchill plan was brewing. "We're going to employ the use of some *charades* to get us down there and beneath their radar."

Where Churchill seemed in a comfortable state or at least able to steady his nerve, Hardy wore a constant expression of uncertainty and reservation.

"Practise the saying," Jack insisted, forcing his participation. "In order to get down there at all, we need to use our brains over brawn, and that means playing the part."

Hardy cocked his eye. "... what are you scheming at, Captain?"

"The plan," Churchill affirmed, an oversimplification. "Trust me. If you can't at least *sound* German, we're dead men before you even get to pull any triggers. Now, speak the phrase. We don't have much time."

Not at all convinced of the advantage given by this master plan, Hardy's raised brow was accompanied with sarcasm. "How do you say *this is a stupid fuckin' idea* in German?"

With dagger eyes, Churchill gawked him. He reached in and handed him the in-tact German stahlhelm he would be wearing as a part of his disguise. "Hold this."

Hardy probed it. "Has this had a dead man's head in it?"

"Probably."

"Fuck meee ..." scoffing after removing his fedora, Hardy examined the inside more closely and was repulsed. He winced, "It smells like a toe."

"Come on. Speak the phrase."

"*Nict ... nicht-schi-e-ssen.*"

"Again."

"*Nicht. Schie-ßen,*" Hardy practised, mastering pronunciation of the sharp S whilst arranging the chin strap of the open stahlhelm as Churchill helped button up the oversized German jacket over his leather jacket, concealing his civilian attire. The fit was slightly large for the five-foot-five American. His dark trousers were already muddy, as were his shoes, and could pass as uniform at a glance. Churchill tightened the smock around his waist with one of the leather utility belts full of pouches, making it seem as though it fit appropriately.

"It's a little big, but it'll have to do," Churchill said as he finalized, taking and plonking the German steel helmet onto Hardy's head and doing the strap up tight. He smeared a bit of mud across his cheeks and over his nose, in his hairline, masking his features a little with hopes that the Germans might not immediately discern his ethnicity—or at least not fully realize his Western appearance and stereotypical *All-American* jawline.

"*Nicht schießen,*" Churchill articulated slowly, and with more sophisticated pronunciation, recalling it from basic trainings prior to their shipment to France. Useful terms for distress were taught to soldiers prior to foreign placement in case of capture by the enemy.

"Nicht schießen," Hardy said again. A passable performance.

"Not bad. Make sure to deliver it with a European tone. The sell is in the accent as much as the pronunciation. Now try this one: '*Gefangene*.'"

"*Jee-fang?*" Hardy repeated half-assed, incorrectly pronouncing the German word. He tried again and again before Churchill corrected him, speaking phonetically. "Geff-an-nee. Gefangene?"

"Like this: *Gef. Ange. Ne.*"

Hardy nodded, a little overwhelmed.

"Remember, for this plan: we're actors. So, *act.*"

Churchill hoped for Hardy to assume a sort of *Dutch courage* with that sentiment; pretending to act a part in order to attain a dutiful bravery; perhaps even kickstart something that resided within most men. Instead, the American expressed doubt and issued it with a whimsical jab.

"Like you act like you know what you're doing?"

Churchill brushed it off. "Just pretend you're in a movie, opposite *Rita Hayworth* herself, and a possible post-scene *shag* hangs in the balance of your performance, eh? Sham a European accent when you speak the German words to your mates."

"Sure thing."

They were out of time.

"Don't worry. You've got this ..." Churchill instilled with a confident nod. "Just think of Hayworth's baps, eh? Waiting for you yond the finish line."

He closed his eyes. "Alright, alright. *Rita Hayworth's tits,* alright. *Ge-ge ... gefangene?"* Hardy almost got it. Then he did, complete with accent, spot on. It surprised Jack—it was as if he became somebody else, acting the scene. *"Gefangene."*

Churchill smirked and gave him a nod whilst he smeared mud and grime all about his own uniform, making it filthy and war-torn. With blade assistance, he tore a sleeve and ripped some pockets. He even cut a laceration across his outer forearm with a knife, not too deep that it would mortally hinder him, but it helped sell the severity. He strapped it up tight immediately following the application of bloody dab transfers elsewhere on his body, smearing the crimson mess across the side of his face and over his ear. It gave the appearance that he had been wounded and beaten, therefore weak and less threatening. Less likely they'd put a bullet straight in his head and want to torture him playfully first.

"Hey, what are you doin', man?" Hardy scoffed aghast and with shock as he witnessed Churchill act like an artist with a palette—a palette that contained only red paint. He dabbed his own blood across his face, his chin, even on his neck. With the outlining of dirt and shadow, he looked a real battle-worn mess.

Jack next applied smears to his uniform tears, making it look nasty.

He informed in quote whilst he applied his make-up. " *'Appear weak when you are strong'.* The Huns will be less likely to predict any chance of resistance if they suspect the prisoner to be already half-spent or unable. They'll let their guards down an inch."

Churchill emptied his pockets and pouches upon his utility belt, leaving them exposed and upturned, as if they had already been thoroughly searched, hence not needing to be searched again.

He took the spare six-bullet cylinder speed-loaders from out of one of the pouches and handed them to Hardy, who hid the sidearm ammunition in a trouser pocket. He felt some of them unlatch, spilling bullets loosely. Churchill next drew his heavy Webley revolver from his leather hip holster and double-checked it was loaded. With his spare palm, he snapped shut the clasp and stepped around Hardy's idle composure, where he tucked it into the rear of Hardy's waistline, just out of sight and under the hang of the smock.

He walked back in front. "It's loaded."

"Why are you giving me all the guns? Shouldn't you keep that?"

"Nowhere logical I can hide it. If they notice a bulge, the jig is up."

Unstrapping his leather quiver, Churchill placed his longbow and arrows in a neat stash upon the base of the foothill. He would not be able to smuggle them into this arena. His claybeg, however ...

He did not want to be improperly dressed for action.

Churchill unsheathed his sword, casting aside only the leather scabbard onto the pile of other dressed-down possessions that he could not bring, intending to somehow take the naked 38-inch, double-edged sword with brass knuckleduster hilt.

"Okay, I'm ready. Give me the biggest gun and lots of bullets. Let's go kill these fuckers," Hardy remarked bashfully, with a heavy sense of savagery within his connotation. It was only natural for him to want rash, abrupt vengeance on those who killed his colleague and friend.

"Oi," Churchill exclaimed, halting him from progressing, noticing that he was now brandished one of the MP38s. "This isn't the time to go cowboy on your mates down there, lad. Devil-may-care and generally neither do I, but I still need you for this. I need regular *Hardy*, not fool*hardy*."

Hardy faced him, clenching the empty Schmeisser.

He was pissed off and ready for war. He wanted to avenge Ny.

"Are you fuckin' with me right now, Captain? Grab the other gun and load up. Let's fuckin' go already!"

"Hold your horses, lad," Churchill stopped him again, staking his blade into the dirt in order to free his hands. "Do you even know how to use that bloody thing?!"

Hardy inspected the unloaded MP38 in his midst.

He knew enough, so replied sarcastically.

"This end's the dangerous one, right?"

Churchill stared blankly, letting him exhume his machismo.

"Point it at Gerry, squeeze here, and hold the fuck on, yeah? How hard can it be. Relax, Captain. I'm a journalist. I am observant. I've watched a few soldiers do battle in my time."

"*Hah,* granted, but are you prepared for the recoil? For the volume? Or the kick of the brunt? It handles differently when you're the one dishing-out the damage."

"I can handle myself."

Jack challenged his self-confidence, suspecting the overconfidence of only masking his bloodthirst for vengeance. "And what about when it runs out of bullets? Or if it jams? What do you do then, eh, tough guy?"

"O.K, well, give me a crash course, then, genius."

Churchill sneered, quickly snatching it from his grasp.

The speed at which Hardy lost possession of the weapon was enough to mildly destabilize his surefootedness.

"Lesson one: hold on to the fucking gun."

Hardy bobbed his head in a touché manner.

"Pay attention," Jack stated, twisting his position to allow for Hardy to better observe the MP38. "It's fully automatic. You get thirty shots fed through a bottom-fed magazine that inserts *here*."

Hardy watched keenly as he held it properly, showing off the mag well, the circular release button, and how to change it when needed.

"Insert *here* and pull this back *here*. Fire. Press *here* and you can rip an empty mag out the bottom if you push *this* in. You insert a fresh, and pinch the fire pin forward again like *this*," Churchill added, instead of allowing for him to perform the reloading procedure, he effectively confiscated the weapon and walked away—but not before throwing him a little inappropriate innuendo. "It's your first time, lad. Trust me when I say you'll blow your load within seconds."

"Hey!—" Hardy protested, following the remark. The outburst was not in relation to the comment about his ejaculate, but because Churchill was again seemingly, again, denying him his madcap revenge.

"It's time to be smart, not stupid. Brains over brawn. You ever heard of *Sun Tzu?*" Churchill interposed. He faced him after stepping over the rest of the unearthed German gear sets which he had spread out. Churchill held onto the gun.

Hardy shook his head a little. It was an impatient gesture barely recognized behind his throbbing sense of resentment and vengeance.

"What about *The Art of War?*"

Hardy shrugged. "Sure, who hasn't."

"Sun Tzu is the author. *'It is the unemotional, reserved, calm, detached warrior who wins. Not the hothead seeking vengeance',*" Churchill dictated from his knowledge of the aforementioned book. "In a world like this, that book *can* and *should* be your bible."

Hardy had sulked and held it while Churchill quoted.

"Be honest, Captain ... I know they call you *Mad Jack,* but are you actually *fucking nuts?*" he exclaimed, irritably. He simply didn't not understand the relevance the way Churchill did. "They're about to make a dessert buffet out of your little girlfriend in there, if they haven't started to already, and we're sittin' here with our thumbs up our asses, quoting some long-dead Japanese dickhead."

"Sun Tzu was *Chinese.*"

Hardy was without words, holding his grimacing face, fuming on the inside.

Frustratingly composed, Churchill expanded upon his correction, reiterating and educating the American. "He's a long-dead *Chinese* dickhead."

Hardy tilted. "Oh, for fuc—"

"Okay, okay. Look, I know, Felix, okay ..." Churchill levelled him out. It was an unneeded reminder of the weight baring on his shoulders. "You're pissed, I get it. I am too. They shot your mate. They're evil sods and they deserve to be put down. Sods like that have killed *my mates,* too, alright? Quite a few of 'em, and they'll continue to do so, again and again, ad infinitum. It's the same with loads of innocent people along the way of their senseless, racial, antisemitic rampage as they take Europe by force like an unstoppable juggernaut ..."

Hardy held his zoned gaze, finally meeting Churchill's.

"That's not to mention the status of Ève and the DuPont family in there ... The truth is, I *don't know* if they're going to be okay, and it pains me to think of it ... But what I *do know* is that we cannot help them if we are *dead* the moment we step out of the gates."

Hardy took a breath.

He seemed to calm.

"I know my art of war, Felix. It's how I survive. How I win. How I outsmart my enemy at every move; stay two steps ahead. It is how I am able to kill them, absent penitence. It is what has kept me alive in situations where I should have perished."

Hardy indulged Churchill, hearing him out.

"Okay then, *Mad Jack.* If not to kill those fuckers, what's your plan?"

"Oh, the plan is we're going to kill those fuckers ..."

It perked Hardy's attention to be quoted, and he looked to Churchill with an askew gaze in time to catch the incoming Schmeisser lofted up at him.

"Just in a style their smooth brains won't see coming."

Finding confidence in Churchill, Hardy concurred with a nod.

"Okay. We're out of time," Churchill stated, extending a stick magazine of nine-millimetre bullets for Hardy's usage. "Are you ready?"

Hardy bobbled his head further, unsure. "Not really, no."

He tightened the latch of the stahlhelm chin strap before accepting the ammunition for the MP38. Before Jack's watchful sterling stare, he inserted the magazine firmly into the mag well and confidently wrenched the bolt, placing the weapon into condition zero.

He was ready.

"One more word to remember ..."

Hardy's bleak eyeline raised onto Churchill.

"*Bellend.*"

That didn't sound as hard to pronounce as all the other German words, and then he realized it was English.

Hardy's brow inverted. "*Bellend?*"

"It'll be our *trigger,*" Churchill further explained, and thereupon saw Hardy's lack of insight. He furthered, "Our *safe word,* if you will."

"What's a *safe word?*"

Churchill rolled his eyes. "You've clearly never visited Amsterdam's red-light district ...?" His tone suggested Mad Jack had certainly experienced some kinky shit whilst touring abroad—before Holland was occupied.

Hardy's stare held tame, blinking ever so unenthusiastically before responding cynically. "Ha-ha, another sex joke. You've probably got a VD—hilarious—but, how's about you explain the *trigger* part, Casanova."

Not biting back, Churchill stabilized their scheming. "We're going to be undercover out there. We can't exactly communicate duress. If you *say* or *hear* that word uttered during our charade, it's the trigger, okay? Once spoken, we unleash both our simultaneous attacks. Someone says it, everything goes to Hell, understand? Everything dies."

Hardy remarked whimsically. "Including us?"

Churchill held a shrug. "Hopefully not right away."

"Why not just simply say '*O.K. go'?* Or something dramatic, like, '*unleash hell!'?*"

"Because the surprise attack is our best weapon," Churchill affirmed. "We're about to become inserted into a circumstance where every nanosecond counts, lad. Contrary to popular belief, screaming *open fire!* before you do so can sort of defeat the purpose if you're catching the enemy off-foot. We don't want to let these bastards gain even a smidgen of cover in this ..."

Hardy scrunched his nose. He stated truthfully, understanding the fundamentals of the plan and the odds of its success.

"For the record, this is a really bad idea ..."

It was time for them to walk up the mound which hid their preparations, becoming exposed to the farmstead and the populous of its German occupancy as they marched insouciantly near it, commencing their *Trojan horse*-esque ruse.

After the keen observation of Hardy's coherent gunmanship, Churchill turned. In wait, his claybeg protruded at hip level from the earth, the empty eyelets staring at him. It was almost symbolic in the way it called to him, and Jack took a step in reverse to collect it fluently before they marched willingly into the jaws of death.

He looked the part of a captured prisoner ... but there was no way Mad Jack Churchill was going to be improperly dressed ...

Tick-tock, tick-tock ...

Every second ticked loudly on the wind-up clock located on the shelf.

The silence was not so much awkward as it was tense and filled with an overdose of fear and distress for the fatherless DuPont family, now held hostage and at the mercy of the invaded German soldiers. This overwhelming trepidation was combined with the lingering despair of their recent loss, a memory looped in their quivering psyches after witnessing their beloved father's execution.

Young teary-eyed daughters Yana and Audréy stood clenched and shivering at the head of the fully dressed dining table, poised like servants. Stripped of much of their attire, as per instruction by the domineering and abuse-threatening Nazis, the barely teenaged sisters were garbed only in their baring nightgowns. The nightdresses were a cause for much undue awareness, intentionally displaying every outline and curve and leaving little detail of their petite forms to the imagination of their disgusting captors.

These same soldiers now sat inside and at the dining table, much alike how the British soldiers did a week ago, only under much different circumstances. Unlike the friendly and respectful British soldiers, the Germans remained mostly armed with their weapons or at least had them at arm's reach. They had slackened their fatigues, loosened their shoulder straps and suspenders, untucked their shirts, and removed their stahlhelms. Jackets and wet smocks were dumped over armchairs, draping the now offset furniture. They had slipped off their large, heavy, muddy combat boots after carelessly traipsing mud and grime through the premises. The cleanliness of their guests' entrance was the least of the DuPont's concerns at the moment.

Tonight was seemingly to be the night for the hard-working Germans to let their hair down. All dutiful regard suspended. All bets were off. They were to enjoy these self-proclaimed spoils of war, as per their feldwebel's orders.

Between those relaxing with a mug of alcohol from one of the late Gérard's homemade port barrels and those on guard outside, the Waffen-SS unit had a rostered turn-taking system of perversion they had concocted, per every French home they saw fit to invade and dictate, before subjugating it from existence and evading prosecution for their sin. Sins that they were immediately absolved of by word of their holy pastor, the *feldbischof.*

The Bishop.

To them, dubbed just *'the Bish'.*

The feldbischof was a high-ranking officer within the Waffen-SS, attaining the rank of SS-Sturmhauptführer of the *14th Company, 3rd Schutzstaffel Division Totenkopf.* This was a position directly beneath the *head storm leader, SS-Hauptsturmführer Fritz Knöchlein.*

Along with his holiness, for these select few tonight it was a session to lay down arms, relax, and be served and then serviced by these gorgeous and innocent captured French women in this beautiful and grossly stocked home. With the expectation of death so foretold, the French would always obey and submit to the needs of the Germans at the very hint of them perhaps sparing their lives.

At the head of the dining table sat guest German Field Bishop with the commanding officer feldwebel of this SS unit, and architect of this particular indulgence of debauchery.

Tonight, like most nights, he lived like their holy king, praised and pardoned.

Smiling and laughing in vast conversation, the men at the table conversed belligerently. They drank from topped glasses of the deceased man of the house's proud port supply, of which if they did not like the selection, they shattered the bottles against a wall in the living room like mindless barbarians. Due to slight malnutrition from a life lived on the frontlines, the effects of the alcohol worked fast. The lot were easily loose, louder, and more abusive than your average Nazi fuckwit.

After the Bishop finished conversing with the young men of the unit, he removed his gloves and placed them with his feldmütze cap on the table. None of the observing French girls could understand as they listened to them speak in German dialect, so they undoubtedly spoke ill and derogatorily of them.

The Bish leant back and glanced to his side, examining the form of the youngest of the DuPont daughters, Yana. Not that it would matter to him or the others who would no doubt partake, but she was a pre-teen barely in double digits. Audréy, to her right, was barely a teenager—both were young enough to be the man's granddaughters.

His tiny, beady eyes glowered over Yana's thin, athletically firm young body as she stood, trembling not from the chill of the air, but out of fear. He smiled wickedly, showing off his set of grotesquely crooked, cigarette-stained teeth.

"Ne crains pas, mon enfant," he said in his best French. "Tout sera bientôt fini ..."

< *'Fear not, my child. It will all be over soon ...'* >

Beside him, the young, scrawny feldwebel took in her form with obvious sexual intent, tenderly touching her on the shoulder with his skeletal pale fingers. The grotesque sensation caused her to flinch in her trembling state. As the delicate touch of his fingertips drew traced down her lower back, just above her buttocks, a tear ran from each of her eyes as she pinched them both shut. Her innocence protected her from the extent of knowledge of what could possibly come.

Behind them in the kitchen, eldest sister Ève and her mother, the recently widowed Sophie DuPont, cast gleams of pure hatred towards the occurrence. They were forced to slave over the sink and stove under the guard of a kitted-up, scary looking soldier with a bald head and no eyebrows.

He watched their every move intently from behind.

They were also dressed down into nothing more than their skimpy nightgowns ahead of tonight's one-sided proceedings.

The set-up was like some sick DIY Nazi *Moulin Rouge*.

Sophie was emotionally crushed by the loss of her husband.

The visible numbness of her crippling vulnerability was only intensified by the second as she watched powerlessly. She had absolutely no control over anything that would transpire this night to either herself or her daughters. She was a helpless wreck, moving like a zombified drone, weeping profusely. Perhaps she had foreseen this outcome all along? She pinched her teary, depressed eyes closed and shied away from her glance at her other daughters in the dining room, who were keeping the other Germans company whilst they prepared their feast.

On the menu, other than steamed vegetables and roast chicken, was severe terror, bereavement, torture, battery, sexual assault, and eventually—at that point, most welcomed—death for dessert.

Beside Sophie over the filled bucket in the kitchen sink, the eldest and more composed daughter Ève slyly inched over after checking on the cooking chicken in the oven. She gently touched her mother's hand as she lent weakly over the sink, chopping potatoes before dropping them into steaming water.

The German soldiers may have been cunts, but they weren't stupid. The drawer which housed the sharp bladed or pointy utensils had been emptied, and all potential weapons confiscated prior to dinner preparations. She was in the process of peeling and chopping the food with nothing more than a basic peeler.

There was not much she could say, due to lack of finding the words, but her gesture was all that was needed to bring her mother to breaking point. Ève leant in to catch her with a firm embrace as she wept and sobbed with sorrow and dread aloud. Within seconds, the bald SS troop guarding them stepped in with his big rifle, poking his attached bayonet between them and hissing at them in fierce tone to shape them up and force them apart. When they resisted, however slightly, he threatened to beat them with the butt of his rifle or a balled fist.

Threats of physical violence typically worked ...

... but this time, Sophie DuPont could take no more.

She challenged the soldier, shoving him away and screaming in his face with a pitch, cursing in French. Her face became as red as the tomatoes she had prepared recently. Her outburst muted the garish banter in the connecting room, and the other soldiers pushed their chairs out, preparing to intervene in gang force ...

The bald guard stepped back in, elbowing the weightless Sophie clear, and she collapsed to the tiled floor against the wooden cupboard with a hollow thump. He raised his rifle above Ève, threatening to butt her in the head, possibly even killing her—

Right as things escalated, there was a shout from outside.

It alerted everyone.

The German voice caused alarm, interrupting the guard's disciplinary action. It halted their commotion in the kitchen, and all men indoors quickly upped from the table and yanked the curtains apart from the glass window, scanning outside into the subdued sunset. Some even grabbed their placed weaponry, becoming increasingly vigilant.

The feldwebel upped from his seat last, instructing the others to calm down and to remain seated inside. To finish their drinks and to relax. He moved past the feldbischof, gesturing that he would sort out whatever interruption had come their way.

Suspenders dangling out of his undone uniform, he, himself, then headed for the front door with his swirling glass of port and reefed it open. He filled the doorframe and scanned into the dusk setting as the many armed troops about the front of the farmhouse began to inch forward, on guard ...

Beside him, the feldbischof allowed for his intervention.

Truth was, the field bishop's biggest fear right now was having another German unit roll through—one not loyal to the abusive nature of the SS, like possibly an honest *Wehrmacht* unit, if such a thing could be labelled as such within the ranks of Nazi Germany. Notwithstanding, a unit who might frown upon their obnoxious ways and maybe even report their actions to their superiors.

With a dozen metallic *click-clack, chit-chit* sounds of rounds being chambered and safeties being disengaged, the soldiers about the front of the farmhouse focused on the direction.

Their attention was on a lone, captured British prisoner as he was escorted by a singular German soldier in the distance, treading towards the farmstead.

Hands upon his head, the enemy Englishman marched under the guard of a friendly, albeit roughed-up, kamerad and headed their way.

The feldwebel reported the news and the Bishop sprouted a smile.

He loved to entertain prisoners of war ...

"Bereite einen anderen platz am tisch vor, Männer," he said over his shoulder in German to his colleagues. "Wir haben einen Englischen gast."

< *'Prepare another seat at the table, men. We have an English guest.'* >

In the kitchen as she attended to her mother, the knowledgeable Ève's ears pricked ...

Now that the ugly bald guard had released his threatening torment from upon them, she had embraced her mother's distressed collapse.

She could speak a little German, at least enough to understand what the feldwebel relayed to his men ...

"*Englischen*," she murmured in her tiny voice, quickly rising from the floor and temporarily leaving her mother. She discretely inched near the window, attempting to gain a look of the Englishman to which the Germans referred ...

... and she *prayed* that it was *him.*

"Fuck, they've seen us ..."

"Fuck, fuck, fuck ..."

"Fuck, this is a fuckin' shit idea ..."

In panicked whispers, Felix Hardy cursed unrelentingly under his breath out of utter nervousness and agitation as he peered out slightly from behind the calm Jack Churchill. The two had walked at an average pace from the outskirts of the farm and towards the house and were now about one hundred and twenty feet out and almost within earshot of the exterior German guards.

With a stahlhelm helmet strapped firmly atop his head and disguised in German uniform attire, the extremely under-qualified American journalist held a tense aim of his weapon against the back of his pretend prisoner: a captured British army captain. Hands on his head, the disgruntled enemy soldier strode hesitantly before him, face down in the dumps.

They each looked and played the part well. So far.

Complete with muddy streaks across their faces, even blood for the 'wounded' prisoner, an artistic detail inspired by Churchill to make him seem even less of a threat, Jack also acted out a bit of a limp and an added grimace to channel a sense of pain and distress. This was in hope of him appearing as even less of a viable threat to the antagonistic German soldiers at the farmhouse.

"Keep your voice down," out and to the side, Churchill replied through gritted teeth, pretending an extension of discomfort. They were trudging steadily across the marshland and to the DuPont dairy farm at gunpoint. Occasionally, he felt the barrel of Hardy's loaded submachine gun press into his back. He would be lying if he said the fact the fully loaded weapon was in the edgy grip and jittery trigger finger of the Yank didn't make him at least *a* little nervous for real.

He cast him a simple reminder. "And keep your finger off the *damn* trigger, will you!"

"*I am!*" Hardy hissed uneasily. "Fuck, I told you, this is a *really* bad fuckin' idea! Fuck! Fuck, fuck, fuuuuck ..."

"Oi, *knock it off!*" Churchill shushed, twisting a little to address Hardy without shouting. "*Stop! Speaking! English!*"

He faced ahead, now a hundred feet out and closing. They were now able to see the defining features of all the German soldiers, which included the black holes of the barrels of their rifles which were aimed their way with a measure of mistrust.

Churchill observed their sceptical behaviour. Although it was only natural for them to react as such and not swallow the bait whole, it was entirely possible that they may have just seen them conversing. If this plan was undersold, it was game over.

"*Shove me.*"

"What?" Hardy hissed, practically hiding behind Churchill.

"*Push me!*" Churchill whispered again, and Hardy complied with a pulled-punch strike across his shoulder blades with the length of the gun in his hands. Churchill overplayed it, acting as if it impacted a lot more than it did. Regardless, it successfully sold the act that he was an abused prisoner of war, and that Hardy was his violent captor from another unit of whom these Gerrys did not recognize.

"*Shout out ...*"

"*Huh?*" Hardy murmured, almost unable to hear Churchill over the thumping of his own heartbeat inside of his head.

"*Do you not recall what I taught you barely ten damn minutes ago?*"

Churchill did not expand further. Could not for risk of ruining the charade. Instead, he let Hardy come across one of the most important parts to this insane plan on his own accord. He trusted he had it in him. If he didn't ... they were both dead.

"Oh ..." Hardy recalled. He inched out from behind Churchill in their slow incoming parade, maintaining hold of his Schmeisser upon his back as they marched. Hardy remained in some semblance of control as he escorted his English prisoner towards his fellow German enemy force by the farmhouse. At the top of his lungs, like he had practised, he informed the armed krauts in a kind and decent accent:

"*Nicht schießen!*"

With each trudge in approach to the heavily guarded farmhouse, Hardy's heartbeat thundered so deafeningly loud in his head he could barely hear himself think.

White-knuckled and clenching, his hands quaked so compulsively that he was sure to retain his finger from the trigger piece entirely in case of premature discharge.

Low-browed, Churchill performed an inconspicuous tally of their numbers as they gravitated closer with each step. Hands on his head in a submissive gesture, he kept his face down, his eyeline gracing the brim of his aslant maroon beret—which, naturally, he kept on even for this ruse.

"Ge ... *Gefangene!*" Hardy finally announced, throwing his voice out for the Germans to hear. There was a heavy tremble in his tenor, evident beneath his accented tone. Thankfully, as a last resort, he feinted a loss of breath, as if he had a hard time capturing and transferring the prisoner under guard and was perhaps even injured, himself.

It was believable.

The improv covered his voice jump adequately and the Germans bought it. They seemed more interested in the British prisoner, paying note to the rank and insignia Churchill had purposely left exposed and undirtied over his breast and shoulder.

He would be a big fish for them to catch.

From the doorway to the DuPont family house, the SS kommandierender offizier gleamed with wide eyes. This feldwebel was still dressed down in his uniform, carrying a rifle and a concerned gleam. Upon further study of Churchill's insignia, he beamed especially happily recognizing that they had just captured an Allied *British captain.*

Such a capture would be handsomely recognized and rewarded.

He relayed something in German and from the house appeared the uniquely uniformed feldbischof, emulating from a peering, mousey view of the discourse so far. His sheepish behaviour exhumed the guilt of his unjust actions, likely fearful of their disgusting antics being found out.

In German, the feldbischof asserted his overall command and ordered something to the surrounding guards, and they fanned a little around the captive Churchill and rearguard Hardy in an arrowhead-esque welcoming party. The partially dressed feldwebel progressed up the middle with his rifle unceremoniously by his side, likely entrusting his men to retain guard of these new arrivals.

In the background, the feldbischof stepped down from the house, first taking the time to slip on his black leather boots by the door.

Acting weak in his movements and his gaze, Churchill raised his angle of focus a little from his down-in-the-dumps expression, his hands weighing his face forward. His blue eyes glared sharply, assessing, absorbing every detail ...

From his view, he could count four SS troops outside the front of the house. There was the indisputably unhinged feldbischof in the doorframe, their feldwebel CO, soon to be amongst them, making six. Two other soldiers were stationed out far by the parked Einheitsdiesel troop transport truck by the barn, neither of which appeared to bear arms, but likely had them nearby. At this point in time, due to his arrival, the five soldiers brought themselves within close proximity: two on either side, and the feldwebel up the middle, reaching between eight and forty feet away from his position. A welcoming party of sorts.

These numbers were not inclusive of whoever else still remained inside the house. Given the prior headcount, Churchill estimated approximately another five or six inside.

Due to Hardy's position directly behind him with a gun trained on his back, none of the SS troops thought to move too far behind his location to form a perimeter. However, they still marginally trained their rifles upon them both at hip level. In that regard, four of the five had their fingers wrapped around the triggers of their Karabiner 98k rifles.

The rifle was a powerful 7.92mm calibre long-ranged weapon, more than capable of killing either one of them with one shot, however ... it was bolt-action and slow. The 98k was gradual firing and limited within close proximity. The fact they were bolt guns was a blessing in disguise. If they fired and missed their target, they could not fire again for a full two-to-three seconds whilst the shooter rearranged one of their hands and pedalled the lever mechanism upon the top of the weapon's receiver to eject the spend shell and cycle another bullet into the chamber.

A lot can happen in two-to-three seconds.

The fifth trooper, who was positioned in the middle beside the front door where the feldbischof was located, held an MP38 submachine gun. Churchill marked him as the most threatening of the lot and, from his position, the submachine-gunner oversaw this entire detention. Even with a half-assed hip-level spray, that soldier could squeeze and swoop his munitions expel, laying waste to everything in front of him at a fully automatic rate of fire. Even if he missed Churchill's fast movements with the first shot, second, third, or even *tenth* shot, the gun was an automatic and held thirty rounds. The soldier could just hold the trigger and douse the area, eventually hitting him.

Churchill scanned past these close five SS troops, noticing the two soldiers over by the parked truck, sixty feet away and near the barn. The two may have been far off and seemingly weaponless, but they were still a viable threat. They were presently relaxed and sharing a match light, sparking fresh cigarettes. They likely had firearms stowed by the truck or somewhere at arms-length and could be armed within seconds if a fight broke out.

Grinding his teeth within his mouth to crush the trepidation and accentuate concentration, Churchill glared about the SS troops. A suppressed utter hatred boiled just beneath the surface, along with the overbearing desperation. It was a carbonated abhorrence, bottled up and stowed by the crate load, now becoming shaken and ready to pop off at any minute.

His focus continued scanning, counting, planning ...

He gained a slightly better idea of those inside of the DuPont residence. Past the feldbischof—the highest-ranking cockhead here—who was now stepping down from the house and into the mud with his unlaced boots, there appeared to be *five more* German troopers. They seemed unarmed and not even dressed in uniform—boots off, helmets off, jackets off, and with no firearms within their possessions. Although, again, they probably had them within a reachable range and would be armed and dangerous within seconds of a fight.

Next ... Jack saw them; Yana and Audréy DuPont.

His eyes lost focus, and he scanned frantically.

Then ... through a part in the kitchen curtains, their mother Sophie and, finally ... Ève.

He made her distinguishable brown stare.

His heart fluttered.

Jack Churchill held his gaze with her in a mesmeric moment.

It was as if time briefly slowed ...

He could read the anguish in her amber brown with a hazelnut blush, honey glowing eyes, as well as a contentment and longing for him, that she simply could not hide. She did well not to break into hysterics at the very sight of the man she cherished.

He saw her eyes widen ...

Saw her mouth his name ...

In her tone of voice and accent, he heard it as clearly in his mind as if she were by his side, singing it in whisper.

The DuPonts each recognized him.

The Germans had toyed with them prior to now.

Tormented them, made them dress in promiscuous nightgowns which they probably giggled at as they flicked the straps from their shoulders, catching an eyeball of skin like right royal perverts in need of a decent spanking.

Churchill's chiselled jaw tensed under the applied dry blood and mud to disguise his condition, and he peeled his gaze away from Ève as her and her brunette family spied past their captors.

They undoubtedly thanked Christ for sending a saviour to them in the form of this man; this soldier, champion, this hero ... he was their only hope.

Churchill prayed for a second that they remained calm. That they continued to be somewhat docile, and not create a scene at the sight of him. They did so, quietly gesturing amongst themselves, expressing their recognition of the British man.

... and then, Churchill's gaze found Gérard lying dead in the mud.

Such an innocent, kind-hearted man, gone.

He was made to beg on his knees, and then shot like a dog.

A fresh dowse of fuel thrown upon his internal fire.

His blood got hot.

Jack felt the rage swell in his chest.

A spark to ignite the inferno.

Churchill and Hardy's motion ceased in their progression, now directly on the muddy clearing before the DuPont home, on ground he had stood on just days prior. They were effectively within the open jaws of death, semi-surrounded by armed SS troops. They, too, halted in their formation, encircling this new arrival.

Time for their agreed signal: the code word.

The situation's tension grew by the second ...

... coming to a head.

"Bunch of bellends," Churchill stated quietly through his gritted teeth. He said the word facing the German welcome party with rifles as if he addressed *them,* none of whom spoke English well enough to perceive the phrase as a signal ...

... however, there was no corresponding action from the secret ally behind him with the gun.

"I said, you bunch of *bellends!"* Churchill stated again, this time, louder and more angrily, as if he wished to provoke the SS troops who each stared him down.

A show of great discipline, they refrained from killing him then and there. Instead, the armed soldiers watched as the feldbischof strode forth in the sludge.

Gradually, Churchill's eyes elevated onto the German military chaplain, taking in the vague blood spatter patterns on his dark leather uniform, red on black.

He grumbled modestly, seemingly content with the prisoner offering made by this lowly German soldier. "Danke, dass du ihn mir vorgestellt hast ..."

The very sound of the German accent pestered Churchill.

"Whenever. You are. Ready. *Bellend."*

Behind him ... Hardy seemed frozen.

The code word they had agreed upon had been issued:

NICHT SCHIEẞEN | **139**

'BELLEND'.

The paralysis Hardy had sustained from the asphyxiating panic of this desperate mission had seemingly overcome him after laying sight upon his fallen colleague, Omar Ny. The late photographer felled face down in the mud, his eyes glued open with a deathly, hollowed, and haunting sideward stare.

Scarily, due to the angle, Ny's vacant stare seemed to home in on Hardy's position. They looked as though he was still there somehow, like a trapped soul in a dead body, watching him from the afterlife.

As a warfront journalist, Felix Hardy had seen dead people before in his line of work ... but never someone he knew personally. This hit differently.

The sight of his departed colleague stopped him dead in the tracks.

"Oi, bellend! *Shit!*" Churchill cursed frustratedly, eyes scanning the surrounding crowd of murderous krauts.

A strange analogy given the high stakes of the present predicament, but Jack felt like a debauched sailor who had gone into the funky sex brothel expecting to hold the power of the scenario, only to find the agreed-upon safe word had no effect. And now *he* was about to be unrelentingly fucked.

Gleaming centre with a degree of foreboding, Churchill watched as the trench coat wearing feldbischof strode in closer, seeming to overshadow him with a sense of grotesque friskiness. He smiled upon his glum expression with distractingly crooked and yellow stained teeth, saying something apparently hilariously condescending towards the British prisoner to his entourage of troops.

Jack heard their shared giggle in operatic theatrical acoustics.

He held his focus—eyes down and forward. Powerless.

In the seconds to follow, Churchill watched the unhinged Hun present a Luger P08 handgun from his black hip holster. It was the same weapon he had used to execute Gérard and Ny not moments ago, and he assumed he was about to be next ...

The German soldiers around the vicinity laughed and sniggered at the comment of their beloved, dear and feared feldbischof.

It was in that instance that Churchill noticed their humour seemed to be accompanied with a slight decrease of their guard duties. He distinguished with his eagle-eyed peripherals that the flanking men with guns trained upon him began to reduce their aim slightly, even just by a few inches, in order to conform. Their tight composures loosened. Some even removed their fingers from the triggers, instead wrapping them around the stocks or trigger guards whilst their barrels swayed ...

Churchill's cunning stare scanned wider than before, noticing the slight changes in the environment as the SS troops relaxed. This would gain a second of delay in their response times when he would attack—*if* he could attack, that was ... since his cohort, Hardy, had suddenly gone AWOL from the plan.

After a prolonged enjoyment of the comedy, the German feldbischof's attention eventually returned onto the captive, and Churchill's blood boiled.

"Fuck you! You fascist fuckwit," Churchill stated harshly in retort to whatever the field bishop had said about him to his comrades in German. "Hope you choke on the Führer's stunted cock, mate."

Calmy, and whilst waving the loaded pistol, the feldbischof issued an order, communicating it in fairly decent English in his thick accent. "Geh auf deine Knies. *Get-on-zee-knees* ..."

It was probably all the Nazi could say and said it frequently, right before he shot whoever knelt in the forehead.

Playing the part, the brooding Churchill dropped.

His knees planted into the sludge muck below.

He did so rigidly and with care not to hunch over or bend too far, intentionally keeping his core tight and straight ...

... keeping his hands behind his head ...

... where his fingertips wriggled downward, grazing the eyelets of the knuckleduster handle groove of the claybeg sword tucked and hidden down his back, beneath his shirt.

"Bellend!" he said again, firmly and with the upmost discretion. It piggybacked as a taunt targeting the feldbischof, who at this moment flaunted the sight of the nine-millimetre pistol in Churchill's face. It was as if the instilling of fear the teasing provoked was somewhat amusing to him and his German lads. Churchill could imagine this moron doing the exact same thing to Gérard, to Ny, and to countless POWs before that. He was probably also responsible for countless other massacres and atrocities thus far into their crusade across France and Belgium.

It had come to Jack's attention that Nazi Germany, or at least the Schutzstaffel, recruited mostly psychopaths as their officers, in a *you-must-be-this-crazy-to-join* style campaign.

Churchill cast a quick glance over his shoulder as the Germans conversed with furthermore hecklings they found humorous, being careful not to reveal the *concealed 38-inch Scottish claybeg* down the back of his shirt ...

Hardy was still behind him, just unresponsive.

He must have choked up after noticing Ny.

Fuck!

Churchill's mind raced ...

Any second ... *he would have no choice but to launch this attack solo.*

Any second ... *this unhinged feldbischof will shoot him in the head.*

Any second ... *and any of the surrounding Germans could notice that the prisoner was hiding something behind the two hands wrapped so tightly behind his head ...*

Any second ... *all hell would unleash.*

V
Carnage

1940, June 2
DuPont Dairy Farm
Nord Pas-de-Calais, France

The German audience snickered at the apparent hilarity of their feldbischof's abusive taunts. The rays of enjoyment swelled about their cracked fascist façades as they dwelled in inexplicable comfort, enjoying in unison the expense of the captured British prisoner of war.

With every chortle, their rifles lowered an inch.

Their devoted Bishop lathered in their ceremony, waving a pistol in the face of the captive captain as he knelt before him; before this false God, overwrought with a false sense of power.

The sun had set so low by now, and all things on this farmstead plane of existence were of a nightscape tinge featuring shades of gold and brown shadows, however the skies were an orange and purple hue. It made for a rather twilight glow setting post-dusk, but still pre-nightfall.

During his supposed roasting by the German overlords, from the low position on his knees, Jack Churchill continuously examined his surrounding environment, preparing his next move. As comfortable as these German mutts were in their self-righteous praise, he was also in knowing how close he was to the edge of unleashing a berserker.

Only, there was a slight spanner in the works ...

The plan had gone dreadfully awry.

Any second now, and he would have no choice but to either receive a bullet to the brain ... or spring forth like a literal *Jack-in-the-box,* pouncing outwards, fighting to the death, prancing before a glorified firing squad.

This martyrdom option would necessitate Mad Jack recalling and utilizing the unique skills acquired during those otherworldly crash-course training sessions in Switzerland six months ago. This was where he had observed and absorbed the specialized fighting manners of a man named

Orde Wingate and his secretive and borderline-psychotic *Aux-Ops (Auxiliary Operations)*. Little was known about the particulars of Jack's time spent with the group, however, the group devoted consecutive weeks of the period focusing on developing a type of enhanced close quarters combat. It was an advanced and more comprehensive augmentation on similar ethics taught in basic training by the British Army—and other armies of the world. It was experimental. Suicidal. Crazy. Mad. *Berzerk.*

Jack excelled.

In effect, the result was acquiring the deplorable knowledge and ability to kill an assembly of armed soldiers utilizing only *melee combat (hand-to-hand combat using weapons, blunt or bladed)*. Such as a sword.

To *go out with a bang* as *old mate* MacLeòid would say.

Spoke too soon ...

"*Aye, dat's et, laddie: go owt wiv a beng!*"

Suddenly, and most inconveniently, the cowering Jack Churchill heard the Highlander haunt's Scottish brogue echo throughout the present dreary tone of snickering laughs and torment.

He searched for him: *the Angry Scotsman.*

Sloan MacLeòid sounded so close, so real, it could not be a memory in his head. It had to be him, here, now, visiting amidst chaos.

Never before had the entity been so desperate ...

"*Walcomed through the iridescent gates of Valhalla where yoo can grab old boy sissy Satan by tha horns an' spank him en his actwel fanny!*" added the tarriance of MacLeòid's voice, quoting some drivel that he had said during a pep talk to the Second Manchester Regiment in Burma years ago—*back when the old goat was still actually alive,* and not a figment of his imagination.

Fighting through the tunnel vision that was the overpowering paralytical fear and bewilderment of certain death, Churchill was able to spot the kilted Scotsman as he stepped out from behind the German feldbischof in his elongated state of luger-waving intimidation affairs.

Jack's vision was starting to blur ...

Outlines were starting to warp and distort ...

His mind starting to play tricks; the wick of the candle of luck beginning to flicker in the wind, hinting maybe it would finally blow out. Curtains closing. Lights out. The end.

"*Git mad, Jackie ...*" the Glaswegian brogue echoed as the blood pumped loudly through Churchill's ears, pressing his coherency. Pure adrenaline coursed through his veins, chasing him to the edge of either blacking out or setting off. "*Dey sey a candle dat burns twice es bright only burns 'alf es long ... dis es yoor time ta shine, lad!*"

"Oi, *piss off!*" Churchill pinched his eyes and shouted upon distinguishing the nuisance of an apparition that haunted his life—persistently tempting his temper.

Outside the delusion, the surrounding Germans took it as a sign of pathetic belligerence towards them, and a verbal explosion out of fear of the torment.

Holding the upper hand, naturally, they shared another laugh.

It was as if the prisoner was so scared, he had lost the plot.

Sadly, they had seen this sort of folly before; when psyches fracture beyond stability or repair. They found it mildly entertaining.

"*Fuck!*" Churchill supported his outburst, breathing heavily under the stress. Voice cracking with desperation he outburst: "Just *piss off* for a minute, eh. I'm bloody sick of your bollocks!"

Recognizing MacLeòid's provocation intentions and identifying the parallel to his own internal combustion overload of tension, Churchill forced composure.

He breathed deep, straining to open his eyes.

He felt his heart rate decrease, and clarity started to return from the edges of his tunnel vision. Everything seemed brighter, more detailed, slower.

The Germans watched quietly for a second following his sudden surge, critiquing his emotional reaction amidst themselves before cackling in laughter at something else the comedic feldbischof said subsequent to the prisoner's small and random, spontaneous eruptions. They belittled him further.

After an extended moment in which Churchill collected himself in the mud, it seemed that the Bishop had finally had enough foreplay. A climax was upon the proceedings, and so his fingers adjusted their wrap around the handle of the Luger pointed firmly at Jack's beret-clad forehead. Churchill tried desperately to not involuntarily shy at the sight of the gun. It was the same pistol that had just killed two men, plus countless more before that. The hollow barrel still echoed with the screams of their taken lives.

The feldbischof spoke in his best English, with a clear intention and attempt to strike fear into the heart of this captive man:

"You zpeak to hoo jus now?"

Still drunk on the wild ride, Churchill beamed, glancing about himself in this wild predicament. He responded truthfully, unafraid of their concern. "A ghost, actually."

"Er *ghost?*"

Jack sneered with a short exhale. "Yeah. He's a real pain in the arse."

The eccentric feldbischof pursed his lips, glancing around playfully and tossing a mockful gleam to his peers. He attempted to relate. "You iz er man o' God?"

His beam subsiding whilst he calmed his heartrate, Churchill shook his head truthfully. "Not really, no."

"Men zink I iz God. Vhen really ... I iz *der Deffil.*"

Raising his muddy face underneath his maroon beret, Churchill eyed him with deliberation. "Oh, you're *der Deffil,* eh?"

From behind the empowerment of gun possession, the Nazi lunatic bobbed singly and with sincerity. This man was a believer and could not be tamed—there was nothing more formidable.

Remembering what MacLeòid had said just now about *going out with a bang* and *going to Valhalla (or Hell) and grabbing old boy Satan (the Devil) by the horns and spanking him on the actual fanny ...*

In the stress, whatever was left of Churchill's collected composure seemed to fracture.

He found the crazy Scot's randomness inappropriately humorous.

He was out of options.

Unpredictability was his last remaining card to play.

Time to show his card ...

He started laughing hysterically.

Surrounded by the armed SS troops, Jack bared his pearly white, winning smile. Still holding on his knees and with his fingers interlaced behind his head, his laughter outburst was authentic, sincere, and rather out of place considering his predicament. Therefore, it shone somewhat contagiously to the assertive SS troops who couldn't resist finding the combination of the prisoner's lark and the fact he was laughing so honestly in such a bad situation, genuinely funny.

One by one as Churchill continued to sidesplittingly chuckle, the troops each cracked a smirk beneath crooked, confused brows, and exchanged a look to one another—all while becoming more and more off-guard.

Wow, this British prisoner had gone mad ...

The menacing feldbischof frowned, not finding it funny like the others. There was only enough room on this stage for one comedian.

This man got off on making scared prisoners think he was some sort of conduit for the *devil* right before he executed them, and he did not appreciate this twisted humour and what felt like insubordination from his men any more than he did the defiance from this prisoner ...

It unpretentiously enraged him.

He finished casting a gleam about the men who encircled him with laughter and brought his view back around to face Churchill from behind the extended pistol hand.

He decided that it was time for him to die.

Without hesitation, he pushed the gun forward and pulled the trigg—

Slish!

Laughter dropped from the air like a lead balloon.

Full-fucking-stop.

The fearful feldbischof had his head turned away for too long ...

Had his eyes off the prize for too long ...

Using his veil of laughter, Mad Jack Churchill had sunk his hand beneath the rear of his neck collar, his fingers wriggling into the eyelets of the specialized hilt, gripping firmly onto the handle of his concealed sword ...

In a swift and speedy action, he drew it from his shirt and slashed forth singlehandedly. He did so expeditiously, the blade of his unveiled sword slashed the fabric at the material lapel on its withdrawal.

Right as the feldbischof finished casting a humiliated look about his encircling men, Churchill threw his shoulder into it. He brought the sword around in a woefully powerful arc, taking off the Nazi's extended appendage at the forearm. The blade lopped through his arm like it was a meaty, sap-filled tree branch, lopping it with a single *chop!*

The weighty indestructible Damascus steel edging of the shrill blade cleaved through the extended limb like a knife through kraut.

Churchill's weighty sword charged with so much speed and might, he barely ended the swipe before the heaviness of the sword struck the mud in the follow-through of the cleave.

The severed hand, wrist, and three inches of forearm landed in the mud, still gripping the pistol tight.

Frozen stiff, the feldbischof held a gaze with eyes as wide as swastikas, examining the shortened stump in sheer shock. After a full three seconds of breathlessness, a streaming gush of warm blood squirted like a severed garden hose from the amputated appendage.

Reeling in shock, the feldbischof kowtowed to his knees in the mud. A waft of heat overcame his body as the wound began to boil, erupting like a gory volcano, followed by a rushing onset of excruciating pain. He retained a hold, cupping it in his chest whilst his composure buckled with a tense grimace as the wave of throbbing agony washed over him like the broken levy of a dam wall.

After this initial attack, Churchill clambered onto his feet from the mud, poising himself in the brief silence of the confusion. Before the surrounding SS troops could recover from the shock value, he picked a target and moved, charged by his own empowerment.

Combining the surprised shock that struck the neighbouring soldiers with an overbearing sense of paralytic horror, there was a moment of hesitation by the surrounding enemy, in which Churchill bared his fangs and released a deep, threatening battle cry. He launched forward with both hands on the brass grooved hilt of his sword as he wielded it, pouncing yond the incapacitated Bishop, like a man possessed.

Channelling his inner *William Wallace*, Churchill bellowed his battle cry at the summit of his lungs, fuelling his charge.

"*AHHHHHHH!*"

He launched his attack, utilizing the full extent of surprise disorientation training from his lessons in advanced hand-to-hand combat in Switzerland, better referred to as a *Berzerker* technique.

In this rapid and charged mentality, the thumping of his beating heart was all he heard beyond the echoic *whooshing, chopping,* and *slashing* of his sword through the air—through human extremities.

Lethal, loud, and crazed, Mad Jack rushed at the two closest SS troops located four steps away on the left flank. Fixated on their maimed feldbischof who was down and out in the mud, his advance shocked them to their cores. They were barely able to react before he was on top of them.

Churchill slashed sharp on the first soldier, cutting a five-inch-deep laceration through his grey uniform, leather belt, belly, and bones with a heavy-handed low-originating upward-diagonal slice. With barely any resistance due to the force of the delivery and the edge of the steel, the sword chomped through at least three ribs on the angle.

The double-edged blade carved an irreparable gash up his abdomen, and the SS troop howled with shock as he split, collapsing to a semi-stifle and involuntarily discarding his weapon.

Vainly, the soldier clutched at the wound just as thick blood poured out of him like a tipping bucket, grotesquely pushing out by his organs as the internals were granted freedom from his ruptured torso. Baring a face of utter despair, the Hun brought up his hands to catch his dropped pink steaming bowels as he leaked and spilled. The sudden jolt at the knees from his collapse caused his innards to pour through the slit in his opened gut with a splash of stinking gorefest.

The Nazi whimpered fretfully and in tremendous discomfort as the whole nine yards of intestines uncontrollably flowed out of him, as if somebody had tugged firm on a well-wound firehose reel, seemingly unending and visually disturbing. Excruciating pain set in, and the man quivered and screamed in a high pitch as he coiled over, likely dead from shock within seconds.

Without linger from the slaughter, Churchill's fluency raged on. He struck the next German soldier with the continuance of the backswing, even twirling his body in-between to gain extra force for the strike across the short distance.

He spun on a pivot in the mud, wielding the deadly double-edged blade to its fullest extent and using all the might in his deltoid to deliver the following incision in a horizontal divide. With a powerful *whoosh,* Jack's spinning tornado attack lopped the stunned soldier's head off at the neck with an effortless chop.

At the very last second of his life, the soldier reacted and raised his three-foot-six rifle within extremely close proximity. However, in this closing moment, he was barely able to even point it in Churchill's direction before letting off a desperate and deafening wide-angled gunshot across the dusking farm scape that missed everything.

The first of many misses.

The soldier's guillotined head was unexpectedly weighty.

Once severed by the sweeping steel, the noggin appeared to levitate before arching forward, stahlhelm still firmly contained within via the affixed chinstrap. Along with a cascade of gushing cherry red blood, the decapitated dome raced the soldier's instantly lifeless body into a collapse in the muck. The blood fountained thickly around the scene, splashing with a wide radius.

Jack did not pause to consider the carnage.

Blood may have spattered across his face, but he was already seeing red before the carnage.

After killing the second troop he only slowed to transfer the might of his attack on another axis, preying on his next opponent in the heat of the desperate melee spree, attacking within close quarters and before anybody could appropriately react. This ruse would only work if empowered by immediacy. He had to outrun their reactions.

Next on the kill order were the two opposite guards, who were now twice as far away from Jack as this dead duo. They were ten feet away from the buckled feldbischof, who knelt winded and debilitated, and covered in his own blood from his amputated hand. Subduing to shock, all this commander could do was watch his men die and his world burn around him.

Churchill's battle cry bellowed a breast-full of dominant and potent exhale as he charged his blast-off departure, raging onwards towards the next targets.

Letting out his roar in Berzerker fashion, he galloped three lengthy strides in their direction, dummying sporadically to dodge any hip-firing aims from their slow bolt guns.

Once cutting in close, he raised his blade and flung himself into a full-scaled flounce in their focuses.

Launching up from his nimble, darting manoeuvres, his mighty hurdle was inclusive of a press-off from the collapsed feldbischof's tilted back, treating him like a springboard. It sent Churchill into the air like a mild gymnasium tumbler, sailing almost four feet airborne.

His prosperous aerial attack was something neither SS troop could have anticipated. Not in a million fucking years. Their eyes grew wide as the range closed ...

The two riflemen finally fired and missed at the incoming sword-wielding British soldier, each backpedalling in a surging panic as they attempted to cycle their rifles for another shot to shoot.

Having gained a clear shot for half a second, the man with the submachine gun by the house let loose with a burst of energetic fire from an MP38. Possibly due to him being the untrained botenmeister messenger who had merely accompanied the feldbischof to the farm, he missed broadly as Churchill catapulted through the air, and he held his fire as he came in close to his kamerad, not wanting to hit his own by accident in this chaos.

Carving crevasses through the slushy mud, Churchill landed hard in the space between the riflemen and immediately performed a shoulder roll in the sludge, predicting new waves of incoming fire.

The two rifle-baring SS troops shuffled apart as Mad Jack landed. Their boots slipped hastily as they separated, parting to force an uneasy distance on this erratic opponent. They were in total and utter fear of this mad man brandishing the medieval blade.

Sloppy with mud and blood, the beret-clad Brit dashed in close between them and acted without hesitation, swinging the heavy sword without mercy and with homing prejudice to the local Gerry.

Churchill took a wide right-arc swipe at the closest man, who he identified as the CO of this Waffen-SS outfit before the Bishop showed up and confiscated the reins, a man holding the rank of feldwebel.

Regardless of Hun hierarchy, It was his time to die.

The feldwebel predicted his wild sword swing and courageously incorporated his lengthy rifle with both hands to block the blade with a cross-T.

With a loud *clack!* the wood-housed metal weapon blocked the steel strike. The walnut wood encasing the German rifle ate the claybeg blade as if it were a block of malleable lard, however the metal components housed within, such as the barrel, seemed to cease the might of the sharp sword, catching it like a vice.

Under their entwined brace, Churchill drove his muddy boot into the feldwebel's core. The action assisted the retraction of the sword with a heave.

Free, he immediately chopped from the shoulder, from over the left and down, and again the cunning feldwebel performed a valiant deflective manoeuvre with the Karabiner 98k. Quickly, Jack subsequently went on a right shoulder attack, still to no avail as the cunning German thwarted each attack. The desperate and frightened soldier somehow happened to obstruct the sword swings each time with his rifle as if it were a bow staff.

The terrified feldwebel shouted with wide-eyed fright as he encountered the full wrath of Jack Churchill and his crazed claybeg, and he cast an eye to his teammate for assistance as the rifleman finally bolted his Karabiner and raised it up, now waiting for a clear shot.

As the sparring soldier collapsed backwards from the fury of the next Jack attack, Churchill quickly switched targets. He twisted on the spot and his nostrils flared, and he noticed the rifle pointed his way.

Jack predicted the rifleman's preparedness to engage with the ranged weapon and so he dashed to duty, strafing in low as though he were weaving under a cordon, and swung his sword in an upward, wide sweep.

The tip of the Damascus steel struck the tip of the 98k rifle with a flint of sparks, dislodging the man's aim. At that exact same second, the soldier pulled the trigger.

With a thunderous muzzle blast, the gun went off. The bullet missed Churchill by centimetres, shooting too high due to the sweep of the sword swing.

Suddenly, from behind him, shouting began to ignite the air at the quiet farmstead with chaos, as the feldwebel who had blocked his attacks with a rifle was now up from the muck, drenched in filth. Slipping as he rushed, he resorted to attacking Churchill from behind in desperate hand-to-hand combat.

The feldwebel wielded his ravaged rifle like a rod with intent to restrain Churchill. With both hands, he hoisted the stick up and over the unexpecting swordsman's head from behind, wrapping around his shoulders whilst his sword guard held low. The attempt to subdue the mad man while his sword-wielding arms were down temporarily bore fruit, and Jack struggled within the firm bear hug.

Over by the house, the messenger with the submachine gun shouted frantically, fretting anxiously. He waved his gun hands, indicating that he wanted all his soldiers to get out of the way and away from the loose, wild prisoner. He needed a clear shot before opening fire.

Locked in a tense struggle with his arms clasped down before him, Churchill remained restrained by this brave soldier's antics of pacification. Their feet lumbered in the sludge.

The feldwebel used his rifle as a hindrance to block and quell whilst the remaining rifleman fumbled dreadfully to cycle another bullet into the chamber of his Karabiner rifle. Having gained a clear shot at Churchill's now exposed and detained deportment, all the anchoring man had to do was dive clear when he was ready and let him shoot.

After a second of tensely bared-teeth and spiteful growling, combat boots trundling in the slick mud below and the flex of tough muscular straining to break free, Churchill did so successfully. He threw his beret-padded head back into the feldwebel's schnozzle. The hard knock dazed the troop, possibly even breaking his nose, apparent by the squelch of red from either nostril as he recoiled.

The soldier slipped in his hold from around Churchill's core, which had been clamping down his sword arms, and the constrained British beast broke free.

In the newly gained distance from the restraint, Churchill twirled the sword out by his shoulder in a flourish, gaining momentum within close proximity with a *whoosh*. After performing what resembled a wild haymaker, he pleated the sword beneath his opposite armpit, stabbing his rear attacker in a retrograde thrust that he barely saw coming. The claybeg impaled the kraut through the lower sternum as he clutched his blood-soaked nose, and his expression dropped open-mouthed and instantly motionless.

Becoming side-on with the soldier after his twist, Churchill drove a balled fist into his uniformed chest, striking above the impalement. The hit acted as a press hold for the hasty withdrawal of his hand, which subsequently allowed the feldwebel to collapse to his knees in the mud, dead or dying.

With a swirl, Churchill brought the bloody-tipped sword back up before him, more firmly threading his fingers through the brass grooves of his knuckleduster handle. Immediately, he rushed the last rifleman as he raised the rifle to shoulder level and fixed his iron-sight on Churchill.

Fresh round cycled in the chamber ...

Finger back on the trigger ...

Target in sight, clear as day ...

Churchill lunged—

He fired.

Bam!

But the staunch and speedy swordsmen had outmanoeuvred the SS troop.

At the last second, Churchill ducked beneath the rifle as his aim tightly trained, and he slid like a batter onto home plate as the catcher caught a throw.

Too high by two inches, the shot missed him under his balling arc.

Jack weaved in from a low stance, reaching up and grabbing a hold of the German's rifle with one extended hand and taking partial control, while with the other, lashing downwards ... bringing his sword in with absolution.

With a wild and robust assail that tore through the air, he brought the blade down where the man's neck met his collarbone. With a grotesque cleave that slurped with suction, it sliced six inches deep. The action resembled a father carving up a family roast with juicy meat cleaved either side of the blade.

Thwuck!

The weight with which Churchill brought the sword down collapsed the German to his knees like he had just been hammered by a pile driver.

The man peered down with unbelieving eyes to witness the horror of seeing himself split like a wood log destined for a fireplace. Blood bubbled up from the wound as with bared teeth, Churchill levered the weapon from the almost quartered body, seemingly propelling the steel from its butchered chasm.

Through a steel, lethal, and now blood-soaked gaze, Churchill watched the downed trooper gasp, briefly attempting words, his mouth popping open and shut like that of a goldfish. His pale frame fell to his right, where his split torso once again combined with a wet, meaty slap.

After completing that first wave, Churchill focused up.

It was time to find who was next on the agenda.

He flicked his blade through the air, purging a layer of thick blood and gore with a slash of droplets.

His stare fixated on the submachine-gunner by the house just as the messenger broke from his opened-mouthed, stunned stare after what he had just witnessed. The dumbfounded kraut suddenly realized that he now had a clear line of sight on the Brit out in the open, and so his fingers wriggled their hold on his weapon.

The man was over *forty feet* away and had both hands on his automatic, targeting Jack. There was no way Churchill could rush this objective as successfully as he had done the others. The German was too far away and held the advantage of preparedness.

The gunner beheld Churchill for an extended moment, still seemingly inhibited by the surprise display of the medieval carnage he had just witnessed. However, after a prolonged moment of realization, Churchill noticed the soldier's intent to open fire ...

And he did.

Caught out and stuck in a bind, he cast a quick glance left, spotting Hardy. The unreliable American was likely still a statue, posing like a department store mannequin wearing a full kit.

Contrarily, Hardy was thawed from his frozen stupor. His entranced stare upon the dead body in the mud of Omar Ny had swung around, and he now simply presented some form of immobilization. Clenching his MP38 tense at the shoulders, he squinted with unease, likely stunned by the spectacle of carnage that unfolded before him as Churchill absolutely cut loose like a recently uncaged animal.

Luckily for him, the Germans had not yet seen him as a threat ... which they absolutely and indubitably would, within seconds, if Churchill fell out of being the focal hostile.

"*Hardy!*" Churchill called out of desperation.

At the house, the submachine-gun-brandishing messenger stepped-to. Even though his wounded kamerads were still partially in the firing line, he saw no other option than to end the madness.

He opened fire.

With nowhere left to run, Jack quickly dived in low behind the cover of the pale-faced feldwebel as the dying man wobbled about in the sludge, somehow yet to fully collapse. In his final seconds, the kneeling feldwebel who had been run-through registered that he was about to become collateral damage, and he raised a single blood-covered palm from his stomach wound in his defence—but it was futile.

The pitching *clack-clack-clack-clack-clack* of the gunner's hip-level MP38 clapped away, missing the targets with the first few rounds but fast correcting course, hitting with almost every bullet after that.

Round after round pelted into meaty gore, striking the fatally wounded feldwebel right as Churchill balled-up behind him, propping him up as a human shield in every sense of the word.

Churchill had no choice but to keep the man upright.

Grabbing him by the back strap that lined his shoulder, Jack temporarily hoisted the dead kraut up like clutching a punching bag while the sparring submachine-gunner threw an amass of unremorseful jabs. Once that faltered, he arranged his claybeg through his lower back—reinserting it through the exit wound of the same stab-hole—impaling him almost through to the hilt and propping him up like a beach brolly.

From the front, the tortured feldwebel, who was now littered in bullet holes, flinched and convulsed from the peppering onslaught. Alive and grimacing for the start of it, one of the last things he would have felt was the protruding blade painstakingly force its way out through his abdomen as he became attacked from the rear as though from the front. The tip of the Damascus steel sliced his covering hand over the wound upon its re-impalement, stabbing him again—through the same hole—but from the other side.

Jack held the dead soldier upright like an umbrella, tilted towards torrential rain as an utter downpour of gunfire struck against the opposite side. The ruthless hailstorm ripped the troop's grey uniform to singed shreds, decaying the undercooked meat beneath like a school of barracuda. The automatic fire grated his dead body to streaks of shiny red ribbon and exposed pale flesh.

Baaaaaaaaaaaaaaaaaaaaang ...

"*Ahhhhh!*" Churchill roared with might over the unrelenting barrage as he used all his might to keep the deceased soldier upright while the fully automatic torrent poured over him, pulverizing and perforating his meat shield. Stray nine-millimetre bullets penetrated the dead man's body, clipping Churchill in the arms and shoulders secondarily. Albeit at a much slower velocity, the through-shoots tore his sleeves and gashed his arms, even gouging him across the neck. Tumbling bullets went whizzing past, flinging wildly into the mud through a multitude of exit wounds.

Thwack-thwack-thwack-thwack ...

The suppressive gunfire chomped into the convulsing body block, eventually overpowering Churchill and decaying his concealment. It was like the rushing water of a flooding river against a failing bank, crumbling piece by piece until there was little left to hide behind.

The dead man's body involuntarily quivered and jolted under the merciless bombardment as the blitz sustained, against all of Churchill's capacity. Finally, right as Churchill and the propped body finally buckled over and slid to the muddy sludge, leaving him exposed to gunfire ... the submachine-gunner ran out of bullets.

The deafening hailstorm of noise ceased.

The *click-click-click* of the automatic firing pin could be heard clicking dry in the troop's weapon.

Soaked through in the blood from the carnage of the shot-to-shit and smouldering dead body on the other end of his sword pike, Churchill peered from his position in the mire, spying the gunner.

In the abrupt silence that followed, the gunner panicked, ripping the stick-mag from under his sizzling submachine gun and searching for another somewhere in his many front pouches. He called to the off-duty soldiers inside the house who were still in the process of obtaining their weapons to quickly join in on the fight. Frazzled out of his mind, this last troop screamed and hollered, demanding they hurry. The situation was somehow still out of control.

Churchill seized the opportunity ...

With a rumble of might, he stood and withdrew his gore-lacquered claybeg. Covered in the claret of his fatalities, Churchill homed in on the remaining soldier with nothing but the craving of his demise upon his wrathful schedule.

An unstoppable warpath. An unkillable Jack Churchill.

The submachine-gunner grew flustered, frantic to reload, unable to do so in time. Realistically, he had enough time to load a fresh magazine within the interval of Churchill being on his position, but the shock that stung him, left him incapable. His fingers were shaking, and he fumbled the resolve, unable to restock his weapon quick enough.

Heavy down beside him as he marched forth, Churchill advanced with his claybeg sword. Closing in, he hurtled without mercy.

The soldier quaked in his boots at his pending death ...

Then suddenly, breaking Mad Jack's charging strides as solid as a brick wall, the half-dressed SS troops from inside the double-storey DuPont home emerged from behind the gunner's position. They stepped straight out into the mud outdoors, either barefoot or just in socks, carrying nothing but their own sets of loaded submachine guns and rifles.

There were three of them, and at least another two or three inside who now approached the windows, gaining optimal fire positions. The men outside fanned out in an evenly spaced link beside their mate and raised their automatics, training them at the unkillable enemy.

Still a notable distance from the target, Churchill slowed and rested his momentum at the sight of the firing squad:

His would-be executioners ...

Unafraid, Mad Jack stared them down with his sterling, steely stare.

The German gunmen posed before this mad British swordsman.

He was clear in their sights for obliteration.

Without much delay, they opened fire.

He had a good run, at least.

No prince or lord has tomb so proud ...

Jack's blue eyes sealed closed, accepting his fate.

Clack-clack-clack-clack!

Out of nowhere, the troops were suddenly raked by a stream of automatic gunfire right as they squeezed the triggers of their own machine guns.

Most unexpectedly, these new shooters became strafed across their chests in a straight sweep from left to right and then back again. Untamed overshoots slammed into the wooden exterior walls of the home, chalking up indentations of damage and clouds of dust.

The sweat-stained white undershirts of the troops exploded with intermittent red hits across their chests, shoulders, and abdomens. They danced on the spot in simultaneous convulsion for an extended interlude, held upstanding only by the continuous strain of automatic fire that hosed back and forth across their bodies for the expenditure of an entire magazine. The slew soldiers managed to let loose a few bursts of gunfire of their own into the mud or into the sky before the shooting all finally stopped, and a dampening silence prevailed the farm.

The Germans were finally permitted collapse and death.

Churchill flinched at the volume, expecting the gunshots to be aimed at his direction. Astonished, he opened his eyes and cast a gleam left, seeing Hardy behind a recently discharged submachine gun. There was an awakened look of utter determination in his eyes and fury upon his plum cheeks. He finally released the breath he had been holding, blowing through the grey smoke cloud rising from his MP38.

He was late to the party, but a welcome guest, nonetheless.

Clenched tighter than Churchill's butthole had been at that very moment, Hardy was edgily gripping the hot steel of his German automatic. He had the look upon his mug that relayed he had no idea what he was doing ... but whatever it was, he had just done it right.

"Cheers!" Churchill declared, breaking the ice of their frozen positions, and he continued his advance, twirling the sword and gaining speed into a fast-paced jog at the initial messenger with the maschinenpistole still left standing after that barrage. The stupe was *still* yet to finish reloading.

Jack engaged, right as *another* hostile opened fire at him, this time, from the house—and he reacted accordingly.

Hanging out an outstretched arm from a covered position in the front doorway, another German soldier fired off rounds from a pistol. He missed with two, three, four of the tiny semi-automatic shots as Churchill ducked and weaved, rapidly changing direction in his progression before Hardy shot back at the aggressor from an askew angle alongside the house. His gunfire seemed to clip the shooter's exposed arm in a stitch of holes along the house exterior and, possibly unintentionally, drilled the remaining submachine-gunner of who Churchill's focus fell upon, effectively stealing his kill.

The botenmeister was struck with an accidental headshot from the extended burst from Hardy at the *other* gunman. The round struck him where he stood with a *ping* that penetrated his steel helmet, and he dropped like a sack of shit to the mud with his fellow deceased Nazis.

Churchill came in low on his knees with a slide, crashing his shoulder against the side of the house, partially concealed by a short stack of chopped firewood below what he identified as the kitchen window. This happened right as more shooters from within the house became active, breaking glass windows with the barrels of their weapons in order to gain sight of him as he disappeared beneath their range.

Hardy was now out of ammunition, and the journalist scrabbled desperately in an attempt to remember how to reload the confiscated German gun.

Now in close to the active shooters, Churchill bided his time.

He remained low and beneath their weapons, his mind racing on how best he could remove the threats and gain access to the DuPont family home which they guarded—

Whiz—CRACK!

Whiz—CRACK!

Out of seemingly nowhere, Churchill unexpectedly came under more fire by a fresh source of aggression on an askew angle.

Tight against the outside wall of the double-storey home, splinters of wood exploded above his position, raining fragments upon his head and shoulders, causing him to dip lower behind the pile of firewood.

The new assault was from the two shooters by the barn in the distance, beside the parked German Einheitsdiesel troop transporter truck. They had taken up arms and now, in the absence of any of their kamerads left standing, had clear shots with their long-range rifles. They had decent concealment if there was retaliatory fire, as they were barely visible behind their locations about the parked truck.

Mid-reload, Hardy also sought cover from this new assault as he came under attack by several potshots from the same outlying men. Several rounds slammed into the side of the house near the rear corner of where he was located. The journalist discontinued attempting to reload the gun in order to duck his head and run away causing him to fumble the action completely, dropping the fresh magazine into a muddy puddle in the stagger. It was now ruined.

CRACK!

After taking another quick peek, Churchill ducked behind his puny concealment just as a round struck, causing him to flinch and wipe wood chips from his ear and beret. Another round hit the pile of chopped wood, causing the heap to collapse and his cover to minimize. He sunk down uncomfortably low, hugging his range-limited claybeg sword and wrapping his knuckles tight through the brass eyelets.

"Whenever you are ready, mate!" unable to move and fuming in frustration, he shouted at his awoken accomplice, salivating for more of Hardy's invaluable assistance. Their double-act may have been spontaneous and unrehearsed, but effective so far.

With that, Hardy leant out from the corner of the farmhouse located near the adjacent chicken coop, squinting a shy but stern gaze. His weapon was fully loaded with his last magazine.

His lack of skill unbeknownst to these stupid krauts, Hardy's steady bursts at the truck off in the distance still affected the shooters' confidence. They sought cover as sparks ignited against the metal chassis of the Einheitsdiesel and the passenger's side window to the parked vehicle shattered inwards above their heads.

"*Go! Go!*" Hardy shouted over the clapping volume of his sweltering submachine gun. Off-shoots by the enemy clouted at him, cracking against the palings covering the walls of the chicken house, causing dust and feathers to float about in a mist. Over the volume of the chaos, he added unconvincingly: "*I've got you covered! ...* I think."

And with that trust, Churchill took the opportunity of their withdrawal to leap-frog the stack of collapsed firewood, emerging out into the open and continuing his advance towards the hostile-guarded front door of the DuPont home.

"Ève, can you hear me?!" Churchill shouted as the distance closed for his unstoppable vengeful and valiant purpose. "Ève! Hold on! I'm coming!"

Inside the house, the volume of the battleground outside was frighteningly restraining for the captive DuPont girls held within the rooms.

The shouting was loud. The shooting was stifling.

From their respective positions throughout the kitchen and connected dining room, they hid low and remained timid.

The particular SS troop who had just now opened fire on the British swordsman with a handgun was of a *rifleman-grenadier* category, with a matching loadout concerning explosive armaments in his harness apparatus.

Typically, the grenadier was armed with an ensemble differing to any of the other men of the German unit. In various dedicated pouches about his webbing and leather housings, the demolitions specialist was armed with an assortment of throwable timed explosives and deployable mines, such as stielhandgranates *(stick grenades,* also known to the British army as *potato mashers,* due to their design*)* and schrapnellmines *(S-mines,* or *bouncing-betty* anti-personnel mines*)*. In separate sections of his pack, he also carried with him raw Amatol and Composition B, for even larger explosions if paired with the appropriate detonators.

With a ricochet wound to his thumb in which he had quickly balled his bloody fist with a rag, the injured grenadier retreated into the DuPont dining room, drawing his only remaining weapon—a dagger—to threaten the two daughters behind him in the corner of the room, Yana and Audréy. Without issuing a verbal command, he gestured for them to *stay put* and *do not move.* Already scared, the defenceless girls complied without hesitation. Trembling, the youngest DuPont sisters held each other in tight embrace, remaining low and shielding their faces.

With an angry grimace and clenching his bloody hand, the withdrawing grenadier writhed in ache. Like the rest of the SS troops who had this night off guard duty, he was mostly disarmed of his gear and his uniform was unbuttoned and relaxed. Since their call to arms due to the arrival of the British prisoner (and his escape), the grenadier had thrown on his utility belts and drawn his sidearm. Within the flap pouches on his belt housed a munitions harness, retaining eight Model 24 Stielhandgranates.

From his retreated position in the back corner of the dining room, he cast view into the recently rearranged living room, where another armed SS troop with an MP38 still remained. There was one last remaining German in a connecting room making three in total; the ugly and abusive bald man, who was also the bishop's right-hand-man. The oaf lurked in the kitchen, keeping guard on the other two women: the mother and the eldest daughter.

The Germans exchanged a look. In this sudden chaos, they were struggling to assess the situation. The one thing that was certain was that their two leaders had been either slain or incapacitated.

Their numbers out there were dropping unbelievably fast.

They were confused and flustered.

What had happened that had gone so wrong?

The grenadier shouted to the overly cautious submachine-gunner in the living room, heckling him to man up and get outside to kill the lone attacker. He hesitantly did so, peeking out of the fractured glass window, and spotting immediate motion. Acting fast, he raised his clumsily positioned automatic and sprayed blindly out the front of the house, shattering what remained of the glass and tearing the veil curtain to strips. The weapon discharge was loud indoors. One for every bullet fired, the ejected brass casings rained down over the timber floorboards and carpeted rug with a contrasting gentle cymbal to the gun's loud clapping drumming.

The movement at which the submachine-gunner fired was at an acute angle, down low and beside the house. The target had been the maroon beret-clad British man with the sword, and he promptly disappeared below the windowsill, out of the gunner's view. Needless to say, he outran the gunfire as the extended burst pelted into the sludge in his wake.

Right at that moment, in the kitchen, the ugly bald German detaining the older female hostages inched over towards the smaller window and peeked in an attempt to gain sight of the commotion outside. The result of his rubbernecking was a lowering of his guard, leaning over Sophie DuPont's cowering shoulder by the sink ...

Discreetly, she exchanged a gleam with her Ève.

The two nodded. The cunning mother and daughter had a sly plan—

Suddenly, there was a voice from outside:

"Ève! Can you hear me?! Hold on!"

It was Jack Churchill ...

He was their knight in shining armour, who was living up to being more than just self-proclaimed.

Their retaliatory plan unexpectedly fell short.

As soon as Ève had heard his voice, all immediate aspirations went out the window—along with her elevated response.

"Jack ...?" she muttered, her attention diverting as she called back in retort. *"Jack?!"*

She was saved.

They were saved.

Upon entertaining her response, the ugly bald oaf of a captor returned his guard upon them, flexing his firm grip upon his rifle. He would be issuing a cease and desist to her retorts—likely, by force.

So, Sophie beat him to it.

In that instant, Ève shielded herself as her brave and impulsive mother suddenly acted, attacking the big German holding the gun, just like before—however, unlike before, she did so this time utilizing a better stratagem.

Using an oven mitt that she had wriggled her paw into, she grabbed the heavy full pot of boiling water and chopped vegetables from the lit stove and quickly poured it over the guard's head, neck, and down his back, scalding their SS captor with sweltering boiling liquid.

Steam immediately filled the kitchen, rising from him.

There was some splash back on both the girls and it burnt, but the collateral damage was worth the gamble.

The German's exposed bald head copped the full contents of the steaming water, instantly applying second-degree burns to his exposed flesh. His pale skin turned lobster-red, bubbling and sizzling.

There was a splash and a sputter, and after a half second delay, the soldier constricted a tight shrug at his shoulders as he bellowed a roar of agony. A reactive kerfuffle ensued.

Hissing vapour poured off his body as he thrashed and toiled, spinning and brutally shoving Sophie away from him before hastily lunging forwards with the affixed bayonet on his rifle to kill her.

With bared teeth and squinting eyes from the sting, he stabbed at the mother as she tumbled backwards in the kitchen, missing her by an inch and impaling the wood of a cupboard door with the tip of the blade as she landed flat on the soaked wooden floor, striking right beside her face.

Predicting a follow-up attack and with the assistance of her daughter, Sophie rolled right and then left while her feet scurried to create any distance from the attacker.

Engulfed in agony, the steaming soldier immediately pulled the bayonet from the wood and stabbed again, missing her again and again with other attempts, likely blind with the heat of the rage and rising blisters that constricted and hardened his skin. The immediate inflammation response had turned his eyelids into puffy mushrooms which he struggled to see out of. With each vicious strike, his bayonet either struck the floor or stuck into the wooden door of the pantry cabinet, missing her by inches as she desperately gyrated and avoided his thrusts.

Ève was fast to react in despairing assistance.

From the kitchen bench by her hands, the eldest DuPont daughter collected the flat-headed potato peeler—the only thing available to grasp—before lunging forwards at the assaultive German. She found an opportunistic moment between his slightly slowing jabbing attacks.

She reached in and raked the potato peeler across his face as high as she could reach. The kitchen utensil glid at first, but then bit into his sweltering flesh as it reached the softer landing below his eye, carving in and stripping off a hand's length of skin as the trooper let out the highest noted shriek he could muster. The peeler dug deep, almost half an inch.

The bald German reacted, spinning with the weapon in his hands, and Ève released her hold of the kitchen utensil in order to catch the tightly clenched rifle with both of her hands.

She was weightless compared to his might.

The two waltzed, whirling about the steamy kitchen confines.

Ève was easily much smaller than the German oaf who practically picked her up as though she was a plaything, spinning around and hitting her against open cupboard doors and other fixtures. Within the close confines of the wet kitchen, they struggled loudly as they wrestled, shattering ceramic plates and glass cups on the wooden floor, creating quite the hazard. Blunt metal cutlery spilled out everywhere with a hundred different instrumental sounds as a drawer was tugged outwards and tipped out.

In amongst the transpiring violence, Sophie managed to clamber to her feet. Her gown was wet, and her hair blocked her face, but she gave it everything she could, and joined in the tackle of the powerful German captor.

Combined, the mother and daughter managed to pull the soldier down to the slippery floor, scratching his already red raw head and face with their nails and bashing into any exposed weak spot, grappling to obtain possession of the weapon.

They fought literally *tooth and nail.*

This was a *fight to the death,* and each party knew it.

Outside the under-siege DuPont home, the extended burst of gunfire from a shooter out a window pelted into the wet mud, springing thin brown geysers that chased Jack Churchill in his active scurry.

He strafed in tight alongside the house, barging his shoulder hard into the wall, faltering in his pace to gain entry inside to save the women. These enemy shooters were pests to his progress.

Finally arriving at the entrance and with his shoulder in-line with the doorframe to the front door, Churchill was unable to get any closer without being shot by the gunner. Remaining concealed, he stabbed his sword into the ground beside his stance and collected the MP38 from beside one of the perforated German bodies as they lay rotting in the sludge.

Quickly, Jack examined the weapon components, for the Schmeisser was slicken with slurry. He accessed the breach, pulled the stick mag clear and reinserted, racking closed and then open again the side-mounted bolt handle to check its functionality. All seemed operational, so he quickly extended the foldable buttstock into him at the shoulder and clutched the weapon with a close, two-handed grip, ready for action.

After a tense breath and a tauter shuffle nearer to the doorframe, he inconspicuously peeked with his eye across the hot zone, spying the movements of an armed troop inside. He also saw a second Nazi—a grenadier—as he attempted to ferry the two youngest DuPont sisters further into the house at knifepoint. They were perhaps going to use them as hostages. The grenadier was bloody and injured, but above all, he was desperate. They all were. And that made them unpredictable and all the more dangerous.

Churchill's ears pricked to the muffled noises of some sort of chaos ensuing inside, in the kitchen area. It was the sound of a struggle, of breaking ceramics and bashing wood. The sounds from within gained his attention. It was possibly a tussle between a German and the other DuPont girls ...

Desperate times. Time that was running out.

Lost for a split-second in overthought, Churchill suddenly snapped back to reality and recoiled as that same armed submachine gun-packing SS troop at the window spotted him through the angle of the doorway, and immediately opened fire with a messy spray.

Whizzes of near-misses passed by his face as Jack rotated back outside with his back against the wall. Right as he pulled away, the wooden doorframe beside his position exploded to splinters with volatile gunfire.

Little had he known, but that previous bombardment through the window and now through the door was about to be followed-up by the injured grenadier soldier ... only to a much more explosive capacity.

Ceasing his movements with the captives, he primed one of his many stielhandgranate stick grenades. After unscrewing the cap in the bottom of the hollow wooden handle, he yanked on the string to start the fuse without a moment's hesitation. He tossed it offhand out the front doorway to the DuPont house.

With a bump clipping against the doorframe, the awkwardly shaped potato masher exited the premises and landed with a *slosh* in the mud right by Churchill's position.

In German, the grenadier accompanied the action with what appeared to be a one-liner: something like *'catch'.*

In that same interval as the grenade arriving, Churchill leaned back inside with his eyes behind his weapon sights, about to boldly return fire on the SS troop. In turn, he caught the passage of the thrown grenade with his peripherals as the stielhandgranate landed in the sludge barely three paces to his right.

Rather than shoot, his focus fell and searched for it.

There was a hint of smoke rising from the device's end.

The fuse ...

It was armed.

Fuck.

The stielhandgranate was a timed grenade. Normally, with the few seconds before it blew, his training would commandeer his body, causing him to grab it up and throw it back inside at the enemy. This time around however, he could not do that safely—not while the civilian members of the DuPont family were somewhere inside, possibly even in the same room. He could not risk accidentally killing them with shrapnel.

"*Shit!*" he cursed, plotting thoughts like a whirlwind.

Acting without overthinking, Churchill dropped his aim intentions and scooped in low to snatch the stick grenade from the mud. Thankfully, it had impaled into the sludge in such a way that the wooden handle protruded. He did so whilst performing a shoulder roll past the open doorframe, narrowly avoiding a follow-up volley of gunfire from the gunner within, who let off an extended burst.

Revolving after the roll and then in an outer-arm throw, Churchill tossed the timed grenade like a trebuchet sling. The top-heavy device toppled in the air, ranging over thirty-feet into the open distance towards the barn direction.

While the stielhandgranate time bomb whistled, flung end-over-end in midair, he immediately jumped backwards, shielding himself from the explosion, for the fuse was surely about to—*BOOM!*

Hurling mud in every direction, the fragmentation grenade violently exploded with a bellowing blast and blinking flash of white light. The blast stomped earth three feet *into* the mud surface beneath the detonation, moulding a smoky crater and splashing brown earth from the impact of force.

Thankfully, the stielhandgranate mostly relied on its ability to detonate a wide-ranged concussion blast. The thin metal container on the head of the device created little fragmentation when compared to the Mills bomb, which was primarily shrapnel.

The impactful shockwave of expelling energy erupted in a circular diameter, rippling outwards, and shoving Churchill's already recoiling body into the hard-wooden side of the house with brute force, quaking the loose panelling. All the windows on that side of the double-storey home completely shattered from the kinetic wave transpiring from the grenade. The ligneous exterior housing was assaulted by fragments of shrapnel, speckling against exposed surface.

The walls and foundation vibrated from the loud detonation.

Thatch from the roof above shook loose and dropped like autumn shed.

And then in-set the ear-piercing pitch of the concussion ...

Strewn across the wet, messy wooden floor of the kitchen, a distraught Ève and Sophie still wrestled their bald German captor.

The man was strong, skilled, and quite formidable. Outnumbered against two smaller women, under normal circumstances he would likely be easily victorious. However, due to the wounds across his bald head, down his back and his eyes, the soldier's capability had become severely hindered.

The explosion went off outside the kitchen window. The three were struggling in tangled anarchy on the slippery, wet wooden floor of the kitchen. The blast blew in a pocket of rushing air through the window and flicked the veil curtain, even dislodging the curtain rod. Glass from the broken pane shattered about their heads, showering them in shards of pointy timber and particles of razor-sharp crystal, littering them in further scrapes and minor lacerations.

Their struggle persisted.

As debris rained down upon them, the two French women wrestled for possession of the rifle that belonged to the soldier whom they were mostly overpowering, trying to pry and even *bite* his fingers from his white-knuckled clamp of the gun. While the desperate engagement continued, during the tussle, Ève by chance disengaged the fitted bayonet from the under barrel of the rifle. After watching it drop to the floor and realizing what she had done, the Frenchwoman collected it and, with both hands, attempted to stab the Nazi with his own blade.

Through the madness of the scuffle, the lobster-red soldier saw the antic and predicted her plan, managing to counter her attack with a free hand by catching her at the wrists. With pure strength, he held her at arms width with all his might.

The tip of the bayonet had halted three inches from his chest.

He strained, exposing his teeth through a grimace.

While all this was happening, during the complication of battling limbs over the Karabiner rifle, somebody inadvertently applied pressure to the trigger and the gun went off loudly, shooting a dent in the metal door of the cast-iron stove nearby them. The entire mounted contraption shifted on its legs as a result, collapsing to the side. An insistent *hissss* could be heard emanating from what was most assuredly a busted gas valve from the harmed connections.

After a further tense trice of struggle, another German soldier entered the kitchen from the dining room. It was the grenadier from the connecting room, and he intervened hurriedly once realizing his kamerad was in distress.

Wet hair and a strain of desperation over her face, Ève adjusted her position over the bald German, collapsing all her body weight into her taut stabbing commitment, causing the blade to sink a little lower. The pointy silver tip almost inserted into the man's chest; however her attempt was subdued at the last second by the new addition to their opposition.

The grenadier reached in and pulled Ève from off the soldier, managing to also parry the bayonet from her grasp with a smack from a stielhandgranate that he wielded like a club in his other hand. With a metallic rattle, the fumbled bayonet scattered across the floor and into the abyss of debris and pooling water.

Although wounded by a bullet to the wrist, the grenadier was still energetic enough to put up a fight. In fact, the pain may have contributed to his wrath. Wearing a scowl of his own, he effortlessly threw Ève into the cabinetry opposite the kitchen with a harsh thud, and then stepped in and swung down on Sophie with his baton as she crawled across his burnt, bald brethren. He laid into her two, three times across the back with heavy *whumps* before switching the origin of his heavy club swings, coming in from the low side and collecting her under the ribs.

With a winded gasp she took the blow, flying over the top of the skirmish and disengaging, launching into the lining pantry door. She hit it so hard that she cracked the solid wood in half. In the aftermath of her collapse on the floor, wet-haired and battered, Sophie became partially buried by falling fillings as the cupboard contents tipped out.

Ève launched herself back into the fray, pouncing upon the bald and dazed German before he could stand. She resumed the attempt at prying the man's fingers from off the hold of the rifle.

Standing over them, the grenadier tucked the grenade club into his belt and collected the bayonet from the floor near his boots. Wielding the weapon like a dagger, he stepped over hunched, and carved an inch deep streak across Ève's grasp. The sting and pain of the slit caused Ève to shriek and release her hold of the weapon into the possession of the bald soldier who, now finally free of the struggle, shuffled breathlessly away from the women across the debris-covered floor.

All members of the tussle spread apart, each eyeing the one who seized ownership of the firearm.

Enraged and disconcerted, the bald Nazi chambered and directed the gun at the two gasping, exhausted, overpowered women.

They had put up a good fight. Sophie and Ève now rested, panicked and motionless against the row of cupboards opposite the Germans in the kitchen. Ève assisted her mother, disregarding her own injury in order to make sure her mother's head was not cracked open from her brutal impact. Sophie may have been slightly concussed from the blow, dazed in her reactions.

Bright pink from his burns and red from his rage, the bald soldier suspended his stare, holding them at gunpoint until they realised.

The ounce of contemplation shown was not of mercy ... *it was only because he didn't know which one of them he was going to kill first.*

He quickly decided.

His sights panned to Ève, and he pulled the trigger.

"*No!*" her mother suddenly aroused and screamed out of nowhere, finding the strength to leap forth and launch another offensive at the Germans just as the gun went off.

Bam!

The gun fired with a blaring blast, shooting her instead. The rifle instinctively swayed towards her in a defensive action, and discharged, point-blank in the sternum as she protectively cut in front of her daughter's execution.

Sophie DuPont took the devastating gunshot with a wince, copping the entire transfer of energy from the muzzle blast of the long-range 98k rifle to her tiny frame. She launched rearwards into a tall pantry door, coiling inwards in a bail of smoke. She collapsed into a slump, lifeless within seconds.

Stunned, Ève's jaw dropped, as did finally a tear from her welting reddening eyes. She was momentarily frozen from witnessing the murder of her mum—now, both parents within an hour. She became paralysed by desolation.

Finally, she lowered onto her mother, hovering above her as she started to pale and quiver, chilled by the sudden overbearing wash of distress of her fatal wound.

The soldier angrily bolted the rifle, in a hurry to shoot again.

With no remorse, he then pointed the rifle at Ève—she was next.

Ève didn't bare to watch.

Her eyes met her loving mother's as she faded.

Bam!

A 98k rifle discharged ... but it was not the bald man.

Another, different gun went off from the adjacent room.

From within the connected dining room, behind the grenadier and through the doorway like a saving grace, a bullet struck the bald German aiming the rifle through the throat.

The German's weapon still went off—but consequently to the interrupting nudge that shook his aim by an inch—and his shot missed Ève by a fraction, striking the tiles on a wall behind her head.

Abruptly losing his stability, the big, bald Hun began choking on his own gore after his neck exploded. Gushing, shiny red ooze fast pumped from his opened arteries, spilling down his uniform and across the mucky floor. The exit wound to the gunshot had critically torn open the German's Adam's apple from his throat, causing brutal, irreparable damage.

He immediately dropped his Karabiner and clutched at his blood-gushing wound, succumbing to the debris-littered floor in a fit of fear, pain, and confusion. Clutching at his bleeding gullet with both hands, he gurgled blood from his mouth, unable to speak as he collapsed roughly into the kitchen bench, sliding onto the floor where he landed on sharp glass and strewn cutlery.

The confused grenadier spun in the kitchen doorway, surprised to see that the other two younger French girls that he had previous secured had managed to evade the distracted machine-gunner and procure and make use of one of the bolt-action rifles stowed on the living room lounge.

The large, smoking German rifle was held between them resembling a cannon for comparison. They quickly started to panic, assessing the big wooden stick in attempt to make it shoot again. Simply pulling the trigger had no effect to the bolt-action rifle.

Looking up in a panic, Yana and Audréy saw the grenadier react.

He quickly squatted low, collecting his dying friend's dropped gun from the kitchen floor. He attempted to bolt the slippery, blood-soaked weapon with his wounded wrist as the two sisters endeavoured to operate the foreign weapon between them.

Baring a grimace of exertion, the wounded grenadier failed to cycle the weapon for multiple reasons, as did the two girls with their untrained, mishandling tiny paws. The whole circumstance became a flustered race of screaming and botching towards a bloody finish line in an awkward comedy of error and struggle.

Predictably, the soldier still beat them to it.

With a muddled, metallic *click ... clack ...* he finished cycling a round into the chamber and then poised, raising the gun at them and about to shoot ...

Yana and Audréy's actions ceased.

Their doe-eyed stares of dread raised onto him, about to witness their untimely deaths when, suddenly, their grenadier captor was tackled from behind by their eldest sister.

In her hand, Ève wielded a metal fork from the scattered cutlery utensils across the kitchen floor, angled like a stabbing dagger.

Latched around his neck with her free arm and her legs over his hips, she gouged at the man's face with the needle prongs as they both collapsed onto the rug-lined floor of the living room in furious and belligerent contest.

The grenadier soldier shrieked in wrenching agony as Ève managed to stab him numerous times in the jaw and neck with the piece of silverware, dotting four evenly spaced tiny spots as remnants. Hoisting onto his knees and elbows with her still mounted upon his back, he attempted to bash her in the ribs with the buttstock of his rifle, accidentally tossing it as a result. After he lost hold of the weapon, he then tried desperately with his balled fists to throw a reverse uppercut at his attacker, however Ève held on tighter than a rodeo rider on a bucking bull.

During this instance, Ève rammed the fork firmly into his face. The piece penetrated deeply into his bloody, dotted cheek, and the cutlery inserted between the grenadier's teeth. He bit it from the inside, clenching tight, and held on with a grotesque internal bite.

The grenadier shifted his stance, pushing up from the floor and attempting to throw his weight into her and against a wall or object in his blind backdrop.

In the action, Ève lost her grip for a second, slipping tensely.

Needing for both hands to hold on, she released the fork in his face in order to grab a better hold on his clothes and shoulder.

Wrapping both her arms now down past his shoulders, Ève was able to hook his extremities lowly. The grenadier was unable to remove the fork protruding from his face, bellowing in excruciating agony and discomfort whilst they viciously cavorted around the living room to the sound of gunshots and war outside.

The scene was an enduring and brutal bloodbath.

VI
Saviour

Discombobulated from the grenade blast, Jack Churchill finally raised his head from the slime of mud.

For a split-second, he almost forgot what day or year it was, however, it did not take long for him to recall recent events; to remember his purpose, and what was at stake.

Rising to his knees, he meaninglessly attempted to block his ears from the lurid pitch that resonated within his head, relentlessly reverberating within the confines of his own skull. The dizzy tone lingered like an irritating insect, buzzing around in his brain. All sound was muffled by shell shock. Even his own coughs, his own breathing.

Churchill squinted to see through the cloud of grey smoke as it blew a gust across him in the outdoor air of the DuPont farm warzone. He spluttered as he collected his head, gradually rediscovering his balance once clambering to his feet in the sticky sludge. His khaki service dress was now shellacked in mud and covered in soot from the grenade blast.

... whiz ...

... whiz ...

Trapped in a subdued trance from the concussion, while Churchill pulled himself from the muck at a casual pace, the all too familiar sound of passing bullets cutting through the air caught his attention. Like awaking from a blackout state of unconsciousness, he cast an unstable look at the wooden wall beside him, witnessing as a slug of lead that was intended to hit him, missed, and struck the side of the house with a discharge of smoke and surface decay.

Whiz—crack ...

Whiz—crack ...

Spaced apart, more rounds from a distant bolt-action with terrible aim struck the house some more, causing muffled impacts. The shots were originating from those same two pesky shooters at the Einheitsdiesel truck by the barn, across the property.

Still dizzy and mildly shell-shocked, Churchill forcefully revived his senses. His awareness quickly returned, and the filthy British captain engaged in an unsteady hobble, carrying him away from harm just as more incoming fire struck the scenery.

Blinking profusely, Churchill wiped an ounce of black mud from his face as the volume of the chaos around the DuPont residence began to restore.

By the corner of the house, he cast an eye to Hardy as he also took fire. Some of the near-missing shots were directed at him, striking the façade of the property by his position as he fought fiercely.

In a fit of action, Churchill watched as Hardy slammed his empty submachine gun to the ground and retrieved the British revolver from his rear waistband, struggling to cock the heavy hammer with his thumb. He needed both hands. Peeking an angle at the aggressors, he released a shot from the powerful .45 as they fired another cluster of shots in his direction, striking the edge of the wall inches from his ducking head.

Hardy boldly preserved his actions whilst under fire, but was grossly unprepared for the heavy recoil of the Webley pistol. The .45 ACP calibre pistol kicked like a mule, throwing his extended arm over a foot in vertical recoil. He almost tossed the thing like a graduation hat.

Between intervals of assiduous and slow retaliatory slugs at the soldiers by the barn, trading fire, Hardy noticed Churchill's new, exposed crisis.

Still with muffled tiding, the American hollered directions at Churchill, shouting between gunshots. Still appearing doped, the flummoxed English soldier could not discern the words over the ringing pitch from the explosion.

Jack concentrated intently, fighting the suppression of his mind's perplexed status and, surely, he began to focus.

Sound returned, like a tuned radio.

A pitch crescendoed into normality, he finally made sense of Hardy's words. The shouting was now accompanied with him shoving a finger in a specific direction ...

He was warning him!

Following the gesture, Churchill's stare scanned lengthways along the house, spotting a German inside the window—right as the submachine-gunner happened to glance out the viewport and distinguish him out in the open through the aftermath of war fog.

The kraut immediately hoisted his MP38 over the windowsill in order to shoot him dead in his partially incapacitated state.

"*Watch out!*" Churchill heard Hardy shout between his loud avenging gunshots. "*Get up, Captain! Move your ass!*"

Hardy fired another round with the heavy pistol before the hammer clicked steel, and he pulled himself behind the corner of the house as it was struck with more potshots from the distant enemy.

Churchill snapped to action!

He took a fast run-up and skimmed in close to the house, right as the gunner inside the window frame attempted to blaze him with gunfire from his balistraria-like position. The extended volley of gunfire missed, tracing a dancing pyrotechnics line through the sludge after Churchill's quick dash and sliding manoeuvre. Mud-spattered eruptions nipped at the heels of his motion as he reached the tight cover of the house, gliding in directly below the gunman's field of view.

In an extended burst, the submachine-gunner protruded his arms further out of the window, bending down at the wrists in attempt to angle the weapon's aim blindly at his elusive target, but still missing.

At the other end of the battle, Hardy was mouse-like with his movements. After retreating to shelter, he now glanced acutely around the edge of the DuPont family home, finding contentment after witnessing Churchill's flee to safety.

Back behind concealment, he beamed down upon his trembling hands as he fumbled yet *another* loose bullet into the mud at his feet. Reloading the cylinder of the slow piece should not have been so hard, but the speed-loaders Churchill had given him prior to their attack had failed in his pockets during the chaos, and it required him to load the slugs single file into the six open chambers.

That dropped golden bullet added to the other three that he had already fumbled into a mud puddle attempting to reload the weighty Webley revolver.

"*Sonofabitch!*" he cursed as his butter fingers let drop the round, leaving only three remaining fresh in his sweaty palm. So far, he had successfully loaded none.

Carefully, he juggled the others with a tinkle in his palm and crevasses of his fingers, struggling to align them as *ping!* the bullet impact from an enemy ricochet slammed into the wall beside his cover ensconce, causing him to jolt and blunder the handful of shells.

In a desperate clutch, he managed to save one round from a watery grave after it caught the slack of his trouser leg on the way down, catching it on the bounce.

Concentrating, Hardy eyed the lone round he now had left ...

After the spray from the gunner in the window had ceased, Churchill leaned out and scooped up a discarded German submachine gun. The thing was lacquered in mud, and he prayed it would still function—*and it did.*

Once rearmed, he allowed himself to pivot backwards into cover, discharging the coated weapon at a fully automatic rate of fire across the distance and at the two riflemen by the truck and barn that were giving both him and Hardy grief. They were getting close with their sporadic rifle fire and needed to be suppressed.

Sparks erupted from all over the metal Einheitsdiesel truck parked in their parallel, causing the soldiers to hide from the onslaught of incoming gunfire. The rest of the truck windshield above their heads completely shattered and the side door fell apart, dropping into the mud. The front tyres burst, and the German troop transport truck sunk low like a tired beast. The metal surface of the parked vehicle became raked by hot embers during the sustained blaze, the side of the exposed Einheitsdiesel fuel tank ruptured from a few poked holes. Diesel glugged, gushing out into the ground below as more bullets from Churchill's counter-attack barrage ignited in sparks against the metal.

Any bullet now would spur a spark to ignite the inferno ...

It would blow big and look awesome ...

And win them the fight!

... and then his gun clicked empty.

Right as Churchill had expected a pellet to stimulate a spark against the metallic frame of the vehicle, inflaming the pouring streams of gasoline as it drooled from the perforated holes along the fuel tank, the weapon in his clutches rudely clicked dry ...

His squinted eyes opened fully, morphing to a confused frown.

Teeth bared in a ferocious scowl through the smoke of his cooked weapon, Mad Jack watched as across the distance, the two soldiers recovered their positions, weapons raised to reengage.

Now reloaded and ready to put an end to this debacle, the two Stahlhelm shooters leant back around from the cover of the Einheitsdiesel and lined Churchill up where he rested, exposed and unprotected. This time, they took their time, aiming down their sights ...

... the apeshit British beret-clad captain was an unmissable target.

Any second now, their gunshots would kill Jack Churchill ...

At that same moment, peeking around the corner of the DuPont family home, Hardy's glance was of a double-take.

He saw the troops ...

Saw the leaking fuel ...

He observed the spilling flow glug and splash down onto the wet soil, and it registered to him, just as though it had for Churchill just moments before ...

Seconds passed like minutes.

Instants as extended intervals.

Hardy's brown eyes blinked, developing a determined sulk.

His view dipped from the distance and into focus at his hands as he finally accomplished reloading the borrowed pistol. With a mind now set to purpose and willpower firm upon his brow, he released the last bullet into one of the empty six holes of the cracked-open revolver and pushed the loaded cylinder to the eleven o'clock position.

Flick of the wrist, he snapped it shut with a stern look of resolve.

Cocking the hammer with his thumb as he brought the piece up past his head, the lone bullet resting within the aligned chamber behind the racked firing pin, trembling in the darkness up the elongated barrel, waited to pop off at the squeeze of the hair-pin trigger ...

Whilst peeking the edge of the corner, Hardy leaned into it for steadiness whilst he extended the pistol with his good arm.

He shut an eye for focus, beaming down the sights as he targeted the fuel tank and bided his time, aiming steady and true ...

All he—they—needed was a spark ...

... just one spark.

Bam ... BHOOF!

With the force of a thousand suns, causing a heatwave hot enough to cause even Hardy to recoil behind cover from across the farm, an orange fireball of high temperature and bright light erupted in the dusk setting.

Across the way, the idle Einheitsdiesel troop transport truck located between the two active German riflemen engulfed into liquid flames, and promptly erupted from beneath like an oil pan on a hotplate.

A single spark caused from Hardy's bullet against the metal chassis of the truck, struck almost directly above the ruptured fuel tank. The flints shot outwards, and the bright flickers of yellow kindled an ignition of the accelerant below, burning the leaking fuel like an arsonist's deliberation.

In an instant, ravenous, hungry fire surged up the soaking stream of highly flammable and combustible diesel fuel, snaking its dazzling way into the pressurized confines of the underbelly gas tank and *bhoof!* an instant outburst of fire accompanied with a strident eruption.

The detonation exploded so raucously loud and so vividly bright and hellishly hot that the remaining doors, supports, and frame of the truck were instantaneously detached and hurtled out in every direction. The burn raised the truck from beneath, as if the force of the igneous fumes kicked it in the guts with the power of a thousand uppercuts.

The two shooters were partially incinerated.

What was left of the German soldiers flung lifelessly ablaze, flailing outwards and into the local ligneous barn doors, which the palings crumbled under the force of their throw. The SS troops were launched off their feet, charcoaled, and carried for yards in mid-air. Upon smashing through the wooden planks of the barn doors in twin puffs of smoke, the troops punched through the wall of stacked hay inside the barn, catching it alight like it was kindling.

The barn itself was quick to set ablaze.

The old wooden structure was filled with highly incendiary contents and was a sure recipe for conflagration. The back end of the barn engulfed into a blinding, breathing inferno within seconds, roasting like a bonfire that dazzled like a lighthouse in the night. A cloud of black smoke swallowed itself, climbing high into the sky, burning a bright brown hue.

A perfectly intact tyre wheel from the Einheitsdiesel shot high into the air, trailed by a finger of smoke. It eventually arced down and bounced in the mud just yond from Jack Churchill sought shelter with his arms over his face from the heat of the fire, causing him to flinch as it landed hot with a *whoosh!*

"Bloody hell!"

Churchill cursed loudly, beholding the glowing remains of the Einheitsdiesel explosion and barn house incineration past the muddy hand shielding his face. The resonating heat roasted his eyeballs.

Entranced for an extended moment, Jack took in the auburn glow and the warmth of the flames. Following the ear-splitting detonation, a fireball had expanded into a small mushroom cloud above the truck before swelling into itself, swallowing into a clouded mass as it levitated, transforming into a thick, black choking smokestack that climbed high into the evening hue.

Snapping out of his hypnotized trance and thanking his lucky stars, Churchill remained low below the window. The German submachine-gunner above him was still lurking, and Jack could hear him trudging around inside. Could hear him swearing, even reloading his weapon.

Jack glanced left.

His trusty claybeg remained bayoneted into the mud, albeit now on a slight angle. He grabbed it, arming himself.

Low and now with his sword back in his hand, Churchill twirled about, resetting this fight. He faced the windowsill above his position, expecting the SS troop to be waiting for him—about to creep out again with his gun and open fire from point-blank range ... and like clockwork, *he was right.*

Churchill predicted the motion of the SS troop's reemergence above him. He prepared his custom claybeg sword, his fingers taut though the four loops of the knuckleduster hand groove and reacted like lightning. Jack upped and grabbed the barrel of the submachine gun with his spare hand, repelling it outwards in order to bring the gunner closer to the window for a clear shot with his closed right fist wrapped encased within a brass-duster handle.

Jack punched the heavy sword hilt.

Whack!

He hit him again and again, and fucking hard, too.

Whack!

Whack!

Punched in the face three times with the solid metal fist grip that encased Churchill's knuckles, the bloodied and now partially toothless German soldier withdrew in a stunned backward fashion before he reclaimed grasp of his resilience.

Somehow seizing it from Churchill and managing to maintain possession of his gun, the stupefied troop staggered into a collapse from the window with a thud on the floor. Still dazed, he immediately hosed with the weapon out through the window space, causing Churchill to vanish instantly.

The sprightly swordsman recoiled, disappearing from sight in the nick of time as an extended, wild burst of Schmeisser diarrhoea shat out the window port, even striking the sill.

Bloody nosed, bleary eyed, and with what was likely a much-needed visit to the dentist, the gunner clambered to his feet and abandoned the room. Dizzy as fuck and most likely with a mild traumatic brain injury from the brutal hits to the noggin, the floundering submachine-gunner crashed into walls and doorframes with his shoulders, attempting drunkenly to reload his MP38 in the process as he fled this bullying Brit.

As he moved, drooling saliva and blood, he kept his focus on the many windows that ran along the front of the house, expecting the British swordsman to attempt another play at any mome—

Movement.

Poking his head up for an instant was Jack Churchill's beret-clad dome.

With his palm, the gunner slapped the stick into the mag well and quickly raised the weapon with a single arm, spraying the window and wall, drawing a wild stitch across the surface. His rounds pulverized the wooden frame to shards, cracking the lumber of the painted wall.

Churchill's head had long since retracted from sight. However, out of pure frustration, the troop grappled the weapon with both hands and then held in the trigger, firing for longer than necessary and scorching the walls where he would have been.

Cursing in German, he shook his head and nursed his aching jaw and split lips. The troop was involuntarily dribbling blood from his mouth like a salivating dog, barely able to even articulate words. His swearing grievance whimpered into a distressed cry of pain as his brow inverted, victim to the immense agony.

After another vertigo spell and colliding with his shoulder into another doorframe, knocking down picture frames and a swiping hanging decorative tapestries, the gunner stepped into the raucousness of the main living room. This was where the remaining German soldier, a Waffen-SS grenadier, was locked in a savage fight with one of the French girls. Judging by the debris and apropos carnage, it seemed as though the two had exploded out from the kitchen and onto the carpeted floor of the dining room, engaged in endless bec et ongles.

The gunner retracted his sights from windows that ran the side of the house and instead aimed in at the desperate hand-to-hand combat as it ensued. Not obtaining a clear line-of-slight, he withheld his shot.

While the DuPont daughter fought the soldier on the carpeted wooden floor, they knocked toppled furniture and smashed ceramic ornaments with loud bumps and shatters. They were both littered in scratches, drenched in sweat and blood smears, and were otherwise completely burgered, trying not to fall apart.

The gunner then noticed the other two younger girls positioned low by a couch, attempting to work one of the German rifles from the piles of gear near there.

Deciding to intervene, he raised the submachine gun towards them and shouted. He left them no time for reconsideration or reaction before he pulled the trigger of his submachine gun—*click-click-click.*

No ammo.

He cursed in German, again, gawping down at his clutched weapon.

His hands acted fast to reload the MP38 and, once again, his actions were hindered due to the overwhelming pain throbbing in his fucked mouth. The British soldier had done some serious damage with the knuckleduster hilt of his battle sword.

Bloody faced and battle-torn, the exhausted grenadier seemingly gained the upper hand during his struggle with Ève, levering her weight and managing to shove the courageous female fighter off him during their tussle.

Ève toppled over the large set dining table, collecting numerous plates, glasses, and set cutlery, before tumbling off the opposite side and subsiding excruciatingly over a fallen chair which she smashed to splinters under her weight, adding to the already rubble-littered floor.

Finally free of the nuisance, the grenadier delicately took the time to harness the protruding fork from his cheek and yank it clear. A spirt of gore followed it out. With a tense grimace, he cupped his face for an extended recovery.

Bloodied and fatigued, he stood tall with the freshly charged rifle, training the weapon at the armed Yana and Audréy. With a shut eye and loose vision, he fired almost blindly at the children—right as the two girls mastered the bolt-action system of *their own* 98k, shooting it at *him* as well.

Almost simultaneously, both weapons discharged.

The bloody-faced grenadier hunched over, having been shot in the lower stomach right above the groin. After doubling-over, he dropped to his knees, trading his grip of the gun to hold his fatal wound and failing to maintain breath. He had felt the exit wound crack his tailbone.

At the opposite end, the grenadier's round had struck young Yana in the centre of the chest, sending the DuPont daughter recoiling.

Audréy screamed loud when the guns went off, but not as loud as when she looked to see that the shot had struck her sister—straight through the heart.

Yana was already dead.

Her eyes peacefully closed within a second of her collapse.

Audréy discarded the heavy German gun in order to scoop her arms under her baby sister, screeching and weeping hysterically, chanting in her tiny, cracking voice for to her to wake up.

From across the room, eldest sister Ève was emotionally winded by the sight. She sobbed in disbelief witnessing the aftermath of the shootout, and crawled bloody fingered through the debris on the floor beneath the dining table in order to assist her sisters, reaching them within seconds.

The two sisters mourned together, immediately bemoaning the onsetting tragedy. They held each other close, oblivious to any other chaos. Nothing else seemed to matter. They became involuntarily submissive.

The remaining submachine-gunner finished reloading after the brief hiatus of action. He, too, had witnessed the totality of the shootout and, a testimony to his underlining, buried humanity, was taken aback. He moved in with his weapon guard to finish them off, likely fighting whatever humanity he had left, instructing him not to be a cunt ... but he hesitated.

His gaze fixed on his mortally wounded comrade as he murmured in pain from the wound to his stomach. Catching his eye, was the motion of him pulling one of the stielhandgranates from a pouch that housed several others, and he began fumbling about the wooden handle of the fuse with his sticky hands ...

In all the panic and noise, the submachine-gunner pleaded to him to desist the explosive action, but the dying man cared no longer for his life—nor anybody else's. His wicked bloodshot eyes fixed on the two remaining girls across the living room, now inactive and backed into a corner of their own destroyed home. This French family had killed this egotistical, evil grenadier, and he fuckin' hated them for it. The vengeance in his deathly gawk was steadfast and absolute.

He was going to kill them all with his dying breath.

Wide-eyed and concerned, the gunner shouted again, about to reduce his guard in order to forcefully disarm his incapacitated madman before he killed them all—himself included.

Suddenly, from behind, a sword-in-hand Mad Jack Churchill emerged, bursting into the room through the bright halo of light shining through smoky residue in the partially shot-to-shit doorway.

As heroic as it was to witness, he pranced inwards with a slight stumble that exhumed humility. Afterall, the man was still a little deaf and dazed from the recent shell shock.

With barely any time to blink, Jack acknowledged the presences within the room; seemingly the only live threat being that of the concussed submachine-gunner. The two witnessed each other's attendance at the same time, and the SS troop immediately reacted to his entrance by turning and raising his firearm.

Jack immediately attacked the soldier before he had a chance to aim.

Indirectly, the automatic went off from an errant trigger pull, and the shots missed everyone and everything bar the floor and a wall.

Across the short distance, Churchill quickly lobbed his sword like a batter out of baseball. The burly *whoosh-whoosh-whoosh* of the spinning sword as it travelled through the air caused for a harsh metallic collision as the medieval weapon whacked side-on against the soldier's coiling body.

The heavy claybeg succeeded in knocking the firing submachine gun clear from the soldier's grip from the blunt impact, and the two items became dispersed across the floor.

The flung blade may not have impaled or even incapacitated the SS troop, but the attempt yielded results. The device averted the gunplay for the second Churchill needed to pounce upon the remaining German from across the room, launching like a human torpedo in a maroon beret, and the two crashed together in a manic tackle.

This brutal horseplay instigated a ruthless and pitiless hand-to-hand fight. The two soldiers slammed onto the heavy dining table, flipping it over and shattering all sorts of breakables about the room ...

... all the while, the mortally wounded grenadier felt about his precious stielhandgranate, ultimately locating the fuse string at the base of the handle. He gave it a firm pul—*crash!*

Out of nowhere and in an energetic dive from a beyond-exhausted girl, Ève DuPont lunged at the wounded grenadier, engaging him in another undertaking. She had realized he was arming the explosive with lethal intent, and the two grappled on the floor over the device as though their lives depended on it.

The weakened duo fought vigorously for possession of the grenade; however the grenadier was stronger in his credence in this, his final cause of devotion. Regardless of his injuries, he shoved the weakened woman clear and *finally* pulled the string of the grenade, arming the explosive.

Smoke rose from the hollow handle ... the fuse was lit ...

Then, he just held it like a torch in the night ... guarded it ...

Embracing it close to his body, it suddenly became apparent just how many other explosive devices this grenadier contained on his person; *schrapnellmines*, even more *stielhandgranates*, and within separate sections of his pack, he also carried with him raw *Amatol* and *Composition B.* Each local device would likely ignite from the detonation of the single stielhandgranate, causing a chain reaction of devastating yield within the confines of this French home.

Across the room, Churchill gained the upper hand in his brawl with the submachine-gunner. The German rode the Brit like a bucking bull. Using pure strength and tactical resolve during the critical fight, he managed to claim hold of the discarded MP38 and pushed off the floor, thankful to use it to end their contest.

Both combatants sprung up. The German held the barrel—but Jack retaliated by dropping his angle—and as he held the soldier with his left hand, he pulled the trigger with his right. Point-blank, the machine gun released a burst through the man and up into the ceiling. The muzzle flashes from the discharging automatic climbed up to the man's chest, shredding him to gory ribbons and killing him dead with a deafeningly loud close quarters volley.

Almost instinctually, Jack felt something else was amiss.

His beret-equipped head tipped against the floor, and upside-down, he spotted the DuPont girls across the room, as well as their situation. Observing with a set of wide eyes, Churchill took it all in within a split-second ...

... *a second that was no longer available.*

... their mother, *Sophie,* lay dead in the kitchen.

... *Yana,* the youngest, was shot in the gut and deceased, and,

... *Audréy* wearily held her seemingly lifeless body.

Covered in blood from the endurance of relentless violence and quivering with tremble, sorrow, and panic, and quite probably shaking off the urge to faint and pass out due to blood loss or concussion from head trauma, *Ève* was in the process of ascending from the furrowed rugged floor. She had been fighting with the wounded grenadier, who held a cooking grenade in his grasp, and had many more strapped within the webbing on his chest harness ...

The five second fuse had since been armed!

Churchill's eyes grew even wider ...

... this meant they had mere sec—

He twisted upright and pushed up, shouting erratically to warn them, right as time ran out ...

His exhalation was cut off by something that literally sucked the air from the vicinity before it expelled it with an unprecedented level of physical and kinetic force.

"*Mov!—*"

The last thing Churchill remembered was dropping the weapon in order to launch himself towards Ève, who was dangerously close to what could be considered *ground zero.*

The last image of her which he saw; she was sitting sort of contently. Peacefully. She had succumbed to her fate—but then again, she had probably done so the moment the Nazis had arrived on the property. She, her family, had been on borrowed time. With each death of a family member endured since then, a remaining shred of life had been stripped from her, again and again until finally, the grenade: a type of ironic mercy.

Ève seemed unable to climb to her feet, not for lack of trying. She was out of breath and out of will, but somehow strangely at peace with it all.

In the nanosecond before the detonation, possibly in the exact moment due to the immersing white light which illuminated her features to Jack's retention like the flashbulb of a camera, she closed her beautiful brown, hazelnut blush, honey-hued eyes for the last time. Prior to their closure, her stare was intently fixed on him. Perceptible through the exhaustion and discomfort and pain, her gaze to Churchill was one without hope and with feeling, one last time, as she accepted her fate; *their fate.*

At that same second, Churchill didn't think. Just acted.

Performed as his training and his heart demanded, that a lot can happen in one second, he lunged forth in a final attempt to save her.

In spite of everything ... *it was simply not fast enough.*

Bo—BHOOM!

The grenade went off in the living room, exploding into a bright white and gold flash of potently powerful light and force.

The detonation instantly set off the other dozen stielhandgranates and explosives loaded on the man's body, practically igniting simultaneously like a super-bomb.

The grenadier was obliterated in an instant, disintegrating into course chunks of black char and ash. An outgoing wave sent his burnt blood across the room like a popped water balloon.

A dynamic blast wave from the housed explosives engulfed everything in the space, violently lifting and hurling heavy furniture whilst simultaneously dismantling it in fragments, reducing solids into particles.

At some stage during the combustible nanoseconds, an element of the discharge caused by the high explosives incited the leaking gas valve in the kitchen, thus igniting the underfloor gas reserve. A bright orange wink flashed between every floorboard, exhorting them like an airburst within a house of cards. Individual planks of wood disengaged from the house walls, backlit by blinding orange heat, propelled outwards. Blown apart like a gust of wind to autumn leaves.

In a nanosecond, the incineration caused the thick rug that lined the wood floor to ripple and singe. Beneath it, the timber floorboards sunk like a crater, tearing apart upholstery, turning timber chairs and tables into splinters and debris.

Smoke filled the entire airspace and puffed outwards.

As he took a single step in approach, the blast wave slogged Churchill away in the opposite direction. He was a leaf in the wind, puffed outwards at high-speed by a gush of exerting air strong enough to launch a human being.

He was dangerously close to the detonation; however, it seemed fate had other plans for Mad Jack Churchill. Protected by measly elements such as the soldier still in his grip and the standing furniture between him and the grenade on the floor to absorb shrapnel and most of the initial power of the discharge, as well as being the farthest away in the room, the blast pocket instead threw him backwards as though he were in an air tunnel.

The blast sent him flying directly out the doorway of the home from which he had originally emerged ahead of the expanding shockwave of force that obliterated everything. He was the bullet from a gun.

Outside, the *bang* and *boom* of the explosives detonating caused Hardy to duck and drop in the sludge as he moved alongside of the DuPont house.

The might of the expanding blast shoved him to his rear in the mud, burying him in hot debris and smoke as the kitchen wall cracked like the foundation of an earthquake, spewing chunks of timber and bricks his way. The top of the double-storey building popped like the lid of a dropped soda, burying all outer surroundings in loose thatch roofing, most of which caught ablaze.

Like a smoking shell from the ball of a cannon, Jack Churchill launched out through the doorway of the DuPont family home in a cloud of smoke, racing a haze of smoulder and destruction as it collapsed and engulfed the household behind him.

In a finger of dust like a missile, Churchill glid ahead of an enclosing cloud of rushing force which followed with a thunderous, trembling eruption and gust.

Endless debris sprinkled about the mud as his seemingly lifeless body slid to a halting stop outside the house, covered in black char, fresh flesh wounds and burns, and a dozen tiny protruding splinters, now completely unconscious—or dead, as he probably should have been.

The indoor and contained explosions rocketed out over the farm, blowing outwards with volatile potency, shooting a gust of wafting flames out of the many windows and doorframes that connected to the dining room, living area, and kitchen in the front section of the DuPont family home.

Alit flames from the thirsty fire breathed out, starved for oxygen. The raging blaze licking through the many fractured sections of house and window, scaling paling walls of the outside of the home before touching the tips of the overhanging thatched rooftop, setting a portion of it on fire with just a mere touch of heat. Some of the flooring collapsed inwards, and an entire section directly above the dining room—the final resting place of the DuPont sisters—caved in on itself with a groan and an echo.

When the reverberation of the walls within crumpling died out, and the dust started to settle, the cracking of the inferno continued to sizzle as the double-storey house kindled.

The wreckage burned bright in the otherwise tranquil dusk setting above France.

Blackness.

"Yoo wanna take somethin' from dis war ..."

In the dark of nothing behind Jack Churchill's closed eyelids as his attention started to stir, the Glaswegian intonation of Colonel MacLeòid echoically resounded, absent origin. He was forever haunting his mentee with his idealistic, albeit often nonsensical wisdom.

"Yoo wanna life beyond tha depths ... wit' dis lassie or tha next ... yoo got' be prepared ta give et somethin' en return ..."

"... Yoo're gon' 'ave ta fecht, und ne'er stop ..."

"... War demands sacrifice ..."

Glimpses of motion were all he saw as he drifted in and out of consciousness. A sample screening of broadening events became sporadically revealed to him as his head eventually lifted, and Churchill reluctantly scanned his surroundings with a sense of displacement.

The sky darkened and distant stars twinkled ...
The DuPont house furiously ablaze ...
A smoke cloud rose, thick and black and impenetrable ...
Rising into the darkening dusking sky high above ...
Orange dots of heat pulsated within the slag cinders ...
Ash serenely drifted down, resembling falling snow of a winter ...
View distorted, a blurred man appeared above his collapsed body.

It seemed a soul Churchill did not recognize at first, but upon further inspection, rattled and beaten, the German uniform-disguised Felix Hardy focused more into picture.

Hardy looked down over him as he lay in the wreckage, baring a new slit across one eyebrow and fresh dark soot smears across his face.

It almost looked as though this white-collar American journalist had been through the wars—because he had.

"*Captain?!... Captain?!...*" Hardy called. His voice was still a distant resonance to Churchill's unwillingly and inattentive, barely responsive ability. The reverberating pitch from the thundering explosion and the harm of the impact on his inner ears were a combination flatline of tone and ruptured eardrums. It blocked everything out except the sound of his own heavy breathing and murmurs of a pain-stricken and bruised body.

"*Captain?!* ..." Hardy continued, appearing above the downed British officer. "*Are you O.K.?!*"

Between long blinks of his heavy eyelids, Churchill watched as the journalist looked about the area for any other valid options, observing absent acknowledgement of the full predicament of their surroundings as Hardy shielded his face from the sweltering orange blaze nearby that illuminated them in the nightscape.

Eventually, he grabbed Churchill's lifeless body, dragging him away from the hot and vibrant glow, moving them both to a safer, cooler distance.

Propped up on something, Churchill finally saw the view from farther back. The view was of the DuPont family home, utterly engulfed in flames. The symbolism that all was lost was found within his mind.

No questions were asked ... he already had the answers.

His red eyes were heavy, and Churchill fought the urge to drift benumbed and fall asleep, succumbing to the concussion he had undoubtedly sustained.

"Hey! Captain?!" Hardy shouted more clearly, causing him to reopen his resting eyes. He stepped into view over his slumped body, stimulating his vision.

Hardy had dragged him almost thirty feet from the hot zone, though the radiance was still hot on their skin. There were two blazes now on the dairy farm, one which had been set alight by the exploding truck and one from the double-storey home, which burned the brightest thanks to the wood stilts, flammable possessions, and thatch tinder.

The entire place showed remnants of a warzone.

With its destruction, this once picturesque locale had now joined so many of its neighbouring French homesteads; a number that grew rapidly by the day to tallies of destruction.

As late dusk slipped into night, the bright orange fires were the only thing that illuminated the area. The fire burned so bright into the nightscape that their low to the earth bodies cast shadows across the flat muddy landscape.

"Captain?!" Hardy called again, propping the stunned Captain Churchill up a little taller and more comfortably. Jack lurched upright with a grimace of aching parts all over his body.

"Jesus Christ, bud. I can't believe you're alive!"

With a wince and a longing pout, Churchill examined his hands. They were littered in nasty splinters and cuts. He even had a four-inch splinter of wood lodged in his hip that had torn through his woollen service dress material, likely timer debris launched from the explosions. He removed it with a roar of pain, applying pressure, however the wound felt somewhat superficial.

The focus of Churchill's starry-eyed stare was lost in the flames of the inferno before them, with just one obvious thing on his mind.

"They're all gone, buddy," Hardy attempted to comfort. "No one got out ... I can't even believe that *you* made it out. I'm sorry, *Jack* ..."

Churchill's eyes were perplexed, frozen upon the flaming furnace as with a struggling groan, the structure's walls gave in and the entire unit collapsed further in on itself, adding more fuel to the fire.

"The sacrifice."

Churchill's muttered word was barely even construed by the exhausted and still deaf Felix Hardy.

"Huh?"

"They ... they were the sacrifice the war demanded."

Hardy remained confused.

Forming a frown, his eyes panned about the area, resting upon the ablaze ruins before them. He shrugged Mad Jack's mad nonsense off to it likely being the concussion talking.

Tears burned his eyes. Churchill clenched them tight.

He laid back into the muddy, grassy recess beneath him and took an extended moment to collect himself.

Time passed.

Hardy watched from his seated position beside Churchill on the flat ground as the unkillable, unstoppable British soldier finally pushed himself up from the ground. He seemed bewildered, as if he had not realized that he had even fallen asleep—or more appropriately, *passed out.*

Aching and in visible pain from his physical wounds, let alone an amass of internal bruising and swelling from being so close to an explosion shockwave, Churchill rose to his feet and limped closer to the smouldering wreckage that had subsided over the numerous hours.

He wasn't sure of the time, but it felt like pre-dawn.

Animals were yet to begin singing birdsong, but the contrast of hue beyond the horizon was casting a silhouette as the sun prepared to ascend as the world turned.

Moving towards the smouldering ruins of the DuPont home with an unsteady footing, Jack gazed upon the cold and deceased German troops laying scattered in the mud. A few of them had been set alight by the fire and burned crisply as charcoal like the rest of the house.

Shielding his face from the irradiating heat of the many internal spot fires, Churchill's advance ceased approximately ten steps from the depths of the wreckage. He gazed upon the black, charred remains, searching for anything resembling a human body within the aftermath, though it was quickly evident during his examination that all organic matter inside would have been blown away by the explosions, let alone incinerated by the blazing inferno that followed it.

Their ashes were buried beneath rubble and char.

Now sure of the DuPont family's entire demise, Churchill peeled his face away from the glowing embers, gaining a view of Hardy in the illumination of the flames as he stood and took a few strides forwards. The man looked exhausted, battle-worn, and beaten. It was a look he had seen a couple hundred times on the faces of soldiers and war heroes ... he never once thought that he would see Felix Hardy under such a different light. But, he did. And he couldn't deny it.

Back upon the wreckage, Churchill's eyes blinked and for some reason, a shimmer of the fading moonlight on a reflective metal surface in the sludge caught his attention. Homing upon it, he glared down at his boots in the mud, identifying his blood- and mud-stained claybeg sword amongst a many broken shards of timber and ornaments that had been thrown from inside the house. The explosion must have blown the weapon outside. The indestructible design of the claybeg had kept it in one piece.

In the eerie quietness and crackling flames, Hardy scanned to his left. A sound had caught his attention over by the toppled German BMW-R71 motorcycle and pod, which had become detached as the bike had fallen to its side. The chromed edges of the jet-black unit glistened and reflected the orange flickers of the fiery house as it burned.

There was movement about it, and the once static item rocked with motion.

"Captain ..." Hardy called, quickly jogging over to the movement after realizing that there was another survivor nearby it, attempting to stand the unit upright in order to flee.

Apparently, the struggle was real with one hand.

It was the German Feldbischof.

The Bishop.

Hardy's run slowed upon realizing who the survivor was.

The enemy compatriot, although gravely wounded, was still a potential danger and one that greatly intimidated him. Inexperienced, Hardy paused in his advance, indicating the threat for Churchill as he saw the lone Nazi survivor on his knees by the bike. Conceivably, the feldbischof was attempting to stand the vehicle upright and escape, a lone one-handed survivor. He had severed limb folded out of sight against his stomach, the other weakly grasping at the handlebars.

In no real rush, Churchill bent down with a stiff grunt.

Clutching at the wound in his side, he collected his sword from the mud. The unit was now entirely stripped of its black paint job and shone reflectively in the flickering orange light of the fire; the Damascus silver and grey blade, the golden brass of the knuckleduster hilt. Ash fell from the surfaces, unveiling its deadly beauty.

The steel was warmed from the fire. Jack felt the heat as he touched it, almost hot enough to burn the palm of his hand, but he of all people, could handle it. He was born to it. The brass trench-knife piece was hot across the bridges of his fingers as they wrapped through the eyelets, almost too hot to hold.

The sword may have been hot ...

... but not as hot as the wrath that still burned within him.

Churchill clenched the sword firmly, embracing the pain of the sweltering heat. Wielding it by his side with overwhelming valour, he strode towards the helplessly crawling and fumbling, one-handed surviving Nazi.

Hardy spectated as Churchill approached from the interceptive flank, unwavering in his resolve. He was a purposed dutyman—nay, an *executioner.*

There was no pending compassion. No sympathy. No mercy.

Tired and hurting, Churchill trod around the dirtied, pale-faced and weakened feldbischof and kicked back over the BMW-R71 motorbike which he had so tiresomely struggled to stand upright in his final attempt to flee.

After resting face down on his elbows, the sunken-eyed, pale-faced feldbischof revolved from his toppled position in order to behold the view of Mad Jack Churchill.

Jack encircled the German at sword point, like a predator cornering his prey. His sterling stare seemed to faulter for a second as he involuntarily envisioned the face of his private enemy, Friedrich Feind.

By complete accident, Feind's facial features were beneath the officer's cap, staring back at him with a bested expression.

"... Feind?" Churchill muttered at the same time as the confusion seemed to vanish. Like the shimmer of a mirage's fadeout.

From the background, Hardy had thought he heard his announcement, but considering the many connotations assisted with it and his lack of knowledge regarding Churchill's past, he thought nothing specifically of it. In fact, if anything, *enemy* was *feind* when translated to German.

Whatever face he had just envisaged, it was all the same to him at this pivotal moment in time. Churchill's focus tightened as his stare intensified on the topic. He gazed upon his previous handiwork—the bishop's severed hand—and noticed that the tough old bastard had managed to pad and wrap the wound tightly, slowing the bleed to survive. He couldn't help but scoff at the tenacity and bollocks it must've taken to do that during the insanity of the tooth and nail battle for this plot of land.

"The Devil, huh ...?" Churchill remarked sniffing back an ounce of mucus from his fight to hold back emotion, covering his potential tracks of delusion from Hardy.

He added fittingly, partingly, and with a steel gaze and a lethal finale, he eyed the bishop. "Let me send you back to Hell, eh?"

With a steel gaze of fury and vengeance, Churchill broke words with the officer from behind the blade. They were English words he had spoken before and therefore understood. Words he *knew* this evil German would understand.

"Get on your knees ..."

The German's eyes seemed to defocus as he heard it.

He understood what it meant, and what was coming ...

Enfeebled and in fear of his life, he waved his remaining hand at Churchill in an unacknowledged plea of mercy, of renunciation.

A moment passed where Churchill stared him down and maintained the glare, making his disinterest for his submission well known before the feldbischof finally complied.

The maimed old man struggled to manoeuvre his knees beneath his weakened state, but those nearby cared little of his hardship. He finally knelt, hunched and depressed before the swordsman: his would-be executioner.

"Iz it worth me zurrendering?" the feldbischof managed to communicate in poor English.

Churchill rested the topic for a moment, still maintaining the same vengeful glower before shaking his head slightly and replying simply and in this piece of shit's native language.

"*Nein.*"

Salivating for vengeance, himself, under Hardy's yearning and watchful eye, Jack Churchill raised his sword out by his side. His hold was firm, his fingers through the eyelets, yielding power ...

But he hesitated.

"Captain?" Hardy questioned from the side. He was unarmed, otherwise he would have finished this himself.

Churchill shook his head an ounce, showing signs of repentance towards this course of action.

His army training talking, he blinked about himself, momentarily confused in this process. "We don't execute prisoners ..."

Hardy shuffled closer, waving an arm at the bright glow of the DuPont home set ablaze. It was all a direct result of the feldbischof and his minions of evil. "Well, this motherfucker does! Think of your woman, Jack. The DuPonts!"

Sensing his hesitation and confusing it for incompetence to perform the execution, Hardy reached in to grasp at Jack's sword.

"Give it here. I'll do it—"

Right as Churchill instinctively furthered it from Hardy's reach, the deemed incapacitated feldbischof made a move.

Pale and sunken eyed, the inebriated German Bishop suddenly retrieved a compact PPK pistol from the elbow fold of his stump, wielding it with his remaining left hand and brandishing it forth, about to shoot the British and the American in their twinkling of judgement.

"*Watch out!*" Churchill noticed the movement and shouted, shoving Hardy clear.

Hardy's brown eyes next witnessed the motion from the feldbischof, growing wider than his macho attitude had ever been in the build-up.

The fact the bishop sported the Walther PPK in his non-dominant hand may have been what saved them.

The extra nanosecond was all it required, and Churchill swung his claybeg with the surgeon's sweep, slicing his *other* hand off at the wrist as the feldbischof pointed the pistol.

Chop!

The feldbischof winced in pain, falling back into his kneeling pose in time to see the aftermath of his barely attached ligament. The sword had performed more as a bludgeon than a blade, however the sharpness of the claybeg had done some damage. His wrist had been hacked and was bleeding profusely, the bone broken, likely severing his veins. His only remaining hand was tethered by what appeared to be a few tendons and loose flesh.

Hardy recovered from the scare. "Holy fuck!"

He stepped out and collected the PPK from the mud, assessing it. The Bishop had collected the thing from the messenger's satchel on the side of the motorbike.

The weapon wasn't even chambered. Hence hiding it, he had likely been unable to perform the cycle due to having one hand. Now, he had none.

Hardy racked the slide completely and eyed Churchill.

"Now are you going to kill him?"

Churchill aimed his sword and stare upon the pathetic German.

Wincing in agony, the feldbischof folded over, tucking what was left of his remaining appendage beneath his opposite elbow fold. Unable to apply pressure to the fresh wound, he would undoubtedly succumb to blood loss and bleed out quickly.

With conviction, Jack lowered the sword.

He parted with, "I just did."

Holding his breath, Hardy watched as Churchill stepped away, walking back towards the flames of the DuPont family home.

In the darker background as the glowing orange illuminated Jack's features, Hardy was visible as he raised the pistol and fired a shot into the maimed feldbischof. His body slumped, instantly deceased.

Churchill did not bother to turn.

There was no judgement. Hardy had stakes in this too, and he was well within his rights to seek vengeance for his departed friend, Omar Ny.

Standing over the fallen corpse, behind a pair of dagger eyes Hardy still trained the handgun.

He seemed unconvinced of his claimed vengeance.

After a moment, he fired again, and again, three more times before the PPK clicked empty, the tiny hammer snapping against hard steel.

Eventually, he threw the spent weapon into the mass of the dead corpse. His expression was one borne of stubbornness, disappointed that it didn't bring Ny back or make him feel an ounce better.

As the fire from the burning house seared in the background to the scene of vengeful execution, Churchill cast his attentive regard onto Hardy for but a moment.

This exchange said a thousand words, however not one was said at the time.

Jack refaced the simmering fire, the glow warmly illuminating his bloodied features in the dimming of the afternoon dusk.

He had courageously embarked upon this voyage in attempt to protect the DuPont family, or at least to save Ève. When finding them captive by the Germans the way that they were, they were unfortunately destined to disaster, traversing towards tragedy regardless of his intrusion.

In a way, even in death, he had still liberated them from an ill fate, to which they were hell bound.

They may have died, but he had still saved them.

VII
Nice Day for a War

'On that same exhilarating day of bloody conflict, painful loss, and suffering, Mad Jack's Merry Men of the Second Manchester Regiment boarded some of the evacuation vessels headed across the English Channel. They were finally leaving Dunkirk. Rex King-Clark rehashed the details to me later in London—not to spoil the plot for you, dear readers—and how he and a select few from the Second Chesters decided to stay in Dunkirk until the very last minute on June 3, in the hope that Jack would make it out in time ...

'Rex, himself, was a keen diarist and memoirist, which served as great source of detail for me and my articles published later in the Battlefront Gazette regarding the topic. Albeit, their accounts from the shores of Dunkirk were nowhere as frenetic as mine or Jack's days for the duration of the retreat. Nevertheless, they were still just as edge-of-your-seat with thrilling and full-to-the-brim tales of valour and heroism, shock and awe. Events and heroes that rightfully shan't be forgotten through history.'

Over 260,000 soldiers had been evacuated from Dunkirk by midday of the 2nd of June as part of Operation Dynamo.

Panic and alarm were a constantly underlining fife, building to a crescendo. The incoming invasion of Nazi Germany could be heard amongst the distant echoic explosions and the aloof rattling of machine guns upon the glooming east horizon.

Closing at any minute, the German tanks would breach the outskirts of the coastal city and it would be all over for those still in Dunkirk, desperately attempting to board a withdrawal boat. And all of that was not to mention the overhead aerial battles high—and low—in the skies. The airspace was a constant contest between fighters of the British RAF and the German Luftwaffe.

Utilizing the combined extraction points of the beaches along the east coast of the city, Dunkirk Harbour was piled up and lined with overheated and busted vehicles due to panicked short-stop arrivals. The British Royal Navy with the assistance of her allies—the Dutch, Belgian, and French Navies—were tirelessly and continuously routing further evacuation vessels for the remaining estimated 100,000 men, trying to get them off the shores in time. Tired, exhausted, battle-fatigued, and drained men of (mostly) British and French armies retreated through the vacated coastal city, stocking the piles of queues and evacuation lines that reservoir the sands of the shores at either end of the shoreline of Dunkirk.

In their numerous overcrowded queues along the shores desperately awaiting the naval ferries, the many tin hat-covered heads bowed over their shoulders, expecting at any minute there to be an armada of German Panzers and Wehrmacht infantry at their rear.

Beneath a sea of brodie helmets on the sand, their sunken eyes would rise to the dreary skies above whenever the harpy's screech of an incoming aircraft would resonate. They would dodge the frequent low-flying German fighters that swooped, targeting the lines of barely armed soldiers and dropping their payloads on the navy boats. The Halt Order was longtime over. Now, the Germans were killing everything and anything as the Allies attempted to get everyone back across the channel in an inequitable time frame.

With the revealed powerlessness and inability of the Royal Navy to perform such a grand evacuation on her own, dozens of civilian ships were now responding to the call for help or being requisitioned for his majesty's navy. The little ships boldly assisted in the withdrawal of the men in Dunkirk as the tidal waves of Nazi Germany occupation came crashing at the heels of those receding the coasts. These civilian captains and skippers were risking their lives for their people. In a time of need, such was the courage and spirit of those standing brave beneath the *Union Jack*.

The escapes were daring and dangerous, and not entirely without fatal consequence, even to the smaller civilian crafts, due to the lurking German submarines and regular Stuka bomber runs. The defenceless vessels were targeted as hostile crafts just the same as the navy ships.

This being said, escaping the shores of Dunkirk was only the beginning ...

The navy constructed three main routes across the English Channel allocated to the vessels: routes *X*, *Y*, and *Z*.

The shortest was route Z with a distance of forty nautical miles, the disadvantage being that the route involved clasping the French coast upon exit. Ships using Z were subject to salvos from German batteries recently situated along the western shoreline, predominantly in daylight hours.

Route X was the next shortest. Though this was deemed the safest route with regard to potential bombardment from the coastal batteries, X travelled through a heavily mined portion of the channel. Ships that took this route travelled over fifty nautical miles north away from Dunkirk and proceeded through the *Ruytingen Pass* towards the *North Goodwin Lightship.* From there, the route veered towards the *Goodwin Sands,* then eventually reached *Dover.* Route X may have been the safest from surface attacks, but the minefields and sand banks meant it could not be used at night—and that route was subject to sneaky U-Boats or other submarines from the Kriegsmarine *(German Navy)* attacking them from the depths like sharks.

The longest of the three routes was Y with a distance of ninety nautical miles of passage. Evacuation ships that utilized this route had an increased sailing time of almost five hours, and double the time required for route Z. Y followed the French coast as far as the *Bray-Dunes* and then turned northeast until reaching the *Kwinte Buoy.* At the buoy and after making an almost 270-degree sharp turn to avoid an expected minefield, the evacuation ships sailed west to the North Goodwin Lightship where they would join passage with route X, heading south around the Goodwin Sands and disembarking at Dover. As their fatalities showed, ships on route Y were the most likely to be attacked by German attack vessels, warships, and U-Boat submarines.

Basically, any route was a run of the gauntlet.

Notwithstanding, the dangers of these routes were all subject to *if* the boats even made it out of Dunkirk Harbour, considering the German artillery was reaching the shores from the east and west by the afternoon of the 2nd of June, and the Luftwaffe were heavily attacking from the skies like birds of prey.

Like a coffee plunger, countless panzer divisions pushed in from the south, squeezing all those who remained in France into the overflowing city of Dunkirk.

The pressure was on, and time was running out.

The body of France—and Europe, for that matter—was officially in
the firm chokehold of Nazi Germany ...

... and Dunkirk was at the head of the body, running out of air.

1940, June 3
Dunkirk
Nord Pas-de-Calais, France

Captain Rex King-Clark and his pile of lining men were exposed on the
harbour queue during the foggy morning at 0900-hours. The forecast was
cloudy with a high probability of drizzle and artillery salvo, but at least the
low visibility might keep the Luftwaffe at bay.

Down by the saltwater spray of thrashing waves by the wooden pier
pylons, the Second Manchester Regiment soldiers prepared to load into
one of the smaller taxiing vessels, a fishing boat, capable of holding sixty
men at a time. However, with time running out, her limits were pushed
to twice that as she disembarked. She was keen to head back out to sea,
where in the basin a navy ship known as the *SS Mona's Isle,* awaited
departure via route Z back to England—a voyage she had made multiple
times over the past seventy-two hours.

The Mona's Isle was the Second Chesters' ticket out of this hell, and
their number was finally up after days of standing in line.

"*Rex!*" the tall Major Dickey Allen called through the chaos as
groups of soldiers pushed into him inadvertently before the bottleneck of
the pier entrance where wet sand met wood. All hierarchy of order aside,
he showed leniency towards the rattled men in these extenuating
circumstances. Everyone was scared and panicked, even officers, and
therefore the regimental CO appreciated their apprehension.

Looking back over the crowd, Allen shouted above the shuffle, the
hum of the boat engine, and the currents that tossed against the pier legs
below rather noisily. He could see King-Clark off the queue, and the two
made eye contact throughout the chaos, thus Allen continued, "We can't
stay here any longer! I'm commanding the unit onto this next barge! I
implore you to do the same *now,* however, I *order* you to do so by
midday! The Mona's Isle will only be making one more trip, you hear?!"

Coasting around in the outskirts of the crowds right now, King-Clark
reminisced about the time he had foolishly purchased general admission
standing tickets and attended an *Artie Shaw* live concert in an overpacked
venue in 1934, right after he joined the *Roger Wolfe Kahn Orchestra.*
One could not even raise their arms up from the pit, the bodies were

huddled so close. In the present crowd, King-Clark was surrounded by a number of the loyalists of Churchill's section, such as Lieutenant Padre Nicholl, Corporal Knocker White, and Privates Wand and Macken. Even Lieutenant Gin Parker, a known adversary of Jack Churchill's leadership elegance, had decided to stay and wait for their captain until the last minute before boarding the last transport ship. Even his haters felt the absence of the fellowship ringleader.

Major Allen concluded with a degree of candour. "I acknowledge your passion to want to wait for Jack ... but we cannot further risk the safety of our men!"

These men were all more than keen to vacate, as was every mother's son in France who called themselves an ally, but the D section family owed a debt of allegiance to Jack Churchill, and they were not cashing it in until the last second. Their fearless leader was worth the risk. Through Churchill's leadership values, they sought endless bravery—at least enough to cling onto the bulwarks whilst the earth beneath them trembled underfoot from a hundred incoming Panzer tanks and a hundred thousand fascist Nazis.

"Understood, Major!" King-Clark responded above the crowds and the action of war surrounding Dunkirk in these final hours. "We're going to wait as long as we can!"

"Captain!" Allen called again, wanting further verification as the crowd he was within started marching in the direction of the pier. As one, they waddled as a slow-moving stampede towards the docking vessel. "The next circuit! Make sure you're on it!"

King-Clark and the loyalists of Churchill's D section surrounding him complied in accord.

"Because after that, and ..." Allen's focus seemed to soften as he scanned the backdrop of Dunkirk in flames and barrage; the coastal city streets imminently about to flood with marching boots and carried swastikas. "... I'm afraid Mad Jack's on his own! God be with him!"

Whilst becoming irrepressibly nudged by a new barrage of men as they attempted to calmly but quickly file into an anchor in the bottleneck kerfuffle, King-Clark shouted aloud the retort to their CO with words spoken as if born from Mad Jack's own mouth. "*Fine-o-fine!*"

This devoted group let the masses pass.

King-Clark faced the crowd of incoming soldiers as they poured towards the piers. It was unlike anything he had ever seen before; a sea of uniform khaki service dresses, brown leather straps and webbing, all with eyelines below brimmed helmets. They shuttled the No. 20 Bergen military sacks high up on their backs, marching in file, pushing into one another—some even jettisoned their gear and weapons, dumping endless supplies in the sand and for the hungry ocean waves to collect as the tide drew inwards and then out. They were just *that* desperate to vacate.

Protruding amongst the ocean of brodie helmets were brown Lee-Enfield bolt-action rifles over the shoulder. But all-in-all, the most identical feature of the mass of British soldiers was the faces ...

Physically, they were pale, malnourished, dirty, and bloodied.

Mentally, these faces spoke of the toll on their minds, sunken eyes propped wide open by exhaustion, anxiety, dread, and defeat.

King-Clark's dirty watch face read *9:10 a.m.*

If the Mona's Isle was departing in approximately thirty to forty minutes along route Z, including roughly thirty minutes to disembark her troops, maybe refuelling, and then a trip back across the English Channel, this would see her here by approximately *3:00 p.m.* this afternoon ...

Additional to that would be a period of roughly thirty minutes to an hour to load up with what would be her final human cargo from France to England—invading forces permitting, as they could very well be entering Dunkirk by that point. This gave Jack Churchill an extended deadline of approximately *4:00 p.m.* at the latest.

"Sixteen-hundred hours ... that's his deadline," King-Clark's gaze raised above the others in their motley merriment of men, turning and scanning the slightly elevated hills on the outskirts of the city to the east, and causing them all to cast longing and hopeful sets of eyes to the southeast yond Dunkirk ...

... right as France started to fall into the shadow of Germany, like a storm over the horizon.

"Do we even have that long?" Nicholl questioned amidst the brave.

Nobody answered.

But they all hoped so.

Due to Dunkirk's shallow nature, the large boats waited in the deeper basin rather than attempt to berth in the harbour, which would have resulted in the evacuation becoming clogged and therefore halted. The use of the smaller boats known later as *the Little Ships of Dunkirk,* trawlers and small drifters, meagre yachts and tugboats, enabled most of the ferrying to the larger naval ships. In the eleventh hour, some even travelled the entire way from coast to coast just to help rescue soldiers desperate to still make it home but unable to ... *so home came for them.*

Charitably speaking, theirs was an extenuating circumstance to stay. While Major Allen and the bulk of the entire Second Manchester Regiment fell into line on the quaky pier towards their boat as it moored, they left King-Clark and a handful of members from Churchill's section in lieu of the scheduled evacuation of their unit. They each embraced the risk and were aware of the high stakes regarding their choice to delay evacuating.

After making the decision to boldly delay their evacuation, King-Clark looked around at the state of the coastline of Dunkirk. Long and straggling queues of varying BEF forces still lingered, from the *Mole* (a breakwater wall currently being used as a makeshift dock) to the beaches, where men now waded out into the shallows to reach the smallest of vessels, rifles held high above their heads by aching muscles. These lengthy crowds still grew to this day, as sections of men lucky enough to return from General Gort's containment lines fell back to join the ranks of evacuees.

The fact that the men accompanying King-Clark could absorb this mayhem, and still choose to wait until the last possible minute for Mad Jack's mad return, spoke volumes about the man; about the loyalty and bravery that he inspired.

Their moment of consideration was broken by a dogfight between dozens of squadrons of German and British fighter planes high up above them. The dreary and cloudy sky momentarily lit up due to an ongoing battle for the airspace, one that Britain was swiftly losing. German fighter planes and dive bombers swarmed like flies above the corpse of a dying Dunkirk, as the diarist King-Clark may later put it.

Dickey Allen and the remaining section of Second Manchester Regiment soldiers—over one-hundred men—quickly hurried aboard beneath the cacophony that ensued in the noisy skies. His section was now mixed with the auxiliary members of Churchill's, King-Clark's, and his own, who were also attempting to board the ships at the same time.

Once aboard the ship, Allen and the majority fruitlessly observed the magnificent display of fireballs and speeding fighter planes as they chased each other down spraying laser lights of pyrotechnic tracer rounds, performing stomach-turning and death-defying aerobatics which caused them all to let out a sigh of awe.

The men ducked and released a joint gasp in astonishment as one of the small German Messerschmitt fighters bit the dust, tail-spinning in a ball of fire and black smoke and came plummeting down into the sea not one hundred feet from their tiny *putt-putt* boat. It was followed by a RAF Spitfire as it, too, was engaged and clipped by another enemy fighter, and came crashing down into the ocean near a banked larger ship of the *Isle of Man Steam Packet Company: the Mona's Isle.*

The Mona's Isle was one of ten vessels in the fleet that were requisitioned by the Admiralty of the British Navy. Eight of the company's ships were partaking in the Dunkirk evacuation. In fact, the Mona's Isle was the first to leave Dover back in May when the evacuation started, and the first vessel to complete a successful round trip of route Z. Throughout Operation Dynamo, the ship had so far been responsible for rescuing a total of 6,000 from Dunkirk on her own—and she was not done yet.

However, it had been at a great cost.

Three of her sisters had perished thus far from the Isle of Man Steam Packet Company family on what would come to be known as their blackest day: 29 May 1940. The *Mona's Queen* had been mined off the coast of Dunkirk along route X, the *Fenella* had been sunk by an air attack whilst attempting to moor on the East Pier of Dunkirk Harbour, and the *King Orry* had been shelled from the coast whilst also attempting route X.

Packed into the ship like sardines, Major Allen stood tall amongst the crowd of British soldiers as it began to draw distance from the Dunkirk Harbour piers. She was a few minutes off reaching the Mona's Isle, where they would then make a dash across the channel.

Where most of the soldiers had their attention in the sky at the display of dogfighting and explosions or at the city of Dunkirk as she received a bombardment shell from the outskirts to the east and west coasts, resulting in buildings collapsing in eruptions of dust or to seep into the sky in thick, black pockets, Dickey Allen's eyes stretched beyond even that ...

With sincerity, under his breath he voiced parting words to those of which he held the upmost respect and admiration. This included the absent Jack Churchill, who he had known the longest.

"Good luck, chaps. Godspeed."

'Jack and I got a few hours rest. Well, rest would imply that it was optional. I know that my body and mind simply gave up, coming down from the adrenaline spike and general fatigue and malaise of battle. My eyes couldn't stay open. I told myself it was only for a moment's respite from the engulfing clouds of smoke and dust that blanketed a sizeable radius of the area.

When I woke in the early hours of the morning, I wasn't surprised to discover that Jack was already up, brooding over the smouldering wreckage of the DuPont family home. I wondered if he had actually slept at all after what had happened, such tragedy. I guess that I had felt a similar degree of grief in respects to the passing of my colleague, Omar. Time and time again we knew that a bullet with one of our names would one day eventually catch us. Existing this close to the frontline of war, death was an occupational hazard.'

1940, June 3
DuPont Dairy Farm
Nord Pas-de-Calais, France

Churchill spoke in a low voice to Hardy as the baggy-eyed American civilian approached him from the rear, coming towards the resonating warmth of the charcoal ruins. He was now dressed back in the comfort of his frayed suit trousers and brown leather jacket. He pushed the folds out of his fedora and asserted it atop of his brown hair.

"Nice day for a war ..."

His melancholy tone slit through the silence of the brisk morning air.

Resting his sword upon his shoulder like an umbrella in drizzle, Churchill stood over the ruins like a memorial statue, revering the simmering remnants of the DuPont home.

Partially incinerated furniture, scattered debris, and singed thatching were strewn about the aftermath, littering the sludge. His pensive stare searched for nothing particular amongst the scorched wooden concaved framework and fractured support beams. Rather, he sympathetically observed the overall demise in reflection ...

... but now, even that had come to an end.

It was time to move forwards, and it was apparent in his tone.

Hardy said not a word as he appeared just shy of Churchill's periphery. The man wondered how it was he even knew he was standing there, shrugging it off to some kind of uncanny cognizance Mad Jack possessed considering all that he had just witnessed Mad Jack accomplish recently. Nothing now surprised him about Churchill.

He was both the wildcard in the draw and a loose cannon on the deck, and Hardy both feared and respected him more than ever after witnessing first-hand his undeniable heroism and intrepidness.

After the shortest of intermissions where the two exhausted men watched over the cinder-radiant ruins, tallying embers that glowed, Churchill finally turned to Hardy. He grabbed his attention like a gasp of air to his lungs.

Blue eyes healing from bloodshot, the gent was buttoned up in his tidied khaki service dress, though still absurdly dirtied from dried mud crust and soot.

"What do you mean by that?" Hardy finally questioned regarding Churchill's rather outlandish statement that it was a *nice day for a war.* Was it a wordplay on the age-old saying *nice day for a walk?* Because contrarily, it was overcast, teetering on rainfall, and it was rather chilly out. Also, given their predicament, it wasn't really a nice day for anything—let alone a war.

"What I mean is, we've got to get back to the coast. Dunkirk is our last chance at survival. It is a *retreat* to *victory.*"

"*Dunkirk?*" Hardy scoffed. "The coast? That's insane! I mean, *from here?* That'd be, eh ..."

"War?"

"I was gonna say *suicide!*" Hardy exclaimed. "Two men against an army isn't *war,* Captain. That's *madness.*"

"Dunkirk is the evacuation rendezvous for Operation Dynamo. Our orders haven't changed. We retreat, just like everybody else. There's been pockets of soldiers holding that corridor open so that everybody could get out ..."

"Yeah, there *was!* ... yesterday," Hardy pessimistically added.

"Granted, it is true that by now, those pockets have folded. Nonetheless, we've still got to try and get there ..."

Hardy threw a carpet-sized saddle on the elephant in what-remained-of-the-room. "Shouldn't we ... you know ... pay our respects to the DuPonts?"

Jack declared with finality. "We will, by winning the war."

"Can't we at least give them a decent Christian burial?"

Churchill seemed quick to move on, as if he had done his mourning whilst the American was still zonked out. "Look around, Felix. There's nothing to bury. This was a cremation."

"Should we say some words, then? Something? Anything?" Hardy said with a hefty tone of guilt about surviving the ordeal when their family suffered so much.

"You want some words ...? All right!" Jack sniffled, his tired eyes glossed over with a combination of strain and loss. "Memento Mori ..." he finally muttered.

"That's *Latin. 'Remember you must die'* ..." the journalist surmised from his college days, also scoffing at the soldier's apparent cold-heartedness. Whether or not it was a façade, he was unsure, but it sure as hell wasn't for him—and he barely knew them.

"Correct!" Churchill bit Hardy. "All of us have our time. Put simply: *this* was *theirs*. I watc—" Jack's voice broke for a moment, and he cleared it. Hardy saw it, allowed for his emotion to fester without scrutiny, as its surfacing was deserving. "I watched Ève die ... And she knew it, in that moment of transcendent acceptance, she realized everything that you seem to be ignoring. *Memento Mori.*"

Hardy fell silent. He simply let the captain continue; to say his piece and grieve—somewhat—appropriately.

"Every glass of vino I savour. Every song I play on the pipes. Every passionately reciprocated kiss from a lass. Every fight ... That is me remembering that I have to die and remember to live while I can. And I intend to fight *and* live. But I can't do all that moping about a bloody farm, now, can I?" Churchill elaborated, fresh in contemplation of the plans for their new day rather than dwelling on the loss that had transpired before him.

Enough time had been dedicated to that now.

Hardy remained silent. He learned something about Mad Jack in that moment. Something very few people probably identified in the man. *That he felt every death.* His eccentricities and enthusiasm for the fight were a way of coping with them, not a passive, dispassionate attitude towards loss. Felix smiled, sincerely, as he'd gotten confirmation that the man who he was seemingly inevitably linked with was human with a soul, and not a genuine madman like the last few days' events might have suggested.

Moving on, Churchill took a few steps away and to where he had gathered his gear, such as his backpack, bagpipes, longbow and quiver of war arrows, as well as a bunch of confiscated gear he managed to obtain from the deceased enemy about the area. The freshly requisitioned German BMW-R71 motorbike with attached sidecar was also accounted for. Churchill had prepped the vehicle for travel; checked the fuel, the water, and the oil. Even given her a spit polish. It was their ticket out of this closing fold.

"*Retreat to victory*, huh?" Hardy muttered, refreshing his mind and considering the hardships of what they had to accomplish today. "What about all the Germans between us and there? They're leagues ahead of us by now—are we just going to *overtake them* on the roads and hope they don't kill us?"

Churchill tossed him one of two upturned grey German stahlhelm helmets. Balled up inside was a polyspot plane tree camouflage smock to throw overtop of their shoulders.

"Not this dress-up shit again."

"Dress that on over your gear and plonk that on your melon, lad. We'll blend right in for the most part. We'll cruise right past them, passing them from the rear. Most krauts won't even raise an eyebrow."

"And if they realize something's amiss?"

"We'll be off like a bullet from the barrel of a gun. They'll not be able to catch us, Hardy," he added with his winning smile, "Not the way I ride."

"Jack Churchill: *the man with a plan.*"

"Now you're getting it."

"And if we get stopped this time? We're deep behind enemy lines— deeper than ever before ..."

Churchill could not agree more and murmured in accord. "That we are. Balls deep."

"Surely, you can't expect us to be able to just *cruise* straight past all of the German armaments and blockades?"

"*Balls deep* and *balls to the wall*, all the same, lad!"

"*Stop saying that! What does that even mean?*" Hardy cussed with a tense frown, unable to translate this mad Brit's outlandish terminology regarding balls.

"Look, Hardy, I know ... but what choice do we have?" Churchill explained as he scooped up his own gear and prepared, layering straps over his shoulders, followed by the German camouflage smock that covered the arrow feathers in his quiver like a hunchback. "Worst comes to worst and the jig is up ... we're going to have to *blast* through them. In this race there is no prize for second best."

Hardy remained, yet to start dressing up and with an obstinate expression and sceptical brow line. "Oh, we'll *blast through 'em?* Captain, there are likely a *hundred thousand* armed and angry Nazi assholes between us and those ships in Dunkirk! We will *not* make it, Captain. Plain and simple."

Churchill squinted as he got ready, contemplating and calculating the odds and numbers. "About *twenty* to *thirty* infantry battalions—that's about *five hundred* men to a unit, plus their scout parties, respectively ... About *fifteen* to *twenty* armoured divisions riding in amongst ... Maybe *thirty* or *so* mortar strike units, armed infrastructure and logistic units with them, moving up and digging in, establishing headquarters, clearing roads and setting up checkpoints, communication relay sockets, radio wire relay teams, newly established command rendezvous points, troop barracks, fuel depots, plus at least two extra waves of reinforcements coming up from Berlin just for good measure. I'd say it's closer to about *one* million, maybe a *one-point-two-five-million armed* and *angry Nazi arseholes* between us and those ships in Dunkirk!"

Disbelief sucked the air from Hardy's lungs.

"That's not including the countless squadrons of airships in the sky: recon, attack, bombers, and their flankers ... Then there's those on the coastlines running parallel: innumerable amounts of submarines, warships, speedboats, gunships, minelayers ... All of that closing in on the beaches as we get there, as well. We're technically behind it all."

"My point exactly!" Hardy finally intervened, chucking the collected German gear back at Churchill. "There are too many Nazi assholes about the place. We need to forfeit, not fight."

"*Too many Nazi arseholes* is exactly why this plan will work," Churchill implored, shoving the helmet and balled paraphernalia back to his tagalong cohort. "Think about it!"

Still unsure, Hardy accepted the stahlhelm.

"These phallus-shaped helmeted bellends are scattered everywhere; hyped up, pumped up, overexcited ... they're winning the war. Everywhere except for the frontline of their push, their guards are *down*. Safeties *on*. The roads are a flurry of activity behind the frontier, which is where their sights are set—not behind them. They won't see us coming."

There was quietness from Hardy. He was still not entirely sold. Churchill caught his blank stare as his eyebrows raised in disbelief. He could sense the impetus within Hardy hit a wall, hitherto whatever amount there was. The journalist shook his head, staring off into the distance. It was all too much. In his eyes, *what even was the point in trying?*

"You can stay if you want, Felix ..." Churchill said after an extended lull. He finished gearing up and aligned his longbow across the handlebars of the motorbike, attaching it with what appeared to be spare shoelaces in a simple yet readily accessible bowknot. "But I don't believe there is a reason this beautiful BMW was sent to us with this God-awful side basket if you weren't meant to come with me."

Hands on his hips, Hardy eyed him and chortled.

Jack Churchill was now sitting on the bike, facing him. He was ready to go, to take on the unbelievable odds of their escape. He holstered his maroon cap beneath the German smock for now, instead sporting one of the helmets to fulfil the ruse of them riding beneath the enemy's noses.

He did the strap up tight under his chin.

"How do I look?"

"Like a stupid kraut," Hardy huffed as he examined the maw of the messenger's side pod attached to the BMW.

Churchill nodded, prepared. With a profound certainty he added, "Right, then. I ride unto Dunkirk, my friend. I will make it there alive ... or I'll die trying."

"Well. Yeah, that second one's a sure thing."

Churchill then went on and added to his case, adjusting the chin strap so it was comfy. There had been one other way he could have gotten this American journalist onboard with him, and he decided to play that drawcard regardless.

"Oi, Hardy ... ever wondered what a story like this would sell for when I get back home?"

For an elongated period, Hardy stared him down before biting.

"... you're going to sell this as a story?"

"Of course," Churchill remarked, playing along with the ploy. "Some reputable newspaper out there would kill for this content."

Hardy's stubborn and immovable stare loosened into a smirk.

He had caught Jack Churchill's subterfuge.

"You better give exclusive rights to *the Battlefront Gazette* ..."

"The what?"

"My paper!"

Jack angled his head. "Lad, I said *reputable*."

Hardy said a laugh. "Ha. Ha."

"*The Battlefront Gazette, though?* Really? I heard the writer was pronounced MIA?!"

Still with a smirk to this obvious duplicity, Hardy shook his head, gesturing an agreeance to go with him by tossing the smock over his shoulders and poking his head through the stitched slot that was now a slightly torn and frayed hole like a cowboy poncho. Even though his cooperation was noted, Churchill still jabbed as he watched him climb into the sidecar of the bike, putting on the stahlhelm so that they both looked the part of German soldiers out and about in a messenger's bike.

Hardy cradled a brown 98k rifle Churchill had scavenged earlier and left in the pod compartment, playing along with the witticism. "*Oh, yeah? Really? Tell me more, sir!*"

"Yeah," Churchill continued, tongue-in-cheek. "He decided to stay behind in France while everybody was bugging out, so he got himself nabbed by the Huns!"

"*Oh, yeah?! Tell me some more!*"

Churchill kicked the throttle. The BMW jolted to life with a deafeningly loud start-up, healthy and vociferous. It was a direct reflection of their spirits at this moment as they literally took on Nazi Germany, about to scale a wall of stacked odds against them.

"Yeah! He now speaks *German* and works for *the Knackwurst Gazettisch* newspaper."

As Hardy threw back amusement, Churchill stomped the throttle and they sped off the mark with power and torque, kicking up dirt and grime in their wake as they peeled off the remnants of the DuPont Dairy Farm and onto the main road, headed north ...

Next stop: *Dunkirk.*

'Riding on the motorbike, the streaks of sweat and blood were dried on our faces by the rushing air. As beautiful in its simplicity as Jack's plan was to get us to Dunkirk, it wasn't without Nazi Germany entanglements. Within minutes of leaving the DuPont farmstead that morning, we came up behind our first German convoy. They were also heading westerly. My heart rate still elevates even now when I think about that moment the blurred dot grew closer. It was a column of four open air transporter vehicles carrying around twenty armed soldiers each. The trucks were obviously travelling a lot slower than we were on the

BMW and, unfortunately for us, they took up the entire road with their convoy body. 'Be calm', shouted Mad Jack as he kept his distance behind them for a bit before insanely accelerating to catch them, even though there wasn't enough room to safely overtake. I screamed at him over the engine and the rushing air, a surge of panic in my voice, questioning what he was doing. He replied with 'rite of passage, old boy,' and 'Relax, and act German'. 'Act German? How does one act German?' I replied, but apparently Jack couldn't hear my question over the noise of his insane plan as it came to fruition.

Shrinking as low as I could into that tiny little sidecar pod, I watched helplessly as Jack sped up quick behind the trucks, gaining the attention of those heavily armed soldiers in the rear tray of the last truck in the file. At least a dozen sets of seemingly unbothered eyes were upon us. I could count the buttons on their uniforms, we were so close. And so, what does Jack Churchill do ...? He beeps the goddamn horn! The madman starts swaying across the road, gaining even more attention. Luckily for us, the German disguises and helmets camouflaged us amongst their ranks brilliantly, and we appeared as nothing more than impatient messengers, desperate to gain ahead. Once we reached the point where they were either going to wave us off or call our bluff and shoot us, just as Jack had planned all along, message got to the drivers ... One after the other, the German vehicles actually slowed and pulled to the side, allowing us to pass. 'Don't forget to wave 'thanks'', Jack shouted as we sped up and slogged it past the trucks. I did so at his insist, keeping up the masquerade with a friendly and appreciative wave and, hysterically so, the Germans in the cabins returned the kind gesture.

This conceited and condescending plan of Jack's worked four more times. Some of the vehicles we even rode up on anticipated our want to overtake, and even pre-emptively inched over before we were close—so courteous these German soldiers were while they invaded this European country. An armoured half-track vehicle with a big gun onboard even peeled off the road for us ... nevertheless, it wasn't until about an hour into our exciting tongue-in-cheek gambit that we encountered our first real delay: an organized and fortified checkpoint.

Certain that nobody could see us and therefore become suspicious, Jack slowed and banked prior to the blockade, and we travelled off-road for aways, searching for an alternate route in the middle of this treacherous swastika minefield ...'

The walls were closing in on the BEF. Time was running out.

There was something in the air. France felt different. Darker.

King-Clark nervously checked his watch again, for about the twentieth time this day. It read *02:00 p.m.*

The Second Chesters surrounding him did not speak aloud about it, but they were starting to weaken in their dedication regarding the postponement of their departure to wait for Jack Churchill.

The withdrawal crowds piling through Dunkirk were thinning out. Most of the numbers coming through towards the pier now were of the French 1st Army and the Belgian Armies, respectively, who were next in line for evacuation after the leagues of the BEF. They were coming down from the eastern side and the direction of *Armentières*, which meant that they had been overrun in their placements beyond that sector and even after displacements, they had been given an all-out retreat order.

The lines were faltering on every front.

The Germans were almost here.

"Captain King-Clark, sir?" Gin Parker questioned sheepishly as reverberations of explosions detonated in the near distance, just over the hills from the east and southeast. It could have been in their heads with the paranoia, but they seemed to be growing closer with each detonation, therefore louder, too. "It's probably getting time to ... y'know."

King-Clark judged him, suspecting out of the men loyal enough to Churchill to stay and wait that it would have been Parker to forfeit first— and it was. And ... perhaps he wasn't in the wrong.

"Feel free to grab your gear and board a boat, Leftenant. Nobody is stopping you," King-Clark responded modestly, personally uninterested in abandonment. Even if the majority of these surrounding soldiers seemed not to contest Parker's notion, he would be steadfast in his resolve. He bowed his head inland, in the direction of the sound of impending doom as the distant artillery grew like a slow crescendo. "Same goes for all of you, gents. I am going to hold out and wait for the Mona's

Isle to return. She'll be one of the last boats and by then, we'll have no other choice but to board. *Until* then, however—"

"But, sir," Parker added, strangely, stepping towards him—his eyes, out to sea. "She *has* returned."

King-Clark blinked and frowned. "What," he murmured, off-balance. He took a step as his gaze scanned the coast. "It can't be!"

He spun back around, checking his wristwatch once again.

He was under the impression Jack still had a few hours to make the deadline ...

Without a word, Parker allowed him to witness it for himself. The ship pulled across the basin, and formations of smaller boats were already en route from her to load up troops for what had been deemed her final evacuation circuit.

"We shouldn't wait any longer for Captain Churchill ... I'm sorry, sir," Parker added, collecting his gear from the cobblestones and leading the rally towards the piers where he was reluctantly joined by Padre Nicholl, Knocker White, and Macken and Wand. The two exchanged a nod to one another, deciding as well to join the evacuation ... for it was now or never.

They turned to follow the others, however their eyelines upon disembarkation met Padre Nicholl and Knocker White, who had had second thoughts and decided otherwise ...

The two stubbornly dropped their bags, choosing to wait.

"No rush, I guess," Nicholl justified, pulling up a section of wall to lean against beside King-Clark.

The men kept their cool as the walls continued to close around them, and the booming of artillery echoes grew closer. They copped many strange looks from sorry-looking passersby as they marched onwards and towards the docks, desperate to get the hell out, seeing as this could be one of the last boats.

Nicholl inclined some justification. "The ferries have still got to make several trips back and forth to load up the Mona's Isle. We'll give him extra time whilst they load up, eh?"

"Sure," King-Clark agreed with that sentiment, glad for the company.

It was just the excuse they needed.

Unenthusiastically, Gin Parker shook his head with doubt, and returned to the men waiting so devotedly for their captain—against all odds.

"Cheer up, Gin. Mad Jack would do the same for us, and you know it ..." Knocker White added, sidling up beside the padre and King-Clark, depositing his gear once again to the dusty street.

"WWJD? Right?" King-Clark asked Nicholl, though, it was not what would *Jesus* do, it was what would *Jack* do? It was an older joke they used to use to burden the lieutenant in Churchill's absence over Christmas when he was in command of D section.

Taking the beating, Parker retorted. "Yeah, for *you*, maybe."

"Thanks," King-Clark acknowledged as the group returned in wait. His thankful smile faded with a truth of certainty. "But, we all know Jack wouldn't wait until the last second if he knew one of us were out there somewhere ..."

The men all leaned in.

What could he possibly mean by that?

But of course, Jack Churchill would wait for them ...

"Sir?" one of the men questioned with a trivial frown.

King-Clark finally concluded after searching for the right words on which to deliver his conclusion, and his opinion about Churchill was fact.

"Jack wouldn't *leave* at all."

1940, June 3
Campagne-lès-Guines
Nord Pas-de-Calais, France

'Mad Jack and I ended up taking a route west of Saint-Omer. T'were a means along back roads and dirt strips, surrounded by heavy forestation that Jack geographically labelled des Caps et Marais d'Opale. We encountered a lot less German convoys and barely any checkpoints this far west. Needing to constantly find alternate routes around occupied towns and crossroads, Jack nervously checked his wristwatch upon every transit delay. I sensed that we were running out of time ...

It was about then the other bikes caught sight of us ...'

The thunderous throttle of the BMW carved throughout the silent and echoic forest that lined the mostly straight road passage.

Barbs of daylight shot through the breaks in the foliage above as their bike sped along the concealed route beneath heavy plantation canopy.

During the journey, Hardy thought it a little strange to see Churchill's distrustful behaviour whilst he drove their motorbike. He recognized that their journey was no longer as uncomplicated, and therefore Hardy followed Jack's over-shoulder gazes. It was as if he searched for something, even allowing their bike to quieten in speed ...

He dethrottled the engine output and they coasted for a stretch through the scenery. The alleviation of the noise was due to the application of concentration by the complicated British captain. It was like the strange sixth sense this grade of soldier possessed was tingling, alerting him that something was amiss.

"What is it ...?" Hardy questioned, no longer needing to shout as loud over the engine's roar now that they idled in drift.

Churchill propped himself upwards, scanning the road ahead, as well as listening attentively to the road behind them, as if he could see something ... hear something ... *sense something ...*

Then ... *they appeared.*

Two bikes.

Intrusive enemy scouts.

Far behind in their rearview, the two single riders zoomed around a bend, seemingly in pursuit of their BMW.

Their engines were loud, resonating through the peaceful French woodland, and increasing in volume as they decreased in distance. The blaring engines bounced from the thousands of tree trunks throughout the forestation south of the French town of *Guînes,* located about four total miles off the coast of France west of Dunkerque; their route via. It was a work-around, but it had gotten them this close.

"Oh, bollocks," Churchill cussed, eyeing them first in the poncey circular side-mirror extremity attached to his handlebar. He parked his rear back down and revved the throttle, causing them to abruptly zip ahead, which made Hardy unexpectedly collapse deep into his sidecar after attempting to rubberneck at their six.

"Who are they?" he questioned loud, his fingers holding tight on the edges of his capsule pod.

"Scouts!" Churchill replied, head low, concentration sharp. So far, their German outfits had disguised them well, though it was only a matter of time before enough holes were poked in the levy to break the dam. This may have been it. "I noticed them parked in a town about a click back. They must have thought our route of passage and speed a lil' strange, and want to find out for themselves ..."

"Oh, shit!"

"Yeah," Churchill agreed. "*Oh, shit.*"

Jack leaned heavier on the throttle and accelerated faster.

However, their sidecar-mounted BMW's top speed couldn't match that of these moto-scouts.

Tensely, every few seconds, his peripherals glinted the small side-mirror. Side-by-side, the twin scouts were gaining at a ridiculously fast rate, likely due to the fact they were single riders and there were no passengers to slow them down.

"They're gaining!" Hardy informed in a shout after twisting in his pod. Down in his lap, running the length of his legs, he wound the bolt on the receiver of the concealed 98k rifle, affirming that a round was chambered. A brass bullet winked at him from the half-exposed cavity, informing him it was ready to shoot at the pull of the trigger.

"Indeed!" noticed Churchill. He decelerated due to an incoming left bend in the road. Upon the realization that there was no way they could outrun this tail, his mind's eye formulated a retaliatory plan on the fly. It would need to be offensive. "Hardy ... they're going to catch us."

Hardy panicked. "What?! Just go faster!"

"I can't! They'll be on us soon ... I'm going to let them come."

" *What?!* "

"Don't make it obvious we're aware of them! Try not to show them that you are holding a gun, it may look suspicious. Remember to act German."

"What if I do it whilst *acting German?* " Hardy's newfound wit replied, finding his sense of humour during these desperate and stressful situations: a direct reflection of Jack Churchill's undying persona.

Churchill had no time to acknowledge, he was so deep in plot.

He announced loud, taking the turn. "Hang on!"

Hardy shrunk low, clutching onto the front lip of the pod and hugging the German Karabiner rifle deep into his chest. He teeth bared as he watched the turn be taken at speed.

"Speeding is pretty suspicious, y'know ..."

His eyes grew wide.

This shit was about to get real.

They took the bend at high speed, though with controllable ease. It was a mere test for the riding ability of Jack Churchill, gaining a feel for the manoeuvrability of the clunky German BMW. He made mental note and would adjust gradations about speed, handling, and balance for the next corner. At the next bend, their extreme swiftness could be increased and perfected.

In the mirror, Churchill spotted the two scouts behind them as they also took the corner at speed. They were just about on top of them now.

The next bend came quickly.

Churchill took this next corner again at high speed. It was one of slightly softer angle and sway, though the lack of weight of the pod attached to the left side of the bike surprised him in a way that he was not prepared.

Hardy and the sidecar lifted from the ground.

With a high-pitched squeal out from the tyres as they took such an angle at such a speed, Churchill felt the weight of the sidecar lift off the ground, resulting in a shift in balance as he stared straight, concentrating on taking the turn and making small corrections.

He caught a glimpse to the left, noticing the pod lift and Hardy flinch and wiggle about with a fretful expression, holding on for dear life, which also added to the change in unsteadiness.

They managed to close the corner, coming back onto a straight, right as Churchill carefully lowered the pod back down to the road and attempted to—

Scree-scree-screech!

As the wheels of the pod planted back down upon the asphalt surface, they spasmed and squawked like a butchered bovine. Churchill wrestled with the handlebars and adjustment of throttle as he regained control.

That had not been the desired result.

They fish-tailed for an instant and lost an ample amount of speed as the suddenly applied braking emitted a vapour of white smoke in their midst.

"Fuck me!" Hardy cursed after bouncing around in the sidecar that bobbled about in the turbulence. It was like an airplane that had scuffed a touch-down on the tarmac. Adjusting his helmet, he eyed Jack, cradling the rifle. "Yeah! That wasn't suspicious at all! Get us there in one piece, Captain!"

"Sorry, ol' boy," Churchill responded, accelerating and making some more mental adjustments to the vehicular manoeuvrability of the BMW and sidecar after that instance. Luckily for them, Churchill had extensive experience driving motorcycles which included correcting balance and mistakes within a nanosecond. It was a talent that saw them still alive and speeding and not a victim of lost control, wrapped around a tree back there on that last corner.

Hardy swallowed his heart back down into his chest and carefully glanced over his shoulder, not that subtlety mattered much after that stunt.

"Oh, shit!" he shouted.

Churchill glanced in the side-mirror with a raised eyebrow of concern as the two moto-scouts finished taking the same bend. From their distance, they would have been able to see everything regarding their swerve and recovery, and they would undoubtedly know that something was amiss.

Now on another long straight, the two pursuing bikes cranked their accelerators, speeding up in a single file behind the suspicious riders upon the BMW. They were so close now that Churchill understood they would actually be gaining speed due to their wake of air water which they carved with their forward momentum.

The first scout effectively slipstreamed their passage, gradually sling-shotting around the side of them on the straight, creeping up on Churchill's side.

Churchill was more than aware of his presence, casting a quick glimpse with his pinched, air-shot eyes and fixed scowl, sure to not slow or react discordantly. He held his poker face even though the die had clearly been cast.

Enveloping both their flanks, the second scout slowly peeled out behind Hardy's sidecar, and he cast him an awkward gleam. The moto-scouts were now on either side of them, boxing them in.

Through wraparound goggles, the first scout examined everything about this strange entity driving the bike. He briefly saw beneath the flapping camouflage smock the rider was wearing; there was a dirty khaki uniform present inconsistent to the grey outfit belonging to any German regimental uniform. He noticed the bloody stains and grazed markings on the attire, and then even noticed the unorthodox branch of bowed wood strapped across the handlebars ...

It looked like a fucking longbow?

The entire attire was unbecoming of a general issue German soldier within the Nazi outfit, and it sent alarm bells ringing.

Through his goggles, the scout's eyes climbed and met the rider, right as Churchill broke words with him, beholding a winning grin beneath his neat pencil moustache.

Jack shouted welcomingly over the wind. "*Gutentag!*"

The scout was mildly dumbstruck. His stare was fixated on Churchill if not quick glimpses of the straight narrow road before them.

Strangely, even though all details within this illustration depicted Churchill and his occupant as anything but German soldiers, the scout replied without hostility. "*Hallo.*"

Churchill glanced left, noticing that the other scout was creeping up on Hardy's flank, and that the journalist's hands down in the pod were exposed to him as he felt for the trigger piece of the bolt-action.

And with that, Hardy attempted to discretely jerk the rifle out from the sidecar, trying to make it able for hostile action ...

This, all under the eyes of the scouts, the combined actions screamed suspicion.

If it wasn't already, the jig was up in *3 ... 2 ... now.*

Calmly and in lieu of his friend's fumbling, Churchill glanced back at the first scout on his right and extended conversation in his best German, of which he knew jack shit.

"Auf wiedersehen?"

Very confused, over the wind and throttle, the scout informed after glancing forwards for a second. *"Zat means goodbye?!"*

"Fucker!" Hardy shouted in panic and frustration as the Karabiner rifle became stuck in the shallow sidecar, and he was unable to retrieve it easily enough to act upon the second scout by his side ...

His neighbouring scout bellowed and performed a signal, alarmed.

Shouting in German to his partner, he braked and backed off an inch in speed. He broke sync widely from the BMW, preparing to bring about the dangling submachine gun strapped to his back with a single hand whilst keeping a hold of the handlebars with the other.

Churchill saw the second scout grow hostile and back off ...

Saw Hardy still fumbling to get the rifle out of the pod ...

And then he casually returned his view to the confused scout on his side right as the soldier suddenly reached across and grabbed their throttle in some vain attempt to halt their transition. Jack's eyes witnessed his rather rude reaction and grabbed the brim of his decorative stahlhelm which he wore upon his maroon beret, and used it as a swat to cripple his knuckles. The helmet hammer worked, causing the scout to retract and hiss in pain, and he banked in a short sweep to gain distance from these strange hostiles.

Armed still with the steel German helmet, Churchill tossed it like a flying disc at the moto-scout. It did nothing but momentarily distract him whilst he reached for what must have been a sidearm holstered at his opposite hip. The scout withdrew it with the speed of a gunslinger, and brought it aroun—

Churchill hunched forth his beret-clothed head and held a tense grimace, applying the brakes of their BMW with a fizzy screech.

The instant tap of the brakes caused the rear scout who had drifted in behind the pod of their bike to instantly react, almost losing control in order to avoid a collision in a cloud of burning rubber vapour. He fumbled his hanging MP40 in the process and backed right off, travelling farther behind them now after one heck of a brake check.

In that same second of action, the first scout had drawn his pistol and fired a shot at Churchill from point-blank range. However, due to the applied brakes, they dropped out of target range and the bullet had missed, firing wildly off into the blurring forestation on their flank. The gunshot was barely audible in the wind current.

The scout blindly fired again and again under his shoulder after realizing they had drifted back and he, too, slowed in order to fall back alongside of them.

As he did so, he exchanged aim with his handgun for better control of the handlebars so that he could align himself beside the BMW precisely, and take another sho—

CHUNK!

Right as the pistol-armed scout's speed slowed and realigned alongside the BMW, Churchill drew and extended his sheathed claybeg sword with his right hand, slinging it out under his hold of the handlebar.

The scout effectively reversed onto the chopping block.

Fingers through the brass grooves for ultimate grip upon its draw, Churchill transferred in might the weight of the four-foot-eight double-edged steel blade, carrying with the momentous strain of wind speed against his extended arm whilst they travelled at nearly one hundred kilometres per hour, into the upper chest of the rider alongside them.

The blade chopped into the scout like an axe into a log of firewood as he passed by them. Although it hacked an inch into him, the blade bounced from off him due to the ricochet of applied forces and motion.

The result was still as desired.

Churchill tilted at the handlebars, straining to hang onto the heavy sword's recoil as they rode at speed, struggling to keep them straight on the road while the winded scout ceased to exist in transit beside them.

Taking the slog like an edged baseball bat to the tee, the scout reverted in a reverse head-over-turkey fashion, flipping over the rear of the motorbike, and throwing his shin-high boots into the air—only, his boots got caught on the handlebars, causing the bike to waver and spiral, losing total control in the seconds that followed his dismissal.

The slashed and broken body of the scout impacted with the road face-first after revolving completely upon himself. With a meaty, bone-breaking, and blistering crunch, he tumbled into a broken wreck somewhere in their rearview mirror. His bike did the same, twisting at the front and causing the vehicle to up-tip and somersault with an overarching *vroom* as the throttle fell out, and it faded into the background of the gross vehicular stunt.

In the background, the out-of-control bike tumbled and bounced at high speed, plummeting askew and into the tree line neighbouring the road. With a sudden *bang!* it exploded into a hefty orange and yellow fireball, clattering hot metal debris through the calm green nature forest.

Overtaking the bike's concluding inferno was the scuffing and thrashing, lifeless and bloody-grazed body of the rider as the dethroned moto-scout finally caught up with the wreckage. The speeding corpse slid into the forestation just beyond his smoking wreckage with a meaty *thump!* swallowed whole by the greenery of snapping branches and rustling bushes.

With bared teeth and strain, Churchill twirled and angled his sword across the handlebars of their bike, able to somehow regain control after that transfer of might.

Careful, and keeping his eyes on the road as well as the remaining attacker in his rearview, he managed to sheath the sword at his hip, freeing up both hands.

He cast a look back, spotting the remaining moto-scout who had somehow managed to survive them braking harshly in his face and also dodged the collapse of the first bike. He wobbled about directly behind them, regaining speed now that he had managed to loop his strapped MP40 from over his shoulder.

The scout cradled the loaded submachine gun in his midst, balancing the barrel upon the handlebars of the bike, setting up a mounted fire angle. He was directly behind them, and the weapon lined up brilliantly to be able to fire upon them whilst in motion.

"Hardy!" Churchill shouted. "Plug this bellend, would you?!"

Down in the sidecar, Hardy was still trying to free the rifle from the peculiar confines of its position in the pod. All the shaking and motion in the meantime had not helped his grip on the situation.

Churchill glanced at his struggle and then back at the rearview mirror, watching as the hind scout prepped the automatic in their unprotected wake, about to shoot them in the back as they sped.

He had to buy time ...

Suddenly, Churchill applied the brakes—not too intensely, so that he could not maintain control.

Their tyres squealed and engine revved.

The unexpected manoeuvre interrupted the pursuit rider's preparation to fire, and he halted speed. However, the scout grew frustrated with this altercation game, and he abruptly sped up in order to correct his steering. Through the trailing vapour Jack purposely created, the bike performed an aggressive rear wheelie, bringing the front end up onto the back of the pod, mounting it with an aggressive skreich. The wheel hit Hardy between the shoulder blades like a schoolyard bully before the scout retrieved balance on both wheels, speeding up behind them afresh.

After that, Churchill was out of magic tricks to buy them time.

"Hardy!"

"Fuck me! I'm trying!" the American frantically replied, finally liberating the rifle with a frown that faded into surprise.

"*Shoot this prick!*"

Acting fast, Hardy twisted on his knees in the pod and gained aim of the moto-scout, tracing him with the sights as he reacted and swayed behind them erratically. Again attempting to position one hand over the handlebars with his gun, the scout sacrificed his speed in order to dodge this shot.

It must have been harder than it seemed.

Hardy shot first.

Bam!

The shot missed, whizzing somewhere past the scout as he ducked low his head instinctively.

"Shit!" Hardy cursed, adjusting his hold in order to cycle the bolt lever. He had to eject the spent cartridge and chamber another before he could try again ... only, the weapon was now jammed. It may have been all the added windage brushing over them or maybe in his panic, Hardy had not pulled the bolt rail back far enough before ramming it forwards, but there was now a crumpled cartridge stuck sideways in the breach.

In utter desperation, Churchill cast him a look as the journalist wriggled down low into the pod, scrabbling the rifle and whacking it with his stiff open palm.

"What are you doing?!" Churchill shouted angrily.

"It's jammed!" Hardy informed, showing him clearly the bent brass shell pinched in the ejection tray of the rifle.

It was their only gun.

"Bastard!" Churchill shouted, reaching out and grabbing the hot brass cell. It was really stuck in there. His frustrations were overpowered by the sudden surge in alarm as the scout caught up behind them, trailing their slipstream again. This time, he surfed their stream out beside Churchill. He did so widely, as not to fall victim to the range of the driver's slashing sword, but also to gain range for use of his MP40 in his lap, which he prepared now to spray them with in a drive-by fashion.

Churchill intervened, tugging at the right side of the handlebar and shoving with the left, bringing them into a side-by-side ram where the two bikes collided and bounded from one another in a mechanical coughing-fit and squawking of tyres. The extreme and dangerous action caused Churchill to lose speed and, almost, total control. It also caused the scout to fumble hold of his weapon. The harnessed submachine gun dropped completely from within his grasp and in a frantic action, the driver caught it by a sling strap at the last second before it fell into the void of blurred road hastening below them.

After the resulting distance of breathing space, Churchill closed in again on the scout, about to ram him a second time—this time, they were so close to the edge of the road that he would probably prove victorious by forcing the scout into the rushing haze of trees that lined their canopy-concealed passage. At this speed, the rider would be obliterated.

The scout predicted as such and reacted.

At that dire moment, he ceased attempting to regain hold of his dangling gun and instead twisted the throttle, speeding up and ahead of the heavier BMW and out of ramming range.

"Bugger!" Churchill cussed, just missing in his heavier ram and watching the scout zoom forwards and out of his reach. Their bike just could not match his speed.

Helpless, they both watched as the scout peeled about on the road in front of them, safe by speed and gained distance. The German scout now took the time to redeem the weapon. In a matter of seconds, he would regain possession and use it by shooting behind, likely wiping them out.

"Fuck me!" Hardy cursed loudly, giving up on the rifle. "It's really stuck!"

"Give it here!" Churchill offered in a shout over the wind.

With a puzzled look upon his face about how Churchill was going to juggle driving as well as unjamming the rifle at the same time, Hardy abided and passed it over.

Instead, Churchill coiled the rifle like a twirling baton in his right hand, adjusting his finger grip and wriggling them about halfway down the length of the wooden Karabiner and achieving a decent balance. He shook it in the air, gaining a feel for the weight of the rifle as well as equilibrium due to the wind resistance.

Up ahead, the remaining moto-scout shifted his view. He now broke out wide on the left, now able to balance and aim his MP40 under his right arm and in their direction in order to effectively cut them down—

Raised over the handlebars, Churchill stood on the generous side footings of the BMW and, with all his might, lobbed the Karabiner rifle forth like it were a javelin.

Like a blunt spear, the rifle travelled with suitable trajectory, spiking into the front wheel of the scout's bike. The enemy motorcycle became instantly skewered within its hollow tyre support cogs. In the same split-second as the wheel rotated, the rifle bayonetted, stuck in the wheel rungs, and raised—caught by the hinge of the tyre. The instantaneous result was the entire front wheel coming to a complete stop at around one-hundred-and-ten kilometres per hour, crunching like a deployed forward anchor.

With a *snap* and *whizz*, the moto-scout's front tyre instantly stopped.

The rear of the motorbike elevated and rotated several feet above the ground, flinging the MP40-toating driver up into the air almost ten feet like a circus catapult stunt whilst at high speed.

The fast-moving bike revolved beneath the launched and airborne rider, head-over-turkey.

The motorbike flipped and touched the road with a skid, bounding from off the coarse surface and gaining even more height like a gymnast performing a vault. The bike somersaulted twice before Churchill and Hardy's BMW overtook the crash scene, partially passing beneath the flipping wreckage as it was in mid-air.

The wreck finally slammed down permanently in a crumbled and broken mess, overturning and crashing into the asphalt in a hail of sparks, hot debris, and hopping springs before slewing off into the shrubbery and exploding into an oxygen-hungry fireball.

The airborne scout finally landed hard on the road on his knees and palms, flattening painfully into a winded skid which would have torn through his clothes and flesh like a cheese grater to a block of cheddar. With a scream of sudden agony, the German rolled and twisted again and again, barging into the solid earth with raw and rough scraping thuds before veering off the road and finishing at a precipitous halt against the solid and unmoving trees, likely stopping at an absolute dead end.

Their victorious BMW flew by at top-speed.

"*Whooooooo!*" Churchill excitedly squawked at the top of his lungs as he and Hardy gazed with eyes the size of saucers at the accident they had caused which had saved their lives.

They exchanged ecstatic looks, both smiling and laughing noisily at the amazing spectacle they had just seen.

"*Yee-haw! Did you see that shit?!*" between genuine guffaws, Hardy exclaimed like a regular cowboy aspirant.

"Someone should call that lad a taxi!" Churchill retaliated excitedly, glancing back in his rearview mirror at the carnage. "He's had enough!"

"A cab?" Hardy hooted, glancing back with a blaring grin, high on excitement and adrenaline. "I think someone oughta call him an ambulance!"

"Mate! A hearse!" Churchill adjusted his seating and took a second to try and see what was left of the scout in his side-mirror. "That bellend is as dead as a doornail!"

Seconds later, their motorcycle punched out of the *des Caps et Marais d'Opale* forestation, speeding north towards the French town of Guînes on a bypass route.

After audibly discerning what sounded like explosions and racket echoing through the silent forest following the reverberations of speeding motorbikes, another pair of idle German moto-scouts had their attentions torn from their chow break.

Candidly, they watched as an out of place BMW with a sidecar flew past them on the backroad.

The occupants seemed to be laughing hysterically ...

Before setting off upon their zippy Zündapp KS600 bikes, one of the two scouts reached down onto a box attached to the rear of his motorbike. The unit was of black bakelite construction with magnetic sheet metal and blackened leather fittings, complete with buttons, dials, and a handset attached via a cable. Just below the dials his gloved hand twisted, read a message impressed onto a metal bracket in red script, saying:

'Feind hört mit' (the enemy is listening).

It was a feld funksprechgerät portable backpack radio.

After radioing the situation to allied German units ahead of where this pursuit was leading, both scouts dropped their canned foods and punched the ignition on their bikes, breaking off after them ...

Up ahead and on the outskirts of the coastal city of *Calais*, a German soldier put down the receiver of his own portable radio unit.

He had just received an important message from two nearby moto-scouts.

Smoking a menthol cigarette whilst overseeing the establishment of their forward fortifications in the recently occupied area, an officer stood nearby him. With haste, the radioman relayed what he had just understood in the communiqué from his southward compatriots. Insighted by the intelligence of the incoming suspected enemy motorbike approaching from the south, the officer stepped outside of the enclosed area and into a wide offset. There he informed the chief of a unit comprised of a further two dozen riflemen and two parked Panzer III armoured tanks of the news ...

With grinding hydraulics, the 37mm KwK 36 turrets of the Panzers buzzed to life and revolved 180-degrees, preparing to engage these newly arriving adversaries ...

The cannons, as well as the barrels of over twenty positioned riflemen, all aimed at the road leading towards Guînes ... waiting to spring the attack.

In the anticipating quiet, they grew to hear the drawing hum of an incoming solo vehicle as it echoed up from the concealed road ...

The trap was set, and they were headed right for it.

VIII
Retreat to Victory

1940, June 3
Calais
Nord Pas-de-Calais, France

In lieu of the evacuation, the French coastal city of Calais had recently been laid to ruin by warfare.

Over three thousand British and eight hundred French troops, assisted by Royal Navy warships out at sea, had held their ground against the belligerent 10th Panzer Division for five whole days, effectively propping open the closing walls for their escaping allies' retreat to victory.

The Germans had taken over Calais twenty hours ago, able to bring forth their armoured forces to a rendezvous at this very town centre before launching a final attack on Dunkirk and those unfortunate enough to remain ashore.

Calais had been trodden to ash and spoil by artillery and precision dive bombing prior to the fall and retreat of the British rearguard. The collateral damage the peaceful town sustained was poignant and depressing to say the least. However, the heavy fighting and sacrifice by the British stronghold did bear fruit, for the German 10th Panzers would have arrived along the Dunkirk perimeter days earlier had their aggressive armada not been stalled at Calais.

But the time had come to advance on Dunkirk, and the 10th Panzer Division, a force made up of eight tanks, a dozen armoured vehicles, and a battalion of infantry troops, had recently received their marching orders to attack east. They had set out to do so with vigour and zeal.

Some of that German unit had lingered for the morning, and had just been given word that a small pocket of resistance had been spotted moving north from Guînes just moments ago. The concept of there still being Allied enemy behind the line was surprising but not unheard of during the chaos of the invasion. These poor Englisch narren were late to the party, is all.

Two Panzer III tanks had been ordered to remain in Calais with a handful of mobile infantries and they welcomed this incoming adversary with cannons and rifles, locked, loaded, and lethal.

"Do you smell that, lad?"

Jack Churchill's question was a shoulder-sided yell to his American journalist passenger riding the pod of the attached sidecar, Felix Hardy. Their commandeered German bike coasted along a quiet back-end road with a consistent resonance that complemented their pace as they sped yond tranquil fields of yellow meadows in the flat French fields. The view scape was mesmerizing beneath the afternoon sun.

He cast a look to his left, eyeing Hardy as he sat calmly in the sidecar of the BMW-R71. His nostrils flared, but he had not the answer.

Churchill nodded, sure of the salty smell lingering in the air.

"That's saltwater! It's the ocean!" he finally retorted. "It means we're almost there!"

From two consistent bookends of thick trees and foliage, the road ahead opened into a clearing seaside scape with a town amidst. The blue of the ocean was visible on the horizon.

Rounding a bend to the left, their view unravelled upon the incoming township: the coastal city of Calais—or what was left of it after all the fighting.

Next minute ...

Tanks.

Churchill's sterling stare zeroed, spotting the opponents in the distance. It resembled a mechanized roadblock.

There were two of them—Panzer IIIs, but what alarmed him the most and caused goosebumps to form upon arms was the fact that they were already looking their way ...

They were waiting for them!

There were also what appeared to be approximately two dozen infantrymen scattered about the ruins of the crumpled buildings and the slants of collapsed rooftops. Jack's squinting eagle-eyed focus briefly saw the bopping of their helmets as they lowered their faces to gain sights across the peaks of their weapon's iron-sights—like the tanks, they were also looking their way on the road.

This was a bloody ambush!

And they were rolling straight into it!

"*Shit!*" he shouted, frightening his reserved passenger, drawing Hardy's attention forwards in an instant. His fingers grabbed the edge of the pod, prepared for anything.

Mad Jack's instinctual senses flared.

Churchill cussed as he felt the heat of the many rifle reticules and more notably, the tank cannons, as their sights brushed upon their position as they cruised up the all-too-welcoming open road to Calais.

The ambush may have been seconds from instigation, just waiting for them to be closer in on the straight and within range—which was about *now.*

Jack acted pre-emptively, decelerating and banking harshly to the right just as two bright flashes emitted from the barrels of the tanks in the distance.

Bl-blink ...

BO-BOOM!

In the nanosecond following the two glints of light sparkling from the tank cannons, two beefy explosions detonated near them along the road from the resulting tank shells.

The thunderous cannons of the partially hidden Panzer III tanks opened fire. Their sights were aimed on the centre of the road—right where their motorcycle *had* been prior to Jack's sudden veering manoeuvre.

Churchill successfully dodged a bullet (many bullets, and shells) by peeling their bike off the road in a severe right-hand arc, almost losing control as the sudden off-road terrain beneath their tyres quaked turbulently. Granted, it was better than the alternative of death.

The asphalt road behind them exploded and cratered, crumpling with a forcefully loud *crack* and *fizzle,* and *bang* and *hiss* all at once. The flattened dirt and bitumen humped and boiled behind them as the explosive shells exploded, creating charred hollows the size of cars and leaving rising smokestacks.

The bike gained a second of airtime after launching itself off the road and curved a short slope, then onto uneven terrain. Along with the new bouncy land beneath their soaring passage, the force from the fierce eruption in their rearview rocked them like thunderous turbulence as the push from the shockwave aided in their launch off the road.

Somehow, Jack recovered the handles.

The warm welcome from the members of the 10th Panzer Division ambush continued with a crackling array of distant fireworks emitting from the many concealed riflemen locations along the frontline of the ruined town side. The sporadic gunfire discharged, tracing the speeding motorbike as it peeled off the main road and beyond visibility of the neighbouring Flanders field, still headed east.

"Ahhhhh!" Hardy shouted, shocked and surprised by the vociferous surprise attack by the Germans in Calais as well as the ceaseless exhilaration of their unplanned off-road detour.

Bullets loudly *whizzed* and *snapped* past their location, some missing by what felt like inches, nipping at the earth below the bike and even lopping down green foliage as they sped past it. Jack was heading them into a tall-grass field for some partial concealment.

"How's that for a welcoming committee!" shouted Churchill.

"How'd they know we were coming?!" Hardy cried rhetorically as he pinned his shaking German helmet on his head, staying low as tall grass ferociously whipped at the sides of the speeding, off-road sidecar as their BMW bashed through the tall grass and reeds of the Flanders field, burying them in uprooted stalks and dirt.

"Hold on!" Churchill demanded as the subject changed. The grass grew taller as their ride began to anchor their speed. He applied power and dropped his head down low, hoping that the meadow would somehow shield them of the Germans' vantage.

This, as well, killed his own view of any obstacles and mounds that may lay ahead in the field. The drag of the harnessed sidecar tore at the reeds like a blunt scythe blade, but their voyage persisted.

"This is going to get a tad bumpy!"

The snapping of weeds and grass was almost as loud as the pelting ricochets from the constant barrage of near-missing bullets as their BMW tore through the field, blindly headed easterly en route to bypass Calais.

Suddenly and all the more unexpectedly since Jack had not intentionally released the throttle, their motorbike began to deliberate and snag. The buzz of the overworked engine began to increase, like the motorbike was mechanically straining and threatening to stall.

Churchill's maroon beret propped up and over, scanning ahead and assessing at the front wheel in motion. Reeds of green grass had wrapped itself around the circular barring, entangling the rotation of the wheel and knotting their revolutions. Smoke rose from the tight, tangled bind as it scorched from squeezing friction.

"Bollocks!"

"What?" Hardy shouted, eyes wide and concerned.

Now that the scrunching of grass had gotten less as their speed slowed and came to a standstill, they could more discernibly hear the bullet-strikes from the German guns as the infantry attempted to blindly smite them in the brush of the field. Quite amusingly from an outside perspective, all the riflemen could probably see was the shaking of the grass tips representing their location. Those who still had an angle cycled their rifles and blindly shot into the field, hoping to get lucky.

"We're snagged!" Churchill responded over the raining barrage of bullets as more incoming lead snipped away at the meadow above their heads.

Chunk!

"*Shit!*" Hardy cursed as a stray projectile chipped the lip of the pod by his fingers. A round also landed close, striking the metal frame of the bike next to the rear tyre with a metallic *ping,* scratching the black paint.

"*We gotta get outta here, Captain!*" Hardy shouted, squirming in his lil pod whilst trying to get as low as he physically could to protect himself from the onslaught of blind gunfire gravitating their way. "*We're sitting ducks!*"

Ding ... whizz, whizz ... snap ... dong!

The incoming barrage was unrelenting.

Just then, as Churchill dismounted to examine the grass caught around the wheel, a stray bullet struck him in the back, knocking him over from the tug of force.

"Captain!" Hardy fretted.

"*Bastard!*" Churchill cursed as he pushed up on his knee, whipping off the camouflage smock that now had a hole through it. There was an impact on his brown leather quiver. It was a through-and-through, undoubtedly damaging a few of the timber arrows housed within. Staying focused, he grabbed at a fistful of weeds and yanked them from the tyre with an arduous tear. Now that he was off the bike and beside it, Jack could also tell that the strenuous whipping he had given the vehicle had also caused the engine to overclock, and therefore overheat. The evident sizzle and hiss could be heard and upon inspection, the valves were boiling hot to touch.

Their unfortunate cease of motion had caused the engine to seize and stall.

Exposed at a halt, it was only a matter of time before the Germans determined their location in the field. The chimney of rising smoke from the burning grass or overheating motorcycle did not help and flagged their location like a pulsating beacon.

Churchill waved with his hands, attempting to cool the singing sections so that the rising smoke would not pinpoint their position, but it quickly proved futile.

"Quick!" Churchill called, squatting low. "Do you need to piss?"

On Churchill's command, Hardy uncomfortably rolled out from the pod and into the crunchy pasture, tripping in the grass and unfortunately ruffling it about like crazy. He scattered, trampling to find Churchill low beside the opposite side of the bike as more random bullets scuffed the dirt near them, rustling reeds and severing blades of grass.

He exclaimed in the pandemonium. "What?!"

"*Do you need to pee?!*" Churchill repeated the question.

"Again, *what?*"

"*Piss! Do you need to make water?! Take a tinkle?! Make urine?! Hang a leak? Sap the lizard? Drain the main vein? Do a wee-wee?*" shouting at the top of his lungs over the loud impacts about them, Churchill fired off numerous synonyms for urination in an argumentative tone as he unlatched his fly and stuck his hand into the front of his pants, apparently about to reveal his trouser snake.

"What the fuck?!"

"Do you need to *piss,* or not?!"

Disgusted and rather confused, Hardy sneered with his reply.

"*N-no?! Why—*"

"We need to cool this engine down—and *now!*"

Repulsed by the display, Hardy abruptly looked away as Churchill contorted in his crouch, fast unbuttoning his fly and yanking his willy out. Mouse out of the house and from an awkward squatting position, Jack attempted to urinate on the housing of the sizzling BMW, hosing it down with bodily fluids—enough to cool the steaming heat and limiting the amount of rising smoke from being visible above the field. Air would now gush against the wet metal, water-cooling it thusly.

"Come on! Help!" Churchill shouted. "Get your dick out, lad!"

"What? No!" Hardy replied. Even if he had to urinate, he doubted he could given the circumstances. He would have severe stage fright.

Jack yelled over his shoulder. "Come on!"

"Captain, I don't want to die with my dick out!"

"We're not going to die! Not if we can get out of here!"

"I can't, alright! I can't just *make myself piss!* Hey! *Hey!*" Hardy objected as Churchill's yellow stream came nearer to his cowering position as he cowered by the hot side of the bike. He crawled away like a revolted survivor, risking gunfire over being peed on.

"Settle down, lad!" Churchill holstered his weapon and squatted back down low after reaching around and obtaining something from a mounted satchel on the bike. Whilst his hand fondled around inside the pack, he took a peek, noticing that there was more than just the one signal grenade he had found in there earlier.

"Old mate was holding out on us. There's a handful of potato mashers in this bag!" Churchill informed as he returned behind the miniscule protection of their upstanding motorbike. More stray rounds ripped tuffs of grass down over their heads as the German infantry loosed round after round into the Flanders field where they had last spotted activity.

Hardy looked over, watching as Churchill presented a wooden-handled stick grenade. This one was different and had a white strip painted around its tin can-looking head.

Churchill twisted the cap in the bottom of the handle and pulled the string, arming the fuse ...

Hardy's peepers widened in fear.

"Relax! It's a smoke grenade ..." Churchill explained, finding it humorous to briefly leave Hardy in the lurch after mentioning that there were explosive grenades in the satchel, too.

Hardy watched with a puzzled stare as Churchill rose an inch and tossed the smoke grenade about fifty feet *ahead* of them. He made sure the arc was low across the field.

"What are you doing?!" Hardy squirmed anxiously, unsure of this plan. He was no military strategist, but there was no way that smoke cloud would cover them from that far out ...

"Any second and those Germans are going to shoot at us with more than just bullets!" Churchill speculated. His plan here was that the smoke would rise there, and hopefully signify to the Germans that they were not where they were currently located.

"Why didn't you throw it *behind* us?" Hardy complained, advising the plan he gathered Churchill had would be pointless by tossing the diversionary smoke grenade ahead of them instead of behind with the goal of obscuring their view.

A few seconds passed and Churchill did not reply.

Instead, he held up a finger.

"Wait for it ..."

Boom ...

Tank cannon.

BHOOM!

The explosive round struck a section of the Flanders field a good fifty feet in front of their locale, sending up a haze of brown dirt and tossed burning grass, steamy with grey smoke.

The shell was spot-on on the escalating smoke cloud, wrecking the shit out of the vicinity where the white cloud had started chugging.

The enemy assumed the riders had progressed ahead.

BHOOM!

Another shell struck the nearby vicinity, sending up another geyser of earth and smoke.

The tanks were unknowingly clearing a path ...

"Jump back in!" Churchill shouted. Remaining low, he swooped his leg over the bike and lurched onto the driver's seat.

Hardy crawled around the back of the bike and toppled into the pod. He cast a glance up and at Churchill in the hope that he knew what he was doing.

Before they departed, Churchill took the time to firmly adjust his filthy maroon beret upon his dome and flattened his pencil moustache with his thumb and index finger prior to tending to the handlebars and throttle stick.

Hardy shook his head in consternation.

It was hardly the time or place to consider dressing attire and appearance, but then again, this was Mad Jack Churchill. The pride of wearing his signature style during warfare was worth the gamble.

Sharing the sentiment, Hardy pulled off his uncomfortable stahlhelm and dropped it into the grass, replacing it with his pocketed scrunched fedora hat.

He mounted it atop of his head. "This is a bad idea."

BHOOM!

Another explosion. This time, closer, at about thirty feet.

The shockwave of the shelling caused them to shake about on the idle motorbike. Smoke and residual kinetic force from a shockwave rushed over them like a gust of wind, shaking outwards like a ripple through the long grass of the pasture. It rained fine grains of black dirt.

Eyes forward through the destruction and Churchill saw through a gap—literally, light at the end of the tunnel.

The tank shells had flattened a path ...

"Hold on!" he called, flogging the throttle and gunning it, even though the bike was still nearly overheating due to the partial reeds anchoring them down.

The BMW, smoking like a cracked chimney, zoomed forwards and reached the crater which the Panzer cannon had made. On the uneven terrain, the rocking motorbike rocketed through the clearing of flattened grass and hilly dirt and into the subsequent crater before Churchill and Hardy both spotted the connecting road leading east out and away from Calais.

"Through there!" Hardy's voice bellowed while he pointed.

"Yeah, yeah, I see it!" Churchill commented, steering them over jagged landscape before having no choice but to tear-ass through what was left of the Flanders field foliage and put them back on the road. "Hold on!"

He revved it, pummelling through the greenery resistance right as tank cannons fired again.

Bo-Boom!

Incoming ...

Churchill pared them on a hard right, steering them up a slight dirt mound before the pasture opened into a clearing and presented a back-end dirt road leading away from this hellish predicament.

They had just found the shortcut to bypass Calais.

BHO-BHOOM!

The Flanders field behind them exploded into chunky brown clouds of dirt and smouldering ashes as the Panzer tanks opened fire at where they predicted movement in the grass.

With high-explosive power, the eruptions discharged exactly behind their travelling wake and beyond the small dirt mound which they had kicked off with building speed, causing them to launch and sail in mid-air and with considerable hang-time for what felt like three whole seconds. The jump lifted them high enough to get back on the raised flat of the road.

The tank blasts covered their exit from the field in an exhale of smoke and singed grass reeds as their bike landed rough on the dry flat of the road.

The wheels screeched and hissed as Churchill fought the handlebars as if he were wrestling an alligator, regaining control of the speeding, squeaking motorbike.

Once in control, he gunned it, sending stem reeds of the grass that had once anchored them twirling and flailing in their wake. They had broken free and escaped the jaws of death.

Over four hundred feet behind them within the city ruins of Calais, German infantrymen upped from their positions and flooded into the stretch of road on foot, forming shooter's stances at either shoulder-level or dropping to a knee. They drew a bead on the escaped motorbike as it sped off in the distance down a connecting road, pointlessly letting off shots.

Bam! Bam! Bam!

Ba-ba-bam!

In a consistent, vain attempt, they fired round after round at the figure as it shrunk into the distance, all squandering and missing their mark.

In the distance, the motorbike and sidecar dipped down a short hill under a tidal wave of screaming *whizzes* and *snaps*, speeding like a bat out of hell. They were headed easterly, likely towards their final destination of Dunkirk where they were *extremely* late for the evacuation party.

The remaining German soldiers were stressed and shouting with rage and frustration.

How had they failed so badly just now?

Whilst they contemplated giving chase after the evading motorcycle or just to let it go, they cleared a space for the rotating tracks of the mammoth twenty-three-tonne Panzer III tank as it roared to life after sitting idly. The armoured beast up-geared, grinding its tracks as it crumbled rubble and entered the strip of road.

The second Panzer followed, one after the other.

In pursuit of the motorbike, the vehicles climbed to their top speed of forty kilometres per hour, which was no contest to the BMW. They would likely need motorcycles of their own to get close to the fleeing—

Vro-Vrooom!

Speaking of which.

Weaving between obstacles and overtaking all other aggressors within the vicinity of the failed ambush, a pair of fresh German moto-scouts on bikes zoomed through the mobilizing space in Calais, thrashing the guts out of their 1938 Zündapp flat-twin engines in hot pursuit.

Goggles wrapped on tight.

Heads down low and focused.

Speed was everything.

VrhoooOOOOOM!

Churchill and Hardy's smoking BMW tore a line through the etching of the war timeline as the walls of the German invasion of France closed in behind them.

In fact, they rode the crest of that tidal wave.

After coiling to the left once again, their dirt backroad merged into *Route des Estuaires*, where they thundered along the coastal strip of road. Exactly point-eight of a mile north was the English Channel, beyond that was ... *home.*

All they needed to do was stay on this—

With such unpredictable gusto, Churchill ripped them off the Route des Estuaires without warning, hanging a left and causing Hardy to clutch onto the edges of his sidecar pod.

Their motorcycle broke left after the French commune known as *Marck* upon the northern Calais city limits. At this point, almost all roads led to Dunkirk, and evidence of the evacuation was becoming more unsettlingly clear as they began to pass more and more abandoned vehicles along the side of the roads. The remnants were eerily vacant. Some were even left idle in the centre of the roadway, becoming obstacles.

In the thick of it now, their voyage was now less than six miles out from Dunkirk and the entire BEF evacuation operation. As they passed Marck, they spotted numerous degrees of enemy activity as the German forces mobilized in and around the perimeter, undoubtedly preparing for their final frontier attack on Dunkirk sometime in the next couple of hours. They had the entire coastal city in a stranglehold, and it was running out of air.

"Jesus Christ ..." Hardy commented as he watched out of the sidecar to their far-out left, watching the hundreds of German soldiers amongst the fresh ruins of French houses and various establishments, preparing vehicles and efficiently organizing, like ants on a dropped quiche Lorraine.

The view included a half-dozen or so slow Panzer III tanks which were driving in a mechanized column along the avenue *du Général de Gaulle:* the widest coastal strip that ran along the edge of northern France between Calais and Dunkirk. It was the most direct route linking two major cities.

They had just caught up to the 10th Panzer Division.

Bypassing their numbers, Churchill and Hardy sped onto a connecting road which, although being parallel to the avenue du Général de Gaulle, seemed to look as though it veered north towards the culmination, linking it up to that road—and eventually the convoy of tanks.

It was a race to the finish line now.

"More tanks!" Hardy informed with a pointing finger.

"Fine-o-fine, old boy. We'll overtake them. This road will take us the ten clicks to Dunkirk via a commune known as *Oye-Plage,* and then after that, *Gravelines.* Dunkirk is the next big town over, a stone's throw away," Churchill announced like he was their in-flight entertainment through the overhead. "You could just about bloody walk it in a pub-crawl."

"And of a German presence?"

"Nay," Churchill disputed on an educated guess. "Oye-Plage is a nothing-town, it's why they mobilized in Calais and not closer. And Gravelines is basically a giant moat around a rock which branches off into a dozen inky canals. Unfortifiable. Really nice beaches, though ..."

"Friendlies there?" Hardy asked across at Churchill as their bike casually plodded along the stretch, taking it easy on this shortcut so as not to attract any unwanted attention from the masses of the German entity.

"Doubt it," gathered Churchill. "Our boys would have bugged out of those towns and headed for Dunkirk hours if not days ago—"

Whizz-CRACK!

Causing them both to flinch, a bullet randomly *whizzed* between them from behind and shattered the rounded side-mirror on the handlebar of the BMW motorcycle.

"Shit!" Churchill cursed, deviating slightly.

He and Hardy threw a glance behind, spotting two new scout bikes closing distance. These guys were not mucking around. They were each equipped with a sidearm in their dominant hand as they controlled the steering, aiming and firing every so often on a straight level at the fleeing BMW.

Bam! Bam!

Whizz! Whizz!

Hardy shrieked and twirled in his pod, shrinking as low as he could in the sidecar whilst Churchill dipped his head low and concentrated on the road. There were very little evading manoeuvres he could pull on this vehicle with regard to dodging any close gunfire, and his exposed back left him with the most to lose.

He up-geared the bike and they accelerated thusly, picking up speed so as to flee from these new and nimbler pursuers.

Crack!

The rear glass teleoptic brake light of the bike took a hit, exploding into shards of broken red crystal and he felt the shockwave ripple to his buttocks. The steel lamp housing suspended lifelessly from its wiring conduit and dangled for an instant before disengaging from its wire thread completely.

"Captain!" Hardy shouted, holding something up from his position low in the rattling pod.

Churchill shot him a glance between gawps at the road where he dodged half a fallen tree which looked as if its trunk had been detonated by a mortar strike. Jack flinched at the sound of the next gunshot, wondered if the bullet chasing him was about to strike him in his exposed back.

The scouts on the zippy Zündapps gained a lot of range before the sidecar BMW reached a higher speed. They were now tailing at less than fifty feet with their gun arms extended and shooting more rapidly as the distance closed, then the shooting abruptly ceased. In his lone remaining mirror Churchill noticed the slides were locked back on their Walther P38 handguns and that the drivers were examining the empty weapons and how to safely reload them whilst riding.

From this moment of clarity, he devised that they were out of ammunition and had to somehow time-consumingly recharge their firearms whilst continuing to ride at speed. Whatever their efforts, it should buy them a few seconds of freedom.

"Do it!" Churchill exclaimed with little thought.

It was all they had.

Remaining low, Hardy shifted within the sidecar, adjusting himself in order to use the devices he had retrieved from the satchel in his pod.

Model 24 Stielhandgranates.

The explosive kind.

"Five second fuse!" Churchill instructed, loud over the rush of the air and the adrenaline of the situation. He had to shout his instructions loud over the wind resistance of their new top speed on this straight.

"Twist the cap at the bottom ... pull the string ..." he advised, keeping his primary focus on the road. "Count down the fuse a few seconds ... and then chuck it!"

Hardy dipped his head in understanding, handling one of the four stick bombs and doing as ordered. This was obviously his first time handling grenades, let alone planning to try and time their detonations just right in order to hit moving targets.

Terrified of the device, he counted fast and tossed early.

The thrown potato masher randomly jumped and bounded across the road in their wake, causing the speeding scouts to not only spot it but avoid it as an obstruction. Seconds later, it detonated in the far distance behind them all, killing nothing.

"Too soon!" Churchill bellowed, steering them around a sizeable amount of fallen brickwork and lumber from a blown-out wall and gate leading to a property on the left side of the street without slowing to properly manoeuvre the obstacles.

"I know! I know!" Hardy defended, preparing another.

The stretch of road ahead of them was becoming more populated by abandoned transportation. Lorry trucks and other vehicles—even an armoured French tank, Churchill noticed—had been deemed derelict along the route by evacuees. The majority of them had been pushed aside and a path had been made between, however most recent additions had been left in the centre of the road resulting in the most inconvenient of circumstances.

Some vehicles were remnants. Burnt-out wreckages, likely having been struck by artillery by distant observers from Germany or strafing runs made by swooping fighters.

The sight of so many empty and deserted vehicles gave them apocalyptic vibes, like something out of a *H. G. Wells* fiction novel.

"How many left?!"

"Three ... eh, two," Hardy explained after rummaging through the original owner of the BMW's satchel. There were another three stick grenades in the bag, only one of them had a white strip around its head signifying non-lethal smoke. He corrected, "One is another smoke."

Churchill hunched a glance at the scouts in his remaining side-mirror. They had both heard and seen the explosion after the discarded item had bounced past them and were both very aware that they might try it again. Thus, they dropped back in distance.

"Try again!" Churchill necessitated, doing the guesswork. "Count to *three,* then drop it behind us. *Drop,* don't *throw.*"

Hardy nodded, upturning another grenade and finding the string in its handle.

"Oi!" Churchill called sternly to him. He understood, it was likely terrifying holding onto a hot potato for that long—and it was. "Three *full* seconds. It's all about timing!"

"Yeah, yeah, I got it!" Hardy replied, holding it out after priming the fuse. "One Mississippi! Two Mississi—*fuck me!*"

His eyes suddenly met the closest scout and saw him latch the slide forward on his handgun with his gloved thumb after reloading a fresh magazine. The rider immediately pointed it and sprinkled gunfire, lighting them up. It may have been inaccurate and at a rapid rate, but the relentless onslaught was a cause for cover all the same.

Bam, bam, bam, bam, bam ...

Hardy fumbled, quickly dropping down low and out of range of the incoming pistol fire and, as a result, cared little for the countdown on the stielhandgranate. Snapping to, he quickly propelled the smoking grenade out the side and onto the road.

The two scouts sped up and swerved around it, observing the device's explosion behind their wake. It was much closer and therefore much louder than the last, but still far off doing any damage to their pursuers.

"Bloody hell, Hardy!" Churchill shouted, dipping his head off to the side and flinching as the nine-millimetre bullets whizzed past all around them. A couple of the small calibre caps even struck the back of the sidecar with metallic *donks,* denting the scratched metal.

Hardy swore. He revolved around in his tight little pod space and prepared the next—final—explosive grenade.

"Give it here!" Churchill shouted—all trust seemingly gone in the capability of Felix Hardy's offence.

"I've got it! Watch the road!"

The American shouted his defence, and thankfully so, as Churchill only just avoided colliding with an abandoned blue civilian car. The doors and trunk were left wide open. They lost an ounce of speed performing the movement.

"Hardy!—"

"Captain! I got this!" Hardy implored with confidence, somewhat angrily, likely in himself for failing with the last two.

"Shit!" Churchill scoffed, firmly grabbing the handlebars and steering them true, dodging another lump of debris on the road from a collapsed stone wall which passed by them in a blur of speeding motion. Their bike shook dramatically as they rolled over some unavoidable fragments.

He shouted the best advice he could give. "Don't cock it up!"

Hardy inched up out of the pod and spotted the scouts.

The one who had fired on them just now had dropped back a little, attempting to reload his empty gun while the other sped up with his pistol up by his head, ready to attack with a fresh load of lead.

Out of sight from the pursuer, Hardy tugged the fuse.

Staying low, his eyes scanned the scouts.

"*One Mississippi ... two Mississippi ... three Mississippi ... four!*"

Churchill's stare intensified, listening to the count.

He was about to scream *what the dickens are you doing it's a five second fuse!* when Hardy lurched up and *pegged* the stick grenade at the pursuing motorcycle, end-over-end.

It was a daring stunt.

He hurled the stick bomb like a throwing axe.

The grenade twirled, counting down that last second in mid-air where it abruptly detonated barely twenty feet in their wake—*RIGHT IN THE PURSUING SCOUT'S FACE!*

The driver was way too close to avoid or react.

Unable to respond or swerve evasively, even brake to clear distance, the well-timed grenade exploded inches from him, bursting brightly into a fireball of dried rose red heat infused with a shockwave of white light. A gust of shrapnel punched into his locomotive force like a harsh air-pocket that the German scout crashed into like a charging obstacle delivered from *Helios* himself.

The scout flew off the bike in reverse, blown to charcoal bits and lifeless. The sheer kinetic power of the detonation would have broken bones, liquefied organs.

The power of the explosive force shredded and singed his leather clothing and skin beneath, cooking and peeling layers in an instant.

The scout's bike also ignited, flipping up in the air and breaking into two main hunks of smoking debris as it scraped off the road in a forking pattern, decreasing in speed as it tumbled wildly out of control. The remnants were an instant meteor of twisted metal, smoking rubber and charred, crumpled cinders, thrashing into the blurred bounds of their passage. A tyre disengaged, flinging almost directly vertically.

A near-miss for the second scout, he somehow managed to avoid the volatile disaster, revving his engine through the heat of the smoke pocket. He then sped up behind them within seconds, loaded with a fresh clip in his handgun and firing fast ...

Bam, bam, bam!

"Shit!" Hardy recoiled within the compounds of his pod as rounds tore through the air, ripping the fabric of sound and also the fabric of his fedora brim. One of the shots angled inwards, hitting the inside of the pod by his tensing legs. "One left!"

"Get the smoke!" Churchill shouted—his eyes noticing something incoming on the road up ahead, giving him an idea, but they hadn't much time. "Pop it ... and hold it!"

Hardy did not argue, just did what he was told.

He had learnt better than to argue with an obscure idea from Jack Churchill.

"Hold on tight! Hold it out!"

Hardy collected the smoke grenade from the satchel and pulled the fuse. He held his breath and closed his eyes as the head of the smoke grenade fizzled and popped, puffing and chugging thick white smoke from its can-shaped tip.

Hardy held it up like a flame torch.

The smoke streamed into a profuse haze behind them, obscuring the last scout's vision ...

The scout pouted his lips so as not to breath in the repulsive white smoke as the cloud chugged out the back of the motorbike sidecar.

After raising his gun and backing off a few feet and even trying to swerve for a fresh air visual, he instead decided to speed up and get aside or even ultimately in front of the finger of smoke in order to gain a clear shot at the adversaries ...

Vroooooooooom ...

His speed increased with a thunderous throttle.

Within seconds, the scout bike started to outlast the smoke cloud, drifting out alongside of the BMW and his now exposed targets, where he gained a clear view.

He aimed the pistol at them, clear as day—

An obstruction!

Debris and ruins were strewn all over the road from what appeared to be a roadblock that the Allies had established to slow the advancing Germans. The road had mostly been cleared through the middle, yet scattered components remained.

They were more than large enough to capsize a motorcycle.

The last thing the scout saw or heard was the occupants of the BMW bike as once finally ahead of the smoke cloud, he overtook them with too much speed. The driver, an Englishman, simply smiled and waved in that split-second announcing *'ta-ta'* as he zoomed past them as they braked, knowing damn well of the unavoidable obstacle up ahead.

The scout realised and braked too late, entering a death-wobble before he hit the scattered bricks and next the timber beam laying across the road.

Travelling at approximately one-hundred-and-fifty kilometres per hour, the scout absolutely launched like a catapult from off the quivering bike, becoming airborne at least eight feet into the sky and sailing before touching down, hard.

Behind them as they safely evaded obstacles, Hardy and Churchill smiled and cheered as they saw the scout stack it amongst the ruins.

Having served its purpose, they tossed the smoke grenade and their BMW sped onwards, peeling left after passing the northern outskirts of Oye-Plage. This road joined them up onto the avenue du Général de Gaulle which had now turned into the *Rue de l'Étoile,* an even more coastal route miles ahead of the convoy of the German Panzer Division they had spotted earlier.

1940, June 3
Dunkirk
Nord Pas-de-Calais, France

Without a word said, First Lieutenant Gin Parker, Second Lieutenant Padre Nicholl, Corporal Knocker White, and Privates Macken and Wand unwillingly collected their bags and rifles from the ground and shifted their weights onto their forward leg.

They could wait for their captain no longer.

It was time to go.

It took an extra second for their substitute CO, Captain King-Clark, to admit the defeat as well. Combined, they had realized the reality of their persistence in Dunkirk overtime was becoming a life-or-death moment. More and more German artillery strikes had increased their range into the city. A payload of bombs had just been sprinkled throughout the southern fringes of the neighbouring coastal towns, laying waste to the outskirts of Dunkirk.

The salvos landed close enough for them to witness.

The sound of artillery whistled through the sky, propelling shells like thrown javelins, arching down into the buildings connected to Dunkirk, reducing them to rubble and dust.

The whole circumstance resembled a high tide, slowly taking out sandcastles as the waves reached further inland by the second.

A shell detonated a busy cobblestone street, exploding dirt and stone outwards, showering the area in smoke and dust. Another strike shredded a group of French soldiers as they marched monotonously in their non-prioritized queue for evacuation at the beach and harbour.

Nothing identifiable remained amongst the remnants of them, other than a few punted boots and tossed rifles. Rimmed helmets rolled in the wake like the hubcap from a tyre.

"This is it, lads. Time to go!" King-Clark announced as more volleys came down. The whistles of the falling shells were hauntingly audible. Pulling rank, he determined that these loyal men of the Second Manchester Regiment could no longer stay and wait for their leader to return, himself included. It was time to leave this continent and finally follow their orders.

Albeit miserable and depressed, the men were silently compliant in their joint accordance to follow his decision, acting without dispute. It was now past 1600-hours, and Captain Jack Churchill was still yet to reach Dunkirk.

Taking complete charge of what little remained behind of Churchill's section in this, their last mission in France, Rex King-Clark instructed the men to stay low and sport their tin hats. Enduring tightly in their retreat, they departed the streets and followed the drippling masses into the harbour: now a bay of flames and wreckages.

Boats were sunken or set alight. Cast adrift. Sharp remnants of their wooden hulls protruded from the flaming debris-littered surface of the waterfront shallows.

A sea foam had been whipped up by the tides, bizarrely dyed green by floating films of diesel fuel and oils from destroyed sea vessels, turning the coast into the frothing rabid mouth of *Poseidon* himself that demanded more sacrifices.

In the skies, the buzzing of an aerial presence was notable.

More often than not, it wasn't friendly either.

On occasion and with increasing opportunity, Luftwaffe Messerschmitts would swoop in like apex predators, performing strafing runs with their machine guns on any targets on the open shores.

"Come on!" King-Clark shouted after their pause overlooking the mayhem that was a war-torn harbour in front of the once beautiful coastal city. He led them east and along the beach dunes which ran along the shoreline, where it appeared countless soldiers had abandoned hope of evacuation via the docks and piers. Instead, men were literally queuing up along the windy sandy shores, some lines even reaching out into the depths and to the little ferrying boats as they came in as close as they could before becoming beached. It was a phenomenal show of despair.

Out of sheer desperation and ingenuity, the engineering corps had scuttled Bedford trucks in a series parallel to the beach, ranging as deep as they could be parked at low tide. They then laid wooden planks and driftwood as far down these truck chains as possible, creating their own makeshift jetties when the tide came in. This brilliantly extended the land as far as possible so that the boats could reach them quicker and easier.

King-Clark's tight half-dozen group stayed close together, navigating through the chaos. They cut through the multitudes of human currents, through the post-apocalyptic tone of abandoned vehicles on the sand, toppled on the dunes, and through the bodies of soldiers seeking refuge in piles, too anxious or uncertain to make a dash from the cover of the dunes and into the water towards the boats.

These men who made the course from the shore to the sea resembled turtle hatchlings needing to run the gauntlet of blinding solar exposure under the hunting eyes of birds of prey in order to make the water. A feat of which less than thirty percent survive natural selection.

The desperation of the evacuation was too much.

It was utter chaos, both on the sand and in the water.

The little ships of Dunkirk were overflowing with khaki-clad soldiers, so much so that some boats were in danger of capsizing as the waves pushed against their sides. Yachts and tugs collided into one another, ferociously clashing and breaking woodwork and stripping lines from their bows. In the incidents of the thrashing tide, people were thrown overboard. Some risked becoming squashed or drowned—that's if they were lucky enough to not be strafed by a fighter somewhere during this survival process ...

German fighters and bombers drifted in flocks overhead, taking dive-bomb and strafing runs at ships full of British soldiers in the bay.

When the planes would strike, the choppy water erupted like it was boiling as fighters unleashed hell on their descent attacks, drilling boats and shredding the unarmed, fleeing men onboard.

The atmosphere was a symphony of waves breaking, planes soaring, and men screaming in the echoic distance of the wind-swept, stretching shorelines.

"Jesus Christ!" Macken blurted as he witnessed the beach scene. This time, the padre did not bother to enlighten him of his blasphemy. There was enough of that happening in the disarray of Dunkirk.

"Captain! Out there!" Knocker White called, pointing through the fog of smoky haze that hovered above the water out from the sands. There was another fleet of brave little ships incoming.

It was now nearing 5:00 p.m., and this would almost certainly be one of the very last ferries to the larger naval boats in the channel.

"Alright, lads," said King-Clark as he stripped off his outer layers and laid his rifle to the sand along with countless others already in a gigantic pile of discarded weaponry. "Let's get wet!"

The others all followed, ridding themselves of anything that would impede their ability to swim and weigh them down when wet, and they begrudgingly trudged into the cold waters of the salt tides.

They walked as far as they could into the cold ocean drink, fighting the waves of the rising tide before they started to swim out in the hope of being selected to board a vessel and get home.

1940, June 3
Gravelines
Nord Pas-de-Calais, France

In the closing distance while they rode the coastal strip, Churchill and Hardy could hear the explosions of falling artillery shelling.

It was Dunkirk.

Their worse-for-wear BMW clapped along the Rue de l'Étoile.

A present for Germany left behind by the BEF or French rearguard, the route seemed entirely blocked up ahead adjacent to a small farmstead, so Churchill navigated them onto an incline that still headed towards the city structures of Gravelines.

Churchill recalled from his mental topographic map of northern France that they were less than three hundred feet from the *Grand-Fort-Philippe* located one mile north of Gravelines and, overall, less than five miles out of Dunkirk.

Aware of just how late they were, Jack dared not check the time on his wristwatch. Nevertheless, the lowering sun beaming behind the clouds to the northwest affirmed that this day was piercing the veil unto dusk.

"Captain!" Hardy called, pointing forwards and to the left, into the setting sun over the ocean of the channel. There were dark vehicles arriving from a very north-most sector of France, practically along the highest point of land before the sandy shores of the beach. "Are they Germans? Should we be worried?!"

Churchill broke his sterling stare from off the road, taking in the mobilizing units on their flank for an instant. They were clearly enemy vehicles given the unmistakable stahlhelm outline upon all of the operators' domes picturesquely silhouetted against the dusky setting over the ocean horizon. The names of the German weaponry and vehicles Churchill could also have accessed from his wide and resourceful database, visible before the backlit vista.

Churchill's brow loosened as he identified the portable artillery units parked along the shore, facing them towards the ocean. He had seen enough to gauge their objective as the engineers and soldiers arranged the cannons northwards and out to the waters of the channel, preparing for imminent fire.

He eyed the road and shook his head, undaunted.

The guns were still ahead of them, but not directly in their route, and were clearly facing the other direction out to sea.

"Not a worry for us, at least. Can't say the same for the evacuation boats trying to tug across the channel in that direction, though."

"What are they?"

"Eighty-eights."

Hardy faced him with a look of question at the military jargon.

"*Eighty-eights?*"

"FlaK cannons," Churchill dumbed down into laymen's terms for the journalist. "*Bloody big guns that can shoot really far.*"

Farther out to sea, they could make out some large vessels. They were barely visible due to the falling light and the hovering fog of the saltwater breeze, but there were definitely some sort of ships out there.

They were the evacuation boats of the navy.

They were going to target the ships!

In the distance, the German artillery cannons fired.

The muzzle flashes at the ends of the 88mm barrels of the FlaK-37 cannons were massive and bright, stretching out at least fifteen feet long in bright white and blue exhaust blooms.

The sound travel of the blasts was delayed compared to the muzzle flashes due to the distance from their route of passage on the speeding bike. The reverberation still shook them to their cores as the blast lateral swept the earth in an invisible wave. They were a fair amount away, but they still felt it.

"*Jesus! Shit! Fuck! Me! Fuck!*" Hardy squirmed, uneasy as the powerful cannons sent a force of shock right through his diaphragm. "Are they shootin' at us?"

"Negative. That's out at sea. Huns are trying to sink the ships!" Churchill explained again, as surefire of the act as the 88s were at hitting the boats.

"Jesus. Will they be able to hit them?"

Churchill bent at the neck with a modicum of doubt.

"Maybe ... probably, actually."

"And sink them?"

"If they hit 'em, then *definitely.*"

Boom—BHOOM!

Abruptly, the dirt and grass alongside the back road on which they travelled at blurring speed detonated, booting up smoulder and debris at their edge, causing severe and immediate alarm.

Receiving a mouthful of mud, Churchill swerved, correcting their course before looking over his shoulder at the next contestant who dared to now chase them down ...

... and this time, it was none other than a tank.

Their pursuer was a Panzer III tank with an active forward thirty-seven-millimetre cannon gawking in their direction. The top turret was clearly fixed and targeting them at the front. Whomever was driving the seventy-millimetre-thick, twenty-three-tonne indestructible beast had her in top gear, attempting a chase like a grizzly after a fawn. The Panzer's tracks clacked away at pace, roaring at forty on the speedometer, hastening straight after them and clearly starved for souls to feed on.

"Yeah, okay!" Churchill announced, peeking back. "That one *is* shooting at us!"

"Oh, shit," Hardy cried as he twisted. "Not again!"

"This is getting boring!" Churchill groaned as he twisted the throttle and sped them up, swerving as much as he could without losing speed in order to make them a harder target for the sluggish tank to home in on. He did so, careful to dodge the consistent blockages and debris on the road that could dislodge their small bike—whereas, behind them, the Panzer just ran that shit the fuck over, perhaps hence how it managed to catch up.

Churchill banked into the corner of a small twist in the road right as another shell came sailing their way with a screeching pitch.

The passage of the shell tore laterally through the fabric of reality like an ear-splitting banshee, carrying on and exploding a still-standing French outhouse beyond their path forrader.

They veered around a corner and were presented with another long straight. Ahead was a clearing before a canal, however the area was flat and absent any concealment. The tank could oversee the stretch in its entirety once reaching the summit of this turn.

"Oh, shit!" Hardy shouted as they rounded the bend and started downing a minor slope. Ahead of them on this path was the *L'Aa Fleuve Canalisé;* a one-hundred-and-eighty-foot canal leading out to sea—*with no bridges.*

Now that they were down the slope and out of the sights of the tank for a few seconds, Churchill brought them to an idling hum, where the struggle of the engine was audible. He considered their options, scanning both ways along the canal obstacle on this detour.

"Where's the ... where the fuck are the bridges?" Hardy commented, sitting up in the pod.

Churchill looked far out north and then south along it, unable to see any route of passage before then edgily looking back over his shoulder. Between breaths, he could hear the metallic growling of the incoming Panzer III just behind the hill. He could hear its tracks squeaking and grinding as she came nearer, reloading and preparing to fire the instant they came into view.

"There is no bridge. It's a canal."

"Canals can have bridges!" Hardy argued.

"Well, I don't know what to tell you. Apparently this one doesn't!" Churchill exclaimed, trying hard to keep his composure.

"What goddamn *sludge river* doesn't have a goddamn bridge!" Hardy added, so mad he was insulting the waterway. "Goddamn brown-lookin' shit water!"

"Crab farmers!" Churchill informed, nudging his head inland.

Hardy silently examined, seemingly perplexed at the information as Churchill continued to speak in their peril moment of dire jeopardy.

"Huh?"

Jack jerked his head as he spoke, both informative of local business and dinery knowledge and entirely fucking useless given their present predicament. "That club over there had the best mud crab and seafood Au Gratin in France!"

Hardy seemed reticent before a sudden outburst.

"*HOWTHEFUCKDOESTHATHELPUSRIGHTNOW?*"

Churchill shook his head, deep in thought.

His eyes were of a steel gaze, looking down the length of the canal and all the way down to Gravelines before there was what appeared to be a bridge—and upon it, a convoy of German trucks passing at present. They hadn't seen them yet, but it wouldn't take long, especially if they travelled any further that way.

Seagulls and artillery cannons sounded off in the ambience of the seaside town. Churchill considered all options, leaving him with one possible to get them over the other side ...

"This is ridiculous! We'd have to go the whole way around the town to get over this shit stain!"

"Sit down."

Hardy complied with Churchill's order, and he revved the idling engine whilst casting a look over his shoulder. He did so just in time to see the summit of the creeping Panzer tank break the horizon behind them. Its creaking engine grew louder as it came into view.

He looked down to Hardy in the sidecar.

"Felix."

"Yeah?"

"Do me a favour ... close your eyes for this one."

"What?!"

"Close 'em!"

"Why, so you can perform some magic spell of levitation to get us across?!" he exclaimed.

"No," Churchill tapped the gear pedal with his boot and twisted the throttle in small jerks, revving the bike as he lined them up on the road now *facing* the tank as it crested the hill. "So I don't have to hear you scream when you see what's going to happen next!"

Hardy's eyes were wide as mud crab nippers.

His face was pale as sand.

"... wwwhat?"

Churchill nodded his beret-clad dome towards the hill—towards the tank. "We're going to need a run up to jump that ..."

"A *run-up?*" Hardy frowned. "The tank is back that wa—"

Churchill cranked the throttle!

The accelerative manoeuvre sent them in a semi-circling skid, now aimed straight for the Panzer tank.

"*AHHHHHJACK!*" the American screamed as he held onto the rim of the sidecar for dear life and possibly harder than he had ever done thus far today.

Jack increased speed.

"*WHATAREYOUDOINGYOUCRAZYSONOFA—*"

Baring his teeth beneath his pencil-thin moustache, Mad Jack Churchill held an angry and determined grimace as he fanged the BMW motorcycle directly along the path and over the mound hill from where they had just come ...

... where they abruptly came toe-to-toe with the German Panzer tank. The stifling bass from the powerful engine rippled for hundreds of feet and the tracks crunched with every revolution.

Their little motorcycle buzzed brave and true, headed straight for the rolling German armour without deviation.

He was playing chicken with a tank!

Whilst Hardy cried, Churchill let out a bellowing battle cry as he charged the tank, as if it were a bout of medieval jousting. They stared down its powerful cannon, waging a bet that the gunner wasn't ready for this.

The droning *buzz* of the 4-speed, 22-horsepower, 750cc flathead side valve engine of the BMW-R71 at almost 110-km/h and gaining had nothing in the way of bass and sound in comparison to the 12-cylinder Maybach HL-120, 296-horsepower, 220 kW engine of the Daimler-Benz built, Panzerkampfwagen III medium tank.

The two closed incessantly onwards, where undoubtedly, the crew of the Panzer questioned just what in the world the two men on the motorbike were thinking making an attack run at them like that ...

The Panzer clued on and sighted the bike, slowing in its march.

The 55mm PzGr turret adjusted for the easy kill, bearing not two hundred feet away and closing on a straight.

Squinting in the closing distance, Churchill saw the tank start to react.

150 feet ...

125 feet ...

100 feet ...

Churchill's eyes pierced the veil.

He stared down the tank; stared down the gunner in the turret.

Any second now, they would be fired upon ...

Not yet ...

Not ... yet ...

NOW!

Churchill rolled the dice and guessed that the cannon would take its shot, and it did.

He tugged swiftly at the bars of the motorbike, so hard in the gambit that it caused Hardy's sidecar to lift from the road as Churchill tore the bike left and then sharply right and steady, holding it firm in a scorching drift on a diagonal angle moto-stunt.

This spectacular act happened right as the tank gun fired as he predicted. A blaringly loud discharge launched in their direction, causing all reality to dull into a high-pitched, deafened ring with a quaky pitch.

Hardy's cry of fear drowned out.

The engine of the bike drowned out.

bhoOOOM!

The rushing of the air ...

The tank hum ...

The purr of the bike ...

The squealing of the tyres ...

All sound drowned out, and Churchill would hear his own heartbeat thumping away in his head, listening to his own breathing, staying sharp where all other mortal men would mentally perish.

In an almost inhuman passage of slow motion time pace, they roared a battle cry on the thundering, tilting motorcycle, and it was at that exact moment they slowed to the point of seeming stationary ...

... wwwWHOOSH!

The 55mm armour-piercing projectile shell rocketed past them in a visually warped and quaking reverberation, spiralling in its passage of motion, trailing with extreme heat from its rear ignition propulsion.

At subsonic speed it passed them in a blink, tugging at them with savage motion of passage with such volatility that it even tore the sleeve from Churchill's arm at the shoulder, stripping the fabric and burning the skin of his arm with a gust of powerful air pressure.

The shell missed them by feet, although the kinetic gravity from the wave of the motion towed at their movement with a rough gust of terminal velocity as the projectile traversed the length of short distance, travelling horizontally alongside the road.

The tank ordinance skimmed the surface by inches where, in the far distance, it impacted in the muddy, shallow canal, erupting into a geyser of brown sludge fifty feet high.

After an extended squeal from the tyres, Churchill twitched the handlebar steering and put the sidecar back onto the road. Their momentum bounded, but he regained total control of the bike in a few seconds, just in time to fractionally miss the rolling Panzer tank in a head-on collision.

This, in turn, was all a part of his plan ...

Screeching and jolting as he reclaimed control at such a high speed, the motorbike drifted in a controlled swirl out beyond the tank, whipping them about. This caused the slow-moving Panzer to stall on the spot as it attempted to veer quickly.

The hydraulic turret buzzed to life, panning around laterally to seek its lost prey. The likely reloaded big gun chasing them whilst the driver twisted the vehicle base at the body to change direction. He accomplished this by yanking the right-side tracks into reverse while keeping the left forward, pirouetting on the spot in a loud shuffle of smoke and grinding steel on the road.

Churchill throttled the accelerator and tapped the gears, now headed *back* towards the Panzer—and the canal—this time, at top speed and with the required run-up he desired to jump it.

Too late. They'd given the dummkopf Panzer the old one-two.

By the time the turret of the confused tank reached the 180-degree mark, Churchill's motorbike raced past them, headed east once again. The tank was now aligning in the complete wrong direction. In the confusion, the gunners operating the turret pursued the nimble bike whereas the driver turned put the tracks in reverse, causing the overall alignment of aim to take twice as long as it had to.

"*Whoooooo!*" Churchill cheered, as they sped past the Panzer for a second time. They passed so close they could have grazed its steel side with their fingertips.

Holding the throttle at top speed as they embarked down the slope and towards the canal, Churchill tossed a glimpse down to his companion, Hardy, finding it hilarious that the American journalist had consciously passed out due to the stress of the ordeal--and quite possibly the G-forces. He laid slumped, lifelessly giggling to the turbulence of the travel, dead to the world. Life would return to him any second. Churchill was more concerned with the yank bouncing out of the sidecar than anything else.

"Oi, Felix!" Churchill shouted over the thrashing gust of wind as they sped, keeping his focus on the road. "Wake up!"

Hardy's eyes fluttered as he gasped for air, finding himself somewhere between a heart attack and wanting to vomit. Instinctively, he clutched at the frame of the pod, head back and eyes forwards, still in a daze.

Churchill placed a hand on his shoulder. "Hold on!"

Hardy's eyes focused ...

They were headed at full speed, straight at the canal crevasse.

Hardy screamed so loud it was audible over the bike's engine.

Their bike's speedometer hit the one-hundred-and-sixty mark as they hit the cusp of the canal edge, sending them over the muddy canal.

After a fifty-foot cruise and a six-foot drop, the BMW splashed down into the murky, muddy water passage shoreline. At low tide, they skidded across the opposite side of the canal, still travelling at speed.

The bike aquaplaned, skimming across the surface and shooting jets of murky water up either side, moving too gracefully swift to sink. They were almost the full way across before running out of momentum and beginning to descend in the sludge like it were a waterhole bog. Mad Jack got them through, and the tyres gripped the sediment rocks and pebbles with traction, able to pull through with a sludgy *rev!*

Mouthful of muck, Felix Hardy fully came-to a few seconds later after blacking-out from all the excitement.

He was both mocked and applauded by Churchill, who informed them that they were away and, once again, Dunkirk inbound ...

IX
Run the Gauntlet

1940, June 3
MV Twente Dutch Coaster
Coast of Dunkirk, English Channel

"Come on, lad! Give me your hand!"

A drenched British soldier pleaded desperately as he and a fellow hapless soldier assisted in retrieving another struggling swimmer from the drink, pulling him onboard their cruising vessel as they floated through the debris of harbour. The taxiing ship was imminently about to thrash the engine and abandon Dunkirk now that she was full of soldiers.

After clambering aboard, the soaked Rex King-Clark met Padre Nicholl, Knocker White, and several other familiar faces from the Second Manchester Regiment. The lucky newcomer received a pat on the back and the group huddled, shivering from the swim out from the beaches and to this boat; a ship known as the *MV Twente.*

Almost forty Dutch coasters had escaped the occupation by Germany of the Netherlands on the 10th of May and were requested by the Royal Navy to assist in Operation Dynamo. The Dutch shipping bureau in London was strongminded to comply.

Due to their size and shallow keels, the Dutch coasters were able to approach the beaches more closely than the larger ships of the Royal Navy.

Numbers were not printed, but a tally done by the captain of the vessel calculated that during his multiple voyages across the English Channel, his little boat alone had saved almost a thousand British soldiers from Dunkirk (and counting).

In what appeared to be a Dutch version of the English translation, the captain shouted ahoy as men made way for him to access the bridge of the small coaster. Dressed in a white woollen jumper and captain's cap, the tall, gaunt Dutchman got behind the wheel and revved the enormously loud and overworked diesel engine of the vessel, chugging thick smoke from its aft. It was time to complete his final trip in the valiant joint collaborative evacuation.

The vibrations of the well-worked engine sent a pair of decorative wooden clogs hanging on the inner wall of the cabin to tock together like a tap dance.

Right after the ship captain keyed the engine, an aerial fighter seemed to home in on their locale, breaking away from a formation grid in the dusking skies, aiming to line them up for an attack run.

Diving with speed and velocity, the Messerschmitt fighter strafed the slow-moving ship with its blinking machine guns, clapping to life with a thunderous chatter.

The ocean water on either side of the ship erupted with lines of tracer fire as it sewed parallel stitches across its target. The seawater surrounding the boat spurted like geysers and in the middle, the timber surface of the floating ship became harshly assaulted by the volley. Splintered deck wood and smoke arose from the sudden damage.

Due to the fighter's descending pitch as it plummeted from the sky, the soldiers onboard were aware of the fighter's incoming charge, however the exposed men were unable to run or hide. Bodies were struck by several bullets and debris fragmentation, as was the bow of the ship, including its engine components through a hollow wooden flooring, being shredded in a single pass. In the wake of the German fighter's zooming flyby, the engine of the Dutch coaster hissed and popped, emitting thick grey smoke from her near-fatal wound.

When the zipping wail of the overhead fighter faded into the distance following her pass, the sound of whistling steam and shouting resonated. King-Clark and Churchill's men from the Second Chesters regrouped to assess their casualties, eager to assist wherever and however they could.

Blood now stained the timber deck as wounded men cried out in agony, clutching at elements of wooden shrapnel that visibly protruded from their bodies. Of those who perished, entire torsos had been obliterated where they stood, like bodies built from sand that had a fist thrown through it. Soldiers who had been unlucky enough to be directly struck by the barrage of high-calibre ammunition and were not killed outright lost limbs and whole appendages.

King-Clark and the others laid witness to the chaos that ensued. Amidst all the commotion, something was damaged in the engine room below, and the Twente was currently unable to push off, even at a coasting speed.

"Oh, no," Padre Nicholl remarked whilst his eyes drifted around them. There was so much chaos in this aftermath he did not know where to best start helping.

Knocker White and the others observed the panic of the couple of Dutch engineers onboard as the sea captain blasted orders and demanded a report. There was panicked shouting everywhere.

In a heartbeat, the Twente had gone from being their saving grace to a giant sitting Dutch duck in the chaotic harbour, the airspace of which was filled with looming German artillery or dive bombers and fighters. They seemed unable to get out of harm's way.

A skinny teenager ran a box of greasy, wet tools down to the engine room access hatch where drenched and shivering British soldiers were chock-a-block. They were insistent on repairs, but lord knew that was never a quick process ...

"We're a sitting duck out here!" Gin Parker stated the obvious as he pushed past Wand and Macken, gripping the railing at the starboard edge, watching out over the sea as the same German fighter banked out wide. The Messerschmitt would likely make another pass at the ships in the harbour, and since theirs was starting to give off smoke, they were probably soon to become a likely target for the pilot who longed to see an explosion somewhere in the basin of limp fish in a shallow barrel.

Soldiers who hadn't abandoned their weapons and gear on the beach or in the ocean on the swim over fumbled to dry and prepare for small arms defence against the planes.

Lee-Enfield rifles were raised and fired in retaliation, some misfiring due to wet ammunition or inundated components. A nearby Thompson submachine gun hosed out blaringly loud cover fire as a squad of Messerschmitt fighters rocketed by overhead, presumably unfazed by the collection of sporadic small arms fire, incurring no visible damage.

With machine guns clapping away, the incoming fighter planes drilled more bobbing targets floating on the coast, for some reason sparing them as a target. At least, for now.

"That's not our only problem ..." King-Clark commented. He was the only soldier amongst the lowered heads and raised weaponry into the sky facing the coast of Dunkirk where he was able to make out the fresh establishment of rather large cannons on the cliff face nearest their beach ...

Their immobilized Dutch coaster was *absolutely, positively, one hundred percent* within their target range.

A few heads stopped and turned following his declaration.

Their stares focused on the coastal hills, realizing the same faraway menace right as if on cue ...

... *bom.*

... *bom.*

... bo-bo-bom.

They fired.

King-Clark's brow loosened as his eyes widened.

"*Incoming!*" a fearful British soldier who had also noticed the FlaK-88 cannons on the coast shouted as in the distance the big guns pumped artillery shells high into the dusk sky above the beach.

Fingers of smoke were visible joining the cannons to the trajectory, and the men were almost able to trace the shells as they arced like thrown javelins into the afternoon sky, arcing in their direction.

"*Incoming!*" King-Clark hurled, spinning and relaying the alert, shoving soldiers down to the deck as he, himself, dropped. "*Get down! Get down!*"

With pitching whistles as the ordinance descended, the men onboard the Dutch coaster, as well as all of the neighbouring vessels adrift in the proximity of the smoke-hazed harbour, stooped and sought refuge as the artillery barrage buckled upon them like a meteor shower.

The water on both sides of the coaster containing the Second Chesters erupted in spouts of white thrashing squall that showered upon their cowering heads as they thrashed about onboard. The Twente was idle, but it felt as if they were navigating a perfect storm.

In the havoc of earth-shattering impacts, men violently collided into one another, collapsing onto the deck and against its solid fittings as the waves of the water surface tumultuously gyrated beneath them like a sick ride nobody was strapped in for. Some men were sent flailing overboard after slamming into the wooden deck railings. In some cases, entire crowds crashed into the perimeter barristers so hard that they broke, dropping piles of men off the edge and into the choppy, debris-filled harbour water.

A fellow soldier-loaded coaster in the bay survived a near-miss. A shell splashed down right beside her, causing a nautical turbulence that threatened capsizing. The boat twisted and gyrated, sending a few men spilling overboard and the rest to hit the deck as she inadvertently spun in the water from the sudden current.

A rocking boat in the harbour to the Twente's port-side was struck disastrously by a direct hit from the 88s. The ship detonated from the strike that collapsed her cabin through the roof, igniting something down below, likely the fuel reserve. Some men happened to abandon ship the second they predicted the impact due to the screaming pitch, just as the ship exploded. Forceful flames shot smouldering wooden shrapnel out above the tide in all directions, launching bodies and brodie helmets. The orange fire was a bright contrast to the dull seascape and a hot gust to the cold sea spray in the air.

The brunt had hit directly in the middle of the tugboat, exploding almost instantly and sending limbless, rag-dolling soldiers airborne—that was if the poor souls onboard weren't cremated upon detonation. The secondary accelerant was the diesel fuel. It ignited within the boat as its fractured remnants dipped into the tide, drowning out the screams of those few who survived with rushing torrents of water.

Like ants in a flood, survivors scurried to mount the floating debris only to have it and the waves around them catch alight from spilled oil as the contamination of the accelerant saturated the salt tide. The floating flames soaked the vicinity like some sort of hellish joke, engulfing those who attempted to swim away and trapping those witty few to attempt diving and holding their breath beneath the watery inferno. Those who managed to outswim the fire, imminently started to drown in a desperate, gargling demise.

Aboard the Twente, the sea captain found his feet at the steering controls of the coaster. He addressed his hand, a mere teenager, shouting again in double-Dutch in order to get him to stop cowering and keep trying to fix whatever was wrong with their engine and the reason they were stalled.

They had survived this artillery barrage.

They would likely not survive another ...

From nearby, an Englishman stepped near, informing that he was an engineer and had half a clue enough to help. They watched as he did so, passing tools and showing supportive spirit during the crisis.

"Jesus Christ!" sopping from the fresh shower of collapsing spouts of seawater, King-Clark scowled in distress. He was still partially shielding his ringing ears, looking up and to the aftermath of their neighbour's ship as it burned bright in the bay. He followed all their glances back towards land, where furthermore German artillery began to sound out in the dusking sky. "Sods!"

Time for another round.

An angry and fuming Knocker White rose to his feet beside him, shaking a wet fist into the sky. He spat out his chewing gum and shouted: "*Just piss off will ya! You absolute fucking bastards!*"

The pitch grew as rounds came in towards them.

... they could do nothing but close their eyes and pray it would miss their position.

1940, June 3
Outskirts of Dunkirk
Nord Pas-de-Calais, France

This German artillery crew had orders from the Führer not to pursue any further than along the outskirts of Dunkirk ... but like hell these angry krauts of Hitler's army were going to let the escaping BEF simply *float away* with their tails between their legs.

Establishing artillery and mortar nests along this elevated cliff overlooking a portion of the bay, this squad of German soldiers were quick to install their bulky cannons. The gear was unloaded from the backs of supply trucks, and ammunition piles were quickly stocked so that they could load their heavy, ship-sinking ranged ordinance. They took aim at the aft ends of the exiting ships as they attempted to flee the harbour and beaches, striving to evacuate as many soldiers from this foreign soil as possible before Dunkirk became blanketed by the swastika on the flat of Nazi Germany. There would likely be an invasion come sun-up the following day.

In the British exodus, the German mortar crews would wave farewell the best way they knew how ... *with a barrage of high-explosive shells raining down fire and brimstone.*

The FlaK-88 cannons and portable Granatwerfer-34 mortars were set up in a row along the highest crest of the hill overlooking the downward slope and beach shore, west of the coastal city of Dunkirk. Their weapons were not so much trained on the mostly evacuated city as they were on the boats trying to evacuate the harbour.

Vanity was behind the reticules of these guns, not integrity.

This was a glorified turkey shoot for the artillery team.

Shouting in German, the assembly and fire-teams barked orders over the deafeningly loud blasts of the cannons all set up in a row. Constant discharges erupted, launching explosive artillery in arcing curvatures of trajectories that bowed downwards and onto the ships in the fleeting distance.

BOOM!

BO-BOOM!

The shelling was thunderous, unyielding, and unrelenting.

Whenever there were hits and a boat sunk, there was vast applause and cheering by the cliffside merry Gerrys as they basked in the glory of what would be a victory against the Western Allies ...

... *not one of them from the established mortar crew once noticed the drumming engine of the smoking and spluttering BMW as it slowed into an idle pause two hundred feet along the road.*

On their way to Dunkirk, Jack Churchill and Felix Hardy arrived discreetly behind the mortar crews, creeping like the very dusk setting that helped shelter their advent. Both men were lacquered in grime and sweat.

"Fucking assholes!" Hardy remarked as their progression halted yet again. They had just hugged the coastline from a westerly approach, however enemy patrols forced them inland several clicks before they could angle back to the coast, meaning another timely detour south below communes *Grande-Synthe* and *Saint-Pol-Sur-Merby,* which would have normally brought them directly into Dunkirk. The enemy had already occupied these towns as well and had them cut off like fingers around the throat of Dunkirk: like a strangle victim about to succumb to the fading darkness which crept in along with the glooming shadow of nightfall.

They were out of daylight, out of time, and seemingly out of luck.

The roads recently travelled behind them were full of countless forms of vacated transportation. Bedford trucks, cars, bikes, even small British and French tanks had been sadly forsaken along the routes this close to Dunkirk. It was easy to imagine that all roads leading to the city weren't just as if not more clogged and congested. Most of the abandoned vehicles had been shoved aside and a small path, big enough for the German tanks to push through, had been made between them. Naturally, if the Panzers could not squeeze between cars, it just ran over them.

The sight of so many deserted and abandoned vehicles resembled a rush-hour traffic gridlock, lining the roads to the devastated coastal city. Now, they had hit another wall and this time, they had never been closer to reaching their objective.

This lot of oblivious Germans had their backs turned and their attentions were out over the coast, and the sun was setting behind their silhouetting water targets. Their blinded mental state could be chalked up to them rushing to burn as much ammunition on the ships while they still had a visual and the light to do so. And so, they were oblivious to the motley pair of belated Westerners on their way to the evacuation.

For Churchill and Hardy, this meant that they could have probably sped right on by them, drawing minimal attention and gunfire before downing the immense and exposed slope that led into Dunkirk ... but strangely, Churchill opted against the easy route of passage.

"We should speed past them while their backs are turned!" Hardy advised, low in his pod, glancing up at the fearless beret-clad, moustached warrior at the helm.

"They'll see us," Churchill retorted, taking a moment from watching the blatant slaughter from these cannons on his own kindred in order to consider a more tactful and strategic plan on getting them down the hill and into Dunkirk. These German soldiers would have been the last ones on the edge of the frontline and the city, presuming they would have some sort of small arms instalment set up along the outskirts with the ranged artillery. Although it was an unlikely scenario for the Germans, they would have still set emplacements in effect in case of an attack from the Allies in Dunkirk, most likely machine gun nests that they simply could not see from this current position. Only moments ago, they had heard the unmistakable drone of heavy machine gun fire as groups somewhere hidden opened fire downwind at the city. That sustained fire had to have come from somewhere just out of sight of the slope with a line on the main road such as the supposed perimeter guards.

Even with a fast-moving run of that gauntlet with a speeding motorcycle, and between the sporadic abandoned lorries and various other jettisoned obstacles, one would no doubt discover these perimeter gun emplacements first-hand eventually.

And then, Jack saw them ...

Well hidden, there was a sandbag barricade nest with a camouflage canopy. Two of them; one on either flank of the main road.

His suspicions were now set in cement.

Hardy added, "We should go now! While they're not looking!"

"We will get cut-down."

"By whom? They've all got their backs turned!" Hardy disputed objectively and utilizing a militaristic tone that he felt he had earned over the course of action on his big day out with Mad Jack Churchill. He wore obvious blinkers towards the exciting fact their final destination was within reach.

"By *them*," Churchill pointed over the handlebars of their humming bike so that Hardy could make out the obscured machine gun turret. It was difficult to find, but their air-cooled ventilated cylindrical barrels protruded from what looked like pale tanned bricks of sand or dirt. There was a net tarp overtop of the nest, erected by wood beams and branches that camouflaged them well with the surroundings from any aerial reconnaissance.

"Oh, shit ..." Hardy commented sitting limp, finally spotting them. There were at least two or three Germans in the nests along with the mounted machine gun pointed at Dunkirk. The barrel of that thing would be up their ass if they tried to make a run for it, hosing them down.

Mad Jack was right; if they gunned it on the bike down that last stretch into the city, they would be shot in the back as they travelled, with relative ease. There was no cover to manoeuvre between on the slope and even in a zig-zag motion between the littered empty cars lining the road, nothing could really outrun the 1,200-RPM delivery of the MG34 heavy machine gun. They would be pulverized, no matter what.

Hardy then made what he thought to be a logical suggestion given the circumstances. "Should we go back around? Find another route?" he suggested logically. "We're running out of light ..."

Churchill eyed the bike between his thighs. The choking sound the engine made helped answer that question. The thing was wincing to breathe, and the fuel gauge had been on empty for a stretch already. He advised with a grimace, "Running out of bike, too. She's about to croak at any minute, I fear."

From his sidecar, Hardy stared at the BMW's damaged flank.

The BMW motorcycle had taken a few hits in their haste today. Mercifully for her desperate occupants, she hadn't yet blown up or keeled prior to now. She had genuinely every right to.

"Repairs?"

"No tools to repair it with."

"What if you piss on it again?" Hardy said sarcastically.

"I'm afraid even *that* could be enough to kill the engine," Churchill responded truthfully. The bike was living on borrowed time. He was genuinely amazed that an idle standstill like they maintained now had not been the final nail in the coffin and snuffed out the engine.

They watched helplessly as the mortar and artillery crews reloaded and fired again, lighting up the dank skyline before they reloaded and repeated, relentlessly shelling the unarmed evacuation ships in the distance as at a snail's pace they hauled out to sea, loaded with capitulated and ceded troops simply wanting to get home.

Those men down there were running out of time, if not out of it already ... these guns had too good of a position over them. And to face facts, they were out of time, also. Even if there were some ships left out in the harbour or along the beaches to the east, which he and Hardy could possibly still swim out to and board, there definitely wouldn't be any evacuation waves left by the Navy—not even the little ships would risk it at night and with nil visibility. Especially not now that the Germans were brimming the outskirts of the city, about to bubble over.

After another ear-splitting battery of artillery fire, an unfortunate little ship down in the basin was hit and destroyed.

Hardy and Churchill both bared witness to the deep, echoic destruction of what appeared to be a stout tugboat out in the distance ...

... and then listened to the celebration by the nearby Nazi mortar crews responsible for her demise.

The artillery crews cheered, even embraced before resuming their craven bombardment. The men reloaded and adjusted to the next target, making the most of what little daylight remained in order to pin-point the ships in the harbour.

Hardy glimpsed to Churchill, keenly observing his brooding simmer as his tensed stare seethed and his teeth grinded behind his pursed lips.

Truth was, there was due diligence anchoring his soldierly soul to the scene, gravitating him to the fray. He wanted an excuse to have to stay. To have to fight.

"What's the plan, then, Captain? What do we do next?"

"I don't have one this time."

"Surely you can think of one?"

"Not a good one, at least ..." cocking his head, Churchill breathed solemnly as he adjusted his sideward maroon beret upon his hay-coloured hair. he eyed Hardy in the sidecar. "... but whatever we do, it's going to involve killing some of these gutless Huns on our way through!"

Hardy also jarred his head. "Sounds like a plan to me."

Germany had orders not to enter Dunkirk.

Instead, they surrounded it with a deathly tight chokehold.

The invading forces established two heavy machine gun turrets in nests along the main road entering Dunkirk from the top of the northwestern hill. There were also various hidden sniper nests scanning the coastal city for any movement.

Between the plethora of arms, anything caught out in the open either attempting to gain access to Dunkirk or spotted moving within the city limits would be completely decimated.

The turrets owned the distance between the hill and the city.

It was no man's land.

On the road along the western route, upon the raised cliff overlooking the harbour and western beaches approximately two hundred feet above sea-level was the location of two active FlaK-37 88mm anti-air and anti-tank cannons. Their goals would soon be to lay their shells on Dunkirk itself, however the operators of the artillery squad deemed the targets on the water fleeing the harbour to be more prudent, effectively shooting the fish in the barrel.

Several small two-man mortar crews had set up their Granatwerfer-34 units between and alongside the FlaK cannons and were assisting in the artillery barrage. Meanwhile, from sources unknown to the southeast, long-range artillery continued to sporadically shell the bare city streets of Dunkirk, razing the coastal city and killing any British, French, or Belgian soldiers still withstanding and hiding amongst the ruins—not to mention French residents of Dunkirk.

The thunderous *booming* of the westerly artillery sounded off along the cliff edge, firing barbs of tracing smoke out over the dusk ocean bay skyline where the shells travelled so far out of focal range, they were nearly invisible until their detonation found a target in the distance.

Shell after shell.

Explosion after explosion.

Nearby, two German infantrymen inside one of the nearest machine gun nests struggled to maintain their dutiful attention on seizing the town at the bottom of the slope. Their interests constantly gravitated to the left and at the coastal view, where their comrades were sinking boats like cheaters on a one-sided battleships board game.

Suddenly, the spotter to the machine gunner noticed enemy movement down within their covered section of Dunkirk, and he was fast to notify his partner with taps on the helmet. The German soldier with the buttstock pulled tight into his shoulder, cheek resting on the bipod-mounted maschinengewehr, was quick to react. The gunner regained his concentration and aimed back down range, spying the motion immediately and tracing it with the battle sights.

What they saw were regarded as previous targets to these turret gunners. There were several presumably pinned British soldiers near a cluster of immobilized transport trucks along the outskirts to the city. These north-westerly machine gun nests had seen the soldiers down in the town earlier this afternoon and fired upon them, trapping them inside a partially destroyed house with extremely limited cover. They suspected at least a half-dozen soldiers, all exhausted, out of ammo, and desperate. They had one way out and into the Dunkirk city, which these gunners and snipers had locked down. They were at a stalemate.

This machine gun emplacement was spot-on and tormenting the escapees. Every time a soldier would try to make a run for one of the nearby trucks to commandeer and bring the vehicle closer to get his comrades safely further into Dunkirk, they would get lit up by a devilish drone from the MG34 and spat at with hot pyrotechnic tracer rounds. That was if one of the many invisible snipers didn't drop them with a single well-placed shot without warning.

Having been issued an active target just now, the machine gunner was fast on the trigger, delivering deafening jolts of bright and bass-filled heavy gunfire down the hill into the doorway of the house ruins. The vivid tracer rounds burned bright now that the light of the day was starting to darken, cutting the trajectory like they were laser beams. The sparkling rounds beamed in an arc as they travelled, raking the already chipped and battle-worn stone wall of the home, kicking up dust and grit as gold jagged lines painted the entire area for a few seconds, evidently turning one British soldier into a cooked red splatter.

In a brandishing of crimson gore, the already deceased corpses near the doorframe copped an additional two dozen more fully automatic impacts from after-shoots. Bullets tore across the cold bodies, defacing and shredding the pink and maroon simmering corpses and leaving them literally sizzling due to the occasional low-power pyro rounds the corpses had absorbed.

One could tell these pricks weren't short on ammo.

The Germans finally ceased their continuous fire, and their Maschinengewehr-34 hissed and sizzled for a moment—the exact same instance the two German soldiers exchanged an odd-placed, baffled glance.

There was another noise underlining the echo of their machine gun's drone ...

Something emitting from elsewhere ...

Something coming to a crescendo ...

Before they had a chance to question the identity of that *other* sound, the two contented gunners realized it was drawing upon them fast and from behind ...

At the last moment, a headlamp blinked on from behind them, illuminating them in a blinding yellow radiance.

It was a motorbike!

Charging at them, full throttle!

The 1938 **BMW-R71**—or, at least, what was left of it's scraped-up, shot-out, dented, and damaged chassis—had been given an extended brunt of gas by its rider, essentially revved up and pointed in a direction, and let go. The rider then allowed the fast mover to coast off-road and over a small set of rickety dirt mounds before powering straight into the built machine gun nest, collapsing it in on itself and squashing those inside.

The thing was a missile ...

... and it was locked on target.

Crash!

The weak makeshift supports holding the camouflage netting above their crouching heads in the nest failed under the weight of the hurtling motorbike as it crashed into them. In a display of dust and debris, the bike and attached sidecar abruptly settled on top of the gunner, crippling him with a painful *crunch* against a sandbag barricade wall in a true testament to the stability of the nests' construction.

The German trapped beneath the vehicle's dead weight was not killed, but he wasn't doing too well either, shrieking and wriggling, writhing in a type of pinned discomfort and ache that made onlookers wince. Grasping at multiple contusions, the man fruitlessly, endlessly struggled.

Beside him, the spotter recoiled in shock, absolutely flabbergasted and a little disorientated by the crashed arrival of the motorcycle. In the quick seconds that followed, a million things flashed through his brain. The thought process was prominent via his bewildered expression.

What the fuck is this?

Was it an attack?

Was this an accident?

What the hell had just happened?

Hands up by his sides in shock reaction and with wide eyes as they scanned the incident in search for sense, he watched as his pinned machine gunner's exclamation for help was brusquely silenced with a brutal impact as a muddy combat boot stomped down from off the pedal of the bike and into his face. The boot drove with an excessive amount of force, seemingly knocking him out cold if not killing him with blunt trauma.

The man's crying shushed with a *thwump!*

Paralysed by the shock, the stahlhelmed spotter glanced up from the stamping event just in time to be *run through* by the perpetrator, for the bike rider and combat boot-wearer wielded a double-edged sword blade and extended it thusly through his breastplate.

The German had no reaction. Not one fast enough, anyhow.

The jabbing blade punctured his chest between the ribs with ease, exiting at the rear two inches beneath his shoulder blade. The soldier cringed in distress for an instant, clenching hopelessly with his hands at the sharp metal of the blade as the warmth of his own bleeding leaked down his body. Winded by the act as air escaped his chest, an involuntary cough sent fluid straight up his throat and blood coagulated the corners of his mouth.

Snarling in his conviction, Jack Churchill leant back and retracted his claybeg with a *schwing!* subtracting his blade from the standing corpse and allowing the grey uniformed Gerry to subside, dead or dying.

With haste, he dismounted the motorbike, kicking into action.

"Now, Hardy! Go! Go!" Churchill shouted now that it was abruptly quiet at this machine gun nest. He quickly holstered his faithful sidearm and brought around his longbow from the handlebars. His stare zeroed at the other machine gun emplacement in the near distance, barely fifty yards away. The two men within that emplacement noticed the mayhem and peril of their neighbourly emplacement and were clearly distressed. They were shouting in German, trying to move their heavy MG34 90-degrees from its advantageous position overwatching Dunkirk and use it on these new attackers. They were too late in their resolve.

Churchill utilized a form of fast drawing with his longbow; at this range he did not need full draw to achieve lethal ability.

With an archer's metronome playing in his mind, he fluently snatched arrows from his shoulder quiver, and loosed an arrow—*once, twice.*

Sch-TOFF ...

Sch-TOFF ...

In quick and accurate succession, both the machine gunner and his partner were each struck centre-mass, bowing out with definitive shots that ran them through and disappearing from sight with subsequent folds. Not even at full force from the drawstring, the arrows carried an incredible amount of dynamic force. The bodkin-tipped war arrows were each fired at about sixty percent power, and they pierced the chests of the men, protruding approximately three to five inches out the back end.

With his third nocked arrow on the bowline, Churchill primed his bow down low and beside him as he examined the exterior perimeter for any more enemy targets with a hunter's focus, scanning both nearby and across the immediate hill of the slope where he knew there to be snipers. He was on the prowl, ready to eliminate any hostiles.

This act also covered Hardy, who on the opposite side of their illegally parked motorbike in the derelict German machine gun nest, had managed to heave and twist the large 44-pound MG34 from off its erected tripod stand and lug it over to the west side. He had tipped its portable bipod out as per Churchill's commands, and dropped it now *facing* the coast ... and facing the row of artillery cannons.

They were turning the enemy's gun onto themselves.

Hardy may have physically struggled to accomplish this feat, but he managed under the pressure and inspiration of Mad Jack's motives.

"Captain!" Hardy breathlessly shouted, thinking the set-up to be ready to fire, and he moved aside to let Jack in.

From behind him in the action, Churchill heard Hardy's call ...

... but his instincts led him to believe that this assault was too easy.

Due to a pessimistic upbringing, he was a firm believer in if something is too good to be true, it probably was. There were ditches and established German defences everywhere, albeit most left abandoned by the BEF in their retreats and were now repurposed, as well as a mess of stalled and abandoned vehicles stacked everywhere. Empty cars clogged the roads into Dunkirk as if this were the dusk of Judgement Day.

In short: it was a sniper's delight.

There had to still be another threat.

There just had to be.

The law of averages suggested it, and Churchill listened.

And then ... he saw him.

A sniper.

One hundred feet beyond the left-side machine gun nest at an approximate fifteen-degree incline, there was an abandoned Citroën Traction Avant, a popular civilian transport which had undoubtedly been commandeered by panicking British troops wanting to make the evacuation at Dunkirk by the deadline. Inside the busted-up vehicle sat rather contentedly a German marksman dressed in beyond-adequate camouflage layers. He had his rifle resting comfortably across the dash of the stalled vehicle, with a firing hole punched through the glass windshield, facing the slope decline towards Dunkirk.

Churchill's panning scowl spied him with an eagle's eye in the distance around the same time that the marksman scoped the disruption of the motorcycle ambush attack. The movement of his attempted displacement of his ranged rifle in his elaborate position to snipe them had been his own demise.

Poised in an archer's stance, true and steady, Churchill calmly drew the drawstring of the longbow, hoisting her back and residing at full power whilst the sniper struggled to gain an offensive position ...

The sniper finally adjusted his pose, lining up his rifle out the driver's side window and spying the enemy just in time to open his eye through his telescopic zoomed crosshair—*THWAK!*

An arrow pierced through the sniper scope!

The last thing the sniper saw was a zoomed-in image of the bodkin-tipped arrow sailing straight towards him.

The pointed tip smashed through the glass telescope and travelled the length of the ten-inch tube, exiting at the rear and thus staking the sharpshooter through his open eye socket pressed against the lens.

With a wet, bloody crunch, the arrowhead obtruded the back end of the marksman's head in a brutal thrust of force, probing out the back of his skull like a harpoon.

One thing was for certain ...

He didn't need a scope to see that one coming.

Slithering like a snake, the thin arrow persisted and tugged its feathery tail end through the tubular telescope and then through the same gaping orifice it had pried open through the man's skull, eventually disappearing from sight after worming a hole through everything. On its bloody exit, the entire missile was a shade of crimson, cock feathers and all.

Finally able to rest, the German's head slumped forward after the motion from the trajectory of the zooming arrow had come to pass, tugging at his dome violently before it jettisoned the victim, staking into the earth somewhere superfluous in the backdrop. Blood leaked out of the gaping wounds and through the busted telescope of which he was now resting upon like a straw for his eye.

Now certain they had enough time to complete their objective, Churchill twisted to address Hardy, however the flattened and previously thought-incapacitated machine gunner had managed to wriggle out from beneath their parked BMW and was now an unexpected new adversary. The man's face was complete with Churchill's size UK10 combat boot tread on his face.

The Hun was pretty messed up, bloodied, and probably only half-conscious, but he had managed to retrieve a pistol from his belt with his broken hand and halfway rack the slide—*CHOCK!*

Smooth and cool as ice as he hopped over the bike, Churchill drew and fired another arrow at almost point-blank range downwards. The arrow punched through the soldier's chest, pinning him like a tac to a corkboard to the sandbag barricade behind him, making it rain grains of sand. With a grimace at the fatal wound, the German expired, finally unmoving.

Placing down his longbow by his side, Churchill crawled in tight beside Hardy. The American journalist had done a good job with the placement of the MG34 and had even brought around the chain belt of bullets, raising them above the ground, prepared to feed them to the gunner like he had noted soldiers doing so from his time spent reporting crisis during warfare.

Churchill wasted not a second. He skootched in alongside Hardy and assumed the available gunner's position, taking the buttstock of the machine gun into his shoulder. Craning his neck so that his eyes were upon the sights, he was able to line up their unfriendly targets by the FlaK cannons on the cliff ...

There was a strange pause before Jack pulled the trigger, and Hardy asked him in a casual tone:

"Do you think they have any last words?"

Churchill uttered. "Fuck 'em if they do."

He squeezed the trigger.

BOM-BOM-BOM!

The initial burst from the machine gun was just a test for Churchill to feel the feedback of the recoil and the weighted balance of the MG34. Of the triplet, two were tracer rounds, indicating that the layout for their belt must have been every second shot, which was rather excessive, but the Germans were anything if not extravagant.

Near the FlaK-37s, one of the crew ducked his head as one of the bullets struck the four-inch steel leg of the turret with a resounding *pingggg*. He turned his head in wonder, but had no time to warn the others before the machine gun came to life again, this time taking no prisoners.

BOM-BOM-BOM-BOM-BOM-BOM-BOM-BOM-BOM ...

In as tight a stitch as Churchill could manage with his minimal heavy machine gun training, especially in foreign weapon accustoming, he maintained fire across the row of German FlaK cannons from their blind flank, enfilade-firing perfectly into their line-up on the hill ...

The German artillery crew were suddenly as unprotected and exposed as the British soldiers were down on the boats.

Instant. Fucking. Karma.

... BOM-BOM-BOM-BOM-BOM-BOM-BOM ...

The machine gun chomped down the unsuspecting enemy soldiers, racking them up to the death tally. The blasts of their artillery cannons had been so deafening, and their ears had become acclimatized during the excitement to the ambient volume of the German-made Maschinengewehr-34 sounding off in the background, they barely even knew what hit them before it was too late. They became wiped out like a squirt gun to a row of plastic soldiers aligned a paling.

The Germans were utterly annihilated.

Cut down in a row.

Standing around with their backs turned, reloading or firing the FlaK-88 cannons, transferring ammunition from the pile, they were like weakened autumn leaves in a gust of wind, blown away by the powerful might of the mounted machine gun.

Sparks ignited whenever rounds hit the metal frames of the artillery cannons as the barrage of bullets collaterally struck them in the continuous stream of emphatic gunfire.

Bright golden tracers recoiled and skimmed from the metallic surfaces like blinking pinwheels, bounding off into the darkening sky high above Dunkirk and the coast beyond. Any shots that made contact with meat simply caused the human target to cease existing.

One particular German artillery operator had just handed his cohort a fresh shell from the stockpile. On automatic, he then returned to the stockpile and collected another, like a conveyor belt, harnessing it in his grasp and rotating at the hips, delivering it to the cohort ... only, the cohort was no longer present. He had been deleted by the machinegun volley, and vanished from sight. Just as the ordinance operator's jaw dropped and he scanned for the death-dealer behind the machinegun, he, too, became deleted from life.

Blinded and deafened by the flashing muzzle of the machine gun, Hardy watched on with a taut squint during the vivid barrage, doing his best to refrain from blocking his ears and closing his eyes from what was possibly the loudest, unremitting, and sustained noise he had ever heard. The reverberation of the shooting bass carved through his body, boxing his diaphragm like it were a speedball. It felt like it had ruptured his eardrums.

The journalist managed to help feed the belt of ammunition the weapon required from the nearby ammo box with an open lid, right up until it ran out from his hands like a fleeing cat's tail, finally reeling into the receiver of the MG34. This meant they were out of ammo.

After almost seventy rounds had been spent, Churchill felt as if the weapon was getting light-weighted now—a sensation and instinct only the most trained soldiers were capable of feeling. He must have been down to his last dozen or so bullets, and so he planted them where they would possibly do the most damage:

An exposed crate of 88x571mm HE shells.

What little remained of the ammunition drained into the crate of explosive shells, hoping for a chain reac—*BO-BO-BHOOOOOOOM!*

Comparable to a close-range fireworks display, the ammunition supply detonated in an escalating chain reaction of vibrant, blaring light and earthquaking trembling explosions that turned the dimming dusk setting into broad daylight.

Churchill and Hardy hit the deck, sinking down as low as they could behind the sandbag barricades and to the floor of the deranged nest as the evening sky above their heads flashed a hot, scorching white.

The blast lifted dirt from the ground in a two-hundred-foot radius of the FlaK cannons, as well as knocked two 17,000-pound artillery guns from their feet, heaving them from its positions in tandem. With a lurid and metallic groan, the first twenty-foot gun raised forward and off its perch, tumbling down the steep slope of which it had been daringly set upon and taking with it a few broiled German bodies. It clipped the second, taking it with it. A small avalanche of dirt embarked in their descents, bringing down bucketloads of sand and fiery wooden planks from the ammunition box. A pair of German gunners who had successfully obtained shelter from Churchill's machine gun brunt were sent tumbling from the cliff with the might of the debris also. The tiny screams of their departure could be heard as a pitch between the deep groans and explosions.

The landslide grew exponentially as the wreckage tumbled down the hill, flinging flaming debris around as the larger FlaK cannons bashed into a series of parked transport trucks and countless other abandoned civilian vehicles. A timpani of explosions detonated throughout the vehicles, shattering glass and contorting metal, sending shards of debris for miles across the beach and into the shoreline of water.

The whole event was visible for miles.

"Time to go!" Churchill shouted over the blaring volume of war as the raucous echo filled the atmosphere. He pushed up off the sandbag barricades, squinting through the cloud of smoke that wafted about the machine gun nest.

"*WHAT?!*" Hardy bellowed, holding the sides of his head with both hands. After that stint of prolonged gunfire, he was temporarily deaf as an absolute motherfucker.

"Hop on, lad!" Churchill exclaimed, rounding the awkwardly parked motorbike. As opposed to Hardy, his ears were accustomed to the audial abuse of war, and so he could hear just fine. Assisting with a visual aid, Jack made a motion with his hand before tugging at the vehicle, eventually persuading it to face the road ... *and then he prayed the bugger would start one last time for them.*

With haste, Hardy tucked his knees into the crumpled sidecar one last time.

Beside him, Churchill cranked a leg and mounted the driver's seat of BMW, collecting his war arrow back from the dead German soldier on the floor of the crumpled nest. He used his boot to pin the man's torso firm as he tugged it clear, flicking it masterfully back into his specialized magnetic quiver over his right shoulder. After the events of late, he had only a handful of arrows left in the cylindrical holster.

"Waste not, want not," he commented at Hardy who was disgusted by the glossy red entrails he had seen snagged on the tip of the arrowhead as Jack holstered it in his cylindrical pouch. Once stowed with the others, whatever magical magnetic device was sewn into the bottom held them all in place and prevented the arrows from shaking out of the holder with any erratic movements—a rather ingenious contraption sewn into the base of the quiver.

Using his body weight, Churchill cranked the pedal and torqued the throttle, bringing the motorbike to life ... but she died almost immediately. He did it again, and she begrudgingly started. In response to the mechanical impudence, Churchill revved the engine a lot harder to resuscitate the bike ...

... however, she died again.

"*No, no-no-no,* don't do this! Not now!" Churchill chattered under his breath while beside him in the pod, Hardy used his fingers to try and dislodge the deafness from his ears and try to examine it. His earholes felt like they were clogged with wax or something.

"Fuck me. Is this normal?" he asked seriously, showing Jack red on his fingertips. His ears were actually bleeding.

"Your first time, lad?" Churchill queried with a laugh after taking a two second break from struggling to start the motorcycle—right as bullets from an unknown location loudly slammed into the sandbags of the machine gun nest they currently occupied. The rounds erupted abruptly, thrashing the collapsed emplacement with chunks of debris and action dust from impacts enough to cause them to shudder.

They were under fire.

It appeared to be sporadic rifle fire from somewhere further along the hill that rimmed Dunkirk, from both the southwest and southeast sections of the outskirt slopes. There appeared to be a half dozen more sandbag emplacements along the slope, some of which had enemy forces ducking behind them. Germans who occupied the turrets behind the barricades overlooking the southern side of Dunkirk were now alerted to the incursion on the south-westerly side and the main road, likely due to Churchill's chaos via the noisy detonation and derailing of a series of FlaK-88 cannons on the ridge. It had been enough to gain the attention of every single person around Dunkirk, and the heat was now on.

With absolute aggression, all those within the vicinity opened fire.

"*Fuck me!*" Hardy shouted as a stray bullet hit the side of his metal capsule. He sunk down lower, shielding his head. "My ears still work! I fuckin' heard that!"

A bullet struck the handlebar of the BMW motorbike, causing Churchill to tug his hand clear and impulsively cuss, and he dropped down low beside it as more rounds tore up the area around them like drops of rain starting to fall before a thunderstorm.

"You want to get your dick out and piss on it again?!"

"Fuck that!" Churchill jerked his chin. "It'll likely be shot off!"

Within proximity, more ricochets struck dirt and cuffed against the hessian sandbags surrounding their nest. The metal frame of the motorbike took another hit as well, igniting a flint spark.

"Rolling start! Come on! Out!" Jack fast shouted over the volume as he dismounted, creeping beside the vehicle.

"Are you fuckin' serious?!" Hardy retorted, staying low after he bravely rolled out the side of his pod and was now face down and safe in the dirt of the nest.

More rebounds struck their barricade on the opposite side, severing the ropes used to construct it and causing the top layer to deflate and topple. Bullets split the remaining sticks holding the camouflage tarp above their heads, and the canopy fell on them like a deflating parachute, dropping like a curtain over a view of the dusking sky, just as Churchill's ears pricked to a *particular* audial detail ...

The sound was an incoming pitch, droning, growing louder.

... and seemingly coming right for them.

Fuck the sporadic riflemen fire—that rather large explosion they had just caused on the frontline had gained the attention of a passing German Messerschmitt Bf-109 fighter.

They had been ousted as an offensive, and he was lining them up, starting the pitch for a dive run attack.

High above the harbour of Dunkirk, a single German fighter plane visualized everything down below, and peeled from the formation of a larger group. Perhaps pride drove the captivated pilot, keen on increasing his inflicted tally by another notch before sundown.

"Oh, bollocks!" Churchill swore as the camouflage curtain fell upon them, burying and partially pinioning them.

The pitch of the fighter grew weary as it closed the distance ...

Ominously, the fighter was zeroing in on their current position, as determined by all the shooting beside the burning spot fires of the destroyed artillery post.

At any second, the fighter's deathly machine guns would roar to life, lighting them up and shredding them to smithereens.

"We have to go!"

"Go where?!"

"Dunkirk!" Churchill shouted at Hardy as he revolved around, drawing his sword from his hip within their tight vicinity. "We need to run the gauntlet, or we'll die!"

Whilst pushing the bike with all his might with one hand, Churchill swung his sword in his other, splitting the fallen canopy in one swift motion as he and Hardy heaved the dead BMW out of the nest under the same continuous assault of gunfire which poured upon them from the distance with extreme prejudice.

More so, this was right as the MG-131 guns beamed to life from the incoming Messerschmitt.

RAT-TAT-TAT-TAT-TAT-TAT-TAT-TAT-TAT!

With massive detonations of phosphorus-tipped ignitions intended to contend with other fighter planes, the larger air-to-air bullets from the German fighter crackled and hissed with fury as it drew a bead up the hill, drawing a straight line yonder their position. The rounds literally melted the collapsed nest behind their evasive progression, setting the ruins ablaze with sparks of kindle.

wwwWWHHHIRRRRrrrrrr ...

In a thunderous gust of air, the fighter zoomed over their heads, peeling off into the dusk sky and almost certainly looping to make another pass at its targets.

Pinning his maroon beret upon his dome as the rush of air from the passing airplane tugged at their postures, Churchill maintained a hold of the handlebars with his sword hand.

Like a toboggan team at a start-up, the two men pushed the shaking and jolting bike onto the strait of the road where the declining slope assisted minutely with their motion. Still under constant rifle fire from everywhere afar, they were fast to leap back onto the bike once the momentum of gravity took over, and the BMW began to roll with the slope assisted by gravity.

"Jump in! Jump in!" Churchill shouted, attempting to holster his sword at his hip whilst his legs cycled beneath him. Hardy did so—gracelessly—*head-first* into the sidecart. His legs poked out the top as he grunted and contorted, rearranging himself to eventually be upright.

Churchill lost time in putting away his sword, exposed to more gunfire as he started to lag behind the rolling bike. He had to run hard to catch up, dancing and fumbling twice before cocking his leg up high enough beneath his dangling doodlesack to mount the cycle's seat, and he corrected her steering to be directly in the middle of the road. With small but necessary corrections, he navigated the rolling bike between a group of abandoned vehicles which had been aerated by the previous strafing runs by aerial fighters.

Bullets poured over them like a hailstorm brewing, striking the intermittent metal obstacles, such as abandoned military and French civilian cars along the road, and even pelting into the asphalt at their following tyres with angry crunches of black grime. Some bullets came so close they whizzed above their ducking heads as near-misses, audible in sharp squalls of pinched air.

Growing in potency, the potshots included extended bursts from a submachine-gunner at long range. The automatic fired in their direction, showering them with small nine-millimetre pellets which chipped away in their circumference like firecrackers and ignited in sparks against the sidecar and bike frame. The glass windows of nearby parked cars littering the road shattered all about them as they navigated between the forsaken stationary traffic.

Sparks ignited everywhere at their sides, creating the illusion of a limelight interval which tracked their ongoing, accelerating trajectory.

Suddenly, the raining gunfire directly raked the side pod, causing a lot of wobbly feedback for Churchill as he dodged low with his beret-clad dome, weaving under bullets whilst trying to steer the deadening roll of the motorbike.

The experienced motorcycle driver corrected the bike's course, whilst also now trying to shock the engine on a rolling start ...

After a few seconds, the BMW cranked, and he revved her hard and long, throttling the absolute shit out of what was left of the abused diesel engine as they gained velocity riding down the slope under constant fire. This would be her final bout.

Picking up speed, the straining motorbike chugged thick black smoke, plummeting like an errant missile.

The *whizzes* and *snaps* of near-missing bullets befell less and less as they rode faster down the slope, collecting speed. Now more exposed, the occasional stray round would spank the metal frame of the bike with a metallic *chink* and *thump* ...

... *but now or never, they had to thrive or die* ...

The BMW thundered down the slope, gaining an unprecedented amount of speed into the city right as a heavy German machine gun from another nearby emplacement repositioned to try and better engage the recent Western assailants.

What seemed like another MG34 in the distance roared to life, spewing deathly tracers in chase behind them. It must have been from a nest far off, around a thousand feet, but they still slung gunfire at the moving target, chasing their exposed descent into the city with a light show of warping golden tracer rounds.

Due to the void in which the machine gun fired across, as well as the momentum at which the bike travelled, the golden tracer rounds visibly arced behind their swiftness, missing them and dragging behind the motion. However, the enemy machine gunner gained the distance behind the bike as the course was steadily corrected and put a lead on his aim ...

The bullets were catching up!

The line of glistening tracers closed ...

Closer, and close, and—

"*Captain!*" Hardy shouted as his eyes grew wide. They were coming in hot and fast into the outskirt houses at the rear of Dunkirk city, travelling so fast they could no longer hear the gunshots that sounded in their direction over the volume of the whipping wind current.

It was just then, inadvertently saving them from the incoming machine gun volley, that the tyre burst on the sidecar, and their trajectory tugged sharply to the right like they had a dropped anchor whilst still traversing.

It was becoming apparent that Churchill could no longer hold the bike steady with it attached ...

"Bastard!" Churchill shouted as the wall of tracers overshot them, momentarily ceasing to correct intervals and range.

He glanced down between them whilst holding their rattling circumstance as straight as possible.

Not only had the pod lost its tyre pressure, but the attachment harness had ruptured and was rattling, shaking apart, meaning that at any second, Hardy's sidecar was about to disengage completely from the motorcycle.

The unit shook fiercely at such a high speed.

Their bike was out of control and now snagging right, pulling straight towards a building along the outskirts of Dunkirk city.

"*Hardy!*" Churchill warned as suddenly the pod disengaged, breaking adrift in a wobbly and turbulent track ...

He was losing him!

At this speed, in the blink of an eye, Hardy could disappear from cooperative existence.

"*Jack! Whoooa ...*" Hardy replied, witnessing the disengagement happen absent his control. He was completely and utterly helpless to stop the impending collision about to severely involve him and his uncontrollable pod.

Before Churchill could even think to suggest it, the American stood in the gliding pod, balancing in the confines of the turbulent cart like an equestrian gymnast, and hurdled from out of the car altogether.

He angled his floundering leap towards the bike, aiming to mount it behind Jack like a tandem passenger upon a riding horse.

It was dangerous and desperate, and was one hundred percent what Jack Churchill would have done and therefore expected and was able to receive, and he couldn't have been any prouder of Felix Hardy's ability in that snap-decision.

Hardy hopped like on a springboard, abandoning the sidecar pod— *just as it completely detached in his wake!*

Jack steered in to catch him, and he landed on the back of the bike like a circus act, pelvis tight behind Churchill's seating and he grappled around the man's waist with intensity. He squashed a nut, but that didn't matter. Both men watched as beside them the pod wobbled and shook like a wayward missile launching into a deathly tumble, at the mercy of momentum.

At their side and still travelling at high speed, the sidecar soon flipped and smashed with such ferocity that it literally tore itself apart. And it would have done the same to Hardy, had he stayed within it.

Churchill grasped tight at the handlebars as the weight of the bike shifted now that he had a passenger, somehow holding their balance and veering them back towards the road rather than obliteration. Churchill failed in the action of putting them back onto it entirely, due to the number of obstacles blocking their path. His peripherals caught a glimpse in the only remaining cracked side-mirror, spotting the golden tidal wave of tracer rounds which again trailed behind them from the distant machine gun. It continued to draw closer and closer, closing in—right as the damaged mirror became shaken off its bracket by the turbulence, and dropped off the handlebar into the abyss.

A ricochet danced off the road surface and bit at the rear tyre of the bike, cruelly snatching away traction and propulsion ability in their most desperate hour. The rubber itself soon lost all form and jettisoned from under the rear guard like dark vehicular confetti.

Barely able to hang on any longer ...

They were at the end of their rope ...

Their voices rattled and shook as the turmoil quaked, out of control.

"I cAan't slOow it d-d-down!"

"WhAat DooO you meAN?! Use thE braAKes!"

"nO!" Churchill shook his head, tensing his jaw and baring his teeth as to not accidentally bite off his tongue from the rampage violently rattling their bones. *"We bRaKe, wE diE!"*

With a scowl of confusion and concern while he wrapped onto Churchill's trunk like glue, Hardy bowed a peek over his shoulder. He spotted what appeared like a giant, razor-sharp golden spinning pinwheel of 7.92mm tracers from a 1200-rounds per minute machine gun, chasing in their wake ... *and it was gaining.*

To ramp-up the danger, the German fighter plane had also returned!

Coming in on approach at their six, it zeroed in on their motorbike to make another attack pass on them since they were a convenient and alternate target to the slow plodding boats far out in the water.

This rogue pilot, clearly a Luftwaffe maverick, wanted a moving challenge rather than a sitting duck like the boats in the bay. He had come back for seconds; to see the job through.

The fighter blitzed them with its intense and destructive machine guns from its synchronized MG-131 guns hanging beneath each wing, and striking bullets erupted like popping fireworks on the road behind their trail.

The large calibre bombardment turned the paved road into dust, shattering the bricks as though they were made of terracotta roof tiles.

Churchill's keen awareness for their pending doom predicted the incoming wave of fire as the beam of glowing lead traced their route, and that it would reach them before they reached the cover of the city.

This was it ...

All they could do was hold the course and pray ...

"FaaaAAark! MmeEEe!" riding the roller coaster from Hell, Hardy grunted in vibrating exhale as he held on with white knuckles.

"Hold on!" Churchill shouted, gripping tight and focusing his stare.

Rounds from the machine gun finally caught their chase, chewing away at the motorcycle chassis in an array of sparks and puncturing damages, including striking their last remaining tyre, shredding the rubber entirely. Their bike briefly skated on skeletal metal, chomping into the city's road like an erred tram track, shooting sparks twenty feet out of their rear end.

Through some act of God or a miracle, the vehicle did not pivot and throw its riders, like how physics compelled. Instead, she stayed straight and true, albeit rocky and looming an entire loss of control.

Regardless of its driver's top-tier skillset in riding, momentum kept them stabilized, and a smashing end was inevitable.

They were a comet charging towards a bastion of the immovable.

Bullets slammed into Felix Hardy's exposed leg on the right side, in two areas. One hit near the shin and was more of a ricocheted deflection. The other more crucially, more painfully, hit him in the meat of the quadricep muscle, tearing it open in a spill of red gore through his trouser leg.

Above all of the chaos, he audibly whelped from the hit.

Churchill also took a bullet, to the left shoulder.

Each of them were unable to place a hand on their wounds lest they sacrifice whatever balance remained of their tenuous ride.

For Churchill, the round was a punch full of force, stabbing him deep into the shoulder joint, seemingly with no exit wound. An involuntary reaction from the wound caused him to balk and involuntarily veer the bike farther left, tearing them even further off-course.

In that instant, the shock of the wound caused reality to become all the more real for Churchill. He grimaced in pain, suddenly succumbing to weakness. His skin went pale in the seconds that followed as the surge of the shock overcame him temporarily, and he fought to retain focus.

Somehow, though, Jack Churchill managed to keep his wits about him, preserving what little control he could of the bike with just one arm, as his grip relaxed completely in his left arm, easing his clamped down fingers like an arthritis sufferer.

Hardy roared loud in agony over the rumbling and quaking of the haphazard, speeding bike as it unceasingly picked up more speed, now driving off even road. Logic suggested that at any minute, they were about to tap a ditch and flip out of control.

He couldn't resist the instinctual pull to apply pressure, and his right hand shot out from holding Jack and gripped hard on his leg. Hardy then pulled in tight into Churchill's belt with the other and shut his eyes, clenching his teeth, and holding on for dear life.

All Churchill could do was lean forwards, taking the strain off the wound to his shoulder, and thus not pass out whilst steering them into what would unavoidably be a head-first crash into this incoming building ruins.

At around eighty kilometres per hour and right as the combined chasing machine gun fire volley and fighter plane gunfire would have—and *should* have—finally reached the speeding target, melting them this time, shredding them to raw human ruin, the BMW motorcycle reached the finish line ...

With a clamorous crash, the charging motorbike impacted into the partially cracked wall of a double-storey French house, most likely killing them both.

In an explosion of dust, all momentum and might seemingly transferred into the wall like a battering ram.

The motorcycle and its riders crashed through the structurally unsound wall with a rumble, vanishing from sight into the particle cloud, embraced by stability.

A dead end.

Boof!

1944, September
Sachsenhausen Concentration Camp
Oranienburg, Germany

Felix Hardy nodded as he scratched away on his notepad, leaving no amount of detail undescribed as Jack Churchill dictated them.

Recalling the events as if they happened yesterday, he muttered sarcastically, "Good times."

Churchill also bobbed his head and took a second to stretch out his left shoulder, pressing in the joint with his fingers. He would forever feel the discomfort of the gunshot—a fragment of a German machine gun bullet forever lodged within his tissue.

He could not agree more—though, for Mad Jack, he was sincere in the reminiscence. "Good times, indeed."

Their entry into Dunkirk was a ride neither one of them would forget anytime soon.

1940, June 3
Outskirts of Dunkirk
Nord Pas-de-Calais, France

Whiiiiirrrrr ...

The roaring thrust of the German fighter plane screamed by overhead, lifting and then ceasing the firing of its powerful machine guns after the speeding target it pursued sought shelter, much like a hawk raising its talons after a failed hunt.

In this circumstance, instead of scurrying into the safety of a burrow, this would-be prey slammed into an immovable object at extremely high speed.

There was an audible *boom* and an eruption of dust almost twenty feet tall after the BMW motorcycle crashed through the wall of the partially collapsed building.

The motorbike and its occupants slammed at high speed into the already shot-to-shit stone wall of the French home, causing it to cave-in after their entrance. The wall had already been so vigorously perforated by previous enemy machine gun fire that it had deteriorated to the point of lesion by the motorbike as it travelled like a screaming comet, ploughing straight through the weak structure with about as much resistance as door-hanging beaded curtains.

The motorcycle exploded through the fortification and continued several more feet on its side, sliding to a complete halt up against a second, inner wall. Debris rained and a cloud of thick white dust covered everything.

Inside and to the right of the crashed vehicle, a group of what appeared to be cowering soldiers in brodie helmets, desperate and on edge, drew lines with their armaments on the two men on the bike. The sights of their rifles scanned through the mist of chalky powder as it puffed all around their untimely arrival.

The beret-wearing driver coughed and spluttered, finally lurching up from his doubled position over the handlebars.

A new slit across his brow and the bridge of his nose, as well as a lung full of dirt, Jack Churchill squinted as he straightened the maroon cap upon his head. He brushed particle fragments from his sleeves like some sort of battle dandruff, sitting up straight.

He took a second to nurse his shoulder and assess the damage, pressing the wound as if it were a mere knotted muscle.

An expert assessment of the wound right now was that *he'd live.*

Doubled-over, Hardy stirred just the same, although clutching at the wound to his leg. He was also amazed at how they were still alive—more-so now, being astonished to have a bunch of weapons pointed in their direction from inside this strange new location and apparent new adversaries.

There was an interval of confusion.

The last thing he had seen was a wall coming at them, and a hailstorm of a thousand rounds of ammunition chasing them down.

Had they died?

Was this Heaven?

With an upside-down frown, he clenched in agony at the wound on his leg, amazed at how minimally they had been injured by such a sudden stop. It seemed that the battle-rotted wall had actually worked for them and softened their point of impact. Broken their fall, so to speak.

As the pallid aroma settled in the air, revealing their surroundings, Churchill spotted the immediate soldiers located within the interior of the house. He registered them as friendlies—the same friendlies he had registered being under fire by the machine gun nest he and Hardy had pancaked with the BMW just moments ago.

They were British soldiers!

The dozen men trained their Lee-Enfield rifles in their faces ...

Eyeing them confident and unphased, Churchill managed to make a remark between splutters—his accent would be the only qualification of gaining their trust not to shoot.

"Got the kettle on or what, lads?"

X
No Man's Land

1940, June 3
MV Twente
Coast of Dunkirk, English Channel

Crac-crac-bhooom.

The FlaK-88 cannons atop the cliff overlooking the basin of Dunkirk Harbour exploded in a bright display of hot orange fire. Even across the distance, the heat scorched so blisteringly bright that the men of the Second Manchester Regiment aboard the Dutch coaster in the bay could feel the warmth upon their faces.

"*Whoa,*" Captain King-Clark mumbled beneath the brim of his wet maroon beret. His blonde cowlick wafted in the current of wind brushing across the water's surface.

Ogling alongside him on the edge of the MV Twente, Padre Nicholl, Gin Parker, and Knocker White all gazed in a drop-jawed stare of awe as the glowing radiance of the fireball lit up their faces. All of the Brits aboard shared the same stunned expression—aboard all of the ships.

They had just been saved.

There was a combined cheer throughout the sardine-packed Dutch coaster as the rest of the drenched British soldiers all witnessed the explosions along the row of offending artillery, as well as the chain reaction of smaller detonations as several parked cars along the outskirts of Dunkirk also ignited. Their applause roared louder than a riot as they watched the metal heap of one of the guns tumbling down the cliff in a cloud of dust and smoke and sizzling flames.

They cheered loud and hard, full of adrenaline, for they were alive due to some random act of *deus ex machina* intervention. Whatever had happened, it had saved them.

Some of the men looked to the skies, attempting to sight and applaud whatever god-tier adversary was responsible for the counterattack that wiped out the big enemy guns ... only, there were no Supermarine Spitfire fighters or bombers in the air space ... there were also no battleships in berth of the harbour who could have been responsible ...

Where had their saviour come from?

Before anyone could question it, Rex King-Clark spotted movement out in the western entrance to Dunkirk, and without a word the corner of his lips formed a smug smirk.

He knew exactly who was responsible for their liberation.

There followed some distinguishable small arms gunfire emitting from the coast near where the guns had just exploded. Whoever that distant someone was, they were still in the thick of it.

"Look!" a British soldier shouted, jumping and pointing out onto the hill as he, too, spotted the motion of note. There was a gun battle kicking off, which meant they still had friends on the coast—the same friendlies who had just saved their collective bacon.

"There!" another called, and suddenly there was a flock of men at the aft of the boat, leaning over the railings for a better glimpse, shouting and pointing.

"I see him! There!" another man relayed and, before long, troops amongst the other neighbouring ships still in the harbour caught on, all pointing and examining the distant escapade of some daredevil in disaster.

As one, the basin of onlookers all spotted the speeding motorcycle and its occupants under fire ...

"It's one of ours! It's gotta be!"

Cheering ensued, egging him on.

"God be with him!"

Applause persisted, loud and proud.

"Who is that fella?!"

"Somebody better bloody buy him a pint!"

Rejoice. Utter rejoice.

Amongst the celebrating and suddenly effervescent, jostling crowd, King-Clark cast a glimpse about his shoulders at the familiar men of the Second Chesters. As if caught in the same moment, they each exchanged a gleam of certainty that expressed a thousand words of comprehension.

These men all knew who that was ...

Nodding, they beamed modestly.

After more ovation and positive cheer, they heard one of the hundred soldiers question who it may have been.

"You all know who it is!" an emcee of sorts, the Cockney song of Private Wand announced in a shout to all those within the vicinity of the Dutch trawler. As he addressed them, their cheering momentarily subsided, eager to learn the name and the answer to the question on all minds. "Who else could it be? You've all heard the rumours of the *mad man* ... the *legend* ... well, lads, they're all bloody true!"

This crowd of men were all covered in nicks and scratches.

They were drenched, depressed, bound with rust-coloured bandages. Each and every one of them sported a drained and pale stare of melancholy, that was right up until now when they were suddenly refilled with colour and vigour. They lingered, longing to hear the title of this icon who had just saved them all from certain demise.

"It's Mad Jack, of course!" Wand finally revealed after much suspense.

It wasn't the response he had expected.

"*... who?*"

"*... yeah, who's he then?*"

"That's bloody Mad Jack Churchill up there, innit!" backing his friend Private Macken added with the same ceremonious cheer ...

... and soon after, every man onboard that boat united in standing ovation, pumping their fists in the air of the smoky, flame-lit, turmoil-ridden coastal town of Dunkirk.

Simultaneously, with a chimney stack of black smoke as she struggled, the engine of the Twente revved and coughed to life, finally starting them moving again.

"*MAD JACK! MAD JACK!*" they chanted.

Their coordinated mantra bellowed across the wreckage and debris-littered harbour, throwing their fists high and mightily into the hazy air with a newfound pride and gallantry.

Those aboard the nearby ships even caught on.

They pumped their fists, and their cheering added to the volume.

"*MAD JACK! MAD JACK!*"

King-Clark remained at first without a word to say to toward the incredible feat. An inspirational quote from one of Jack's favourites, Dryden, came to mind, and he finally muttered it aloud for his friend:

"*'For they conquer who believe they can',*" he nodded with a grin, becoming slightly inundated in the wild celebrations of those jumping around behind him. "That's *you,* old boy. *This* is for you."

1940, June 3
Dunkirk
Nord-Pas-de-Calais, France

"Once again, who are you?" one of the British soldiers questioned, only just lowering the sights of his Lee-Enfield rifle. He bore a nasty lateral split across his chin.

An ominous silhouette, he stepped closer from the shadows of the confines and to where the motorbike had just erupted through an outer wall of their refuge, engaging the rider in person.

The crash had caused a minor cave-in of the upper level, making a seal behind them from the enemy vantage points and conveniently protecting them from any further volleys of gunfire, locking them in like a closed blast door.

Now that the identities of these two men had been established as non-hostile, these concealed British soldiers lurking about the dark and enclosed confines of the French home revealed themselves in full. Releasing their guarded stances, they de-cocked the hammers of their sidearms and lowered their trained rifles, retracting to their slumped positions in the depressed dark and dust. Their team of last-minute misfits had been pinned down in this house for some time now, contemplating a permanent residence considering they were unable to safely reach Dunkirk and join the evacuation.

The rider on the bike, a man of mid-height, sporting a maroon beret and a pencil moustache, dismounted the ruined BMW and approached the apparent leader of this group of lost evacuees with the upmost pleasantry in this moment of despair. A fresh bullet wound lacquered the shoulder opposite the one sporting a leather quiver full of feathery arrows.

Masking a wince of pain, he extended a hand.

"Captain Jack Churchill. Second Chesters."

The man with an ugly, deep gash across his chin, said with a raised brow of wonder. "A *captain?* This far back in the evacuation?"

Even as a mere corporal from some sort of infantry outfit, his question stood to reason. Why would someone of such high rank within his majesty's army not be among the first transports back across the English Channel days ago?

With that resolve, the corporal shifted his view and took in the appearance of the civilian in the background as Hardy attempted to dismount the crashed bike. He did so in a hobble, noticeably wounded, and showing it through a grimace of agony. This was unlike Captain Churchill, who acted as if the bullet lodged in his shoulder was a mere stain on his uniform.

"Yes, well, any *good* captain is the first on the battlefield and the last off it," Churchill stated with certitude.

"Sir, you've been wounded ..." interrupted a soldier from the vicinity.

Churchill assessed the gunshot wound as if it had just only now been brought to his attention. Confused by the captain's unconventionalism, the corporal did not shake his extended hand, but rather bypassed the gesture in order to imply sympathy towards the injury. "Medic?"

"Nonsense," Churchill remarked discerningly, waving them off. "'tis nothing but a graze."

"But ... you're bleeding, sir?!" the corporal added, once again stuck on understanding this fellow. Ignoring his nonsense, he called, "Can I get a medic over here, please?"

"I haven't the time to bleed today, I'm afraid."

"Fuck that, I do! Medic, come here! Hey, medic, over here!" the American cussed desperately as he limped on his favoured leg. In the foreground of them all what was left of the BMW-R71 fully collapsed and its front tyre trundled off the axle, completely wrecked and steaming. She had endured a valiant run carrying them back to the frontline.

Churchill and a few of the others cast it a glance as the bike caused a ruckus one last time as she finally let go and collapsed amongst the rubble, smoking and dead.

"Rest in peace, old girl," Churchill solemnly remarked. The verbal semblance was rather odd to those in the room he had just met. He returned his attention back to the present, making the introductions. "I beg your pardon, where are my manners. This is Felix Hardy, a journalist for some chip-wrapper back home ..."

The men assessed Hardy, who took a second between grimaces to at least force a respectful nod gesture in their directions.

"He's a Yank but don't hold that against him ..." Churchill added in whisper and a wink, but then immediately felt bad, and stood up straight with his gaze cast upon the American before the British soldiers. "Hardy by name ... seemingly hardy by nature, it appears."

Hardy's face met Churchill's.

He nodded, appreciatively.

The corporal remained perplexed—at their entry, at their situation, their askew mindsets on the present situation and overall debacle of missing the evacuation, but especially at Churchill's attitude considering just how screwed they all were. They were hanging by the skin of their teeth and his sense of jubilance about it all was received without appreciation.

"Um, yeah, okay ... I'm Corporal Jim Hill, 4th Infantry," the soldier finally identified. "Sorry for the surprise, Captain. We, eh ... we weren't expecting to see anyone else make it *this* far, *this* late. Even most of the French that made it in behind our boys are trapped in the wake of scattered ruins. No other elements of rearguard can get past that new

German perimeter. They've propped up a fence around the whole coast. Even we thought the gates to Dunkirk were closed ..."

"Oh, they are. The net has indeed been cast, Corporal, *Hill*, was it?"

"Sir."

"What seems to be the hold up here? Why aren't you lads at the docks waiting to board a vessel out of this impending doom?" Churchill asked as he pivoted, taking in the numbers of those occupying the home as a medic briefly saw to Hardy's wounds.

There were around fifteen to twenty men inside the dimly lit house, most of which appeared to be treated for wounds of varying intensity, wrapped in white bandages. It was as if they were once a mobile triage station long since left behind. There were a few immobile on stretchers, almost all with bandaged or splinted limbs—some of those limbs were even missing, now enfolded to stubs and tied off in dressing wraps. About four of the soldiers upstanding were not combat fighters, they were combat medics who had taken up arms, evident by their red cross insignia on both their arm bands and painted helmets.

Churchill put the jigsaw pieces together before Hill even had to show the rebus. The deserted row of trucks crashed and collided outside may have been a part of a medical convoy, bringing troops in from outskirt areas for the Dunkirk evacuation. On their late entry to city, they had been snagged by the built-up abandoned vehicles blocking the way and then pinned down by the enemy whilst trying to move the wounded. The outskirts of the city were as close as they could get—possibly ever.

"Sir?" Hill asked as though it wasn't obvious enough. He was still rather thrown by Churchill's sprite attitude on their whole situation. He had noticed the quiver of arrows on his back and watched as he collected a longbow from the bike wreckage. There was a sword on his hip, also. The contemplation of asking him which outfit he was a part of arose, as Hill didn't realize the army still had an archer regiment.

Hardy had two bullet injuries to his right leg, of which the top one was the worst. As a 4th Infantry medic attended to him, Churchill assessed his own situation, as he had felt an impact across his shoulder blade during the crash. He delicately removed his arrow quiver from over his head.

Disarming for a munitions check, Jack removed the final remaining arrows from inside the quiver. Due to the violent crash and bullet hole, many were broken. Some shafts were even shattered wood splinters, and he shook their twig remnants from the leather housing. The majority of his munitions had been spoiled.

"A tragedy," Churchill breathed as he partook the damage. He seemed more interested in assessing his belongings and the harm done to them than that done to his own body.

In amongst the remnants of his medieval ordinance, there appeared to be but five good arrows left.

"*Ah, fuck,* watch it, *ahh-haahaa!*" Hardy whinged as the medic tore his pants in order to assess the wounds.

"Hush now," the medic shooshed.

"Yes, Felix, *hush!*" Jack reiterated with a mischievous tone.

Searching his medicinal bag for supplies, of which, the duffel bag seemed exceptionally light and near empty, that same medic evaluated, "Lucky, I don't think the leg's broken. The bullet passed through the meat."

"See, Felix," Churchill remarked. "Just a graze!"

"A graze?!" Hardy exploded.

"I'm out of dressings ..." the medic informed. All the bandages he and his colleagues had were currently on the other wounded soldiers in the room. They had no more field dressings left.

"Here," Churchill said, taking a second from assessing his arsenal and tearing the shredded remains of his torn sleeve that had been undone somewhere during their war run and handing it in ribbons to the medic.

Hardy squirmed and shifted but the medic forced the khaki makeshift dressing upon him, tying it off tightly.

Churchill brought up a sixth non-fractured wooden arrow and assessed it. The bodkin tip of the war arrow had been broken off on this unit. In total, a half dozen functional arrows survived the crash. One was without its bodkin-tipped head, but it may still prove useful if Jack had time to fashion it into a point.

"There's a countdown, Corporal. You boys are late to this party—even later than us, which I didn't think was possible," Churchill finally elaborated to Hill, back on topic and noting the soldier's perplexity regarding the topic of the evacuation. "Your lot have reserved seating, but those ships won't wait around."

"Of course, sir," Hill retorted, assisting a struggling soldier nearby redo a bandage around his injured forehead.

"Who is in charge here?"

This corporal could not possibly have been the head of the hierarchy. Following the question, Churchill stood up straight, now carrying his longbow and arrows back in their quiver. The men all took in the sight of him; of his current armament as well as the sword holstered at his belt. Unquestionably, they were all a little bewildered at the sight of Captain Mad Jack Churchill.

"4th Infantry ...?" Churchill introspected for a moment, eyeing the floor of the dark and dusty structure. "It had better not be that *Collins* bellend, from Wiltshire? That guy was about as authoritative as a wet fart that followed through."

The decision Sergeant Collins of the 4th Wiltshire Regiment had made to leave L'Épinette undefended in the eleventh hour of an enemy advance still left a bad taste in Churchill's mouth. Orders were orders, but logic and common sense should have prevailed for that man, and seemingly his negatively received judgement calls weren't exclusive.

Hill responded, adding in-kind. "No argument here, sir. But our CO wasn't Collins. He and his unit are probably halfway across the channel by now. He ... sort of, left our guys behind ..."

Churchill scoffed. "You're pulling my leg?"

"Afraid not. The wounded were slowing down his mission ..." Hill expanded. "Like you said, those ships aren't waiting around. And he wasn't about to miss out on his medal. He took their guns and gave them a white flag to wave."

Churchill was without a word to say.

He suddenly felt for Hill and those stragglers that he had been cursed with escorting to the evacuation. Moreover, he felt like a bit of a dickhead for having acted slightly egotistic towards their predicament.

"*That* was our CO: *Sergeant Briggs*. And *that's* our second-in-command, *Dalton*, out there by the first truck, in the mud, dead."

Churchill stepped over so that he also could see outside via the hole in the wall, past the rear doorway that had been chipped and riddled with holes and scolded by the machine gun nests up the hill. He saw the two dead bodies between their building and the rear end of the parked convoy of trucks. The commanding soldiers had been gunned down as they attempted to commandeer one of the transport trucks to get the wounded out in a last-ditch effort.

Churchill's eyeline dropped.

He felt like a real dickhead now.

Hill articulated with a due sense of sarcasm. "So, blimey, sir, I guess that puts me in charge then. Unless you wanna assume command, which by all means, please do ... because I don't know how the bloody 'ell I'm gonna get everybody out alive past this point. Leaving the wounded is not an option for me. I know some of these kids. We been through a lot of shite together."

In the pause that followed Hill's inspirational speech, Churchill nodded glumly.

He was modest enough to admit when he was wrong.

"Of course. Apologies, Corporal."

The reticence that followed assumed that Hill granted Churchill such, and the battle-weary corporal continued telling his tale with sombre detail.

"... Briggs got cut down trying to get the rest of the wounded out. Dalton got hit trying to get back to a truck to get us transport out of here. We need at least one functioning transport to carry this lot out, some of them can't walk or even stand. But I've got a feeling none of those engines will turn over after the grinding those machine guns gave 'em. Those bastards literally melted through each bonnet with that sustained fire."

"Bollocks," Churchill turned and faced the men in the room. He had paid note that even though most of them were from the 4th, there were several stragglers Hill must have collected on his retreat from several random units left behind. These men were a direct result of combat loss.

"We're at a logjam, Captain. We can't get out of here without being shot at by those nests. They have a clear line of sight from advantageous positions presenting overarching lines of fire. If the machine guns don't cook anyone they see fleeing, the snipers will pick 'em off ... Oh and, before I forget, if you take a step around that next street corner into the city, the French rearguard will light you up thinking that you're a Gerry finally invading the city."

Churchill's brow fluttered.

They were caught in the eye of a perfect shit storm.

"We're out in *no man's land*," Hill concluded. "Every man for himself."

Quietly, Churchill acquiesced, now fully understanding the stalemate of this new situation. This had evolved greatly from where he was ten minutes ago; out of the frying pan and into the fire.

Hill furthered, "We can't retreat ... We can't advance ... And we're too shot-up to try either avenue without falling apart. We took a vote after Dalton died; the krauts aren't far off a total invasion of Dunkirk now that the last of our boats are bugging out. By the time night falls, they won't risk return voyages for anybody remaining. When that happens, the Germans will move in and secure the city. We're going to wave white flags, let ourselves be captured along with the frogs in town."

"*Let yourselves be captured?*"

"To hope for the best is all we have left."

The surrounding men were as much in a functioning order to hightail it out here and make a run for the harbour as Jack Churchill was inclined to leave them for death or capture. It was a beautiful yet torturous paradox.

Their last remaining position regarding surrender was unfortunate but true, and night had already begun to fall. Regardless that they were out of time, Churchill could not give up nor could he leave a man behind—not even mentally in his decision-making process.

"Corporal ... time to trade that skirt for a kilt."

Hill gulped, not expecting a shout of discipline right now.

"Excuse me?" he wobbled his head, confused and a little on the defensive backpedal.

"We all know the field we're playing on, and we all know what can happen in the course of a contest. You lost men, Corporal, and I get that. You lost morale, I get that too. If you were unprepared for all the potentials in this game, then you shouldn't have stepped foot on the field in the first place."

Hill shook his head.

This was preposterous, but Mad Jack Churchill was not finished with this pep talk yet.

"You need to bring this *home*, Hill. Bring *them* home. It's your duty as their leader, understand? You can never stop fighting. Otherwise, in this game ..." Churchill bobbed at the men behind him. "They're already dead. You're already dead. You all saw the genocides on the roads on the way in ...?"

Hill nodded, recalling the scenes.

"These Huns aren't accepting surrender."

"Captain?" Hardy questioned from the floor, propping himself up into a standing position. Judging by the tone of his voice, he didn't seem too enthusiastic about taking the risk of trying to carry anyone else across the finishing line. After he failed to elaborate, Churchill stepped in nearer for a more confidential discussion between them where Hardy added in a whisper, "We're so close here ... maybe we should just, y'know ... go."

"We can't just leave them," Churchill replied, giving Hill time for that boost of confidence to sink in. "I can't."

"They've made their choice! They wanna wait and surrender—and that's fine. You have to play the cards you're dealt, right?" Hardy argued after Churchill had already turned around, examining the wounded. A few prying ears were privy to this open air conversation; however their absence of disapproval only cemented their standing to surrender to the enemy.

"Captain? *Jack?*"–*the use of his actual name causing Churchill to acknowledge Hardy*–"We don't have time for this repartee! Let's *go!* Let's *get out of here* while we still can!"

"Felix, *wheesht!*" Churchill scolded like an old Scottish mother, then turned to face Hill and the wounded men of the 4th Infantry within the shadowy dumps of the vicinity. Hill and one of the medics had a quick discussion of their own, and now Jack was awaiting a response.

"So, what do *you* say, Corporal? This could be your last chance to be truly brave. You're already in the deep end, we all are ... the question is, do we *sink,* or do we *swim?*"

From the crowd, Hill faced him. He clearly had nothing specific to say ... but he was at least open to suggestions.

Hill eyed him exhaustively, soaking in the rays of positivity that Churchill emitted like a macho pheromone.

"You're the captain, Captain."

Churchill smirked, proudly assuming command.

"Fine-o-fine."

1940, June 3
MV Twente Dutch Coaster/ SS Mona's Isle
Coast of Dunkirk, English Channel

Out to sea ...

Having finally reached the mothership and moored, *the little Dutch coaster that could* currently bashed against the ballast side of the taller armoured boarding vessel known as the SS Mona's Isle during a rough tide. Her and a great many of her larger brothers and sisters were cruising in holding patterns just out of artillery range of the Dunkirk coast, on the cusp of the English Channel.

The Mona's Isle was at full capacity now that the Twente and several other little ships had returned from their ferrying voyage bringing soldiers aboard, and soon it would be time to return to Dover via the preordained passage of route Z.

"Who is in charge?" King-Clark called as he pressed the crowds aboard the top deck, still sopping wet along with all the other men currently disembarking from the lower harnessed Dutch Coaster and onto the larger Royal Navy Mona's Isle.

There were literally over 1,500 troops onboard the navy ship. Saying that it was *packed like sardines* was an understatement. Men were up on the railings, hanging from masts and even up along the bolt rails of the twin smokestacks looking down, not to mention the entire interior was stacked wall to wall. Men even filled the hanging raised life preserver boats and even hung from their cranes for the voyage, wherever there was space.

King-Clark questioned again raising his head above the masses, barging through the horde of sailors and soldiers alike. Tailing him from off the coaster were the others from Churchill's section, such as Padre Nicholl, Knocker White, Gin Parker, Wand and Macken.

Wading through the crowd of army men, King-Clark halted on his warpath after discovered a pair of uniformed sailors. He raised his voice, cutting above the bodies. "You there! Who is in charge of this vessel?"

"A gent named *Dowding*, sir," a seaman replied.

"Where is he now?" King-Clark hollered, peeking over many heads to address the fellow. The sailor replied with a finger at the raised compartments which housed the bridge as a blinding white searchlight upon the bow brushed over the domes of the overcrowded soldiers.

King-Clark and the *Merry Men* of the Second Chesters pushed past the evacuation mobs on deck as well as those clogging the thin staircase. They upped metal flights, gaining access to the bridge of the ship where there were slightly less bodies but a more intense atmosphere.

"*Oi, boarders aren't allowed on the bridge!*" from the flank, a loyal sailor sternly advised, placing himself like a bouncer in the hatchway. He physically pacified King-Clark, preventing him from entering any further with a hand across his chest.

"I'm looking for a man named Dowding?"

King-Clark's question resonated for an extended moment.

"I'm John Dowding," a man in a raised neck woollen jumper responded. He was wearing a naval captain's hat with his arms crossed, brooding upon the nightscape view of open northerly waters. He stood focal amongst the other navy soldiers around the bridge who were manning radios or control consoles. A minority of those standing held binoculars by the saltwater frosted glass windows, scanning the dark horizons.

"I am Captain King-Clark of the Second Manchester Regiment," he informed for what it was worth, designating his place in the pecking order. That chain of command didn't seem to exist onboard the ships of the Royal Navy, let alone during the evacuation. The ladder of military hierarchy had all been excused.

"Congratulations, Captain," Dowding replied with haste, well knowing what this officer was about to ask: a question, which would in some way, shape, or form, deviate from his own order to some degree, hence his reluctance.

King-Clark seemed a little miffed at his management.

He exchanged a look with the sailor blocking his path, not overly making an effort to retaliate right now on the implied mistreatment.

Over his shoulder, the noses of Knocker White and Padre Nicholl peaked, intrigued with the operations of a bridge. This was all new and uncharted waters for them, lest they ever get the chance again to witness an active naval command.

"Is there a reason you are intruding on my bridge?"

Breathless from the flustered search and race to the command centre of the Mona's Isle, King-Clark persisted, choosing to overlook Dowding's arrogance and tone for the time being. "Yes, sir! Did you happen to see or hear the artillery cannons along the coast?"

"I saw them be destroyed, yes."

"Yes, good. The man responsible for that ... he's coming into Dunkirk *now* as we speak!—"

"No."

"*As we speak,* sir!"

"No, Captain!" exclaimed Dowding whilst shaking his head, already predicting where this conversation was headed. He took a sudden stride across the bridge and closed the distance of King-Clark to address him face-to-face in the hatchway. "I know what you're going to ask, and the answer is *no.*"

Emphasizing his resolve, King-Clark pressed against the firm security of the sailor guarding the doorway.

"We have got to go back!" he pleaded, watching as Dowding lowered his face and turned away, halting before entering a doorway leading into another part of the ship. The corridors were tight and packed full of soldiers leaning on walls, smoking, talking, wrapped in blankets and shivering.

"Captain!" King-Clark shouted with desperation.

"Absolutely not!" Dowding returned fire, matching his shout. It appeared that this naval captain had been wound just as tight as he was. "I need to get this ship moving! I need to get these men home!"

"I agree! I'm asking you to wait ..." King-Clark proposed. "I'll go back in a little ship and get him, then meet you back here! Where it's safe!"

"Nowhere is safe!"

King-Clark huffed, eyeing the naval captain.

Dowding said nothing, hearing him out.

"Give me an hour!"

"*Only an hour?!*" Dowding scoffed, humouring King-Clark from his posture halfway through the connecting hatchway. Truth was, it would take about that to get the ship moving under all this weight. "Mark the time, Captain. We're already several hours past the deadline. I've got orders to return to England when the ferrying ships return, and they have. My men and I have been dodging submarines, fending off aerial attacks, and weaving through surges of artillery shelling for over twenty-four hours straight. It's time to bring all *these men* home."

"And I understand that, but—"

"No, I don't think you do," Dowding called him out, terminating his exodus through the doorway in order to fully address King-Clark and the others trailing behind him. He stepped up close, staring him in the eyes. "Let's get one thing straight if you want a lift home with them, I am the captain here. You do as *I* say ..."

King-Clark exchanged a low glance with the Second Chester men within the close corridor. Where men like Gin Parker and Padre Nicholl were reserved and submissive of the naval captain's orders, men like Knocker White, Wand, and Macken wanted to defiantly punch him in his melon head. It itched them below the surface of their resolve.

"If your Godsend of a mate is still in Dunkirk, then his time has already run out. May the Lord have mercy upon his soul," Dowding added with slight remorse for his harshness. "I appreciate what your fellow did along that coast. I really do. We all do. But we can linger no longer ... it is time for us to go."

They all watched as Dowding finally disappeared through one of the many doorframes in the dimly lit interior, and they reassessed their situation.

"What do we do?" Nicholl questioned in a harrowing tone, not prepared to give up yet. Clustered in close, none of them were.

"What *can* we do?" Knocker White shook his head, deep in thought. He looked to Gin Parker, who was also still surprisingly keen on saving their treasured Captain Jack Churchill, even just for the sake of honoured veneration.

A few seconds of silence passed, and the men looked about themselves and about the ship and its unsystematic array of passengers from all walks and ends of the BEF.

"We're asking the wrong question," clued King-Clark, coming to life amidst their huddle. "The question is *what would Jack do?*"

He pushed past them—an idea on the tip of his brain.

The men all exchanged a glance before shrugging and squeezing through the gaps, following King-Clark through the crowds, the group headed back towards the lower decks ... towards the moored boats ...

1940, June 3
Dunkirk
Nord-Pas-de-Calais, France

Now with Corporal Hill and the majority of his able men seemingly onboard with the idea to move out to the coast, Churchill properly evaluated their situation to formulate a plan. God knows they'd need a good one to get everybody out alive—to smuggle everyone out of purgatory past the devil.

The semi-destructed home which the medical convoy had taken refuge within only had the one entry or exit via its exposed southern side. Through a connecting room, a wall had caved in due to artillery shelling by the enemy, probably long before they even sought shelter within the French cottage on the edge of the city of Dunkirk.

Churchill did a head-count.

There were eight heavily wounded soldiers who needed assistance, two of which were unconscious and required direr medical attention of a hospice grade in order to survive any movements whatsoever. Four of the wounded who were wrapped in squalid blood-dappled bandages were mostly coherent, but nowhere near close to being combat efficient. There were four medics, undoubtedly with minimal combat training, and Corporal Hill. Then, there was Felix Hardy, who was wounded *as well as* combat inefficient.

The odds were not in their favour.

In their position along the outskirts of town, they had no able vehicles within reach and no real safe avenue leading them north towards the Dunkirk coast, where the evacuations *may* have still been leaking out across the channel. But, honestly, Churchill had glanced at his watch several times since, noting that they were so far into what could be considered *overtime* that if there was a chance of them making a craft across the drink, it would be due to that vessel's own delay ... otherwise, everybody would—and should—be long gone by now.

"... the engines are most likely dead," Hill informed from over Churchill's shoulder as they rounded a few dark, caved-in rooms at the side of the dusty war-torn house, managing to worm beneath some partially collapsed structural supports. This gained access to a bedroom which housed a window overlooking some of the other vehicles from the derelict Bedford convoy out on the street. The first truck contained two dead soldiers in its cabin; they had been shot dead by an enemy machine gun on their entry into Dunkirk. The hood and sides of the truck had been punctured by heavy machine gun fire which tore holes through the metal cassis. The truck convoy had been lucky enough as it were to have trundled down the hill and still manage to stop short of crashing down by the houses the way they did, not to mention unload the wounded in such a timely fashion whilst under fire, further losses notwithstanding.

The rear truck trays were loaded with several other departed souls; those who had probably survived as casualties up until the enemy had lit them up on their escape like cutouts from target practice.

"Good God, lad," Churchill breathed, taking in the horrible sight and gathering a better understanding of the hardships Hill and the medics, and the wounded soldiers, had faced in getting as far as they did.

"Our numbers in the convoy were originally up around the thirties ... and then the Gerry machine guns cut us off. Bastards set up nests right outside the city limits, just waiting for straggling units to lure in."

"Yes, we met a few first-hand."

"Apparently the defences killed hundreds of French soldiers upon their retreat and rounded up thousands more in camps north of here. There's still a large portion trapped within the city streets, unable to make the evac ... pinned down ... and now, likely deserted to the Gerry engulf," Hill eyed Churchill. "Like us."

"Poor bastards," Churchill muttered. The British had, in many ways, fallen down in their support of their ally. As far as Operation Dynamo went, the French were not even informed of the evacuation until the eleventh hour. By then, the venue was clogged with the armies of the BEF. The ships, too. Most of the French did not make it past the German ordnance which invaded the land at the speed of wildfire. The ones that were fortunate enough to make it into Dunkirk behind the British were now stranded without direction or transport. They would hide out in the ruins of the harbour only to become eventually captured or killed by the Germans when the forces entered Dunkirk ... which would likely be at first light.

"We should have seen that the Germans were ahead of us ... we should have *expected* it, but we ... we could see the ocean ... we could smell the saltwater. We were too glad to be finally out of harm's way that we let our guards down and gunned it towards the finish line. We had tunnel vision."

Churchill took a breath, imagining the scene; they had trophy eyes, rushing like a rugby forward to the try line, as if nothing else mattered. Regrettably for them, the Germans were utter cunts, and knew no bounds. Their tactics were tasteless and merciless. They slaughtered prisoners of war, the wounded, as well as innocent civilians. Right now, Jack could not hate them any more than what he already did, but no matter what, he could still upkeep a sense of honour for, at the end of the day, not all Germans were *actual* Nazis. He prided himself in staying humble of that.

However, in 1940 Europe, and at the tip of the vanguard, most of them appeared to be.

"Relax, Corporal," Churchill comforted. "You could have been *on guard* and those MG34s would have still turned your trucks into Swiss cheese all the same ..."

Churchill pressed his face against the windowsill, eyeing as far as he could up the cobblestone street and into what had now become the ghost city of Dunkirk. It was hollow and haunted as its eerie smoky haze suspended over its partially war-torn streets. The only echoic ambience was comprised of distant gunshots and bass-hungry explosions, the occasional reverberation of a mortar detonation, and the shaking earthquakes of multi-storey houses collapsing to ruins somewhere in a neighbouring street.

In the obscure serenity, Churchill's stare found a partially buried vehicle up ahead: an armoured, heavy vehicle. It was familiar, one of theirs.

"Whose tank is that?"

"It wasn't with our convoy," Hill informed and elaborated his intelligence findings regarding the busted and partially buried cruiser tank on the corner of the adjacent street. "It was already here when we stopped short. It's driver and gunner likely ditched during the evac ..."

Churchill eyed it curiously.

Half a building had fallen on the beast, pinning it like a crab in the sand protected wholly by its armoured shell, but trapped under the immense weight rested upon it. It was entirely probable that whoever was manning it for the rearguard bailed at the first sight of insolvency, claiming it as deadweight.

"Got a partial look at it when we arrived. It appears to be disabled, I know that much. She was giving off smoke pretty badly when we pulled up. The hatch was wide open, too. Looked as if it had been recently abandoned, just like the rest of the codswallop leading into this Hellhole."

Churchill's resolute gaze intensified upon the cruiser tank, examining its exterior as the light bulb inside his head began to glow brighter. The tank had sustained an indirect hit, possibly over its rear shell. As a result, the nearby building collapsed upon it, burying it in rubble.

"She was probably on rear defence, combating the Germans that staged up on the westerly hills, trying to buy the evacuation time," Churchill conjectured.

"It appears to be an A9 cruiser," Hill admired, tenderly padding the deep gash on his chin.

"Nay," Churchill corrected. His advanced studies in warfare and technology overshadowed Corporal Hill's. His eyes opened wider, realizing as he studied. "She's a Mk. II A10—the new model. That only came out of development a month or so ago. Poor girl would have only been in France for a couple of weeks. Days, even ..."

Hill bobbed his head, clearly not as astonished or as emotional about the vehicle as Churchill apparently was ...

Quite disenchanted, Churchill quantified. "... she barely even got to see the war. Tossed aside like a used rubber johnny."

The depressing mood of Churchill's demeanour about the vehicle made it seem as if he was legitimately personifying the tank. As if it were a solider, like *himself* or *Hill*. As if it were a life that mattered—a wounded soldier who required rescue, like any of the other men in this neglected unit.

Hill added in an *an-y-way* tone of voice, "Right, well ... as I said, after the Gerrys lit us up on the way into town, the drivers managed to fang it down the slope and pull up once the first trucks' engines gave out. We got the wounded off and tossed them into the house for cover while the guns continued to pour it on us. They would have spent at least a thousand rounds. The snipers took their time—waited for gaps in cover, picking off the slower targets ..."

"You did well, Hill. Eighteen men of the 4th Infantry in there will testify to that fact. They wouldn't be alive if it wasn't for your quick thinking and heroism," Churchill commended him with emboldened sincerity.

Taken aback, Hill replied to the compliment. "Thank you, Captain."

They started to walk back through the dark house.

It was now around 1800-hours and darkness had set in, making it difficult to see in indoor areas without light sources to illuminate.

"Now, we've got to come up with a plan that gets all these men—and ourselves—to the docks and onto one of those boats before it's too late."

"The docks?" Hill stopped. "You haven't heard?"

Churchill stopped and frowned, his split and bloody brow askew.

"The harbour is a floating graveyard," Hill informed. "They started loading up there initially, but too many ships got shelled trying to get out of the bay. The docks and boats that sunk clogged it all up. Whole ships were marooned in the harbour, therefore no other boats could fit or manoeuvre through without risking becoming beached themselves. The French army is still held out throughout the wharfs to the west because they're still standing absent shippers. But those main docks are completely gone ..."

Churchill's view unfocused.

This had been the last locale where he had left his men of the Second Manchester Regiment the day before last. A lot must have happened since then. The scenery was likely unidentifiable after that nautical nightmare.

This complicated things.

Hill continued, "By now, there'd be nothing more than a tangled faggot of driftwood and bloated corpses. The BEF resorted to loading up along the eastern shore and along the sands, using smaller vessels in the shallows and makeshift docks made out of deserted cars and trucks. Soldiers reportedly spilled out across the beaches from the city limits. Men were even swimming out to the boats in the pandemonium ... God knows how many would have drowned ..."

"We can't go west from here, we're too far south. Plus, the Germans will most likely see us move in that direction and pick us off, which leaves just the one option ... the east coast," Churchill premeditated, straightening out his moustache. He felt it in need of a trim.

"And what of the wounded? They wouldn't be able to make such a length?"

"They'll make it," Churchill bobbed. "Let me worry about transportation. You just get them ready to move when the time comes."

"Fine. What are you thinking, Captain?"

"Well old chap, either way we are going have to retreat north and through the city, then peel off east and onto the beaches if we are to make one of the last ships from Dunkirk."

"And how do we push away from the Gerrys on the immediate slope behind us? Not to mention find a way to inform the frog rearguard not to cut us in half the second we step around the corner into Dunkirk. They're going to think we're the German infantry, and they'll shoot on sight each with itchy trigger fingers ..."

"Let me worry about warning the French. And if we can get far enough into the city, the German gunners will lose sight of us. There's a whole city of real estate between here and the coast. Their view will be obscured by obstacles, night, and the fog of the smoke from their own artillery barrages. Once clear of Dunkirk, the dunes of the beach must be what our boys are using for concealment from the Hun infantry and guns along the coastal positions. We must at least reach the shores by daybreak, then all we need to do is hitch a ride ..."

Hill nodded along with the plan.

It seemed simple enough when Churchill laid it all out.

"Hopefully, there are still some ships loading up with our boys. Otherwise, we'll truly be left to perish here with what's left of the French Army ... with France ..."

Hill yoked forwards, deep in dwelling thought on Churchill's plan whilst the enigmatic captain endured the dwelling silence, likely contemplating formalities and unforeseen contingencies.

"Sir, if I may ... even if we get out of the machine-gunner sights and sharpshooter scopes behind us, a retreat through the city is still no easy feat. The city is a warzone. The streets are a maze. Artillery has razed almost all landmark structures within the city centre, and has existing districts targeted for further strikes ... that's if the lanes are even accessible after all the shelling Dunkirk has already sustained. Even before the blitzing, the roads were clogged with abandoned military vehicles like you wouldn't believe. It's like something out of *the War of the Worlds*."

Churchill nodded in total understanding, recalling the abandoned, apocalyptic state left in the wake of the panicked evacuation into Dunkirk. "I can imagine. We saw that along the roads on the way in."

"Yes. It's a crumbled labyrinth, buried in rough stone and twisted iron rods. We'd need a tank to get over it—"

An idea pricked Churchill's mind.

"—The empty streets are veiled in smoke and in dust and now dusk is upon us. It will take us too long to navigate there ..."

Churchill threw Hill a raised brow and sarcastic inquiry, staying the course of rationale for their would-be plan. "You sound keen to meet the knackwurst-noshers, Corporal!"

"No, sir," Hill sneered. "I just want you to know what you're planning for. Previous COs attempted to stride forth, knowing not of what was to come ... one way or another, they never reached the shores—or the ships. You gave a good speech earlier ... I'd hate to see it go to waste."

"Let me ask you something; do you want to take something from this war, Corporal?" Churchill asked as their quiet and contemplative stroll entered the main vicinity of the house. "All of you?"

All focus fell on Mad Jack as they entered the void of the main room.

Hill gave him three winks of disconcerted silence.

"Survival?" Churchill questioned, standing focal and out before them. "You want to live? The war is not going to allow you to take something without some form of a sacrifice. You and your men need to be prepared to give it something in order for it to fulfil your wishes."

Hill's view grew askew.

Churchill's personification of the war was an odd one ...

"You want to live? Then you've got to get up off your arses and fight for it."

The atmosphere amongst the motley group of wounded men and medics was still mostly one of opposition against Churchill's war. The medics still firmly believed that moving the wounded from this state would kill them—if a German bullet didn't beat them to it.

"If you don't understand that, understand this: though this all, the darkness will be our ally ..." Churchill added grimly and with a degree of enticement. "The darkness, and hopefully a pinch more from my old friend, *luck*."

'I don't really remember much of that conversation. All I mostly recall was how much my leg hurt. Nevertheless, for what I make up in lack of attention to detail, Corporal Hill made up for in his after-battle report where he singled out Captain Jack Churchill in his war diary, commenting on this extraordinary figure.'

"One of the most reassuring sights of the embarkation from Dunkirk, was the sight of Captain Churchill passing down the beach with his bow and arrows. His high example and his great work were a great help to the 4th Infantry Brigade."

Scampering like a mouse in the eclipse of war, Jack Churchill stayed low and unnoticed as he made his way out from concealment and into the area designated no man's land circumnavigating the outskirts of the city of Dunkirk.

From within the dark recesses of the French house the 4th Infantry were holed up in, he braved north and towards the city, venturing as far as he could without being spotted by the surrounding hawk-eyed Germans, and also as close as he could before running into any of the French Army guard. There existed a tightrope and Jack was on it. On either side, the risk of being shot on purpose or by accident was high. He had to maintain his balance for now, eventually getting past it.

Inching around a cobblestone street corner in the shadows of the ghostly town, his trained eye spotted an element of the French rearguard at a fortified emplacement. He could make out their nationality due to the recognizable curvature of their M26 Adrian helmets. They had set up defences within a partially destroyed building which retained an advantageous line of sight up the street and beyond where Churchill was currently located. Stacked sandbag walls blockaded most connecting avenues, fortifying their defences. The battlements were visible beneath the blue moon beams. Nothing could enter the city along the main roads without them seeing.

In the darkness, Churchill spied them from a dangerously close proximity. Judging by the preparedness of their nervously twitching silhouettes in the gloom, they were on edge and arranged defensively, ready to destroy anything that attempted entry via means of several bipod-mounted FN machine guns partly hidden within the rubble or protruding between sandbags.

Returning south in the bleakness, Churchill silently prowled through rubble under the cloak of a blue shade evening like an experienced feline. He neared the row of Hill's neutralized trucks in the street to the south-southwest of the building. Due to the drape of inky darkness over the landscape, the German shooters on the south-westerly slope with the panoramic view of the city outskirts could not easily, if at all, see any of his miniscule motions of reconnaissance.

Eyeline below the brim of his affixed maroon beret, Jack slyly surveyed about in the shadows of the ruins, searching for crucial elements for his brewing masterplan to get them all out of this debacle alive ...

Sword sheathed and his bow firmly looped around his neck and shoulder, Churchill kept his head low as he darted quickly between the gaps of the disabled Bedford transport trucks, moving only when he felt the time was right.

Corporal Hill was not wrong when he had said the German machine gun bombardment had aimed deliberately to disable the vehicles. The engines and tyres had been specifically targeted, along with the driver's compartment, and all the parked transport trucks had been absolutely obliterated. Their brutal machine guns had ruthlessly carved and gouged the metal hoods of the trucks, collapsing engine components beyond repair, and even caved-in the top halves of the unlucky souls riding within the cabins.

Forever entombed within the confines of the resting truck compartment, the bodies were stained with dry blood and charred indentations.

Carefully, Jack checked the trucks one by one.

Underneath the automobiles, the fuel tanks had been punctured and had drained into the earth beneath. By some miracle, the highly combustible fuel had not ignited and exploded beneath the poor wounded chaps, engulfing them in flames as they scurried to flee the machine guns. Instead, in the truck's stony standstill, the penetrated petrol reservoirs had simply glugged out fuel, resulting in a deluge across the dirty cobblestone street beneath it, pooling in the dusty gutters.

Even Churchill's iron stomach turned upon him quietly cracking open the closed driver's side door, witnessing yet another British soldier inhumanely shot-to-shit and torn-to-shreds, buried in glass fragments from the shattered windows. On all the past trucks he had checked, the doors had been littered with exit holes from the machine gun onslaught. The metal edges were torn and rough from at least a dozen bullet punctures which had passed through the vehicle chassis and the men inside. The doors were rickety on their warped hinges and some of them disengaged entirely.

The only scent stronger than the spilled petrol fumes was the metallic smell of iron from the dried blood spatters across every cabin surface.

He could tell this next cabin was going to be as nasty as the others he had just investigated, as even before he had opened the door, the red ooze of gore was dripping from the bottom of the frame.

Churchill tensed and opened her up, checking the situa—

Breaking the deafening silence of his reconnaissance, an internal weight against the door suddenly heaved it open upon him when he disengaged the handle latch. With a gasp, he shuffled clear as the deadweight of a desiccated body came tumbling out before him, dropping gear and a weapon from his lap. The deceased British soldier free-fell four feet to the road before Churchill with a sickening *thump!* The poor sod wore unidentifiable facial features due to the brutal and grotesque machine gun facial he and his passenger had received upon their leisurely drive into Dunkirk.

Tense and still as a statue, Churchill paused for an extended moment following the surprise ruckus, quickly wondering if any of the machine gunners or snipers had heard or seen movement due to that body falling out of the truck. Cautiously, he eventually climbed the tray of the lorry, peering over to peek the slope of the northerly hill. Luckily, it appeared that they had not noticed.

"Blast," Churchill commented, remarking that this truck, like the four others crashed in close behind it, had a seemingly destroyed broken console panel and gear shift. This truck's steering wheel had been detached from the column, and it was strewed across the pool of glass glittery red on the floor. Upon further inspection and with the upmost irony, this was the only vehicle that *did not* have a steering wheel but was the only Bedford truck of the group that *still had* six good tyres ...

Out of annoyance, Churchill shoved closed the door with a punishing thrust, remaining as discrete as possible from the dozens of lurking enemies.

Frustration befell him.

The odds were stacking up higher.

He was so sure that at least one of these transports could still operate and could therefore conceivably tow another, hence his certainty of getting them out of here. Hill was right in his pessimistic outlook regarding the trucks and now, finally, Churchill could see why he wanted to surrender to the Germans. Without a means of transport, there was no way they could get the immobile wounded soldiers out of here, weave through the city streets, and down to the coast.

... his eyes rested upon the A10 cruiser tank along the connecting road, towards the city.

There was no way the thing could carry twenty people. Not the vertically challenged, gurney-ridden wounded, anyhow. They would not even be able to funnel down the top hatch.

Further assessing his severe lack of other options, Churchill decided to check her out anyhow. Remaining low and noiseless, he discreetly ventured the long way around to the ruined tank to avoid being spotted.

Once in close, Churchill examined the cruiser like an animal conservationist approaching an injured mammal in the wild, and he saw the damage done to it from the shelling.

The steel was still warm on her bonnet.

"Young lass, what have they done to you, eh?" Churchill whispered in a passive tone, softly touching the metal as if he were stroking the belly of a beast. She had full canisters of reserve fuel in her outer webbing, known colloquially as jerrycans (funnily enough, invented by the Germans but now standard issue for the British and even American armed forces). The webbing also bore a surplus of entrenching tools, mechanic tools, and levers that they could perhaps use to free the rubble from off her back half. After Churchill rounded the cruiser, he paid note to a new addition the A10 had over the superseded models; a retractable lever winch. The cable was lightweight and probably a steel weave, complete with a wicked heavy-duty junker's hook on the end.

Judging by the seep leaking from the neck of the damaged turret, there was no way the hydraulics functioned on the gun turret. The QF 2-pounder itself had even been ruptured from the same barrage of shelling she had received. The tracks on the exposed side seemed intact and from what he could gauge beneath the rubble on the buried side, they were fully functional.

"Well, that's just not on," Churchill stated judgementally. The reason for this beauty's abandonment was purely due to her offensive gun turret becoming compromised, and because the building next to her had a wall tumble atop, pinning the tank down like a crustacean under tow.

Otherwise, the cruiser seemed to be in impeccable mechanical order. She merely needed to be unrestrained. Given the fact there was a dozen tools and they had a dozen free hands that could assist to some degree, they could get her out in no time ...

Just then, an idea sprung to mind.

Churchill donned his winning grin as he laid eyes upon the A10 cruiser. She may have just been their saving grace in all of this.

"Sit tight, old girl. I'll be back to free you, I promise," Churchill whispered, taking the time to scrape his fingertips across the armoured hull one last time as he rounded the front of the tank, where he suddenly halted ...

His stare squinted as he spotted a marking on the exterior, and he waved aside some hanging netting and insistently scrubbed some grime from battle-scorning to expose a hidden artistic element.

It was a painting.

Pilots in the air force refer to it as *nose art.* Unauthorized but common by militaries in nature, the works were considered folk art and was typically a type of decorative painting or design usually highlighted on the frontal of an aircraft, generally chalked up on the obverse fuselage, the graphic was a form of glorified graffiti.

Churchill's maw blossomed into a smile.

Whoever this tank was identified as was a good-looking lass: a brunette, and almost disproportionately endowed in an unbuttoned uniform blouse that barely housed a quarter of her bursting, luscious bosom.

His hand rubbed at the bottom of the art, revealing some sort of slogan or a name: *Busty Barbara, Bang-Bang.*

Jack couldn't help but erupt in a boyish snicker out his nostrils. Whomever had pencilled the nose art on this cruiser tank had a rather adolescent humour, and the type of fun that menfolk like Jack Churchill relished.

This tank had an identity.

"Pleasure to meet you, Barb. You shall ride again. See you soon ..." Churchill offered ciao, planting a kiss from his lips to the picture via his fingertips before getting back to work and devising his plan to get them all out of this mess and across the chaos that was later known in history as *the Battle of Dunkirk.*

He lent across Barbara's tank tracks, becoming completely exposed. Luckily, thanks due to the darkness of his location, he was confident that no German up on the hill could discern him.

From this spot, he could see the whole situation; the French house that housed the two dozen wounded men of the 4th, plus Hardy, the damaged convoy of lorries they had ridden in on, plus the slope to the south that was scattered with German machine gun nests and probably a couple of squadrons of itchy-trigger-finger snipers.

Then, the idea came to him like a light in the darkness.

Cue the medley.

If there was ever a time for a *Slavko Vorkapich*-style montage along Churchill's historical warpath, it was now.

Snapping to work, Churchill removed the spare fuel canisters from the exterior webbing of the buried tank. He then disengaged the towing harness from its rear, raking the coil of wire so that there was at least twenty metres worth of slack in the spool that curled on the ground. Unlike the A9 cruiser, the A10 had been equipped with a retractable winch, possibly due to her extra weight in armour plating suggesting a higher risk of the tracks becoming bogged in certain terrain. This item would prove pivotal in Jack's plan to get the dregs of the 4th Infantry to the coast.

Remaining persistently low and sticking to the moonlight shadows, but acting fast in his concealment exposure, Churchill ran the heavy jerrycans and the winch cable to the row of trucks in crashed convoy along the connecting street. The locale points were approximately seventy yards apart with the French home and their point of origin amidst and by the truck end. Once there, he dropped the coil of line in a heap and freed his hands to handle the jerry cans.

Inside and out, Churchill poured the fuel over three of the four stalled convoy trucks. He shellacked the rear trays and the sadly deceased souls within—and was quite apologetic about it—making sure to soak the cabins' material seats. This fresh accelerant would blend into the streams of existing fuel pooling around the location. He ran a clear trail across to the next truck and did the same, dowsing the vehicles and creating one great, long daisy chain of extremely flammable gasoline. In combination with the already immense pool of petrol spilled out across the cobblestone road beneath the vehicles from their ruptured tanks, it was fair to say that they were a spark away from complete incineration.

Once done and with both jerrycans emptied, Churchill drew his sword from his hip and touched the pointed tip of the steel blade against the fuel tanks that hung exposed and below the trucks. With a careful thrust as not to strike a spark, he ran them through with deep scraping punctures. Though most had been split already, this relieved the gas tanks of whatever remaining petrol they had left inside them, soaking the street below with even more highly combustible fuel which lined the gutters. The coursing liquid slowly travelled down the cobblestone street and towards a blocked sewer grate where it pooled.

With the last truck in the convoy line, Churchill crawled beneath and tied the strong wire from the tank's winch around the forward axle bar. The truck may have not been able to steer, but it had four good wheels and an intact disengageable brake.

Covered in filth from crawling around beneath the trucks and reeking of gasoline, Churchill lastly returned to the infantrymen inside of the home. The atmosphere was rightfully anxious.

He addressed the men whom Corporal Hill had successfully prepared for movement, rallying the troops. Those who could of the wounded were upstanding, either propped against walls or on crutches. Some were on stretchers, others were even being carried between less mortally wounded soldiers.

"Ready, lads?" Churchill asked, finally sheathing his petrol-greased sword before their pondering sets of wide eyes.

"We are," Hill confidently remarked, gently caressing the gash wound on his chin. It had stopped bleeding long ago; however the horrid wound was so deep it impacted the way he articulated some words. It would undoubtedly leave a nasty scar.

Jack moved aside, guiding them in the direction of the exit and watching to ensure that the coast remained clear.

"Captain, the majority of these men won't be able to move more than ten paces at most," Hill reiterated. This was a suspicion he had ascertained once getting the men ready to move.

"Lucky for us we're only going about nine paces then."

"The trucks? This is crazy," in a quarrelsome tone, one of the background medics remarked verbalizing his disagreement. Albeit, he abided the command to move, this esteemed combat surgeon was all but too cynical about the plan—and probably more so about the man with the plan: one Mad Jack Churchill. He implored to Hill, "Jim, you need to reconsider following these orders ... this is preposterous."

"*Preposterous?*" Churchill frowned, mildly offended.

"Yes! With all due respect, Captain Churchill, we're soldiers, not *Looney Tunes*," the medic continued, seemingly pertaining to some knowledge of some of the particulars of Churchill's master-plan. Jack found this humorous as he had barely even told Hill of the finer details, meaning this bloke had arrived at his conclusion based on whatever he had spied of Jack's mousey actions outside with the cable winch and fuel cans.

Come to think of it, it was rather looney.

"But, you haven't even heard the best part yet?"

The combat surgeon faced Churchill directly. "It never ends well for that little *Bosko* bloke, does it?"

Jack didn't know this guy. Didn't know his name, or rank.

Didn't care to.

He made his own nickname for the twat.

"The conspicuousness of this action is what makes this so concealed to the enemy, *Bosko*. It's like hiding in plain sight; the Huns are looking everywhere *but* the peppered vehicles from which you arrived. Their sights are on the rear of the property and scanning the paths between all the nearby real estate, waiting to catch eye of a sliver of movement as you all undoubtedly crusade away and towards the city ..." Churchill expanded, moving through the crowd of bandaged and bloodied men and finding Hardy. "Felix: do you hold a current driver's license?"

"Uh, yeah, sure ..." Hardy retaliated, rather affronted. "Of course, I can drive!"

"I thought the trucks were destroyed?" a different member of the 4th overheard and questioned as they prepared. The same defiant, insolent medic overheard the query and put in his two cents, answering for Churchill:

"They are. The trucks, themselves, are not drivable," Bosko said.

This naysayer certainly had his doubts, hoping to sway Corporal Hill. At this stage, Hill may have also had his doubts about Churchill, but at the same time he had a creeping suspicion that through his senselessness laid a type of genius, and he was willing to take a gamble. Something about Churchill's confidence sold it for him.

"Who said anything about driving the trucks?" Churchill eyed Hardy and poised the question. "Think you can drive a fifteen-tonne tank named *Busty Barbara?*"

In the background, the insubordinate medic scoffed at the absurdity.

Hardy blinked inanely hearing Churchill's elaboration.

"Uh ... whatever, yeah, sure," Hardy shrugged, too defeated to even further question where this plan was going.

"Good," Churchill smirked his winning grin. "Corporal, did you stockpile all explosive ordinance from your men like I asked?"

"Affirmative," Hill obliged. "But like I said before, other soldiers during the evacuation robbed these guys blind of ammunition—*especially* hand grenades. All we came up with was a couple of Mills bombs and a matchbook."

Churchill slanted his head. "It'll have to do, then."

They watched as Churchill dropped the hand grenades into an oversized pack and slumped it across his shoulder. Whilst doing so, another idea sprang to mind as he witnessed a wounded soldier take a gulp from a glass jar filled with the remnants of water from a shared rationed cantina.

"You there," he said, stepping over. "I need that jar."

The wounded man's eyes widened, eyeing his medic.

"Drink up. That's it. Come on! Skål! Skål!"

The wounded soldier seemed apprehensive as Churchill assisted him by tipping up the rear of the jar so that he drank the entirety. It spilled from the rim of the jar down his chin. Once done, Churchill confiscated the clear pickling jar.

"That's it. Good lad," he said as he placed it in the grenade bag along with the other ordinance. Like everything else, the glass jar had an impending purpose.

At this stage all the witnesses were baffled, but the only thing stranger than Jack Churchill stealing the wounded man's beverage was the fact that nobody seemed to verbally question the act.

"Hill, prepare your men by the side door. One by one, I want you to take them outside, low and behind the trucks. Start loading them into the forward-most truck in the convoy, for that is the one we'll be taking."

Hill gestured a complying nod, listening well.

"I've opened the side of the tray for you already. File everybody in, lying down as flat as possible, as not to be seen by your cranky mates up on the slope. Be discreet, be deliberate, and be brave, men. I will have you all out of here in a jiffy."

Hill shook his head but agreed. "Yes, sir."

"Good luck, chaps. Load in, stay low, and don't forget to *hold on.* Hardy, you're with me," Churchill stated, helping up the limping American journalist. They moved to a rear door exit and stepped outdoors after a quick peering, making sure the coast was clear. The streets were empty, dark, and hazy with a blend of lingering smoke and fog.

On the summit of the hill overlooking the outskirts, the enemy had now set up powerful, large-scale searchlights. The white beams were mostly scanning across the city and into the water, searching for boats in which to target their artillery. However, some of the smaller searchlights were now scanning the dead streets of Dunkirk, attempting to give sharpshooters a target to mark.

Of the several beams of light shining across the city from over two hundred yards away, one of them was the most prominent searchlight, and it proved an unexpected nuisance of illumination.

"I've got a really bad feelin' about this, Captain," Hardy quantified a second before they started progressing. It was right as one of the searchlight beams just happened to sweep over the darkened street they were about to step into, turning it into a glow brighter than daylight.

"It's war, lad. You'd be plain *wrong* if you had a good one."

Per Captain Churchill's instructions, slowly but surely—but most of all, carefully—Corporal Hill managed to successfully commence the operation of transporting all the wounded men from the abandoned French house into the open air tray of the specified Bedford truck.

Like Churchill had advised, he utilized the cover of darkness to safely move the men *back into* the disabled vehicle that had brought them to Dunkirk, right under the observant gawks of their overwatching aggressors.

It proved a delicate and difficult mission, loading the incapacitated men with their heads down so that they were low behind the two-foot tray guard of the rear tray of the transport truck, nevertheless they succeeded. For most of the injured bound to stretchers, it was just a matter of sliding them up and across the flatbed, lining them like sausages on a low grill.

"*Stay down ... Stay down ...*" an assisting soldier alerted in a stern whisper as the familiar incoming threat spanned their way like a carousel of illumination.

All partially exposed men suddenly lowered themselves an extra inch as the patrolling searchlight beam swept across the area, searching for any movement resembling a prison yard. When the vivid beam shone into the street lanes, it radiated brighter than the sun.

After it passed, they unfroze and continued loading the wounded aboard one by one.

"*That's it!*" *Bosko* the medic hissed. Left to load up was just him, Hill, and one other mobile soldier with a head wound who had been assisting in loading the wounded. "*What now?*"

"*I don't know,*" Hill stated truthfully as he tensely clutched his pistol, crouching down beside the tyre, searching the dark and gloomy connecting street for Churchill. They had not seen him since he broke right around the street corner, disappearing with his American friend towards the cruiser wreckage.

For the moment of limbo, the three of them remained low and quiet behind the truck in the darkness, hearts pounding. They shared the same glance up the street and at the cruiser tank, where they had seen Churchill embark with the other section of their escape plan.

"Jim, is this guy straight as a die or what?" the defiant medic took the time to comment, again questioning the legitimacy of Churchill's forthrightness. "I mean, he's carrying a bloody bow and arrow for Christ's sake."

Hill shrugged. "He seems to have gotten himself this far ..."

"He's a fruitcake!"

"He's brave. Has conviction."

"*Brave?* Nonsense. It's *blind luck* behind the wheel ..."

"He's a highly trained officer in the British Army," Hill argued sternly ... and then they saw movement from the cruiser as Mad Jack Churchill came moseying back, exposed as all hell and seeming to not give a single damn. He trotted straight across the street, wandering at a casual pace with his bag of explosives like a kid searching for his bus pass before boarding.

"On second thought, he may just be bat-shit insane."

"*Oi, Captain! Get down!*" a medic hissed from behind concealment. There was no impending light near them at present, his apprehension was due to overcaution.

"Relax, lads, staying low was just precautionary. If they could see us in the dark from this range, they would have shot at us by now," Churchill confidently commented as he trundled near, bringing the bag of explosives about. It was now filled to its tensile threshold with 40mm HE *(high explosives)* shells leftover from the cruiser tank.

"And what if Gerry's been eating his carrots?"

"Nonsense, he's too busy poking them through his and his mate's balloon knots," Jack broke the tension with humour. "Relax, Bosko. Gerry's eyes are everywhere but *here.*"

"Fuckin' hell!" the medic commented quite fearfully as he watched Churchill haul the heavy bag near and plant it down with a *clunk* in order to adjust his maroon cap. The weighty bag made a metallic sound as the brass cylindrical highly explosive shells all clinked together.

Mild outbursts were emitted.

"*Oi, watch it, mate! Be careful!*"

"*Sir, are you bloody insane!*"

Hill asked, "What are you planning to do with all of that?"

Churchill eyed the three after they flinched at the sound of the placed bag of heavy ordinance, and he scoffed. "This? This isn't even all of them."

Meanwhile, over at the partially buried cruiser, Felix Hardy sat on the edge of his seat inside the dark confines of the tank belly.

Seconds ago, Churchill had set him up at the controls and left him to wait.

Ignoring the surging pain from the strapped wounds to his leg, he lurched forwards, reiterating to himself what Jack had just instructed to him with regards to the many tank control mechanisms. Ever-confidently, he had given Hardy a crash-course on what little he actually knew about how to operate the A10, based on having seen a trained operator drive an A9 *(the previous model)* from the outside, approximately a year ago at a military tattoo parade.

"Okay, okay, you've got this," sitting lonely in the cold and dark belly of the armoured beast, Hardy coaxed himself. He clapped and rubbed his palms together, psyching himself into the mood to take control.

With the engine off, he grappled onto the levers and release triggers and nodded his head as he catalogued through the instructions one last time, practising.

"*Ignition. Ignition key lock. Gears. Steering; forward, back, left, right,*" he said under his breath before looking down past his feet, spotting the numerous pedals. "*Brake, clutch, accelerator* ... See, you got this! Nothing to it! We're all good!"

Hardy gulped.

Driving the tank was one thing ... Churchill's plan on freeing it was something completely different altogether, and what was truly bringing down the beads of sweat across Hardy's temple.

"*'Hold this',*" one minute ago Mad Jack had said to him, passing him the Mesopotamian variant No. 36 Mk1 Mills bomb: the standard issue British hand grenade. He had simply shoved the cold unit into Hardy's frozen stiff hands and cupped them around the Baratol-filled, time-delayed pineapple-looking explosive with a seven second fuse ... and then he yanked out the pin, arming the device. He tossed it away, discarded somewhere in the dark abyss of the cold tank belly.

Beaming that grenade, Hardy's eyes were as big as the bulbs of the searchlights above their heads.

"*'Hold still and don't let go of the spoon, lad','*" Churchill had said calmly, bringing around a glass jar. Carefully, he took the unit from the fearful American, being sure to clench the lever so that the fuse did not ignite. He then carefully pushed the grenade into the clear glass jar, which also encased the spoon for them. He held it up and into view with a smile of triumph.

Upon question, Jack replied: "*'We just turned a seven second timer into something I can detonate with a well-placed arrow'.*"

That *grenade in a glass jar* was now atop the stack of rubble outside the armoured tank ... atop of even more explosives ...

... Hardy glanced to his left and he let his mind wonder about the stack of the remainder of the 40mm HE ammunition and Mills bomb hand grenades Mad Jack had set up against the outside of the tank wall, buried and placed in amongst the collapsed rubble pinning the tank down. The plan was to excavate the vehicle from the heavy ruins like TNT to a cave-in.

Hardy shook it from his mind.

He was inside an armoured vehicle. Safe and sound.

"Not to worry ... Not to worry ... Oh, fuck, he's gonna blow me up! Fuck! *FUUUUUCK!*"

From outside the steel cruiser tank, his displeased tantrum was barely even audible.

"What's next, Captain?" Hill asked, remaining affirmative and surefire, trusting Churchill's risky plan to get them off the outskirts and safely into the city.

"Climb aboard with the others," Churchill nodded, still as confident and assured as ever. "Lay down flat and get ready to hold on tight at my signal ..."

"This is great," the same sceptical combat surgeon commented as he complied. "If the Germans don't shoot us leaving, the French certainly will the second we round the corner."

"That's only if we don't blow up first," Hill furthered, paying note to what it was they watched Churchill do next ...

Last onboard, the medic followed their gaze to the other trucks parked in the convoy ...

From the bag, Churchill was tipping the ordinance of shells into the pool of fuel behind the other trucks. He started kicking the shells out with his feet once they were poured out, dispersing them thusly. They rolled against the gutter and danced across the cobblestone, reaching far out behind the Bedford trucks. Churchill even tossed a couple in the truck trays and scattered the 40mm shells about.

With the bag now empty, he balled it up and tossed it aside, pausing as he passed the trucks only once to disengage the handbrake of the only vehicle they needed.

"Hah! That'd help!" he remarked derisively as he lent into the cabin and unlocked the stationary park brake. He whispered loudly so that all those prone in the rear tray could hear. "See you gentlemen once we're in town."

"Captain?!" Hill breathed, catching Churchill before he could dismount from the cabin, unsure of how he could possibly signal them while they were in hiding. "How will we know when to hold on?"

"Oh, you'll know."

Squashed and packed, the men exchanged an awkward look.

Nobody quite knew what Mad Jack meant ...

... that was until they heard the signal ...

The skirl.

Dodging the pan of bright white glowing light as one of the searchlights swept his way, Jack Churchill's casual saunter quickly strafed in tight behind the corner of the French home, placing his shoulder against the wall and out of sight in the nick of time.

Everything was set in motion, and he was now in position.

He brought around the Scottish bagpipes from under his arm, placing the blowstick between his lips whilst his fingers found the airholes. He took his time, slowing his breaths, making them deep and stretched, able to release mellifluously. He tensed his lungs accordingly, as did all professional bagpipers for their preparation ... and then he blustered, red cheeked, and as vigorous as the connotation of the tune itself.

Scotland the Brave.

The skirl sliced through the cool night calmness.

The pitch of the bagpipes started off unobtrusive in tone, soon expanding in volume as it did in familiarity to those who were scattered throughout the vicinity. Nevertheless, the song was world renowned to all ears who heard it.

The ears of the city in ruins ...

The song inspired a mindfulness, a comfort.

It instilled a warm familiarity and to contrast the abhorrent discomfort of the destruction of Dunkirk. Volume inundated every locale with the sound of the purr and skirl, flooding the streets.

It travelled through entire building hollows, destroyed or collapsed, filling like a current across the air. The sound penetrated the thick dusty residue clouding the streets, the resonance of the bagpipes was not only heard, but it was also vehemently heeded.

The ears of the French rearguard ...

In sporadic locations throughout the ruins, the brave souls of the French Army who had made it into Dunkirk for the evacuation inched up from behind the holds of their gun turrets. Beneath their Adrian helmets, they each frowned and exchanged a look of inelegance upon hearing the Scottish instrument, accepting the possibility that there were still British soldiers attempting to get into Dunkirk.

The fallen and the deceased ...

The sound reached the soul of the ambience and all those within it, drew emotion of those killed and fallen in the wake of war, littering the streets ...

Not a soul was spared from the inspiring tune.

The echoic skirl beaconed a radius wide in the war-torn night of the Dunkirk outskirts, travelling far and true. Even almost reaching as far as the harbours and the beaches of the shoreline ...

For miles across the coastal city, those crooked souls held up in the ruins perked their ears to the soothing resonation, suddenly cognizant and inspired to be brave, as the song intended.

Hope refilled.

Faith restored.

A plan for survival was somewhere in motion.

It inculcated morale for those had lost it.

Peering through the haze of dust-settling streets of Dunkirk in search for the source, broken men everywhere raised and became upstanding. Cracking stiff bones and scraping dry blood from wounds, scattered astray soldiers were suddenly reminded of home and of their mission ...

Men gathered, collecting the fallen.

They woke the rested, becoming stronger together.

For heroes everywhere it was time to continue their march to the coast ...

Towards the evacuation ships ...

Towards salvation ...

Inside the rear tray of the Bedford truck primed for improvised transport, Corporal Hill and his surviving 4th Infantrymen each heard Captain Churchill's doodlesack melody.

They were at first marginally confused as to why Churchill would stray from their plan and blow a song from his bagpipes at such a desperate time as this.

But then after a while, they realized why ...

They comprehended the importance and appreciated the tune, and men laying within that packed tray of survivors suddenly felt a relevance beyond their existence.

It was the sound of home.

Tears swelled in the eyes of the wounded.

A warmth washed over them, comforting them.

A few men who were able even brought their right arms up and across their breast, over their heart. This was their fight song with which they were about to charge into battle. The men listened intently and sensed the harmony, allowed themselves to become imparted with gallantry and virtue. Reminded of the reason they were here fighting in the first place, as well as the reason they needed to make it home.

As much as the sound was the signal for their escape plan, the Scottish bagpipes were also a much-needed boost of morale and encouragement. The British soldiers did not realize how much they needed it until the skirl fell upon their eardrums like musical stardust. It was euphonic to their ears.

"Men," Hill held back overwhelming emotion. "Whatever happens, it has been an honour to serve by your sides ..."

His arms laid back by his side, finding the guard rail ...

... *and he held the fuck on.*

Over in the squashed A10 cruiser tank, Felix Hardy's eyes fell out of focus as in his moment of preparedness, the muffled sound of the bagpipe tune fell upon his ears from outside.

He had thought he was ready for anything before hearing it ... but now, he knew not only that he was ready, but that he could handle the responsibility placed down upon him by Mad Jack.

After casting a gaze over his shoulder in search through a view hole for Churchill on the street outside, Hardy returned his eyeline across the many levers and controls before him in the driver's seat.

This was the signal Churchill had told him to listen for ...

With a gulp, he hunched inwards and set the ignition, cranking the tank into gear and revving life throughout the abandoned armoured vehicle.

A deeply toned engine sound grumbled alive, barely audible over the deafening hum and the carving skirl of the shrill Scottish bagpipes outside and filling the eerie streets of deserted Dunkirk.

In the distant outskirts of town, the German infantry became aware of the faraway activity as the screaming pitch travelled up the slope, flooding over them like a delayed shockwave.

The troops could all hear the audio across the distance and although they did not understand its relevance, they were precipitously made more aware and prepared for anything.

Due to the range and the volume emission of the foreign musical instrument, they could not identify the exact origin of the source emanating the skirl of the Scottish bagpipes.

Infantry spotters more actively scanned the streets with their portable searchlights, sweeping in fast and erratic motions over the ruins below. The powerful beam cast heat onto the areas that it illuminated. From afar, it resembled a child tormenting ants with a magnifying glass.

Men combed the shadows with their pupils acute as optic lasers, skimming for anything resembling a target. Their awareness dialled in, sifting through the darkness for detail.

Machine gunners with powerful attached spot lamps swept the many vacant streets, tracing the foundations and boulevard corners. They cracked their necks and gripped their buttstocks firmly against their shoulders, ready for absolutely anything.

Snipers and sharpshooters prepared their rested eye, primed for night-vision scanning ...

... their alertness because of hearing the bagpipes, all a part of Jack Churchill's master-plan.

Up on the incline, the hundreds of strewn about Germans waited, attentive, anxious, and on edge. Their assortment of heavy machine guns, rifles, both telescope or iron-sights, aimed downrange and around the vicinity of French homes—especially the one that they had seen the soldiers flee into earlier that day ...

    ... their fingers were on the triggers, ready for anything ...

    The bagpipes ended.

    Silence echoed.

Flaming-tip of a war arrow ...

    Nocking point of the bowstring ...

    Longbow carried out beside him freely ...

    Jack Churchill boldly trod into full view, leaving the glowing flames of the entire matchbox discarded and ablaze, casting bright behind him.

    He was exposed and fearless in his strides, taking steps out into the quiet open street with the fire burning bright in the darkened space. Mad Jack paced unafraid and with the confidence of a courageous, imperative purpose. One too important to fail.

    Once fully unmasked and with his target insight, Churchill became stationary out in the open and pulled an archer's poise, arcing his bow to anchor point with the flame arrow drawn.

Beyond the licking fire at the tip of the dead-shot arrow was but only the momentousness of his sterling blue gaze as he squinted ...

    ... he drew a bead on the target.

    He was about to re-ignite war.

XI
Pride and Extreme Prejudice

1940, June 3
Dunkirk
Nord-Pas-de-Calais, France

Scotland the Brave was played in its entirety.

The piper exhaled his final breath.

Jack Churchill stowed the mouthpiece and tucked away the chanter, stowing the trusty slung bagpipes around his side.

It was go-time.

Without a care to the shadow games he had been playing with the likes of the German forces perched upon the perimeter, Churchill revealed a matchbook in his midst. He struck the open heads against the coarse brick wall beside him, igniting the phosphorous sulphide tips of the entire packet which he in-turn let drop onto a small nest of kindling.

The flames grew into a small spot fire at his flank. The orange flare illuminated him in the dim of the vacant street corner he occupied, casting bold shadows on the evening-lit walls around him, the radiance around the corner would have been visible from the enemy-occupied southeast slopes.

Now that all ears around the vicinity of the echoic and war-torn Dunkirk outskirts began to empty to normality—absent the wail from the skirl of the pipes—the idling *hum* of a British tank known as *Busty Barbara* could be heard, purring like a tame lioness.

Churchill prepared in his fire-lit stance, gazing left and towards the cruiser tank. He hoped that the lone occupant inside, Felix Hardy, had not only heard the pipes *(the signal)* but had also put on the pair of gunner's earmuffs as instructed. This next part of the plan was going to be a little loud ...

The archer in the shadowy dominion drew a single bodkin-tipped arrow from his shoulder quiver and with pure muscle memory, notched the feathered rear and drew back on the drawstring to take aim.

His target in the dim fire light: the buried A10 cruiser tank.

Drawstring pressed against his cheek, one eye closed to aim ...

He raised his aim an inch to slightly above the dormant tank, where resting amongst the rubble of the crumbled stone of the destruction partially burying the vehicle was a purposely exposed target ...

A glass jar housing a hand grenade.

In the shine of the housing, he saw the reflection of the spot fire glint winking at him.

Churchill loosed the arrow true with a quick *lash.*

Like a loosed bolt, the arrow struck the glass object encasing the timed explosive with a shatter and chime. Pin removed from the lug, the Mills bomb inside became allowed to flex its fuse, thus tossing the anchored spoon lever with a metallic *whip*, igniting the purposely extended seven-second countdown.

7 seconds ...

6 seconds ...

Following the shattering of the glass jar, the grenade spun on its weighted axle for a half rotation before it toppled and fell amongst the charred ruins beside the armoured tank ... and amongst several other explosive devices scattered in a demolition-rig alignment in a contour encompassing the buried vehicle.

5 seconds ...

While the seconds counted down, Jack next selected a special arrow that he had set aside. The feather stick had suffered damage upon their crash-landing through a wall into Dunkirk, and consequently the arrow without a head now had an improvised purpose. Around the wooden tip of the projectile, torn breast pockets been bound tight, pinched firm in crimpled wire. The covered tip had then been soaked in highly flammable accelerant when he had been by the trucks. This weighted the projectile enough to sufficiently fly, and would also aid in keeping alight through the wind resistance.

Jack waved the arrowhead above the spot fire. The material drenched in ignitable fluid brandished across the heat, combusting with a tiny *whoosh.*

The arrow shaft in Churchill's hand resembled a giant matchstick, struck alight on its sizzling end.

4 seconds ...

Flaming arrow pitched and now also at nocking point of the bowstring, longbow carried out beside him freely, Jack Churchill stepped into complete exposed view.

He was endangered, yet fearless.

Taking steps out into the open street with the fire burning bright in the darkened space like a torchbearer, Churchill paced audaciously, burdened with an imperative purpose ...

3 seconds ...

Once fully displayed and with his downrange target in sight, Churchill halted and pulled an archer's side-on stance, cranking his device to anchor point.

Drawn so firm that the burning tip of the flaming arrow singed the flesh on the index finger of his bow hand, Jack's composure and form remained disciplined. He focused past the pain; the glint in his stare only sharpened as he squinted, marking his objective.

2 seconds ...

Sch-TOFF...

Like a struck bullet from a gun, the flaming arrow loosed from the hundred-pound draw of the longbow.

Because of the powerful forward momentum thrust upon the charging projectile, the glowing tip of the arrow appeared more like a tracer, drawing a line from Churchill and towards the target:

... the trucks and the hidden members of the 4th Infantry.

The still hazardously and highly explosive array of trucks.

It was only moments ago, before he had played the tune on his bagpipes, Churchill had abetted more leakage of the already ruptured fuel tanks beneath the crashed and abandoned transport trucks. The cobblestone streets and gutters beneath the deflated tyres of the vehicles were soaked in the flammable petrol fuel. Churchill had also coated the rear trays of the trucks furthest left in fuel, as well as sprinkled all but one of the vehicles with spare 40mm HE shells from the tank like he was decorating a cake.

1 second ...

The flaming arrow hurtled like a lightning bolt towards the trucks ...

He didn't watch it ignite the fuel source, but had no doubt it would.

In a jerking motion upon loosing the projectile trigger, Churchill reefed himself back behind the cover of the French house and into the illumination of the tiny spot fire. He pressed in low against the wall of concealment and covered his ears ...

0.

Boof!

First, there was a concealed impact detonation from within the partially destroyed building structure across the cobblestone street away. It coughed up white dust and smoke from within the rubble, barely causing the fifteen-tonne sleeping cruiser tank to even flinch a muscle.

Then....

Bo-bo-bo-boom!

Like mining charges at a tiny quarry, the externally placed 40mm HE tank shells and other random explosives that Churchill had buried amidst the rubble discharged in a chain reaction of detonations, dislodging the wreckage in a quake of activity.

Dust haze plumed outwards from the force of the blasts.

Spotlights from up on the hill twitched and focused light on the area, drawing in the attention of the massive searchlight. The beam concentrated on the source of the explosion, illuminating the new solid smoke and dust cloud as it wafted from the rubble, rising into the alley.

The light beam was so white through the dust that everything went bright as day. There was no real target and as such the many shooters perched upon this overwatch did not open fire—*yet.*

Quick to pull his head from his hands, Churchill caught a look at the cruiser tank known as Barbara. Commanded inside by Hardy, she stirred in the smoke and raining stone as it speckled in shards about her coated armour chassis. Glowing elements from within the structure, such as wood beams and strips of wallpaper rained down slowly, breathing life into the smoky nighttime airspace with further ash, tinder, and activity.

Protected safe inside the cruiser, Hardy followed the instructions Churchill reiterated earlier: to lean on the accelerator the second the explosions start sounding off beside the tank in order to break free.

There was no way a hand grenade or unchambered shell could puncture or damage the outer hull of an A10. Unharmed inside the heavily armoured vehicle, Hardy was safe and sound, albeit his ears would undoubtedly be ringing from the detonations outside.

"*Yes!*" Churchill shouted, up tall and raising his longbow above his head in celebration as the tank came to life. "*YES!*"

Just as he had planned—as always—iron tracks screeching, the cruiser tank managed to tug itself free from the ruins with the assistance of the disruption of rubble, bursting out and onto the street.

What little obstacle wreckage was in front of her, Barbara just mounted with her flowing tracks as she kicked up dust on her acceleration.

"*Yee-haw!*" rocking about within the confines of the cruiser tank, Hardy cried at the top of his lungs.

Riding the adrenaline rush and flushed with the excitement of their escape, he crunched the gears and levers, pounding the pedal in order to steer the tank onto the amber-lit street before following Churchill's specific instructions for what came next: *drive like a bloody demon possessed.*

Thanks to the German searchlight, the road ahead of him was lit up like Independence Day. The road ahead illuminated better than any functioning headlights could have done.

"Be free my beauty! Yes!" Churchill shouted as Hardy somewhat clumsily grinded the gears, getting a feel for driving an armoured tank. He had instructions and he was following them to a T.

On the street as the cruiser passed him with an obnoxiously loud and motorized metallic ambition, Churchill's stare collapsed down into the rubble where the movement of the attached winch cable became taut, visible in the bright light of the enemy spotlight.

The tightening of the line was expected and part of the plan, and from the edge of the building Churchill's eyes traced its connectivity to the furthest right truck—the one with all the soldiers stowed onboard. The cable had been attached beneath, wrapped firmly about the steering column.

As the wire spool unwound with the steady march of the cruiser tank up the street, Churchill relied on just one more thing other than the successful harnessing and tow of the truck behind the tank.

The fireworks distraction.

Speaking of which ... *the trigger was late.*

In all fairness, he had expected mostly a simultaneous explosion along with the freeing of the cruiser tank. Jack's curious view climbed and focused on the flaming arrow that he had loosed at the pool of flaming petrol and explosive debris ... *and they widened with horror.*

Churchill's steadfast gaze of confidence swiftly drew a blank and they broadened and lost focus.

He could see the arrow he had released ...

The flame had gone out.

There would be no ignition, as he had intended.

Like planned, the cable grew taut from its slack spool and began to snag and eventually tow the loaded truck full of surviving, wounded British soldiers like a train carriage on a locomotive.

The activity down in the quiet street was growing enormous, due to the necessary sounds and action. Now, without the crucial distraction and smokescreen Churchill had devised for them in this portion of the escape plan, they would become fish in a barrel to the plethora of nighthawk machine gun sights and eagle-eyed snipers watching them at this current moment.

The pride he took in his fortune had been his downfall.

This setback was a devastating blow. It was a linchpin to the entire plan and would probably cause all the men aboard the exposed hauled truck to be shot to death. Within seconds, they would be perforated and decimated, now that they were completely unprotected without that distraction ...

As the ass fell out of his plan, Churchill sneered.

Perplexed, this was something he expected to see transpire as it had from a *Robin Hood* movie, which admittedly had initially given him this whacky idea.

"Well ... That never happened to Errol Flynn!"

Every pair of German eyes in the surrounding area were locked onto the motion and activity down in the quiet Dunkirk street. The bagpipes had stirred awareness. The explosion had acted as a beacon towards the motion, and now ... *all sights were set.*

Countless machine gun turrets locked onto the moving tank and the exposed towed truck and engaged with extreme prejudice.

Even from over two hundred yards away, enemy shooters could discern the development. They could clearly see that the truck had an open tray and that within that space, there appeared to be concealed enemy British soldiers.

The many handheld searchlights spotted out the targets for all to mark, bright as day.

Snipers zeroed in on the score, tracing the movement through their scope attachments. Via their zoomed enhancements they could see the helpless members of the 4th Infantry Division, see the woe in their fearful faces.

Itchy fingers on hairy triggers, Gerry's stares had been down the sights, *waiting* for a target ... and now they had it, offered to them on a silver platter.

They opened fire.

Whizz! Whizz!

Prang! Snap!

At devastating velocities, stray rounds spiked everywhere about the proximity as the range of sharpshooters attempted to hit live targets within the truck tray once it sprung to life, forcefully yanked in hops and bounds behind the departing tank. The A10 cruiser rounded a corner towing the Bedford—gaining distance and with it, a lengthy slack of the winch line.

Minus any control, the transport truck reeled tangent without much grace. Its reel nipped at snags and ditches in terrain imperfections along the stretch of road, pulled after the grunting, armoured brute.

The scraping tyres of the Bedford made rubbery yelping sounds as the wheels disputed their rotation. The whole act resembled a disapproving canine cogently dragged on a leash by its owner.

The great big searchlight atop enemy positions painted the truck with vivid luminance, lighting it up as though it had been selected for rapture. The bright beam tracked them, locked on, arresting all onboard with pure hot white radiance.

Ping! Tonk! Ping! Ping!

An array of sparks ignited from the metal frame of the tray of the truck, puncturing the cabin roof, tearing it to shreds. Without the knowledge that the vehicle was being towed and not driven, intelligent shooters concentrated their fire on the unoccupied forward compartment in order to stop the vehicle's impetus. Little did they know, the driver of this vehicle was a fifteen-tonne cruiser tank named Busty Barbara.

It did not take long before one of the exposed wincing soldiers within the open tray abruptly convulsed, tragically struck by one of the hundreds of bullets pouring down upon them like a concentrated hailstorm.

An already wounded soldier cried in agony as a different bullet hit him in the shin where he lay, grotesquely breaking his leg in the process. He lurched up, grimacing in excruciating pain and clenching at the wound with an already bandaged hand and head.

"Stay down!" Corporal Hill shouted through the chaos, witnessing the tragedy of the event unfolding. Now upright, his man was more exposed. Hill's voice bellowed as more noise polluted the air in the form of hot 7.92 Mauser lead sporadically striking a metal chassis.

"Private get down! Now!"

Condemned by his Hippocratic Oath, an able combat surgeon lurched forwards in the pandemonium and attended to the flesh wound with a fresh pair of hands. It was Bosko, the same disgruntled medic from earlier. After this cock-up, he would presumably have some more negative things to say about Churchill's plan.

"This is fucked! We're all dead!" he shouted. *"We're turkeys in a shoot down here!"*

"Get down!" Hill shouted over his hurling argument. Thankfully, though, his aid caused the wounded soldier to lay down flat. *"Get! D–"* *whiz-DONK!*

Through the white and red medical logo on his steel brodie helmet, a lethal round struck and killed Bosko the assisting medic right before Hill's eyes, and he slumped dull and lifeless over the wounded soldier, becoming a forthcoming human shield. His voiced disagreement ceased like a snap of the fingers as he went from being alive to dead in an instant.

Automatic machine gun tracers began to assault the dusty cobblestone street about the area, inaccurately raking the vicinity with impacts raining lightning and brimstone. In controlled volleys, the Germans in the far distance hosed at the side of the truck tray as the vehicle tugged into a pile of rubbish along the side of the street. She snagged briefly, breaking free with a taut hitch. The sudden skip in fluent motion just so happened to save them from an onslaught of arcing machine gun fire across the distance, causing them to inadvertently evade the incoming barrage. The absent area they previously occupied became decimated, striking a couple dozen pinwheels of flowing sparks in their wake as they skidded clear, almost tipping.

The searchlight surrounded them like crooks in a jailbreak.

It dropped a pin on their location, like a beacon on the radar.

The shooting intensified.

"No ..."

Still hypnotized by crippling anguish, Churchill exhaled from his street corner cover, watching the pandemonium unfold.

"No, no, no ..."

Auspiciously, the winch supported the weight well for such a thin cable. The tensile strength of the wire was quite robust.

He watched as the lifeless transporter truck hauled, towed by Hardy in the cruiser tank, heaving them to safety ... however, without the required distraction, this was nothing more than a pyrrhic victory for these few brave Brits. With every passing second, the non-action potentially inflicted mass casualties.

Churchill flinched from a stray round as it struck the stone wall near his grimy face whilst he gazed upon the chaotic scene of the truck occupants becoming lit up under the German searchlight.

His face peered more into the street of exploding ricochets and occasional bouncing tracer rounds, and he laid eyes upon the row of other trucks, lying in wait for ignition. They were covered in ordinance and flammable substances, but his prayers went unanswered for a convenient eruption of the combustibles by the enemy fire. The many sparks from the many gunners' off-shoots and ricochets missed them by miles, too focused on the big picture.

Beneath the thundering anarchy, Jack caught a glimmer of reflective light in one of the many puddles of petrol, just asking to be sparked.

That was it ...

His mind's eye spied the requisite last-ditch effort.

If he could light that fuel ... he saved them all.

"Come on," he whispered, regathering his pride.

He raised his longbow and took a breath. Suffering all that he was accountable for, Churchill stepped out into the ballistic shooting-range of intermittent gunshot impacts and explosive volume, concentrating on the targets downrange from him ... and praying for a miracle.

"Give me a spark, you bastard!"

He quickly drew an arrow from his shoulder quiver and released it at the steel frame above the pools of combustible liquid.

The hocked-back arrow launched from his longbow clench with the upmost supremacy, striking the metal tray beside the depository with more kinetic power than a bullet. The war arrow sprang off with a flint of smoke, disappearing into the abyssal shadows of night.

Spying no detonation, he immediately drew another promising arrow, loosing it with another rushed draw at the target. It struck the metallic framework beside the deflated tyre, mere inches above the pool of petrol. The bodkin head of the war arrow caused a brighter spark than the one prior, but only flinted for an instant before becoming dowsed by a gust. It was not enough to ignite the fuel, dissipating before it reached the pool.

That wooden arrow fractured on impact, showering the area in splinters from the breakage: an exact symbolization of this failed, broken, and hopeless plan.

Growing anxious quickly, Jack took another arrow from the quiver, nocked and drew his string, when—

Crash!

Stray large calibre rounds had lashed out at a nearby awning, whipping chunks of brick towards Churchill's face. Instinctively, he tucked his face into his shoulder, and in doing so, his pained left joint gave way, causing a wasted stray shot, which alarmingly looked to be headed towards the troop carrier. It missed.

"Come on! Just one bloody spark!"

He reached to draw the next arrow from his quiver, freezing for an instant upon realizing it was his last ...

Bollocks.

"Just. One. Spark."

His gaze zeroed, muting all noise around him.

Drawing the bowstring, he aimed for a patch of dry cobblestone surrounded by shiny, glistening oil puddles. The course nature of the stone promised better odds in igniting a bright and hot enough spark to ignite the fuel—

Suddenly, the bright blinding light of the searchlight found him in the madness, leeching from off of the passing truck.

It blinded him, feinting the draw.

Crac-crac-crac-crack!

A volley of disconcerting machine gun fire drew a destructive stitch line parallel to him, assaulting him with close ricochets across the stone street. The bullets were so close the velocity tore at his clothing, strafing Churchill in his exposed stance, and causing him to instinctively react in a pivot.

Infuriatingly, he had been a microsecond from loosing his drawn arrow on the target, and the shot had felt precise. Felt certain.

Just as the machine gun strafe beamed yond him, Jack impulsively desisted the draw and collapsed his held arms in recoil, pulling himself towards a closed doorway in the side of the French home. With a thud Jack barged through the door, averting sudden death by countless gunshot wounds as the volley passed him by in a flurry of golden tracers.

Tucked away for a second longer than he had hoped as the machine gun fire raked the walls past his position, Churchill quickly lent out into the street in a tight peek.

Behind the pointy bodkin tip of his arrowhead, he brought about his firm bow hold, searching for the same target beneath the trucks ...

... however, the blinding searchlight from afar illuminated his inching frame, including his sterling blue set of his eagle-eyes. His vision burned as it intensified, searching for the target zon—*SMASH!*

The doorframe an inch above his head detonated as a distant sniper attempted to target him through his zoomed crosshair. Debris from the wooden frame showered upon Churchill's stained maroon cap, and the desperate archer had no choice but to again abruptly withdraw.

This time, however, his last arrow clumsily escaped from the pinch of his fingers and dropped out onto the exposed warzone of the street. It remained in one piece, just discarded.

A fraction of a second after, another distant sharpshooter fired at where he had just peeked, resulting in another loud near-miss alongside the doorframe. Making matters worse for his upshot, he was now a target and was pinned down.

Tracking its fall through the chaos from mid-air to the cobblestone as it rebounded, Churchill spied through the raining pandemonium, and sought his last botched arrow as it settled on the stone street. Amongst piles of debris chunks and accompanying dust, the wooden arrow was taken dancing around by the reverberations of sporadic gunfire impacts and sprinkling chips of stone.

In this moment, the arrow was fragile and vulnerable, imminently about to become struck by a stray round from the inbound machine gun sprays, resulting in a bouquet of splinted wood and, more severely, a lost cause of irreparable resolve ...

This had gone from bad to worse, to completely fucked.

The motion of everything decelerated.

The intensity of the anarchy drowned out as Churchill's heartbeat became audible within himself.

... smoke sizzled from ricochets.

... stone crumbled from stray rounds.

... ash and dust fell from the blasts that had set the tank free.

... the skimming tracers of automatic machine gun fire blazed the street space as they chased after the slow-moving truck, visible due to the dust pollution beneath the bright searchlight.

The shock of deafening bedlam within the abrupt war-zone was paralysing ...

The dial of war cranked to eleven ...

Mad Jack's favourite volume for the soundtrack to his life.

Chit-chit-chit-chit ...

Even in this time of slow-moving motion, the fire rate of the distant droning machine gun as it sprayed downrange seemed lengthier. The spewing stream of golden tracers arched over the district, chomping up the cobblestone streets and carving the walls of the structure ruins like daisy-chained firecrackers.

Through his grimacing stare, Churchill scoured low. He cared only for the wooden arrow—a master key to unlock the seizing of their exodus.

His stare attentively watched as the thirty-inch arrow hopped perilously on the road, inadvertently under heavy fire almost as if it wasn't by random chance, and that the Huns knew of its worth, specifically targeting the projectile for termination.

Rising past the breakdancing arrow amidst the bullet impacts in the stone, Jack's focus rose onto the taut winch cable as it towed the immobilized truck into view. It was about to be passing his position, still constantly assaulted by gunfire by the Germans.

In those fleeting seconds, Jack spied it from his precarious position.

Somehow, the occupants inside were not all dead yet.

There was still a sliver of hope!

Still holding on, they hadn't given up.

That was the spark he had been praying for ...

The *real* spark.

It reignited his courage.

From the view of the passing chariot, Churchill's eyes rolled into the back of his skull, deep in not only thought during the peril but realization that *this* was it.

Forlorn by nature, Churchill recalled the Thomas Francis Meagher quote *'no prince or lord has tomb so proud, as he whose flag becomes his shroud'*. It spoke to him.

This was the moment. *His* moment.

While his raised heartbeat drowned out all other volume of war, Jack Churchill trundled out from the concealment of his French house as it became sustainably pummelled by at least three consecutive heavy machine gun nests, causing the stability to falter. The house became so consistently drilled by automatic bombardment that some of the walls and supports inside structurally collapsed, resulting in a cave-in coincidentally as Churchill lunged clear, escaping the clutches of death once again.

This additionally prevented any attempt for him to resume cover, though it no longer mattered. Jack had not planned on returning to seek shelter.

Now out in the warmth of the searchlight-lit war-zone and steering frantically through a laser grid of machine gun tracer bullets, the beret-clad archer was centre stage for a sold-out audience to marvel at.

Amidst entering the chaos, Churchill completed a shoulder roll on his painful side. During the tactical manoeuvre, his hand collected the lone arrow as he revolved, happening to duck between volleys of continuous rapid-fire as it hosed across the area and pulverized the house behind him. In a noisy fit of floating fragments and a potent exhume of dust, the structure subsided in his wake like a crashing wave.

Orbited around in his stance and returning vertical, Churchill dropped to a knee, scraping it hard as he halted the slide, and brought the arrow around. Upon collecting the projectile, he made sure to clutch near the fletching, able to nock.

He twirled and manipulated his fingertips so that the feathered end was rear, and he fastened the bowstring, raising in his crouching stance to an appropriate brace height ...

Whizz ...

Whizz ...

Whizz ...

Endless torrents of machine gun fire tore through the street air around Churchill's illuminated figure in the spotlight. It was amazing that nobody had yet hit him.

The haze of bullets resembled an insect swarm in a floodlight.

The zone was a tornado of receiving gunfire, and he was in the eye of the storm.

If it were a normal rate of time, the entire incident would have happened over the course of a few seconds, but to Jack it felt like an eternity.

At normal speed for an instant the volume of gunfire was at this point mistakable to the would-be soundtrack of Armageddon. The wave of gunfire ripped through the very fabric of existence, possibly even enough to relay particle tachyons backwards through the preserved continuum.

Halted in his skid on one grazed knee, Churchill closed an eye as he drew a bead on that same patch of dry stone beside the puddle. The razor-sharp tip of his war arrow aligned perfectly. It was time for him to take the shot, changing the course of their history ...

Suddenly, the gaffs of bright golden tracer rounds which were carving up the vicinity of the street painted a beam of concentrated fire towards Churchill ... but not before cutting across the two stationary trucks at the end of the street.

Glorified touch-off-detonations.

The tracer rounds from the spray chomped away at the bare cobblestone before steering a line into the convoy metal trucks, splashing like gumboots in rain puddles at the fuel deposits and kicking up more sparks than what Churchill could do with a hundred well-placed arrowheads striking steel framework. Before the machine gun could drag its consistent fire up higher and onto Churchill's position in the spotlight, the fuel seemingly portended to catch light in several different places.

The orange flames began to swirl and expand.

The short fuse had been started.

The split-second before Churchill could release the draw on his final arrow, his gawk watched as the string of machine gun fire sprinkled a glinting hail and spurs across the lifeless ruins of the abandoned trucks at the end of the street, igniting the fuse in several places for him.

The igneous puddles were ablaze in seconds, about to blow big.

Seeming almost sentient, the bright conflagration traced inescapable routes of the flammable liquid both horizontally and vertically, climbing and covering all coated connecting outer surfaces. This included the areas where the explosives were located.

Within seconds, the ravenous fires had surged across the entire saturated area, rising in livelier and brighter sweltering flames, creating a wall of fire. This caused a thick curtain of smoke to rise, illuminated by the powerful searchlights in the distance creating an impenetrable barrier for vision.

The light.

That pesky searchlight.

Beyond all, the large and most prominent searchlight was an unexpected nuisance ... and so in the spur of the moment Churchill had one final idea.

In lieu of the rising fire, he raised his unused draw higher.

... much higher.

By about three and half feet.

... and released.

After releasing the shot, Churchill was suddenly back in the evacuation game, not even caring to spectate his loosed arrow.

He tucked another evasive shoulder roll to his left and out of the path of an incoming machine gun strafing that raked a vicious line across the stone past him and chased sprinting after the towed truck.

Churchill was sure of that shot, more so than he had ever been in his entire life about any other archery game.

His arrow would quest on that target.

220 yards for distance ...

He had raised his shot an additional 36 degrees.

Windage, north-easterly, approximately 3.5 knots ...

At 220 yards, he had moved his aim approximately 3 inches to the left ... and without a second thought and barely a first, he had released.

After dodging the incoming stampede of gunfire, he upped and ran in revert chasing the truck as did the multitudes of malicious machine guns.

Longbow by his side, Churchill was in pursuit of the truck for two by-now obvious reasons. The first, to escape into Dunkirk with the others. The second, *to get as far away as possible from that big line of fuck-off explos—*

Ka-bo-BO-BO-BOOM!

Amidst the convoy of ruined transports, the scattered explosives in the blazing pools ignited in quick succession and in a growing chain reaction.

40mm HE shells ...

Mills bomb hand grenades ...

Countless random rounds of small arms ammunition ...

It all went off together, all at once!

It resembled a Chinese fireworks display, shooting into the skyline mushrooms of hot red fire, fingers of thick black smoke, as well as smaller javelins of spiralling spurs throwing jets of fire high up into the night sky in all directions.

A bit late, but the perfect distraction, nonetheless.

Screeching barbs of munition ignited and launched upwards and outwards in every bearing, blinding all onlookers with the heat of ordinance radiance ...

Smaller bullets crackled and fizzed along the line of vehicles constantly popping and tossing sparks amidst the inferno streak like pinwheels and pyrotechnics.

Shortly after, the fuel canisters and grouped 40mm shells underneath the lorry trucks sought enlightenment from the sizzling molten they were stranded in. When they went off in amongst it all, they went off big. Their path of least resistance shot flames out from under the bellies of the parked lorries. Once the explosives ignited the pressure had no place to go except vertical. The compressed fireballs heaved and lifted the vehicles up into the air, carrying them approximately six to ten feet before tipping them over onto their sides.

Alit fuel in the rumbling street, that had absorbed dirt, and the grime surroundings became a weighted incendiary that, once flung, clung to perpendicular surfaces. Rather than disperse sparsely or extinguish all together, the ignited substances carried themselves outwards, falling like lava from a choking volcano.

Fiery pastes coated many exteriors with an orange glow, scalding exteriors with a murky tar for almost fifty yards.

In that moment, over a thousand rounds of ammunition were fired north into the outskirts of Dunkirk ... but only one projectile in revert.

And it was dead-on target.

A Parthian shot of sorts, the lone war arrow sailed through the night sky after Churchill had loosed. The bodkin-tipped shaft arced brilliantly in its trajectory, briefly becoming illuminated in the beam of the searchlight as it closed in the said target: smashing into the thick glass magnification lens the same second there were distant fireworks down along the cusp of the city limits.

The light shattered inwards and flickered, fizzing as its bulb imploded with the weight of the glass. The light died.

The single German operator immediately recoiled from the impact, instinctively taking cover from what could have only been retaliatory fire by the enemy down in Dunkirk; however, upon a second glance, he had to remove his helmet in order to make sense of the scene: a single arrow fletching protruding from within the centre of the massive five-foot mouth of the damaged searchlight.

His attention to the fact was short-lived as the fireworks display of explosive eruptions down in the city made every soldier wince and cover their faces from the heat.

They ceased fire as the flames burned bright and the smoke from the fire rose into the night sky.

The beams of a dozen hand-held spotlights shone bright into the thick climbing pillar of smoke, unable to penetrate the veil. Whomever was moving beyond the wall was long gone.

Not unlike a leaf in a lateral gust, Jack Churchill was uplifted from behind as the wave from the blast carried him as if he were weightless.

Like the rising flame of a hot-air balloon, Churchill galloped into a spike as the scorching air struck him from behind, collecting him like a train, shoving him into a horizontal freefall. Back flexed concave and his limbs stretched wide, the blast sent him soaring like a cannonball.

He had been only seven or eight paces from the trail of the rolling transport truck and jumped at the precise right second to become uplifted and sent like a glider into the back of the rear tray by the heat of the shockwave.

As he gracefully soared like an eagle almost ten feet in the air, he got a good look at her condition and their path; conjoined via cable to the cruiser tank fifty yards ahead and up the street.

Longbow in one hand, holding down his sheathed sword with the other, he dropped in hard with a painful rough landing upon a few soldiers all at once.

The wounded men in the tray were stacked sideways, and were still shielding themselves from falling debris and the tidal wave of heat behind their retreat into the city. This brace suitably protected them at the right time, thus involuntarily assisting in breaking Churchill's landing aboard the open tray.

After an extended grimace at a dozen aching pains from both fresh and elder injuries alike, Churchill planted upright and took in the new view of the upward growing smoke wall behind them.

The obstruction covered their escape brilliantly and as initially planned.

He glanced around as the British soldiers realized they had not been landed on by falling debris per se, but Mad Jack, instead.

After a slight pause and as more and more of the wounded soldiers realized what had just happened and who had just unconsciously joined their ride, and before any of them could come out with something first and spoil the moment, Jack came out with:

"Beg your pardon, gents. Was this seat taken?"

Churchill had not intended to live through that act.

Metaphorically, he ascended only to be sent back down.

The war wasn't done with him yet.

XII
Ride of the Valkyries

1940, June 3
SS Mona's Isle
Coast of Dunkirk, English Channel

Moonlight illuminated the calm, tranquil ocean.

Aboard the full-capacity, lamplit SS Mona's Isle Packet Steamer, Rex King-Clark and his inherited devotees from Churchill's section sauntered the peripheries of the outer deck. In a hustle, they conversed with the various civilian ship captains whose little ships still moored from her sides, transferring troops from the Dunkirk evacuation. Now that their jobs ferrying soldiers from the beaches were done, these little ships would soon escort the naval-acquisitioned Mona's Isle on the final return voyage back across the English Channel. They were moments away from setting sail.

With the same relative goal, the men all split up, searching for a rite of passage back to the fray.

"*Oi!*" port side, Knocker White shone his flashlight off the deck railing at a pair of English sailors threading rope aboard two smaller fishing vessels. The illumination disturbed their practice and with squinting eyes they looked up into the beam. "Either you lot fancy another trip back?"

"To where?" one asked, holding up an arm to block the shine.

"Dunkirk!"

"You fuckin' what?" the sailor replied with a frown and open palms of question, as if it were some sort of joke.

"This guy havin' a laugh?" the other glanced with a scowl of displeasure. "Very funny, git."

"We're already sailin' back across the channel, ya dalcop! Ain't anybody goin' back to bloody *Dunkirk!*"

"So, that's a *no,* then?" confirmed White with an attitude to remain positive of their prospect. In the solid couple of seconds that followed the question his torch light skimmed between the two men like a tennis match as they stared back at him blankly.

They finally replied.

"*Fuck no!*"

"*Piss off, ya fruitcake!*"

Along the starboard side of the Mona's Isle, Padre Nicholl and King-Clark questioned some other ship captains. One of them was the same Dutch captain who had transferred them to the Mona's Isle, still down aboard his coaster known as the Twente, repairing the engine with his engineer.

In double-Dutch, King-Clark managed to get out of him a promising rejoinder, in that he would have been keen to attempt another return run into the hostile waters of Dunkirk harbour if it meant rescuing a soldier, but unfortunately his boat was ruined. She was now at the mercy of the Mona's Isle in order to get her back across the channel.

"Blast!" King-Clark cursed at the bad luck, pushing off the railing and away from the coaster. There was another boat attached to the Mona's Isle, hitched up the other end. Some sort of pleasure yacht, it was the very last ship along this side—and it could have very well been their last hope if the others struck out.

Gin Parker, Wand, and Macken reappeared after being absent for a stretch. They seemed disillusioned from this quest's lack of success, now congregating with Nicholl as King-Clark's desperate gawk intensified onwards towards the final yacht and final option.

The frustration of the desperate situation receded as he was lost in thought. King-Clark lingered in his stare, watching the captain and his two young ship hands toss ropes around, detaching the yacht from the side of the mother ship. The Mona's Isle was preparing to build speed now and head north back to England.

The ship seemed as content at staying the course as most of the others. King-Clark sighed helplessly, not bothered to even ask.

Nicholl appeared at his side, still willing to ask.

"Excuse me, good sir?" the well-mannered padre shouted down to them over the loud thrashing of the Mona's Isle's engine propulsion and now that they were in motion, a building wind current. Nicholl waved his small angular flashlight, signalling. "I say, hello down there!"

"Hello!" an Englishman responded, looking up from the collapsing wet rope around his hand and elbow.

"Oh, at least he speaks English," King-Clark said under his breath. Their last conversation with the Dutchmen had tested their patience.

"Nice boat, eh," the padre added, finding it difficult to segue into requesting such a large favour from a stranger, like King-Clark and the others had been attempting to no avail. He was not a man fond of querying nepotisms, and therefore had little confidence in the field.

"That's it," Knocker White appeared running up behind them, looking over the railing at the yacht. "This is the last guy with a boat that we haven't asked ..."

"Hullo there. My name is Captain Rex King-Clark," he intervened, butting in to take charge and adapting Nicholl's enquiry strategy in a desperate attempt to gain acceptance of his proposal. "Thank you for your service here today. You helped save a great many men."

"You're very welcome, lads," down below, the captain replied wholesomely, going about his business with his small civilian crew. They seemed exhausted.

"Ask him," Knocker probed after a slight pause. "Come on."

King-Clark leant against the railing. "Say there ... how would you and your lot feel about, eh ... returning to Dunkirk?"

The captain did not seem fazed. His response, both in body language and verbal retort, were both not what any of them were expecting.

After an extended moment of incommunicativeness, he looked about himself and his ship, then back up at the men along the railing. "Yeah, alright then."

The response took a second to sink in.

Knocker White promptly exploded with ecstatic laughter, immediately turning back around and excitedly shouting out to the others in the background. "*Gin! Gin! We got one!*"

Gin Parker tapped Wand and Macken respectively on the shoulders, luring them over.

Nicholl intrusively grabbed King-Clark by the arm.

The men were dumbfounded.

"R-really?" King-Clark queried, surprised.

The captain shrugged. "Yeah, why not. What's the job?"

"Rescue mission."

He nodded, still winding the wet rope. "Who?"

Suddenly, in the far distance of Dunkirk, there were multiple, bass-filled explosions erupting in an audible continuance. They were larger than the impacts of erratic artillery shelling and were quite the focus of attention.

The sound originated from the back of Dunkirk, far south and at ground level. The bass in the air and the heat of the orange glow turned a lot of heads on the many boats evacuating the harbour. The sound carried across the dark glistening of the flat-water surface, chasing the distance after them with a delay from a bright flashing and blinking somewhere on the fringe of the coastal city, along its outskirts.

King-Clark nodded afterwards. "Him."

The sea captain and the crew all heard the distant detonations, and they exchanged a glance, already preparing to detach from the Mona's Isle. The captain of the yacht looked up, back at the willing soldiers along the railing, each retaining the same yearning to return into the fray.

As King-Clark addressed, Padre Nicholl, Knocker White, Gin Parker, and Privates Wand and Macken appeared behind their substitute captain and along the deck railing.

The yacht captain jerked his head towards the sound.

Towards Dunkirk.

"Friend of yours, eh?"

"The very best."

"Well, leave no man behind, eh?" he waved welcomingly. "C'mon then! All aboard *the Sundowner.*"

1940, June 3
Dunkirk
Nord-Pas-de-Calais, France

In the wake of a crumbling tidal wave of action, the British cruiser tank rumbled down the dark and dust-fogged streets of war-torn Dunkirk. Towing behind it via winch was a decommissioned Bedford transport truck, packed with a motley group of wounded soldiers all equally as keen to make the coast in the hope of getting transported.

The night air was cold, and the joining streets were quiet.

The radiance of action was still strobing from the massive fireball Mad Jack had just set off behind in their wake.

A bright and sweltering veil of heat and light distorted any view of their fleeing escape and blocked out most enemy fire.

When the fireworks of detonating ordinance began to dissipate in the aftershock of their planned escape, the wall of smoke lived on, billowing thick and tall and further obscuring the enemy's view on the southern end of the coastal city.

Inside the rickety metal confines of the A10 cruiser, controlling the course of their new tank/truck cavalcade, Felix Hardy finally took a breath and removed the sweaty earmuffs from his head, stowing them loosely on their designated harness above the forward viewport as he drove.

Now that they were nearing four whole blocks away from where they had started, he began to slow as the volume of their assault began to lessen into nothingness.

"Oh, fuck. Oh, shit. Oh, fuck ..." like a skipping record, the man whimpered under his breath, still amped on an overdose of adrenaline from their loud exodus.

He looked helplessly around at his feet, at the many gears and pedals, struggling to search the handbrake now that he had allowed for their acceleration to slow into an idle drift, just like how Jack had instructed. They were now out of harm's way.

The cruiser tracks slowed to a steady grind, barely moving them forward while Hardy searched for the means to stop them completely or cut the engine.

"Fuck me, where ... which one is it ..." he mumbled to himself, barely audible over the loud engine. His complete attention was down and around the lower console.

While he tipped his head, attempting to gain a better look for another pedal that may have been the brake, Jack Churchill's beret-attired upside-down head poked inside from the above hatch, and he shouted:

"*Oi!*"

"Fuck!" Hardy flinched and jolted in his seat. He jumped so high he bumped his head on the roof of the tank. His crushed and filthy fedora did little to soften the blow.

The tank had been cruising so slowly just now that Churchill had been able to dismount the dragging truck and run up to the tank, leaping aboard to find the top hatch.

"*It's there! Next to the throttle!*" Churchill pointed, shouting loud above the roar of the engine boom inside the steel beast. At this angle on the tank, his ass would have been high in the sky as they cruised. "*You have to squeeze it! Then disengage the ignition!*"

Hardy scanned about at his hands, feeling around the driving levers. One of them resembled a push-bicycle handle. He found it and squeezed, and a loud pitch gave out as the crank brakes slowed the grinding tank tracks outside and they finally came to arrest.

"Fucking thank God!" Hardy whispered with an exhale, finally feeling in total control. The audio notably reduced now that the axles inside were not rotating, and the left and right tracks weren't clunking away outside.

"Bank us via left!" Churchill ordered now that his voice was more audible. Hardy nodded, yanking the left lever as he allowed the unit to coast, still dragging the truck behind them.

The cruiser tank twisted and veered into a connecting street on the left, now well out of range and view of the outskirts.

Hardy finally pulled them to a complete stop.

The lugged truck behind rolled a few extra feet before jolting still, and those few men aboard began to stir and lean out to gain a view. This was the furthest they had ever made it into Dunkirk.

Upstanding on the turret of the tank, Churchill stood tall and hollered, "Stay in the truck!"

Below him, Hardy's fedora-clad head emerged. Moderately deafened and now covered in an extra layer of soot and sweat, he peeked around at their surroundings now that they were successfully within the eerie city.

The tank had dragged the truck onto a cobblestone street framed with ruin and clouded with a dust haze that was thick enough to taste. They were completely out of view of the chaos along the outskirts from which they had just escaped and, at least for a moment, they were safe.

"Hill! How are we?" during this breather, Churchill called across to the attached vehicle. In the rear of the tray, he could see the 4th Infantry corporal moving about, wincing from a fresh bullet gash across his hairline. He had suffered an awfully close near-miss during that whiffed escape.

Half-heartedly, he replied with a thumbs-up gesture ... but the gesture faded into concern as his attention swayed, as did everyone else's ...

Once the cloud of dust they dragged in behind them settled, all the men suddenly became aware of movement within their proximity, in all vectors. From the street buildings parallel and on either side of their position, noises would be heard.

Rubble disturbed in some positions, causing rocks to fall.

Running footsteps trod across dusty concrete, shuffling debris.

From inside the broken and bombed buildings and structural remnants, dark figures aroused and surfaced from many vantage points and out of infinite crevasses, enveloping their new cavalcade.

They were on them in seconds.

These unknown figures all had weapons.

Potentially hostile, the numbers surrounded them.

They said not a word as they dispersed and positioned.

"*Contact!*" one of the wounded 4th Infantrymen shouted as the movement startled him, and he retracted back into the tray of the truck with his sidearm extended above his head.

Other men found their weapons, unknowing of which target to aim towards, as the more they prepared, the more movement seemed to encircle their position, even high in the second storey of the buildings. Whoever this was had tactical advantage of the higher ground.

"*Watch out!*" another shouted, huddling in close.

Heart rates elevated.

"*Defensive positions!*" said another instinctively, recalling their training. A bandaged troop raised a Lee-Enfield rifle, heroically dismounting the tray in order to use it for partial concealment whilst scanning the walls over his iron-sights, standing his ground in the face of a numerically superior force.

Nobody fired.

It was a stand-off.

"*Hold your fire!*" Corporal Hill shouted as he dropped behind the protection of the truck tray. With his Webley up by his shoulder, he waved his spare hand at the others, attempting to contain them from instigating a bloodbath. The odds here were tactically very much not in their favour.

Erect and exposed upon the tank, Churchill remained.

He did not shriek or wince upon their subtle ingress from the dusty shadows of the battle-torn environment. He made no sudden moves, watching calmly as their cavalcade became surrounded.

"*Hold fire!*" another British soldier repeated. Their voices echoed throughout the post-apocalyptic empty street. "*Hoooold!*"

Appeasing the shadow arms as he stood focal atop of the cruiser tank, Churchill raised out his palms wide to show his utter renunciation unto them. His gaze sharpened as the closest figures finally emerged from the woodwork, and in many ways fulfilled his suspicions.

The unknowns were like statues come to life, each covered in ash and grime reminiscent of an excerpt from a shaded oil painting. They materialized from the grimy walls all around, like *Morlocks* to snatch the *Eloi.*

Not that he had shown any fear prior to the realization, Churchill held his non-threatening pose as an overabundance of assorted firearms were pointed his way. He could feel the heat of the bulletheads recessing in the shadows of the countless gun barrels, prepared to blow him away at the slightest pull of a trigger.

"*Bonjour,* lads."

Jack's announcement in French broke the ice of the intense silent stand-off between the two forces. His suspicions were confirmed by the sheer numbers, the location, as well as the fact he caught glimpses of various Adrian helmets, that the unknown combatants were none other than the French rearguard—*or what was left of them at least.* This far back in Dunkirk, the poor bastards had been exposed to non-stop artillery shelling, explosive barraging, and unrelenting aerial attacks from sweeping fighters trying to pick them off. They had been dodging bullets, bombs, and collapsing buildings for the past twenty-four hours straight, wondering if the evacuation boats that left were ever coming back.

As the dust about the vicinity settled Churchill could finally make out what appeared to be an established French aid station in a shattered shop front, and a machine gun emplacement over some arranged sandbag barricades at the corner of the street.

"Bonjour, heh-hello?" one of the unknown soldiers finally spoke as he approached the vehicles from his position in the rubble.

Churchill's attention quickly concentrated on him. Hopefully, he was the leader of this squad. From the top of the tank, he gazed down and through the dissipating vapour cloud at the fellow.

Jack bowed before carefully dismounting the cruiser.

When he did, Hardy's head shyly reemerged to look upon these scary fellows. When he laid eyes upon their battle-worn and flat, hollow expressions, he realized that there was one right up against the side of the cruiser, staring straight at him with a bayonet-fitted rifle. It startled him immensely.

"*Parlez vous Anglais?*" Churchill asked after dismounting and representing their lil motley group of latecomers, taking his extended hand in embrace now that he was on ground level.

"Oui. A little," said the Frenchman. He spoke with a heavy accent, taking in Churchill's insignia on his uniform collars. "You-eh the one who mak-eh the song?"

Churchill followed his gesture to the hanging bagpipes slung on the rear side of his hip. He returned his eyeline and heartedly bobbed his head. "I am."

In the seconds that followed, the Frenchman seemed to allure to his men a sense of relief. He signalled to them and then gestured, lowering their combined offensive stances.

The British followed suit and everybody relaxed.

Their collective hearts finally slowed their excessive beating within their chests, and they all caught a breath.

"You com-eh very lat-eh to your ships, Cap-ti-on."

Churchill's focus fell upon his man's uniform, paying his rank note since he had done the same upon observation. It was torn, discoloured, frayed, and stained. Whoever he was, he and his unit had seen a lot of action fighting the Germans, probably even before reaching Dunkirk and sustaining the bombings. They were lucky to have fallen back to the city in one piece.

"Well, better late than never," Churchill remarked, half-wittily. He knew any humour would likely fly right over the head of the Frenchman for lack of translation. He was also distracted by the realization that they were probably going to encounter more stranded French army soldiers on their way to the beaches than he had expected—none of which, were officially prioritized to come with them across the channel. This obviously was not a decision Churchill shared with those calling the shots, but he understood that the evacuation of the British Expeditionary Force came as first priority. Many of the French were pulled out, but many would unfortunately perish at the hands of Nazi Germany.

He felt pity for these abandoned souls, and he was not capable of leaving a single man behind. He had come this far.

"Well, all aboard the evacuation bus, *mon ami*," Churchill said with a welcoming gesture. He wasn't exactly sure how he was going to fit another three dozen soldiers aboard their tank/truck convoy, but it could be attempted. Even if those able marched out.

"Non désolé, ami," the Frenchman regarded, shaking his head ever so slightly in non-compliance. Around him, his loyal servicemen cradled their weapons and what little ammunition they had left. They were war-torn and battle-hardened, indefinitely set to purpose.

Churchill tilted his head at the response as the Frenchman elaborated. "Our duty is to get-eh you people out safe. We will hold. We will complete this duty. We will hold-eh the Germans back, as you have done so long for us ..."

Churchill's view reeled, taken aback.

Their courage was overwhelming.

"Until our last breath, we will hold-eh Dunkerque."

"*Dunkirk?*" Churchill pouted and his brow inverted with earnest sincerity. "My friend, Dunkirk has *already* fallen. France has fallen. It is time to leave."

"*My friend,*" the French soldier reiterated with a hint of defiant stubbornness in his wayward tone. "We *will* hold."

Churchill gazed at him, taking an extra second to process his decision on behalf of his men. With a glance around at the devoted Frenchmen, he could tell they were as dedicated as their leader in holding their ground, even in these impossible odds.

There was a contrast in attendance.

Where the British were dying to get out of this country, the French would die to defend it.

"You are commendably brave," Churchill commented sincerely. "Merci. To you and your men for your service here."

With that, Jack nodded to the few around him and mounted the cruiser tank as Hardy preserved the cue to start her back up again, preparing to move out.

"Cap-ti-on," the Frenchman bellowed deeply, calling Churchill's attention one last time from atop of the tank. He eyed him dead square and spoke on behalf of all his men and people. "Thank *you*, and *your* men."

It was then Churchill remembered. Remembered they were here for them in the first place. It was an ideology that escaped his conscience, as helping people in need was genuinely second nature deep seeded within him. He always leapt without looking. Although the defence of France had not worked out, they must have been grateful to the British for their valiant effort.

After a moment's pause, Churchill gave a solemn nod in retort to the French soldier as the rearguard retracted back into the darkness, into their fortified positions.

There then grew an increasing pitch in the night sky ...

It was a sound all too familiar—more so to the French.

... *wwwwhiiiiiiiiirr* ...

"Oh, bollocks."

Churchill's view dropped down to the Frenchman as he added with haste to his tone.

The Frenchman remarked, "Germans! It's anoth-eh wave of bomb-ehs. They hit Dunkerque from-eh the skies. You and your English-men must hurry. Get to the beaches! Get to the boats!"

"We will. Good luck, my friend!"

"You, too," he bobbed, gesturing to disperse his troops, as well as Churchill and his tank and truck full of wounded Brits.

Dropping down into the belly of the A10 tank, Churchill immediately addressed Hardy. "Punch it, Hardy! Now!"

"What's that sound?" he attempted to ask.

"You don't want to know! Now, lad, go!"

"I don't like that sound!" Hardy bellowed as he shook his head, reluctantly performing his tasks. He grinded the gears and caused the A10 to perform a bunny-hop before stalling.

Churchill stood back up and poked his head out of the top hatch, searching the night sky for the incoming Luftwaffe planes. The growing pitch sounded like an armada coming for Dunkirk, likely an assortment of close-range fighters, medium and light bombers, maybe even some heavier ones, since it was night-time and there was less risk of RAF defence or counter.

"Come on!" Churchill shouted at Hardy, who was struggling with the tank.

"I'm trying!" Hardy argued, frustrated.

"It's been five minutes, have you already forgotten how to drive this thing?"

"Yes! Alright! I have!" Hardy exclaimed. "Doesn't help that she's a hussy and won't start!"

"That's no way to speak to a lady," Churchill retorted, remaining composed as the sound of the incoming air raid increased in volume exponentially, making every man's ears feel like they needed to pop. "Barbara's taken a few loads ... she's exhausted."

"Yeah! I think she's had one load too many!" Hardy shoved the gears, looking back. The explicit sexual innuendo seemingly went straight over his head, lost sailing above the cloud of frustration the American was blinded by.

Churchill squatted down inside and leant in, pointing to the many levers and pedals. His soothing hand on Hardy's shoulder calmed him, focused him.

Together, as it came back to Hardy in a disarray of befuddled mess, they shouted in tangent: "*Ignition. Ignition key lock. Gears. Steering; forward, back, left, right. Brake. Clutch. Accelerator—*"

"Alright, yeah, I got this!" Hardy shouted, cranking the pedals and getting the cruiser cruising.

Churchill stood once again, protruding from the open hatch.

His eyes scanned the night sky before they rested upon the dragging Bedford behind them and its exposed soldiers who were all aboard. There was no way they would survive in that open tray if a fighter locked onto them from the sky and lit them up, let alone a bomber dropping a payload. Even those able to pile within the tank would barely survive that, if not only to be entombed in rubble.

Deep in thought, he retracted back inside and readdressed Hardy. "We've got to get these lads off the streets and under cover somehow!"

"What?"

"Just while the blitz is upon us!"

"How, though? Where?"

"Just gun it for now. Get us balls-deep into Dunkirk as fast as you can, before those birds get overhead!"

"O.K.!" Hardy nodded, cranking the levers and grinding the gears. The tracks on her shoulders chewed sternly and the tank lunged forwards, gaining speed and reaching its maximum along a straight street, now headed north once again. The only time she showed signs of slowing was when Hardy steered her between obstacles, or needing to barge some as they blocked the road.

Behind them in tow, the loaded lorry punched through an overhang of rubble that the tank missed, exploding through a cloud of dust vapour like a grass tuff from a punted kick-off.

"We need to make as much ground as we can!"

"Got it! Then what?!"

"We've got to find shelter of some kind. Wait for this air raid to piss off."

Hardy looked over his shoulder as they rocked about. "Captain, what *shelter?* There are no goddamn buildings left standing as it is, let alone one big enough for us to park our little daisy-chained convoy under. Those doors are all locked, buddy."

"Well," Churchill spoke as he contemplated and with a twitch of the jaw. "Lucky for us, you're driving a master key."

1940, June 3
M/Y Sundowner
Coast of Dunkirk, English Channel

The gentle hum of the 72-horsepower Gleniffer diesel engine puttered as the yacht skimmed the sea, driving towards the hazy and dark Dunkirk harbour that gloomed upon the night horizon.

The coastal city radiated utter destruction from what was visible in the night. From afar, the coastal city wore a golden glimmer from the couple of thousand spot fires. Backlit structural skeletons were all that remained of some buildings after the bombings. Smoke pillars still climbed in stacks from countless glowing conflagrations and flickering embers.

The ship graveyard left in the bay of the harbour mimicked something out of the epilogue of the *Battle of Salamis*, only every floating, capsized remnant of a boat belonged to the same team.

There were abandoned ships set ablaze, drifting lifelessly, as well as charred floating debris from ships long gone to the bottom of the channel. Oil slicks would have discoloured the sea in patches, indiscernible currently due to the nightscape.

The Sundowner yacht cruised at a mild pace through the floating naval wasteland. The men aboard gawked quietly off into the lapping water, sometimes shining their shortrange flashlights upon the driftwood debris in search of survivors. Most times, they became engrossed in disarray at the amount of drifting dead corpses. Like buoys, they were a surefire way to tell if the tide was going in or out.

Up front, Corporal Knocker White supervised their forward travel with vigilant eyes and a loaded rifle while Privates Wand and Macken rode on her bow armed with long prodding sticks. They were given the duty of respectfully pushing clear the deceased bodies in the water and parting their way, so that they did not unpleasantly bounce off the keel of the boat.

Staffing the yacht were the captain (or skipper) by the name of *Charles Lightoller*, a fellow navy man now in his 60s, and his two crewmen. One was the eldest son of the captain of the ship by the name of *Roger*, and the other was his friend from England, an 18-year-old sea scout named *Gerald Ashcroft*.

The plan was to flow in along the beaches headed east, and then drift the Dunkirk harbour-side—where accessible—in the hope of spotting the man they were rescuing. In their mind's eye, they hoped to simply spot Jack Churchill standing there on the end of a pier as if waiting for a taxi, and he could just jump aboard the yacht and they could be on their merry way.

On the way over, King-Clark and Padre Nicholl had engaged the ship's skipper in conversation. They had learnt a brief summary of the vessel's history; that it was launched in 1930 after Lightoller and his wife purchased it for £40. They learnt that the hull of the boat was originally recovered from the mud at *Conyer Creek* east of the *River Medway*, southeast England. She was fitted with two masts and ketch-rigged with a jib, mainsail, mizzen, and a mizzen staysail. Because his wife was Australian, they named the yacht *the Sundowner*, which was Aussie lingo for a *hobo*.

"Well spank my arse and call me Charlie ..." the silver fox skipper of the ship, whose name was in fact *Charlie*, made comment upon witnessing the aftermath of the evacuation in the harbour as he steered his motor yacht back into the fray. The low tide had dragged a lot more debris out and into the sea compared to when he had last been this close. With a sudden realization, he spoke pardoning to the military chaplain aboard. "Excuse the French. I've got the foul mouth of a sailor because I used to be one—retired in 1919."

"Relax, skip," responded Padre Nicholl from the doorway behind them in the cabin. "This is your ship. A sailor's swearing gets right of way aboard the sea, ex-service or not."

Lightoller gestured a respectful nod at Nicholl.

They had been chatting for a while now, but he was yet to stop wondering how such a young-looking man becomes not only a military chaplain in service, but a second lieutenant in the army.

"Thanks, *Padre*."

"Where did you serve?"

"*The Great War*. I was *Lieutenant Commander* of the *HMS Garry*."

Nicholl nodded as he listened—the title triggering a recollection that dwelled and lingered furthermore inside his mind like a splinter. He breathed the words, trying his dandiest to recall. "*The Garry* ..."

Whilst Nicholl pondered, King-Clark took a good look at the floor of the cabin, noticing again that it seemed very polluted with loose brass from recently spent shells. In fact, there were bullet casings absolutely everywhere. They had been swept into the corners of the cabin and lined the many crevices of the timber deck joins. For the most part, they had obviously been swept from the floor of the cabin and into the drink.

King-Clark made comment as he kicked a few brass casings with his boot as they tinkled and rolled about the wooden boards as the drift of the ocean tipped their latitude like a tilting gyroscope. "Seen some action of late, skipper?"

"Sure did," Lightoller nodded to a hanging M1928 Thompson submachine gun resting on the console before the glass of the cabin. It was complete with a wooden streetsweeper-style foreword grip handle and loaded with a one-hundred-shot drum magazine. "Took a few defensive squirts up at them German fighters yesty."

King-Clark scoffed. "You don't say?"

Lightoller smirked and shrugged. "I was never a good shot."

"Heavy piece of machinery for a light ship?" Padre Nicholl questioned, following up on his intrigue. His line of investigation seemed slightly targeted to those who knew his passive demeanour, such as King-Clark. He gawked ever so slightly upon the padre, wondering about the tone of his enquiry towards the skipper.

"Alright, boys, you caught me," Lightoller raised his hands briefly at the question as if it were an interrogation. He placed them both back down on the wheel after demonstrating his playfulness. "I'm a spy for ol' boy Adolf."

Nicholl and King-Clark exchanged a look for a second in silence.

"No, really, we are spies ..." Lightoller further explained, not so playfully. "... just, not for Hitler—the cunt. That bit was for a laugh."

"What do you mean?" bearing a fresh frown, King-Clark cued elaboration. In these dark times, throwing around such allegations to strangers within the military was not typically taken lightly.

"I guess none of it matters now, but the Admiralty hired us as a civilian vessel last year. We survey the coasts and report to the British Navy."

Nicholl and King-Clark each cast raised chins of admiration.

If so, that was mighty courageous of Lightoller and his crew, and it's entirely plausible they would have been lawfully deputized because of it.

Lightoller continued, "Myself and young Ashcroft there, who comes from a navy background. It's why we are geared. No way we risk running into a kraut party without the means to defend the ol' Sundowner."

King-Clark tipped his head at Nicholl, who did the same with an acknowledging pout. "Fair enough."

After an extended moment of calm cruising, Lightoller shook his head. This view scape was disastrous, but his tone did not seem as much surprised or shocked as it did merely concede to the fact of war, making it even more obvious that he was a veteran. The view had definitely changed a little now that the ships had all finalized their ferrying through the debris. It all had time to settle and rise to the surface. "Would you take a look at this place ... Padre, could you step out and tell everybody to be on the lookout for any survivors in the water?"

"Sure," Padre complied, leaving the cabin and relaying the sea captain's orders to the two crewmen, as well as the four other British soldiers onboard the yacht, as well as remaining on deck to partake.

In the cabin, King-Clark stepped in close and levelled his attention at the scene through the sea salt-assaulted glass. Stray and abandoned boats were still smouldering afloat, aimlessly drifting in the coast of inky black. Shipwrecks of a few bigger vessels were marooned in the shallow harbour, poking upright and partially sunken. The elements of debris clapping lifelessly against the hull of the yacht.

In the background of it all, mostly a silhouette in the darkness, alit by the glow of smoke and fog beneath the moonlight, was the coastal city of Dunkirk in devastated ruins.

Even in the absence of his knowledgeable friend, King-Clark had to speak the Shakespearian quote aloud: " *'Once more unto the breach ...*"

Lightoller's focus drifted in his panning view and onto him as he spoke barely above his own breath. Lightoller's brow raised as he listened to King-Clark. He already considered him looney for wanting to come back to Dunkirk, this just cemented it.

"*... or close the wall up with our English dead.'* "
Okay then.

The skipper said not a word, but King-Clark felt his contemptuous gaze. He didn't debate it. It was true that he was more cultured and literarily in-tune than most men.

"*Henry V ...?*" he explained futilely, and Lightoller bobbed his head, politely, wordlessly acknowledging. King-Clark added pointlessly, "*Shakespeare ...?*"

Again, Lightoller nodded. "Sure."

After a full moment of silence, King-Clark waddled his head and commented to himself with a yearnful tone. "Jack would've gotten it."

"*Jack?*" Lightoller mentioned, keeping his eyes on the water. "That's your friend, yeah? The one we're rescuing?"

"Jack Churchill, yes. Though, if it were him wording what we're doing, we wouldn't so much be *rescuing him* as much as we are *giving him a lift.*"

"Aye, I know the type. You reckon he's still alive in there?" Lightoller questioned, starting to turn them port side and in a sweep adjacent to the coast and onto a passage that would allow for their small yacht to cruise through the distilled harbour.

"He's alive," King-Clark responded with utter certainty. "I've come to believe that over the years Mad Jack Churchill is unkillable."

"*Unkillable,* eh?" Lightoller chuckled to himself. "That's what they said about my last ship."

King-Clark faced him, waiting for the revelation.

"*The Titanic.*"

"*The Titanic?!*" King-Clark glowered and stared. "You were on the Titanic?"

"Aye, Second Officer," Lightoller waggled with pride.

"*Lightoller, Charles Lightoller,*" King-Clark whispered to himself before shaking his head, finally understanding where he knew this man's name from: the Titanic disaster of 1912. "Bloody Hell, man, you're *the* Charles Lightoller. You're notorious."

"Well, I don't know about that," he responded modestly. "I was the most senior officer to survive. With the utmost discipline, I enforced the *women and children first* protocol. It saved a lot of lives overall. I saw all boats leave her, filled with passengers. Even had to cling to the Titanic when she went under as I was sucked against an exhaust grill. I held on until I was deep under the water, beneath the suction of her drag ... Then, when all hope was over and my life flashed before my eyes, I was blown from the grill plate by a rush of warm air from a boiler that exploded on the underside. I hugged atop a capsized boat with thirty other poor sods until salvation came hours later."

"Remarkable," King-Clark himself remarked, and his eyes drifted away from the infamy and back into the reality of the ruinous harbour. He suddenly realized why Lightoller had been so audacious about embarking in this crusade back to the coast. "So, none of *this* must faze *you* then ...?"

Although Lightoller's steel gaze remained dead-straight, he knew to what King-Clark was referring; the amass of lifeless carnage outside their boat and hovering in the harbour tide. To the war, even.

Charles Lightoller served as a naval officer of the Royal Navy during the previous war. He had been present during many battles and was decorated for gallantry, and therefore the Titanic wreckage had not been his only experience of death.

His eyelids softly blinked. It was the only facial expression that accompanied his desensitized response. "Not really, no."

As the motor yacht now steered parallel to the beaches five-hundred-feet offshore and towards the disastrous main harbour, their gazes all scanned the coastline.

By aid of binocular zoom, they could spot numerous survivors still seeking shelter in dark places. They were men of the French and Belgian armies, who had missed out on the great Dunkirk evacuation.

More ships were supposedly planned to return at dawn to recover more of the Allied survivors, but these poor souls would have to wait out the night and survive the countless strikes of artillery shelling, aerial bombings ... and pray to God that the Germans did not invade the town for at least another day.

Some of the survivors spotted the silently drifting yacht as it cruised beyond the shallows.

There was not much life left in them.

They were huddled up and exhausted—almost too exhausted to even shout or wave for saving.

"This is crazy ..."

Out on the deck and with his face glued to a pair of binoculars Gin Parker made comment to Nicholl with a disheartening tone. The two men stood at the starboard-side railing gazing upon the evacuation aftermath. Scanning the groups of French soldiers, they could see that there were also some civilians in amongst the remains. They had no choice but to wait patiently for the next evacuation order, die, or surrender to the Germans when the time came.

"We should save some of them ..." Parker announced, this time, aloud. He turned and faced the two young crewmen.

"We can't," one of them responded.

"What do you mean?" Parker frowned, slightly melodramatic. "We can fit a dozen people on here, maybe two. Just tell him to get in closer. We'll pull a few aboard—there will still be room for Captain Churchill ... *if he's even out there,* that is."

Nicholl snorted silently at Parker's undying distaste for Mad Jack Churchill. Honestly, he was surprised Parker even came along on this unsanctioned rescue mission.

"*We can't!*" the young crewman informed, again.

"You don't know what it's been like!" exclaimed the other one, who was the son of the boat's captain. "They just about bloody capsize the boat!"

"It's been a bloody free-for-all trying to get even just the *British* survivors aboard. At least we can communicate with them and tell them to remain in an orderly fashion. Pandemonium sets in, and men turn into animals ..."

Parker and Nicholl listened intently.

"Yeah," the other crewman added. "We'll get swamped and risk overturning if we get in too close. These men are desperate to survive."

"Not to mention the time it takes ..." Roger Lightoller stated logically. "We want to be out of here as quick as possible. It's suicide out here during the day ..."

"Why?"

"The Luftwaffe ..." Ashcroft regarded. "They pick off boats like target practice."

They watched as Roger eyed the cabin and made eye contact with his father, who obviously had had to force his son to develop a thick skin with regard to this evacuation. He had recently come to understand that not everybody was going to survive. There was a history there.

Lightoller wordlessly acquiesced, proud of his son.

It was a tough situation, but finally Parker understood the hazard potentially involved if they opened the doors to these crowds.

"We stick to the mission," Nicholl regimented in a disciplinary tone over the raised voices of the exchange. He planted a hand on Gin Parker's shoulder, the heart of kindness that laid within did not go unnoticed. He was not an evil man, and therefore felt he deserved some recognition. After all, there had to be some underlining reason as to why he had tagged along in the attempt to rescue Jack. "We find Jack, and we save him. Maybe ... hopefully ... we can save a few others on the way out, too. But the captain is the mission, here."

"Is that true?" King-Clark commented inside the cabin, overhearing the commotion outside about rescuing panicking survivors capsizing boats.

Still at the helm and staring into the distance, Lightoller nodded grimly before he elaborated. "The first few trips weren't that bad. We were still loading up at the harbour piers, back before they got clogged and then blown to smithereens by bombers. Men were orderly. But once the artillery started hitting the city and the threat of invasion grew more imminent, panic and chaos proceeded. People started pushing. Men were falling into the drink, getting crushed between boats and piers, even drowning. It was bedlam, especially considering the Royal Navy insisted in principally evacuating all VIPs and officers first. All that was left after that were scared and reckless NCOs who just want to survive. Survival instinct is a hell of a thing. There was not much formation remaining once the first shoe dropped ... it was every man for himself trying to beat the other."

King-Clark shook his head at the likely truth.

Padre Nicholl quietly stepped back into the rear of the cabin, holding onto the doorframe for stability against the tide they sailed across. He listened acutely to the conversation as Lightoller continued ...

"... It was like being back onboard the bloody Titanic again, except there were no *women and children* to board first," Lightoller analogized. "And then, the harbour got hit; aerial strikes, carpet bombings, fighters strafing the lines on the beach. Never seen anything like it after the piers collapsed in the harbour. Men were in hordes, stretched all the way down the beaches, neck-deep. They formed queues of bodies, from the sands all the way spanning out to the big ships that could not get in the shallows. Desperate men even drove cars onto the sands, sinking them in the water, all in attempt to cut the lines and make it to a boat first. Trust me when I say, we're here to help ... but the first people to help are yourselves. You can't underestimate the tide of a crowd of desperate men ... and I'd seen it happen before. I've seen boats capsize. I've seen people die because of *pandemonium.* People get drunk on fear. They get stupid."

"*People* do," Nicholl agreed, with a degree of dispute. "But these are *soldiers* ..."

"Soldiers are people too, son," Lightoller bobbed his head, eyeing the younger, albeit judicious padre. He may have been an old geezer, but he was still shrewd, and caught onto the undertone of the padre's nature of questioning.

He cast an eye back towards him with precision, and it was in that moment of exchange that Lightoller read Nicholl's mind—he recalled the history about the Garry ...

Lightoller faced forwards, not about to play coy.

"I didn't *shoot 'em,* if that's what you're getting' at?"

In a brief space of awkward censorship, King-Clark's ogle drew a blank, and he gazed from Nicholl and then back to Lightoller and back again, utterly lost.

"... eh, sorry, but what is happening right now?"

Nobody said anything for a stretch and King-Clark grew paranoid.

"Padre!" King-Clark demanded.

"Charles Lightoller," Nicholl asserted. "Captain of the HMS Garry. In 1919, there was an involvement in the massacre of shipwrecked sailors—*German* sailors. He shot them all dead."

It had all come back to Nicholl during his stroll back out onto the deck to clear his mind. The bodies in the water had helped solidify the memory claim. He recalled reading published 1933 memoirs which accused Lightoller of ordering his crew to open fire on the unarmed survivors of the German U-Boat *UB-110*—a depth-charged, rammed, and sunk submarine off the Yorkshire coast. With revolvers and machine guns, they apparently executed the adrift survivors instead of taking them onboard. During the ensuing massacre, the German captain who reported the supposed war crimes stated in great detail that he watched the skull of an 18-year-old member of his crew being split open by a lump of coal hurled by a Royal Navy sailor, as ordered by Lightoller.

"Alleged," Lightoller distasted. "You're quoting a connotation published by *Kapitänleutnant Fürbringer's* recollections, aren't you?"

Padre Nicholl stood tall with conviction.

"Let me tell you, Fürbringer would've been the first one in line for all this Third Reich bollocks!"

"*Alleged?*" Nicholl responded in-kind.

Lightoller removed his eyeline from the waters, facing Nicholl and King-Clark. "Padre, myself and my men were later made exempt by the JAG office and decorated for gallantry. I would never harm an innocent person, let alone taint the brave soul of a soldier—Allied, or Axis."

... wwwwwwhir.

Halting Nicholl's response, the course of the topic changed.

A distant pitch filled the highlights of the night's ambience, and almost all at once all the men outside addressed them in the cabin.

It was a welcome save from the heated confrontation.

"Captain, you hear that?" Gin Parker shouted from outside the glass windows of the cabin, overly concerned.

The two 'captains' replied simultaneously.

"*Aye.*"

"*Yea—*"

Lightoller and King-Clark exchanged a quick look.

"It's the Germans," Parker exclaimed, running in and entering the rear of the cabin. "They're coming back!"

"*We got incoming, lads! Turn all handheld's off and keep her dark and still!*" Lightoller then commented specifically at Nicholl and, by extension, King-Clark who was understandably concerned but yet to take a side. "You may have to put your money where your mouth is, Padre.

You may not trust me, but it's because of that I was the only ship captain crazy enough to taxi you lot back across the channel and into harm's way. Deal with it like how I forever deal with the scrutiny of Fürbringer's allegations."

"I hope so!" Nicholl exclaimed, leaving the cabin and searching the night sky with the others.

"You, of all people, should have a lil' faith in the truth!" Lightoller shouted after him.

"Another air raid?" King-Clark elucidated with a longing stare that faded out into the coastal city ruins through the sea-salt assaulted and frosted glass. They had experienced the last couple of minor bombing runs that had strafed the city during the day, bringing down buildings and wreaking havoc ... this one, however, felt like a *motherload* compared to what the already ruined city had suffered. The ominous drone made it seem like it was an incoming aerial armada.

"We're out of time on this," Lightoller remarked, eyeing those aboard his ship. "We got lucky with the last few trips. I doubt we'll be lucky, again. We're going to have to head back. That sounds like a squadron of bombers ... without any naval countermeasures, they will lay waste what is left of Dunkirk."

The men each exchanged a look.

Tactfully, it may explain why the Germans had not yet invaded the city ... they were going to blow the fuck out of it first.

King-Clark's look was one of unwillingness, so Lightoller reiterated. "I'm sorry, but your friend ... even if he's alive, he won't be for much longer. We, on the other hand, need to head back if we want to stay that way—and now! If we stay here, we will become a target. Those things do not discriminate between land and sea."

"Alright! Alright!" King-Clark moved forward, fast collecting himself. His heart was breaking. He thought that this would be the chance to save his friend, Jack Churchill ... but it had failed. He cast a view into the scape of Dunkirk one last time to wish it goodbye.

"Sorry, Jack ..."

He faced the few Second Chesters who were hanging on his gallantry. Each one of them was hesitant, gazing upon him with puppy dog eyes.

"*Let's go!*" he commanded, stiffening his upper lip.

Lightoller scanned the faces of the dispirited British soldiers briefly, contemplating something daring. "Look ... we've got a few minutes before they're above Dunkirk. It'll be unlikely they'll see us if we stay away from the bigger landmarks and don't act rash or alive, or moving."

Lightoller's suggestion sparked life into the chests of the Second Manchester Regiment men, and they tuned back in.

"We'll cruise through the harbour dead stick ... I'll navigate us through the shipwrecks ... we can scan the shore, and at least that will give your mate half a chance if he's waiting."

"Thank you. Half a chance is all Jack needs!" King-Clark stated gratefully to the skipper, onboard with this motion.

"Oh my *God!*" Parker shouted, moving away from the cabin. "We need to fucking get out of here! Do you fellas hear that?! We're going to be fucking fish food!"

"Oi," Nicholl remarked, silencing him, bringing him back to earth. "You're worried about us out here? Think about all of them stranded in *there!* There's *nowhere* they can run!"

Gin Parker stared out into the coastline, seeing the crowds of French soldiers stir in the night as they, too, undoubtedly started to hear the growing pitch of the incoming blitz impending overhead like a thunderstorm. Only, instead of risk of getting wet, they were at risk of getting dead.

"We'll be fine out here!" Nicholl instilled. "You've just *got* to have a little *faith!*"

In the cabin, Lightoller gazed at King-Clark discreetly, and referenced their previous argument involving the discussion of the human being and the survival dramatic. This man, Parker, was a soldier, but in the line of incoming disaster, acted desperately ... stupidly. "See what I mean?"

"What?" King-Clark held a frown before searching Lightoller's eyeline towards the starboard deck; to Parker. The soldier's first response had been panic and the desire to cut and run, as Lightoller had explained the desperate soldiers had done to them earlier.

Suddenly, an electronic crisp screeched from the CB radio built into the console of the yacht. There was a degree of static interference and the hint of a French voice as they accidentally intercepted another frequency.

"Damn, I thought I turned that off," stated Lightoller, quickly turning the knob to resort to silence. "We're picking up the French signals because we're coming into the ports. German ones, too, if you can speak a bit of pig Latin."

"Not the Navy?"

"Negative, they use a different frequency."

Nicholl stepped back into the cabin, observing their conversation. He seemed reformed and peaceful, forgiving in his demeanour regarding Lightoller. He elaborated with his knowledge on radio waves.

"That's right," he agreed with the skipper in a sign of olive branch-extending, which seemed to be reciprocated through Lightoller's additional response expansion.

"We use encoded frequencies. These are mostly open air channels. Wide. Public."

"Is it possible, though?" King-Clark questioned, suddenly with a growing idea. "Could you reach the Allied frequencies? Existing land channels, I mean?"

Lightoller shrugged. "Probably—if there are any left out there. Your lads were scuttling everything your boats couldn't get back across the channel. Why?"

King-Clark stepped in close, assessing the controls and picking up the hand-piece for the attached radio.

"I've got an idea on how to shorten our search for Jack."

"Oi, wait just a minute, now," Lightoller raised a finger lieu of advising him of his thoughts regarding the potential outcome. "If you get on that thing and broadcast that we're out here in the water, we'll get thronged," Lightoller exclaimed through genuine concern. "How on God's green Earth are you gonna get just *your man Jack* on that thing, and not the whole city?"

"We'll ... just *ask* for Jack?" King-Clark replied daftly.

"You do that, and you'll suddenly have a thousand people on the other end who are claiming to be *Jack Churchill* and cashing their ticket out of here."

King-Clark eyed Nicholl and then Lightoller with a gleam of hidden confidence.

He had a plan.

"*Have a lil' faith.*"

The planes came from the southeast.

Materializing alike the beginning of the third act in *Die Walküre,* the second of the four operas by composer *Richard Wagner* and a score known better as *Ride of the Valkyries,* cloaked in the darkness of the night sky arrived the behemoth squadron of Luftwaffe bombers. They were in an enormous formation, planning to once again blitz Dunkirk.

If it wasn't for the already dark night-time atmosphere, then the fleet of planes would have blacked out the sky like a plague of locusts.

On a whole other level, the combined whine of the aircrafts drowned out all other volume on the ground like a sound turbine. The collective and synchronized mechanical pitch of a hundred propeller engines reverberated through the airspace of Dunkirk and along the coast, rumbling the surface like an earthquake from the sky. So much so, the seismic activity would have been felt through the Eurasian tectonic plate four-hundred-miles beneath the earth's surface.

Amongst the vast ruins of the coastal city, all heads raised and turned with peepers the size of beamless searchlights, gawking the pending vertical doom as jaws slackened and dropped.

Positively bursting at the seams within the multiple ships evacuating Dunkirk via the English Channel, the circular brims of the distinguishable brodie helmets worn by the soldiers everywhere tipped upwards, glancing into the night sky to the southeast in search for the incoming wave of German fighters. They knew the sound well and dreaded it.

It was the forthcoming death from above.

There was nowhere they could turn.

Nowhere they could hide.

Nowhere they could run.

Churchill and Hardy both stared with a focused glare out of the forward viewport of Busty Barbara.

Their partly decommissioned A10 cruiser tank sped down the cobblestone streets of the deserted end of Dunkirk, bursting through obstacles such as abandoned vehicles and dust-piled wreckages as though they were driving a battering ram. Some of the roads were blocked like a rush hour traffic grid, and so a decent amount of force was applied to gain passage.

They were mindful of their objective to gain as much distance towards the coast as they possibly could before that air raid arrived above their heads. And so, they charged forth, the tank pulling the truck along like an excited dog on-leash with its owner.

Maintaining speed, they mounted a sturdy stone canal bridge, shoving an abandoned mini charabanc off the edge and into the murky debris-littered shallows below. The vehicle launched like a child's plaything, clashing down into the brink.

The other side of the canal bridge was packed heavily with a gridlock of ditched vehicles. The congestion was getting thicker as they reached what must have been the centre of the coastal city.

"*Hold on!*" Hardy informed in a shout as they rammed violently into several criss-crossed parked civilian cars which had been left with open doors in the street by desperate soldiers attempting to reach the Dunkirk evacuation hours ago.

Crashhh!

The armoured A10 punched through the frameworks, bending steel and throwing bumpers into collapsed and partially destroyed real estate that lined their route.

One section of a stalled vehicle was hit so hard that it bounded from off a raised kerb, gaining air and slamming into the already destructed storefront of a butcher's shop. It brought down the upper levels of the double-storey building, crumpling like a landslide into the side of the tank and under the wheels of the tailing open air transport truck behind them. The dust cloud enveloped the men of the wounded 4th Infantry as they passed, shaking and bouncing as the cruiser dragged them through.

"*Whoops!*" Hardy murmured.

"*Love your work, chap!*" Churchill commended, holding on tight to handlebars within the tank's armoured steel belly. Their ride was unsteady and turbulent as the tank tracks climbed over debris and barged through obstacles. They were unstoppable.

"*Don't thank me! I don't know what the fuck I'm doing!*" responded Hardy.

"*Neither do I half the time!*" just as truthful, Churchill responded. "*Just roll with it!*"

Churchill stood and mounted the hatch, checking once again that the Bedford was still intact behind them, dragging through some of the left-over debris. Its tyres at times skimmed like a water-skier on a rough current.

Hardy let off the acceleration as he assessed their road ahead. It was absolutely clockablock clogged multi-layered with vehicles, stacked from kerb to kerb. The positioning of the abandoned cars resembled an unending pile-up.

Churchill felt the decline in their gearshift, and he rotated forward in the hatch of the tank. He upped it fully and stood like he was surfing a fifteen-tonne wave, gaining an even better view.

Holding a strengthened gaze, he gauged their route.

They pushed in deeper along a congested main road, unbeknownst to Churchill as being the *Boulevard of Alexander III,* a place he had been through before. Unrecognizable due to the damage, it wasn't until through the hazing fog of dust that he saw the monumental statue of *Jean Bart,* in what was once the town square, that he knew precisely where they were.

"*Ah!*" he jeered with a smirk as he realized, offering a hand in welcoming gesture towards the landmark. "*Hullo, Bart!*"

"*Jack ...*" Hardy shouted from inside. His voice was barely audible over the roar of the heated tank engine, the clattering of the steel tracks, and the all-encompassing tidal wave of German aerial armada cresting their night horizon. Their countless dark underbellies were now visible as they passed by under the white clouds beneath the moonlight.

"*Yeah! I see 'em!*" Churchill responded, rubbernecking hard to formulate a new plan as they rolled along the main street, vibrating underfoot. Still riding the tank like a surfboard, he braced his footing as they shoved their way between steel obstacles. The A10 tracks shoulder-barged cars, crumpling them like tin foil if they did not roll or thrust clear.

... WHIIIIRRRR ...

The *hum* of the aerial engine's reverberation was becoming stentorian now; painful and likely damaging to the inner eardrum. So much so, the peaking reverberation broke Churchill's concentration, almost incapacitating him. It felt like someone had put his head in a vice and proceeded to tighten the lever.

The noise caused him to pivot around and stare into the sky as the moonlight intermittently eclipsed due to the fleet of fighters.

Armageddon was upon them.

"*Bollocks!*" he mouthed, but his voice was not audible at all, barely even to himself. He shouted it again just to see if he could hear it, but without chance.

Upon the steel roof of the tank he spun, seeing no choice left to make. They would have to go *through* the town square, which was at this point absolutely jam-packed with abandoned trucks and cars like an ocean of flat chassis rooftops, Churchill recalled the last time he was here that there was a rather large and abandoned multi-storey department store front across the way. From memory it was rather hollow and sound as a structure. They *might* fit inside ...

"*What do we do?!*" Hardy bellowed, screaming so loud he risked laryngitis. His words were simply no longer perceptible below the pending air raid. "*Jack!? JAAAACK?! Fuck me!*"

The cruiser rolled to an idle pause in the street approaching the blocked town square. The dragging truck rolled to a stop, slackening the winch cable into a spool on the stone street. All the men onboard could do nothing but stare helplessly at the night sky, blocking their ears as death finally arrived for them from above.

Directly above Hardy, Churchill's head appeared through the open hatch. "*The building!*" he shouted and pointed on their diagonal right. "*Across the square! Go!*"

Hardy's hands waved as his head shook, eyeing forwards.

Fuck it, he thought as he gunned it with a kangaroo hop, pushing into the cars before them and ploughing the way for the hauled Bedford.

Churchill still rode exposed from the hatch.

His eyes climbed into the sky, resting one hand on his holstered claybeg and the other upon his filthy maroon cap while he watched the clear night sky turn to metal as the storm of Luftwaffe began pulling a steel shroud over Dunkirk. Below the larger heavy bombers which were imminently about to deliver their payloads, smaller fighters began to scout the city ruins, marking targets and searching for survivors to strafe with their mounted machine guns.

Just then, less than three hundred feet above the ground and about four thousand beneath the floating armada, a lone Messerschmitt scout plane zoomed in low. It must have spotted their cavalcade's movement from above and rapidly attuned his flight path, aiming in low on an attack run with its twin barrels charged.

No way it was the same bloody plane as before?

"*Bastard! No!*" Churchill bellowed to himself as he saw the fighter change course and bank, headed after them like an overconfident and starved predator in the wild.

It was likely another fighter, but something about this circumstance was awfully reminiscent to his and Hardy's arrival into Dunkirk, where they were chased down by one of these yellow-nosed bastards.

Unfortunately, the main turret was immobilized, and the A10 cruiser had no small-arm mount that could have provided cover for their convoy. Churchill made himself thin and dropped through the open hatch. He could do nothing but pray for the safety of the men of the 4th Infantry in the open air troop carrier behind them.

RAT-TAT-TAT-TAT-TAT-TAT-TAT-TAT-TAT!

The lone fighter whipped in with furious speed.

Its underwing machine guns blazed, peppering the slow-moving convoy as the steel plough cultivated through the field of rigid steel carmageddon.

Phosphorus-tipped tracer rounds speared into the carnage like sprouts of lightning as the speeding fighter swooped down in a low attack run.

Luckily for the men in the truck, it appeared that the fighter's main target seemed to be the bigger damaged cruiser tank, desperately shoving its way through a path across the town square.

The discharged bullets were designed for aerial combat, and they splashed hard against the armoured walls of the cruiser, causing little to no damage compared to its flying brethren, when the line stitched across the path. The attack seemingly target practice for this Luftwaffe maverick.

Again, Churchill subliminally compared this fighter to the last one they had encountered on the way into Dunkirk. The pilot had shown the same level of tenacity and enthusiasm when gunning them down, therefore, he intuitively marked it as one in the same.

There was a personal vendetta forming ...

Of that same barrage, rounds tore through the metal of the dozens of parked vehicles in the town centre, shredding them with pint-sized holes and shattering glass windows. Sparks sizzled in the night across the metallic surfaces like new year's fireworks.

wwwWWWWWWHHHHIIIiirrrr ...

The fighter rocketed by, extremely low-slung.

Two abandoned civilian vehicles within the target line exploded as their fuel tanks were punctured through the metal chassis and ignited, erupting in rising fireballs of hot orange. The force of the shockwaves tossed one of the small civilian vehicles over and onto its side, flattening another like their chassis were made of tinfoil.

The cruiser tank barged through the flaming vehicle wreckages, causing them to burn even brighter on impact as they were shoved clear.

"*What's your problem, huh?!*" Hardy shouted within the cruiser, dipping his head as the plane shot overhead in order to spy a glimpse of the fighter.

"*Keep going through!*" Churchill bellowed from over his shoulder, pointing through the view port slit.

"*Nah! I was thinkin' about stoppin' here!*" retorted Hardy sarcastically. He added with much frustration, "*Fuck!*"

"*No, I mean through! Not around!*"

Hardy glowered, eyes forward and upon the town square.

In its centre: the concrete pylon housing a large copper statue of Jean Bart. Even though Dunkirk was bombed to the absolute shit house, the monument still stood strong and intact.

"*Sorry, old boy ...*" Churchill rhetorically apologized as he climbed back out of the tank and into the noise of the air raid, searching for that nuisance of a German fighter as it undoubtedly circled around to make another pass. He tracked it almost instantly beneath the iron sea of bombers. The Messerschmitt loomed in the near distance beyond some buildings, angling this time to attack from the northwest.

It would be on them again in less than thirty seconds.

Churchill brought his attention forwards along their path just in time to immediately react by ducking. His focus widened and his head dropped through the hatch as their tank rammed at speed, smashing directly into the concrete base of the mounted statue de Jean Bart.

Barely losing an ounce of speed, the charging cruiser rammed into the bolster base of the raised heavy copper monument. The concrete housing and rebar supports beneath the mount exploded like a detonation, and the tank pushed beneath with little to no resistance.

Somehow, the vertical-standing copper statue of Jean Bart remained balanced and vertical, dropping slowly like a lopped tree only to be caught perfectly by the extended turret of the cruiser tank, hitched and now along for the ride, remaining vertical. Some of the flat base of the statue fell over the front of the tank—including the view port. The unit stayed attached due to the turret barrel protruding from between his legs, upright like a firm erection—enough to make any adolescent giggle.

The copper incarnate of Jean Bart rode the tank like a bold conquistador, sword tip aimed towards the sky, the barrel of an inoperable 40mm cannon rigid between his legs.

"*Shit!*" Hardy scoffed. There was now a lump of copper and stone crust blocking most of his view, and he could not see where they were driving. Let alone that, but they were likely now a much bigger target. "*Jack!?*"

Within the confines, Churchill looked about and winced with laughter, immediately recognizing what had just happened. "*Looks like old Bart wants out of Dunkirk too! Can't blame him!*" he remarked wittingly, climbing up and taking a better look from the hatch. He did not have to look far, as the statue leaned over the access.

Churchill laughed again, attempting to give the unit a shove clear but it was far too heavy. His laughter was silenced suddenly as the German fighter in-came with its machine guns blaring, strafing across the tank once again.

God only knew what the pilot thought upon making the pass and witnessing the statue of Jean Bart now mounted upon the tank, rolling through. He undoubtedly had to double take from the side of his clear canopy on his low flyby—which he did, leaning his forehead against the glass of the cockpit to get a good gawk.

... was zum teufel?

< What the fuck. >

Sparks ignited with high-pitched ricochets as they struck upon the hollow copper statue, sounding like a bizarre all metal electrified double bass being played. The rounds ceased bombardment after the fighter swooped past, climbing back into the space between the ruins of the Dunkirk city and the travelling armada of airplanes at around four thousand feet. Squadrons of other fighters travelled within the space between, though all seemed disinterested in divebombing a single ground target, unlike this random maverick pilot in his short-ranged fighter.

He appeared rogue and undeniably out for blood.

... vvvROOOM!

The German fighter rocketed overhead, shaking the land.

It then peeled off again into the distance, banking right and performing some skilful aerobatics in the clear airspace. He barrel-rolled at a tight angle, gaining some distance to the south to come back around again for another pass at them.

"Piss off, you scallywag!" Churchill shouted after watching the maverick's manoeuvre. He paid attention to the fighter's particular markings, recalling what the designations represented from theory elements of his officer's training. From what he could tell, this fighter was a part of a squadron or a *jagdgeschwader* or *fighter wing*. He had markings that suggested he was a scout: a finder of target designations for pre-blitz raids, as well as sweeper for after when survivors of bombing sites would roam the open grounds. The only real *gruppe* marking he could spot in the motion and in the dark distance was that the plane had a yellow or a white nosecone. This guy was clearly overzealous, shooting at targets beneath the bombers ahead of the payload's fall.

He was all about notching up that war tally as though it added inches to his dick.

Jack's eyes dropped to ground level and the road ahead beyond the hitchhiking statue of Jean Bart.

The cruiser tank began to do just that: cruise.

Churchill realized the absence of grunt and retracted below.

"*Hardy!*" roared his voice, leaning back into the tank body. "*Keep going! Punch it! Go! Go!*"

"*What? Where?!*" Hardy responded, waving a hand at the clogged viewport before his face. "*I can't fuckin' see, Jack!*"

"*Just drive straight! Full-throttle!*"

Hardy could not quite discern what Churchill meant at first, but he soon added a splice of eccentricity to what he gathered from his words and drove their tank *into* the wall at the end of the street, making their own doorway through it.

As he set heavy on the accelerator rather than brake, he tugged hard on the ripcord of the air horn, blasting it even though it was barely perceptible over the incoming air raid.

Pushing through the solid stone brick wall, the tank barrel charged like a jouster, collapsing the brickwork like hail down over them and the mounted copper statue as they busted inside. They were enveloped in a pouring stream of white dust as the brickwork collapsed and they entered the hollow space inside.

Inside the tank, the falling bricks slamming onto the armoured roof were barely audible below the air raid.

Churchill ripped the hatch closed over the second the tank shook violently from the brunt of impact, barging through the solid wall like an uninvited guest.

The cruiser pushed through with ease, choking slightly as the poised statue of a man holding a sword upright latched onto the lip of the wall, finally beginning to dislodge from Busty Barbara. However, the copper hitchhiker was more solid than hand-placed brickworks and so, Bart pushed through along with them.

It seemed almost like the wall was made of nothing more than stacked building blocks. There was barely any structural resistance.

With a crash and earthquaking shake, the tank drove into the open space of the department store building, which—through the falling debris and erupting cloud of dust—appeared to be a clothing store, once upon a time. Furniture, crates, and racks filled of stock were thrown about the floor and destroyed as the tank drove inside, coming to a standstill as it reached the outer wall which led back out into the street. The cruiser tank involuntarily skidded out a few feet as it braked, finally tossing the five-tonne statue from her back and onto the floor where it took out a row of naked display mannequins.

With not a second to waste, Churchill shoved open the heavily debris-covered hatch with might and exited the cruiser tank. He jumped down into the dusty ruins and found the winch at Barbara's rear, immediately retracting the winch via its manual lever crank.

The semi-exposed truck which hung half out the destroyed wall began to drag inside and beneath shelter, pulling slightly more brickwork down upon it and showering the men on its tray. Those who were able covered a nearby wounded comrade and sheltered them from harm. Once in, many jumped overboard, seeking refuge somewhere inside the building.

"*Get inside!*" Churchill shouted, his voice perceptible now that they were indoors. He assisted a limping soldier after the winch retracted and pulled the rear end of the truck beneath cover just as the German maverick fighter passed by as low as it could in order to squeeze off a few dozen rounds through the hole in the wall behind them. "Come on! Go, go!"

It was like a shark swooping in one last time to try and bite at the swimmer's feet as they were lifted out of the water and into the boat, just in the nick of time.

The machine guns blazed, chewing up the stone street and tracing the route they had just taken from outside. The shots munched up the dusty floor and even pinged from the rear of the metal truck, assaulting the steel body in an array of sparks before the plane peeled off again, passing by quite low above the infrastructure as if he had a death wish. It passed so low that the updraft blew out spot fires like candles on a birthday cake.

This time appeared to be the last assault from the fighter.

It didn't bank around like it had every other time.

Instead, it headed away from the city ... *which meant only one thing.*

All of the men did as Churchill ordered, remaining low-slung and moving into a safer section of the building as the air raid high above Dunkirk unquestionably reached zero hour.

Bombs were dropped.

Very high-pitched whistling in the sky high above them escalated like a thousand boiling kettles. The pitch only grew louder as the hundreds of bombs plummeted from above, freefalling towards their targets.

The carpet-bomb layer sailed aimlessly down and upon Dunkirk in streaks, drawing dot lines as they fell to earth.

The men all limped and scuffled indoors and below concealment, collapsing painfully on top of one another. Hardy's head peeked from the hatch of the cruiser. His view hovered over the commotion within the dusty and trashed storefront of which they now occupied, bounding over more wounded soldiers of the 4th Infantry as they sought refuge.

Hardy's view locked onto Churchill in the chaos as he assisted carrying two struggling men in each arm, and they plodded along and discovered a space beside the tank.

He couldn't help but watch Jack's efforts; an awe-inspiring hero.

Even in the eleventh hour of the face of death, he did not ever leave a man behind.

And then ... Hardy saw the stragglers.

Out beside the troop carrier, Hardy spotted one of the medical officers struggling to dislodge one of the portable gurneys from off the rear of the tray. It was somehow stuck, and the wounded soldier onboard seemed too hindered to help. His cries bellowed out for assistance, but due to the deafening air raid four thousand feet above Dunkirk, nobody could hear their pleas.

Hardy puckered his lips and leapt to it.

Trying his best to ignore the pain as it surged from the wrapped bullet wounds in his leg, he launched himself from the tank, full of zeal and inspired heroism. He jumped down onto the uneven brick debris that littered the floor, kicking up a cloud of dust. Favouring his wounded leg, he quickly jogged over and started to assist with the snagged gurney.

Most of the other men who had already retreated crowded by the side of the cruiser tracks, between the tank and the fallen copper statue. They tumbled in on top of each other, absent comfort, piling up the wounded and running back for more, dragging stretchers forcefully from off the tray and running them all over.

They sought as much refuge as they could from the blitz as the pitching incoming bombs dropped blindly above them, imminently about to cave their heads in from above, either exploding them or indirectly burying them in building-sized rubble.

Churchill set down the two wounded soldiers. They collapsed into each other on the way down, but it was a necessary cruelty as time was not of the essence. Before joining them all in the space between the collapsed copper statue and the cruiser tank, he took a panoramic glance around the room, spotting Hardy, the medic, and the wounded soldier on the gurney.

Churchill took a step to—

... *wiiiir-bhoOOM!*

Explosions shook the stability of the earth beneath them, causing Churchill to tread awkwardly and collapse full to his side. A gargantuan gust of wind in the form of a shockwave passed laterally across him, shaking his balance further.

More detonations about the city centre went off, several of which were out in the town square. It lit the outside area up like sunrise having a seizure.

The space outside the hole in the wall flashed like the eyelids of an epileptic's fit.

"HARDY! MOVE!"

Boom. Boom. BOOM. BOOM!

BO-BOOM! BOOM! BOOM! BOOM!

Louder than Krakatoa, the blanketing carpet bombs fell towards them, coming in closer and closer—the view from their position inside of the abandoned store saw the explosions out in the open, erupting like a volcano, pouring molten flames, stone and debris for miles, filling the street with the vapour of unbreathable thick soot and dust.

Cars flipped and ignited into fireballs, tossed around like they were as light as feathers. Chain reactions of detonations continued in every direction, covering the outdoor surfaces in fire and brimstone.

Craters were dug into the township, sending huge spires of stone, dirt, and metal shooting into the air. Buildings caved in.

Storefronts like the one they occupied collapsed like avalanches as bombs dropped in through their roofs, blowing out windows and walls.

"HARDY!"

Churchill's shouts were inaudible.

... and to think, just as he was starting to like the Yank ...

His last view before a destructive shock-wave of dust from outside shot into their vicinity like a tsunami torrent was of Hardy and the medic finally dragging the wounded soldiers free from the tray. They began to share the load of the gurney and run with it between them as the power of the force hit them from behind, wafting inside and blinding everything.

In the darkness and haze, more explosions went off right above them. So loud and fierce, Churchill himself thought that this was the end.

There was the thunderous sound of walls falling, brickwork shifting and dropping like spikes from a cave ceiling.

Men were shouting, screaming, briefly before what appeared to be the roof above their heads collapsed inwards like a house of cards.

It buried them alive.

The view from afar was surreal.

As the sea of bombers and fighters above cruised at high altitude, the bombers simultaneously released their payloads over the already seething coastal city of Dunkirk.

The high pitches sounded like a thousand steam whistles, all at once reaching boiling point before—

... bom-bom-bom-BOM-BOM-BOM!

The numerous explosions detonated across the city in upsurges of smoke exhausts and oxygen hungry fireballs, reaching tall for the night sky.

The battered city smouldered like a wildfire inferno in the darkness as literally thousands of impact shells discharged in tangent, like a giant chain reaction, collapsing buildings, carving craters in streets and roads, exploding hundreds of abandoned vehicles and reducing entire structures to ruins.

The coastal city was razed.

Countless lives were lost as soldiers sought refuge within ruins and in vehicles, but nothing could protect them from the destruction. French and Belgian soldiers were crossed out by the dozen-load as the bombs fell, chalking up thousands of lives lost within seconds of the air raid.

This was not to mention the hundreds of civilians who had not been evacuated from their homes within Dunkirk. Cowering within their houses and desperate for survival, families of men, women, and children huddled together were undoubtedly shown no mercy by the bombing that flattened their households, crushing them to dust and cinder.

For most of those wretched souls, the reality was there would be nothing left but splinters, crumble, char, ash, and bone.

XIII
Long Live the King-Clark

Under the pallid moonlight, the view of the coastal city of Dunkirk was one of disaster, despair, and utter obliteration.

The payloads of over three dozen German bombers had just been distributed across the already partially destructed cityscape in way of a saturation bombing, reducing edifices to ruins.

What had ensued was absolute annihilation.

A day ago, Dunkirk was a thousand-year-old French coastal town, built up from a fishing village to a privateer base with a port, to a functioning city. In the year 1940, due to constant bombardment by the Luftwaffe by order of Adolf Hitler, a millennium of European community evolution had been reduced to crumbled stone and ashes.

Hollow skeletal remains of buildings reached for the sky where they should have buckled, protruding from the hovering vapour which veiled the vicinity. The lingering mist hazed the remnants, resembling deciduous trees through the fog of a winter morning. Only instead of fog, it was smoke and dust and ash from the mass destruction.

Once their payloads were delivered, the aerial armada vacated as quickly as they had arrived. The noise of their thunderous formation dissipated as they grew in distance, returning to the motherland.

All structural textures and exteriors were coated in charcoal and char, as if it were scorched in a brief exposure of Hell itself. Like the door to damnation had been opened a crack, just enough for doom in the form of an inferno to exhale onto our plane of existence, extinguishing life like a gust of air to a candle flame.

Ash softly fell upon the city's frayed, scalded, and fragmented remains. In the fading echo of the withdrawing air raid, weightless cinders fell like winter snowflakes—noiselessly and feathery— coating the land in a layer of stone-grey powder. There was a resemblance to Pompeii in the wake of the bombing.

1940, June 4
M/Y Sundowner
Coast of Dunkirk, English Channel

"Well spank my arse and call me Charlie ..."

While Charles Lightoller declared his state of bemused wonderment from behind the wheel in the cabin, Rex King-Clark barely paid attention, completely lost in his own reverie while his eyes stared entranced by the event that he had just born witness to. Like everybody else onboard, he was completely captivated by their view of the coastal city from the Sundowner.

Zombified in his trance, King-Clark stepped out from the cabin and joined the ranks of Mad Jack's Merry Men at the railing.

Padre Nicholl, Gin Parker, Knocker White, Wand and Macken ...

The men of Second Manchester Regiment D section were awestruck, mouths agape, leaning against the polished wooden kicking of the drifting yacht as they passed by along the expanse of the coastline. Even across the distance, they could feel the resonating heat from the bombing on their faces.

The two members of Lightoller's crew; his son Roger and family friend Ashcroft, were also both in mild shock after viewing the demolition. They had seen a lot of destruction since they embarked upon this mission from England ... but nothing like this.

This was something else.

This was almost biblical.

All men aboard stared onwards, slack-jawed and in awe.

Helplessly, they had just witnessed from a front-row seat the most breathtaking and terrifying display of firepower they had seen in their lives.

Dunkirk was in devastation.

Residual temperature from the bombing radiated from within the glow contained by her dark and shadowy silhouettes. The city in many ways right now resembled a jack-o-lantern, heated from a core within shining out past the bordering structures. The glowing pulsated from within her city centre like a dying soul. Hotspots breathed heat with flames and singed rubble, exhausting stacks of smoke for miles into the night sky.

Behind them all in the cabin, Lightoller keyed the engine of the Sundowner, roaring the ship back to life from her silent and inconspicuous drift along the outer rim of the floating debris from the harbour. It was time to go.

The activity caught their attention, and Nicholl and King-Clark reared towards the cabin. The glow of burning Dunkirk reflected upon the salt-fogged windshield, but Lightoller was still visible within.

Leaving her idling, the ship captain stepped about the cabin in order to address the men. The circumstance of watching Dunkirk be laid to ruin had not only probably squashed their friend, Jack, but also quashed their goal of rescuing him. They were momentarily directionless.

Lightoller addressed King-Clark—addressed them all:

"*Unkillable,* you say?"

King-Clark said not a word. Nobody did.

Instead, he faced the coast, finally uttering a response.

"I did say that, yes."

"Do you still believe that ... after what we just observed?"

Pondering the man in the taciturnity, Rex King-Clark nodded sternly, bringing his face back around to Lightoller.

Unequivocally, he nodded. "Yes. I do."

1940, June 4
Dunkirk
Nord-Pas-de-Calais, France

Enfeebled yet endlessly enduring, Mad Jack Churchill arose from the remnants, like a symbol of hope. A phoenix from the falling ashes.

Survived.

Inexorable.

Unkillable.

He was the definition of persistence and the very quintessence of a modern-day crusader. That, or simply neither kingdom wanted his residency yet.

Within the surrounding area of the ruined department store, survivors started to stir beneath the rubble and ash, choking on powder and dust. From beneath a miracle of shelter that had somehow concealed them from the collapsing rubble that the bombing brought down around the town square, their conjoined view fell upon the figure of a lone survivor upstanding in the mouth of destruction. Illuminated by the refractions of a dozen spot fires against the sheer sides of topple rubble, Captain Churchill stood strong and unwavering, assessing the damage around him.

With his hands on his hips and around the knuckleduster hilt of his holstered claybeg sword, Churchill had to squint to count the heads of the

4th Infantrymen awakening within the rubble. More survivors started to rouse throughout the hovering haze as it began to calmly descend to a layer, dwindling to earth. The thicker scatter started to settle but the ash hovered in the atmosphere, constantly falling like a whiteout winter.

The clamour of the German Luftwaffe in the skies began to fade with distance now, replaced with a spooky pitch of nothingness that ringed in the ears of every survivor at Dunkirk.

"Someone must be watching over us, lads," Churchill stated aloud as men started to emerge from the ashes and debris around him. His hoarse voice was audible now that the aerial armada in the night sky faded into the distance and dominating timbre.

As their group of BEF soldiers started to reconvene by the A10 cruiser tank, they realized the full extent of what had happened during the bombing. The blitz had reduced half the city square to rubble, visible now where it hadn't been moments ago as a gigantic hole in the wall now existed.

A result of the bombing had caused a close explosion outside the department store, throwing the immobilized Bedford transport truck up and over top of them where they had cowered for shelter beside Busty Barbara: the A10 tank. The truck had landed directly over top of them, wedging like a sheltering parent above the tank and the copper statue of Jean Bart, who had acted as a propped shield for the rubble that should have buried them alive.

All the men beneath it were miraculously protected, safe and sound. Those around the edges of the tank or around the general vicinity were also unharmed and further uninjured, albeit now covered in soot, and avid collectors of the minor nicks and superficial scratches the vacuum of air from such close-ranged explosions cause.

Even Churchill had accrued a few more of his own which were pasted in dust, including a nasty one across his left jawline that bled. The laceration had already been clogged with grey dust, acting as a blockage agent.

After another extended moment of observation by him of the turned-over troop carrier, Churchill suddenly remembered that Felix Hardy wouldn't be amongst those safe and under the shelter. In fact, the last he had seen of the journalist was of him in grave peril, risking his life for others as the explosion had hit ...

There was a disturbance in the rubble nearby and Churchill put two and two together, locating the yank immediately. He was lying next to the medic from the 4th Infantry and a wounded soldier still partially laid on a gurney board. They were slightly more worse for wear, but alive.

Churchill grinned, genuinely pleased of his friend's survival.

He hid it quickly, revealing nothing more than mild concern.

"Felix, are you okay?!" he questioned, dropping down and assisting Hardy as he lurched forward, coated in dust. Churchill brushed it off him, and the American coughed and spluttered, wiping caked grime from his eyes. The brim of his trusty fedora was torn off and limp, and he finally discarded the piece of attire.

"Fuck me," he barked, rather hoarsely and partially deaf.

"Here," Churchill informed as he brought around what was left within his canteen.

With a trembling hand Hardy accepted the welcomed tepid beverage and took a swig, which discoloured his chin from the pale of dust when he made spillage. He said afterwards, holding up his limb and attempting to squeeze a clench with much unease. "Fuck! My wrist ..."

"Wanker's cramp?"

Hardy grimaced. Legitimately hurt, he ignored Churchill's witticism for now. It was a cheap shot. "I think it's broken."

"Can you make a fist?"

He tried and failed—painfully.

"Nah ..."

"It's likely broken, lad," Churchill stated, tearing off another peel of clothing in order to bandage a splint for his loyal cohort. His eyes glanced about the surrounding dust-layered rubble in search for something thin, sturdy, and straight to support his potentially broken wrist, and his stare immediately honed onto something familiar nearby. An uncanny appearance to say the least, a bodkin-tipped war arrow that was embedded into the tyre tread of the truck had, by some miracle, been preserved from the earlier failed attempt: tip, fletching, and shaft. Churchill found it quite ironically humorous—it was almost a providence. Jack smirked as he reached over and tugged it from the deflated rubber tread, using it to run the whole way up Hardy's forearm and hand, strapping it thus as a makeshift split, tying it off.

In the minutes to come, Churchill checked out everybody else as those who were able climbed to their feet. A few of them seemed to be standing on drunken legs as they navigated through the dusty debris and shook clear their shell-shocked minds.

Churchill spotted their leader. "Corporal Hill. Are you okay?"

With a new slit upon the bridge of his nose, Hill looked over to Churchill, nodding. "I think so. You?"

"Fine-o-fine. Any new casualties?"

Hill took a second to reply, attempting to make a quick headcount. He spotted a few soldiers as they stood from behind the cruiser tank, nursing extremities and reapplying bandages to wounds. As a whole, they weren't exactly better off, but they were alive.

"I think we're okay. That was a close one."

"A close one? Lad, we just got shat on by Satan himself and lived to tell the tale," Churchill relatively agreed as he approached Hill with a positive note and ironic chuckle, reaching up and touching the flipped over truck which leered over their position. The metal was still hot from receiving a bomb blast under its rear end and flipping head-over-turkey. Churchill shook his head in utter amazement.

"It was close alright."

"A little *too* close," Hill denoted in reference to the illegally parked truck and beat Churchill to the punch, giving a logical order. "Everybody clear out. We don't know how stable this is."

While the two dozen survivors of their motley BEF section attended to those who needed assistance, Churchill and Hill took a moment to devise the next part of their journey.

"What now? We can't possibly continue after that?" said aloud Hill, following Churchill as he paced a step back and forth, hiding his expression on the inevitable and most probably *favourable* topic of submission. "The men ... we're all *buggered.* We have no transport ... no drive ... no morale ..."

Churchill paused to eye him, and a smirk crept into the corner of his mouth beneath his dusty upper lip pencil moustache.

"Morale, you say?" he asked rhetorically at Hill.

He turned to address the men as they finished exiting the ruins of the department store, taking up seats or standing in awe in the foggy ash of the city square. They were coated in soot and dust, dry mouthed and exhausted.

"We just survived Armageddon, lads. Hitler just came at us with everything he has got! No, really, *everything.* Take a look outside ... What's that say to you? You all still see surrender? I see a reveille. We're the *defiant little shits* in the eye of *De Führer* right now ... do you really want to give ol' toothbrush head what he wants, and admit defeat?"

There lingered an eerie silence.

It was probably due to exhaustion.

"I didn't think so ..."

"What are you saying?" Hill exclaimed, breathless.

"We stay the wayward turds, Corporal! Keep defying the odds. Steer upon our drive, our path, and reach those beaches! We reach a vessel and vanish victorious from these shores as the world turns black, white, and red beneath our very feet!"

There was still a tranquil silence.

Churchill was faintly perplexed by the lack of enthusiasm that usually followed a speech of his, especially one so full of praise and elevation in a dire time of need.

What more of a sign from the king did they need?

(static) "*Stand and unfold.*" *(static)*

Between garbled intervals of electronic static discharge and pitching white noise among the deathly still ambience in the aftermath of the blitz, an English-speaking voice began to emerge through a crackling wavelength via the short-range wireless receiver aboard the A10. It called to them over a distance, audible via the hollow acoustics.

(static) "*... stand and unfold yourself. Repeat: stand and unfold yourself...*" *(more static)*

Emitting from the belly of the cruiser tank radio, the voice was heard by a few of the men, and they exchanged a look of incomprehension. Churchill was included amidst that puzzlement.

Standing focal amidst the apathetic and shattered survivors, Churchill's brow tweaked at the voice unlike any others—as if he recognized the man on the radio as well as deciphered the context of the sentences' obfuscation.

"Do you hear that?" he questioned as more white noise hashed away, and a soldier glanced about himself with a shrug. They all heard the crackling voice yet cared little for random nonsense spiking on garbled radio waves.

"Sounds like a nutcase talking gibberish," Hill finally responded on behalf of his tired and weary men, hands on his hips.

"Nay," Churchill smiled. "It's the king."

Hill and the other men frowned with confusion.

"If you lads all needed a sign ... then *this* is it."

Still centre stage and very much the spectacle, the eyes of the group watched as Churchill stepped back into the ruins and towards the resting tank, upping the tracks to gain access to the cruiser's hatch where he could reach the hanging radio hand-piece.

"Sir, what are you talking about—"

"*Shh!*" Churchill paused and shooshed as more transmission hashed across the radio waves. Whatever words were to be admitted, they were crucial to the game.

This time they all rested and listened, hearing out the voice behind the electronic hash and humouring the claptrap—because Jack said so.

Had this bloke's brains been scrambled during the air raid?

As if they didn't have enough reason already, these men were really beginning to understand why he was known as *Mad Jack*.

"Listen ..." Churchill remarked, holding up a finger in ellipsis.

(static) "I say again, if you're listening: stand and unfold yourself..."

The voice repeated, somewhat enigmatically.

The way the sentence was structured by the speaker did score a cryptic undertone. The fact Churchill seemed to have cracked that code already was rather intriguing, and so their stares befell him with a quiet attentiveness.

Once the challenge was offered, Churchill dropped in through the hatch and snatched the attached handie-talkie piece of the CB radio, standing and hanging out of the cruiser so that he could speak with everybody present.

Although mildly interested, the scattered men of the 4th were still undramatically aloof in this communique regarding *'the king'*.

"As I said, it's the king," Churchill regarded finally before responding over transmission. "The *King-Clark*."

Hill retorted quoting nonsense. "It's a bloody fruitcake, that's who it is ..."

"Actually, it's *Hamlet*," Churchill educated with a glimmer of hope and happy acknowledgement, as if he had solved a puzzle. "It's a countersign, like what we use today."

(static) "I say again, stand and unfold yourself..."

"Watch," Churchill advised before pressing the button and transmitting his next words. "I say, who's there?"

The phrasing changed, accepting of his response like it unlocked a new avenue of transcendence. Some of the men became instantly intrigued while understandably others remained sceptical.

"... nay, answer me. Stand and unfold yourself."

Amidst the men, Corporal Hill appeared incredulous to this gamble but was honestly somewhat intrigued, as were several of the other men who had turned in their seating amongst the rubble in order to face the tank in the department store ruins. They had all eyes on Churchill, wondering what the secret code word response was after the challenge phrase.

Churchill glanced over them before he spoke the answer:

"It's *Bernado*," he said with a thousand-yard stare of confidence. He followed it with the infamous phrase from the literature, albeit slightly altered as a part of an inside wordplay between the two intellects:

"Long live the King-*Clark*."

1940, June 4
M/Y Sundowner
Coast of Dunkirk, English Channel

(static) "*Long live the King-Clark ...*"

Across the city, adrift in the Dunkirk harbour, the Sundowner bobbed in the calm and silent moonlit current.

A smile crept over King-Clark's mouth. It may not have been evident through his speech over the radio, but his expression indicated a sudden sense of contentment. "Jack?!"

King-Clark's peepers searched those in the cabin of the yacht.

His explosive excitement attracted Padre Nicholl and he appeared in the doorframe, leaning against the frame. He smiled with delight, hoping, too, that it was Churchill.

"*He,*" via the radio speaker from afar, the unmistakable voice of Mad Jack Churchill responded with Shakespearian content.

Beside them at the wheel, Lightoller cracked a sneer at their success. They were nerds and this was a stretch, but holy shit: it had somehow worked. The skipper nodded with glee, sincerely glad that the main objective of their mission had been identified.

King-Clark exploded in joyous response—an emotion he couldn't help but contain. "Jack! It's you!"

(static) "*Hullo, Clark!*"

1940, June 4
Dunkirk
Nord-Pas-de-Calais, France

"*Jack! You're alive! I can't believe it!*" the static-encrusted tone of King-Clark exclaimed, sounding both parts surprised and ecstatic that he had managed to find him on the radio.

Churchill brought the radio transmitted before his pencil-thin moustache and dimple chin. "Of course I am! Why wouldn't I be?"

(static) "*Because I just saw what appeared to be one of the ten biblical plagues rain down upon your head!*"

"Oh, *that,*" noted Churchill, acting coy. "Nonsense, Clark. 'tis nothing but a graze."

(static) "*Tell that to the city.*"

"Are you still waiting somewhere out there for me, old boy?"

(static) "*Indeed I am, and with a boat of chaps as mad as you are! Mad enough to return to Dunkirk, that is. Hence the coded message to make sure I got you and no one else.*"

"Silly boy, you should be long gone by now."

"*The thought had crossed my mind.*"

"Fine-o-fine. Where shall we meet ...?"

(static) "*The question is* how *shall we* communicate *this meet ...?*"

Churchill sulked, eyes down and focusing on the radio. While he did however, there was a slight surge in optimism amongst the group of survivors. They all understood that they had a ticket out of Dunkirk *if* they could make it to the coast. This was *half* of their mission done.

"Come again, Clark?"

(static) "*We are but a small yacht, Jack, and this is an open channel. Crowds of pandemonium could ensue if you were not quick enough to the extraction ...*"

Suddenly, Churchill realized what they meant. There would be thousands of desperate soldiers still trying to board any ships crazy enough to attempt re-entry into Dunkirk for evacuation across the English Channel. To some extent of self-preservation, they would have to be careful and limit the amount of broadcasting ado their rendezvous whereabouts. Undesirable attention was their counter objective, of either Axis or, unfortunately, Allied impediment.

(static) "*We wish we could take them all ... but that is an unfortunate impossibility.*"

"Understood, Clark," Churchill responded candidly, recognizing the current level of clandestine undertone over the open broadcast. A shoutout to the location of the last ship from Dunkirk over an open throng of desperate soldiers would definitely result in chaos.

And it was with that realization, an idea sprang to mind ...

In late September of last year when the Second Manchester Regiment had landed in France, they had arrived an hour earlier than expected. While they waited for their orders, Captains Churchill and King-Clark had advanced on a wander easterly and along the beach. Back then, the civilian lifestyle of Dunkirk had been thriving. There were numerous small businesses and residential housing that aligned the road parallel to the shore, among which they discovered a well-maintained tennis and squash course venue. Even though the British Expeditionary Force was pouring in by the boatload, the owner was more than fine with allowing the two English chaps to have a quick game session. It was easterly along the beachline, and a landmark Churchill hoped his dear friend would recall as they had numerous times joshed about playing another round as they finished one for all, a third for match point.

Churchill's sterling stare tightened, and a smirk formed upon his maw, concocting the perfect protocol for their predicament.

"Clark ... fancy that rematch?"

(static) "... *I do, Jack. We'll wait a drift for you there, stay in touch.*"

"Will do, friend," Churchill released the talk button, eyeing Hill and his surrounding men who had all gravitated towards the tank. A few located on stretchers were even sitting upright, listening intently, watching from under bandaged foreheads.

"A *rematch?*" Hill questioned.

"Squash," explained Churchill, heaving up from the tank hatch and sitting on its armoured side. The bullet wound to his shoulder was beginning to give him grief, stiffening his movements.

The gathered men were absent words.

They vacated the lip of the rubble surrounding the tank in order for Churchill to descend, and Jack examined their transport situation, or lack thereof. Their Bedford transport truck remained upturned and now completely wrecked thanks to that carpet bombing, though they were grateful. Its sacrifice had protected them upon its upturn. Ol' Busty Barbara, the cruiser tank, wasn't doing too good either, with smoke hissing from her agitated engine. Its side had been again buried in rubble from the blitz downpour, and the track that ran along its right side was detached at a clasp, and now lined the floor exposing the metal wheel chassis.

"Bollocks," Churchill stated, realizing the gravity of their transport situation post air raid.

"*Some miracle,*" in a disgruntled tone, one of the soldiers in the background muttered. "*We gonna bloody walk to the shore?*"

"We've got a boat waiting for us," Churchill stated. "That was the hard part."

"*The hard part?*" another from the crowd of wounded repeated sarcastically. "*I thought the hard part would have been surviving a trek across Dunkirk!*"

Another piped up in his defence while Churchill stood idle and in deep contemplation.

"*We're alive, ain't we?*"

"*Barely. Those of us who weren't already wounded, are now! Are they really going to wait for hours on end out there for us to walk to the bloody coast—a coast we probably can't even reach.*"

"*Oi!*" a prominent voice shouted from a downward trajectory. It was a badly wounded fellow lying in a stretcher, who had painstakingly lurched forward. Churchill eyed him, along with everybody else. Until now, this fellow had been quiet, possibly unconscious or heavily incapacitated. Apparently now he was at his wit's end, and it was in Jack's defence. "*He's gotten us this far, hasn't he? And he's right: do you really wanna give up after living through all that! I sure as fuck don't, but I need at least two of you cunts to realize that so that you can carry me out! 'Cause me legs are fucked!*"

A quiet pause resonated following that outburst.

However, before anybody could respond from their silent reflections, the sound of an incoming engine caught their attention.

Churchill's ears pricked ...

"*Shh!*" he shushed, silencing the men.

Through the stillness of the echoic bombing aftermath, flickering spot fires and the distant quaking of tumbling rubble, there was the gentle hum of incoming multi-wheel land vehicles. Heavy vehicles, more than just one.

"*What the bloomin' 'ell—*"

"*Oh, what now?!*"

"*Is it the Germans?*"

"*Shh!*" Churchill hissed more vociferously.

This was cause for alarm and there was the sudden surge of panic. It suddenly occurred to the men that maybe now that they had carpet bombed the city, the enemy forces were invading.

It made for sound logic.

"They sound like bloody tanks!" in a whisper, Hill remarked, getting down low with his men and drawing his revolver. He was one of the only men still possessing a firearm after the craziness of that blitz.

"*Jesus Christ!*"

"*Shh! Shh!*"

The men stirred, all wide-eyed and full of dread.

Hill turned to Jack in the crowd of stressed soldiers, unable to hide, fight, or run from whatever was coming around the next corner. "If that's the Germans invading ..." Hill shook his head. "It might be time to wave that white flag, Mad Jack."

"Stay calm," Churchill silenced them again, passing through the standing crowd of beaten and wounded soldiers. With bollocks of steel, he drew the claybeg from his hip and climbed the brick mound, approaching the giant hole in the wall that led out into the burning status of the destructed town square. Harsh orange heat blared in through the haze of dust from a dozen spot fires out in Jean Bart Place, where bombed cars burned vividly.

The men cowered, watching the sword-wielding wit seemingly engage an unknown force of unknown numbers ... with a claybeg.

Churchill fearlessly stood tall in the yawning mouth of the building, fully exposed as the rumbling of the incoming vehicles rattled louder, now pretty much on top of their location as they downed one of the main drags. The roads through the town square were all mostly blocked with stationary vehicles. They knew this first-hand, which meant whatever was coming was about to traverse the same route they had taken.

"What is it!?" Hill called as men around him squatted down as low as they could go, preparing what weapons they had for close quarters combat and defence.

"Jack?!" Hill repeated, his concern growing cumbersome.

A smile happened to grow upon Churchill's face, and he revolved around and sheathed his sword at the hip. He seemed unafraid. Happy, even.

"It's your *miracle*, lads!"

Just then, they all watched past Churchill as a convoy of several British Bedford transport trucks rolled along the road within close proximity of the shop, rolling to a stop as though somebody had ordered a pickup. The in-tact Bedfords were not fully stocked with troops, and each had around three or four soldiers in the rear of each unit.

One of the trucks passed the opening into the building before stopping, the second stopped right in front of the hole in the wall, having seen and gestured at Churchill's standing poise, with a third truck halting behind that. There was even a fourth transport vehicle, pulling up just out of sight of them and around the corner.

The men aboard were all British and all armed.

"Hullo there!" Churchill acknowledged them, still holding his position about the rubble hill of the department store and appearing like a coalminer compared to this lot.

"Hello!" the voice of one of the men hanging out the window of the cabins replied, dismounting from the passenger's seat of the truck and stepping forth to greet Churchill. He was a captain within the BEF ranks, and one that Jack had never had the pleasure of meeting, until now.

The soldier and his men had clearly seen some action on their retreat from Dunkirk. The captain himself had a slice across his cheek and a tattered uniform, albeit not as discoloured as any of the men of the 4th Infantry Division after surviving the blitz.

He had an exceptionally large and round jaw and spoke with an Irish accent as he demurely addressed Churchill, peering beyond him and at the others through the hole. "I would ask *how do you do*, but I reckon I already know the answer."

Arriving up close, he extended a hand.

"*Captain Marcus Ervine-Andrews. East Lancashire Regiment.*"

Churchill firmly took his embrace, replying in-kind.

"Captain Jack Churchill, Second Manchester Regiment. How do *you* do, Marcus?"

They were both a sight for sore eyes for one another.

"Just surviving," was Ervine-Andrews' only response.

"Know the feeling," replied Churchill. "Are you running as late for the evacuation as we are?"

"Indeed, we are. Got held up at the *Canal de Bergues*, southeast of Dunkirk. Me and my lads here had to fight our way out of a German stranglehold. Took us bloody forever and a day."

Churchill shared a glance to a few of the other men from the East Lancashire Regiment. They each looked baggy-eyed, dishevelled, and exhausted.

Jack locked eyes with one and nodded respectfully.

The troop returned the gesture.

"The enemy is not far off a complete invasion of Dunkirk," Ervine-Andrews added in reference to what he and his men had recently witnessed, though it didn't take a first-hand account to work that one out.

"I can imagine. My civilian cohort and myself ran into a convoy of 4th Infantry transporting their wounded from the rearguard, who had gotten themselves pinned down by the enemy along the outskirts. We got them out and travelled this far ... managed to survive that air raid, too."

"Yes, us as well. We hiked it into the city in chin-high canal, avoiding enemy fire, followed the *Quai aux Fleurs* canal to a dry-dock south from here. We were delighted to discover these stashed lorries inside one of the buildings where we hid from the blitz."

Churchill nodded, entertaining his story.

"Anyhow ..." Ervine-Andrews moved them along, halfway acknowledging the others amongst the ruins. "You lot fancy a ride to the coast or what?"

The men were overjoyed.

Ervine-Andrews returned his eyeline to Churchill.

"Let's just hope we can get further than the beaches, yeah?"

"Captain, if you can get us to the coast ... I can you get you *home.*"

Ervine-Andrews read the sincerity in Churchill's eyes.

He bobbed his head, gesturing to the men in the trucks to lower the trays and prepare to receive more occupants. They systematically jumped down and did so, also assisting the wounded men of the 4th and making new friends.

Together, they bonded.

Once aboard, they raced through the dawn and the rising sun, hoping to reach the shoreline before daylight did ... for with it, the day brought a formidable scourge in the form of a swastika.

'By the time our newfound convoy neared the beaches along the northeast coast of Dunkirk, the light of morning was breaking beyond the horizon. Needless to even say, it had been a long night and even longer few days trying to get out of France. However, those near-death adventures with Jack Churchill, I will never forget until the day I die.

As history will read it, the 4th of June 1940 was the last day that any successful evacuations were made across the English Channel from Dunkirk. Within twenty-four hours, 35,000 French and Belgian soldiers, including a few dregs of British soldiers who missed the initial waves of evacuation, would be forced to surrender to Nazi Germany as the enemy stormfront arrived. The Axis would finally invade the coastal city in wake of Hitler's controversial Halt Order, which in many ways allowed the British to <u>retreat to victory</u>. Hitler would state publicly: 'Dunkirk has fallen! The greatest battle in the history of the world has come to an end!' With further exaggerations of detail which included rounding up the totalities of captured soldiers and inflicted losses to the Allies and that of the Axis, the Führer announced the event as 'The greatest annihilation battle of all time' against the British by strategic hand of the Oberkommando der Wehrmacht (German armed forces high command), and placing credit to the force.

'The road we took was a congested one. They all were. The blocked route was chosen by Jack and new collaborator Captain Ervine-Andrews. The eight

Irishmen of the East Lancashire Regiment were new additions to our motley evacuation drive, and they brought into the fray able bodied men to assist with the wounded, guns, and most invaluably, vehicles for transportation. As per the rest of routes into and throughout Dunkirk, abandoned vehicles lined the roads in an almost post-apocalyptic tone. What avenues weren't chock-jammed with cars were blocked by the rubble of destroyed buildings, but somehow, we managed to push through ... and drag with us an armoured A10 cruiser tank by the name of Busty Barbara—Mad Jack's wishes.

Before we left Jean Bart Place, Jack hitched the four transporter trucks together using the winch cable on the rear of the tank so that combined, the big trucks could drag her in tandem. Diffident as they were in wanting to drag the fifteen-tonne incapacitated vehicle with us, Jack informed them that strategically they required her for her onboard radio communiqué and to up-keep communications with those upon the Sundowner vessel. The convoy of Bedford trucks had not a CB unit between them, and Barbara's was welded into the armoured console.

Perhaps a method to the madness. Perhaps not. Having known Mad Jack Churchill better than most, I knew it was out of sheer romanticism that he wished to save her. He'd go to hell and back again for a busty broad of such high calibre ...'

Their fresh heterogeneous convoy headed directly east and along a road known as the *Rue Paul Vancassel.*

This orienteered direction took them all the way to the north beyond several city blocks, eventuating on a road parallel to the shoreline. The route was far less congested by vehicular traffic due to it being an indirect route from the city centre and to the harbour.

It was a longer route but, in this case, was the quickest. They were so close they could hear the waves of the ocean.

"Up ahead, next left. Take it one block and then turn right, then left again. That'll take us all the way to the coast and to the rendezvous point where we should meet Clark's boat," riding in the tray of the leading Bedford truck, Churchill informed the driver through the open slide window behind the cabin. He put away his crumpled officer's map of the Dunkirk docking zones for they were miles outdated, however still laid out the streets well enough to navigate.

The driver, a battle-scarred soldier from Ervine-Andrews' section, nodded to comply, apprehending the instructions clearly over the deep and droning bustle of their convoy. There was a constant bouncing along the uneven terrain of which they cruised at a relatively high speed, the four trucks daisy-chained together via winch cable, pulling along Busty Barbara on her squeaking track wheels at the rear. They looked like a bunch of horses hauling a big, armoured carriage.

Churchill revolved around in his seat in the rear tray of the first vehicle alongside the battle-worn Ervine-Andrews. Along with them in the open air troop carrier was one other occupant, another loyal Irish rifleman. Evidently, he had also seen some action, as had every man within the unit.

All vehicles were driven by members of the East Lancashire Regiment. In the second and third vehicles, they had loaded up the wounded members of the 4th Infantry, as well as Corporal Hill from their unit. Several medics standing in the trays attended to all the wounded soldiers as they cruised, most of which were laying down flat and with a lot more luxurious space than their previous transportation.

In the last truck tray of their convoy before the attached cruiser tank that rolled along smoothly behind the carriers, was Felix Hardy by himself. Pen and notepad in hand, the American journalist had a moment in which he could reflect and write. Even with a possibly fractured wrist, his pencil scratched away in the dim radiance as dawn slowly climbed upon the distant horizon. He found solace in doing nothing else.

"I beg your pardon," finally commented Churchill seated beside the Irish captain of their saviour unit. "Do continue."

Riding in the tray of the first truck, he had been in the middle of exchanging his war stories between Ervine-Andrews and Hill to date when Churchill had addressed their driver to aid with navigation.

Captain Ervine-Andrews was telling Churchill about his unit's last few days in the Nord-Pas-de-Calais leading up to Dynamo's finale. Like the Second Manchester Regiment, the East Lancashire Regiment had also been tasked with befalling the rearguard and holding open the passage for the evacuation.

He had mentioned in detail that during the night of 31 May along a waterway known as the *Canal de Bergues,* south of Dunkirk, the company set up a defensive line. They were under intense artillery, mortar, and machine gun fire for over ten hours whilst they held their own against vastly superior enemy forces. Heavily outnumbered and outgunned, the Lancashires held out until the very last bullet.

Ervine-Andrews commented that his low numbers now were not due to enemy-inflicted casualties, but rather he sent most of his men to Dunkirk to make the evacuation during stages of the battle, getting as many out as possible whilst the rest propped up the closing walls. He and a select few volunteers stayed back to hold the line a few hours longer, to guarantee the majority of the BEF's retreat and evacuation.

"... we rushed to a barn nearby and from the roof shot at least a dozen of the enemy. We were running low on ammo, so we lulled them into a false sense of security, drawing them in nice and close," he chortled with a perception of vanity hiding a more sincere sense of mourning for those fallen men whose lives they had taken. His expression seemed to deadpan upon recalling the scenario.

"Poor bastards, eh," Hill scoffed with absolutely zero sympathy towards Nazi Germany.

Ervine-Andrews pursed his lip, nodding.

"You played the hand you were dealt," Churchill reassured respectfully. He understood how Ervine-Andrews was feeling more than most. The situation of being outnumbered and running out of ammunition during a fight aside, the successful strategy enacts as per what he described, however dishonest of an ambush manoeuvre as it may seem in the swelling of survivor's guilt that befell the victors, was simply just good tactics.

"They were all out in the open, taken by surprise. They must have thought we kept on running to the coast ... We shot them all dead, and kept shooting until we clicked dry. The less bullets we had, the lighter we were to run," Ervine-Andrews further explained. "Soon after, we bailed and fully retreated. All we had left was a couple of Bren guns which we used in a withdrawal method to cover our retreat while Gerry kept trying to give chase. They eventually backed off ... for whatever reason, Hitler's not letting them go past a certain boundary. We got lucky."

Churchill listened intently, comprehending in great detail how they utilized this military manoeuvre with two main guns; one machine gun would set up somewhere low and with a suppressive line at the rear. They would open fire past a column of retreating men and engage at the pursuing enemy with bursts until it was their turn. After an agreed amount of ammunition expenditure, the latter gunner would then fall back under the concealment of the former, alternating that same suppressive with the machine gunner who was now further along the line to likewise cover their retreat. They would do this again and again, like a waltz sling, until a safe distance was managed. That way, the team would make haste and pace their retreat but also never turn their back without some form of cover, all the while keeping the enemy at bay.

"The barn got shot to shit, shattered, even set on fire by some kraut wanker by the time we finally legged it. We made it across open ground before we sunk into the canal as artillery fire surrounded us, as did an overarching machine gun emplacement from another direction. We swum up the waterway of this filthy canal for miles ... that's how we got into the city. My men were exhausted, treading water for hours. The murky shit stunk too, lapping under our chins for hours."

Ervine-Andrews and the rifleman sitting opposite him were content on the topic. It had obviously been a difficult firefight, and an even worse couple of days spent getting back to Dunkirk.

"We waited out a few patrols as they sped past and even duped a scout patrol, eventually managing to get back on dry land again and collect ourselves. We reached the outskirts the following day in the afternoon. Waited until late at night to venture in, as there were enemy units setting up along those same outskirts."

"Sounds familiar," Hill remarked snidely.

Churchill felt Hill's glance land upon him.

They knew them all too well.

"They would have been the same lot we encountered."

"Yeah, we broke through, though. I still don't know how. We managed to survive the air raid and at the same time stumbled across these few trucks ... then across *you* and *your lot of strays.*"

"Glad you did," Churchill responded gratefully. "I don't know how we would have made it to the beach without use of your transportation, Marcus. Going to have to shout you a scotch or two when we're back home."

"A ride back home would be payment enough, Jack," Ervine-Andrews took Churchill's hand in promise. "... and maybe a wee dram of whiskey as well."

Churchill snickered as he ascended to his feet in the open tray of the rocking and turbulent voyage, facing the next vehicle in the convoy behind them. The trucks were all latched via winch harnesses through their axles, the second lorry was but a bee's dick in distance. He slipped his strung longbow over his head, positioning it comfortably across his shoulder, the drawstring running across his uniform with the diagonal strap of his leather quiver.

While Hill wasn't surprised, Ervine-Andrews and his rifleman both watched him precariously as if he were going somewhere ... and he was.

"Going somewhere?"

Balancing on the rocking platform of the truck tray, Churchill glanced over his shoulder with his shouted response. "Going to check on my lads. I'll be back in a jiffy."

Ervine-Andrews and the rifleman exchanged a look.

Is he serious ...?

The vehicles were in-motion!

Before they could barely shift in their seats or pose any opposition, Jack Churchill leapt from the tray of the truck and onto the nose of the truck behind as it drove in tandem. The driver through the window raised his hands from the wheel, absolutely astounded. With wide eyes and bared teeth, he and a passenger shouted something imperceptible through the windshield.

Churchill upped from a kneeling landing and gave a partial salute to the occupants in the cabin before climbing up and over the cabin with several *thumps* and *dongs* along the hollow metal roof.

Inside the cabin of the vehicle, the two Lancashires looked out past where they had just seen Churchill disappear over their heads. Their view in the forward truck was of their own captain in the forward truck, wearing an equally as bewildered look upon his face.

It was misplaced anxiety.

This was child's play for Mad Jack Churchill.

"You get used to it ..." unphased, Hill remarked to Ervine-Andrews.

"How do you do, lads," Churchill commented as he dropped down from the roof of the cabin and onto the tray of truck number two of the convoy. The wounded men all glanced up to see him, rather surprised at his sudden appearance upon their vehicle while they were all still in rickety motion.

They nodded and observed as he passed between them and around the wounded, lying flat.

"Just letting you all know we're about ten to fifteen minutes out from the beaches," he informed as he steadily manoeuvred through the wounded lying along the open air tray of the truck in an array of aligned gurneys and the medics attending to them.

Under their anxious eyes, Churchill approached the rear of the truck and propped a leg on the rear tray door. With the slightest of pauses which resembled a form of disinclination, but was merely just cunning, he leapt from the truck and onto the nose of the next truck.

Same as before, Churchill saluted the drivers and upped the truck cabin, dropping down into the rear tray and catching a medic by surprise.

"Hullo there," Jack calmly remarked as he relayed the same notice and briefly checked on the wellness of the men as they rocked around on their gurneys in the tray. Seconds later, right before their eyes, Churchill leapt from the rear of the rambling vehicle and onto the final truck of the convoy.

With a calm signal, Churchill gave a gesture to the stunned driver, who hovered his hands above the steering wheel in order to signal his shock, horror, and confoundment at what he had just done.

Churchill upped the compartment and his boots thudded into the empty tray of the rearmost Bedford truck, issued with a view of Busty Barbara in tow. His boots landed loudly right beside the American journalist, who seemed deep in thought as he stared at his notepad and twiddled his pencil, however Felix Hardy did not jolt upon Mad Jack's surprise arrival. It seemed that he had acclimatized to the eccentric man's practices.

He balanced his notepad against his knee with his injured hand that had been splinted with one of Jack's arrows. The sharp tip of the arrow poked out the front almost like a nasty-looking medieval wrist blade contraption. Logic may have suggested to break off the bodkin-tip, however Hardy had opted to leave it in-tact for the possible collector's value, for it would make a prized souvenir if they got out of this hell hole.

"Captain," he instead announced as he took his time to apply a visual address, looking up. "Had a feeling you'd be paying me a visit."

"You should have gone with *dropping in*, lad," Churchill remarked, balancing tall before Hardy in the wobbly open tray. One hand was on his hip, the other on the knuckleduster hilt of his stowed sword. The pose could not have been any more Errol Flynn-ish if he tried. "I thought you writer types were supposed to be more capacious with your vocabularies."

Hardy's brow raised an inch as he accepted the critique. "Truth is, glossary expanse is usually upon publication. Publication and imagery in draft notes are not quite one of the same."

"You mean, *not on the same page?*"

Hardy eyed his paper for a whole second before returning his blunt stare upon Churchill.

"I could do metaphors all day, lad," Jack coyly remarked as he finally took a seat in the tray, holding his longbow. "Perhaps *I* should be a writer? You know, publicize my adventures here in France, such as today. Make an absolute killing. I could retire young."

Hardy smirked with a candid glimmer beneath a cocked brow.

" *You? Retire?*"

"Yeah, you know ... one day. When we're old men, Felix. Get all this etched in history before bloody Clark does in *Free For a Blast: Chapter-* bloody-*ten*."

Hardy held a drifting gaze which Churchill caught in linger, and therefore the silence that followed as they bopped about in the back of the transporter truck demanded explanation.

"What?"

"No, nothing," Hardy failed to deflect, so he expanded his thoughts. "Well, it's just most men I've met in war times, like you Captain, are all *rampage* and *recklessness* in the sense that they've come to terms with death. Men fight either afraid of dying and therefore ultimately cower and hide, or they're accepting of their fate: that they are *already* dead. That they undertake combat anticipating that fateful bullet with their name on it to eventually find them and send them home. *You* on the other hand, you're at war, but ... you're somehow ... in the middle somewhere."

"Felix ..." Churchill inhaled, seemingly to prepare his retort in this moment of utter bromance, their first without pending warfare or whilst under a veil of raining lead. "... call me *Jack*."

They laughed.

"Honestly, you've got nothing to add on that? I thought we were finally opening up, as if you actually *like* me or something."

Churchill judged him. "Did I not just say you could call me *Jack?*"

"You know what I meant."

Churchill took an extended second.

It was rare that he peeled back a layer deeper than what you saw on the surface. Ever.

" *'No prince or lord has tomb so proud, as he whose flag becomes his shroud',*" Churchill quoted, and Hardy interpreted the meaning.

"Sounds like *dulce et decorum est pro patria mori.*"

"Same but different," Churchill agreed. The romanticism was shared. "But *Owen* copied *Meagher.*"

"Then *Meagher* copied *Horace*," Hardy replied, surprising Churchill with his intellectual knowledge of historical quotes.

"It's funny, I picked you as more of a *movie* guy than a *book* guy ..."

"Hey, hey, I know how to read," Hardy defended, but then realigned their discussed relative sentiment. "Regardless of the origins of context of platitudinal literature; you want to die for your country. I get it."

"Felix, I don't *want* to die here. Not in this war or the next war, or the next one after that. This battle will be over and another on a different front will begin, and I'll be there to do this all over again. It's my duty, it's who I am. Like you said, there may be a bullet out there with my name on it—another one, I mean," he made reference to the wound in his left shoulder, "and perhaps even one day it may find me, but it's not a moment that I fear. It's just another obstacle in my path."

"A *path?* To where?"

"Anywhere war takes me. It's my *warpath*," Churchill ideologized. He nodded his chin at Hardy's notes, liking what he had just expressed and wanting to coin it. "Write that down."

"And you," scoffed Hardy again, snagged on a fundamental part of Churchill's plan. He jeered again, "A *writer?*"

"Pardon?" Jack remarked with playful offence. "You don't think I could master the pencil and paper had I the time?"

"I don't think you have the patience for it," Hardy said with validity. "*That*, and a story like this, even professionally researched and *however* well phrased, paced, and written, you may as well call it *jack shit*. Begging all pardon, being honest, I don't think anyone would believe your tale, Mad Jack."

Churchill cocked his head in agreement, bringing his eyeline before them and out the back to the fifteen-tonne A10 cruiser tank named Busty Barbara presently being dragged behind their combined two-hundred-and-twenty horsepower fleet of winched Bedford OYDs.

"God's honest truth there, lad. I barely believe it myself."

The view of the road past the dragged cruiser tank changed angle as their convoy slowly snaked around another corner. They were now alongside the beach side, adjacent as a sand strip.

To their right (northeast) was the bloom of a dawn-lit horizon, breaking over the smooth and distant flat of the ocean. To the left (southwest) was Dunkirk city. They passed several congested routes leading inland. Up ahead and tracing the coast was the sight of the harbours. They still smouldered from aerial assaults. Thick, dark smoke plumes climbed into the dawn sky.

In the back of the rear truck tray, Churchill upped and clung to the exterior of the cabin, scanning the road ahead of the convoy.

Dawn was rising upon France quickly this morning.

The sensation occurred to Churchill in his tired state, however he quickly rejected the thought, reminding himself of basic science and of the Coriolis force. The earth's rotation cannot happen quicker than on any other day. As a result, he considered that perhaps it was simply due to how long the night had felt. Maybe even the glow from the burning city after the blitz bombing had cloaked the glow of the rising sunlight until now.

Without even checking his watch, Jack could feel the auric sunrise radiance of dawn upon his tired face, feel it strain his stare as he looked towards the horizon of the seascape. The light pricked his irises like needles.

Their convoy weaved between a few abandoned vehicles along the road, and Churchill spotted the bolted-up sports venue of relevance to their right. The coast here was the point at which they were to rendezvous with King-Clark and his boat.

"We're here!" Churchill thumped on the roof of the cabin, and the driver let out a short double-tap of the car horn to notify the others in tandem.

The daisy-chained truck convoy chauffeur gradually braked to a halt parallel to the establishments; shops on one side, the beach sands on the other. Men immediately dismounted with weapons drawn, scanning the perimeter. They were at the furthest point possible away from the

German forces on this landmass, and therefore should have felt safe. However, this was still a foreign land, and all signs of life were quite absent. It was eerie and desolate, and made for an understandable temperament of discomposure.

Up by the front truck, Ervine-Andrews stood tall on the rear tray, mimicking Churchill aboard the last. The two exchanged a look, and Jack gestured to him that on the right was the rendezvous point. The Irish captain then signalled to the others, relaying fresh orders to his men to hold the position for whatever came next. They timely dismounted the vehicles, probing about.

Churchill's view panned along the dark coast, panning into the light and towards the sunrise portion. The waters were clear and vacant, albeit for obvious signs of floating ship wreckages and washed-up debris.

There was nothing.

No sounds, no people.

Waves calmly crashed upon the sand of the shore.

The beach sand was thrashed with old indentations, both vehicular and by footsteps. Some of them had been washed away by the tide. Only a day ago had these shorelines been stacked with queues of British soldiers, thousands of them, all waiting in line for evacuation by ship across the English Channel.

There were some vehicles still left abandoned in the sand dunes. Some were even out in the water, half drowned and partially entombed in wet sand. It was the remnants of the man-made jetties, improvised during the kerfuffle by the engineering corps—the epitome of a desperate measure in desperate times. Soldiers had literally driven them into the swells, abandoning them once they took water, swimming the rest of the way out to sea in the hope of salvation.

Lapping against the shore in the incoming tide there was much debris. Mostly splintered and decayed wood, frayed rope, and chunks of coal from the bombed piers and ships. Most heart-wrenching, though, amongst the floating drifters were a great number of dead bodies; once desperate soldiers, now departed of life. They had either drowned during the pandemonium or been killed on a ship in the harbour, perhaps a little of both.

Lifeless corpses lined the blood-laced and oil-slicked seafoam, some partially buried in the new sandbank the tide had founded. They were prisoners of the current, now softly caressed by the gentle waves of the shoreline.

Festered pockmarks lined the sands of the shoreline, caused by machine gun sweeps by the Luftwaffe the previous day. The larger and deeper charred craters were made by bombers.

An overturned Bedford truck barely one hundred yards from their position still smouldered with embers from an explosion. Bodies of killed soldiers who had sought it for refuge from a raid were long deceased, fanned out and away from the blast like flower petals. Face-down, they were each singed at the back, likely having been unable to outrun the explosion.

Evidence of the war carnage only thickened as the coast stretched west and towards the Dunkirk harbour, where the piers were located. It was a horrible sight to see.

"*Captain Churchill?!*" an East Lancashire soldier announced from his position within the top hatch of the towed A10 cruiser tank at the rear of their convoy. His brodie-helmeted head emerged from the circular hatch, and he had to shout over the windy breeze sweeping over the flat surface of the beach sands.

Apart from laboured steering and braking, this soldier's only other duty had been to answer the phone should she ring, and she just had. The soldier was holding out the handheld of the CB radio.

Breaking from his harrowing stare of the shoreline destruction, Churchill dismounted the truck, threw his longbow back over his shoulder so that he was hands-free, and jogged over quickly. He built up speed and mounted the track of the cruiser, attending to the hatch. The radio line extended to its fullest, and Jack brought it before his maw.

"Clark?"

"*Jack!*" King-Clark's voice boomed. The signal was much clearer, with marginally less static interference—that meant that they were much closer now. "*We see you on the beach! Look to the sea, pirates ahoy ...*"

Churchill and the soldier both scanned to the north, as did Hardy from the rear tray of the closest truck. At first, all they saw was a bland dark nothingness beyond the slithery, slick waves of the post-dawn shore.

Then, they saw the beam of the searchlight as it subtly blinked at them from the vessel, cloaked in apparent plain sight.

The yacht was approximately five hundred yards out and bobbing on the surface of the calm seascape.

"The only pirate around here is you, Clark," Churchill joshed.

"Need this?" Ervine-Andrews questioned as he trotted in close, holding out a copper-coated signalling flare gun known as a Very pistol. The thing was an odd shape, with a one-inch diameter barrel. Hill was in tow, listening intently.

Churchill responded by shaking his head, still engaged on the radio communiqué. They did not require any visual confirmation.

"*What light through yonder window breaks?*"

Churchill grinned. "Roger that, Romeo, I see you."

"*Does that make you Juliet?*" King-Clark jested.

"Depends on if you buy me dinner first."

"*I, eh ... see you've found some friends, Jack?*"

Churchill bobbed his beret-donned head, eyeing the boat in the distance as if he were speaking to King-Clark in person. "I have. It's more like they found me. They're coming too."

There was a brief quiescence on the other end where, undoubtedly, King-Clark relayed the information to the ship's captain and likely argued the point, negotiating their passage.

"*How many?*"

"Two dozen."

More silence.

Churchill's eyes dropped to the sand, staring blank.

"Clark?"

"*Two dozen, roger. Agreed, Jack. Bring them aboard.*"

Jack's stare focused.

Beyond relieved that they could be accommodated for, he had just had the sudden fear that the ship captain may deny their voyage ahoy.

"Thank you," he said genuinely. "How close can you *scurvy dogs* come to shore?"

"*Captain Lightoller here says not close enough for you to board. The boat has a low-hanging keel, and this coast is a shallow ascent to shore. He doesn't want to risk becoming beached and thus marooned in Dunkirk.*"

"It'd be one for the history books at least."

"*We can get within a hundred or so paces. Might have to take a dip if your men swim to us by chance?*"

"Negative, I've got wounded lads amongst. Most can barely walk let alone swim," he relayed to King-Clark before releasing the transmit button on the radio, then to Ervine-Andrews who nodded silently in accord. "We're going to have to figure something out ..."

"Might wanna make it soon, eh?" Ervine-Andrews remarked, casting a look about his shoulders. "I've got a feeling the full force of Nazi Germany is riding into town with this rising sun."

Churchill concurred.

It was a high probability, at least for another aerial display.

Ervine-Andrews was almost certainly right in predicting the German advance at first light. Invasions usually filled the wake of bombing raids. That, and they had left Dunkirk alone in this Halt Order for long enough. The timing suits, and pilots would have visual advantage in the daylight and were likely well rested and hungry for more target practice.

"*Understood. Jack, we can see that there is a small wharf left standing towards the harbour to the west,*" King-Clark's voice relayed from the skipper of the yacht. They could probably spot the location from the sea, but all they could see from the convoy to the west was a partially collapsed high pier and boating shed, still smouldering from a recent bomb blast. What King-Clark referred to must have laid beyond that structure.

"*If you can make it there, depending on recessed debris from sunken ships, we could perhaps get in close enough to collect you and your flock from the end of the wharf.*"

While Churchill listened, the heavens parted, and he saw their new distant objective. The billowing black smoke from the destroyed boatshed behind a collapsed pier suddenly wafted by a gust of air. Beyond it and along the west coast there stood a wharf, still seemingly operational. At her sea end, there were multiple destroyed wreckages protruding from the water.

The BEF evacuation had probably used this in the early stages of the evacuation, however the pier had fallen target to aerial bombing. Large ships had fallen prey to the shallow recesses of the coastline beach. Any ships who found themselves beached during such a manic time were undoubtedly shot to shit by the enemy flyovers. There was a family of destroyed and partially sunken ships at the end of the wharf making her unusable for any further evacuations, however, their smaller yacht *may* fit if Lightoller could navigate her between the wreckages. He must have been confident to have suggested it.

"Fine-o-fine. We'll meet you there," Churchill said as he shoved the talkie back to the hands of the man in the tank. Beside him now was Ervine-Andrews and two of his East Lancashire men. The rest had all fanned out into a partial perimeter defence around the convoy. Hardy had also dismounted from the tray of the truck, using the cruiser tank to balance with his one good hand and limping on his injured leg. After the ride in the truck, his leg had succumbed to the inflammation of his injury site and grew stiff and sore. He collected from the ground a soldier's discarded and empty Bren machine gun, slightly chocked with sand from the beach. It wasn't exactly lightweight, but Hardy managed it, burying its thick brown buttstock under his arm and using as a crutch to lean on.

Churchill was late to finally accept the offering of the flare pistol from Ervine-Andrews. He cracked open the chamber, seeing the brass puckered asshole of a resting red signalling flare inside, ready to be stricken.

"Where'd you scavenge this?"

"Was left in the glovebox of the first truck," Ervine-Andrews explained bringing back around his wooden Lee-Enfield. "One of the only things the troops didn't strip from the trucks when they abandoned them."

Churchill closed the cap and tucked the signal pistol into his belt. It seemed they didn't need it, as King-Clark already knew where they were. Nevertheless, he explained with astuteness, "May come in handy."

"To the wharf, then?"

"Affirmative. Hopefully we can access it and jump aboard ..."

"Sounds simple enough."

They spoke too soon.

Right at that moment, as all the men came to exultant terms and understood what the feeble final step in obtaining their retreat to victory entailed, their ears all pricked to the underling high-pitch squeal in the sky of distant plane engines. The droning sound began to flood the dark and echoic dawn sky from the south, and from the direction of *Germany.*

Soldiers amongst the convoy heard the pitch, making panicked remarks and suddenly becoming alert to what they assumed would be another wave of aerial raids—one surely this time they would not survive.

It wasn't fair! They were so close!

However, the wail of these incoming engines sounded different to last time. These did not sound slow and cumbersome, unlike the bombers from the last big raid.

Ears pricked, attentive as the others, Churchill gathered that due to the frequency of the sound that they were smaller Luftwaffe fighters. Though this time they were not escorting any bombers and were thus approaching the coast at top speed.

They'd be upon them in seconds.

The hopes of the men aboard the trucks physically sunk.

Their shoulders slouched and their chests dropped with an exhale of despair.

"Shit!" Ervine-Andrews cursed as the two captains made eye contact—their looks said it all.

They both knew their mission.

Get to the pier!

"*Mount up!*" Ervine-Andrews exclaimed as he turned and ran at full pelt under the tone of more incoming fighter planes, shouting his harried orders to his men as he got back into the first truck in the convoy. His men all did the same, mounting their vehicles and keying the monstrous engines of the Bedford truck convoy.

"Oh, not again!" Hill remarked, breathless and shaking his head with despair. The level of despondency crippled him. His shoulders sank. "Oh, bloody hell, not again!"

"Man up, Corporal!" Churchill exclaimed, verbally slapping him in the face.

"We can't survive this again! Not again!"

"Oi! Get inside the tank!" Churchill shouted, helping Hardy with his injuries to mount Barbara's track where he forced the assistance of the tentative Hill, partially erasing his anxiety from the pitch of the pending air raid. Hardy hoisted with him his makeshift Bren crutch, likely needing it to move anywhere on the ground. The two of them climbed into the tank for safekeeping.

Once seeing them safely in and while the rest of those mobile redispersed about the convoy, Churchill's eyes climbed to the dark skies to the southeast and the origin of the planes. Away from the morale of prying eyes, he emoted desolation. His unassailable confidence dipped an inch at the sight of the incoming aerial armada.

After Hardy and Hill vanished into the tank, Churchill reached to grab the dangling radio piece to communicate with King-Clark and the yacht. He did so with small amount of trepidation present in his voice—a rare occurrence for Jack Churchill.

"Clark?"

"*Yes, Jack, we hear it ...*"

Churchill hesitated in his concern before speaking.

"... Clark, you should just go."

"*Jack, zip it a second!*"

"Pardon? Clark, bring your boat about and get out of here!"

Churchill's left brow rose as his blue eyes beamed upon the hand piece as it let out a soupçon of static following the last response.

Out in the bay, and aboard the Sundowner yacht, the growing pitch of the incoming aerial assault elevated the already heightened moods of the men onboard.

"*Please, Clark, you must leave!*" the imploring voice of Jack Churchill charged the CB speaker, offering a rather selfless striving towards his friends' own survival. "*Turn around and gun it for the open sea! You may still survive this!*"

"Jack, stand-by!" King-Clark beckoned through the radio as he addressed Captain Lightoller once more, referring to whatever it was they had just been discussing. "What do you mean?"

"I mean, it's sink or swim time, lad!" Lightoller commented, putting the motorized yacht into neutral and he took to the wooden cabinet in the corner of the cabin. "Even if we run for the English Channel, we won't outrun *that.* We're too close inland and the sun is up. They'll see us, and we'll be a sitting duck."

"So ... you're saying we stay?" King-Clark publicized in question.

"We have no choice! We fight!" Lightoller turned and yanked open the panel to a concealed ceiling cabinet in the cabin, revealing a small arsenal of suspended modern weaponry.

"*Clark! We're too late, we won't survive it this time—*"

"Jack, please, zip it!" King-Clark pinched the radio handpiece, waving for those out on the deck to come in. Gin Parker, Knocker White, and Privates Wand and Macken met Padre Nicholl simultaneously in the doorframe. Their jaws dropped at the display of weaponry. Even Knocker White's mouth opened, losing his gum somewhere onto the deck.

Two more submachine guns; both Thompsons, the 1928 *Chicago typewriter* models with wooden groove forward grips and one-hundred-shot drum magazines. The lumber frame was polished, and the steel looked freshly blued and greased. And,

Two bolt-action rifles; one was the familiar and current service-style Lee-Enfield rifle No.4 Mk I, and the other was its outdated predecessor, the Lee-Metford, which had been out of service since the 1920s. The Lee-Metford was a darker stain and looked well-maintained considering her age.

On a lower shelf were several boxes of ammunition for all weapons, as well as four spare .45 ACP drum magazines for the Tommy guns. There were two hanging flare pistols between the leaning primaries, as well as bandoliers loaded with spare flares.

"Take what you think you'll need to defend this ship at all costs!" Captain Lightoller ordered, reaching in first and collecting his armament: a Browning Hi-Power; an expensive and modern nine-millimetre semiautomatic handgun with a thirteen-round capacity. It was housed within a brown leather chest holster which he slotted around his shoulder before facing King-Clark with an explanation as he did up the harness, positioning it centre and for easy access.

"Told ya we worked for the Admiralty," he said simply to King-Clark as he watched Gin Parker and the sea scout Gerald Ashcroft from Lightoller's crew reach in and collect a submachine gun each, loading up with the heavy drum magazines of .45 ACP bullets just outside the cabin. Nicholl stepped in next and firmly grabbed both of the remaining rifles, passing them out to Wand and Macken. Knocker White refrained from accessing the armoury since he still carried his own Lee-Enfield, however he was glad to receive some extra ammunition. They didn't have an endless supply of bullets, but they had enough to put up a valiant defence against a Messerschmitt if it started buzzing around their vessel like a bothersome mosquito.

"I didn't doubt it," King-Clark retorted as Lightoller stepped forth to the wheel and clutched the other Tommy gun that had been placed atop of the console. He dropped the mostly empty drum that was currently loaded and engaged a fresh, pinching the pull-pin back and then dropping it in King-Clark's able arms.

"We surveyed the coast to report back to our navy. We were prepared to defend ourselves against Kriegsmarines a long time before Winston Churchill sounded the horn for retreat for our boys."

"Good thing," King-Clark responded, finally putting aside all prejudice he may have held against Lightoller regarding Fürbringer's allegations against him. In his mind, they were definitely allied now.

"... *Clark?*" Churchill's voice cued from the radio, cutting the swooning rush within the cabin.

King-Clark juggled the big, heavy Thompson in order to reach the handpiece and press the transmit button by his maw.

Ashore and by the gearing idling convoy of Bedford trucks, Churchill finally received a response on the CB radio.

"*Jack, we're not leaving!*"

Churchill's eyes rolled as he prepared to plea further with a deep sigh. "Clark, I—"

"*Even if we wanted to make for home, we can't outrun an aerial squadron of that size ... Captain Lightoller agrees we'll be more of a target at sea.*"

Jack eyed them out on the water.

They were all in this together now.

"*We've taken steps to prepare a defence ... Jack, we're going to cover your retreat. Get to that wharf!*"

XIV
Evacuation

1940, June 4
Dunkirk
Nord-Pas-de-Calais, France

Rather than even attempt a U-turn on the two-lane coastal road, the four daisy-chained flatbed open tray Bedford OYD transport carriers and towed A10 cruiser tank mounted the pedestrian strip. The trucks subsequently burst through the stubby lumber pylon and chain railing guarding the beach sands, officially off-roading their charge to the evac point.

Low in the morning skies, the growing drone of a couple dozen incoming Luftwaffe planes washed over the city scape and all trapped souls within. The fighters were thirsty for targets to blaze and buildings to raze, and their exposed, slow-moving convoy would be of impeccable candidacy.

The tied trucks dragging the fifteen-tonne cruiser tank detonated through the wooden pedestrian guardrail lining the coastal street, hurdling the kerb with a coarse climb before dropping down onto a small overgrown grass slope. Eventually, the convoy carved like a derailed train into the cold damp sands of the beach, tearing up the shoreline.

One after the other, the closely connected trucks touched down, shaking and rocking with rough turbulence. The A10 tank behind them carved deep through the grass stretch, then even deeper once it became towed into the sands, almost sinking like an anchor. The haul resulted in a definite loss of speed due to the heave.

Despite the deceleration, the attentions of the men seemed not to dawdle on the flaw in their rapidity. Rather, all wide sets of peepers were to the navy-coloured sky as it brightened with the day, focusing on the incoming death from above as the enemy air raid now reached the airspace above Dunkirk.

Spreading out into multiple smaller squadrons of a half-dozen per squad, both of high and low altitude formations, the Luftwaffe fighters began scouring the landscape like airborne predators.

"*Here they come!*" shouting out of the passenger side window of the first truck, Captain Ervine-Andrews commentated after scanning the skies.

The driver beside him, a trusted veteran from the East Lancashires, held his concentration tight on the sloping coast out before them as their convoy bounded outlandishly across the sandy surface, navigating naturally formed dunes as well as deep craters in the sand made by artillery.

They beelined it for the wharf. It was all or nothing.

Lugging the load, the trucks steered in formation between formidable obstacles along the beach such as abandoned overturned cars and trailers from the evacuation lines, some of which even still simmering in flames from previous air attacks and bombing runs. At their persisting pace, doing so required an extra amount of focus so that the sluggish trucks did not slide out and risk T-boning the towing convoy.

Riding in the rear tray of the last Bedford in the convoy, Jack Churchill stood tall and stout-hearted, balanced with a leg cocked upon the cabin roof. His squinting eyes in the rushing air were unlike the other soldiers. Rather than up in the air at the pending doom encircling the airspace of the city in their rearview, his concentration was locked forwards, seeking the designated wharf.

They were now closing in on the position and coming in hot.

Churchill took a dismayed gleam.

The landmark of the mostly destroyed boathouse passed by on their left, and they now had sight of the slouched pier objective. Further out to the water from the boatshed and between two thinner and partially destructed piers were the remnants of several little ships lapping idly in the water. The rising morning tide had brought the mess in from the ocean with seafoam like food trapped in the spittle of a slavering beast. Most of them were shot to shit from German blitz runs and were therefore all unseaworthy, some were even partially sunken with their nose tips pointing diagonally from out of the water. Debris bopped and drifted, all clogged and amassed by the inward current against the shore.

Thinking nothing more of the inundating sights of destruction, his stare scanned ahead through the misty morning sea mist, focusing upon the lengthier and sturdier elevated wharf that King-Clark had been talking about. Beginning at a declined slope into the sands of the shoreline, the wooden dock then inclined and extended out into the water, surpassing the length of the neighbouring piers. The end of the wharf had seen a harrowing end in the action of the previous days, and seemed as though it had received a direct hit from a Stuka. In the hazy distance, the pier appeared to prematurely slope into the ocean, now sunk low enough to be abused and thrashed by waves. Perhaps now inaccessible by any of the larger ships of the Royal Navy to berth, the remaining interval was at least enough for the smaller Sundowner yacht to moor on the side midway along—at least, that was their plan.

The convoy was now closing in ...

On the land-attached side of the extended pier, the wharf housed a few boatsheds, much like the smaller exploded one they had just passed on the sand. And much like the previous sheds, the ligneous civilian structures were all just about blown to smithereens by previous German air raids. All that remained were partial walls and struts, coils of knotted, strewn rope, and other broken, charred remnants surrounded by what was once a rooftop. Smoke still faintly ascended from their remains.

There was an amass of abandoned military vehicles all driven up close to the wharf, rammed into one another like a gridlock. Some cars were even driven *into* the water, reaching out to sea. Only the tops of the vehicles could be seen looking like submerged rock bars.

"*Watch out!*"

Suddenly, some of the pitches from the overhead flock of German fighters seemed to sharpen upon their position, flying gracefully overhead like a hawk. One fighter from the sweeping formation seemed to home in on their position upon the bare wet sands of the shoreline, stalking them like locked-on prey.

The yellow-nosed rogue broke formation and peeled off from a squadron tracing high above the coastline, coming at them from a mostly head-on passage of trajectory.

The tyres of their convoy sculpted indentation lines in the sand running parallel to the incoming hightide and therefore would have been an easy target to mark from an aerial vector.

The pitch cut through the cool dawn air. An unmistakable declaration that the single incoming Messerschmitt Bf-109 fighter plane selected them to pick on.

Whiiiiiiiirrr ...

On a sharp decline, the fighter lined up an enfilade machine gun strafe upon their travelling cavalcade, engaging the string convoy with its 1200-round per minute synchronized MG-131 machine guns at fully automatic rate of fire on a diagonal degree pass.

RAT-TAT-TAT-TAT-TAT ...

7.92mm tracer rounds punched tambourine-sized holes in the sand before the passage of the first truck in lead-up, tracing an unrelenting perforation column across the defenceless Bedford with a cluster of tightly grouped, concentrated hits on target.

With sparks and smoke, the rounds effortlessly chewed through the metal of the bonnet. The truck took a salvo of brutal hits, turning its chassis frame and cabin roof into Swiss cheese, shattering the glass windshield.

The men onboard the convoy shouted, shielding themselves in contorted positions as hell peppered brimstone upon them as the strafe of fighter fire continued across the open air tray. Two exposed soldiers on the rear of the truck sheltered themselves and hid low, hoping for the best. They got lucky, receiving nothing more than flesh wounds from surface ricochets and flicked splinters from shattered wooden supports.

The driver on the other hand ... not so lucky.

A bullet the size of a pocket flask punched through the cabin roof, striking him in the collarbone and neck. The round tore through his entire torso, exiting out through his hip and then rebounding out the driver's side entry, shredding the metal and causing the door to open. As a result of the violent exit wound, the force of his convulsion flung his smoking, bloody carcass out into the sand. Lifelessly, he rolled and tumbled like discarded roadkill.

Ervine-Andrews had been lucky in the passenger's seat, doubtlessly due to his quick reflexes. When the plane had started its descent run, he had instinctually gripped onto the door handle, ready for anything. Once the rounds struck their vehicle relentlessly and painting them the bull's eye, he had rolled his ass and ejected himself fortuitously.

After diving clear of the truck right as sparks emitted all around him from the attack and somehow evading death, Ervine-Andrews landed with a grunt in the sand beside the wheel indentations. He was still clenching the cabin door, which had taken a hit around its frame and hinge, disengaging it from the vehicle and assisting in his fall from the vehicle.

The plane peeled up and headed off into the distance after drilling their truck, bringing the convoy to a slow roll and eventual idle rest.

WWWWWWWWWHHIIiiiirrrrr ...

The fighter plane rocketed overhead, followed by another few wingmen from the squadron that followed his lead on the attack run.

No doubt, they would return to chalk up some more dispatches for their tally. This convoy was a sitting duck and an easy kill.

Ervine-Andrews upped from the sand, nursing a severely bruised elbow. He was not sure how, but he had banged it pretty bad. It was leaking blood from a deep laceration, likely from slicing it on some of the ripped metal from the door after the bullet ricochets tore it to shreds.

Behind the grinding halt of the forward truck, the convoy of Bedfords each bumped into themselves, each grating to a standstill now that the first vehicle was smoking and out of commission resembling uncoordinated unbuckled train carriages in a decelerating row.

Whilst clenching his arm, Ervine-Andrews jogged around the front to assist his jettisoned driver. It was a soldier he knew well—now a thoroughly deceased casualty in the sand.

He stopped when he saw the aftermath ...

He felt the loss hard as his eyes rested upon the KIA soldier.

With a grimace, Ervine-Andrews traced the planes in the skyline.

Churchill performed an aerial dismount from his vehicle as it bashed into the butt of the subsequent transport truck, immediately entering a jog on the wet sand.

He passed several other soldiers as they also leapt from the trays of the stalled convoy and onto the soft, mushy sand. Their eyes were in the sky and attentions alert, tracking the overhead squadron as they banked in the sky above the shoreline.

Churchill fast appeared by Ervine-Andrews' side as he examined his casualty. It was pointless to check his vitals.

"I'm sorry," Churchill uttered after the cessation of the passing. Ervine-Andrews nodded as he respired, staring off after the fighters as they peeled away over the ocean. They were arcing out to the right in a tight formation, circling back around to the beach ... *no doubt* what they had in mind was another run.

Churchill announced with a level head, "They're going to make another pass! We've got to move!"

He stepped in and took a good look at what was left of the first truck after the strafing run. She was in just about as good shape as the deceased driver on the sand. Thick smoke hissed from several large holes drilled across her shredded hood, and the engine within was undoubtedly shot to shit.

Following a look at their stagnant situation, he pouted with much dismay. "Bollocks."

After a few seconds of assemblage around the suddenly inoperative Bedford cavalcade, a few of the men, including Churchill, measured the light of the dawning sun to the distant eastern horizon. They could see the flaking German birds as they circled wide and then back around, about to be following the coastline westerly and straight towards them like tracing a limelight.

This time, they would fire upon their mark in defilade.

They would draw a line across the entirety of their convoy ...

Churchill glanced about the shoreline and the wharf.

There was still a lot of distance to close.

They could either run on foot in an attempt to make the evacuation zone or they take their chances seeking shelter by the arrested convoy.

Either way, their odds were dog shit.

Out on the water, the rising morning sun peaking upon the Coriolis effect of the planet caused for a hundred thousand sparkles to glisten upon the ocean's surface. The skies were brightening, and the enemy fighters were more clearly visible as they circled the shoreline above the friendlies like vultures, picking off defenceless game.

"Jesus bloody Christ," Lightoller stated from the cabin of the Sundowner whilst they cruised parallel to the coast, observing the bombardment from the seaside and the now inert procession. "They're coming back around to have another go!"

He, Rex King-Clark, Padre Nicholl, Gin Parker, Knocker White, the two deckhands, Roger Lightoller and his friend, eighteen-year-old sea scout Gerald Ashcroft, as well as Privates Macken and Wand, had just witnessed Churchill's convoy be mercilessly heavily assaulted by a fighter plane, and it wasn't over. Next time there were going to be multiple planes, and they had a much better run-up from which to aim at the target.

The soldiers wanted to help by shooting their small arms at the planes but the experienced sea skipper insisted against the option. At this point, all it would accomplish was drawing fire onto their boat also.

Outside the yacht cabin, they watched helplessly as in the air behind the stationary convoy, the squadron of incoming Luftwaffe fighters swooped down low in an arrowhead formation. This meant that instead of one frontal ship firing whilst the others provided support, they could all fire with a clear line of sight. They could almost annihilate the trucks with a single pass.

The open air trays of wounded soldiers would be wiped out.

Those out on the sand had minimal cover.

This was it.

They would be dead in seconds.

"We've gotta do something!" disclosed Knocker White, cradling the rifle across his chest whilst nervously gnawing on chewing gum—his coping mechanism.

King-Clark eyed him, noticing that this corporal within Mad Jack's army was not as cucumber cool as he usually projected. White was tensely hugging his rifle, watching on, unable to help. Standing beyond him were Macken and Wand. Their fingers were wrapped tight around their rifle instruments, intent for action.

Whilst tensing his jaw and baring his teeth, yearnful to act, King-Clark's focus drifted onto Jos Nicholl. The padre was young and was anything if not an advocate for passive sensibility and prolonging life, and an entrusted figure of much enriched counsel ... *and he nodded.*

King-Clark scanned across the men. They were each keen to intervene, and to attempt to save their friends from utter annihilation, absolutely throwing caution to the wind—even if it meant putting them in danger.

His breathing intensified ...

King-Clark faced the coast and screamed:

"*Second Chesters! Light 'em up!*"

Forming a line along the boat, guns pulled tight into their shoulders and eyes down the sights, the men formed a firing line aimed at the line of fighters currently closing in above the travelling convoy.

Before Lightoller could shout anything to dissuade their actions for the sake of beaconing awareness, the men selflessly engaged the enemy in an attempt to do what they could to save their brethren—and he had to admit, the sensation of heroism they disseminated was aspiring. Whatever this *Mad Jack Churchill* had infected these boys with, it was contagious. These guys weren't runners ... they were fighters, balls to bone.

Bolt-action rifles clapped away intermittently long-range, shooting deafeningly loud. The combined submachine guns roared to life, spewing in short and controlled bursts at the distant targets, leading their fire with precision across the distance.

The soldiers maintained their stances, gauging their shots and calculating the distance. They allowed estimated lead-times for the moving, speeding aerial targets. Thankfully, their training and experience set in at an instant.

Their small arms salvo from the sea was accurate and true.

Bam! ... Bam! ...

Baaaaaaaaaaaaaang! ...

There would have had to have been some hits on target.

The muzzle flashes in the dim morning light lit up the starboard side of the boat as they cruised towards the west wharf, battling a choppy tide. Their rounds shot out of the coast and into the distant air.

Together, the controlled small arms fire was enough to at least deviate the aim of the squadron of fighters. A few stray rounds struck the armourless aluminium frames of the Messerschmitt fighters, frightening and distracting the pilots who had slowed to hold a tighter reticule on the convoy. Their deceleration added to the amount of small arms fire they received, making them an easier target from the ground.

Taken by surprise, two of the six planes peeled away from the attack run, accelerating and making evasive aerial manoeuvres. Of those who remained, the targeting of their accuracy at the convoy would have been substantially decreased by the abrupt attack on their flock. Nevertheless, the gunners still managed to dose the idle trucks with hot lead to some extent.

Multiple lines of their heavy tracer rounds drew lines across the sand and over the file of stopped vehicles. Sparks ignited from the rear of the cruiser tank and loud volleys of metallic ricochets brightened up the dawn-lit sand like a fireworks display.

Bullets pierced through the truck cabins like a hole punch to paper.

The open air trays were drilled, sadistically slaughtering already wounded men who laid across them in beds. A few of the wounded who could move got lucky by painstakingly throwing themselves overboard of the trucks and onto the beach sand outside, landing agonizingly hard to survive a gruesome alternative.

Whereas most of the soldiers dropped and rolled beneath the truck underbellies. Some of the soldiers outside who attempted to use the trucks for concealment were smiled upon by the gods. Bullets impacted near them with bass-filled *thumps* in the wet seashore as fingers of smoking shells buried themselves ten feet deep in the earth, kicking up grains and coating the surrounding soldiers with powdery white sand in the aftermath.

Blazing piercingly overhead, the squadron of planes flew low over the stalled convoy after hammering it with a multi-machine gun assault. It was like stitch work, dragged through a press.

Thankfully, nothing containing flammables exploded. However, immediately after, Churchill did notice that the Bedford he had rolled under had been punctured through from the top, and its fuel tank had become ruptured in several places, glugging vile petrol into the sand beneath.

Tragically, several men in the rear trays were slain.

Already wounded soldiers from the 4th Infantry within the middle of the file were unfortunately finished off. Churchill had been their saviour since he encountered them upon the outskirts of Dunkirk, and now lost them so close to the end of the line—inches from reaching salvation. In their already incapacitated states, lying on or strapped to their gurneys, mummified in bandages and splints securing their wounds to an almost paralysing degree, they could do nothing but close their eyes and quake with trepidation as the passing flock sprinkled tracer rounds upon them.

Churchill energetically rolled out from beneath the truck.

An eyeline full of scorn, he beamed upon the flock of persistent aerial assholes, teeth bared, and fucking pissed off.

This line of assault was diabolical and cruel.

He was as dismayed as he was utterly disgusted.

Their obtuse defensive of small arms gunfire at the fighters ceased as they swooped overhead of the trucks, dissipating yonder. The fact they broke formation meant that their barrage had at least upset the pilots to a degree.

Perhaps it wasn't as much fun when the ground targets shoot back?

From their small yacht out in the bay, they now risked making themselves a target for the German fighters in the sky. This was in exchange for prolonging some lives within the convoy line. It had been a valiant attempt, one that bared some fruit considering they had made two of the six fighters take evasive manoeuvres away from the pattern, as well as potentially causing the remaining Luftwaffe flyboys to falter their aim.

"Bloody hell!" Gin Parker exhaled after their blaring hail of gunfire. He raised his smoking Thompson out by his head, recovering from the full-body shakes from all the sustained recoil.

"Did that actually just work?" through his scowl, Knocker White shouted surprised after believably protecting the convoy, or at least minimizing the damage. They had successfully blindsided the fighters.

The course was continual for the four fighters after their attack run at the convoy, disappearing over Dunkirk somewhere unseen in the distance. However, the attentions of the soldiers returned forwards as the two fighters who had previously peeled away from that same squealing squadron seemed to be now heading straight for them from a flanking approach ...

Before they fully realized it aboard the yacht, the machine guns beneath the wings of the fighters crackled away as the sea wind pitched beneath their annexes.

Without communicating a word, the gunmen raised and extended their weapons and fired at full force, attempting to defend the yacht as the yellow-nosed fighters passed by low overhead, bubbling the water around the boat with a hundred skyward geysers from overshoots.

The two fighters landed a few hits across the Sundowner's deck, splintering wood and cracking one of the side windows to Lightoller's cabin. The wailing of their overhead swoops was absolutely ear-splitting in pitch, screaming directly down their earholes as they rocketed past, dangerously low in altitude.

"Reload! Reload!" King-Clark shouted as he snapped free the mostly spent lug one-hundred-round drum magazine from his smoke-hissing submachine gun. The fresh drum was easily three times the weight of the empty one he had just discarded, and he struggled to hold the heavy gun and load it without burning himself on the sizzling metal surfaces of the Thompson.

The men around him did the same.

Some of them had collapsed onto their backs on the deck when the planes had flown overhead, shooting in a 160-degree arch that tracked the flyby, arching vertically. It was unknown if they had landed any hits on the fighters, not that they expected to inflict much damage at all with the small arms against the nimble Messerschmitt planes.

Hundreds of empty brass casings rolled about the wooden deck and tinkled under their footsteps. Empty clips and magazine housings were discarded from the weapons in favour of fresh ammunition. The men quickly collected themselves, loading open gun chambers with metallic *clicks* and *clacks*. Their eyes became instantly wide and focused on the sky, searching for the birds' rapid return.

"This is why I said don't shoot unless they've seen us!" Lightoller bellowed from the cabin, fuming and with red in his cheeks. This circumstance was his concern. They were now marked for death.

"They've gone, bruvs!" Wand made comment with a hint of contentment in his Cockney undertone, finishing loading individual rounds into his bolt-action.

"Oh, don't you bloody worry," Lightoller remarked glumly, stepping out from the cabin whilst they coasted dead stick for a moment. "They'll be back, and from any course. Probably in a tighter formation that will bombard us from afar. We'll barely see 'em comin'!"

The men on the boat deck exchanged a series of glances, next scanning the skies, ready for anything.

King-Clark brought about his Thompson and used the railing with his elbow to assist himself from a kneeling position. As he did, he glanced out to the coast to observe the aftermath surrounding the shoreline.

There was some movement around the convoy of trucks.

They seemed to still be alive.

With his peripherals, he paid notice to the destroyed smaller piers that the trucks had just passed. The docks were destroyed, and the area was a minefield of floating debris and sunken ships and oil spills. Their existence, and the existence of the debris fields, severely prevented them from getting anywhere near close enough to pick anybody up from the shallows.

"We're almost there!" Macken stated above all their cowering heads, eyes forward as their yacht coasted towards the length of the pier. "Look!"

All the men took a moment to cast their attention forwards, eyeing the wharf as they drifted through a cloud of hovering fog and blowing sea mist.

The wooden jetty was in view and closing fast.

Waves crashed against the raised pier legs as the current of the tide began to take a nasty turn, thrashing about in the wind.

The gusting wind also affected the current somewhat, blowing some of the nearby oil spill dangerously close to where the yacht needed to travel. With heavy steps, Lightoller gave a concerned gleam overboard, now rather wary of their surroundings as he navigated.

Needless to say, the Sundowner's engine choking on oil right now would be severely less than ideal for making a prompt getaway.

"Look sharp!" Nicholl announced. Emerging from the sea to the northeast, the larger group of four fighters had banked wide from over the city and were advancing to dive-bomb them from the rear.

They came in hard and fast, lining them up before engaging. They would be swooping in low above the water. This time around, the pilots were aware of the small ship's small arms countermeasures and defences, and clearly did not fear taking another run at the vessel.

Aboard the ship after Nicholl's alert, the gunners were barely able to react before the deck was assaulted by the distant, low planes. The formation of Messerschmitt fighters even slowed in their attack upon lining them up, now able to deliver a constant and more ferocious torrent upon the small floating yacht.

Round after round chomped into the wood of the yacht, violently assaulting it with a continuous and unrelenting string of firepower.

The tracers perforated the Sundowner.

Wood from the decking shredded to shavings.

Holes the size of tin cans pocked across the polished surface, drilling a stitch of jagged lines across her, aft to stern.

The strafing run pulverized the coasting yacht, taking her from fully functional to nearly lifeless and dead in the water within seconds.

The soldiers did what they could to take cover, dropping and sliding away behind the cabin front, clumsily crashing into one another, losing hold of their tin can helmets and weapons.

The planes rocketed overhead climbing high once clear.

A few shots got released by rifles and even a burst from one of the submachine guns, but the men were forced to immediately seek shelter from the aerial barrage too early to form an organized defence.

King-Clark, Gin Parker, Knocker White, Ashcroft, and Lightoller's son, Roger, dove in low behind the cabin, where Charles Lightoller, too, hit the deck as rounds completely shattered the salt-stained windows, showering them all in pointy glass shards that caused lacerations over any exposed skin. The mechanical console around the driver's wheel was dotted, primarily resulting in the destruction of the CB radio they had been previously using to communicate with Churchill and the truck convoy. The compass, fuel gauge, and other various ship vitals displayed in a series of instruments and indicators were now completely useless.

During the chaos, Nicholl prayed for the best and clung onto the rungs beneath the lumber railing and, as a result, accidentally lost a Tommy gun over the edge as he slid between the ropes. His feet dangled for a moment off the boat for an instance before he struggled and pulled himself back onboard, resting breathless in the aftermath.

Out on the exposed deck, Privates Macken and Wand became the first unfortunate casualties of this heroic rescue mission.

Loyalists to the end for the Second Manchester Regiment, the two young Cockney soldiers had been struck by the Messerschmitt barrage of bullets during the aerial bombardment.

Wand was killed outright. The lad was hit in the centre of the chest.

His best friend, Macken, collapsed in tandem alongside him, struck in the leg by a round and hand by a ricochet, was left bleeding and writhing in pain.

Out the other end of the thunderous chaos, Macken called for his friend, ignoring the sting of pain from his wounds. There was no response from Wand. It took him a second to realize that his mate's stare into nothingness was a lifeless one.

The man ignored his own pain to mourn, clutching at Wand's face with his own blood-covered palms. Tears stung his eyes, and he pressed his forehead against Wand's. He wept unconsolably for the sudden loss of his best friend.

Wooden splinters still rained about the deck. King-Clark was slow to regain his footing beside the cabin. He rubbed at a sting in his face which burned from a half-dozen lacerations made by broken glass fragments, with countless more in his hairline behind his ear. In a grimace, his eyes cracked open upon the sight of two of Churchill's men lying on the deck, shot to ribbons.

Beside him, Gin Parker and Knocker White quickly recovered.

They flocked over to assist Nicholl climbing back aboard. Luckily, the padre had managed to hang onto his spectacles, though now a lens was cracked.

King-Clark climbed unsteadily to his feet due to the concussive sound from the deafening incident. He saw in the perforated cabin that Charles and his son Roger were alive and okay, minus a few scrapes and new bruises. Ashcroft was also accounted for, more shell-shocked than anything else and trying to catch a breath.

He shouted over the ringing. "You lot all right?!"

Breathless, those nearby nodded.

"We won't survive another pass like that," Lightoller hollered at King-Clark as he and his son left the cabin to check on the damage done to the yacht. Plumes of smoke now hissed from the peppered deck above where the engine components were located. Some damage was done to the ship, to what extent they were yet unsure. If they were sinking, it wasn't serious thus far. A slow leak was patchable.

King-Clark looked to Lightoller and nodded firmly.

He was honestly surprised that they survived *that*, let alone another.

Before he could even come up with a response, Roger shouted a sit-rep for the skipper on the extent of the damage done to the boat.

Gin Parker, Knocker White, and Padre Nicholl now assisted in dragging the injured Macken and sadly deceased Wand clear and positioned them up against the front of the cabin. The deck was now smeared with crimson stains.

Roger's overbearing holler was a whole bunch of nautical jargon that King-Clark did not understand, but judging by his tone and Lightoller's response, it wasn't positive. He stepped over to take a look himself, still clenching the weighty Thompson out by his side.

Charles Lightoller assisted his son in hoisting open the large access hatch that covered the engine access. The wooden panel had at least a dozen puck-sized holes stitched across it.

Looking down after they had flipped open the damaged hatch, a cloud of scorching vapour steamed their flesh.

Fanning it clear, Charles and Roger Lightoller climbed down into the compartment beside the engine and accessed the destruction. It was obvious that the machine had been damaged but to what extent they were unsure.

Lightoller upped and got clear, attending to the steering wheel in the cabin whilst he shouted out instructions to his ship hands. Ashcroft dropped in fast to assist with the repairs.

While the chaos of relaying instructions and naval gobbledygook was hurled at one another, King-Clark's view drifted back upon Private Macken as Nicholl strapped his new wounds. The young soldier who was never separated from Wand would now embark doing so for the remainder of his life—however long his, and theirs, would be. His empty eyes drew a blank stare out to sea. He may have been in shock.

Suddenly, the gentle hum of the boat's lively engine choked and seized shutting off completely. The atmosphere of the machine was replaced by the hiss of smoke pouring like a chimney from its engine.

"Fuck!" Lightoller shouted from inside the cabin. He turned over the engine, attempting to restart it and failing constantly. After a few more attempts he cursed colourfully and exited the yacht cabin, strolling furiously out and to the deck.

They were dead in the water.

He glanced to King-Clark. "I think we're shagged, mate."

There was no response to give. King-Clark stared onwards whilst beside them, Gin Parker eyed the sky while manning one of their last ready weapons.

"... ol' *Mad Jack, fuckin' Mad Jack* ..." Parker muttered under his breath, both scared by and frustrated at their predicament.

King-Clark cast his view onto him.

His stare said a thousand words.

Gin Parker was particularly hot and cold with regards to the topic of Jack Churchill. It wouldn't be a far cry for him to place the blame of this circumstance wholly upon him.

"He's fucked us again!"

"You volunteered for this mission, Lieutenant!" King-Clark stated. The heat of the quandary was suddenly starting to get to all of them. Their frenzied discussion increased in volume to subjugate that of the Lightollers and Ashcroft as they communicated with their faces over the engine.

"*Mission?* Is that what this was?" Parker replied, lowering his guard in the face of their futility. "Because it feels more like a *fool's errand.* I'll give you one guess who the *fool* is?! I'm surprised we can't hear the bloody bagpipes from here! You really think he would have gone through all *this* for us *voluntarily!*"

"You know that he would!"

"Death?"

"Definitely!"

Suddenly their arguing voices faded out, as did the engine talk done by the Sundowner crew over the open fumes and all their attentions honed at the sound of another incoming aerial assault.

"... what is that ...?" Lightoller commented, pushing up from the grease pit and strolling towards the railing, as did King-Clark and Parker *side by side* and in unison.

What they saw was mesmerizing enough to silence their quarrel ...

Furthering his argument, Parker asked. "What about *that?*"

All King-Clark could do was gulp.

Eyes wide, Lightoller shook his head, absolutely beside himself at what he saw ... at what they all saw ...

Coming their way.

This was the end.

Inside Busty Barbara—and not in the way Felix Hardy hoped it to be—he and Corporal Hill exchanged a look. They, too, could hear the incoming sound of Armageddon.

Hardy eyed him in the dark depths of the A10 confines.

"I vote we stay here for a minute."

Hill nodded. "Agreed."

On the beach Ervine-Andrews was leaning against the side of the smoking carnage of a fried truck, nursing his injuries when a sand-soppy Churchill joined him in viewing the situation.

Naturally, Jack Churchill took a second to brush as much sand as he could from his uniform and even straighten up his cuffs with orderly fashion.

"What do you think they're doing?" the Irishman questioned.

Churchill's sterling stare squinted as he spied the skies.

He could see those same two fighters linking up with the other section of the squadron, forming an even bigger mass. They could hear over the skies of Dunkirk that there was more shooting, more razing. There was much small arms fire being fired from the ground from the French rearguard up at the Luftwaffe planes.

Anyone still holed up in the city was fighting for all they were worth.

Those planes seemed to not only leisurely bank out and around the back of Dunkirk to the south, but they also seemed to link up with several other scout fighters, forming numbers for an even bigger assault ...

... Churchill's eyes widened.

The noise from the fighters scrambling above Dunkirk like flies over faeces was beginning to become drowned out by an even louder, more bass-filled reverberation.

Something big was coming from the south ...

"Do you hear that ...?" Ervine-Andrews observed, cocking a brow.

Churchill fearlessly strayed from the cover of the convoy.

Facing the city, he backpedalled out to the open sand of the beach in order to obtain a better look at what it was that was coming their way.

He reeled in reverse, all the way to the breaking waves of the morning current. Water rushed into his pant legs. He ignored the sensation. His gleaming blue stare was fixed upon the skyline to the south, scanning ...

He stopped after a few wet paces, listening to the sound as it travelled in the wind. Other than the hum of the distant fighters gracefully scouting the air above Dunkirk, and the waves of the shore crashing softly in the background, there was an underlining bass growing beneath it all ...

Surely it was not another carpet bombing?

Right then, like spots of black against the white cloud under the dawn skyline, they started to see the incoming armada of Luftwaffe bombers and more fighters flanking them.

"It's another blitz ..." Churchill breathed to himself, somewhat calmly. He strolled back, comfortably resting his hand upon his sheathed sword while with the other, he caressed his pencil moustache. His eyeline dropped, observing the others by the exposed Bedford cavalcade.

Ervine-Andrews' eyes closed, and he faced the ground, utterly defeated. The other two dozen of the men nearby all did the same, realizing that they were now at the end of their rope.

If those bombs were coming for the harbour ... which, it had to be, since there were no other targets left ... then this was truly the end.

The bombers were above them before they knew it.

Before they could even contemplate running or hiding—not that either would help them if the bombers released over the shoreline.

They would not survive another carpet bombing.

All hope was los—

... boom ...

... boo—boom ...

Suddenly, lifting their morale, remote explosions detonated in the distance—but not the type they expected to hear as the bombs fell upon their heads.

Rather, these were above.

Far above the armada—above the clouds, even.

All their faces raised and looked towards the skyline high above.

It sounded like thunder ...
It struck like lightning ...
It was as if the bombers were being *bombed ...?*

"What the fuck is that?" Ervine-Andrews questioned, stepping out from concealment. His attention was short-lived as fast and incoming German fighters suddenly blindsided them, making another attack run at their position and emerging from out of the peripherals of the shoreline. They came in low and from behind the city.

"Move! Get down!"

Men about the convoy all reacted instantly as another strafing run applied about their location and the sands erupted everywhere.

Churchill tore his view away from the distant skies.

He desired to know what act of God had come to save them from the bombers—but right now, he had to evade a more sudden death.

Mad Jack ducked his beret-dome and hustled, getting in close to their idle truck convoy as it were assaulted on the opposite end by a vast array of tracer rounds from their squadron of aerial nuisances.

Out on the water, those aboard the yacht also heard the explosions echoing from high above the clouds, and were equally confused for the moment.

While Knocker White remained behind with Macken, King-Clark, Gin Parker, Nicholl, and Lightoller looked out and up from the deck railing. Behind them, Ashcroft and Roger's appetites were whet, and they took a break from attempting to fix the boat engine to take a peek. They peeled their faces upwards and to the blue hue of the morning sky, where the rising sun chased the dawn afar.

There were flashes of distant white light.

Detonations.

It was from behind and above the German air raid ...

Approaching from behind their location, from the English Channel, and the direction of the rising sunlight for the brand-new day, what happened next was almost symbolic.

The tables turned.

"Look!" Nicholl shrieked, lungs *full* of enjoyment and cheerfulness in a depressed and anguished frame of mind. He pointed towards the sky as though he had just witnessed his lord and saviour—because he had.

Aboard the yacht, they all spun and saw behind them as an aerial fleet big enough to match that of the Luftwaffe came in from the ocean.

It brushed over them like a breeze of fresh air ...

British Flyboys.

A whole armada.

"*Yes!*" Nicholl shouted and whistled in applaud, upstanding. He raised his arms and punched the sky as he hollered, praising the lord and the Royal Air Force.

A smile the size of a child's entering an amusement park formed over King-Clark's gob, and they all grinned ear to ear and leapt with joy to see that the air cavalry had coincidentally arrived.

It was the full force of the RAF.

WHHIRRRR ...

An overload of noise filled the airspace about Dunkirk.

The titans of two nations' air forces were about to clash.

Rumbling bass caused everything to vibrate beneath the constant resonation as over a hundred Royal Air Force planes journeyed in from over the waters of the English Channel.

Amidst the formations were such familiar aircrafts as Brewster Buffalos, Supermarine Spitfires, Hawker Hurricanes. The whole nine yards.

The assortment of RAF and RAF Navy fighters and bombers soared in regress of the German aerial attack, zooming in above and at a mix of varying altitudes.

From the opposite direction of the incoming German fighters orbiting the motionless shoreline convoy and those trapped within the proximity, at least four or five whole squadrons of RAF fighters shot by over the water to intercept, so close they swayed the yacht at water level.

The deafening racket of their charge drowned out all other noise, including the saved souls aboard the Sundowner below as they sung their hearts out.

The men cheered the glamour boys on, leaping on the railing and even exchanging a few embraces with rejoice.

On the pale setting of the dawn-chased beach, Churchill's view of the incoming German fighters baring down on their position altered. From the direction of the sunlit ocean, a sudden flurry of different coloured tracer rounds speared out like barbs of horizontal lightning, discontinuing the reign of the German fighters who attempted another strafing run over their immobilized convoy.

One of the Messerschmitt fighters detonated mid-run, exploding into an instant orange fireball amongst the other fighters in their tight formation.

Reacting quickly, Churchill ducked and recoiled back under cover as a flock of RAF fighters raced into the fleet of German fighters, clapping away with their roaring machine guns and spearing tracer rounds into the opposition. The two opposing forces crashed into each other, exchanging twisted metal and blasting fire.

In the nick of time, this was the perfect counter-attack.

The enemy airplanes were suddenly too busy to care about the soft targets down on the beach, and a busy and chaotic dogfight ensued in the skies above the shoreline and the coastal city of Dunkirk. It was as if a freak storm had set in, tearing streaks of thunder and flashing beams of lightning during a twisting and tail-spinning tornado of activity.

Finally believing his eyes and what had just happened, Churchill cracked his winning smile. This intervention was almost too good to be true. The RAF had saved them at the absolute last second.

Ervine-Andrews and his men along the side of the convoy collectively cheered, beaming in grins of pure contentment. They assisted each other from the sand and watched for a moment as the skyward skirmish proceeded above Dunkirk.

The action was resounding and energetic.

At high speeds and performing death-defying stunts whilst engaged, energetic planes arced at unbelievable angles in the air, engines screaming, guns rattling. As they zipped about, the crafts let out screeches of air in wails of dangerous descents, swooping in perilously low.

Aggressive aerobatics from pursing events such as evasions and the dodging incoming fire raged on as machine guns continuously sounded off and explosions echoed across the dawn cityscape. Ignitions boomed as fighters were struck from the atmosphere in infernos of falling twisted, smoking metallic fuselages, plummeting down to earth in a whirl and pitch.

They had been saved—but the war was not over.

"We've got to move! We're not out of this yet!" Churchill announced from beneath the action, drawing his claybeg sword from his hip scabbard with a metallic *shinggg.*

He then used it to single out the wharf ahead before revolving around on the beach beside the idle convoy, and he addressed all the men. "Mount up!"

"*Mount up!*"

"*Let's go!*" he heard other voices relay as the manic movement set about their crowd and they were put to final purpose. Everybody left piled into the remaining two trucks, filling them to the brim.

Churchill stepped in behind the first truck, spotting the winch cable that lassoed them together in the daisy-chain tow. With a bare-teethed raging roar that was audible above the chaos, Mad Jack brought his single-handed indestructible sword in on a left-upper strike, slashing the steel winch cable with all his might.

A bright flint of sparks emitted as the Damascus steel of the claybeg cleaved into the woven steel of the cable, severing the line from the bumper of the Bedford. It freed their convoy from the dead weight at the front of the line like an axe in a lop.

"Go! Go!" he shouted as he sheathed his blade. He took a second to watch the sky as a German fighter attempted to chase down a small British Brewster Buffalo overhead. The flying Hun was tagged by another Spitfire as it banked in to save the day, and the German fighter barrel-rolled out of control in a smoking, flaming heap before detonating into a fireball as it struck the sands barely one hundred and fifty yards east of them. It was loud and bright. The fiery remnants stretched a line from the grassy hill to the incoming tide of the waves.

Churchill grabbed onto the tray frame as a truck passed him and hauled himself up like a cowboy mounting his horse. The vehicle convoy all pressed on towards the wharf beneath the anarchy of the live dogfighting.

Barely two hundred yards off the coast by the Dunkirk beach, the Sundowner still idly bopped in the choppy sea tide.

"Try it now!" Charles Lightoller shouted over his shoulder, his head still over the open deck and exposed engine. Grease now coating his wrists and chin as did sweat on his brow.

His son, Roger, was in the cabin, awaiting his command to twist that key and turn that engine over now that his knowledgeable father had resuscitated the damaged yacht.

He turned the ignition.

She choked ... nothing.

"Slag!" Lightoller grunted, grabbing another tool from the open tray of utensils beside the galley and reaching back inside the deep hole hiding in the rising steam-stack.

King-Clark looked away from the repairs and back on guard duty along with Gin Parker and Padre Nicholl. The three of them possessed the last three weapons after the last disruptive attack, and they kept a guarded eye to the busy sky. Since the RAF had inadvertently showed up to fight the Luftwaffe, the atmosphere above had been a lot less hostile towards them down in the water.

"Come on, lads," he whispered under his breath as he faced the coast. He could see Churchill's convoy. At least three of the four trucks plus the dead tank thing seemed to be on the move again.

Now that the German air raid above them was kept busy by the RAF counter-attack, everybody involved had the time to recollect themselves and soldier on. This could have been the distraction they needed to get out of France.

King-Clark announced their development.

"They're on the move again."

"They'll beat us there at this rate," Nicholl responded in a low tone after taking a step closer and viewing the coast, as not to aggravate the busy seamen frustratedly kerfuffling behind them.

"Yeah, you're not wrong ..." King-Clark responded throwing a look over his shoulder. Lightoller was still cussing and bashing away on the engine. He was red in the face and drenched with sweat after being held over the spit of that frying engine.

Nicholl took in a deep breath and held it while they observed Churchill's convoy as it snaked along the beach, now less than one hundred yards out from the designated wharf and closing. The tables had now turned, and it would now be a result of their delay in the boat.

From beneath a frown, Nicholl finally released his thoughts.

"Captain King-Clark, did Jack happen to mention why he is bringing us a tank?"

Perhaps unbeknownst to Churchill, Busty Barbara would be the one survivor to make it to the shoreline and not fit onboard the yacht.

King-Clark shook his head, unknown.

"Because he's Mad Jack Churchill, that's why ..."

"Okay! Try it again!" Lightoller bellowed out to his son in the cabin, regaining their attention from the dogfight in the distant high skies over Dunkirk.

They all eyed the cabin and watched as Roger Lightoller keyed the switch one more time.

She choked ... nothing.

"Poofter!" Lightoller shouted, pegging his metal shifter at the machine with a series of loud clonks, losing it into the crawlspace abyss.

Upping from his old knees, groaning, he was approached by Nicholl who attempted to calm him before insisting that he take a look at the engine instead.

"There's no point!" Lightoller exclaimed between breaths as he wiped down his forehead with a pocket hanky. "She's cooked, lads. We got the leaks sorted but she's burnt out. The filter supplying water to the engine has been damaged by the fighters, and it's let oily water into the pipes. As a result, she's overworked and croaked it. I've flushed it by hand, but I don't know how to cool it down to at least get her started ..."

Nicholl was Johnny-on-the-spot with suggestions. "Can't we just get a bucket and scoop some seawater—"

Lightoller deterred with certainty. "Nope. Too much oil in the water."

"Canteens, then?"

About them, the men sought their water bottles. They were all empty except for one, which contained a dribble.

Upon hearing their effortlessness, King-Clark's frown released, and an idea sprung to mind. He paced nearer to propose his idea—well, it was *sort of* his idea.

"We piss on it!" he stated sternly and with a deadpan delivery. He immediately placed down his Thompson on the deck and was undoing his button fly.

"*What?!*" Lightoller questioned rather confounded and with a lurching frown.

Nicholl and the others just stared, dumbfounded.

"What Would Jack Do, right?" King-Clark responded. Having heard way too many cases of Mad Jack Churchill resorting to doing this throughout his life, he figured why not give it a g—

"Hold up, lad," Lightoller remarked seriously, halting his draining of the main vein. "If you think I'm gonna let you take a piss on my deck, then you're having a proper laugh ..."

"It'll work!" King-Clark replied surely, then in a low and uneasy follow-up: "I'm pretty sure ..."

He unbuttoned further and reached—

"*Oi!*" Lightoller shouted again, holding him up. "Don't make me shoot you, mate."

"The metal gets wet and air-cools. This will fix it! I'm being serious!"

"Me too!" Lightoller tapped the pearl grip of his holstered 9mm pistol. "You pull it out, and I'm shootin' it off."

Before King-Clark had another instant in which to even attempt to plead his case, Roger Lightoller appeared by his side with a canteen of water from the cabin galley of which to use in cooling it down.

"Can't we remain civilized, chaps," he remarked quietly.

King-Clark observed the water tank. "Oh."

"Here I was thinking you were the respectable one of this lot ... You're a bloody savage, mate," Lightoller remarked as his son upturned the canteen over the searing engine, making it froth and sizzle. He tipped the contents slow and all over, cooling it down dramatically.

When he watched it happen, feeling slightly embarrassed, King-Clark buttoned his fly. As he did, Nicholl passed him with a hugely dubious eyeball under a raised eyebrow and through cracked glasses.

"Sir," the padre stated in-kind. "I fear you've been hanging around Mad Jack for too long."

King-Clark rolled his eyes. "You're probably right."

"Try it now!" Lightoller called as he stood after emptying the canteen over the engine centre.

She choked ... ON.

Through the windowless cabin Roger Lightoller's smile beamed as he revved the engine, keeping it alive until his father could return to the wheel after kicking shut the deck hatch.

"We're back in business, lads!" the skipper shouted as he assumed control, quickly pressing buttons and adjusting dials on the console. This included pushing forward some levers and then preparing to yoke back on another: the accelerator.

"Hold on to your backsides!"

Lightoller put her into a harsh throttle to make up lost time, tearing through the water towards the wharf, weaving about some foreign debris and skirting a reaching spill of dark oil.

With a few jolting barges and scraping shoves, the convoy of Bedford trucks nuzzled their way forth through the sand mounds, finding the path of least resistance through the accrue of abandoned vehicles clogging the entrance to the wharf.

"Here?" the driver of the truck commented to Ervine-Andrews who rode shotgun in the passenger seat of the quaking cabin. They were severely running out of dry land of which to drive upon.

Ervine-Andrews agreed with a nod and prepared to open his door—

"*Not yet! Go all the way up!*" Churchill's voice shouted after thumping on the roof of their cabin. The eccentric Second Manchester Regiment captain had just frog-leapt across the externals of the moving trucks again in order to make it to the front one, leaping across the daisy-chained vehicles like a railroad bandit across train carriages in a western movie. "*Push through there!*"

"Jack, are you sure this jetty can hold our weight?"

Churchill examined further.

He had absolutely no idea.

He nodded confidently. "Of course it can!"

"Okay, keep going!" Ervine-Andrews added to his driver, heeding Churchill's recommendations.

From his position above, Churchill leant over the cabin of the first truck like he was riding the first cart in a roller coaster. Under his order, they floored the accelerator of their transport truck fleet, ramming a parked civilian lorry from off the entrance to the pier. The prodded empty vehicle trundled awkwardly in reverse off the slope, rolling down into the waves of the thrashing tide with a tremendous splash.

Their truck convoy upped the short slope, leading them onto the raised wooden wharf. The revolutions of their wheels sounded wildly different now on this surface, tapping across the many timber floorboards that showed immediate signs of strain beneath the weight of their heavy convoy.

The waterfront ran approximately one hundred and fifty feet out to sea where, hopefully, the water was deep enough to dock the Sundowner yacht and collect them.

The wharf was chock-a-block full of abandoned civilian automobiles and dumped supply crates that the BEF were attempting to evacuate early on. Most obstacles located on the thin dock were in the way of the pier access, so they took to them like a battering ram, sending them effortlessly and dissolutely into the drink.

From both sides of the pier, vehicles and crates stacked with food rations, ammunition, and medical supplies, tumbled off the edges with a splash, adding to the floating debris and mess already down in the basin.

"That's it!" in a shout Churchill apprised as they rolled to a stop: the width of the Bedford OYD troop carrier barely fit on the wharf, she was so wide. Any further along and they risked sinking the entire pier.

The wharf groaned and rumbled ...

Creaked and shifted ...

There was certainly a maximum weight limit for the wharf, only nobody knew or cared what it was. Logic suggested it was probably a lot less than the weight of three Bedford transport trucks dragging a tank, but, when in Rome, right?

The gentle hum of the decelerating yacht pulled into the wharf as the men all began dismounting the transport trucks.

"Hullo Jack!" King-Clark hollered with his hands cupped around his mouth as the Sundowner slotted in alongside the pier. Young Roger tossed a rope like a lasso, mooring them to the side and hauling them in tight.

All men from the Bedfords carefully dismounted and formed a line towards the yacht in the background. They each assisted where they could in getting the wounded from the rear trays in order to carry them aboard.

The soldiers watched graciously as their ticket out of France welcomingly arrived.

"Clark!" Churchill replied, jogging close and stepping on the breach of a pylon in order to reach out and receive the man's firm handshake. The shake developed into a hugging embrace when King-Clark used it to launch himself onto the wharf from the boat. He stepped on what was effectively dry land for the first time in hours, experiencing mild mal de debarquement.

Once given a few pats on the back Churchill withdrew, wincing slightly, and it was then his friend noticed his shoulder injury. His uniform was stained black from dry blood and dirt.

"You're shot?"

"Yes, but only a little bit."

"How does one get *a little bit shot*, Jack? Look! it's dripping off your fingers!"

Churchill examined the stickiness on his fingers. The blood had travelled from the fresh wound in his shoulder under his sleeve. The bandage he had over it must not have been as constrictive as he had hoped, and at some point, during all this activity, it had leaked through.

"'tis nothing but a graze, darling. How are the men?" Jack responded, deflecting his concern for a possibly serious wound. He waved at the other men onboard the shot-up boat whom he recognized from his section. "Boys! See you had the same visit from the Huns as we did?"

Nicholl and Parker trod up from the boat to the wooden pier.

They nodded, solemnly glad to see their commanding officer yet remained reserved and to the mission. Nicholl gave Churchill a pat on the back as he passed, and Churchill saw Gin Parker. Of all the people within the Second Chesters D section he expected to have come back for him, he didn't expect to see this bloke.

Churchill nodded in respect—which was mutually returned.

"Most of your section made the initial evacuation yesterday. A few volunteers and myself decided to come back and see about rescuing you."

"*Rescuing me?*"

"Oh fine: *collecting* you, then. Not all of us made it, we suffered a casualty, I'm afraid."

Churchill changed into a serious gear, searching past King-Clark onto the boat. "Who?"

His stare loosened as he saw his men Wand and Macken propped up against the cabin, soaked in blood. It was recent, too, likely from the dastardly, yellow-nosed Messerschmitt.

"Oh, no," Churchill moaned.

"Wand was strafed. Macken is hanging in there," King-Clark explained as Churchill leapt from the pier onto the deck of the yacht, tending to them as best he could. He gave a solemn nod to the skipper, Captain Lightoller, as he boarded, who stared at him plainly from behind the console in the cabin.

The two did not say a word.

Their respective bowing gestures said enough between the two war veterans.

"Captain," Macken whispered with a left-handed handshake, still nursing his injured side.

Knocker White was situated beside the downed men by the cabin. He reciprocated a wordless nod of appreciation by his CO.

Churchill asked rhetorically as he took a knee before them. "What have you boys gone and done to yourselves, eh?"

Macken was without words to say and still clearly in much disarray about losing his friend.

"Thanks for coming to get me, lads. You saved me. I'm very sorry about Private Wand ... he was a brave soldier."

Tears swelled once again from the meaningful words told to Macken by the most esteemed man he admired most in this world, his commanding officer. Macken's chin quaked, and he nodded after hearing them, offering his captain a hand which Churchill gripped without hesitation. The two steadfastly held embrace as the emotion of both the compassion and the grieving seemed to overcome the young soldier.

Meanwhile, Knocker White offered a vocal respite of relief to the ever-growing silence. "I ran out of gum," he informed Churchill, causing his captain to tenderly beam within the circumstances. Delirium seemed to have finally taken hold of the bloke, and Knocker White guffawed with an amalgam of laughter and a snotty choke from holding back bottled-up emotions. The sleep deprivation, malnutrition, constantly heightened nerves over several days, and the fact that they'd met their objective in finding Jack happened to culminate in the man's mind, and he experienced an overwhelming combination of relief that his brain simply couldn't process in the moment. So, he just cackled and walked away, unsure of the words that had just come out of his mouth.

Churchill stood after giving Macken another assuring pat on the shoulder, and he came face to face with the captain of the ship. Their eyes met properly through the non-existent window of the cabin.

"Charles Lightoller," the skipper finally introduced with an extended paw, reaching through the makeshift hole.

Spying the damage done to the yacht which included this shattered glass window, Churchill reached in and firmly took his hand.

Lightoller was an older fellow. He seemed experienced and well-versed in warfare, as many of that generation were. He may have already seemed the part, but Jack could smell it on him.

"Jack Churchill. Thanks for the ride."

"The *rescue*, you mean?"

Churchill kept shaking his hand for an extended moment of pleasantries which all of a sudden steered towards a sour dismount, however he allowed for humility to prevail.

"Sure," he responded, for the most part accepting that this was in fact a rescue—and that it clearly stimulated Lightoller's ego. "Let's go with *that.*"

Lightoller snickered through the teeth of his held smile.

The expression suggested that maybe the old geezer was merely testing Churchill, and that he had passed.

The two kept shaking while they seemingly assessed one another. It was getting awkward for those around them, and then finally Lightoller said his peace and released the handshake.

"You're everything you've been cracked up to be, Captain. Your reputation precedes you."

Churchill bowed his maroon beret sincerely, looking the man dead in the eye with a customary respect that Lightoller returned.

"Thank you, sir."

"Jack?!" King-Clark interrupted from his position on the edge of the pier. It was in reference to the incoming wounded men of the 4th Infantry Brigade as they started being carted onboard, escorted by those who could stand and function along with the few surviving members from the East Lancashire Regiment. Ervine-Andrews was amongst them and had been one of the first to jump down into the boat to donate the most assistance.

After a rapid introduction, the Second Chesters assisted in helping to get all the wounded aboard. Parker and Nicholl helped the medics get the gurneys from the truck and carried men over, supporting in loading them into the yacht.

All hands were on deck. In an orderly fashion, and as the battle still boomed busily in the brightening dawn sky above Dunkirk, they managed to transport all bodies from land to sea. It was almost time to finally get the fuck out of France ...

They had more than half inside the yacht by the time that King-Clark finally caught back up with Churchill, guiding his attention elsewhere.

"Glad you decided to ditch the tank."

"Pardon?"

"What were you going to do with that thing, anyhow?"

What did he mean by ditch it?

Confused, Churchill glared upon the query before cranking his neck to examine the string line of Bedford trucks along the wharf ... behind their convoy, there was no longer an A10 cruiser tank where it was supposed to be.

A surge of panic overcame Churchill and his attentiveness darted out into the distance, retracing their route from the last time he had seen the armoured sinker on their line.

This whole time since they had stopped on the beach, they had not been towing the tank. Churchill was under the assumption that the tank was still in tangent with their convoy, and that they had successfully dragged it all the way up the wharf with them.

"Good thing you didn't try and drag it onto the pier like you did with the trucks," King-Clark added, unaware that the tank's lack of presence was actually unintentional. "I don't think it's going to last long with all that weight as it is. And she sure wasn't going to fit on Lightoller's boat!"

"Bollocks!" Churchill cussed, leaping up from the yacht deck and back onto the pier right after they got the last few men aboard.

"Alright, *all aboard!*" Lightoller yelled, revving the engine to life. The propeller thrashed and steamed in the water at the rear. Out of the boat, the skipper's son Roger, flicked the knotted tether from the cleat hitch on the edge of the pier so that they could get away. This happened just after Churchill leapt out of the yacht and back onto the wharf.

"Wait!" Churchill appealed, holding up a hand. He looked back at the abandoned tank. "We've left someone behind."

King-Clark rolled his eyes a little, aware of who that *someone* was. "Jack, it's an asset. It's not a *real person* that needs saving. It's a bloody *tank*."

"I realize that—and, by the way, her name is *Barbara*."

"Pardon me?"

"*Busty Barbara!* She has a name!"

"Please! Jack!—"

"Clark, no! I mean *inside* the tank!" Churchill explained. "Corporal Hill and Felix Hardy!"

From the boat, all those who could gander a look out to the early morning coast were able to spot where the tank had been left on the beach. The top hatch was open, and Hill and the injured Hardy were hanging their top halves outside, waving their arms and probably shouting at the top of their lungs that they had been accidentally left behind. Across the distance their voices were inaudible over the waves of the incoming tide thrashing against the wharf pylons and the racket in the sky above Dunkirk.

Churchill turned and eyed King-Clark.

"I've got to go back for them!"

"No! No, no, no, no! You can't! *We* can't!"

"*I have to!*"

"Jack, *we've* got to go! This boat is our last chance, and her engine is on the brink of death! We simply cannot idle any longer. It's time. I'm sorry."

"Last call!" Lightoller informed seriously, turning the rudder in preparation for departure, and out into the channel. There would be no coming back this time. He had overheard some of their predicament, and had something to say about. "Ten seconds and I'm out of here ... with or without ya, *Mad Jack.*"

"Jack."

Deep in moral contemplation, Churchill looked at King-Clark, and at Nicholl and Parker behind him. They stood on the boat, whereas he stood on the wharf. There was a symbolism present, and they all felt it. He found in the crowd of men on the boat more familiar faces that were blank in counterargument to his barney; Ervine-Andrews, his loyal men of the East Lancashire Regiment, the soldiers of the 4th Infantry that he had conversed with, even the two seamen and eventually Charles Lightoller himself. Their faces all stared anxiously at him, imploring him to *please come aboard* so that they could finally depart. Their longing stares begged him to cut losses and allow for them to escape and succeed in this mission. To retreat to victory.

"Sorry, lads!" Churchill remarked, disappointing the masses. "I can't leave a lad behind."

If he did, none of them would be there.

If heroism was an addiction, he was an addict.

Lightoller could already tell Jack's answer by his hesitation. Before Churchill had even finished his response, Lightoller already revved the engine and begun to peel the Sundowner away, preparing to power them clear from the wharf.

"*Oi, Jack!*"

"See you in England, Clark!" Churchill announced as he started to move back along the waterfront—back *towards* Dunkirk.

"*Wait! Jack!*" Clark called as an uneasy distance started to grow between the friends. He climbed the railing rung, not to jump, but to relay one last message as closely as possible. The notion captured Churchill's attention before he vacated.

King-Clark caught his breath a second. With it, an idea seemed to formulate ... a last-ditch effort that proposed the salvation of them all.

His view panned to the side, following the direction.

"*The destroyed pier! To the east! We'll pass by it in a few minutes! Be ready!*"

Churchill heard the impromptu plan.

Understanding, he cast a gleam across the waterfront and over the water and to the east, eyeing the shorter destroyed pier they had passed on the way over.

He had no idea what King-Clark's plan was, but he probably had more than enough time to make it to the tank, get Hardy and Hill out, and make it to the pier, thus he accepted it all the same.

He saluted with a finger to the brim of his beret.

"Fine-o-*fuck!—*"

RRRumble!

The timber floor beneath Churchill's feet trembled fiercely—enough to scare him. He threw his arms out for balance.

Near his location on the pier, Churchill glanced right and saw as the flat deck of the wharf was clearly bowing under all the newly arrived weight and, as a result, the parked Bedford trucks had begun to slide to one weakened, slanting side.

There was a loud groan and what sounded like lumber cracking and splintering. At first there was ample confusion as to what was causing the destabilization that distorted the permanence around him, but then it was suddenly obviously clear ...

The wharf was collapsing.

"*Run, Jack! Run!*" Churchill heard King-Clark bellow.

From the water, they all noticed the pier decline.

The loaded Sundowner yacht had pushed off from the volatile and trembling wharf and Lightoller was giving it power, growing farther and farther away by the second. There was about to be no dock left to reembark to, even if he wanted to.

Their position back at the pier had the best overview. The middle of the extended jetty where they had loaded up was bowing savagely under the heavy weight of the trucks and was concaving more by the second. A few of the other men who were watching were also able to see the wooden girders of the dock crossbeams start to falter under the burdening weight. The stilts were not loadbearing to this extent.

They all stood on the yacht and approached the deck railing, shouting back at Jack with concern.

"*Run!*"

And Jack did.

Quickly collecting his balance on the pier with concentration upon his brow, Churchill contorted and faced the shore. His boots climbed across the crooked wooden beams now like he were manning an obstacle course at basic training, briskly returning him towards the stable end of the wharf.

With another shift in surface angle that threw him mildly off balance, Churchill was fast to pick up the pace, leaping up and onto the hood of the first truck as the whole thing slowly plunged on a defective beam beneath him.

Deciding to go up and over the parked convoy rather than shimmy his way along the side of the vehicles, especially if they were to slide off and into the water, potentially knocking him over and then crush him to death, Jack ran as the floor literally gave out beneath his boots.

Churchill heaved and pulled himself up the cabin, dropping into the tray. He carried two hard-out strides before leaping through mid-air onto the next truck. As he did, the far end of the pier buckled with an audible groan and crack of splintering timber. One of the main support pylons of the wharf must have given out.

With a bone-torquing thundercrack, the thick loadbearing lumber stilts exploded into fragments, failing to support the weight set upon her docks. The ocean end collapsed into the drink like a failed drawbridge, splashing loudly into the thrashing tide.

Droplets from the heavy splash hit the Sundowner as she rose and fell upon the choppy waves of the hightide. Of all those onboard, all nervous eyes were as wide as lifebuoys upon Churchill as he tackled the remaining sections of the unsettled wharf.

From the far end the entire dock began to slope as more of the stilts had much of the weight shifted upon them and they, too, began to waver and fracture with a hundred thousand snaps and crackles.

Churchill slid on his rear upon the roof of the second truck cabin, landing with speed on his flat boots in the rear tray. After three or four quick steps he leapt clear out of that, as though he was jumping hurdles, skidding across the roof of the third truck and into the final tray—but it was too late. The docks beneath the trucks gave out, and an entire partition of the wharf collapsed down into the water with a plummeting weight.

Jack took the final step before the truck he was rushing across dropped like an anvil, nose first. He pushed off with both feet at a harsh incline and jumped with all his might, sailing upwards through the air like a gymnast fighting gravity. His boots and knee hit the decking floor of the sloped section as it all came splashing down into the ramped water below, spraying up at him.

His fingers treated the slanted and hanging dock like a ladder and the tips of his boots found footing enough for him to scramble similar to a racing rock climber, reaching the summit where the wharf had detached from the instability. Churchill's hands and elbows found level floor as the panel behind him finally dropped loose, joining the rest of the barge and the three trucks in the toxic drink of sharp debris and thrashing waves.

Jack pulled himself up and rose to his feet, brushing some grime from his knees. He straightened his attire before continuing his jog along the pier, towards the tank and those left behind.

Onboard the Sundowner, all the men on the ship had just witnessed Churchill gallop and outrun the falling portion of the wharf, and they applauded and carried on loudly.

Amongst themselves they smiled and cheered, releasing all that angst they had bottled up from the intensity. They shouted out over the water at the courageous hero as Mad Jack Churchill barely slowed in his journey towards rescuing those left behind on the beach.

Joining in on the ovation, King-Clark shook his head while wearing an ear-to-ear grin, ever envious of that man's luck and brazenness.

XV
Lifeline

The skyline battle taking place above the coastal city was ferocious and immense in volume. The spectacle of the fast-moving mechanical birds swooping and weaving through various altitudes was a compelling view from ground level.

Ear-splitting aerodynamic whistling, the contending belligerents of the German Luftwaffe and British RAF were locked in fierce aerial combat. Glowing tracer rounds lit up the vista with a vibrant exhibition as full squadrons of RAF fighters reasserted themselves in the war.

The British had successfully outmanoeuvred the proposed bombing raid by the German armada hovering in slowly at five thousand feet above Dunkirk. From above the morning haze, the flyboys had accosted the enemy position, scraping the atmosphere in their manoeuvre. The surprise trajectory tactic caused their inclination to pivot vertically at the last second on a death-defying descent attack, blitzing the bigger German bomber's topsides and vertically outflanking fighter aircrafts from above, striking down upon them like bolts of lightning sent from Olympus beyond the clouds.

In the cunning gambit, RAF planes were able to successfully shoot down an entire third of the larger and slower bombers, sending them back down to earth as plummeting, smoking cadavers. The shrill pitch of their heavier descents wailed loud above the rest of the tussling fighters. The eruptions of their explosive-filled remains as they dropped from the sky sank like a fiery curtain backdrop of the lower Dunkirk dogfight.

As the dawn sky brightened into day, the skirmish raged on.

Fighter planes screamed and zoomed across the atmosphere, swooping low and executing lateral rotations, performing all sorts of sensational stunts and aerial finesses whilst chasing through one another's contrails. Their heavy mounted machine guns chain-fired unrelentingly, loaded with bright tracer ammunition, lighting up the morning sky with booming echoic explosions and the vigorous sound of dubious battle.

Down below the mechanical storm and on the ground, Jack Churchill disregarded the raging battle above his head. Running at full pelt, the maroon beret-attired, faded khaki-uniformed, bloodied soldier finally made it across the wooden wharf and back to the wet sands of the beach, retracing their vehicular passage.

Dashing as though he was being preyed on from above, he sought refuge beside the destructed boatshed on the beach in order to take a second to witness the awesome overhead display with a wide-eyed glare of absolute wonderment. The warzone sight was unlike anything he had ever imagined. He suddenly felt miniscule and inconsequential in comparison to this chaotic conflict.

After an extended moment of gawking at the fireworks in the morning air above, his attention lowered and drew the shoreline, searching his goal. Following the blood-washed waves of the contour of the hightide along, he traced their tyre treads leading to the unmoving cruiser tank.

The lard sat there on the sand like a beached whale.

Churchill could basically hear the distressed screams of the wounded Felix Hardy and Corporal Hill, still hunkered down inside.

Beneath an inverted brow, Churchill's attentive stare homed in on the damaged and smoking A10 cruiser tank right as a rogue fighter plane passed by low overhead, pelting it with another stream of armour-piercing tracer rounds. Maiming it like a wounded beast, kicking it while it was down.

The German Messerschmitt Bf-109 fighter was one with awfully familiar yellow markings, and clearly the Luftwaffe maverick pilot must have carried some sort of egotistical vendetta against this particular convoy.

Carving air currents, the screaming fighter nosedived dangerously short to pelt the halted tank on a lateral engagement, bombarding it with a bright array of sparks before yanking on the yoke and zooming yonder, most likely banking up and out wide to make yet another pass ...

This pilot was clearly determined to destroy this tank.

After the slipstream of air gushed across the smoking cruiser tank, Churchill noticed that low in the sand around it there was evidence of trickling flames.

Upgrading from a frown of mild concern towards one of severe anxiousness, Churchill's lips pouted. He squinted hard upon the vehicular distress, examining the scene from behind the corner of the burnt-out boatshed. He was able to spot the glistening orange combustion as it began to burn taller and brighter, licking the iron tread on the coastside and gradually clambering up the exterior of the tank. Wherever there was a texture laced with oil or spilled fuel, the yellow fire snuffled the surface and multiplied like an infectious disease, quickly coating the entire side and back end of the cruiser.

An eventual rupture had obviously been caused by the constant aerial assault made by the plane. The persistent barrage of hits had finally punched through a section of the tank where the fuel was stored, and a spark flint of a tracer against the steel side had now ignited the flammable liquid.

That tank was about to go up in flames and then explode.

They had seconds to act!

"No ..." he breathed with concern as he watched. He wrestled the sudden wave of futility as it washed over him, anchoring him behind cover. There was almost nothing that could be done in the time it would have taken him to reach the occupants trapped inside of the immobilized cruiser.

The endgame to his seemingly futile sweeps made by this maverick pilot upon the armoured target suddenly became apparent. The cruiser tank would eventually ignite and possibly explode, if not nastily simmer the occupants inside. The thing was practically a cauldron.

Churchill's crest glanced up and into the brightening easterly sky. It was the direction in which the maverick had pitched in incline to clearly veer around and make another pass at the burning tank ... likely a final one.

His loose stare tightened after he spotted it.

It was distant. He had sixty seconds, maybe less, and the cruiser tank was a one-hundred-yard dash across open sand ...

The flames grew more vivid by the second as the northerly wind gusted across the water, now spanning 180-degrees around the circumference of the beached vehicle. It was then that Jack noticed that the climbing flames looming about the open top hatch, attempting to gain access to those inside, were being arrested by the harsh wind. This could potentially buy him valuable seconds.

"No rest for the wicked," Churchill exclaimed, barely able to catch a breath. Longbow looped tight around his shoulder via its razor taut drawstring, he pushed off from the partial cover of the boatshed and into an all-out sprint across the open sands towards the tank.

Right as he did so, the overall volume of the aerial dogfight looming in the skies above Dunkirk seemed to increase.

A British Spitfire rocketed by overhead, dipping in close to the coastline to the north during the all-out scrimmage while being pursued by two Messerschmitts. Both MG-131 machine guns of the German fighters were blazing, chasing. Side-by-side, the trailing fighters squeezed the trigger on their stick, spearing javelins of barbed golden tracer rounds at the evading RAF target as he attempted to shake his pursuers, slicing air and passing inadvertently across the airspace of Churchill's gallivanting position down on the shore.

zzzzzzZZOOOOMMm!!

The plane thundered by atop and traversed beyond, passing within fifty feet of the flat beach closely enough to lift sand and debris with its drag.

Churchill covered his face and performed an instinctual shoulder roll as the powerful gust from the wind current assaulted his clothes and jolted his sprint.

Furthermore, the overshooting bullets from the chasing German fighter sprayed into the sand about him with tough impacts, dispatching grey wet beach clay six feet up like jet spouts.

ZZOO-ZZOOOOMMm!!

The pursuing Messerschmitt wailed after the Spitfire.

Ignoring the near-death collateral, the sandy Churchill upped to his feet from his bowl, grimacing tensely at his injured shoulder, and pressed on in his unstoppable dash.

A few paces out, he glanced out to the sky over the sea as those three planes fought on and performed intertwined rolling scissor aerobatics like playful birds of prey, playing with their food as they dawned upon the lone British plane.

RAT-TAT-TAT-TAT-TAT!

Out of seemingly nowhere, a second RAF fighter came sharply into at their skirmish, dogging out a pursing German fighter with an accurate volley of machine gun fire. This caused a thunderous *boom* as the Messerschmitt became an instant fireball, exploding with bright orange fire in midair. Its wings and flaming tail piece tossed aimlessly into the shallows further along the coast as the rest of the wreckage sailed in a flaming heap resembling a meteor, splashing down in the waist-high water of the shoreline.

The saviour RAF fighter bellowed through the heat of the explosion, its throttle loud as it peeled off to rejoin the battle and find a fresh target in the skies above Dunkirk.

It was absolute airborne chaos.

Churchill pressed forwards, beginning to shorten in breath from the sprinting and overexcitement. His attention was never too far from tracking the position of that rogue, yellow-nosed Messerschmitt who was out on a wide bank, setting himself up for another attack run at Barbara. Afar, the Luftwaffe maverick was currently straightening out a bend, now on approach and lining them up for the strafe ...

Churchill collected his focus, speeding up his already exhausted strides in order to reach the finish line before the fighter did. Hopefully, he could seek shelter from this incoming assault.

... *wwwwwhhhir* ...

He heard and saw the Messerschmitt angle its approach.

The pilot undoubtedly saw him out on the sand.

Heart beating deafeningly within his ears, Churchill bellowed with wrath as he pushed himself harder than he had ever done.

He charged in and dropped low just as the fighter's distant machine guns clapped away, pummelling the sand around the stationary armoured target with earthy wallops. When the beams levelled and hit the target, a firework display of sparks erupted against the armoured chassis.

Churchill slid through the sand, carving deep with his boot. His glide ended painfully as he bashed hard into the immovable cruiser tank right as the beach detonated around him with sharp *snaps!* and beefy *thumps!* The tank exterior became loudly assaulted with stridently brash metallic impacts as the fighter shot by, soaring with a dragnet of air that tugged upon every surface. Unfortunately, the gust of air helped spread the existing fire of the petrol spill in the wet sand. The undercurrent and flux blew like trick candles on a birthday cake, pushing the flame spread across the terrain, which included Churchill's position tight under cover.

He rolled away just in time to not become completely engulfed by liquid fire as it splashed his way, licking at him like a hissing snake. With a grumble, Churchill attempted to swat some flames from his wet fatigues as it crawled up his trouser leg. He must have touched some unignited petrol-soaked sand in his arrival.

After patting it out, he stared with a grimace of utter hatred at the German fighter as the wit showed off, performing aerobatic aileron rolls, reeling out to sea to take another lavish pass at them.

"Oi!" he shouted, bashing on the steel side of the tank with his balled fist. "You hear?"

"*Who's there ...?*" a sheepish voice responded.

"Who do you bloody think?! Come on! We've got to go! Get your arses out here!" Churchill bellowed, eyes guardedly to the sky.

The top hatch abruptly slung open and Corporal Hill's head emerged, searching for Churchill down below.

"Jack?" Hardy's voice called from within Busty Barbara's echoic armoured belly and he, too, upped and had a look outside.

"Come on! Your mate'll be back at any second, Hardy!" Churchill added in reference to the annoying Luftwaffe maverick piloting the rogue Messerschmitt who seemed hellbent on destroying their tank—and probably now, *them.*

"I noticed! What the hell are you doing back?!"

"Saving your lily bellend, lad, let's go! *Now!* I'm no chef, but you guys seem to be cookin' with fire here!" Churchill hunched, catching a breath. His face panned right, spying the maverick out over the ocean. The pilot banked a perfect circle, arcing around to face them once again from the other direction.

Dropping sight of it for an instant, Churchill dropped to a knee and scooped up two handfuls of wet sand, tossing it upon the flames in an attempt to extinguish them. He did this over and over while Hill dismounted the tank tracks and promptly assisted as the fire started to grow at the rear, completely consuming the armoured reserve tanks.

Churchill's eyes grew wide. "Hardy, come on, we got to go right now! Busty Barbara's going to pop her lid!"

Hardy roared with agony as his sore leg touched down in the sand, and he used the tank as a support to stand upright. He winced, fatigued and drained from the pain and drained of energy, barely able to manoeuvre the empty Bren rifle beneath his arm to use as a crutch to walk. "I can't ... I can't ..."

"Yes, you bloody can!" Churchill argued confidently. "Come on, lads! We've got to head for that dock! We got one attempt at catching the last ferry across the channel."

The three men aligned, stacked along their burning concealment, and prepared to move before Churchill stopped them with a call, decisively preventing them from dashing from cover. "Hold!"

"Oh, shit," Hill called with a tossed look over their shoulders. "The tank's on fire!"

"*Hold!*"

"*We've got to go, Captain! It's gonna explode!*"

"*Hold up! Or you're going to explode!*"

Up above, it became clear why Churchill was anxious at not exposing them just yet. The Luftwaffe maverick had dived deep, lining them up for another death run almost parallel to the shoreline strip.

If they had moved then and there, they would have been fully exposed and easily shot to ribbons by the incoming Messerschmitt. They had to wait until the very last second to avoid being anywhere near those tracing machine gun lines ...

A distraction for their flight wouldn't go astray, of which Jack had an ace up his sleeve.

"Wait for my signal, then move fast!" Churchill stated as he crept out, drawing a small snub-nosed brass pistol from his belt. Acting fast, he unclasped the cap of the Very pistol and blew the sand from across its top in short bursts before snapping it closed.

Behind them, the flames growled noisily and crackled as they climbed alit, spanning across the entire back end of the cruiser tank. The encased reserve fuel jerry cans along her rear were now well and truly on fire, the contents about to reach ignition. They had mere *seconds* before the pressure eruption ...

The Messerschmitt targeted them, shooting from afar as it sped with a downward pitching soar. His machine guns clapped to life and blinked intervals of white muzzle flashes, drawing a line through the sand before climbing and drilling the tank with dazzling sparks ...

By surprise, Churchill strafed diagonally in the sand, aiming the flare pistol with a steady hand and a closed eye.

Pufff!

From Churchill's signal gun discharge, an intense and vivid bright red spur shot out with blinding, flashing pulsations. The bright flare soared straight towards the path of the incoming fighter as it flew low, skimming the beach.

A fruitless endangerment, as even with a direct hit, a signalling flare could do little to no damage to a Messerschmitt Bf-109 fighter plane. Albeit, it was a distraction, nonetheless.

As expected, the pilot was at least a little surprised to see the blinking, hot object travelling like a javelin towards his cockpit windshield, and he reacted instinctively by tugging the yoke and pulling up from the target pass, prematurely ending the volume of the strident machine gun barrage.

His vacancy was their cue to run.

"*Move! Go, go, go!*" Churchill shouted hastily, discarding the flare gun and assisting Hardy's movements from under his arm.

The three men hobbled as quickly as they could away from the flaming A10 cruiser tank as the fire crept up along her turret and through the combustible hydraulics, reaching the internal space of her belly. Fire now breathed out the hatch that they had recently occupied like a smelting furnace.

They were barely clear when she exploded.

BOF-BOOM!

Oxygen-hungry fire burst at the rear end of the British tank.

Raw force and power jolted the stationary fifteen-tonne unit, and Busty Barbara shifted violently in the sand. Flames spewed out about the beach area around it, exhausting in the wind like a fiery kiln. With a loud metal groan, the A10 cruiser became a blistering steel carcass, roasting hot and raucous.

Barely outrunning the inferno that claimed her life, the three escapees rested a moment, and Churchill looked back in sorrow as they ambled in their retreat.

He muttered glumly, "Rest in peace, old girl."

"Could you please go slower!" Rex King-Clark pleaded.

Over the starboard railing, he nervously observed Churchill's progress on the shoreline of which the Sundowner yacht cruised on the parallel. He spoke to Captain Charles Lightoller directly via the shattered cabin window, and certainly didn't need to shout as loud as he did. That was due to anxiety.

The desperation in his tone was with regards to the skipper's apparent contempt in applying any more time to this mission, indifferent towards abandoning Jack Churchill. Notwithstanding, they had been on borrowed time for a while. Overtime, even. They should have been like any other one of the Little Ships of Dunkirk by now: long gone and well across the channel. Out of harm's way and out of range of the Germans.

With his eyes glued on the northern horizon, Lightoller shook his head. Due to the angle of the peeking morning sunrise, the surface of the water was shimmering, therefore becoming more difficult for him to see obstacles that may beach their vessel.

"Please?!" King-Clark added with despair, urgently attempting to buy his friend more time. They were only a minute out of passing the broken pier and the last point of which Jack Churchill and his two hobbling friends could make the jump onto the fleeting boat ... and they weren't anywhere near ready yet.

They were still on the sands.

They weren't going to make it in time.

"That's a negative, Captain," Lightoller stated, steadfast and surefire.

"C'mon, Charles!" King-Clark exclaimed, pushing through the new crowd of quiet and reluctant saved souls onboard. Even though they undoubtedly owed Jack Churchill a debt of gratitude, the exhausted and wounded infantryman did not argue King-Clark's point. The desire to remain home free was too alluring.

"You've just saved the lives of over two dozen soldiers on this run. You've already got that medal of valour in your palm ... how's about you let Jack get his."

"Like I said before, we're rat shit. If I idle this engine again, she may never rev back into gear, and then we're stranded here. We will barely make it across the channel as it is. Now, I am truly sorry, but that is a risk I can no longer take—and that's not speaking for my *medal of valour* either," Lightoller spat condescendingly and letting it sink in. He even took his gaze off the water in order to stare directly at King-Clark, and he saw how serious the skipper was. "If we wait, we die. We came back for one man, we left with twenty. Take the win, Captain."

King-Clark frustratingly turned, facing the beach. "Bollocks."

Their boat was travelling analogously to the beach and in the same direction Churchill was moving. Whilst under fire from that pesky German fighter, they had all just excitedly watched him successfully make it to the incapacitated tank, rescue the occupants, and get them clear mere seconds before the armoured vehicle exploded into flames. The only thing that had been missing from this front-row action epic was the popcorn.

To reach his objective and make the jump aboard, Churchill still had to make it all the way along the wonky, partially destructed pier with his wounded men. And he still somehow had to do this without drawing too much attention to the ship by the enemy fighter plane, which may have been impossible.

King-Clark lurched forwards from his defeated slant against the cabin, and he grappled the railing. There was something coming up in the lapping water of debris that caught his eye, and sparking a truly great *WWJD?* idea.

"Rope," he uttered just as Padre Nicholl found him in the crowded yacht. Gin Parker was there also, still with a weapon in hand. It was like Churchill's D section were subconsciously assembling, attracted and gravitated towards something resembling a Mad Jack-level plan.

Facing them, King-Clark elaborated with excitement now that there were ears for his words to fall upon. "We get one of those long ropes from the stow, throw it down into one of those drifting dinghy boats or canoes that aren't sinking. If we tie it off, it can be eventually dragged behind."

Understood, Nicholl nodded, as did Parker.

It was simple enough. Worth a shot.

"That could work."

"How long is this?" King-Clark questioned, grabbing at a coil of rope that was hung beneath the cabin window.

Roger answered in his father's seeming absence of any further assistance to the men. "That spool is about a hundred metres, sir."

"If we tie it off and let it unspool, how long do you think one hundred metres of slack will buy my friend?"

Roger shook his head, deep in mathematical estimation. "Eh, I dunno, sir, maybe ... five minutes? Probably less?"

"Two minutes!" Charles Lightoller interrupted, slightly more educated in nautical guestimations. "Maybe two and a half."

They all looked at him, the idea now set in stone.

"Alright, then," Nicholl asserted, taking the rope from King-Clark's hand. "Step one, let's try and lasso one of these boats that aren't full of holes."

"That one!" Gin Parker hailed their attention, pointing enthusiastically overboard and singling out what appeared to be a small, four-man fishing dinghy. One of the edges was splintered, likely damaged from one of the many airborne assaults the coastline had persevered in the previous days, but the bow and bottom seemed fine in its floatation. Completely adrift, the boat was oarless and motorless, but most importantly, it appeared lightweight and easily towable by the Sundowner.

They watched as Nicholl hurriedly fashioned a knot in the coiled laid rope, and they prepared to lasso the small hump at the centre of the depressing dinghy.

Before they started, Nicholl gave King-Clark a look.

"What Would Jack Do, right?"

"Oh, I'm not beseeching Jack for help with this one ..." replied Nicholl as he readied himself for this incredible feat: one that only Jack or Jesus would probably pull off first go. "I'll ask the other guy I serve."

"Give him some space, boys," Gin Parker announced, clearing a section of the deck from the rubbernecking passengers of the 4th Infantry and East Lancashire Regiment. They ogled on as time ran out.

Padre Nicholl attempted to channel his inner cowboy, winding the lasso up and over his head for an instant before throwing it out and into the water beside the boat as the Sundowner drifted past it.

Quickly, they retracted the wet line and tried again, managing the next time to overshoot the boat completely.

Time ran out and the dinghy was now too far to land a line.

"Blast!" King-Clark shouted as they finally retracted the wet rope, however, this time, was unable to even prepare to toss the line out again, they had missed their opportunity.

In the cabin, Lightoller couldn't help but evilly grin at their misfortune. His humour was not for the sake of them failing to attempt the rescue of their friend, but more so that it seemed so idiotic to begin with.

"Here! Try this perry buoy!" Roger said, pushing between wounded infantry onlookers with an adult-sized orange and white painted lifebuoy. It was a floatation device designed to be thrown overboard to fallen sailors in the water, to provide buoyancy and prevent them from drowning. "Tie it on. It'll add weight."

Cleverly, the skipper's son elaborated his idea just as the strategy developed in King-Clark's mind. Padre Nicholl was already on it, tying the loose end of the wet rope through the big hole of the doughnut-shaped flotation device. They promptly leant back over the railing, searching for the next viable drifting dinghy.

"There!" Gin and Roger both shouted, as did a couple other of the 4th Infantrymen aboard who were now onboard with their plan to try and buy Mad Jack more time to make the evacuation.

Every pair of eyes onboard watched them as they hauled the anchored lifesaver over the edge. The buoy landed perfectly into the tub of another adrift dinghy boat, which luckily happened to be on their path as Lightoller navigated the yacht towards the edge of the damaged dock ... perhaps even subconsciously angling their voyage in tighter to better the odds of their valiant endeavour.

"Yes!" King-Clark shouted, balling a fist in the air.

There was praise and merriment as the men aboard joined in a celebration of the successful attempt.

With a smile still on his face and praise for the lord in his lungs, Nicholl took the wet lasso end of the rope and latched it firmly onto an available sturdy aft cleat on the decking of the yacht. As the yacht would vacate the vicinity of the docks, headed away from Dunkirk and across the English Channel, the dinghy would eventually become dragged behind it in tow ...

With delicacy, they hauled the dinghy boat close behind the Sundowner and better affixed the line so that the knot would hold against the drag of the tide.

"What's next?" Padre Nicholl asked as he courteously moved through the standing array of infantrymen and positioned himself back before King-Clark and the armed Gin Parker, who was still gripping a tight hold of the Thompson submachine gun, in case the fighter got cute and decided to try and sink them again.

"I'm going to mount up," King-Clark deliberated.

"Y'know something," Lightoller regarded as King-Clark planned his final preparations before boarding the deadweight dinghy in the hopes of baiting a big British fish. "You're as stubborn as your friend ..."

"Thanks."

"That wasn't a compliment."

King-Clark jeered with a smirk. "Let's hope I am as lucky as him, too."

Upon wafting through the parting crowd towards the aft of the yacht to board the dinghy, King-Clark was surprised to see both Padre Nicholl and Gin Parker already seated within, raring to go.

Considered an element of floccinaucinihilipilification at the time, Nicholl tapped with his toe a small crate of heavy contents beneath one of the passenger's seats in the dinghy.

The Padre then announced, gesturing a hand to the vessel.

"All aboard."

Once reaching the eerie indoors of the ligneous barebones boatshed, Churchill, Hill, and Hardy collapsed in a breathless heap upon a stack of loose beams, strewn netting, and other superfluous fishing tackles.

The shed interior was bleak and shaded, however strips of morning sunlight shone through the damaged ceiling and missing planks in the wall and cast luminescence on a small workbench opposite them. Its extensive tool collection appeared to be nothing more than a rusty hammer next to a vice. Spools of rope and other nautical-esque netting lines coated the palings.

Their breathing finally began to lessen from the dash across the sands, and the three men were able to hear the wailing soar of the pesky Messerschmitt in the skies above the shoreline.

The fucker was circling back around for another pass.

And it went without saying that this boatshed shit shack was a lot less armoured than the A10 cruiser tank had been.

Whilst the other two grunted and stirred laying upon a thousand black charred shards of lumber and collapsed roofing, Churchill became hurriedly upstanding. He revolved around and spied through a missing paling towards the northeast sector, able to see the German fighter against the looming glow of the sunrise. There was one hundred percent certainty that the pilot saw them cross the sand and enter ...

He attended to the others, remembering the plan to meet the Sundowner on her pass; to reach the end of the pier in time. That time was running out.

"Come on, we've got to keep moving, otherwise we're truly doomed in Dunkirk."

Churchill's impatience was noted while he helped Hardy, handing him his Bren gun crutch.

Hardy poised a moment, examining his hand.

Something protruded his finger and halted his progression, and the waylaid, wounded American raised it into view before himself and Churchill. "Fuck me. I got a splinter ..."

When he moved from his collapsed position, Hill suddenly screamed rather piercingly, stunning them both. Churchill looked as the corporal turned, presenting the source of his newfound anguish: a seven-inch sharp wooden splinter protracting from the back of his thigh, having fallen on it.

"Jesus Christ!" Hardy exclaimed, taking a look. "What the fuck is that?!"

Churchill contemptuously remarked, "*That's* a splinter."

With a grimace and hesitation, Hill gripped at the skewered fragment with intentions to yank it out like a plaster strip. Instead, the unit seemed snagged within his tissue, and he winced in agony.

Concentrating on his breathing, Hill immediately retried and slowly began to withdraw the—

He failed, collapsing back and rolling onto his side, pounding the debris-scattered floor with his fist out of extreme discomfort and suffering. He was in total distress from the puncture wound, unable to even think clearly.

Quickly, Churchill ducked in low, locating the giant shard and wrapping his hands firmly around it. They did not have time for this and there was no way Hill would make the trek with it embedded within his thigh.

He would count to three, but they didn't have time for that.

"Corporal, we've got to move!"

"Just go!" Hill spat, frustrated. Defeated. "Leave me!"

"Not a chance," Churchill responded calmly. "I'm going to pull it out. Are you ready?"

Hill nodded.

"On three, ready? One ..."

Shlish!

With all his might, Churchill yanked it free and immediately applied pressure as the warm red blood gush began to flow. It was a considerably deep protrusion. In an alternative scenario, it would have been prudent to wrap the leg with the instrument still within, but they didn't have the time or the resources. Jack needed Hill on his feet and moving, and there was no way that was happening if the poor sod had a six-inch-long piece of wood hanging out of his leg.

Churchill tossed the wooden barb to the mountain of rubble, assisting Hill to strap his own wound with a torn article of clothing to forge a temporary makeshift bandage.

"Sounds like that asshole is coming back around ..." Hardy remarked in disbelief as he hobbled unsteadily in the darkened shed, able to discern the incoming pitch. "Fuck me, he won't stop!"

"No shit! This bloke is bloody obsessed!" Churchill responded with emphasis as he leant in, tying off Hill's bandage with as much pressure as he could muster. Notably, his energy was now starting to drain from the severe lack of sleep, physical beatings, and blood loss from the bullet hole in his left shoulder.

Outside and in the early morning sky above, the German fighter commenced its attack run. The Luftwaffe maverick seemingly ignored all other appropriate aerial targets, swooping through the mayhem in order to target the partially destructed boatshed with its heavy mounted guns, aiming to drill those inside.

As it fired upon the helpless trio, an abundance of suppressive small arms fire unexpectedly emitted from the waterside, somewhere just past the partly sunken docks connected to their boatshed.

The canopy of the unexpecting Messerschmitt took a few abrupt hits from what must have been a submachine gun at medium range and on ground level, and he peeled away impulsively from his attack run, performing some evasive aerobatics to create distance.

The deterrent successfully prolonged the lives of those contained within the boatshed like lambs to the slaughter. After the bout of sporadic gunfire, Churchill, Hardy, and Hill each swapped a confused look.

They thought they were the last men in Dunkirk?

Traipsing inwards from the wet dockside, two pairs of combat boots came trotting inside with a low-slung weapon. The two familiar British soldiers entered the boatshed carrying a smoking machine gun between them. After entering, they paused.

It was Rex King-Clark and Gin Parker.

"Hullo again!"

Churchill was perplexed. He was under the impression the Sundowner was unable to moor amongst these shorter, debris-littered piers. "Clark, what the Devil?"

King-Clark bypassed any further questioning with resolve. "Come on! We scared him off, now let's go! The Padre has got a boat on the end of the dock!"

"He'll be back!" Churchill responded, presuming Captain Lightoller had decided to wait and park the boat by the boundary of the dock somewhere pending their eventual escape onboard and also hence King-Clark's arrival. "We won't make it far in the yacht with him around!"

"Eh, about that ..." King-Clark started to explain—

—however Hardy elaborated the former point with an ounce of exasperated frustration. "The fucker keeps circling back. The entire battle is happening right now above Dunkirk, and this bastard is focusing on only us! He's *John*-fucking-*Barrymore!*"

"Who?" King-Clark grimaced. He assisted Jack in standing the American up whilst Parker peeked through the doorway and assessed the skies with his Thompson at the ready, guarding their exodus.

King-Clark was smart when it came to literature, but with film and Hollywood culture, not so much. Hardy's film reference had him at a question mark.

"The actor?" Churchill quizzed—and it was at *that moment* an underlining idea sprung to the forefront of his cognizance, only he could not convey it entirely without more to jog the splinter of his mind's eye.

"Yeah, from the movies!"

The idea fogged Jack's temporal lobe. He required more to get the juices truly going. "Yes, I know who he is! But why did you say that?"

"He's from *Moby Dick!* Y'know, he plays the obsessed sea captain hunting the white whale!"

Churchill wallowed, even deeper in thought. This referencing further tripped an idea in his brain; an idea that may just be the key to getting rid of their pesky maverick friend.

"You're referencing the character of *Captain Ahab?*" King-Clark caught on, recalling from his knowledge from *the book* of Moby Dick known as *The Whale* rather than the film starring John Barrymore. "I'm confused, though. Are you're saying that *we* are *Moby Dick* in this analogy?"

"Nonsense. We're not lard whales, Clark. A bunch of dorks, on the other hand may be up for debate ..." Churchill interjected with mild humour amidst the topic deviation. "Gents, I believe that I have an idea stemming from this digression. The tables will soon turn on this maverick Hun."

During all of the underlining chaos, the group watched Churchill as he began rummaging alongst the ground debris with his hands and tracking a piece of rope that had tripped him up seconds earlier. It appeared to lead to nowhere and was rather short to act as a component in Churchill's newly formulated and rather eccentric idea.

"Jack, we don't have time for any of your longwinded shenanigans! We've got to go!"

"Go *where*, Clark?" Churchill upped and turned, mildly frustrated. "Old mate *Ahab* up there will be back any second to blow us off the dock—or worse, he'll spot the yacht and sink it, and kill everybody we've tried so hard to save!"

"About that ... Jack, Lightoller has already left."

Churchill glared at King-Clark, motionless.

"Pardon?"

"He's heading back to England. We have a lifeline attached to his yacht. It's tethered to a small boat at the end of the pier just outside, the Padre is waiting there for us ..."

Churchill blinked, bewildered.

This more than mildly complicated things.

"As I said, we haven't got the time for this! It's why we've got to hurry, Jack! We've got *seconds* before the line runs out and tows off without us," King-Clark unnervingly explained, outlining their time frame.

"How long is the line?" Churchill asked, frozen in action.

"One hundred metres ..." King-Clark calculated direly, seeing that Churchill was attempting to calculate in his head how long that gave them to procrastinate before evacuating. "We've got seconds, Jack! Not minutes! We've got to take our chances and make a run for it! Now!"

"We *cannot!*" Churchill exclaimed indignantly. "Not while *Willy Dieterle* is out there dogging us like a yellow-nosed mutt."

"*Who?!*" King-Clark exclaimed at Churchill with a scrunched frown.

"The *German* John Barrymore!"

... there was silence ...

"They made a German film version of Moby Dick," clearly more of a movie buff than he was and the only one picking up the obscure reference that Jack had put down, Hardy informed finally in King-Clark's ear as a form of exposition.

Adding to the awkward tranquillity in the face of the fast-paced nature of the situation, he eyed Churchill in a momentarily quaint tone. "*Deep of the Sea* or something, right?"

"*Demon of the Sea*," Churchill informed at a foreign guess, nodding and strangely calm for an extended moment—a moment they absolutely *did not have*.

King-Clark exploded, breaking the moment.

"Gentlemen! We are out! Of fucking! Time! I did *not* come all the way back here to talk about foreign cinema! Jack, what do you propose?"

Churchill focused resiliently, devising yet another magical *Mad Jack* plan with a relevant *Moby Dick* theme.

Like an oven bake timer chiming *ready*, his piercing blue eyes focused and his winning smile curled.

"We *harpoon* him!"

" *What?!*" King-Clark retorted, bewildered.

"About a minute left, boys ..." Gin Parker informed gently in the background, keeping guard with their only offensive weapon. Uncontainable nervousness was breaking his calm.

"We've got to swat that nuisance out of the sky, otherwise, even if we make it to the boat, we won't get very far," Churchill explained as he scrounged about the debris in the boatshed, searching for the necessary tools to implement his grand idea. "I'm suggesting we make *him* the dork in this story! Not us!"

"Fine!" King-Clark shrugged, conceding. "How do you propose to do this, Jack?"

"Don't worry about it, I've got a plan," Churchill said bobbing his head and casting them a gleam. "You mind?"

Hardy traded him a gawk, sighting his desire for possession of his empty Bren gun crutch.

"Eh, O.K.?"

Churchill collected it, leaving the wounded journalist under the support of King-Clark's hold.

"You lot just get ready to make a run for the boat once I run out towards Barbara's smouldering remains. I *guarantee* you that he will be aiming for me and not you."

Through the doorway, Churchill's stare from the shed was of the familiar roasting cruiser tank out on the wet sand ... and the uncoiled steel winch cable laying in the sand around it.

"That's it?" King-Clark scoffed, quoting his mate's odd and possibly misplaced judiciousness. He quoted something Churchill had once cited of someone's misguided wisdom regarding war and sacrifice. " *'War demands a sacrifice'*, so, after all this, you're going to surrender yourself?"

"Nonsense, Clark, I'll be along," Churchill discarded.

"I'll cover you," Gin Parker added with a gallant posture. His emitted level of selflessness was most unexpected.

Churchill's eyes met his. In a fraction of a moment, Jack questioned Gin's motives here; his newfound undying devotion to the cause, to the war, maybe even to him.

In all the time he had known him, Parker had never been Churchill's biggest supporter, and thus it came as a surprise. Parker said simply Jack's motto—perhaps it had grown on him. "Never stop fighting, eh?"

Churchill nodded, most appreciative.

... wwwwwwhhir ...

The pitch grew in the air.

He was back!

"Alright, lads. If we're going to do this, let's do it ..." King-Clark informed, preparing them to move. "Ready?"

"Doesn't matter anyway ... you lot hear that? He's incoming," Hardy pessimistically yet accurately informed as they all heard the unambiguous pitch of a Messerschmitt fighter engine dwelling on descent for another attack run. They may have been within cover, but those bullets would punch through the burnt wood of the boatshed walls like it were made of twigs.

"It's showtime, lads," Churchill voiced definitively, referring to their cinematic discussions of late. Jack began to remove the barrel from the Bren gun; the ends of the barrels of this machine gun were known to splay out and warp from continual use, and this one in particular was no different, having seen plenty of action in the fall back into Dunkirk. The black rifled barrel was well worn and quite weighty. It was effectively a straight, hollow, twenty-five-inch steel tube—and precisely what Jack needed right now.

Along with it, Churchill's busy hand rifled across the nearby work bench, knocking about items strewn across the dusty surface until he located something that he knew he'd need to formulate this quick plan: a mallet.

Tools in hand, Churchill stepped out from the shade of the boatshed, out into the morning light and onto the cold sand, heading towards the flaming tank wreckage on the beach.

"Oh, Jack?!" King-Clark snagged his progress one final time, stopping him as Parker stepped into position near the door, guarding the airspace range with the submachine gun. From a trained pilot's perspective—something Jack often forgot about his friend—King-Clark had noticed a possibly vulnerable weakness this German pilot held. With a twinkle in his eye as he deemed the intelligence useful in the last second, he relayed it to Churchill:

"... he banks to the right. Always *right.*"

Churchill took the intel onboard, firmly bowing his head prior to continuing in his run out in the open and across the sand toward the hot burning wreckage.

Since their time spent holed up inside the shady boatshed, daylight had filled the land. Visibility was much higher now than it was before and the sudden change in brightness stung at Churchill's retinas.

Churchill ran with his longbow in one hand, a hammer, and the barrel from the Bren light machine gun Hardy had been using as a prop in the other.

While on his descent, as expected, the Luftwaffe maverick spotted the exposed human target out on the shore, scurrying from shelter. He engaged thusly, aligning Jack and clapping away with his synchronized MG-131 guns. The bullets drew parallel lines of tracer bursts across the flat sands, ascending towards Churchill and about to cook him alive.

With thick wallops, bullets impacted in the sand all about Churchill as he competed in his race on foot, trying his hardest not to deter his strides as he knew countermeasures would soon be in effect from his help by the boatshed.

At that instant, after biding his time for decreased distance and therefore increased accuracy, Gin Parker returned fire with his fully automatic submachine gun in his midst. Like a demonic typewriter, the .45 ACP Thompson crackled to life with droning bass, striking several destructive hits on the fighter.

However, rather than deter his fire entirely, the airplane veered sharply left, deciding to engage the offensive boatshed target instead.

Gin Parker saw this and at that same moment the gun unexpectedly ceased firing, clicking dry and out of bullets ... *his eyes grew wide.*

RAT-TAT-TAT-TAT-TAT-TAT ...

The sand erupted furiously out before the doorway, drawing a line straight up the beach and into the boatshed where he was standing, claiming Gin Parker's life with a direct hit to his torso. The wound was big and gory, punching a hole almost the size of a tyre through the man's chest and exploding him to red ribbons.

As the follow-through overshoots of machine gun fire tore up the wooden boatshed above their heads, King-Clark, Hardy, and Hill all witnessed the tragic fall of one of their own in the aftermath of the strafing run.

In an almost slow-motion reality, Gin Parker bared his teeth, clenching his lids closed, and grimacing from the carnage. His chest had exploded violently with crimson gore, and his body was left dancing on the spot by the salvo for a whole three seconds before slamming down onto a pile of charred timber panels, completely dull, bloody, and dead.

A moment of shock passed as the three men witnessed the slaying.

"Let's go! There's nothing we can do for him now, we need to move!" King-Clark stated with Hardy's paw wrapped over his shoulder, tearing their fixed view away from the back of the small shed as they left it on cue.

Set to purpose, the three men hobbled out, trotting along the wooden dock panels until they reached the end where the small dinghy remained docked. Padre Nicholl was hiding down low, feeding the rope into the drink as the Sundowner yacht faded into the misty distance of the English Channel to the north horizon.

With the process of the unravelling rope naturally dispersing on its own as the Sundowner grew in the distance, he dropped the bulk of the coiled rope down in the boat in order to assist them to get aboard safely, concentrating his balance to keep the dinghy stable.

Nicholl spied the improvised splint the American had strapped to his arm, jokingly implying that Churchill had finally had enough and put an arrow in the journalist.

"Did Mad Jack finally shoot you?"

Hardy flaunted the injured wrist. "It's a splint."

"Uh-huh," Nicholl regarded as he helped the limping American into the boat, and they all found seating around the dinghy.

"How much of the tether is remaining?" aware of their ever-draining countdown, King-Clark quizzed whilst he gestured at the orange and white buoy with the lifeline tied around it. The thing was wedged under a sweat to anchor it down.

Through his damaged lenses, Nicholl eyed the coiled rope.

The wet line was still unspooling out into the water from the boat. "Still a little b—"

Spoke too soon.

In that instant, due to a knot somewhere along the one hundred metres of supplying rope left drifting from the yacht in the distance, the buoy became prematurely yanked into the water along with the remainder of the coil. Knotted at some interval during the generous ditching of line, their lifeline had been snatched, and the lump disappeared overboard, and thus yanked with it the buoy from under the seat.

Nicholl failed to catch it in time.

With a *plop,* it splashed into the depths, instantly drawn away from them before the float even had a chance to fully rise to the surface.

Four complete sets of open hands almost tipped the boat as they extended at once, all just out of reach.

Tragically, the lifeline towed from view ...

"... no! *No!*" Nicholl exclaimed fearfully as he allowed for himself to slink overboard and into the water, swimming futilely after it, but it was too late and unable to even get close. It was gone.

The life preserver plucked away from an unseen force, just out of his grasp like some sick joke made by the universe.

"*Oh, God, please no, no!*" he muttered as he futilely paddled.

All King-Clark, Hardy, and Hill could do was watch in complete and utter dread.

Hanging from the dinghy, King-Clark scrunched his face with exasperation as he splashed the water surface with anger.

That was it.

Their only chance.

The lifeline had expired.

They were stranded in Dunkirk.

"*No!*" Churchill's voice bellowed.

Upon a glance whilst he darted across the wet Dunkirk sands, he bore witness to the distressing sight of the fatality. His long-time second-in-command Second Manchester Regiment section lieutenant being shot dead.

Another victim claimed by the nuisance Luftwaffe maverick in the pesky Messerschmitt fighter with the yellow nosecone.

Involuntarily, Jack slowed in his dash to watch to the upsetting loss.

Momentarily transfixed by anguish, Churchill's eyeline traced into the sky as the enemy fighter pulled up and, like King-Clark advised, banked right before arcing around for another distant pass at the fish in this warzone barrel.

Churchill's eyeline drifted back down and onto the aftermath.

He could make out Gin Parker's deceased body in the doorframe of the boatshed and the sight haunted him for a longer time than expected. Whether it was just the sight of his friend's death that had shocked him, or the overwhelming sense of loss Churchill felt drown his spirit, something transcendent had thrust down upon him like a darkness. A gloomy shadow of failure had befallen, causing him to suddenly lose hope.

Then surged something almost as powerful as faith.

Rage.

Revenge.

A newfound determination.

An all-too-familiar Glaswegian brogue echoed as the blood pumped stridently through Churchill's ears, pressing his coherency.

"*Git mad, Jackie ...*"

With furthermore utter hatred towards this German pilot circling the skies as he stood exposed out on the shore, Churchill traced the airplane in the air for a while longer while he refocused his purpose.

Eyes trained low, Jack started jogging again.

Reaching his objective at the burning tank as it crackled and hissed in flames, Churchill began sifting through the sand for the steel winch cable as the heat from the glow heated his skin.

Taking a knee in the soft beach by the burning wreckage he reeled in the tow cable, creating a makeshift spool beside him in the sand that could easily be recoiled. The line was still affixed to the winch at its closest and that was attached to the heavy tank wreckage, but the farthest frayed end was askew along the shore. It had severed from the rear of the last truck in their towed convoy at some point during the last stretch of transit and remained untethered. After unlooping almost two hundred feet of thin high-tensile cable, Jack discovered the severed end and immediately brought around the hollow Bren gun barrel, feeding it through as though he were threading a barb to do some oversized needle-pulling.

Churchill fed it all the way through to the other end of the hollow barrel and then he laid it flat on an exposed part of Busty Barbara's armour plating. Jack brought the hammer around swiftly, and like *Hephaestus* and his anvil, he delivered mighty blows down upon the end as if he were fashioning a weapon for the gods.

Giving Barbara one last good and proper banging.

Timing being of the essence, he really put his shoulder into it, driving it with all of his—

On the third strike, the head of the defective mallet detached, shooting into oblivion and leaving Jack holding the puny handle with a perplexed look upon his sweaty brow beneath his putrid maroon beret.

Shit.

His stern stare scanned the device. It wasn't ready, and still needed at least one or two more good hits to close the mouth and properly hold the cable line.

In the interim of thought, his focus had tracked the enemy plane as it circumnavigated the beach in the sky. The yellow-nosed fighter was preparing another pass ... and he was out of time.

But then it occurred to him.

He *had* a hammer ...

It was on him always.

Churchill stepped back an inch in order to draw his trusty claybeg from his hip; his fingers through the many eyelets of his knuckleduster handle and asserting a firm grip before—*whack!*

He drove his closed fist into the barrel piece, striking it metal to metal. Not yet satisfied, he did so again, this time noticing results from the energetic punches, done as though he were punishing it.

The resounding blows echoed from inside the mighty metal lass and rung like the death toll for the antagonistic German pilot.

Ensuring that the ends of the barrel crimped down and clamped onto the cable evenly, Jack flipped the tube over after each strike. Finally satisfied with one side of the improvised weapon, Churchill brought up his bladed end this time instead. Pulling the cable taught out of the open tubular end and to the side, he delivered a well-placed strike across the circular opening with his Scottish broadsword. The immensely sharp weapon only bit into the edge by a mil, but that was all that was needed to make a nock.

His creation was now complete—and good thing, too ...

... for he was out of time.

Ready, his beret-clad head again tracked the Messerschmitt in the sky. The fighter was now closing in on his attack run ...

Regardless of how this played out, it was likely a final one.

Mad Jack stowed his claybeg, preparing his longbow and improvised harpoon ammunition.

He was completely exposed out on the sand of the coast ...

... and it was right where he wanted to be.

With a whip and a flick of the cable so that it was untangled as best he could semi-coiled, Churchill placed his bow down width-ways in front of him on the flat sand, so that the drawstring was facing away from him. He was aligned beneath what he presumed would become the fighter's flight course for his final attack run given all previous angles of trajectory as well as it being lateral to the shoreline.

Churchill stepped over the bow.

This was a peculiar archer's poise ...

He shifted his boots an inch in the sand, positioning rationally behind the longbow grip so that he could perform the exploit that came next, and he then placed the barrel of the Bren gun—the improvised harpoon barb—upon the resting bowstring. The sword-hacked slit sat snug on his makeshift nocking-point.

And like *that* ... he stepped away from the positioning.

Churchill took some strides out into the open area of the beach where he waited, brushing the soil from his palms while his sterling stare squinted into the clear morning sky, locked onto his target.

"That's it ..." he murmured under his breath as he watched the plane begin its attack run, lining him up faultlessly. "That's it! Come and get me, you yellow-nosed bellend!"

Without making the temptation too obvious, Churchill waited an extra few seconds, staying exposed on the beach sand whites before, all of a sudden and when the timing felt purposely dire, he turned and absolutely *sprinted* back to where he had laid in position his prepared and loaded longbow.

Taking the bait, the fighter zeroed in, targeting him ...

The circular battle sights mounted upon the nose of his canopy would have lined up the little man on the sand perfectly ...

Locked mark, his finger felt for the trigger button on the stick of which he strangled, and the machine guns clapped away, tracing his quick, sandy scuttle ...

The faceless goggle-wearing maverick behind the stick of the fighter started to engage. He did so almost playfully at first, sketching parallel lines in an artistic zig-zag rear Churchill's boots as he bolted, tossing sand like thrashing water along the shore.

Needless to say, it still effectively made Jack run quicker.

The cocky pilot fired in extended bursts as he slowed his nosedive. Sadistically, he did this in order to spend an extra few seconds turning this pedestrian into red paint.

He wished to savour the moment.

Savour and torment.

Each time he'd shoot a burst, the bullet drizzle climbed closer to the soft target before he let go of the trigger. He would fire again after dropping aim, starting again back behind the soldier on the sand, before pulling the stitchwork of the ranged bullets closer, and closer, nipping at his heels ...

This was it. Time for the kill.

The pursuing bullet stream finally reached, about to turn Churchill's khaki clothes to crimson gore, when—

Dodging sharply and to the right of his predictable sprint passage, just as the plane closed in on the final kill, Mad Jack avoided the volley of chasing tracers by inches, performing a strafing stride, drastically changing direction.

In what was effectively a long-jump leap, he drove both feet onto his positioned longbow, mounting the wood on either end of the leather grip handle. The jump slightly resembled a game of jump rope, only, he aimed for the rope.

Above and behind, the dominant fighter charged in with the thunder and barrels of lightning, now deciding to target him for real.

... wwwwhhhhhiiiirrr ...

The maverick was inbound and about to fire again, this time dead on the exposed target.

As the whistling pitch of the incoming fighter tightened, Churchill's sandy boots trod on the wood of the resting longbow, and he fell into a controlled collapse opposite the concave arc of the weapon. Jack's ass hit the sand and he immediately engaged his core, inclining forwards with both hands, where both sets of fingers gripped onto the drawstring. He then rowed backwards as though he wrangled a well-tucked bedsheet, whilst holding the specialised shaft in place.

In a drawing style known as a *double Mediterranean draw*, he used three fingers on each hand to clasp the string; his thumbs centred the edge of the Bren gun barrel resting on the bow string.

... wwwwhhhhHHHHIIIR ...

Sinking low onto his back, then oddly revolving to balance on his shoulder blades in the sand, Churchill raised his legs to the sky forming the human equivalent to a medieval ballista.

... his body was now the anchor point.

Tensing all his core strength and conducting some sort of callisthenics regime not unlike one would expect to see made by a circus performer, Churchill wrenched hold of the drawstring with the heavy barrel and steel coil at an improvised nocking-point. With all of his leg muscles extending the draw of his longbow, he pulled tighter, harder, stronger, past the point of strain and tremble from around his knees as they fought the desire to buckle. This method was unlike how he had ever trained before.

As he pulled, the yew wood of the longbow stressed ...

The fighter was arriving loudly.

He needed a few more seconds—*timing was everything.*

... WWWWWWHHHHHIIIIRRRRR ...

Outstretched, he gave a roar of might as he held the draw ...

Further than what the springiness and flexibility of the longbow could naturally provide, Churchill held his legs at full lengthening, pulling the line into his chest for a draw much further than what the device was ever intended ...

The wood of the longbow started to jitter and split ...

Out from either end of the leather binding of the bow handle, the timber was fracturing, fraying into splinters at the core ...

... WWWWWWHHHHHIIIIRRRRR ...

RAT-TAT-TAT-TAT-TAT ...

The machine guns of the incoming fighter roared to life one last time, now directly on Churchill's position, about to bury him in dead-on kill-shots.

... Churchill held the shot.

Exposed, lying on the beach, he withstood the barrage.

Tracers struck the sand of the shore with deafening volleys of clapping gunfire, missing him all around—by inches in some cases.

Round after round pounded the soil, dotting the edges around him, even causing him to sink.

... and yet, still, he held the shot.

The earth detonated like raindrops in a hailstorm, impacting him with painful ricochets of damage inflicting kinetic force.

Bullets got close.

Tears of fabric split at his sides and hot tracers grazed his thighs, nipped his triceps and elbows, scraping and scratching his posture as he held taut the drawn line.

"AHHHH!" Churchill roared while sand and smoke showered all over him as the beach became fully tattered by a constant chain reaction of automatic gunfire as the sights dragged a line all over and around his bodily circumference.

The wood of the bow was beyond tensile limitations.

Losing all pressure, the bow finally brok—

The plane screamed by overhead!

zzzZZOOOOMMM!!

In a gush of downward shaking wind, the fighter screamed in low along the beach, possibly even lower as he ever had before with his strafing passes.

With thunderous fury, it rocketed overhead, shaking the shoreline like an earthquake, absolutely blasting the sands with a downward riptide of air current.

... and like he always did with his strafing passes, the maverick pilot banked *right.*

... Churchill held the shot no longer.

He loosed his hold on the harpoon, propelling it upwards.

... and due to a last-minute tip from a trusted friend ...

... pulled slightly to the right.

Like a proper harpoon launched from a mariner, the blunt barrel loosed from between Churchill's boots via the longbow draw, impelling it skywards with the strength to drag with it the steel winch cable.

The line of the cable trailed behind the sailing projectile, slithering like a snake from the sandy coil, climbing up and up with speed and force and ...

The harpoon line shot out perfectly in the path of the dive-bombing German fighter as it banked to the right, intentionally missing the plane itself but dragging the steel cable hazardly into its flight path.

Like a grappling line, the cable tangled around the fighter's right wing alongside the canopy, reeling tight within a split-second with the transferring of intensity due to the upward launch and that of the lateral travelling airplane.

In the blink of an eye, the cable looped the wing a half dozen times and knotted, wrapped tight.

The line was instantly tied off.

With an inhuman amount of towing influence, Churchill caught a glimpse beside where he laid as the slack of the winch cable was suddenly pulled razor taut, anchored down by the flaming wreckage of the burning A10 cruiser tank.

The German fighter, although designed to be aeronautically weightless and therefore unarmoured in dexterity, was suddenly dangerously awry in flight.

The wing, surprisingly, did not sever.

Instead, most probably due to the angle of the plane's flight combined with the skilful maverick pilot attempting an evasive manoeuvre and at a relatively low speed, the yellow-nosed Messerschmitt managed to maintain airlift, albeit at an influenced angle.

At a sharp regression, the plane pivoted and banked in low, glided by the limitations of the attached line. It was now tethered to the earth by a stem, and there was no possible way this was going to end well for him.

Fastened to an immovable object on the ground and aerodynamically bound, the pilot quickly attempted to tug loose in his aerial swerve, though immediately and consecutively failed.

Within a few seconds of struggle, the panicking fighter pilot arced the airplane to the left, pulling at its farthest distance from the anchor point of the cable, however, he couldn't get away. At risk of stalling, he instead initiated another circle loop that was in keeping with the direction limitations.

Churchill became upstanding, witnessing the mayhem unfold from his position on the sand as the Luftwaffe maverick wrestled with the grapple of the winch line, unable to break free, unable to land ... *unable to live.*

Encircling the angle of his capture from the anchor point, the plane zoomed in lower and lower before eventually losing control and colliding into the sand in an attempted controlled crash-landing ... however, this maverick's luck had run out.

Instant fireball.

Like a skimming stone off an uneven surface, the aircraft forcibly bounded before the winch line disengaged its hold, sending the fiery wreckage into a sandy dune bar nearby, where it exploded on impact with a loud strike.

Bhoom!

It was unclear why Jack approached the engulfed remains.

Maybe the most rational explanation was that he wanted to ensure that the enemy maverick pilot within the smouldering crash had actually been terminated.

Perhaps the simplest reason was that Churchill wanted to spit on the grave of the sadistic antagonist, taking solace in the revenge.

Without shying away from the radiating heat of the sizzling Messerschmitt Bf-109 fighter wreckage as the housing and scattered debris scorched across the sand dune, Churchill watched the fire for a few seconds before the shouting voices of men calling his name caught his attention, bringing him back to the present. The voices reallocated his priorities and reminded him of the time-sensitive nature of their present situation.

Bruised, bloody, shot, sliced, burnt, and sleep-deprived, the longbow-wielding Churchill instantly picked up the pace, jogging towards his friends at the docks.

When he came in close, he noticed the dismayed expressions to go along with their hysterical shouting.

Slowing in his run along the damaged docks as he finally approached the small dinghy they had secured for this last-ditch gamble, Churchill saw a drenched Padre Nicholl as he slopped back into the boat from out of the drink. He was mortified and breathless, maybe more so than he had ever seen the military chaplain. Next, he saw a depressed King-Clark throw his maroon beret down into the bow of the boat with a gutted frustration, and saw Hill and Hardy both silently distraught.

Hardy gloomily raised an arm, indicating out into the sea ...

Their lifeline was gone, as was their hope.

"What is it?" Churchill probed as his concerned brow followed their gestures out and to the ocean.

He saw the bobbing life preserver fading in the distance.

The line that was attached to it was knotted and tangled, though had begun to unspool on itself now that it was free sailing behind the distant yacht.

"We shagged it," King-Clark impassively muttered. He was kneeling in the dinghy, absolutely gutted. "That was our only hope. That was our lifeline."

Out of time and out of luck ... *they were stranded.*

1944, September
Sachsenhausen Concentration Camp
Oranienburg, Germany

"*The end,*" a slightly older and imprisoned Jack Churchill stated as he lurched backwards from his leaning position.

"*The end?*" Felix Hardy exclaimed, pausing in his scribbling motions in order to cast his storyteller a wide-eyed expression of distress and doubt. As far as he was concerned, leaving them stranded in Dunkirk was neither truthful nor a decent way to end this chronicle. "What do you mean *the end?*"

"*The end,*" Churchill remarked again. "You want this to sound more like a story than a documentary, don't you? Wasn't that the goal? What's better than leaving your audience with a cliffhanger. Leave them salivating for the next issue."

"That's hardly the case here," Hardy gestured in contempt. "It's based on a true story ... the readers are going to *know* you get out of Dunkirk before the invasion. Anyone with half an understanding of history reading this after the fact will *know* that you get back home. I already even published an article once we were home in late 1940, don't you remember?"

"Eh, yes, the *Dunkirk Jack!* issue ..." Churchill recalled. "That brought me great fortune with the ladies. And you ... not so great fortune at all."

With pursed lips, Hardy bobbed his head.

He wasn't wrong.

"The issue was *well* received, at the least."

"I'm pretty sure I found it filed under fiction, next to *Archie, the Shield, Superman,* and various other colour-filled comic book sorts designed to lure children."

Hardy defensively corrected, "Excuse me, when I saw it, it was amongst the newsstand with *Daily Mirror, Morning Star,* and *the Guardian.* I remember picking up a copy from besides *the Daily Telegraph.*"

Churchill nodded after the playful digress, preparing to arrange his sleeping quarters for slumber.

"Let's get some rest."

"No, we need to finish this chapter," Hardy demanded. "We can't leave it here."

Tired and weary, Churchill emitted a long exhale as Hardy twisted his arm.

"Please, Jack. At least an encore of sorts ... for the readers."

"Fine," Churchill reluctantly sat back down, leaning forwards and facing Hardy from across the barrack bunks while the journalist quickly indecipherably scratched away at his notepad, preparing to note take. "You ready or what?"

Hardy made a sound with his mouth and finished his lead inscription. "O.K., go."

ENCORE
The Upshot

1940, June 4
Dunkirk
Nord-Pas-de-Calais, France

Churchill's view tightened on the trailing rope as it slithered across the water's surface, reeling away from them into the distance, towed by a force unseen (the Sundowner was but a spec on the horizon).

He squinted beneath his frown.

His blue sterling stare performed some mindless calculations as he observed the bounding buoy in the ocean. Perhaps the curse of an overactive archer's mind, forever focused on targets, Jack's brain performed trigonometry, algebra, and calculus on autopilot. He accounted for the windage, the distance, the instantaneous movement by the current of the tide, as well as the vertical limits of the sea as she rose and fell. He tracked the motion for a moment, observing his findings ...

"Jolly good work with the fighter, though," slumped down in the boat with the other defeated men, harmonized King-Clark while trying desperately to find a bright side in this unfortunate desertion. "Hopefully the Huns won't hold it against us when they invade Dunkirk and take us prisoner."

"Nonsense, Clark ..." Churchill distantly remarked whilst assessing his longbow still in his grasp. A plan was formulating in his mind. The conifer yew had shown signs of breaking just now when Jack had mistreated the ol' stick and string, shooting something other than a perfectly designed arrow and at a much heavier draw than intended. The flexible lumber was splintering beneath the leather bind in the centre and showed signs of fracture along the stern, however, she may hold together for one last shot ...

With that motive, Churchill remarked to those about him:

"We'll be long gone by the time they get here."

King-Clark didn't bother to reciprocate his friend with that quip. He just giggled unto himself while Hill, Hardy, and Nicholl wallowed in sorrow as the dinghy lifelessly lapped against the edge of the pier, absent their tether; their lifeline.

At the present, Churchill fired off a lively question after examining his longbow. "How far do you think that perry buoy is?"

King-Clark eyed him attentively, dismissively, observing as Mad Jack took a few mad steps to the right almost as if his attention pursued the current—and the conceived long-gone drifting life preserver and lifeline to the Sundowner.

Nobody seemed to want to play his game.

Their heads were already in the gallows, dreading about what was coming next at the hands of their prospective captors, Nazi Germany.

Thus, Churchill answered his own question, and humoured his own contemplation. "About forty ... maybe fifty yards? I'll guess forty-five, forty-six to be precise, eh?"

King-Clark's eyes blinked about the others sitting with him in the small dinghy. They were clearly mentally tumbling down the rabbit hole, passing through the five stages of grief while somehow, Jack was able to hit pause.

One by one they seemed to recognize hope as Churchill elaborated upon his own questioning—how he had the energy to do so was beyond them. They eventually looked up and to him on the pier, listening to his drivel as he spoke to himself like a madman.

"What about windage, Clark?" Churchill continued as he jumped across a body of water from one of the docks and onto a broken and disconnected section of the other wharf. It was mostly sunken due to damage, though stable.

"About four knots westerly, you say?"

"Jack?" King-Clark following him with his eyes, as did the others from the rootless boat.

"Here!" he shouted and ignored the plea of sanity. Churchill reached down into the floating debris and tossed them in the boat a coiled line of wet rope. Jack kept the end of that spool. The reel was decently long, maybe eighty or so metres.

In the dinghy King-Clark caught the rope, becoming splashed with murky water by the soaking, heavy coil. His brow rose. "No matter how good of an archer you are, Jack, you still need an arrow. I count none."

Churchill smiled audaciously. He had a plan.

"Hang onto that! Give me the slack!"

King-Clark looked about the line, confused.

"Jack, what are you thinking?" His face scanned across the others in the boat. They couldn't contain their hopefulness, though, they seemed as equally as puzzled as he was.

Churchill added at a whim. "Oh, and, eh ... don't let go this time, yeah?!"

The men in the dinghy exchanged an offended look.

At the risk of tumbling down that rabbit hole, they were expectant of this magician to pull a rabbit out of a hat at this build-up.

"Hardy, give me your hand."

From down in the floating boat Felix Hardy cast a confused glance up and to Jack. He was visibly confused as to how in his injured state he would fit into whatever plan Churchill had right now, but all-the-same he offered him his remaining, functioning hand—

"No. Your *other* hand," Churchill corrected, wanting his splinted paw rather than his good hand.

After an extended pause of consideration, Hardy again complied and offered his bandaged and splinted wrist ...

... the arrowhead of that wooden splint pointed towards Churchill.

They had an arrow after all!

One. Last. Arrow.

And with that, Jack Churchill sprung to action.

He collected the arrow, pulling it firmly out from between the makeshift bandages so that the feathered end brushed past Hardy's palm with ease. Once clear, Churchill returned the arrow into his magnetic quiver housing and stood tall, eyeing the ocean. With the slackened wet line still within his grasp, he leapt forward over more water and onto another floating obstacle yond their dinghy, gaining himself precious metres towards chasing the tide-absconding Sundowner buoy.

The onlookers observed with bewildered stares.

It got serious enough for them to adjust their slouches, pursuing him with their eyelines.

Churchill's wet boots squeaked onto the hood of a submerged truck hood that protruded the watery wasteland of abandoned rubble sunken along the bottom of the shallows. In the dozen-foot depths of the mostly destroyed wharf, the truck cabin canopy barely breached the surface during the hightide and was slippery as moss.

From off it, being sure to untangle the line from any snags, Churchill next pranced right in a hurdle, and reached another floating piece of debris slightly further out. This car roof was barely able to stay afloat with the extra weight of him aboard, so he quickly jumped from it and onto another, onto a large, angled portion of a sunken tugboat wreckage.

During this impromptu journey, he used the protruding debris in the depths of the shallows like stepping stones, gaining more and more distance out from the pier ... and obtaining a better angle on the away drifting buoy.

"Jack?! Wh-what are you—?!" King-Clark's confused voice bellowed after him as they all watched him go, playing hopscotch across floating debris whilst carrying a rope out from the boat.

Beside him in the unhitched dinghy boat and acting quick to obey the idea, Padre Nicholl took the coiled line and threw it into the water overboard. He held its end, tying it off around the seat in the centre of the dinghy.

With a stern gaze he eyed King-Clark from his position amongst the others, sitting in the boat. It was a snowball's chance in hell, but it was the only one they had.

He spoke with the belief that he finally knew what Mad Jack had planned. "Something tells me that you might want to get in and sit down for this ride, sir."

1944, September
Sachsenhausen Concentration Camp
Oranienburg, Germany

"Do you remember that day, Felix?" Churchill asked from his bed in the dusty and musty prison barracks. "The smell of the ocean ... the beautiful sunrise action ... the way the flames from the burning spot fires along the debris of the coast warmed our wet skin?"

"I remember I was going to keep that arrow as a souvenir. I remember my leg was fucked from the bullet wound in it, and I remember feeling terrified that we were about to be stranded in Dunkirk as the Nazis came pouring through the streets behind us," the more cynical and sardonic Felix Hardy remarked, still with his pencil in between his fingertips from chronicling Churchill's life story as he retold it: with much suspected falsehood and elaboration to detail.

"Our last session, do you remember when I told you about *Oslo?* About my idea for the closing ceremony if I had taken the gold?"

Hardy recalled. It was many chapters ago.

Churchill expanded, "I said, it would have been awesome if I lit a flaming arrow with the fire of the Olympic flame, and I loosed it from afar at the wreath to ignite the ceremony."

Hardy bobbed his head, finally recalling Jack's telling of the idea which never came to fruition. The war interrupted his athletic aspirations.

"Sure."

"Well, that's how it felt that morning in Dunkirk ... only, instead of a wreath during the closing ceremony at the Olympic games, it was a perry buoy bobbing in the outgoing current of the Dunkirk coast," Churchill described with vivid commemoration. "But the *upshot* was just the same."

'In a traditional game of archery, the last play was referred to as the upshot—the final shot of the match. It was fair to say that Jack had seen his fair few of them, but at this juncture, the last time he had an up-draw on an upshot with stakes as high as what they were, he had choked in front of a stadium full of onlookers. If he failed again, those onlookers would be comprised of a great many more Germans ...'

As child, the competitive Jack Churchill was always proficient at the kid's game *the floor is lava.* Good thing.

There would be extremely few instances in adulthood where such a skill may prove useful to have mastered. Perhaps never?

With a wet skid and lapping splash, Churchill hopped from sunken boat and onto element of adrift debris, leaping like a frog amidst lily pads.

Elevated across the water's surface up ahead, he discovered almost ten feet of wooden plank left askew between two sets of floating dock ruins like a bridge. He quickly crossed it, treating it like a balance beam at a gymnasium.

Once across and much farther out to sea, Churchill dropped down onto the partially flooded deck of an abandoned half-sunk ship, moving hastily across the afloat obstacles whilst he raced the clock of his drifting target's exodus from the Dunkirk shallows. He upped the bow of the angular wreckage, reaching the summit, where he positioned himself in the rays of the rising sun.

The sharp morning light assaulted his retinas.

Two days without sleep, his eyes were bloodshot and languid.

They painfully throbbed as the brightness stung his eyeballs.

Squinting and struggling to attempt focus across the choppy tide, he finally discerned the bobbing buoy on the sparkly surface flat.

Out in the open of the current, the floating circular life preserver boogied amongst the serene body of water that flickered in the sunlight like the scales of numerous fish.

Their lifeline.

Notably, the buoy was being towed farther away every second, pulled on the end of a one hundred metre rope attached to the Sundowner yacht as it ventured across the English Channel back home. The target shimmered as a blotch hovering above the sea spray of the ocean waves against the blinding horizon alit by the rising sun.

Taking a moment to feed his dinghy line through the debris-littered waters around these decommissioned docks, Churchill flailed an arm like whip crack. The rope seemed to be fortunately clear of any rubbish entanglements, and he could now focus on making this shot: the upshot to win the match.

Reminiscing from his competition era at the Oslo World Archery Championship, Churchill announced beneath his breaths as he attempted to catch them after his morning hopscotch. "*Up next we have John Churchill for Great Britain ...*"

As he broadcasted to himself, he prepared the end of the rope line by tying it off around the base of his final war arrow. Acting fast, he pressed the wooden body of the arrow firm against the edge of a rough corner of the sunken tugboat and began to scrape an indentation line around the circumference of the shaft, just underneath the bodkin point arrowhead. He did so not too deep, but deep enough to slot a rope knot in the groove for added truss and bind. Once a petite gouge became sculpted across the arrow body, he wasn't sure how best to fasten the band or what knot to tie. Time was not of the essence, either, so he went with a constrictor timber hitch that inserted into the lateral groove hitch he had just carved. He pulled firm, making extra sure it was fucking tight. There may have been many other better suited ties for the practice, but that knot *should* have been enough to carry the line through the air.

"*... scores an ace panel in the fore and hind. All that remains is a bullseye for the win ...*" a moment of clarity overcame Churchill, and a more serious tone befell him. His throat gulped. This was it. "Please let it be a bullseye."

Calmly, he eyed the drifting life preserver as it bobbed up and down in the ocean. He had clambered as far out into the harbour as he could physically reach after chasing the buoy, and the buoy was about to become towed too far out into the ocean for him to see.

Jack raised his face into the morning glow ...

Closing his eyelids, he felt the air ...

Sensed the temperature ...

Guessed the current of sea breeze; the direction, the knottage ...

He became one with this moment of existence.

By the time he reopened his eyes in the calm ocean air, he felt marginally rejuvenated and primed.

Bringing around his six-foot-tall yew longbow, Churchill nocked the arrow against the bowstring, making sure the attached line ran beneath his alignment for less resistance during the pitch of flight. He raised a boot onto the railing rung of the tugboat to brace his pose, facing out over the ocean.

Without even tensing the drawstring of his bow after nocking, he could feel that she was in some pain after being mistreated to launch the harpoon takedown of the fighter. The wood directly underneath his hold, within the leather-bound handle piece, flexed with a hundred fraying splinters beneath his fingers' grasp as the ends pulled taut.

Churchill suddenly fretted that the bow may not even be able to loose another arrow ...

... guess he was about to find out.

"Come on, lassie. I know you're aching," he spoke, genuinely pleading to his trusted and loyal, beloved conifer yew longbow. "Just one more shot, eh? Just one more ..."

Rolling his injured shoulder to loosen it, he prepared to brace a steady shot. He pushed the throbbing agony of the bullet wound lodged in his meat into the back of his mind, playing it zen.

He wiped his forehead on his arm, calming his psyche ...

Blinked his eyes, refreshing them ...

Cracked his neck, lessening the tension ...

Prepared in his stance, Jack performed some last-second calculations as his anchored draw of the longbow increased, tensing with unhealthy resistance.

As he drew taut, pulling the poundage, she tensed and groaned.

... cr-cr-craaack ...

The wood of the folding yew sung a song of fracture. Of rupture.

... the life preserver floated sixty metres out, headed north-east ...

... towed at a variable rate ...

... the knotted rope gradually disentangled, causing mild mishap ...

... wind resistance four knots westerly ...

... temperature approximately fourteen degrees Celsius ...

... minimal mist upward evaporative rise from the ocean ...

... the inward tide equating drift plus wind resistance divided by distance plus additional weight of the rope, plus drag through the water plus additional weight of the rope being wet ...

In that nanosecond, Jack's brain was a clusterfuck fluster.

But through the reckoning, Churchill's eyes drew a sterling focus.

Suddenly, whatever knotted the rope attached to the life preserver snagged free. For an interval, the floating doughnut was now dragged at the same pace of the yacht, approximately ten knots, directly northeast. This changed *all* of his former calculations in a heartbeat.

Fuck.

... the drawn bow still creaked and budged within his firm grip, inadvertently distracting his aim allurement ...

Churchill took in the shift in variables with the blink of an eye.

There was simply no time to readjust his premeditated aim.

He had to act. And NOW.

... he raised his shot a fraction ...

... craaack ...

The yew wood of the bow began to break in anchor of the draw ...

Churchill's hand clenched tighter, clamping the wood together.

He was completely out of time.

Churchill refocused slightly in his aim, and loosed, just as—

CRUNCH!

In a slow-motion traverse, the final arrow pinched against the taut bowstring became loosed from the archer's fingers; from the one-hundred-pound draw of his longbow, propelled in an arc towards the morning sky.

Like a rippling effect in the almost still-motion spectacle, and as the arrow launched with a *whip* and *snap* through the air, the shock from the released drawstring traversed down to the vertical tips of the damaged yew bow. The force met in the middle and suddenly contradicted the forces, unable to remain sustained and intact any longer.

Sailing true as a chaos detonated in its wake, the arrow launched from the erupting splinters in Churchill's hand as the longbow *exploded* with pressurized force behind the catapulting vigour.

Once released, even the discharge of burden from the bow could not retract or interfere with the trajectory or power of the launched arrow. The propulsion had set its aerial course to purpose, and the arrow (and attached rope line) soared true.

Like a miniature harpoon, the war arrow shot out into the seascape towards the open waters, towing the thin, sloppy wet rope from the water in a spit of spray, resembling the strike of an attacking sea snake.

Still viewing as a slowed rate of passing, Churchill's cobalt stare tightened as the longbow in his tense draw inadvertently released. The pressure of the bent wood was like an explosive charge detonating, bursting a rupture of tiny splinters in all directions. The entire unit recoiled violently as the drawstring retracted after launching the last arrow it would ever loose.

Fragments of wood bounced from all surfaces as they shot out like a porcupine, pricking into the sideburn and cheek of Jack Churchill's maw, even foraging at his clothing. His eyes rolled closed just in time to avoid splinter damage.

With his gaze pinched tight, he grimaced as the surface of his face became assaulted by barbed kindling, though through desperation and desire, he would wrench open his tensed eyelids in order to search the travelling upshot through the flailing kindling particles ...

Over in the aimlessly drifting dinghy, Nicholl, King-Clark, Hill, and Hardy gawked open-mouthed and in wonder, watching the travelling arrow as it climbed into the sky, chasing the disappearing buoy.

The arrow towed the rope from the water as the valiant missile arced in divergence against the melancholy contrast of the sky.

Poetically, it carried with it more than just the tether ...

It carried their hope, prayers, and their very survival.

Like a needle loop and a thread, the tailing war arrow angled downwards and pierced the doughnut of the floating life preserver with a *plop* in the waves.

The view from beneath the water saw the arrow penetrate the crystal surface and through the circular opening of the buoy, striking a bullseye.

The rope still firmly tied about its wooden shaft, the arrow lost all travelling power once it became submerged, spearing through the circular opening, swallowed like a button through an eyelet.

As the timber arrow rose to the surface within the confines of the circular life preserver, pulling against the ring of the buoy, the contraption formed a taut toggle button-eyelet formation. The weight attached to the end of the towline acted as a latch to hold the side-ward arrow in the circular float.

Sitting anxiously in the dinghy boat, the soldiers all ogled the rope line ...

Under the constraint of the tide, the arrow dragged the loosened rope from the water, causing activity until it moored in the distance. Within seconds, like a fish taking bait, the line became pulled as target distance journeyed, pivoting towards the current and towards the direction of the yacht and steered buoy.

It was a firm tug of resistance.

They were attached.

In the small boat, the soldiers resembled fishermen patiently awaiting a catch, intently watching the fishing line. With a small tug followed by a growing pull, the line dragged them along with it, towing them out and towards the ocean to the north—towards the English Channel.

Up front, Nicholl used a block of wood he collected from the field of floating debris as a prod to remove any obstacles that may get in their way. They could not afford to become snagged.

"Jesus Christ!" King-Clark scoffed, unable to even smile at first, he was in such utter disbelief. "He did it! Jack bloody hooked it!"

Sitting in the back of the dinghy, Hill and Hardy each swapped a similar look of revelation, overcome with joy. They cheered and grappled hands with excited embrace, taking in King-Clark's handclasp as he repeated with such enthusiasm.

"He did it! He bloody did it!"

"We're going home!"

They praised and applauded ... but it wasn't over yet.

They were still missing one passenger.

The man, himself.

Over on the partially sunken tugboat, Churchill stood tall and proud after making the winning archery shot. He could be seen holding his injured shoulder as he nodded in celebration.

Down by his side, he finally discarded what was left of his faithful longbow and unravelled string into the debris of the Dunkirk tide.

He took in the profound moment as the dinghy full of his friends drifted by his position, about to pass him by now that it was tethered to the ferry buoy, which was in turn hitched to the Sundowner yacht, by now over a thousand feet out at sea.

They had successfully created a daisy-chain connection that would drag them away from France and back home to England. To victory.

A beam of sunlight cleft between the cloud motion, illuminating some warmth upon his skin, and Churchill shut both his eyes. He beheld his winning smile as he perceived the cheers of the men onboard the dinghy as they towed happily behind the buoy—and the yacht—headed finally out into the channel.

Churchill took a concluding farewell glance back at the coastal city as it smouldered and crumbled in ruins behind them. Dunkirk looked hugely different now than what it did several months ago when he and his men of the Second Manchester Regiment had first landed ashore from England. She was a representation of symbolism regarding the German advance and the crumpling fall of Europe.

"Oi, Jack!" King-Clark shouted as their dinghy drifted uncontrollably *beyond* his location, around thirty feet from where he was located on the recessed tug. Their speed was constant, unwaivable, and unstoppable.

There were no brakes or control upon that ride.

It suddenly occurred to them all that if he did not actively jump and swim over to them now, he wouldn't actually be able to make it aboard in time. Their distance was growing thusly, already reaching the point of no return.

And with that ...

Jack Churchill ...

... knelt and took the time to loosen the shoelaces of his tall size UK10 combat boots.

"*Jack!*" King-Clark shouted, fretful and rotating in the boat. As did Hardy and Hill. All occupants within the dinghy became immediately overanxious, rubbernecking his locality.

Once loose, Jack sprung from his standing position within the boots and dove into the drink, sending him spearing beneath the surface and out towards the trajectory of the dinghy.

Eventually up for air, fixing his now saggy and drenched maroon beret, Churchill performed some timely freestyle strokes as he had done countless times in the pools at *King William's College* and again later in the *Royal Military College*.

Not realizing exactly how much the wound to his shoulder would hurt performing a physical act such as swimming, Churchill battled the tide, becoming unexpectedly fatigued almost immediately. He raced the towed boat and raced the clock as the time expired, and the distance expanded almost unrecoverably ...

He traced the stream of the boat, checking between breaths as he desperately pursued, hearing the voices of the men onboard as they cheered him on. Overexerting much quicker than he ever could have anticipated, he felt his speed start to decrease as the pain in his shoulder joint became almost too much to bare. The agony was so bad that it not only caused his rotations to diminish in paddle, but it sapped him of all energy and will to continue chase.

All that kept Churchill afloat, kept him swimming, racing, was his will to escape Dunkirk. To be victorious. His will to fight, and *never stop fighting ... only ...*

He was done.

About to clock out, Jack struggled to breach the surface for air, he was sinking, drowning, being pulled under by a magical force—

Right as this happened, Churchill was happily surprised when he felt three sets of hands hanging from off the back of the boat reach into the water and collect him.

Breathless, sopping wet, and in immense pain, his exhausted body became hauled painfully aboard the rear of the travelling dinghy, where he collapsed wet, drained, and exhausted.

After a moment, he used all that remained of his energy to heave himself up and slump onto the lumber seat amongst his fellow survivors and friends.

Seated upright now, Jack felt the most comfort he had felt in months.

A fishy, damp towel that must have been found lining the bottom of the boat was donated to his posture, guaranteeing an indulgence of sorts. The men aboard, all of them wet and cold, felt in unison that Jack was the most deserving of such luxury.

Churchill's view was met by an array of smiles and wordless gratitude.

Padre Jos Nicholl, Captain Rex King-Clark, Corporal Jim Hill, and American journalist Felix Hardy had been through the most hellish of scenarios over the past few days, and they should have had nothing to smile about ...

These men were shot, cut, bruised, and bleeding.

Exhausted, malnourished, and sleep-deprived.

They had taken lives and suffered losses.

Accepted defeats and embraced the sacrifices of war.

But in that bliss and as it all caught up, every single one of the men wore an ear-to-ear grin, strangely regretting not a single second of it.

In the wake of their great last-minute escape, the fading view was of Dunkirk as it crumbled, burned, and fell victim to the occupation of the invading Nazi Germany.

Battles still raged on within the coastal city as the French rearguard defended to their last bullets against the invading Germans. Buildings were bombed, targets became air raided. The echoes of the warfare boomed out behind them, fading in volume as they faded in visibility across the surface of the saltwater ocean.

"What an absolute tragedy," they all heard Churchill muttered, seated behind their view and calling their attention from the devastating coastal spectacle. Mistakenly, the diminishing view was *not* what he was commentating about. They looked to see that Jack was holding his set of wet bagpipes afront. The Scottish musical instrument had been shot up, scuffed, and now drowned. It was in no way able of being performed ...

... but Mad Jack Churchill tried anyway.

It didn't go so well, and the men just observed with a smile.

Churchill attempted to puff a breath of air into it once more before casting it aside. A wet and spongey puff of air emitted rather flatulently and, at first, nobody acknowledged it.

He couldn't help but find a consolation in his inability and decided to lift their spirits with some humour instead.

He remarked, placing it on the floor between their boots. "Pardon the toot, lads."

While the Brits giggled at the term, full-well knowledgeable of the popular British expression, Hardy questioned, "... a *what?*"

"A *toot* ..." King-Clark explained while the others snickered like schoolboys, taking a stab at the American's lack of conception before ultimately explaining the term so that he, too, could engage in the hilarity alongside them. "A fart, lad."

Having pulled the pin and tossed the funny grenade into the fray, Churchill's exhausted mind wandered for an isolated moment while the others discussed more educational explanations on the colloquialism of the term. During that background noise, the isolated vocalization of a familiar Glaswegian growl sounded in his ear. It was his highland haunt, Lieutenant-Colonel Sloan MacLeòid, and he offered a warning:

"*Storm's still comin', laddie ...*"

Déjà vu stuck Churchill. Paralysed him. His stare defocused.

"We just went through the storm ..." in a whisper unto himself, Jack affirmed resolutely. If the metaphor of the storm was the war, then Dunkirk was over with. They had passed through and were well onto better weather.

"*That?*" upon MacLeòid's maw at Churchill's open ear, his crooked smile beamed. "*That was a warm-up. Yoo ... got ... no idea ... what's comin' next ...*"

Breaking the hold MacLeòid temporarily had on his sonorization, Churchill's toes accidentally tapped the top of a wooden carton stowed beneath his and Padre Nicholl's shared bench. At first, he considered jettisoning it for the sake of haul weight, however, something much more attractive dawned upon his gleam.

All attention was brought focal.

Jack's eyes widened.

"Lads ... did we die and go to Heaven?"

His strange question prompted a pause to the praise, and all attention focused on Mad Jack as he reached into the wet carton and withdrew one of the half-dozen bottles of liquid contained in packing shredded hay within. They contained a red liquid with a somewhat coagulated consistency and distinguishable sediment residue consistent with the fermentation of red wine.

The unlabelled bottles of pinard were clearly a form of discrete exportation of rations owed for French soldiers. Whoever had owned this dinghy must have abandoned the endeavour.

The carton was full of Vino.

Hardy frowned. "Is that wine?"

"Such spoils of war," Churchill proclaimed, handing out the corked bottles to the men. Before long, each soldier within the towed dinghy held a bottle of wine to himself. It was a cause for celebration, and Padre Nicholl raised his first to salute a respectful toast to the fallen.

"For *Gin.*"

Each man held their own bottle of crimson booze.

Each man had their own reasoning for tribute.

"For *Omar,*" added Hardy.

"For *Dunkirk!*" Corporal Hill declared, well-rounded.

Seated adjacent to Churchill, King-Clark eyed his friend.

Rather than toast anything specific, the two men simply raised a bottle in the air and mentally chinked. They grinned.

"*Chin-chin?*" King-Clark proclaimed lifting the bottle, however Churchill dawdled towards the cause, his thoughts obviously lingering on what he had lost these past dreadful yet exhilarating days.

The savouring of the drink meant it was time to move on.

A clean slate as such.

While all men drank, his gaze wafted beyond them and to the backdrop of France ...

He had much more personalized reasons to toast his drink, however, simply, Jack Churchill knew not where to start.

While the men each turned to watch the coast fade in the distance, he finally saluted a toast beneath his breath. "Chin-chin—"

The bottle was snatched from his grasp.

Stealing the Vino from his lips, a hand outstretched from the cloth sleeve of a dated Queens Own Cameron Highlander's uniform. The hand snatched the bottle from outside of his peripherals. It came as a surprise considering there could be nobody else left on the dinghy but them five survivors, and they were all in front of Churchill's vision ...

Who was this sixth?

When the man at Jack's peripheral came more into view, he noticed that the uniform was complete with a heavy Scottish kilt patterned with regimental earthly colours of the Cameron of Erracht. It was none other than his highland haunt, Lieutenant-Colonel Sloan MacLeòid, complete with his pom-pom bonnet aslant. He had materialized for Mad Jack now.

MacLeòid nodded, eyeing the smoky shore.

"Chin-chin, indeed, laddie."

The view of their travel raised, seeing the five (and a half) men off towards a rising sun over the stillness of the ocean, finally across the English Channel.

Towards home.

"... that's the closing of this chapter," in the darkness of their confined prison barracks, Churchill concluded to his scribe as Hardy jotted it down in his notes.

The passing of a clock's hands may have been almost meaningless in the life of a POW, but the time was roughly an hour or two past midnight, and it was time for slumber.

He added, "I'm going to get some shut-eye."

While Hardy finalized his biographical transcriptions, Churchill prepared his bed space with a thousand creeks and squeaks of the savage wire framing beneath his double-folded rag mattress.

"Just ... for today though, right?" Hardy asked, concerned. Coaxing the modest Jack Churchill to open up about his life the way that he successfully had tonight, and in the detail that he had divulged, was a virtue in and of itself. Up until today, drawing blood from a stone would have been a more accomplishable feat. Naturally, the reporter feared that this had been a one-shot, and may rest incomplete. A tale of incarceration discovered in the right time and place. The warpath until Dunkirk may have been all he would ever get from the great Mad Jack ...

Churchill was quiet, getting comfortable.

It was a struggle that seemed endless at the Sachsenhausen.

"Because ... there's more to this story, right ...?" Hardy lured persuasively. "*Måløy* and *Vågsøy* ... *Sicily* and *Salerno* ... *Brač* ..."

"*Brač* feels like yesterday," Churchill remarked. "Do you want my life story or an after-action report?"

Hardy thought hard about his answer.

So far, everything Churchill had fed him he felt could be taken with a grain of salt, with a handful of respectful exceptions, especially those segments where he was present. Those times he could vouch for personally.

"I'll take whatever you're willing to give me."

Churchill sighed. "Stop being so melodramatic, Felix. I said end of the *chapter*, not the end of the story. Get some rest now, lad."

Hardy bowed acceptingly, still scratching away at his papers in order to properly wrap up what he had written. "And just so I know where to put the pin ... what *is* next, Jack?"

There was silence.

Hardy's scribbling stopped after an extended interval and the journalist glanced up after not gaining a response, and he peered over at Churchill as he lay on his side in his bunk, facing away. The soldier must have been asleep.

Hardy snorted softly. He couldn't believe the way Jack's lights blinked out at an instant. It was machinelike. He was jealous as it was like Churchill and many others of these soldier-types had access to a switch in their brains, from *on* and to *off* in a flick. It was probably a byproduct of years of conditioning and regimental training.

He wished he could do that.

Sinking quietly back into his own wiry crib, Hardy took the time and finalized his literature ...

'I'll admit, something I failed to fully appreciate during the events of the Battle of Dunkirk was the extent of Jack's emotional suffering, and it is something I've come to realize only now, during a revisit. Camouflaged in combat and concealed by a chauvinistic attitude and the intrepidness of warfare, it was hidden, I believe even to himself. During the already unendurable situation with the hardship of the evacuation of the entire BEF from France, Mad Jack was compelled to react based on his overwhelming emotions for Ève DuPont, only to fail and have her be taken from him before those feelings could ever truly blossom. It wasn't until later it dawned on me with the way he acted around Busty Barbara—the cruiser tank—and his desire to save her. Appealing to his inescapable weakness, she was another damsel in distress and in needing of rescue. Given his failure with Ève, he didn't want to leave her behind. It was a second chance, and in some strange psychological way, perhaps Jack's way of mourning her immediate loss.

This exhumed courageousness is just another trait of this incongruous hero soldier.

Even now as he leaves me hanging in suspense as to what avenue we shall stroll down in the tour of his life story, I can't help but speculate as to what direction we might take next on ...

'The amazing adventures of the brave ...'
'No.'

'The incredible saga of the valiant and heroic ...'
'No. That's not it, either.'

'The unstoppable warpath of the unkillable Jack Churchill.'

'Yes.'

While Hardy's pencil scratched away in the quietness of the prisoner barracks, a secluded view fell to Churchill's appearance as he lay on his rolled side, facing away the shadows ...

... unbeknownst to Hardy, his eyes weren't closed.

In fact, they were wide open, and none too proud of what chapter came next in his biography. Dependent on how much he would feel like sharing come tomorrow, it could prove quite the exposé for his journalist companion if he elaborated in full.

MacLeòid had been right that day; in that dinghy boat.

There was a storm still on the horizon ...

... only the word *storm* was an understatement.

What was coming was a goddamn tsunami.

The battle that came next in Mad Jack's story was a solitary one.

A war with himself.

EPILOGUE
Dunkirk Jack!

1940, July
Western Approaches Command, Plymouth
Devon, England

This lieutenant-colonel's army office may have been small but was rather quaint and homely. There was a degree of permanence present in what was likely a superfluous positioning.

Alike many of the workplaces built into the headquarters of the *Western Approaches Command* office established in the port city of *Plymouth, Devon,* this multitude of work quarters was converted from a repurposed facility for the manufacture of munitions during the Great War.

At this late hour, the building was nigh empty.

The halls were darkened, and most doors were closed, even locked.

The only lights still on were near the elevator lift, the fire exits, and the lamp on the corner of his desk in his far wing office enclosure.

Following the lightning advance of the German juggernaut across Europe and through France, and the ensuing Dunkirk evacuation, the British War Office had put out a call for volunteer units to carry out attacks along the coasts of occupied territories. It was about to be time to take the war to Germany.

This high-ranking colonel had recently been promoted (brevet) and was able to convince his commanding officers to recommend him for the new and unconventional special force that was being raised to perform these raids, the first operation of which, his men were about to embark.

Beneath his lampshade moustache, the colonel peered down upon his desk in his lampshade-lit office with an attentive gawk. On the tabletop was an array of open files and documents, black and white intelligence photographs, maps, and stationery.

Casting a shadow, he anchored down upon them, examining some focal paperwork. Placing his glass of neat scotch down, he then used his hand to push aside a particular sheet of paper and exposing another, which contained a degree of colour stamped across its header.

In red, it read in capitals:

OPERATION: AMBASSADOR.

There was a strange new insignia upon his battledress outfit, and it matched that upon the file notes, as well as an odd new unit title that read Comm—

Appearing suddenly in the open doorway to his quiet office was a recently promoted major (also a brevet promotion) by the surname of *Tod*. His presence didn't startle the colonel; however it did immediately tear his attention. "*Ron?*"

They were two freshly promoted commanding officers, born of a freshly created special forces unit known as Comman—

"Burning the midnight oil, eh, John?" Tod asked, gesturing towards the fact his CO was still present at the Plymouth base so late after everybody else, deliberating over the operational footnotes whilst sipping on a tumbler of whiskey.

The colonel by the name of *John* bleakly eyeballed him from above his thick lampshade moustache.

"We've barely even begun training the men ..." he pondered whilst shaking his head with a sense of uncertainty, still hovering over the collage of typed correspondence. "And now the War Office wants to throw them straight into a fight."

"They're in a hurry to hit back."

"They're setting us up to fail ... *again*."

"They're angry—"

"They're delusional!"

Ronnie Tod stepped closer into the room, curtly adding to the piles of manila folders on the desk with some more documentation. This time, the article was in the form of a newspaper and furthermore portfolios of recruits.

The colonel received the additions unenthused.

He barely touched the new stuff, however his eyes glazed across the letterhead of a newspaper, attracted to the bold headline.

Atop of the pile was an issue of a local newspaper known as *the Battlefront Gazette*, and its illustrations caught his eye as did the front-page headline: *DUNKIRK JACK!*

There was an artist impression on the cover of a British soldier in a beret, armed with a sparkling sword and an English longbow. This character appeared overly exaggerated, with carved chest pecs exploding from a war-torn battle blouse. The paper obviously had a rather large issue on some sort of poppycock BEF standout and was probably all bollocks, knowing the type of content which *Hardy & Co.* published.

"Could be an interesting candidate if you want a wildcard," Tod assumed at the extent of a laugh. The paper was obviously something he had picked up on his way over here from a local Devonport newsstand.

"I said I want soldiers, Ron. Not show ponies."

Tod held a smirk as he gestured towards the exit. "Come on, John. Let me buy you a pint."

This arrested and superficially brooding colonel had no argument.

He downed what remained of his stiff drink beneath his lampshade moustache and reached under his desk lampshade, turning off his light. On his way out he grabbed his coat and faced his desktop one last time of consideration before exiting the building ...

... and with a swift motion of declaration, he swiped the issue of *the Battlefront Gazette* featuring *Mad Jack Churchill* off the desk surface and into the wastepaper basket aligned beside it—where he believed such rubbish belonged.

The door to the personalized office closed, labelled:

Lieutenant-Colonel John Durnford-Slater.
'No.3 Commando.'

The unstoppable warpath of the unkillable **Jack Churchill**

will continue in ...

There's No Place Like War

About the Author.

Benjamin Blackie was born in Camden, New South Wales in 1987. Growing up, he often found more comfort outside of everyday life in watching shows and movies, reading books and graphic novels, playing games, and generally exploring the vast variety of creations and art forms made by others, as well as developing and practicing his own imagination. Still does.

He currently resides in Sydney with his wife and daughter, and remains close with friends and family who enrich his life with love, inspiration, and encouragement every day.

Acknowledgements and thanks.

My beloved proofreaders, Laura, Candice, and Grant. Thanks again for your time. Your feedback was contributory to the creation of Nice Day For a War, and your flow of positive criticisms and just appraisals helped churn this action-packed sequel. So, once again, I thank you.

My editor, Andy. The book is all the more good lookin' due to your good works, and I thank you for your efforts and well wishes along the way. Thanks for coming back to take on the job.

Once again, the good fellows of the community associated with the Commando Veterans Archive. Your reservoir of collective knowledge is absolutely second-to-none. Thanks for keeping their memories and the history of their sacrifice alive. Those pictures are black-and-white, but you helped me and many others to see them in colour. I appreciate all answers to the enquires I asked over the years. The intricacies of my probing was likely annoying for some, but hopefully you understand now why I asked those types of questions ...

Joe. I wrote you a nice enough acknowledgement in the first book, so I don't know what you're expecting here? I kid. You know how much you mean to me, and how invaluable you were to the creation of The Unstoppable Warpath saga. I still don't know where to start articulating the recognition befitting how much you helped me achieve the vision. To the stars or to the abyss, shotgun on this slow-travelling and rickety wagon is still - and will always be - reserved for you, no matter where this madlad venture leads.

Once more I would like to thank all those who I bored over the years talking about my seemingly endless endeavour about Mad Jack Churchill. Friends, here's some more of it. I hope you enjoyed.

www.ingramcontent.com/pod-product-compliance
Lightning Source LLC
Chambersburg PA
CBHW020822030726
47496CB00001B/55